A Treachery of Shadows

THE NULL WAR
PART I

First Editon 2026
First Edition © Sean Van Damme

Cover illustration by Keturah Rose
Editing by Nicole Evans

ISBNs
Ebook: 979-8-9947523-0-2
Paperback: 979-8-9947523-1-9
Hardback: 979-8-9947523-2-6

For Elizabeth,
Without her none of this would be possible.

Contents

SEAN VAN DAMME

Cold Open

The *Ishimura* was doomed.

It was a line that people had been telling Captain Jeffery "Trap" Trapper for the last ten years. Every time he took the ship out, somebody would comment that he didn't have enough money to take care of it, or a large enough crew to run it. Each time, he would wave them away, reiterating that *this* was going to be the big score. *This* would be the job that would set him up for life, allow him to give up his life of almost crime.

Trap never considered himself a criminal, just law abiding adjacent. No matter how many times he said this was going to be the last mission, the last score, something would always happen to get him back out in the cold darkness of space aboard his baby the *Ishimura*. On good days, it was because a job ended up not paying enough—or life happened, and he was forced to step up and take care of things. Trap was not convinced that child on Tripoint Station was his. Still, he couldn't prove she wasn't. So back to space he went. On bad days, he and his would escape by the seat of their pants, with hopefully enough credits to eat for a few days and patch their wounds before space called them back once more.

The last job had been one of those. It was supposed to be a simple cargo run with some unmarked boxes. Trap never asked where things came from. He just put them in the cargo hold and avoided the authorities. This time, though, his morals had gotten the better of him. The broker had loaded *his* ship with biological weapons. The manifest said they were medical supplies, but when a vial started leaking and killed his second-in-command, well…

Well, nothing. You did what was right. They killed one of yours with those horrible things, and you made sure nobody else would suffer that same fate.

But, because of his sudden embrace with morality, they were out here in the ass end of the Confederation: the Doldrums. Systems with no jump gates, just parsecs of empty space.

Trap flicked aside his long purple coat as he came sliding down the ladder from the crew deck to the mid-deck. His boots hit the steel of the floor with a satisfying thud. He turned, pulling his brown gloves on tightly and started walking toward the command deck. He flicked his coat to the side, tucking it behind the holster of his plasma revolver. Trap didn't think there was any danger on his ship, but after years of being on the edge, he liked to always be able to easily place his hand on the butt of his pistol. She was a good gun. They had been through almost as much as he and *Ishimura* had.

The lights around him started to flicker. *Damn, just another thing I need to replace.*

"I'm sorry, girl. *This* time. This time we can get you into a real dock and fix what ails you," Trap said, stopping for a moment, placing his hand on a supporting girder of steel that was open to the hallway. He could feel the ship creak, the stress of years in space without a good repair, without proper maintenance, sounding off. The Confederation didn't work for everybody, and if you ran afoul of them, they never forgot. But it was the life they had chosen, and he was going to make sure it worked out in the end.

"Sitrep, Mister Brush," Trap said as he walked onto the small command deck. They called it a command deck, but it was mostly just a glorified cockpit. There was a large round window at the front of the room. Through the glass, all Trip could see were red and purple clouds rippling with energy and electrical storms. Spread out in the middle was the pilot's station, behind which were two other computer terminals that were modular and could be used for any number of systems. The one to his right was broken, and had been for almost five years.

"Looking about as good as we can, Cap," Mister Brush said.

The pilot turned to look at him. He had on a brown jumpsuit with a red vest. The short man had a ratty, green knit hat doing a poor job of holding back his orange hair. The cap had a small pin belonging a long dead resistance group—red, white, and green stripes with a hammer and olive branch—on its center.

"Details, Mister Brush. I pay you for details," Trap said, sitting down at the broken computer station. He had turned it into his de facto captain's chair.

"Meaning no disrespect, Captain, but you haven't paid me in going on five months," Brush said, giving his shoulders a shrug as he turned back to his controls.

"We have been in space the last three months, just the four of us. What are you going to use credits on?" Trap asked.

"I don't know. We could have come across a really good floating restaurant or something," the pilot said.

"You are always thinking about food," Trap said.

"When all your meals are freeze dried or from expired cans, it kind of becomes an overriding desire," Mister Brush said.

"Most men cooped up on a boat well off the jump gate paths are usually thinking about finding a comfortable bed and a nice woman to spend some time with," Trap said.

"Have you given Mister Brush here a look over? He would need to upgrade his entire style to even be allowed into a half reputable pleasure house," a woman's voice said from behind.

Trap turned and saw the *Ishimura's* medic, Sarah Jene, walk onto the Command Deck and sit down. She was a handsome woman. Tall and curvaceous, with long black hair and silver eyes that held secrets. Secrets that he had tried to get out of her night after night in their bunk. Like Brush, she had on a brown jumpsuit, but her vest was blue, with two faded white snakes wrapped around a red cross over her heart.

"I do alright with the ladies. A good meal goes far," Brush said.

"A shower and a fresh outfit go even further," Sarah said.

"It's a manly musk. You know the shower in my cabin is broken," he responded.

"Yet somehow Harrison manages to not smell nearly as ripe," Sarah quipped back.

"I don't have to sit here and take this. Right, Captain? I don't have to take it?" Brush asked, looking from Sarah to Trap.

"How you like to take it is between you and whoever is throwing. Right now, though, you *do* have to sit there. I do believe we were talking about details? Things I need so that I can take care of that back pay you like to keep reminding me about?"

"Wait, we are getting back pay? I want back pay," Sarah said.

"I think Captain is giving you plenty of back pay," Brush said. Sarah gave him a dirty look, narrowing her gaze, giving him only the silver of her eyes.

"I can't help it if the walls are thin and he is a screamer," Brush said, throwing a thumb toward Trap.

"I don't scream," Trap said defensively.

"Fine, grunter. It's still loud," Brush said.

Trap turned to Sarah and just gave her a shrug. What was he going to do with Mister Brush? There wasn't a better pilot on the rim—at least, not one that he could afford. Sadly, this was a fact that everybody on the ship knew, and so there wasn't much that Trap could do except just let him talk and get them out of sticky situations.

"You had a report; something about details?" Sarah said, letting out a sigh and leaning back in her chair.

"Fine, fine. You are no fun," Brush said.

"I think you are plenty of fun," Trap said to Sarah. She shot him a death glare. He just held his hands up and chuckled.

"Boys," she muttered.

"I'm all man over here," Brush said, waving his hands in front of himself.

"Men take showers," she snipped back.

"They also answer the questions of their damned commanding officers," Trap said.

"Double teaming was not the backpay I was looking for," Brush said. Both Trap and Sarah rolled their eyes at him. "Right, so *details* and not just, 'we are the same as we have been for weeks.'

"We arrived at the rendezvous point last night, after two months of hard flying through the dark nothingness. Mister Harrison reports that we should have enough juice to get us home, provided your contact is on time. I've parked us as close to the Barrier as I feel comfortable," he said, motioning to the mass of red storms that dominated the command deck's viewport. "That should keep us hidden from anybody that isn't looking for us. Though honestly, anybody who *is* all the way the fuck out here is probably looking for us."

"Good, so now we just wait," Trap said. He reached into his pocket and pulled out his watch, flicking open the small, tarnished gold faceplate. The screen was cracked—like everything else in his life, it had seen better days. Doing a quick calculation in his head, he closed the watch.

"They should be here in four or five hours. Cutting it close," Trap said.

"I already pushed the old girl to get us here. Next time, explain to your contact about the size of space, and how it's really big," Brush said.

"I'll keep that in mind, though I think they know, considering how far out we are," Trap said. "Well, just keep me up to date. I'm going to check on a few other things."

With that, he stood up, flicking his purple coat and exited the command deck. Trap could hear Sarah stand up behind him and follow. The two of them exited into the narrow hall of the mid-deck. One ladder led back up to the crew deck, the other led down to the cargo hold and the drive section.

They were not even halfway down the walkway before Sarah put her hands on Trap's shoulders and pushed him against the wall. He wrapped his hands around her waist as the two of them started kissing.

"He thinks I'm loud," Trap said as he pulled away from her full lips.

"You are," she said, kissing him again. He could feel her body against his. She was warm and smelled of lilacs. Everything on this ship was dirty and cold, except for her. One of these days, Trap was going to be able to fully choose her over the *Ishimura*. The two women in his life.

Just... not yet.

"Trap, you can't keep letting him talk to you like that," Sarah said.

"What do you want me to do, have him lashed?" Trap asked, frustrated. He wanted to lean in for another kiss, but Sarah pushed him against the wall, keeping him stationary.

"That seems a little drastic—and pulling his jumpsuit off might be more a punishment for us than him. No, just... The buyer is almost here. We need to look like we are running a tighter ship than we are. I just worry that they won't take you seriously," Sarah said.

"I don't completely take myself seriously. It's hard to think the crew will," Trap said. She let him go and not in a way that allowed him to kiss her again. Which was a disappointment. His eyes remained focused on her lips. He could taste them, feel his against hers.

"Men who take command are twice as sexy. Just keep that in mind," she said, turning and walking over to the ladder that led up to the crew deck where her small sickbay was. She swished her ass as she walked. Trip hated for her to leave, but didn't mind watching her go.

Right, be more commanding. Put on a good face for whoever it is we are supposed to meet out here in the cold darkness. He enjoyed a healthy rapport with the crew and didn't want to be the kind of captain that he had served with in the navy as a youth. That style of command was just exhausting. Also, that style of commander would never let the crew know he was shacking up with the Chief Medical Officer.

That kind of commander also has a bigger ship, Jeff, Trap thought as he walked to the ladder leading downward.

The lower level of the *Ishimura* consisted of a large—and often far too empty—cargo hold, and a small room that had access to the ship's reactor. Jumping off the ladder, his boots made their required *thump* on the metal. Trap really did love that sound. It made him feel important—more important than the captain of a beat-up, rundown cargo ship, at least.

In the hold, there were a few crates of provisions, what they would need to get back to civilization, and a large crate. The crate was about half as tall as he was but twice as wide. It was made of wood, which was strange. These days, most things were made of steel, so that they could be sealed against a hard vacuum. Every time Trap got near the box, he felt cold, like it was cursed. Not that he believed in curses. He was an old sailor at heart, but not *that* old. He was sure it was just some kind of coolant system surrounding something stupid and organic. A wave of nobles in the Unaligned Planets were trying to push a fresh food in space agenda. Maybe that had caught on with some far-flung Admiral or titled explorer here up north in the Confederation.

You don't ask questions, Trap. That is why people keep hiring you. Even when they fuck you over...

He turned away from the strange single box of cargo that would soon be off his ship and moved toward the engine room.

"Mister Harrison, how is my old girl's heart this morning?" Trap asked.

Inside the hot, stuffy little engineering room filled with consoles and hanging wires was a man who always made Trap just a little uncomfortable. Harrison was of average build, his black hair slicked back. His face was always turned away, even when all he was doing was giving a report on how the thrusters were working. At first, Trap had thought the man was hiding something. Now, he just figured he was a bit off. Like Mister Brush at the helm, Harrison was the best at what he did, within Trap's meager price range.

"She is doing well, sir," Harrison said. As expected, he didn't look at Trap. "I fed her this morning. It was a little more than normal, but enough to get the water recyclers working."

"Thank goodness for that. I was thinking we were going to have to space Mister Brush to get rid of the smell," Trap said.

"I've taken to sleeping down here. Burnt fusion oil smells better," Harrison said. There was a quiet moment and then Trap chuckled. He wasn't sure if the man was being serious or telling a joke. *Touched, for sure,* Trap thought. Didn't matter, because he kept them in the air, and didn't whine about backpay.

"Seems a bit cramped, but I can't fault your logic," Trap said.

Again, there was silence. So, not a joke. Just as he was looking for something to say to get him out of this conversation, the comm unit on his belt chirped. Trap reached down and picked it up.

"Go ahead."

"Captain, you are going to want to get up here PDQ," Mister Brush said from the Command Deck. There was no mirth, only worry in his voice.

"Rodger, on my way," Trap said, putting the communicator back on his belt and flicking his coat so that his revolver was free. He then turned and, moving swiftly, was back at the ladder and climbing up.

Back on the bridge, Trap had never seen a ship like the one he was looking at. It was painted a bright crimson and shaped like an arrowhead. It was half the size of the *Ishimura* and looked angry. That worried him, but it was what Brush had said about how it arrived that worried him more. Sarah ran into the command deck and cocked her head at what was hanging in space in front of them.

"Tell her what you told me," Trap said.

"This... arrowhead thing just appeared. There was a flash of light and then it was right here. Scanner readings are consistent with the radiation you would see from a ship exiting a jump gate," Brush said, worry in his voice.

"Have they tried to contact us yet?" Trap asked.

"Negative. I sent out a hail but got no response."

Klaxons went off in the ship, the lights flashing red. Proximity alarm. Trap slid over to the working computer station and pulled up the radar. Three more ships had just appeared on their scopes. Well, at least within range of the radar, but more could certainly be out there. The radiation scanners were spiking.

What in the Confederation fuck is going on?

More images were coming in. The new ships were of the same build as the one in front of them. All three were moving in a wedge formation, arrowheads shaped like an arrowhead. It felt like the tip of a spear coming for them.

"Hail them again, I don't like this. I don't like this one bit," Trap said.

Brush started pressing buttons and sending out another hail. Trap walked over to a locker off to the side of the Command Deck. Pressing his thumb against the pad, the locker clicked open. Inside were plasma shotguns. They looked like the pump action weapons of old and fired a scattered, plasma-infused buckshot. They worked like all other plasma weapons in that they mimicked kinetic weapons, even throwing slugs. Only these slugs burst into plasma fire before hitting their targets, doing horrible amounts of damage.

Trap pulled one out and threw it to Sarah. She set it down next to Brush and expertly caught the next one that Trap threw at her. He grabbed the third and started loading plasma shells into the feed tube under the weapon.

"Ah fuck!" Brush yelled, pulling the headset off his head. Trap could hear the static coming through the earpiece. Jamming.

Why jam us all the way out here? There is nobody for parsecs?

It didn't matter. Trap had seen enough action to know what was coming next. Right on cue, the *Ishimura* shook from three angles. The new arrivals had taken up holding positions along their side and hit them with grappling hooks. The next step was for one of them to latch on and start boarding.

Trap grabbed the comm from his belt and started turning a small dial. The interference cleared.

"Harrison, we are about to be boarded. You know what to do," Trap said, calmly and quickly. Before he could finish the message, the jamming kicked back in. He hoped that enough of that had gone down to the drive room. He was not about to be taken prisoner.

"Confederation out this far?" Sarah asked. "With cloaking tech?"

"I've never seen any ships that look like that before. Confederation or otherwise," Brush said.

"And they didn't cloak—that's impossible. Somebody has figured out how to independently jump again," Trap said.

As an old spacer, he understood the implications of a ship that could jump into Null space without the aid of a jump gate. The kind of advancement in technology would change how life operated in the Confederacy. To his—admittedly limited—knowledge, Trap couldn't think of a single group that was anywhere close to having such tech. Especially not a group that would be messing with the likes of them.

"A jump engine, on a ship that small? That's as impossible as a cloak," Brush said.

"Well, it looks pretty possible to me," Sarah snapped back, slamming the last of her slugs into the shotgun and sending one home.

"Right now, I don't give a fuck about possible or impossible. They are here," Trap said as the ship shook again. He expected to hear the sound of a torch on the other side. They were clearly coming, so...

The sound of steel hitting steel rang out, before a sound he never wanted to hear: the heartbeat thrum of a star-steel blade.

"What are the Host'ire doing here?" Brush asked, crouching behind his chair and leveling his weapon forward.

"I don't know, maybe we can ask them," Trap said. He finished chambering his weapon and pointed it down the hallway. Another rattle, and smoke filled the room. Sarah fired. The super-heated plasma burned blue-white as it cut through the smoke. Boots were on the deck. The sound that had brought Trap so much joy in his life, now filled him with dread as it signaled what was very likely that life's end.

Green light filled the hallway. He fired, the light moved, and his rounds evaporated. Sending another slug into the chamber, he fired again, as did Sarah and Brush. The green light swished with each of their shots, causing the blue-white of their plasma to vanish into nothingness.

Then the hallway returned fire.

Trap heard the triggers being pulled and threw himself to the ground, reaching up and grabbing Sarah. She fell down on top of him as the Command Deck was ripped apart by fully automatic plasma rifle fire. Mister Brush wasn't so lucky. Trap didn't see the rounds hit him, but upon glancing back, he saw what was left of his corpse. The jump suit was full of holes. His face was gone. All that was left was a gaping hole of burned and melted flesh. The threadbare green beanie hat was on fire, the revolutionary pin already starting to melt.

"We are going to get killed if we stay here," Trap whispered. "Lay down some covering fire." He pointed his shotgun forward and started pulling the trigger and pumping.

The weapon clicked empty. There was no return fire, no sounds.

Did we... Trap thought apprehensively. No, they couldn't have won; couldn't have driven them all off. There was a Host'ire with them.

Quickly, he slipped another clip into the shotgun, racking the slide sending a plasma slug into the chamber. Motioning to Sarah, he stood up and started walking forward, the smoke from the weapon's fire retreating from where he stood. Sarah was right behind him. The hallway was empty.

"I'm going to get my medical bag," she whispered, reaching the ladder. Trap nodded as she started to climb.

The ring of the shot echoed through the ship. Sarah fell. hitting the deck. her head flopping to the side. Trap tried to scream, but nothing came out of his mouth. They were above them, hiding, luring them out. He couldn't stop looking at her. She was trying to say something, her lips moving as the light faded from her silver eyes.

Trap jumped for the ladder going down. Pain erupted from his lower leg. It bloomed and cascaded through his body; he'd been shot.

His foot slipped on the last rung of the ladder, and he hit the deck of the cargo hold. The ground was slick with blood from where the stump—that was once his right foot—bled. His breathing was getting ragged, and already Trap could feel his attachment to the world of the living fading. Reaching out, he began to pull himself across the deck.

Was that whimpering? He turned his head and saw Mister Harrison crouched in the back of the drive room, his legs pulled up to his chest. The man was crying. He was supposed to be defending the cargo and he was crying! Rage would have filled Trap if there had been enough energy for it. As there was, he could barely pull himself forward.

The box. It was in the center of the room. They were coming for it. At this point, he was going to be damned if he let them take it. His crew had died protecting this thing and he would rather see it destroyed than allow them to have it, whatever *it* was.

He pulled out his pistol and shot at the lock on the box. The first round missed wildly. The second was close enough. The third melted the lock.

Crawling forward, he dropped the weapon and grabbed the edge of the crate, pulling himself up. The sounds of men behind him coming down the ladder were getting louder. *Well, at least they'll put an end to the whimpering.*

Grabbing the edge of the box, he thew off the wooden crate. Inside was a stasis pod. The small window was frosted over. Trap blinked for too long, his brain having trouble registering what it was seeing. A stasis pod, and an old one, too. There was no power nearby. How was it...?

Questions don't matter anymore.

He reached over and with the blood-stained sleeve of his purple coat, he wiped away the frost.

Inside was a child.

Boy or girl, he couldn't tell. They were young. Their hair had been shaved off and golden light cascaded around them like vines. Was that...? Was that Null energy?

A child. Trap had smuggled plenty of things in his day, but never people, let alone children. He knew that, regardless of his questions, these people couldn't have the child. His employer, he could deal with later—if there even was a later for him. Right now, he was the only person standing between that kid and whoever was killing his crew.

Trap reached for his pistol, only to then remember he had dropped it. He turned to reach for it when a round of plasma smashed into his chest. He stumbled and fell to the ground, leaning against the crate, clutching his gut. The smell of his own burning flesh filled his nostrils.

Through the smoke, that same horrible, sickly-green light was shining, with that heartbeat thrum. Out stepped a man. He wore black from head to toe: long leather jacket, gloves, and sunglasses. In his hand was a star-steel blade, the energy weapons of the Host'ire. Wizards.

What were wizards doing here? What were those tendrils of Null energy? Who was the child? Ships could jump again?

Why us?

So many questions raced through Trap's mind as the life drained from his body. The man with the green blade walked up to him. Trap raised an arm and tried to form words. Nothing but a few incoherent mumbling sounds came out.

Then his world went dark.

SEAN VAN DAMME

EPISODE 1:
Specter of the Past

Antiga Prime Shipyard, Erik

It had been six months but Erik Cordova, third of his name, was finally free to feel space beneath him once more. Six months of leading repair details, six months of cleaning up, six months of classes at the war college on Antiga Prime where the Dreadstar *Fury* was in dry dock. He had spent so long away from his Rapier doing other things that a few more days without space beneath him and his flight status would have lapsed. It would be unseemly for the Air Group Commander of one of the last remaining Dreadstars to lose his flight status. Plus, Erik loved to fly. It was the only time that he truly felt free; like his life was in his hands, and his hands only.

Flying also came close to getting him killed; had almost gotten *all* of them killed. He held the flight stick with one gloved hand and his accelerator in the other. The battle of Hyroncore was still fresh in his mind, even though they were half a year removed from burying their dead in the void of space. That the pirate clans thought they could destroy a Dreadstar was bold. The fact that they actually tried was hubris. That they almost succeeded was luck of the highest order.

Their survival weighed on Erik's mind. So many had died, and yet still they were here, and he was forced to spend six months not in the cockpit but managing repair crews and learning about logistics and supply lines.

Anything outside of his cockpit bored Erik. He was working on changing that as he grew older, though his mother would have still called it a failing; would have said that a Lord needed to know how to do everything on their Dreadstar. His Mother—the Lord-Admiral of the Dreadstar *Fury*—said many things these days and vanishingly few were nice.

Thirty thousand kilometers from the shipyard was a large asteroid held in place by the system's gravity and the occasional thruster burst from a single engine strapped to it. The asteroid's dead, pockmarked surface had been used for generations as a bombing ground. A place where fresh young Confederation pilots and gunners could practice. Today, it was his planned destination.

This was a quick trip. Dart from the dry dock, pick up as much speed as possible, and then sling shot around the hunk of rock. The speed from the sling shot would be enough and he could make a return to *Fury* without having to use his afterburners. He would need to time the sling shot and his thrusters perfectly, so that he would only need the lightest tap on his thrusters to slow down enough to land; a sign of a pilot who was one with their ship.

The asteroid was coming up on him quickly, so he pushed the throttle even harder. The fighter's frame started to shake. Rapiers were light interceptors, not bombers like the Broadsword or Star Superiority fighters like the Katanas. They were small and fast, using their speed and maneuverability to shake off foes. That was the kind of flying that Erik enjoyed. It was the kind of flying he didn't get to do enough. As CAG, he never got to really get into the mix of a fight, unless things were going poorly.

Like at Hyroncore.

He had gotten into the mix, had racked up double digit kills.

And it still hadn't been enough.

Clicking the peddles at his feet, Erik pulled off the speed, hit his maneuvering thrusters, and gave the fighter's stick a turn. The little ship came close to the surface of the rock. Looking out of his canopy, he could see the thousands upon thousands of craters that had been punched into the gray dirt. There were wrecked ships there, too. Evidence of cocky pilots who had gotten too close, or gear that had been dropped there to be blown to bits. Taking his hand off the stick, he let the small fighter move under the power of nature. Rounding the asteroid, Erik could see the Antiga Prime shipyards far in the distance. The shipyard hung there in the middle of deep space. The planet of Antiga Prime was on the other side of the system.

There was a buzz of static from his radio, almost as if somebody was pretending to make the sounds of static with their mouth. Erik turned, looking up and behind him. That was when he saw the second Rapier flying above him. The slender fighter was no more than an engine, a cockpit, and two guns strapped to wings that pointed angled out to the side. On the belly—under the cockpit—was a black chimera on a field of gold, the sigil of House Cordova.

"Beautiful morning for a flight, cousin," Erik said into his radio. There was only one person that could catch up with him and would pretend to broadcast static over their comms.

"Cutting it close this time, big coz," Bella's soft voice replied over the radio. The two of them had the easy rapport of children who had grown up together. They had been raised close as siblings. Bella had been on his wing from the moment Commander Blackfire, the ship's previous CAG, had put both of them in the cockpit. Bella would take over the *Fury's* fighter wing one day. *When mother dies, when I take command.*

"Who can find the damned time anymore, these days," Erik said. Bella's ship, like his, zipped forward toward the shipyard only under the power of inertia.

"I was told if it was important, you make the time. Sir," Bella japed back at him. Erik knew those words. They were his, what he said to every young pilot who didn't want to put in their simulator hours before hitting vacuum.

"You wound me, cousin," he said. There was silence and then Bella's fighter spun, coming damned close to his, before ending its roll above him. Looking up, Erik could see Bella looking down at him. She hadn't used her engines to make that maneuver or match his speed. Bella had always been the better pilot. He was practiced, she was *natural*. No amount of breeding or title could ever get her to give up the cockpit of a fighter. He dreaded the day that they needed to try and find a match for her, somebody that would be advantageous for the family.

"I wound, but I also bring glad tidings," she said.

"Go on," Erik replied. They could use some good news these days.

"The *Crimson Sky* is twenty minutes out from the station."

The transport ship was early. They were not supposed to arrive until this afternoon—hence why he had scheduled his flight now. The ship was bringing in the last of their replacements, save for their Host'ire Ambassador. The important passenger, though, was not a new member of the crew, but family. His brother, Alexander, home for a quick visit before going on ahead of them to NovaTerra for Festival week.

"Damn. I guess I had best hurry, then," Erik said, putting his hand on the throttle. Bella rolled her fighter over and came up on his wing. She gave him a little two finger salute and punched her afterburners. Erik followed, pushing the little ship to full speed.

Quickly, the shipyard started to fill the view from his small cockpit. It was a massive complex, stretching over a hundred kilometers from one end to the other. Antiga Prime was the only yard left in the Confederation that could work on a Dreadstar. Closer and closer, Erik could see the smaller tugs and sloops moving around, flying from berth to berth, servicing the ships of the Third Fleet, under the command of Admiral Gaius.

The Third Fleet was one hundred ships strong, their weights ranging from a handful of giant, three-hundred-gun ships of the line to the smallest corvettes that were barely bigger than two Broadsword bombers sewn together. Admiral Gaius, in the grand scheme of things, was subservient to Erik's mother, as he was only an Admiral, the son of a cobbler, and not a highborn Lord-Admiral. This was his sector of space and Erik understood that out here, title didn't matter nearly as much as rank. Admiral Gaius was a widower, and a single good match would make him a power player not just in the military, but Confederation politics.

In the back of the yard, not in a standard berth, was the Dreadstar *Fury*. She was a massive ship, ten kilometers from stem to stern, packing seven hundred guns. From a distance she looked like a massive upside down "T" with a small serif on the bottom. The large section of the "T" housed the ship's engines, marvels of technology that had not been matched since she was commissioned almost a thousand years ago. All along the center were guns and landing bays, while at the front were more guns and communication equipment. Her dark hull had three blisters that each housed a corvette. Two of them were original to the Age of Chaos. The third was a spry two hundred years old.

In all the Confederation, there were only five Dreadstars left, relics from the Age of Chaos a thousand years ago. A ship filled with lost technology that present day engineers could barely operate, including the ability to jump into and out of the Null without a jump gate. This had made them targets for pirates and rival houses for the last five hundred years since the Wayfinder wars. It was a ship made to last a lifetime, and she had endured. Erik had been born aboard *Fury*, and was sure he would die there as well. The last five generations of Cordovas had commanded the Dreadstar in the name of the Confederation, and God willing, he would be the sixth.

Heading toward the landing bay, Erik was going to have to slow down. Bella had gotten far ahead of him, pointing her ship right at bay three and coming in at near full speed. On the radio, he could hear the deck officer yelling at her.

"Slow down, if you please!"

Bella, of course, ignored the old man until the last moment and then threw her space brakes and killed the fighter's speed. The maneuver would leave her with belt bruising, but she never seemed to mind that. Erik came in at a much slower approach, not looking to stress out the deck officer any more than he already was. Those kinds of stunts were the things that Bella could get away with while he, as the heir and CAG, could not. Still, Erik would need to give her a talking to about it later. It reflected poorly on them, and made the younger pilots think they could get away with the things she did. Commander Blackfire would have given both of them a week of hard duty for what she just did, but Blackfire was long dead, and Erik had a lighter touch than the old man.

It took ten minutes for Erik to land his fighter and be taxied to his berth. Halfway though, he cracked open the cockpit and pulled off his gloves and helmet. His long auburn hair was pulled up in three clips. Removing the clips, Erik ran his hand through the thick sweaty tangle of hair so that it fell just past his shoulders. Just as he slid the small Rapier into the berth, a ladder was rolled up to it, followed by the deck gang who had come to take care of the weapons and fuel. Behind them was his squire, Young Joe, a lad of fifteen. He held Erik's blues, the uniform an officer was expected to wear while aboard ship.

Standing, Erik slid down the ladder and walked over to a short pudgy man who time had not been nice to. He had on a gray jumpsuit with a gold vest trimmed in black and stuffed with tools.

"Chief, capital work on the ships. She still controls like a beauty," Erik said, giving the old man a cap on the back of his shoulder.

Chief Hassan turned, giving Erik a sour look. The kind of sour look that only the most senior of enlisted man could give an officer who also happened to be highborn. It was the sour face of a man who had seen too much in his seventy years. The kind of man that didn't need compliments from the young pups of lordlings.

"Of course she controls that well, my lord. I tuned her myself," Hassan said before he turned and started to bark orders at the rest of his deck gang. Erik walked over to where Young Joe stood with his clothing.

Erik pulled off his leather pilot's jacket and button-up field shirt, which was covered in small gears and switches to monitor his life signs while strapped into the fighter. His hairy chest was covered in sweat. A towel was the first thing that Young Joe handed him. Erik dried himself. It wouldn't do to change and still be moist to the core. The towel had been perfumed with rosemary and lavender.

"Has the *Crimson Sky* landed yet?" he asked as the squire passed him a heavily ruffled white shirt with a high stiff collar.

"Yes my lord, she is in landing bay seven," the young squire said.

Next, he handed Erik a yellow satin vest, much like the ones that the deck gang had on. His, though, was embroidered yellow-on-yellow with the chimera of House Cordova. At a glance, you could tell the vest was expensive, but not why.

"Then we should make haste," Erik said, turning and starting the long walk from Bay Five where they were to seven. Young Joe handed him a black cravat. Erik started wrapping and tying it about his neck. Just as he got the large knot where he wanted it, Young Joe had the small pin ready for him. The pin was a golden chimera holding a ruby. The ruby was to signify his rank of Commander. Erik pinned the Cravat in place and kept walking.

"My brother is arriving today. Were you aware?" Erik asked.

"Yes sir, I was told by Lady Hanna this morning," the young boy said, referring to Erik's younger sister and twin to Alexander. Next, Young Joe handed him his sword belt. Erik wrapped the brown leather belt around and clapped the iron buckles keeping it on his waist. On his left was the golden hilt of a saber rattling at his side in its silver sheath. On the right, attached to his thigh via magnets stitched into his pants, was a holster with a plasma pistol.

"Perfect. Once we are finished here, I want you to find electrician Windsail. Send her my compliments and let her know that Alexander has arrived. We have been holding his visit close to the vest. You understand?" Erik said as the squire handed him his jacket.

"Of course, sir," the young boy said. Erik took the heavy woolen blue jacket, trimmed in gold with a single epaulet over his right shoulder and spun it, slipping his left arm in and then his right. The jacket fit snug and hung down to the tops of his boots, which were just two inches shy of his knees. It had a high starched collar to match his shirt and, pinned to the side opposite the epaulet, was a silver eagle holding arrows. Lastly, the young man handed him a yellow ribbon that Erik used to tie his unruly damp auburn hair into a ponytail.

Finally, he looked the part of a space lord upon his own ship.

Clutching the hilt of his saber, Erik picked up his pace, a happy jaunt in his step.

Olympus Ares Research Facility Apartments, Grace

The alarm buzzed with the certainty and finality that it did every morning, signaling the end of sleep and the start of the day. The end of that usually joyful time when logic gave way to impulse and random connections of memory and desire. When a person was truly free but also constrained within a world where the rules did not stay the same. A world that Doctor Grace Goodspeed both loved and loathed in equal measure.

Her hand reached out from under the cover and slid across the glass screen of the clock, silencing the shrill blast echoing in her ears. She took a deep breath and rolled over, not ready to face the day. Sleeping in was not something that Grace was known for, and on most days, she would have bounced from the bed as soon as the clock went off, if not a few minutes before it. Yet the night had been fitful, and her sleep broken. Her dreams had been filled with numbers that would not add up, equations that sat on the edge of a knife and refused to be balanced, no matter what she did; alongside, always in the background, a burning whisper gnawing into the back of her skull, like a stranger sitting too close behind you.

Emily could have balanced it. She would have solved things.

The buzzing would go off again in three minutes and this time, she would have to walk across the room to shut it off. A holdover from her—no, *Emily's*—college days when she would stay up late reading and then have trouble waking up for class. Grace and sleep had always shared a contentious relationship: her body wanted sleep, but her mind found it a true waste of time. Over the years, she had trained herself to go to bed on time as opposed to running ragged until her body shut everything down and forced sleep upon her. At least that way, she had a bit more control over how much time it took from her.

Last night, though, she had been up too late reading a book on archaeology , about the mysterious ruins on Ross II.

A decade ago, researchers had found a dead city buried under an ocean, signs of a cataclysm in its past. An advanced civilization that seemed to have vanished in the blink of an eye. There were hundreds of worlds like this pocketed throughout known space; worlds that had known life and now only knew death. Or ones that flirted with civilization before violently returning to the natural order of things. She found this fascinating and hoped that it might obliquely contain a clue to the problems that she worked on today.

While Doctor Grace Goodspeed had a degree in Xeno Archaeology, it was her four degrees in astro and theoretical physics that she used for work. The archaeology degree had been something Emily had earned on a lark so she could be closer to a boy. It had seemed so frivolous, then. Now, though, she understood just how important seeing where a civilization had been was regarding looking forward to where they were going to go. Where *she* was going to help take them. The questions of the past were the answers of today.

The second alarm went off. This one louder and more obnoxious than the first, she wouldn't have been able to ignore it even if she had wanted to.

Kicking off the light cover, Grace stood up and stretched, rolling and cracking her neck. She quickly scanned the room. The second alarm was tied to a hologram and never spawned in the same place twice. An evil invention designed to make sure you were awake and just a little annoyed, enough so that you would get out of bed, but not so much that your day would get off on the wrong foot. The small hologram, shaped like an orange cat, was sitting on top of her laundry basket.

Grace stumbled over and gently stoked the orange illusion from head to tail. The hologram sent back a feeling of soft fur as the sound changed from the blaring of the alarm to the purring of the cat. Grace knew that it wasn't a real cat—she hadn't seen one of those since before she left home—but it was still a calming force, a happy way to start the morning.

Everything about you is designed to calm, to assuage, the whisper in the back of her head thought. After a moment, she stopped petting the holographic feline, and it vanished, replaced by the lights in her room slowly starting to come on, increasing in intensity by five percent every ten seconds.

As the lights came up, the stark, bland whiteness of the small dorm room assaulted her eyes. Bed, desk, shelf, kitchenet, and bathroom. The facility didn't spend extra on comfort and Grace never spent enough time in her room to worry about it. Aside from filling her shelf and desk with books, there was nothing in the room that displayed her personality. She had been told to leave most of it at the door when they hired her, and she had. No posters, no pictures, no journal, not even her diplomas. Just her books. Though, to be fair, having printed books, in this day and age, was considered something of a personality quirk. How interesting it was that the only personality in the room belonged to the one she'd been meant to leave behind.

Emily and her books.

It was time to get started, today was an important day. Grace dropped her night clothes into the hamper. Next to the hamper was a small coffee pot, which she got going before heading to the bathroom. The water in the shower was warm when she stepped in. On the wall, the timer started. The Olympus Ares Research facility was completely self-sufficient, recycling everything, so things like showers were tightly controlled and timed. A researcher could request longer ones as their luxury item—everybody was entitled to two. Grace didn't need to sit and think under hot water—at least, not at the expense of her books. Their weight alone had constituted a luxury item, something both extremely important to her and completely frivolous at the same time. Many of her fellow researchers' luxuries were food or booze. Her lab mate had brought with him a quilt that had been in his family for ten generations, burning climate credits to keep his room cold enough to always sleep with it.

The timer for the coffee and the shower went off at the same time. Grace flicked a switch that started blowing hot air on her body. Wringing out her long black hair, she made sure every drop of water made it back into the drain—the last thing she wanted was to be accused of wasting it. A minute later, the blowing stopped and she was dry.

Stepping out of the shower, Grace walked over to her closet that had rows and rows of the same outfit: khaki pants, a blue button up shirt, and white lab coat. Quickly, she dressed and then poured the coffee into her steel travel mug that was emblazoned with the symbol of the Olympus Ares Research Facility. Current styles and fashion were not something that the organization running the facility worried about. She knew that this uniform was horribly out of style, by a hundred years, if not more. Yet she enjoyed the simplicity of it all.

Some things did not need to change.

Today was the big day, the day that they were going to turn on the gate, to see if they could stabilize it before drawing too much power and shutting the facility down again. The scale of what they were doing weighed on her mind as she sipped her coffee. Reaching into her pocket, she pulled out her pad and started scrolling through messages; looking to see if there was anything that stood out as important, that she should address before heading in, that might be too sensitive to look at on the tram.

Everybody at Olympus Ares had ocular implants that prevented them from seeing things they were not authorized to see. The feeling of needing to keep secrets in an analogue way was a holdover from her university days. No school, save for the military academies on the most affluent of worlds, could afford this kind of technology. Unless you were in the Confederation, where technology like this was unheard of. Those poor backward people. Grace had met a few citizens of he Confederation, and they were always impressed by the most mundane things. If it didn't help you sell shit or kill people, their scientists were not terribly interested in it.

Emily would have fit right in, Grace thought ruefully.

One of her alma maters, Khornburge Collage of Math and Science, had done some amazing research but instituted lackluster security protocols. The year after she graduated with her second PhD, their systems had been compromised. Decades of research paid for by the Free Worlds Alliance leaked onto the net. All because a mid-level researcher had checked his messages after spending a night with a conveniently affordable escort. After reading about that debacle, she had started to be extra careful, even as the universities she worked at became more and more secure, leading to Olympus Ares, which was so secure that most people didn't even know it existed.

Today there were no messages of high clearance that required her attention, everything appeared set. But still, a strange feeling persisted inside Grace's gut. There would be a second wave of messages to check once she got in, ones that didn't leave the lab. Only then would she feel better.

Looking up from her cup, Grace could see the equation from her dream. The one that was perched on a knife's edge, wobbling from side to side, refusing to balance itself, no matter what she did. The numbers hung in front of her, written in a golden wispy hue. Reaching her hand up, Grace moved an integer and changed an exponent. The formula still hung in her view, refusing to balance itself, changing and mutating like something was wrong with it, as if it existed in a world where the laws of math and physics as they were understood did not exist. Grace closed her eyes and shook her head, erasing the vision from her mind. Most days, the ability to visualize mathematics was her greatest asset, but when there was something that triggered her anxiety, the equations she saw would always be wrong, unsolvable.

Where was Emily when she needed her?

Everything is fine, the gate is going to open. You don't need her, Grace thought, pushing the insecurity away as she finished her coffee and put the cup into the recycler to be cleaned.

Flight bay, Dreadstar *Fury*, Alexander

Alexander Cordova, first of his name, stood at the top of the transport ship's gangplank looking out over the large hanger bay. It had been over a year since he had last been home. No matter how long he was away from *Fury*, returning made him feel like a schoolboy again.

If anybody outside the family asked, he was still in school, going for a second degree in physics. In reality, Alexander was on a research team whose work was so secret, so compartmentalized, he couldn't even tell his family about it. Even a family that included a high-ranking member of the admiralty. A family that controlled one of the last Dreadstars in existence.

He, of course, wasn't here to *only* keep secrets. A part of Alexander relished the idea of having a secret that even his mother didn't know. Something related to the military that was strictly for him, a civilian. It had caused friction last time, though, spoiling the fun. He hoped that had passed so that they could enjoy the fleeting moments they could spend together. Eventually, Project Far Step would come to light, and he would be allowed to tell them everything.

Secrets aside, Alexander was here to see his family before catching another ship to NovaTerra for his tournament. Festival week was upon them all. A time when all NovaTerra and her child worlds came together to elect the Minister of the People. Yes, it was a purely political affair to elect the minister, but everything around it—the feasts, the card games, the balls—*that* was what festival week was truly about. A time when everybody came together and put aside their grievances and remembered that they were one people, one Confederation. After the week was over and the banks and schools reopened, they could return to the normal, petty squabbles, but for that week, it was time to have fun. Perfect for him, as whenever Alexander wasn't at the research lab—times which were fewer and fewer, these days—he ensured that fun was top of mind.

Alexander tugged on his black vest, inlaid with blue holographic chimeras, and started to walk down the gangplank. Everybody else on the ship was in military blues, but he cut a fashionable swath, with his black vest and cravat over a white shirt. His jacket was a bright vibrant banana yellow, the piping and buttons silver. His pants were a deep navy blue, like the jackets that the rest of his family wore daily, coming just below his knees where his white stockings took over. On his feet were black shoes with golden buckles. Holding his long, jet-black hair in place was a yellow ribbon tied in a fancy bow, hiding the metal claw clip that was actually doing the work.

Looking out over the crowd, he saw a figure walking quickly toward the ship, the busy deck hands parting as he walked by. Even from a hundred yards away, Alexander recognized his older brother. He wanted to run to him, to embrace him with a large hug. That was not proper, though. No, he would just have to match his brother's quick and joyful gait. Down the gangplank he went, bobbing and weaving through the crowd. While he might have been third in line to inherit command of *Fury*, he was not as well known here as the rest of his family. The older deck hands who never left the flight deck might still remember him as the little girl who ran around the ship with her twin sister, causing chaos. That was a long time ago, and he cut quite a different silhouette these days.

It took only a few minutes for them to reach each other.

"Brother!" Alexander called out, stopping and throwing his arms wide. Anywhere else and this would have been too much of a faux pas of etiquette. The *Fury* was theirs, though, and a little leeway was allowed. Erik closed the ground and embraced his brother.

"It has been far too long, brother, far too long," Erik said, clapping him on the back. There was silence and then the two brothers pulled themselves apart. "You are striking quite the style, I see."

"This old thing?" Alexander said, looking down at his outfit. "We don't get to accessorize on project, so when one travels, one must go in style."

"You shall get no argument from me. The family colors always did look good on you," Erik said.

"We all bleed the same black and gold, brother," Alexander said. There was a pause. "I was much distressed to hear about your dust up at Hyroncore, much distressed. Word didn't reach us until just two months ago."

Erik looked down, taking a deep breath, his hand falling, gripping the hilt of his sword. His ungloved hand almost turned red as it wrapped tightly around the gold and ivory of the hilt.

"I have hit a sore subject, I see," Alexander said.

"The wounds of that day are still raw. There was no way for you to know, sweet brother. The reports of that battle have been downplayed. We can't let the whole Confederation know just how close those rogue space lords and their corsair allies came to taking down a Dreadstar," Erik said. He leaned in close. "We lost many—and mother, she has not been the same since."

Alexander was taken slightly aback. Mother had always been the rock that held the ship together. If a battle had shaken her to the core, it must have been quite the row. It *had* put the ship in dry dock for the better part of a year.

"Does she still keep her council with Tiberius?" Alexander asked. "I know he will help with perspective."

"Ambassador Tiberius was killed in the engagement," Erik said. "Caution, dear brother. Do not speak lightly of that day. Mother is still raw at you for leaving. Now, I fear her wrath might be heightened. She was not interested in speaking of your visit."

"Then I shall go and present myself to her presently," Alexander said. He might not be a warrior, but he wasn't one that ran from hard conversations. Had he known the true extent of the battle, he would have dropped his research instantly and come to his family's side.

"I would advise against that. We shall all see each other tonight. Dinner is at the same time, as always, in the family chambers," Erik said. Alexander read the graveness in his voice and didn't press the matter.

"Well, then, I shall just have to keep myself occupied until then," he said.

"On that front, I might be able to help. I had the deck crew find Fox to let her know you were home," Erik said. Alexander laughed and slapped his brother on the back.

"Brother, you read my mind. I know my old friend well enough that I should be able to find her on my own," Alexander said.

"I shall leave you to it then, brother. See you tonight. Do not be late. And perhaps a slightly less garish outfit. You know how mother feels about holographic needlework," Erik said.

"Yes, of course, of course. My stateroom is still free?" Alexander asked.

"I had them make it up for you yesterday, and the ship's boy knows to take your sea chest there," Erik said, giving his younger brother a bow and a flourish before turning and walking back into the throng of activity that was the flightdeck of a Dreadstar.

Alexander watched him go before turning and walking his own path. There was a small electrical closet on Hanger Deck Three. That was where he and Fox had always met up. Where together, they had lost their virtue.

The electrical closest was easy enough to find. He had been coming here for years and years. If somebody had asked Alexander Cordova to find something on the flight deck of *Fury* aside from this single room, he would have been lost. Dreadfully so, much to his mother's dismay. Here, though, this was a place he knew how to find and where he was most comfortable on the ship.

The door was locked. Alexander pressed in the four-digit code and crossed his fingers that it hadn't changed in the last few years. The mechanism clicked. He took a deep breath and spun the wheel on the door and pushed it open.

The small room was cast in shadow, the only light coming from a small red emergency bulb. It provided just enough light for him to see the edges of the four walls that were lined with shelves and filled with an absurd number of boxes full of cables.

She was on him before the hatch even closed.

Fox Windsail was a waif of a woman. Just under five feet tall, she had short brown hair and a hard angular face. She wore the same deck crew overalls as the Chief, but her tool vest was green, denoting that she worked in the electrical department. As her lips locked with his, the sparks flew as if they had not been apart for over a year. With his back foot, he kicked the hatch the rest of the way closed. It clicked, bathing them only in the dim red light.

Alexander didn't need light to know what Fox looked like, or how to move his hands across her body to pull off the uniform. She also didn't need illumination and was faster. He fumbled with her vest for just a moment, going for the one-handed unbuttoning. She pushed his hands away and slid down to her knees, quickly working the buttons of his trousers. A moment later, his cock was in her hand, and then between her lips. He took a deep breath as her tongue moved across his member. Placing a hand on her head, he ran his fingers through her damp and dirty short hair, pushing her into him.

After a minute, when she was satisfied with how hard he had become, she pulled away and took a step back, giving him a beckoning motion with her finger. Alexander followed, pulling off his jacket and slipping his legs out of his trousers. He was on top of her almost instantly, their lips locked again. This time, he pressed her against the small bare patch of cold steel wall. His hands quickly worked the snaps on the front of her vest. Pushing it aside, he grabbed her jumpsuit's zipper and pulled it down. It was only another finger flick to free her small breasts from the bra they were in. Fox moaned as he took her nipple into his mouth. She ran her hands into his black hair, pulling it slightly.

He couldn't move his head, and didn't want to. His right hand ran along her other breast. The electrical room was cold, and her other nipple was already stiff. Alexander slid his other hand down into her jumpsuit, rubbing the edge of her cunt, which was already wet and needy. Fox pulled his head away from her nipple and kissed him deeply, then shoved Alexander to the ground. She kicked off her boots and climbed out of the jumpsuit. Before he knew it, she was naked and had taken his throbbing member inside of her.

Thrusting, he enjoyed feeling her around him, the soft warmth of her. Reaching up, he pulled her down so that they could kiss again while still coupled. She let out a soft moan and then rolled them both so that Alexander was on top. A few minutes of rolling and thrusting before both of them reached climax, doing their best to keep the sound down, lest one of the deck officers walk in on them.

"It has been far too long since I'd had you inside me. Let us never do that again," Fox whispered into Alexander's ear as they lay together on the steel deck, using his yellow coat as a blanket.

"I shall try not to. Not having your touch while away has been the biggest burden of all," he said. "I wanted to talk to you about that, while I was here."

"Not now, Alexander. Can't we just enjoy the moment?" she asked.

He knew this conversation was going to be a pain point, but also knew that it was something he had to get off his chest. He and Fox had been infatuated with each other since before they understood the concept of love, and lovers since they were able. Station and geography were always what kept them apart, what reared its ugly head time and time again to dampen their love.

"I don't have much time before I head out again," he said. "I talked to my administrator. He said as long as you pass all the checks, you can get hired onto the build team. You can come join me at the facility," Alexander said. He figured that would cheer her up. He had found a way that they could be together, and both follow their dreams.

"I can't leave. My place is here on *Fury*," she said, pulling away from him and sitting up. "I can't just leave them, not after what we have been through; the blood we have spilled together."

Alexander huffed and sat up behind her, wrapping his arms around her, running his hands along the gooseflesh that was forming on her back.

"They would understand. Nobody would fault you for leaving. Leaving for an opportunity to do good things, amazing things. *Leaving for love.*" He whispered the last part into her ear, nibbling on her lobe as he finished.

"It is not that simple. This is my home. I was *born* here. I've never known anything else. I don't get to go to parties and balls, galivanting across civilization like you. These people here are all I know," she said, leaning into his touch.

"You would have me, though. We would be together. Sure, there would be an adjustment, but you would excel at what we do. Think of the things you could build. It would be more important than rewiring another Broadsword or the lights on the starboard fire control postern." He kissed her softly on the neck. She pulled away.

"That is just it. I love doing this, I am *happy* here. This is my home," she paused and tentatively bit her lower lip. "*You* could always come home. Come home and be with me."

Alexander recoiled at the notion faster than he realized he had, sitting up with his back ramrod straight. The thought was black in his mind, and the next words were ash in his mouth. Spoken in the kind of haste that they could not be stopped, even though regret followed before he was done speaking.

"And be what? A grease monkey like you? Some assistant to Dr. Friedrich? No."

"Of course not, because what I want isn't important. I'm just some grease monkey that you enjoy fucking." Fox stood up and started pulling back on her uniform. "It's always what Alexander Cordova wants. It is always *your* plan for *your* life. You asked me to wait and I *have* waited. But waiting implies that you are going to come back for more than just a few days every year." She put on her vest and boots.

"This is the best move. You don't want to be stuck here forever; you are too smart for that," Alexander said, trying to appeal to the intelligence he knew she was proud of. Fox wrapped her hands around a small badge on her green vest and pulled it forward.

"I am an electrician's mate third rate. Only three master electricians on the ship are above me. In another two years, I can take my Master's boards. I've already been approved. One day, I will be in charge of all this." She walked over and put her hand on a clump of wires that were running through the room, all neatly coiled and color coded. "I can feel the hum of power in the wires in this place. Why would I want to leave it?"

"Because you love me," Alexander said. It wasn't a question; it was a flat statement. His irritation was starting to bubble up from under the surface. "I went out of my way to arrange a job for you on an ultra-secret project, so that you could be with me forever. Instead of saying thank you, you just throw it back in my face, like it's just some petty little offer you aren't interested in. So you can... what? Stay here and toil until you are killed in some pointless engagement and forgotten?" His voice was loud, just under a yell. At some point, his hand had wrapped around Fox's arm, holding her in place.

"Let go of me," she said, pulling away from him. "I don't want or need your charity. Since that is all it is. Just a pity job so you can have steady cunt." Fox spun the wheel on the door and pushed it halfway open. "I see having a cock has really gone to your head." With that, she slipped out and slammed the door shut, leaving Alexander alone in the red darkness.

Well, that didn't go as I was hoping, Alexander thought bitterly as he stood up and readjusted his outfit, so he didn't look like he had just laid with a woman in the back of an electrical closet. There was a second door that exited into a service hatch and then out into the main walkway. It was why they had chosen to use this as their rendezvous point for all these years.

Picking up his yellow coat, he thew it over his shoulder. Walking up to the door, he put his hand on the latch and paused.

Go back for her, you moron...

His hand started to slide off the latch.

No, she made up her mind. That was clear enough.

Taking a deep breath, Alexander pushed open the door. He didn't want to be here any longer. It was time to move forward.

The hallway was empty as he started walking. Then, from the corner of his eye, he saw a young man with blond hair dressed in a fighter pilot uniform, dark trousers, and an open space jacket. Pilots on standby duty were not required to wear their blues, lest the ship get called into rapid action.

"Ander Stormwind, you villain!" Alexander yelled out. The man stopped and spun around on the heel of his large boot. There was a look of anger and surprise on his face that melted away as soon as he saw Alexander. The two men walked over and embraced in a hardy and manly fashion.

"How has university been treating you, old boy?" Ander asked. He had a deep northern accent compared to the more proper Novagrad speech of the Cordovas.

"Quite well. They keep us terribly busy."

"What is it that you are prattling away the years on again?"

"Theoretical physics. Math that is far, far over your head, my friend," Alexander said.

"In one ear, out the other, I know. Give me a solid fighter over anything else," Ander said, rubbing his nails long the edge of his jacket where his flight badge was. Alexander stifled a chuckle. Ander Stormwind thought he was the best pilot aboard *Fury*. That honor fell to his cousin, Bella, but Ander had the confidence to think he was that man. Nobody was terribly interested in telling him otherwise, and Alexander knew deep down that Ander knew that he was middling at best. He kept up the bravado by flying mostly with green recruits, so his reputation looked intact, most days.

"Men like me make sure those fighters keep moving forward. Otherwise, you would just be floating, dead once the magnets flung you off the ship," Alexander said.

"I guess that is true," Ander said, glancing at the way he was going. "I don't suppose you have your deck on you?" he asked.

Ander reached into his jacket pocket and pulled out a small silver box that he slid open. Inside were thirty richly illustrated playing cards covered with numbers and text. Alexander cocked his head to the side, giving his friend a look, mixed with a little shock and disgust.

"Who do you think I am, man?" Alexander asked, reaching into the inside pocket of his yellow jacket and removing an identical silver case. Inside was a deck of thirty cards for Peculiar Pentagon—the most popular competitive card game across the entire Confederation.

"In fact, I am only here for a quick stop before heading to NovaTerra early to play in the Festival Tourney," Alexander said.

"Then you are in luck, sir. I was heading to a pickup game with the flight squadron, and we can always use an extra if you are looking for some practice," Ander said.

"That sounds like a smashing idea. Lead on, good sir," Alexander said, motioning forward. He fell in behind Ander Stormwind, throwing on his yellow coat with a flourish. If he was going to show up to a card game full of pilots who he was about to beat bloody—allowing at least *one* thing to go his way, since Fox had rejected him and his mother was still angry with him—he might as well look smart doing it.

Space, Lucas

Up is a relative term, Lucas Brandice repeated to himself as he kept his head pointed down. All around him, the stars taking on an elongated form as space rushed by. Far ahead, still only a pinprick, was his target: a luxury cruise ship—the *Sequin Dream*—that had been taken over by pirates. Negotiations had failed and now it was down to his team of Host'ire Rangers to recover the ship and save the passengers.

The pirates had been getting more brazen now that hijacking massive cargo ships had lost its profitability, since shipping companies had started bio-tagging all their cargo. So, if the cargo was taken off the ship without the right scans, or reported stolen, the containers would destruct on the inside, ruining the cargo. Everything was insured so all that was lost were shipping crews, and nobody gave a damn about them. So, pirates had turned to hijacking ships. Companies might not care to recover cargo, or their crews, but rich passengers were another matter.

Thus, they had sent Lucas and his five-man team. The plan was simple: they'd drop from their ship, which was outside of the *Sequin Dream's* scanner range. They would traverse through space using the inertia from the rockets on their suits to reach the cruise ship. While she might be a big ship, her scanner package was lacking in robustness when it came to detecting things like five wizard knights flying through space toward them.

Up is a relative term, he reminded himself again. There was no up in space but what you said was up. As such, he had determined that the ship they were falling from was up and the one they were heading toward was down. It kept everything clean and focused. As soon as you forgot what was up and what was down in the void, you were lost. It was an axiom that also applied to life. Lucas knew all too well about having trouble knowing up from down, right from wrong. Life as a Host'ire Knight could do that to you.

A memory tugged at the back of his mind. Something unknown, a light feeling of déjà vu. He discounted it, kept moving forward.

They were getting close now. Lucas took a deep breath and activated the heads-up display on his visor. The ship came into focus, as did their angle of attack. It was a series of red arrows superimposed upon the vacuum of space. Even with a computer assist, the landing was going to be tricky. That was why they were not going to use the computers. This was one of the moments when being a Knight-Commander of the Host'ire rangers came in handy.

They were not normal warriors, or ambassadors. No, they had the ability to see beyond into the Null, the place between the material world and whatever lay beyond. Their connection to the Null allowed them to exert great control over the material world. Some people called it magic, and to those who lacked understanding, it was.

Lucas, having now confirmed everything through the computer, switched it off. He raised the blast shield over his helmet. The stronger the Host'ire, the harder it was for them to block out the Null, because it was always seeping into the material world like light coming through a poorly sealed door. To limit their exposure, most days they wore sunglasses, while in space, they kept down their blast visors. Right now, he needed his connection without any interruption or barrier.

The *Sequin Dream* shone brightly through the Null, all the energy and life that was aboard the ship turning it into a small star. Closing his eyes, Lucas could feel the four other rangers behind him. Their blast visors were up as well. Their minds had reached out and were wrapped around him like cords of rope. They were relying on him to guide them in. Their chosen landing point was a small platform on the side of the ship, close to an engineering hatch. The radiation from the ion engines would hide them from anybody that might be watching. They had been given the command codes to the hatch by the ship's owners so they could enter without triggering any alarms.

Lucas closed his eyes for a moment and focused on his hand, creating a rope inside the Null that he could feel and see. Once he had the rope in his hand, he opened his eyes and again focused on the point where they were going to land, pushing his vision further than even the camera on his suit could go with any clarity. Once he had the landing point in view, Lucas threw the rope out, guiding it with an unseen hand, clamping it to the hatch of the door. He gripped the rope with both hands and pulled himself forward, making sure he always knew which way was up. Once they reached the landing pad, it was time to enter the ship and get to work.

"Everybody ready and steady," Lucas said, looking over his team. Each of them nodded an affirmative. Lucas placed his hands on the wheel that had the door locked and gave it a solid turn. After a moment, the door was open. The knights filed into the small airlock and Lucas quickly went through the venting and pressurization protocols. The red light above them turned green.

Flicking a switch, he pulled off his helmet and took a breath of fresh, recycled atmosphere. There was a hint of orange and lavender hanging in the air, a demonstration of how rich those who traveled aboard the *Sequin Dream* were. Lucas flicked his head to the right and then left, letting some of his long black hair fall out of the tight bun that it was in. Reaching into a pocket, he pulled out a pair of dark glasses and put them on, quieting the sound and vision of the Null around him.

The rest of his team followed in kind, pulling off their helmets and gloves. Their suits were designed to operate as both space and combat suits—only the gloves and helmets needed to be removed. Each Host'ire Knight still had on their standard black leather gloves under the heavy space gloves.

In a wedge, the four knights stood around Lucas. There was Hobbs, a large man with dark skin and locs, a scar across his dead right eye. Next to him was Sellers. She was shorter, with a series of tightly coiled buns containing her pink hair and had opted for Null dampening contact lenses as opposed to glasses, causing her eyes to look like black voids. Jung-jae had a strong jaw and kept his black hair short and styled so that it was connected to the pencil-beard that ran along his jaw line. He had a custom pair of glasses, one lens was Null-darkening-black, and the other had the ability to change color, allowing him to focus on different aspects of the Null, such as people, energy, and emotions. Lastly, there was Miller. Nobody knew what she looked like. Even under the heavy space helmet, she wore a mask with a rebreather and flat glass cover. She didn't speak, only motioning with her hands and sending feelings through the Null to her comrades.

"Okay people, the mission here is simple. Hobbs, Miller, you will head to engineering, eliminate any hostiles there and take control of the ship via secondary systems. Sellers, Jung-jae, and I will head to the lower level where they are keeping the hostages." The team all looked at each other and then at Lucas and nodded.

Lucas cracked his knuckles and reached down to his belt. Haning there was a sword hilt, missing a blade. It was a fancy hilt with an ivory handle and golden cross guard. On the handle was a small button that would activate the star-steel blade as soon as there was trouble and not a moment before. Each member of the team also had a blade hanging on their side, ready for battle.

The *Sequin Dream* was populated by ghosts and flashes of previous violence. One group of dead were the ship's under-prepared security forces, killed making an ill-advised last stand. Another was a passenger who had been made an example of. Both were grizzly sights of over-the-top violence that made Lucas's blood boil. He was not against the use of violence, but only in a measured way, against those who were capable of doling it out in return. Those who were innocent were to be protected at all costs. These pirates were no better than animals in his mind.

He had seen violence like this before. Hollister 9. The Fellowship.

Lucas breathed in and out, centering himself, moving those memories to the dark places in his mind where they belonged.

A sound caught the edge of his ear, the pitter-patter of bare feet, followed by a child's laughter. Lucas held his hand up in a fist, stopping the group behind him. Something was wrong. There shouldn't be any children on this ship.

Taking a deep breath, Lucas closed his eyes and tapped into the Null, reaching out to look for the child. He could hear the feet again and a gruff voice yelling at the child to stop running. Returning to the real world, he slowly took another step forward, creeping around the next corner. Just on the edge of his sight, he saw—or thought he saw—the shadow of a young boy running, his laughter turning sour as he faded from view, a shadow with one arm following him.

"Did you feel anything strange?" he asked, turning to Sellers and Jung-jae. They both gave him blank looks and shook their heads.

Nothing, then. Remember which way is up, Lucas thought, signaling the group to move forward.

There were always echoes of the past, pockets of emotion that didn't leave a place. Some Host-ire were more sensitive to them than others. This was a bad time for Lucas to be sensitive to the echoes. Last time Lucas had seen shadows, he pinched off his connection to the Null and let them fade. That wasn't an option, not with this mission. There was only one way forward. He would be fine, as long as he remembered which way was up.

Entering the room, Lucas saw three pirates—three dead men.

The star-steel blade came to life with a heartbeat thrum; the searing green blade of energy grew from the hilt in Lucas's hand until it was a meter long. A pirate heard the sound, starting to spin around, living just long enough to realize his life was over. The blade came smashing down into the top of his head, turning the man's face into a melted ruin before Lucas's blade exited through the dead man's jaw. The body hung there for a moment before crumpling to the deck like a rag doll.

The other two pirates were quicker on the uptake, getting their plasma pistols out and firing. Lucas side-stepped the first bolt of plasma and lazily deflected the second one back with the blade of his sword. The super-heated plasma round smashed into the chest of the pirate that had fired it, burning through him. The energy and life faded from his body, his shoulders going limp first before he fell. The third pirate dropped his gun and threw his hands into the air. Prisoners were trouble, but once they had surrendered, Host'ire rules of engagement dictated that violence could no longer be inflicted upon them.

Lucas signaled to Sellers, who reached into her belt and pulled out a zip tie and a bag. A moment later, the pirate was on his knees, his hands tied behind his back and a black hood over his face. Anybody who surrendered would be immobilized and left where they were. It would be up to the Confederation authorities who would come through later to decide the surrenderers' ultimate fate. If it was one of the more enlightened houses, it probably would be jail time. If it was one of the houses who used private military security forces, then Lucas and his team were more than likely condemning these prisoners to the cold vacuum of space. That was the way of the world and there wasn't much he could do to stop it. Actions had reactions. Up was up, down was down.

"The ballroom ahead is where the majority of the life signs are coming from," Jung-jae said, pointing in front of them. Lucas sauntered forward, taking off his glasses.

What came next was why people feared and respected the Host'ire.

"Watch my back and keep the rules of engagement in mind," Lucas said.

With that, he pushed open the door and walked into the ballroom as if he owned the place. Sitting on the floor were thirty civilians. All of them were dressed in fancy clothing, Confederation style formal wear: long coats, vests, tight pants and cravats, flowing dresses created from the best holographic fabrics that NovaTerra had to offer. These were not the kind of people Lucas ever interacted with, his entire experience with the Confederation capitol being the few times he had been called to the Host'ire temple. He didn't understand them, but that was not a requirement to save them.

The rough armed pirates walking around in their patch work outfits, he understood *them.* Twenty years as a Ranger on the edge of civilized space had given Lucas an affinity for the broken and the downtrodden, if not a good understanding of them. It was why he had joined the Rangers instead of becoming a Host'ire Knight for hire to some random noble house, killing at the whim of the rich and powerful while reporting their every move back to his masters at the Temple and Citadel. That life did not appeal to Lucas. There was something wrong living that way. It did nothing to make civilization better, and if that was not the goal of people who had power, then what were they even doing out here?

"Afternoon, fellas. How are we doing today?" Lucas asked as he walked into the room, holding his hands in the air.

The pirates raised their guns. Lucas could feel the tension spiking their emotional state causing them to glow deeper in the Null.

"Woah now, let's calm down, shall we? No need to get itchy trigger fingers. I'm just here to talk," Lucas said, motioning with his fingers for them to lower the weapons, while keeping his hands in the air. The pirates didn't lower their weapons, but they also didn't shoot him, which Lucas considered a win.

"Which one of you has the ability to speak for the group—or are you all just kind of hoping that somebody over the radio will save you from having to make any decisions?" Lucas asked. There was no point trying to talk them down if none of them had any power to affect the rest of the ship.

Thankfully, one pirate stepped forward. She was a tall woman with dusty skin and long green hair tied into braids adorned with golden bangles. Clipped to her belt was a mundane saber and, in her hand, an antique plasma revolver. She definitely had the markings of a leader, if not *the* leader of this group.

"I speak for the Thrown Circle Clan," she said, leaning the massive pistol against her shoulder. "You can call me Chartreuse." Her accent was thick. Lucas couldn't place it.

"Well Chartreuse, I'm Knight-Commander Lucas Brandice of the Host'ire, but I suspect you already figured that out. I'm here to take these people off your hands," he said.

"Over my dead body—unless you and your order have started paying for normal folk," Chartreuse said.

"The corpses of you and yours are well within my operating orders, but if we can prevent that, I would prefer it," Lucas said. There were plenty of corpses at his feet already and there would be plenty more. Anything to lessen that number was appreciated.

"We are in House Rook space. Surrender makes us as good as dead," she said, taking the pistol off her shoulder and tapping the long barrel in her open hand.

"Extradition is the best that I can offer you. There is no money to be had here today. You know that, and I know that," Lucas said.

"I don't know... Maybe we should just capture ourselves some Host'ire. See if your order will pay for you?" Chartreuse said, gesturing with the weapon in her hand. It made Lucas uneasy, but he held his ground and kept his hands up. He was going to have to trust in the Null to alert him to any coming violence.

"You are most certainly willing to try, but I wouldn't recommend it. There is less money in that than..." As he spoke, Lucas heard the pitter-patter of children's feet again. This time, there was no laughter—just yelling, fear, and anger.

He whipped his head around, trying to gauge where it was coming from, turning his attention away from Chartreuse briefly. Another child's voice joined in, adding words, but he couldn't make them out. Worlds that were lost in time, in memory.

"Than what? Our star-steel melted and mangled corpses?" Chartreuse demanded, breaking Lucas out of the daze. His eyes darted around the ballroom. There were no children, nowhere for them to run. It was just him, the pirates, and their hostages.

Something about that feeling hung in his mind. It tasted like a long-ago memory, the kind that was more feeling than anything else. Diving into the Null, he tried to find that feeling, but there was nothing; no residual energy, not even an echo. Null echoes, though, were not his specialty.

"Null got your tongue, Knight?" Chartreuse asked. The gun was pointed at him again, irritation washing across her face. Whatever echo he'd felt was gone. All that was left was a jumpy, pissed off pirate that he most definitely was not going to be able to talk down. Especially not after his distraction.

Lucas knew that this was where he was supposed to say something smart and quippy, but his mind was no longer in the moment, lost to whatever strange sounds he'd heard. The situation was just a hair away from being beyond his control, and Chartreuse did have a point about the brutality of justice under House Rook. The hilt of the star-steel blade was in his hand and arching through the air before anybody heard the heartbeat thrum of the weapon coming to life. The green blade sliced through the plasma revolver in the Pirate leader's hand like it wasn't there. She dropped the weapon, jumping back.

"Kill them," Chartreuse hissed, drawing her sword.

It was too late for the pirates, though. Sellers and Jung-jae had positioned themselves on the other side of the room, dropping out of the shadows, the purple and red from their respective blades driving away the darkness. Chartreuse charged Lucas, swinging her sword. He stepped to the right, then the left, giving her ground each time. He was able to see the third swing coming, a forward echo in the Null giving away the move. He reached up, grabbing her arm, and then rammed his blade through her gut. Life drained from her eyes as the smell of burning cloth and flesh filled the room. Lucas let go of her arm and the pirate leader fell to the ground. Less than thirty seconds after the violence had started, it was over. All five pirates were on the ground in bloody piles. None of the hostages had been harmed.

With their leader dead, the rest of the pirates of the Thrown Circle Clan folded, giving themselves over to whatever justice they would find from House Rook. His team secured them in the ship's morgue and Lucas returned control of the *Sequin Dream* to her remaining crew, and as quickly as they had arrived, the knights of the Host'ire were gone, leaving nothing but bodies and stories in their wake. It was how Lucas preferred it. The fewer people who knew about how they operated, the better. The mystic of the order was one of their most powerful weapons.

After a quick debriefing, Lucas returned to his quarters, stripping off the heavy armor and setting it in his closet. Clad only in his long sleeping pants, Lucas lit two candles and sat down cross-legged on the floor. He had been trying to shake the strange vision of the laughing and screaming children, yet it had refused to leave his mind, hanging there, trying to take root, but only finding stony soil. The voice had been familiar, but from where, he couldn't say. And none of the words stood out enough for him to remember them.

Closing his eyes, Lucas pushed into his mind where he kept his memories in an ordered fashion, filed away by years, feelings, and key words. It wasn't complete, especially for his early years, but it was a place to start. Just as he was about to dive in, a small beeping pulled him from his trance.

Lucas opened his eyes and saw the light beeping on his communication station. Taking a deep breath, he stood up and walked over, pressing the key. He had a new message. It was from an unknown address but encoded with Citadel encryption. The actual message was garbled like it was a cypher or code that the computer couldn't understand. All that Lucas could read from it was the word 'Help' and the signature.

It was signed 'Hyacinth'.

A sudden feeling of unease filled Lucas, as he could hear the children screaming again, their voices punctuated by a wet thumping sound. It made his skin crawl, sending goosebumps across his arms in a visceral, violent way. Lucas stumbled back from the computer.

The children were screaming again. This time, he understood the words.

"Get away from her!" the child's voice yelled.

His voice.

Dreadstar *Fury*, Cassandra

Lord Admiral Cassandra Cordova, first of her name and commander of the Dreadstar *Fury* and all its relevant holdings, was in a foul mood. All her moods of late had been foul. The things that had given her joy were gone, turned to ash. All that was left was duty and keeping up appearances.

Like her, the tram was moving painfully slow this morning. The alarm had gone off and the melancholy of being awake had replaced the comfort of dreams.

Play on, my love.

She pushed his voice away with a sigh. Nobody was on the tram, as she sat on the couch in the back. Her sword was sitting in her lap and the long blue coat with its golden braiding was spread to her side.

Lord Admiral Cordova was not one for fancy uniforms or fabrics. She believed in dressing for the station of her family and not what the rest of them aspired to be. She was a commander of a ship of the line. It was the biggest ship, yes, but still just a ship that owed its allegiance to the Confederation. Too many Space Lords, in her opinion, dressed like they were landed lords, draping their coats with holograms and lights, actual metal in their braiding and fancy fabrics. Her coat was wool, her shirts and pants linen. There were things she spent money on and quirks of flourishing, but her uniform outside of an official function wasn't one of them.

This was the last day she was going to be able to give into her malaise. During the six months that they had been in dry dock, on days when she didn't feel like being perceived by the crew, or even family, staying in her cabin was an option. There was always paperwork to be done. Cassandra preferred to do paperwork when sad, since then it couldn't foul up one of the few good days.

However, they'd all been bad days since the battle of Hyroncore. The battle where she had walked them knowingly into a trap. She had not thought the pirates in possession of forces able to stand up to a Dreadstar. They didn't. But with the two rogue houses, Tok and Cannon, they had put up a good fight and almost won. She should have known that the cruise liner was bait. It'd been bait she couldn't afford to ignore. They had saved a few people that day, but the liner never stood a chance. There was no way to fight off the attackers and protect the civilian ship before the bombs went off. With no good choices that day, she hoped that the ones she'd picked were the least bad of the shit provided to her. History would decide that fact, once her body had been returned to the cold dark void of space.

Play on, my love; something new, something happy.

He wasn't supposed to be in her waking thoughts anymore, yet always there he was.

The tram came to a gentle gliding halt, the magnets driving it switching polarity. The doors on both sides opened with a hiss. A single man walked in. He was tall, a little younger than her, mid-fifties, and gaining size in the midsection. His coat was white and trimmed in black. His pants and undershirt were also white, while his vest was yellow and cravat blue. Pinned on both sides of his high collar were golden caduceus. He didn't wear a sword, but in his hand were two metal mugs.

Her younger brother, Doctor Joseph Cordova, walked over and sat down next to her, handing her one of the drinks. She could feel the liquid's warmth through the stainless steel. The smell of fresh coffee wafting across her nose.

"You missed our breakfast this morning, dear sister," he said. His tone was too familiar in public. If it had been anybody besides her younger brother, she'd have had them clapped in irons for the afternoon.

That's harsh, Cassandra. Don't let your pain make you that person, she thought.

"The melancholy came again and turned my stomach," she said flatly. The smell of the coffee was welcome, reminding her that she hadn't eaten anything even though it was already high morning. Far past time she should have been in the CIC.

"You know, there are people you can talk to about that. You needn't suffer alone; we are all here for you," Joseph said in a soft, pleading voice, the voice of a man who healed and listened. That wasn't what she needed right now; wasn't what she wanted.

"I will not submit my mind to your brain butchers," Cassandra said quietly, taking a sip from her coffee. It was fresh and had just the correct amount of sugar and cream. If this couldn't help her mood, then there was no hope for the day.

"Brain butchers... That sounds like the name of gang from lower Terra. Fine, you don't have to talk to one of them, but you *should* be talking to us, your family. That is what we are here for," he said. Joseph raised his hand to comfort her. She glared at him. He pulled it back.

"Those of you that are here," she bit out under her breath.

"That isn't fair. You couldn't expect him to stay. There was nothing here for him," Joseph said.

"*We* were here," she said quietly.

"A boy needs to find his own way in the world. That is what he is doing. You should be proud. Mother and father would have been ecstatic if either of us had gotten onto a project that was so secret that they didn't know what it was," her brother said. He was right, but she didn't want to hear it, didn't want to be pulled out of the foul mood she was in. The morning had been trying to tell her something, that there was no point finding comfort today.

"Honor, duty, family. Erik and Hanna didn't have a problem understanding that; didn't have a problem finding that here," Cassandra said.

"Erik's a pilot and your heir. Where was he going to go? And Hanna, she is nothing like her twin, except they have the same nose and eyes. She is just a shorter version of you, sister," Joseph said. "What could you have offered Alexander here? Working on the deck, navigation?"

Cassandra didn't want to talk about Alexander. His absence made her sad, and that emotion always dovetailed into anger and resentment. Too many had been lost already. So, she said nothing, and took another sip from her coffee.

"His ship arrived this morning," Joseph said.

"I am perfectly aware of that fact, doctor. I approved the flight logs and manifest. There are no secrets from me aboard my own ship."

Cassandra took another sip of her coffee. Something no longer sat right with her. She closed the lid and set it in the small cup holder beside her.

"Are you going to send for him, have a talk?"

"We will see each other at dinner tonight. That will be sufficient," Cassandra said, standing up. Clipping her sword to her belt, she walked over to the door. She had to sway with the train to keep her footing without grabbing any of the handrails. A Lord Admiral could not be seen holding handrails, even if the only person in the train car was her brother.

"The new Host'ire Ambassador arrives tomorrow afternoon on the last transport," Joseph said. Cassandra's face bunched up into a scowl. Even with her back turned on her brother, she suspected that he knew what expression was on her face. He had that frustrating habit of knowing her better than herself somedays.

"We shall see about that," Cassandra said as the tram came to a stop and the doors opened.

Gripping her sword with her right hand and placing her left at the small of her back, she smartly walked off. The stop for the command deck was crowded but everybody made way for her before packing into the train.

Library, Khorn'tosh Academy, Joanna

"I'm sorry we don't have any more copies of that in right now," Joanna Pike said, not looking up from her computer.

"Look," the young man started. She glanced at him over her sunglasses. He had on a tight leather vest, puffy white shirt and green cravat, his red hair pulled back. "If I don't get a copy of that book, then I will fail Doctor Martin's class," he said. His voice reeked of boredom and entitlement.

"That isn't my fault. You should not have put off getting your texts until a week before Festival," Joanna said, finally looking up at the young man from where she was sitting at the intake desk.

"Listen, bitch. I'm going to make it your fault," he said, pointing a gloved finger at her. She didn't have time for this.

"Okay, I am going to stop you right there. I am a graduated and trained Knight of the Host'ire Order, and you are…" She was going to say something rude, but her supervisor had warned her to stop antagonizing the students.

"I am your better. Do you know who my father is?" he asked, placing both hands on the intake desk and leaning forward, hovering over Joanna.

Children. She could stand up. If she did, she would be at least a head taller than the young man. But she didn't want to get in trouble, *again.*

"We leave our families behind when we join the Order. We are all equal under the light of the Null," she said, repeating the words.

"Maybe for you base-born, Citadel-trained scrubs. Say that again when you have a name that matters," he said.

"Well then, if you are so important and your name matters so much, might I recommend you go and find that book at one of the shops on High Street?"

"I'm not going to spend that much on a book," he scoffed.

"Have fun explaining to Doctor Martin why you need an extension on your paper. Now, if you will excuse me," she said, standing up. As Joanna suspected, she was a head taller than the young man. She cut an imposing large figure—not sporty or gangly, just large.

Picking up her leather jacket, she pressed a button and turned the window of the intake desk black, signaling that they were closed. *Entitled highborn brats.* She didn't have the time or inclination to find their books for them. Library studies was a basic class here at the Khorn'tosh Academy. Of course, that meant that they didn't pay attention to it, if they even bothered to show up.

The Khorn'tosh Academy was where highborn Host'ire were trained. The order preached equality among members, but Joanna knew that to be one of the most egregious lies they told. All children who showed any aptitude with seeing the Null were, by law, taken into the order. In exchange for your child, the Confederation would give you thirty silver crypto credits. For a poor family, that was a decade's worth of money—if not more. For a rich highborn family, it was nothing. How then were the Host'ire to get rich lords to possibly sign over their heirs and children, if money was not an option?

Thus, the two schools were born. Poor children were sent to Icarus and The Citadel to be trained in the shadow of the Barrier and the Eye to Hell; beaten, broken, and turned into weapons. The rich and well-off were sent to Khorn'tosh to learn the same things they would have at any expensive elite academy, only this one also indoctrinated them into the Host'ire order. It crafted them into ambassadors and advisers; people close to political power while also being wizards. Some were even allowed to retain their titles, which Joanna thought was just a complete hypocrisy, but then, so much of what went on here was hypocrisy.

She was able to see the dichotomy because of her rare situation. Joanna had not been born into a rich family. Her father had tried to turn away the money. The kidnappers would not take no for an answer. So, she ended up at the Citadel. It was not a place for an overweight bookworm to be, but it was where she landed. In the end, she had made it work; worked enough that she now served at a library finding books for rich brats that didn't want to study. At least it usually left her some time for her own projects.

"Get away from them!" she heard the faint voice of a child scream.

Joanna spun around. There was nothing but rows and rows of books. Lost in thought, she had wandered deep into the stacks. She knew the great library well and sometimes her feet operated independently of her mind. A chill ran up her back as she took a tentative step forward. There shouldn't have been children here. The stacks were closed off to the Academy's younger wards.

Each step she took moved her toward where she had heard the voice echoing in the cavernous concrete void. The sound cascaded off the rows and rows of old books, the collected history of humanity tucked away for only a few to see. Joanna rounded a corner, just in time to hear more footsteps—*children's* footsteps. On the other side of the corner was the main walkway that led a person from one set of stairs to the other, down past the rows.

There was a chill in the air, and she pulled her long leather jacket closer around her. Reaching up, Joanna pulled off her glasses, closing her eyes for a moment and pushing her eyelids against her corneas. She created two little starbursts of light in the darkness of her closed eyes, before opening them again. For normal people—mundanes, as the order called them—this was as close as they would get to the Null. For a fully trained Host'ire Knight, this was just the first step in opening your mind when looking for something. Now, there were pockets of bright light all around, places where the Null was leaking in; spots of great emotion, some even from books that had power threaded into them. She looked around, stepping quietly forward. There was nothing to see, nothing out of the ordinary.

"I said get away from them!" It was a boy's voice, this time, coming from behind her.

Joanna spun around again, her coat whipping against her legs. Her eyes darted between energy spikes. There was nothing. She took a deep breath and shook her head. She was too deep in the stacks for it to be actual children.

It's stress, Joanna. You are letting these punks get to you again, she thought, giving the area one last look just to be sure. Still, there was nothing. She wasn't going to chase ghosts in the stacks today.

The watch on her wrist buzzed. Joanna's focus was lost. Putting her glasses back on, she raised her arm and pressed the green call button on her watch. The Caller ID said that it was Archivist Moore.

"This is Pike, go ahead," she said.

"Libarian, we need to talk. Now," the angry voice said on the other end of the line. Joanna let out a sigh as her shoulders slumped down, and her eyes rolled back in her head. *Another pointless meeting*, she thought.

"Is this about that student that was trying to check out something we were out of?" she asked, figuring the spoiled brat had already gone and complained instead of trying to find a better way to get his assignment finished.

"No, but I suspect that's something I will have to deal with tomorrow. My office, now!" he said before the line went silent.

Joanna huffed and let her arm fall to her side. With all these interruptions, she was never going to be able to get any research done, let alone any writing. Her mind, full of irritation at her superiors, dismissed the strange voices she'd heard, falling away from her thoughts. Joanna turned and headed out of the stacks.

***

"Did you not read the ten messages you were sent?" Archivist Moore yelled at her as soon as she arrived. He sat behind his desk, a cigarette burning in his hand, his long gray hair hanging to his shoulders. He had a close-cropped beard and, with his small spectacle sunglasses, looked very much like a Glacier Park radical. Which was as far from the truth as possible.

"I looked at them," Joanna said, leaning back in her chair.

In reality, she had no idea what messages he was talking about. She had not checked her official messages in the last few days. There was never anything important in them, always meetings and policy changes that she was going to forget or ignore. Everybody that worked with Joanna Pike knew that if they wanted to get in contact with her, they needed to just ping her watch or leave a message with her AI calendar that kept her on task. Research had a tendency to consume her at the detriment of any real-life concerns.

"The messages that talked about new leadership, about not opening research into heretical topics, particularly during operating hours?" Moore asked, taking a long drag of his cigarette, holding the smoke in his mouth for a moment before blowing it out through his nose.

"You approved this line of questioning three years ago," she said, blinking. "They left thousands of pages of prophetic text to comb through."

They were the Wayfinders, a sect of humans that had the ability to chart faster-than-light travel through the Null. They had built the jump gates that held civilization together, and five hundred years ago, the Host'ire committed genocide against them. The official line was that humanity, with help from the Host'ire, fought a horrible war that ended with the death of every Wayfinder, but the documents she had been finding—those that were buried away—told a different story. One she was determined to pierce together.

"Not stopping you is far from giving you my approval," Moore said, shoving the cigarette down into the ashtray. "You were going to do it anyway."

"You made the correct choice and let me do my job and follow my research. I commend you for making one of the few good choices of your tenure," Joanna said. The Chief Archivist, like all forms of authority, brought out the snarky side of her. Some said it was the worst side of her, but she wasn't so sure about that.

"I avoided a fight, which is now at my doorstep because you couldn't accept your win with grace. No, you had to keep fighting with students, keep poking the system," Moore said, picking up the cellophane package and staring at it, as if contemplating pulling out another cigarette.

"But now, you are no longer my problem," he continued, picking up a folder and throwing it across the desk. Joanna reached down and picked it up. They were reassignment papers. She was being moved from her position in Research Assistance to Collections Management in the annex building, on the southern continent. Effective immediately.

"The hell is this?" she asked, dropping the papers.

"Something you can't ignore like an email," Moore said flatly, pulling out the smoke and flicking his lighter as he turned his chair around to look out the window.

A child screamed in the background, but Joanna couldn't focus on it. She let it fade away.

***

The whole thing was bullshit. Joanna threw the reassignment papers onto her apartment's table. She had so much work still to do at the main archive. The Wayfinder room hadn't even been opened to her yet. She wasn't going to go. They couldn't make her.

They can, you know they can, she thought, looking at the piles of papers in her office. Years of notes, with copies of many of the strange prophetic writings that the Wayfinders made before they were defeated in the war. She was convinced that if they had been able to see into the Null to guide ships, that they possibly could use that to see through space and time. She just needed to be able to prove it.

"Joanna, over here," a young boy's voice called. She whipped her head around so fast the braid of her purple hair hit her face. There was nothing to see, but the voice had been familiar. She couldn't place it. When was the last time she had even interacted with a child?

While there was no child to be seen, there *was* a blinking light on her workstation. A message. She took a deep breath and walked over, tapping the screen. The last thing she wanted was to open her email for once and find some kind of snide, 'sent-to-all' message from Archivist

Moore about her transfer. *Effective immediately, Joanna Pike is no longer staff at the central library.* She could see the words in her mind.

That was not what the message was, however. Instead, it had no address, no sender. The base of the text was garbled, and she could only make out a few words: 'Help, below, Heaven'.

It was signed, 'Hyacinth'.

Bits of memory came flooding back to her. A childhood spent under the thumb of people worse than Moore. Joanna took off her glasses and pressed her hands into her eyes, pressing away tears.

"I won't leave you," the child's voice said from her memory.

Pain and disappointment pushed through the callus exterior that she had spent the last twenty years building. The childhood owner of the voice locked into place: Lucas Brandice. They had gone to the Citadel together. She had followed him around like a lovesick puppy, even more than the rest of them. Feelings she lost in the haze of time and human memory came flooding back to her. Feelings that she didn't want to feel, but which moved her.

"I won't leave you," her memory repeated. Deep behind it, there was a wet thump. Joanna shuddered as the noise repeated in her mind, causing her to breathe faster and shed more tears.

Lucas had lied. He had left. *She* had left; all of them had.

Images of children standing covered in blood returned to her mind, shattered and broken; names and faces she hadn't thought about in years; the only friends she had ever had.

Joanna knew what she needed to do.

The Citadel was calling...

Black Hollow Stellar Observatory, Naomi

The Black Hollow Stellar Observatory was always breaking down. Corners had been cut building it and too much equipment had been rammed into the station. Still, through grit and determination, the Host'ire had been keeping it running for the last hundred and forty-seven years.

The observatory had been built for two functions: to observe and study the Barrier that cut off humanity from a large swath of what was assumed to be a larger galaxy and to keep an eye on the Unaligned Planets outside the Confederation. The Host'ire had a stranglehold on people who were sensitive to the Null inside Confederation space, but outside of it, from the Demilitarized Zone all the way to the event horizon of the Fissure, they had far less control. The order existed out there, but the patch work of governments, worlds, and even species made exacting their control much harder. And so, they watched, and waited, gathering all the data that they could for the day they eventually would make a move and gain control over those mundanes as well.

Naomi Perkins knew all these facts and did not care a lick about any of them. Her job on Black Hollow was to keep the station working. That task took all her energy, leaving no time to question the broader implications of what the Host'ire might have been doing with it. Naomi had been with the order her entire life, so even if she had taken a break to think about it, a contrary opinion would not have formed. The order had taken her in as a child after her parents died; fed her, educated her, taught her technology, and most importantly, helped hone her skills in the Null. Skills that were extremely useful to an electrical engineering repair tech.

"Mister Wood, could you pass me the hydrospanner, if you please?" she called up to her assistant.

Naomi was currently three levels down in an access tube covered in wires, a soldering gun clinched in her teeth and diagnostic tools attached to each of the fingers on her left hand. The imaging lens was acting up again. She had spent the last week working on the actual lens trying to track down the problem. The head researcher, a man by the name of Quinn, had insisted that something was wrong with the lens and its physical appearance. Naomi had disagreed. He overruled her and a week had been wasted taking measurements on refraction angles. She had seen the images in question, and it was clear to her then, and doubly clear to her now, that the problem had been inside the electronics of the imager and not the lens itself.

So, now that she had convinced Quinn of the *actual* problem, she was free to finally fix it. It had taken another week to get even to this point, fixing bugs and gremlins the whole way down, as the observatory tried to rip itself apart.

All in all, it was a standard Tuesday on the Black Hollow Observatory.

"Pray tell, which one is that again?" Wood's voice came from above.

Noami took a deep breath. He was far from the assistant that she wanted, but he was all the Host'ire would give her. He didn't know his tools apart and insisted on speaking like he was a highborn from NovaTerra. She knew he wasn't, but didn't have the heart to confront him about that fact. So, she played along, hoping that perhaps one day he would just take the time to learn the toolbox or read one of the manuals. She had rewritten most of them to be, in her opinion, far more user friendly.

"Long neck, green lights; it should be two down from the sonic drill," she said.

While waiting for the tool to be passed down the small shoot they had set up, Naomi went back to her wires. She could see where the problem was. The circuit board was fried in three places, and the power rot was moving toward three more boards. Now that she had found the issue, fixing it would be simple. Just cut off the affected board and shunt the power other places around it. There probably wasn't a replacement, so she would have to build a new one from scratch—a tedious process, but one she would rather do than trust another stock replacement. At this point, she had rebuilt half the guts of the station trying to bring it to a working baseline.

There was a clink and the hydrospanner landed next to her hand.

"Thank you, Mister Wood," she called up. Naomi grabbed the tool and turned it in her hand, so the head was facing the panel as she got to work.

"My pleasure, sir," he responded back. At least he wasn't calling her 'Knight Perkins' anymore. That was a habit he'd held onto tightly, the formality. While she appreciated how it made everyone's standing clear, it just took too much time.

It took Naomi another two hours of delicate work to remove the damaged board and reroute all the systems around it. Now, for the truly hard part: explaining to Quinn why he wasn't going to have full use of his telescope for the next few days.

Naomi made her way to Quinn's office. The station attached to the observatory wasn't big, the halls just tall enough for a person to stand and wide enough for two to walk abreast. You had to walk with mag boots here, because gravity plating would have interfered with one of the old scanners on the array. A scanner that they could replace these days, but wouldn't, even though Naomi had filled out reams of forms to try and make that happen. She was sure it had something to do with Quinn trying to prove something to people above him. Naomi didn't understand all the interdepartmental posturing and wasn't about to start trying now.

Quinn was in a meeting and so she stood outside his office and waited. She paced, rubbing her bald head in anticipation of the conversation she didn't want to have. Naomi just could not understand why he refused to listen to what she had to say and follow her advice. It was always right, after all. He would quote back to her old books and regulations that didn't have any useful application out here, which was just frustrating.

Quinn, unlike Wood, was from a middling-ranked NovaTerra family and thus thought himself better than everyone. He wasn't, though. Happenstance of birth didn't denote intelligence or aptitude for a job. One day, Naomi would be in charge and could dispense with all these family connections—or, at the very least, she would eventually find a head researcher that would just *listen*.

The light over the door flashed green, signaling that she could come inside. Naomi took a deep breath, readjusted her glasses and walked into the room. Quinn, a middle-aged man with thinning hair and a protruding jaw, sat behind his desk, typing away on an old-style keyboard, the click-clack echoing in the small office. He had on a pair of VR glasses that were halfway down the bridge of his nose, allowing him to both see her and see his work without compromising any security.

"Report?" he asked without even looking up. The tone of his voice was cold. He already knew what she was about to say and wasn't pleased. Naomi didn't care, though, because it was the truth and she couldn't sugarcoat it for him, even if the man refused to learn anything about the technology that ran his station. *I'm just going to have to write the books better next time so that people like him are interested in them.*

"One of the circuit boards in the lens housing is fried. I've reworked the power so that you can still use the imager, just not at the same clarity that you could before," Naomi said. Just as she was taking a breath, getting ready for the next part of her report, Quinn held up his hand, still not looking up at her.

"I don't want to hear a long, detailed explanation. I just want to know how long it will take for you to fix it," Quinn said, the irritation in his voice not even contained. Naomi huffed lightly, trying—and failing—to hide her own frustration. She didn't do anything that wasn't long and detailed. That is why all her repairs worked for years afterward, until the substandard parts broke again.

"It's going to take me a week to rebuild the board. So, you will have to go to Wood if you need anything else fixed in that time," Naomi said.

"Unacceptable. I need that lens working at full capacity in three days," he said. This time, he finally looked up. His eyes said that there wasn't to be any backtalk. Naomi had seen those eyes on her superiors often enough that she had finally learned how to read them. Some people, people like Quinn, were easy for her to read. Most, though…

Well, she was learning, slowly but surely.

"Okay, well that is not something that I can make happen. Rebuilds take the time that they take. Unless you have a secret device in your desk that makes time not linear or maybe speeds it up. Well, at least in a local area. Making the whole universe go faster seems like it would take too much energy. Or do you—?"

"Knight Perkins," Quinn barked, snapping Naomi out of the babbling spiral she'd fallen into. She did that too often, especially when she tried to use sarcasm. There were too many options, and she never could lock down on an idea.

"I do not have a temporal device, I just have a tech that is incapable of managing her time," he said, putting his elbows on the desk and folding his hands together with the index fingers up like a steeple. "Would you agree with that, Perkins?" Quinn asked, pointing his connected fingers at her. Naomi swallowed and lightly sucked on her teeth. She didn't agree, he knew she didn't.

"No sir, I would not. I said it will take a week to rebuild the board and it is going to take a week to do. Two, if you insist on not using Wood for small problems," she said.

"Both of you work on it, then," he said, looking back down at the keyboard.

Naomi took a deep breath and put her thumb to the bridge of her nose and pressed. She was already on thin ice, she knew that, but at the same time, saying yes and then failing to deliver on time was going to net a worse reaction from Quinn. If he had just listened to her last time, or the time before that, then these problems wouldn't keep happening.

"It isn't a matter of hands, sir. If you had—"

She stopped herself. That wasn't going to be the right course. The logical, personable part of her brain knew that, and it almost stopped the side of her brain that just talked and was constantly frustrated by people who wouldn't listen.

"If you had read any of the manuals that I gave you, you would know that rebuilding a board requires time for setting, time for installation, time for trouble shooting. You are asking me to rebuild from scratch with hand tools a ten million credit part. It takes time..."

Quinn held up his hand. "Yes, it takes seventy-two hours. Dismissed, Knight Perkins."

With that, he went back to his typing. The conversation was over. She would have to work day and night, only to have this same fight again in three days. Naomi dreaded it, as she turned and started walking back to her quarters. There, at least, it would be quiet, and she could start the work. Working in her quarters met that napping could happen while code compiled and welds set. That was the only way it would get done, and that was only if the station cooperated with her and didn't fall apart during those seventy-two hours. It would, though, she knew it would. It always did.

Naomi was glad to be back in her room, her safe place. There were no middle managers to tell her what to do here, or how to do it. The small room was laid out exactly how she wanted it, for optimal functionality.

The bed was to the side and made, with her desk across from it and the chair rolling between the two. Her tools were laid out like she was a surgeon, each one in its place, organized first from big to small, then by function. On the wall over her desk was a large set of small drawers, six rows of ten. Each one was labeled. Next to the storage unit was a slip of paper with a key so she could quickly find what she needed—though Naomi had long ago memorized what went where. From stem bolts to eitherscrews, she could find anything with her eyes closed. Above her bed was a shelf with all the station manuals that she had rewritten over the years. All perfectly detailed, all better written than the originals, and all still waiting for wide publication.

At the foot of her bed was a small computer station, the only place she was able to send and receive messages on the station. A small red light was blinking. Naomi walked over and pressed the button. A message came up. It was garbled, but she could make out a few words. 'Remember, friends, Rostov.' It was signed.

'Hyacinth.'

That name sparked memories in Naomi, things she had not thought about in years and years. The Citadel.

"Rostie, we have to go!" a voice of a young girl echoed in the back of her mind. Naomi recognized her own voice. The name, though. She grasped for it, reached into her mind. It dove into her memory, trying to escape from her. A wet thump filled the back of her head and her gut dropped like the station had just acquired a full G of gravity.

She swallowed and sat down in her chair. Flashes of the Citadel tower ran through her mind: teachers yelling, children and their jeers. A young girl on the ground, weeping. She heard the wet thump again. This time, it filled her with resolve. There were things that needed to be done, things that were not rebuilding a circuit board for Quinn.

Zeta Lab, Grace

The tram ride had been uneventful. Grace had read over the morning paper to see what was going on in other parts of the base and had worked through her new equation a few more times. It was going to work, she knew it was. The golden numbers had stopped wobbling on the knife. It was a dangerous balance, but they seemed to, for the moment, be stable. It felt good to think outside the box without needing Emily; doing it alone, moving forward. The tram came to a lurching stop. Grace grabbed the handhold to keep herself in place.

"Arriving at Zeta labs. This is the end of the line. All passengers must exit the train," the calm female voice of the tram system said over the speaker. Grace grabbed her bag and exited.

The landing was cavernous and empty. A huge steel door blocked her path from entering the labs. Standing next to the door was a man in a long, black leather coat with his hair pulled back into a ponytail. The tram station was cloaked in low light, and yet he had sunglasses on. Grace recognized the arrent Host'ire Knight that the base's security team had picked up. She couldn't remember his name at the moment. He was looking at a diagnostic pad, his fingers sweeping around at a holographic readout that she couldn't see. Every time she saw him, he seemed strange—out of place. This wasn't where warrior monks belonged. But then, nobody here was exactly what they appeared. Grace was sure that he had an interesting story, they all did. Nobody ended up at Olympus Ares without one. A facility that stripped you of your old name and gave you the moniker of the person you were replacing? That policy attracted all manner of rogue and scientific vagabond.

Grace ran her access card over the reader. The Host'ire was watching her with interest. Emily, from deep in the back of Grace's mind where she lived, gave him a strange look. Grace pushed her down. There was no time for the past today. No time for Emily's paranoia.

The door beeped. Nothing happened. She cocked her head and then swiped the card again. This time, the card reader beeped, and the doors started to open. Two large cross beams moved first, the top beam going to the right and the one below moving to the left. The sounds of the heavy steel gears echoed in the large chamber. Then, the round door started to roll. It was nothing more than a massive gear on a track. On the other side of the door was a small room and another door.

"Morning, Doctor Goodspeed," the Host'ire said as he walked up behind her, holding out his diagnostic pad toward the card reader and starting to press a few buttons.

"Morning..." Grace said, turning to look at him, leaving open the pregnant pause so that she could get his name. Maybe this time, she wouldn't forget it.

"Essex," he said, looking up at her and giving a small smile. There was something off about this man. He shouldn't have been here. Why was a Host'ire Knight running diagnostics? Essex brushed a lock of blond hair from in front of his glasses, tucking it behind his ear.

"People don't usually remember us security types," he said, turning from his work and looking her in the eye, his glasses having slipped down the bridge of his nose. There was a warmth there that she wasn't expecting. The Host'ire were supposed to be cold fascist wizard monks—or at least, that is what she had heard. The magical arm of the Confederation, nothing more than thugs with powers.

"Not too many ex-Host'ire Knights running around here," Grace said wryly, stepping through the doors that were already starting to close.

"Freedom is that illusive elixir for most of us, sitting on too high a shelf." Essex paused, like he was considering saying something else. Perhaps giving her a cryptic part of his backstory that would hang with her all day or disappointing her with an inspirational platitude. Instead, he said neither of those things.

"I hope whatever you are doing in the test chambers goes well today. Get good data," Essex said as the door closed.

"You too," Grace said, pointing to his pad. As soon as the doors closed, Grace scrunched her nose and shook her head.

Don't flirt, we don't have time for that, Emily thought in the back of Grace's mind. That small voice from her past, the voice of who she had once been. Olympus Ares had made her Dr. Goodspeed, relegating Emily to just a whisper that sometimes reached the surface. Annoyingly today Grace agreed with her and pushed away any thoughts of the attractive Host'ire Knight. Flirting was dangerous—it got people killed.

The second door opened, and Grace walked into the lobby of the Zeta lab. There was a large desk with three people working behind computers. It was a sparce room, not like the lobbies on the higher levels that were filled with motivational posters and videos telling them about the great work they were doing. Those rooms were cold, sterile, spotless.

This room in the Zeta labs had a grunge about it. It was a place where people worked, where real science was done, and where occasionally, things got dirty. That wasn't to say it was not clean—just old and beyond the eyes of people who worried about aesthetics over results. Grace liked that about this place. She had spent many years in spotless labs while working on her PhDs. Good science never got done there. That was where money changed hands, where people who liked the idea of funding research went. Down below, past prying eyes, was where she liked to be. Where people would just leave her alone to do the work.

The desk contained the last security check point she had to go through. A bio scanner, just in case somebody with a changeling cloak had gotten this far. She shook her head at it while gladly submitting to the test with a smile. This was the price for getting to be on the bleeding edge of physics.

"Morning, Doctor Goodspeed. We are running a bit behind today—glitches in the system. I had a message for you from the Spectrometer AI, but the damned computers won't let me back in," the secretary behind the desk said. Her face was red, and Grace could tell she was flustered by the whole thing.

"Don't worry about it, Deb. I'm sure if it was something important, Beckett would have woken me up in the middle of the night. Despite programing Artificial Intelligence for thousands of years, we still can't seemingly create one that understands the concept of sleep," Grace said with an easy, forgiving smile.

"I'm sure you are right," Deb said, pressing a few keys. Grace put her hand in the small box. There was a slight burning, pinching sensation as the laser scalpel removed a layer of her skin a few microns thick. A moment later, the computer beeped green. "Looks like you are still you today, Dr. Goodspeed."

Oh, are we now?

"Well now, that is a relief to hear. Are you seeing that cute boy from Astronomy again tonight?" Grace asked, turning around after passing though the checkpoint.

"Tomorrow. I think it's going to work out for once—though you know work relationships," Deb said with a chuckle.

"Not like we have much of a choice. Good luck!" Grace said, waving as she walked into the locker room to suit up before going to the test chamber. She was happy for the secretary. Nobody should be stuck here for the rest of their lives without finding some kind of love.

It's a myth that is just going to hurt her, Emily thought from the dark places.

Combat Information Center Fury, Cassandra

It was a calm morning in the Combat Information Center of *Fury*. That, of course, meant that thirty people were all bustling around, moving from station to station, looking at reports, punching keys, and turning dials.

The round room was large, stretching a hundred feet in any direction from the center. The center of the room, the lowest point, housed a large glass map table, covered with charts and reports. While in dry dock, it served no purpose but to be a place for the Lord Admiral and the ship's captain to collect papers. Arrayed around the map table, in three tiers, were a bevy of stations: navigation, weapons control, damage and environmental control—the list went on and on. At the top ring was a station with a large wheel and a bell. The helm where the ship was driven from, and a bell to keep the time. An anachronistic and honored tradition.

"Lord Admiral on deck!" the boatswain called, before playing a quick tune on his whistle. Everybody in the CIC stopped what they were doing and stood at attention, as Lord Admiral Cordova walked down the stairs to the central map table where her daughter, Major Hanna Cordova, second of her name, and Captain Rackland stood.

As Cassandra started walking, low music began to play, violins and pipes. It had a vaguely highlands sound to it. An original composition she had written years ago, theme music. Cassandra Cordova was fond of music and had been composing for most of her life. Were she not a Space Lord, she would have liked to be a composer.

There was comfort and power in music. Whenever the ship went into battle or deployed—or really, whenever she felt like it—the Lord Admiral would pump music through the halls of *Fury*. In the last thirty years, she had compiled quite the original score for her house and ship. There was no greater honor than having the Lord Admiral write you a theme.

Play on, my love.

When she reached the bottom step, Cassandra turned to the boatswain and gave him a crisp salute, the palm of her hand turned away from him. He returned the salute and played another bar on his whistle. On cue, the theme music faded into the background. With that, the crew was at ease and returned to their work.

"Sitrep, if you please, Captain Rackland," Cassandra asked, pawing through the papers that were on top of the map table. Personal reports, supplies, mundane things. All reports she had already signed last night. The insomnia had come before the melancholy, and thus she had turned to the mundane reports. Reports that were costing them millions of credits, credits that House Cordova barely had.

"The last of the station's repair crews mustered off ship last night and the second-to-last personal transport arrived this morning. Our stores and armory are stocked, and the air wing and marine detachment are at full capacity," Rackland said.

The captain was a short, pudgy man with a clean-shaven head and truly ugly face. His uniform was well attended to, but it still managed to look unkempt upon him. It gave the captain the image of a storm that was not quite under control. It was a useful look and one he employed often with the crew. In confidence, and with those he trusted, Camron Rackland was a soft giving man.

"We took over Combat Air Patrol from the station this morning and are only waiting for the ambassador to arrive tomorrow before we can begin shake down," Hanna said.

Major Cordova was the spitting image of her mother. Both women were tall, lanky, and if invited to a soiree, could not have filled out a ballgown. While the Lord Admiral was in blue, her daughter was dressed in a red jacket, with pants and cravat in black. The jacket had gold piping that ran up the shoulders. Hanging tight from her neck was a silver gorget with the crest of House Cordova. Hanna was the head of the marine detachment aboard ship.

"Damned late is what they are," the Lord Admiral muttered. She wasn't looking forward to this new ambassador. The Host'ire didn't sit well with her; wizards that held their power over people, quietly making decisions in the background that affected billions. Looking for signs and portents to fit with whatever their dusty old tomes told of the future. Cassandra had little trust for an organization that full of secrets. An organization that, with government sanction, stole children. An organization whose machinations had both founded the Confederation and damned them to never move beyond where they existed.

She felt his hands on her shoulders, warm and calming. Cassandra turned, half expecting to see him there. There was nothing. Of *course* there was nothing. He was the exception to the rule and without him, nothing was left.

"Alexander arrived this morning, mother," Hanna said. There was excitement on her face. Of course she was excited to see her twin. Cassandra could not hold that against her.

"Yes. So everybody keeps telling me," she said, turning and walking over to the steward who stood at attention in the shadows off the side of the map deck.

"Mister Buckland, bring us a coffee service, if you please," she said. The young man nodded and disappeared into the bowels of the halls and alcoves that surrounded and supported the CIC. Before she could return to the map deck, Captain Rackland was behind her.

"A moment, if you please, my lord," he asked in a whisper. She nodded and the two of them stepped away from earshot of the rest of the crew.

"Not to be too forward, but go see your son. You never know when it will be the last time. *Trust me*," Rackland said, dropping that last part quietly. His only child had died in battle fifteen years ago now. The boy had been a midshipman aboard a frigate in the Second fleet. A fleet that was lost during some pointless boarder war with one of the Unaligned Planets.

"I will see him at dinner tonight," she said briskly. "That will be all, Captain."

"Cassandra," Rackland said, using her given name, burning a small amount of the social capitol that they had built up over a thirty-year working relationship.

"I said that will be all, *Captain*." This time, her tone brokered no rebuttal.

"Aye, my lord," he said, giving her a salute and walking past Major Cordova and up the stairs.

Hanna gave her mother a questioning look and Cassandra moved her hand in front of her, signaling that the conversation was over.

He wouldn't have agreed with this, wouldn't have liked what you have become, she thought as Mister Buckland brought out the coffee service.

"You left me here alone. I don't know how to *do* alone anymore," Cassandra said quietly to nobody.

You don't have to be alone. They are here for you. Go to them, the voice in her mind said.

Cassandra took a deep breath and picked up her coffee, dropping in a cube of sugar and quieting the echo of the dead ambassador that only still lived in her mind.

Lynch II Space Port, Lucas

On Lynch II, Lucas had managed to find a cargo ship heading to Icarus, the small moon that held the Citadel of the Host'ire. It was the last ship heading that way before Festival and he *needed* catch it.

"I just need to get on this ship. I am a Knight-Commander of the Host'ire and have important business on Icarus," he said to the cargo ship's captain in the landing bay.

Lynch II was a small world, filled with tall trees that made strange sounds at night. The only thing of note there was the minor spaceport where cargo ships refueled before heading through one of three jump gates that were in the system.

The captain wrinkled his nose at Lucas and pointed toward the cargo ramp.

"Lots of that going around," he muttered, turning back to his work of scanning the last remaining crates.

What the blazes does that mean? Lucas wondered as he started to walk toward the ramp. The cargo ship was cramped. The entire rear section was filled with unmarked crates, as was Host'ire style. Sickly red light bathed the interior of the ship. Along the wall sat a line of mesh jump seats. These were something Lucas was very familiar with, from spending years jumping out of spaceships.

What he was surprised to see were old friends.

Joanna and Naomi were already seated and strapped in, talking to each other, gesturing wildly with their hands. A smile crossed Lucas's face as he saw the two of them. Of course they were here. If Hyacinth had sent him a message, she would have reached out to the rest of them. But now that he'd considered it, he realized there were only three, when once, a lifetime ago, they'd been five. Where was Rostov? Where was Essex?

Lucas had lost track of all his friends from the Citadel. That time in his life was hazy in his mind. The feeling of comfort and friendship, though, had never left him. Life in the Host'ire had dragged them apart, and seeking out old friends was usually impossible with how compartmentalized information got on most Host'ire bases, but time had just made the heart grow fonder. And he had to admit, he was feeling something for both of them that he didn't remember from when he was a child—a comfort, an attraction.

Before he could say anything, Naomi noticed him and started waving.

"Lucas, it has been far too long," Joanna said, unstrapping from the jump chair and wrapping him in a bear hug. Joanna towered over Lucas, even though he was not a slight man. He remembered that she had always been tall, but figured somewhere along the line, he would have caught up, which was apparently not the case.

"It has indeed, it has indeed," he said, wrapping his arms around her and squeezing. Lucas felt a comfort in her arms that he hadn't felt in years. It had been so long that he didn't even realize it was something he missed. He didn't want to let this moment go, didn't want it to end, but like all good things… Joanna released him. Lucas turned and hugged Naomi, wrapping his arms around her and squeezing tightly. She felt a little more uncomfortable with physical touch, from what he remembered of her.

"I like what you have done with your hair," he said, motioning to her shaved head.

"Ya," she said quietly. "The locs went against some old Host'ire space station code that my last supervisor was very strict at following," she said, her voice getting low.

"We haven't followed those codes in over a hundred years," Lucas said as the red light started to flash, indicating that they were getting ready to take off. "If you give me his name, I will look into it. Being a Knight-Commander does have its advantages," Lucas added, tugging on his long leather jacket.

In that moment, Lucas felt the strangest sensation like a child playing at being an adult. As if everything he had accomplished hadn't happened and he was a child again, hanging out with his friends pretending to be knights. He put his hand down, cutting off the bravado. The sensation passed as quickly as it had arrived.

"Quinn over on the Black Hollow Stellar Observatory," Naomi said. "But you didn't hear that from me. In fact, I'm not even here. Nope. I'm just back in my room toiling away rebuilding a circuit board in seventy-two hours that should take a week. I told him it was going to take a week, but you know middle managers, they—" She stopped, looking around, clearly realizing that she was slipping into a rant. "Sorry, I still over explain things."

"Never apologize for being you," Joanna said, reaching to put a hand on Naomi's shoulder before pulling it back. "And always stick it to those fools that don't know what they are doing. I work for a head archivist who wouldn't even be managing the branch of a backwater colonial library if he didn't have a connection to the Null and a fancy last name."

As a high-ranking commander, their conversation made Lucas feel a little uncomfortable.

Do the people I lead talk about me like this behind my back? No, I don't take their skills for granted, I'm not a manager. I'm a leader, he thought, stopping just short of reciting an affirmation of confidence he had learned in one of the many leadership classes he'd taken over the years. Next to him, Joanna and Naomi laughed at their shared dislike of managers as the three of them strapped back in. He loved hearing them laugh. It was a sound that he hadn't thought about in decades, but instantly upon hearing it again, he knew it was something that had been missing from his life.

The launch was rocky. Old ships always punched out of the atmosphere like they were strapped to propellant rockets. Once they had cleared Lynch II, things smoothed out. Twenty minutes later, they hit the jump gate. Lucas took a deep breath as the Null surrounded and brought them into its warm embrace.

"So… you both got messages as well, I take it?" Lucas asked, looking over at Joanna and Naomi, who had started talking about some book they both were reading. "Messages from…" he tried, before trailing off.

It still felt strange to say her name. The childhood friend that he had forgotten about, who had once meant so much, but whose name he couldn't even remember until it had been presented to him. Her face, her voice, any adventures they had gone on together—those were all still a blur to him, and he didn't know why.

That was something he was for damned sure going to figure out.

"Hyacinth," Joanna said quietly. Even though Lucas hadn't seen her in twenty years, he could read the look upon her face. She had the same feelings that he had; the same broken memories that were flooding back in fits and starts.

"I couldn't read most of it. The text was garbled and broken. Just a few words…"

"But even then, I knew it wanted me to go to the Citadel; needed to be there as soon as possible," Joanna said, finishing Lucas's sentence for him. The two of them took an uneasy breath together.

"What do you remember of her?" Lucas asked.

"So little, so…" Joanna paused, her words drifting away, her hand grasping at the air, trying to bring them back to her. "She was frail, small; needed our protection."

"Something happened, with her. With…"

Lucas closed his eyes, tried to bring back the flashes that he had been seeing; the actual memories and not just the feelings. But they wouldn't come.

"Essex. The two of them were always close. I wonder if that has to do with why he isn't here," Joanna said.

"Maybe," Lucas said.

Again, he could hear that wet thump in the back of his mind.

"He could already be there. I know we are missing something in those messages we couldn't read. I just knew I needed to come, that she was in danger, but…" He couldn't finish the sentence, and instead just balled his gloved fists, hoping to maybe squeeze out the answers.

"Um, I guess I'm the odd one out here," Naomi said, holding up her hand. Lucas and Joanna both looked over at her.

"Because I just translated the message. It was in a bi-fractal, polyhedral algorithmic code. Not too hard to pull apart once you recognize what you are looking at," Naomi continued, her voice getting higher and more excited as she went into what kind of code the message had been written in.

"Of course, why didn't I see that," Lucas said, putting a hand to his head.

He was trying to be funny, but he saw Naomi's face fall a bit. She had been excited by something that he didn't even understand, and his first instinct had been to mock it. He felt horrible, like a child; like a stupid boy who was making fun of a girl that he liked because she dared to talk to him about something she was interested in.

"I'm sorry, that was not nice," he said, folding his hands in his lap. Joanna shot him a look of approval for the apology, but one that also said to be quiet for a few minutes.

"It's fine. I do ramble, and not everybody sees… sees what I do," Naomi said, starting to retreat into her shell.

"Don't listen to him. Boys never know a good thing when it is right in front of their face," Joanna said. Lucas noticed that Joanna's hand wanted to move and be supportive, but she was holding it in place. "Tell me about this code. I didn't see it, either, but then math was never my strong subject."

Naomi smiled again, taking a breath, her eyes rolling up a little and darting around as she worked out how to explain things in a way that would be both factual and easy to understand.

"Hyacinth rolled two codes on top of each other. I noticed it when the two words that I could read from the start didn't line up with any cyphers that I was familiar with. So, I just wrote a little program that started putting algorithms on top of each other, and eventually I brute forced the message out. It wasn't too much work, really," she said. Lucas suspected she would be beat red right now, if her skin wasn't already so dark.

"I'm impressed," Lucas said. Joanna nodded in agreement.

"What did it say?" Joanna asked.

"That is the frustrating part. Nothing more than I had already gleaned from just reading three words and the feeling that it unlocked inside of me. She wants to see all of us; there is danger; come now," Noami said, shrugging her shoulders. "I guess, in the end, it was a waste of time."

"No, not at all! I see what she was doing now," Joanna said. "The cypher was just an extra layer of security, in case somebody who isn't one of use looked at the message."

"A Null Cypher," Lucas muttered.

Host'ire who had deep connections to each other could impart their feelings into blocks of text, so that even if the presented words were gibberish or coded, the knight that they were intended for would be able to understand the meaning and what the message was trying to convey on a deeper level. A level that would be hard to put your finger on, especially if you couldn't really remember the woman who had sent you the message.

"Exactly," Joanna said. "We would have been the only people in civilization that could read it. Well, besides Rostov and Essex. I thought I would see them here," she said.

"Maybe they are already there," Naomi said.

Rostov and Essex were the other two members of their little group from back during their days training at the Citadel. Like Naomi and Joanna, Lucas had lost track of them both, even though the three boys had once been thick as thieves.

"Perhaps. There was no separating Essex from Hyacinth. And Rostov..." Lucas said.

"Rostov always had something sharp to say. Even worse than you," Naomi said, motioning at Joanna.

"I always have a well-reasoned argument, he just..." Joanna started.

"He agitated, fought just to fight, sometimes," Lucas said.

"I hope they are both there. I miss Rostov," Naomi said quietly.

"I'm sure he is already there, causing trouble," Joanna said.

"We will know soon enough," Lucas said.

The Citadel awaited them.

Stateroom *Fury*, Erik

"You secured a spot in the Minister's tourney. That is quite a feat," Erik said, holding a glass of wine up in toast to his brother.

"There were a few moments there where I didn't think our team was going to make it in. They have a tendency to look down upon qualifying rounds that are played remotely. But O'Hair's lord father pulled a few stings and made it happen," Alexander said, picking up his glass and tapping it against his brother's.

"You know Lord O'Hair? The third minister of the whole Confederation?" Hanna asked. Alexander chuckled as he took a sip of his sweet red wine.

"No, no, just his fifth son. We work together. Once the election is over, when we are all on NovaTerra, I shall have to introduce you all to my fellows. Thrace, O'Hair, Hoben, MacGuffin. All great and fast friends," he said.

The family dinner had taken on a lively tone, Erik thought, even though his lord mother was trying to sour it. The whole family was there. His mother sat at the head of the table. Flanking her were him and Hanna. Next to Erik sat Alexander and next to Hanna was Bella. She was tall and slender, like all the Cordova women, with hard features, while her jet-black hair was streaked with neon green. Next down the table was Bella's father, Joseph—the ship's chief medical officer—and her younger brother, Baxter, a boy of thirteen who was training to follow his father into the medical field.

Across the long table there was a healthy spread, the kind of feast one throws before a campaign or to celebrate a return to action. In the center, there was a large prime rib roast, bones and all. Each of them had carved off a slab and still there was more to spare. Potatoes mashed in rich cream, butter and white cheese, sprouts coated in bacon and balsamic, warm fresh black bread with creamed garlic butter, string beans, and a gelatinous berry jelly that Erik didn't care to try completed the spread. Chef, as per usual, had outdone himself, and Erik had already eaten his fill.

They were on the wine course, where everybody was picking at the remnants of dinner and polishing off the bottles that were spread across the table. Then, dessert and an after-dinner aperitif would soon be brought out. Erik didn't know what was in store for dessert, but he suspected something with apples, as those were Alexander's favorite.

"I shall enjoy getting to meet all of them. Learn who it is that my twin spends so much time with these days that he can't even sneak in a letter," Hanna said, looking from Alexander to her mother. Erik saw and knew what she was doing. Asking the question for their Lord Mother so that she and her sour mood didn't have to.

"I do heartily apologize for my absence upon the page. The last few months saw us working on a project that had the whole base locked down to no contact. We squeaked in the two card games. I do wish I could say more," Alexander responded. "But yes, I shall be more aware of my duties in matters of correspondence."

"See that you are," muttered Lord Admiral Cordova. The comment hung over the table for a moment like somebody had passed wind that nobody wanted to claim but everyone could smell.

"Alexander, pray tell, what details about your work *are* you at liberty to divulge with your family? Keep in mind we all hold quite high security clearance," Uncle Joseph asked, as he signaled for one of the pages to cut him another slab of beef off the bone.

"Uncle, you know better than to ask," Alexander said, taking a sip from his glass.

"Does he? We all have noble access here—and aside from you, all warriors," Erik said, throwing his uncle a bone, despite knowing the answer to the question before he even asked it.

"Alas, the project is beyond noble access. Even I am only cleared to know about my own work within it and not the full scope," Alexander said.

Both brothers exchanged a glance. They needed to quickly find a new subject. Dinner had been moving from lively conversation to deathly silence at far too rapid of a clip. Normally, at a family dinner of this size, the conversation would be guided by their mother. Yet, she rarely joined them anymore for supper and when she did, this was the mood that usually prevailed.

Erik knew that he was going to have to bring this subject up with her soon. This thinly veiled irritation at her continued existence that she was holding was all well and good in private, but now that the ship was back to full capacity and not filled with repair staff, a more positive face needed to be established.

He wished she would compose again. There was still no victory theme for Hyroncore. Yes, it would need to be tinged with sadness, but a victory was a victory, and the soundtrack of *Fury* was currently incomplete.

"Cousin Bella, I trust you are still outflying my brother with one eye closed?" Alexander asked.

"At this point, I'm not sure I even need a single eye open to run circles around him. This morning, I was able to buzz him without even being challenged," she said, giving Erik, who served as her wingman, CAG, and cousin all in one, a sly look. Lord Admiral Cordova scowled and the sly look on Bella's face vanished.

"It just shows that we need to get the training of the squadrons back up to snuff," Bella said. She lightly kicked Erik under the table as his mother nodded in approval.

Good, the attention is back on me and my failings, small as they are, he thought, returning Bella's jab. He would find a way to make her pay for calling him out. She, alas, was not easy to discipline, as Bella took nothing that happened outside the cockpit with any real seriousness.

"In fairness to your brother, he hadn't been behind the stick in half a year. That three-month elective at the war college and repairs were keeping him busy," Bella said, serving the conversation shuttlecock back to Erik.

"Indeed, indeed. Such a riveting elective about logistics and supply lines. Kansays's World is working on a new strain of wheat that they claim is rot resistant, even after being milled into flour. Also," Erik said, motioning with his wine glass, "I can now tell you facts and figures about every port in the Confederation that can support a Dreadstar without going out of business from it."

"How does that work? If we pay for everything, how would they still go out of business?" The question came from Baxter, who had been quiet the whole meal.

The young man had been taught by his father to rarely speak up when the adults were talking. Erik did not share his uncle's opinion that children should be seen and not heard. He was always happy when they asked questions. It was the only way they would learn things. His uncle could teach Baxter everything about running an infirmary or treating wounds, but his knowledge base outside of the medical was lacking.

"Well, little cousin," Erik started, lowering his voice into an educational baritone. "If we buy up everything that a small port has to offer, while they might have our credits, in the time it would take them to bring in new stores, the ripple effect across the sector would be detrimental. There are some starports out there where the whole world pooling everything together still couldn't support a Dreadstar. Our arriving there for a resupply could consign those people to death, even though their accounts would be flush with credits. Then, there are the medium sized words that have the supplies, but if we take them all, there is nothing left for them. So again, rich but hungry."

"We are lords, though. The smallfolk of those dock worlds owe us their allegiance," Baxter said, parroting the standard line. Uncle Joseph flicked the boy on the ear to quiet him down. Erik held his hand up, signaling that it was fine, he wanted to answer. These were the kinds of things that lords had to explain to their families, and it took a family to raise any child of noble birth.

From the corner of his eye, Erik saw a steward walk into the room and whisper something to his mother. She stood up and walked out into the hallway for a moment. Whatever it was, he was sure she would let them know at a time that fit her dour mood.

"They do, but it is still our responsibility to be benevolent and not leave them in ruin. Otherwise, what are we even protecting? Always remember, Baxter, that our power comes *from* them. Not this huge ancient technology, not our ability to bring death, but *theirs* to bring life. As somebody destined for the medical field, you would do well to keep that in mind," Erik said.

"Yes Cousin, I will do that," the boy said, looking back at his plate, chagrined, returning to his quiet existence.

"So yes, those were the things that we were learning while I was being rudely kept away from the cockpit of my Rapier," Erik said back to the rest of the table.

Lord Admiral Cordova walked back into the room, going to her chair and placing both hands loudly on the ornate black wood of the table. Everybody put down their forks and napkins and quickly pushed their chairs back and stood up. Etiquette dictated that if the Lord of the ship had something important to say, everybody must stand, and could only sit once released, either with a command or by the Lord Admiral taking her seat.

"I regret to inform you all that dinner must be cut short tonight. Timetables have moved up, and we are shoving off within the hour," the Lord Admiral said. "Alexander, I suggest you return to your ship, which will need to find a berth somewhere else for the night. Unless you have suddenly found an interest in honor and service. That will be all," she said, excusing them. The family murmured for a moment and then started to depart.

"I shall see you again soon on NovaTerra. It is Festival and we shall enjoy ourselves," Alexander said, patting Erik on the back.

"I look forward to that, brother. Until then, stay out of trouble," Erik said.

"I make no promises," Alexander retorted. He pulled away and went to talk to Hanna. Erik's eyes fell on their mother. She had retreated into the back part of the dining room that led into her quarters. Erik picked up his sword, clasped it to his belt, and followed her. There was something going on more than just her sour mood.

"Mother, we need to talk," Erik said.

"No, Commander, we do not," she said flatly.

If he had been anybody else aboard the ship, that would have been enough to send him running away. Unfortunately for her, Erik wasn't anybody else.

"What is going on, Mother? We were not scheduled to leave until late tomorrow after the new ambassador arrives," Erik said, pressing forward.

She turned. There was thinly veiled anger on her face and the hint of a tear. She passed him a slip of teletype paper. Erik quickly read the message. In short, it said the new Host'ire Ambassador was arriving in the next hour and to be ready for him.

"I will not have them upon my ship. They think to replace the unreplaceable. I will not have it," she said, pulling off the fancy blue dinner coat and hanging it up.

That was when Erik realized that they were always going to leave before the ambassador arrived and the only person who knew this was his mother. He knew it should have surprised him, but with a moment of reflection, it didn't. His mother did few things impulsively, and from the way she spoke, Erik could tell that she had been mulling this idea over since the moment the Host'ire had sent over the orders. Only now happenstance had moved up the timetable.

"I agree, we do not need another of their ilk right now. But did you have to be so curt with Alexander? You haven't said a kind word to him since he arrived."

"And why should I?" the Lord Admiral said. She didn't turn to look at her son, taking off her black vest covered in golden chimeras, hanging it up and replacing it with a more modest black duty vest.

"Because he is your son," Erik said, shocked that they were even having this conversation.

"My son," she spat, turning around to face him, "would not have left us in our time of need; would have stayed and understood service. My son—" She pulled back, biting the rest of her words and swallowing them, unspoken. Erik took a step back.

"Commander, I believe you have an air wing to take care of. We shall be in need of a CAP as soon as we exit Null Space," she said, pulling a blue deck jacket from the closet.

"Mother," Erik started.

"That is all, *Commander*. You are dismissed," she said flatly.

The conversation was over.

Taking a breath, Commander Erik Cordova turned smartly and exited the room, his hand gripped tightly around the hilt of his sword.

The Citadel, Lucas

"Would I be correct in assuming that neither of you took leave to come on this expedition?" Lucas asked, looking down at his watch and then up at the girls. Both exchanged a look and then averted their eyes.

"I'm supposed to be reporting to exile at an archive of no importance," Joanna said.

"And I'm rebuilding a motherboard for the next three days," Naomi said. "Though I told Quinn it would take five, he just didn't listen."

"Why am I not surprised?" Lucas muttered.

"Because you know us. What about *you*, Mister Knight-Commander?" Joanna asked.

"I do not put in for leave, I approve those kinds of thing," he said with a little huff.

"Got it. So you also just up and left, but rank makes it acceptable for you. Cool," Joanna said, giving Lucas a sarcastic thumbs up.

"Regardless, it poses a small problem, because none of us should be out here, and without some kind of cover story, there will be questions," Lucas said.

"I figured we would just filter in with the novices and see what happens. It's not like the Citadel is a quiet place bereft of people. Even during Festival," Naomi said.

"I agree. But we will eventually need access to floors that we are not coded for," Lucas said.

"Oh, this sounds like he has a plan," Joanna said, excitement creeping into her voice.

"A bit of one, yes. Just follow my lead if they ask," Lucas said as he laid out his simple plan.

***

The euphoria of being at faster-than-light speeds inside the Null passed as the ship came out of the jump gate and made its final approach to Icarus. The ride got bumpy again as they entered the world's atmosphere, and the pilot made a hard landing. The crew of this ship was far from the cream of the crop. The surly shipmaster came out from the front section and motioned toward the door. They had work to do and no time to deal with passengers who had already been unexpected. The three of them grabbed their bags and headed for the gangplank.

Reaching the edge of the ship, Lucas was greeted by the massive structure that was the Host'ire Citadel. The place where they trained all the lowborn children who were able to touch the Null. Where they taught them to fight and kill, to become weapons for some shadowy purpose. The landing pad was just inside the curtain wall, but far enough away that the concrete structure dominated their field of view.

It was a series of rectangular floors. Each one looked like it had been constructed on its own and then placed on top of the one below it. Each of these rectangles was slightly offset from the one below, creating the appearance of a round spire even though there were only harsh right angles in the construction. The gray concrete was still rough, even though it had been battered by storms over the five hundred years that it had been standing. There were windows, a row of them on each side, making the massive, not quite cylinder-shaped, building look like it was covered in eyes. It was a monumental testament to an architectural style that had long gone out of fashion, replaced by a return to the older ways that had swept through the Confederation well over a hundred years ago.

Looking up the spire of The Citadel, Lucas saw the sky. It was not blue, but a churning mess of red, orange, and purple. Icarus orbited a small dying star that was extremely close to the Barrier, so close that it dominated the day and nighttime sky. There were no stars to see from Icarus, only the reminder that they were trapped in this section of space next to Hell itself.

Standing waiting for them was a young knight. He had on a long black leather jacket like all the Host'ire did, buttoned up, his utility belt on the outside, along with the standard black gloves and sunglasses. His brown hair was tied up in a topknot, and leaning against his shoulder was a star-steel spear. Lucas recoiled for a moment seeing the weapon, memories flashing of sparing and abuse. The young guard held up a hand as they approached.

"The Citadel is closed. We are not taking any visitors at this time," he said in an accent that Lucas was not familiar with.

"We are here on official business. I am Knight-Commander Lucas Brandice. I was sent orders and told to report post haste to Administrator Fel," Lucas said, coming to a stop. He puffed himself up and fell into a parade rest, letting his arms cross behind his back.

"Nobody is allowed entrance..." the young knight started again. There was uncertainty in his voice. Lucas had heard that before. He was green. This was most likely his first assignment; probably hadn't gone on more than a few missions away from the Citadel. Plus, he couldn't have been that old—the topknot had only just returned to being in style.

"Yes, I heard you the first time. I am not nobody. I am Knight-Commander Lucas Brandice, and these are my associates. We are to report to the Administrator as soon as we are planet-side. It would be a shame if I had to note in my report that you hampered our arrival." He threaded in a few strands of class conflict in his voice. Lucas understood this man, he had been in his boots before. Now he had rank and privilege, and what good was rank if you didn't throw it around from time to time?

"I have my orders," he said meekly.

"Yes, we all have our orders. You call up to the Administrator while we go. You can let her know that you did your duty and to not hold you responsible for being unaware of our arrival, as it was not on any of the books."

This time, he didn't give the young man a chance to say anything. He just motioned for Joanna and Naomi to follow him. They walked past the befuddled guard, who started walking quickly to his gatehouse and the radio that would allow him to call his superiors.

Lucas scanned across the parade field. The one-armed shadow from the *Sequin Dream* was still in his mind, still following him. Was he here? Or had time taken its toll? The yard was empty, and Lucas picked up his pace. If the man he was worried about was here, their façade would crack in a moment. Best to keep moving.

"We don't have orders to be here," Joanna whispered as they walked up to the large doors of the Citadel tower.

"Just walk like we do. We will be upstairs by the time anybody realizes what is going on," Lucas said.

"Well, this is exciting," Naomi said, raising her eyebrows and putting a little pep in her step.

The entrance to the Citadel was grand, a large lobby that led to a series of elevators. Stretching through the lobby, from the massive steel doors to the elevators in the back, were large columns of marble.

Carved into them were the history of the Host'ire, from their founding during the Age of Chaos a thousand years ago to their glorious victory over the Wayfinders, up to the present day. The walls behind the columns were covered in flags and tapestries, all of them showing the grandness and pomp of the order.

There were guards stationed at the doors and by the elevators, but that was it. There were no people. There *should* have been people. Novices milling about, knights coming and going. The young man outside had said that nobody was allowed in, but Lucas found it odd that it seemed nobody was even here. Never had he seen it so empty before.

"Something is very wrong, super big bad wrong, the feeling is… off," Naomi whispered to the group, the cadence of her speech slowing and speeding up as she searched for the needed words to express how she was feeling.

Joanna looked from Naomi to the empty foyer of the academy and then at Lucas and nodded. They were all in agreement that something very wrong was going on here. The letters from a friend they didn't remember until just a few days ago. The feelings of connection and longing attraction, even though they hadn't spoken in twenty years. The emptiness of a building that should be bustling with people. A pile of strangeness.

The guard at the elevator didn't stop them as they entered and headed toward the administrative floors.

The tower of the Citadel was broken into zones, and the elevator had to stop at each zone, scanning who was inside, making sure that they had the correct clearance level to proceed farther. The first level were classrooms and the library. Any Host'ire could enter this level. The second were the Dormitories. Only Facility and novices could enter this level. The third level were training rooms, gyms—all the amenities that would be needed to build one's body and mind for war. This level was open again to any Host'ire, as many members of the order took pilgrimages to Icarus so that they could bathe in the light of the Barrier and reflect about how it and the order protected the civilized world from the demons the lay beyond. Lastly, at the top level, there were the administrative offices open only to those who worked or had business there. Lucas hoped that the guard had called ahead, and somebody had cleared them. Otherwise, even his rank wasn't going to get them to see Administrator Fel.

The elevator reached their destination. There was a beep, laser lights moving through the small elevator car. Then, nothing, before another quiet beat. Lucas looked at Joanna and Naomi, and took a deep breath. They looked back at him, then the doors opened, revealing another empty floor.

This was a bland section of the Citadel. Hallways of concrete with maroon carpeting from wall to wall. Hanging between the doors were posters with slogans about staying the course and fighting for the future. Each door had a placard with a name. The fluorescent light overhead gave the whole thing a sickly glow.

It wasn't until the trio reached the end of the hallway that they saw anyone. The hallway broke into a T-shape. There was a large wooden double door. In front of it was a desk where a young woman with thick sunglasses and green-black hair sat, working on her computer. Off to the side vacuuming the floor was a janitor who paid them no mind, just quietly humming as he worked.

Lucas stared at the man for a second. He could swear it was the same man who had been cleaning the floors when he was a novice here, and he looked the same. There wasn't time to reflect upon him, as the secretary started talking, her voice flat and even.

"The Administrator will see you now, Knight-Commander, Knights," she said. She only looked up from her work for a moment, just long enough to push a key opening the door and waving them toward it. They rounded the desk and started walking toward the office. Lucas had never been to the Administrator's office before—hell, he had never even been to this level of the Citadel before.

Well, there is a first time for everything, he thought dryly.

The office was at the end of a small hallway. This was the most inviting room that they had seen since entering the base and it was still formal and austere. The floor was covered in the same maroon carpet; the walls were paneled in wood and covered with shelves of books and memorabilia. There was a large desk at the far side and beside that, a window that bathed the room in the natural red hell-light of Icarus.

Sitting behind the desk clad in a black suit, with a tie instead of a cravat, was a middle-aged woman, pushing sixty, if Lucas remembered correctly. She had a strong angular face that, while cold, was striking in its beauty. Her trim figure was perfectly accentuated by the tailoring of the suit. Her hair, black as night, was tied up in a baker's braid. She wore glasses, but unlike most Host'ire who wore sunglasses to keep out the brightness of The Null, she wore a pair made of transparent plastic, giving her the appearance of having on normal corrective lenes. When she spoke, her words were pointed and biting. If not for her demeaner and reputation, Lucas would have found how she sounded extremely alluring.

"Speak quickly, Knight-Commander. What business is it that you have here? I am extremely busy," Administrator Fel said, setting her pen down and folding her arms on the desk.

"It really doesn't look like you are all that busy," Joanna said before Lucas could say anything. He pinched his brow and muttered a curse under his breath. This was something he had forgotten. The trait about her that he both loved and hated in equal measure: her inability to stop picking fights with those in command.

"Excuse me, Knight Pike. You will address me with the respect that my station warrants," Fel said.

Lucas and Naomi both looked at Joanna as she did exactly what they knew she would do. All his memories of the times they had spent together were fuzzy, but he didn't even have to question what she was going to say next. He knew it deep down in his soul and so did Naomi.

"It really doesn't look like you are all that busy, *Administrator* Fel," Joanna said, making sure to hit each and every syllable of her title, making them as crisp as possible.

"Knight-Commander, might I advise you keep a tighter leash upon your subordinates? What you see, and what is going on, are two different things," Fel said.

Joanna was about to open her mouth again—her cute mouth that said the worst things at the worst times. Lucas shot her a look, and she backed down, falling into an easy parade rest.

Cute mouth? Lucas, this is not the time to be thinking like that. Get it together.

"Yes, Administrator, I shall keep that in mind. We are here on a fact-finding mission. Highly encrypted messages were sent from this base. Host'ire special intelligence intercepted a few of them and sent us to investigate. We were supposed to be acting as visiting instructors, but there seems to be a lack of novices," Lucas said, looking around in mock befuddlement. He had spent most of the trip here coming up with a lie that seemed plausible, simple, and that would let them snoop around. Now it was time to see if he could sell it or not.

"I was not told about this. The student body has been sent away to enjoy Festival and get a start on the spring deployment. You will find there are very few people to teach or staff to question," she said. "You will also find that there are no ships leaving, or coming back, so I would advise you to enjoy your stay." With that, she turned her attention back to the papers on her desk.

"We were expecting to meet two more of our party here: Knights Essex and Rostov," Lucas said. There was a quiet moment and then Administrator Fel had to stifle a small snort.

"I see that Host'ire Intelligence is as oxymoronic as the military variety. I find it interesting that your *investigation*," Fel dripped the word in condescension, "would require a failed student who has been consigned to the re-education levels and a vanished knight."

She paused for a beat. "Knight-Commander, do not lie to me again. Keep your secrets to yourself, but know that I will learn them. We always learn them. There are no more ships leaving, so feel free to investigate. I'm sure your friend will be happy to see you, if the madness allows it."

Her voice was cold as ice, and yet Lucas felt as if there was a nasty chuckle underneath. Administrator Fel flicked her wrist at them, signaling that they should be gone. Caught off-guard, the trio didn't argue. They just bowed their heads respectfully, turning to leave the room. Whatever latitude Lucas had hoped to gain with the story had been shattered. Now. every move they made would be conducted under the distrustful eye of the Citadel's Administrator.

"One question, before we leave," Joanna said, turning around. Lucas could hear a soft snort from Fel.

"Why are all the ship's grounded? It can't just be for a Null storm?"

"Oh, a storm is coming, Knight Pike. Of that you can be sure."

Lucas put his hand on Joanna's shoulder. He could feel that she wanted to say something else. The two of them locked eyes. She sighed, and they exited the room.

Re-Education Cells, Joanna

Re-education. The word sent a shiver down Joanna's spine. It was such a nice, pleasant-sounding euphemism for what happened in the lower levels of the Citadel.

The Host'ire as an order were steeped in rules and dogma. Traditions and conventions that were followed to the letter. Stepping outside of those presets was a sure-fire way to earn a trip to the lower levels. Minor infractions might just get you administrative punishment— another fun phrase that they liked to use; where they would beat you every morning and then proceed to grill you until the words of the creed were all that you could hear in your mind.

If that didn't work, they moved you to re-education.

Joanna still vaguely remembered Rostov, the memories of their little group strong but hazy. She remembered he was the joker, the one who would say the first thing that came to his mind. He would do anything for a laugh. Rostov must have said one too many things to the wrong people to lose his knighthood and end up in re-education. The prospect scared her.

How close to this fate have I been before? How many times have I been saved by somebody just not wanting to pull that trigger?

The elevator was authorization-coded going down the same way it was for going up the tower. From the outside, the Citadel looked like a huge tower with a few outbuildings and a curtain wall. In reality, what was above ground was just a fraction of the complex. There was a immense labyrinth of floors and rooms and facilities underground. Not all of them were in use and without express authorization, almost none of them were accessible by knights who were not also faculty. Administrator Fel had given them authorization to go into the lower levels, and so they rode the elevator down into the darkness.

"I thought we were in trouble back there," Joanna said, finally breaking the silence.

"I was sure Fel was going to throw us in a cell," Lucas said.

"Why didn't she?" Naomi asked.

"Something is going on here," Lucas started.

"No shit," Joanna said before he could finish his super serious brooding leader talk.

"I'm being serious. I have an incredibly bad feeling about this place," Lucas said. "Fel is hiding something, but is also backed into a corner; overextended, in some way. She cut us loose because she lacks the resources to deal with us," Lucas said.

"Do you think it's connected to why Hyacinth summoned us?" Joanna asked.

"I would be shocked if it wasn't. We have stumbled into something, my friends. I just wish I fucking knew what it was," Lucas said, crossing his arms and looking very grim. The elevator fell silent again as the numbers kept ticking down.

"What do you think he did to get re-education?" Naomi asked.

"He was a joker," Joanna said.

"He was insolent, and talked back; said things he shouldn't have," Lucas said.

That seemed almost too harsh, like he was drastically condemning him. Joanna hated the rules and chaffed against those who followed strict adherence to them, but at this moment, coming from Lucas, it was strangely attractive. An odd feeling to be having as they were heading into the bowels of the Citadel.

That is just an old schoolgirl crush, push that to the side, Joanna. Focus on what is going on right now, she thought, chiding herself.

"Re-education, though… That seems harsh for just a joker, even an insolent one," Joanna said.

"And they took his knighthood," Naomi added in.

"A part of me doesn't think he graduated. There was something in the way that Fel said he was no knight," Lucas said flatly. There was an uncomfortable pause. "But yes, I don't remember anything he said ever being worth re-education. Administrative punishment, maybe…"

"Narc," Joanna whispered in a sly little voice.

"What did you say?" Lucas asked, spinning around, confused but still self-serious. The schoolgirl crush wanted to win out. Joanna had to push it away.

"You were always a rule follower, Lucas. Always looking to get in with authority," Joanna said lightly. It wasn't much of a dig, especially compared to what she could say. She didn't want to cut too deeply.

He left us, a small voice said in the darkness of her mind.

"I just wanted to protect us; somebody had to. Otherwise, he…"

"He was going to come for us. Abuse us," Joanna said quietly, fear moving through her body, the playful ribbing banter falling to the side.

"They just let it happen. Encouraged it," Naomi added, looking away from the rest of the group.

"That is why I had to protect us. The order wasn't going to do it," Lucas said.

That felt as close to a condemnation as she was going to get today. *He is so close to coming back around,* Joanna thought. She let it be, thinking before she spoke for once. They rode the rest of the way down to the re-education level in silence.

Deep down, Joanna expected the doors to open to a horror show, to reveal the true naked evil of the order. To instantly prove her right for distrusting them, for not wanting to put up with spoiled brats and ambassadors who thought they were the true power in the Confederation. To her disappointment, the hallway was as bland as every other hallway in the Citadel. Just more concrete walls, lined with metal doors that each had a number on them. The floor was flat, cold, lifeless steel. The carpet on the floors above was one of the only things that gave the Citadel even a modicum of warmth and humanity. Down here, there was none to be had.

Two guards stood at the end of the hallway, their leather coats open and flowing. Strapped to their hips were small kinetic assault pistols, along with their star-steel blades. Their faces were blank, and any expression that might have been read from their eyes was obscured by their glasses. These men, unlike the rest of the guards that they had encountered thus far, would not give you a chance. They shot first and asked questions later. In this tight of a space, there was no dipping into the Null to stop the bullets or dodge them. You would just be sliced to bloody ribbons. Then they would wash down the hallway and pretend that you never existed.

The Host'ire were very good at making people and things vanish.

Did that list include memories?

You don't even remember one of your best friends, somebody that you spent time with. Only when she reaches out, in trouble, do you start to remember—and even then, it's more feelings than memories, Joanna thought.

It wasn't just Hyacinth. She had seen academics vanish, their works removed and scrubbed from existence so completely that it almost felt like she was gaslighting herself when she went to look for them.

Was Rostov next? Was this all just an elaborate ruse to vanish him—or perhaps all of them? She didn't know. There were far too many questions, and not enough answers. The answers that she knew were all frustratingly locked away in her mind, hiding under... under what, she wasn't sure.

"Halt!" the guard on the right said, his hand sliding down to the grip of his weapon, the threat of violence not even vague. Lucas stepped forward, flicking open his coat to show his own star-steel blade before raising both of his hands. It was a sign of respect among the combat wings of the order. It was a 'you show me yours, I show you mine, then we can talk' kind of mentality.

"I am Knight-Commander Brandice. Administrator Fel gave us leave to talk with prisoner Rostov," he said. His voice was even, powerful, commanding. The more Joanna wanted to chafe against authority, the more she felt attracted to Lucas.

There was a moment of stillness from both sides as they looked at each other. Joanna hadn't drawn her blade in over a decade, and only then because she had to requalify to carry the weapon. If you did not carry a star-steel blade, you could not be a Host'ire Knight, and if you were not a knight, then you got nothing but scraps from the order that you couldn't legally leave. That dearth of experience left her wondering if Lucas was fast enough to draw down these two guards before they fired their weapons. Maybe. She knew he wouldn't risk it. You did not become a Knight-Commander specializing in hostage rescue by being reckless. They were on the same side after all, right? The two guards lowered their guns, and Lucas followed suit by lowing his hands and closing his jacket.

"You may enter," they said, opening the door. Both men reached onto their belts and pulled out truncheons. The guards entered the room first, while the three of them followed close behind.

The room was stark white, on one end there was a bed, a desk, and a toilet. On the desk was a single book. Joanna recognized it instantly as the Codex Host'ire. The book of laws, dictates, and dogma of the order written by High Lord Cavill. She knew the book well, and after how long he had been in re-education, Joanna suspected Rostov knew it cover-to-cover. On the steel floor, there was a white line.

Huddled on the bed, clutching his legs pressed to his chest, was Rostov.

He was gaunt, his skin a milk white. Rostov's chestnut hair was streaked with gray and white. As they entered, he looked at them. At first, his striking blue eyes showed fear. Fear of the guards, fear of the people who usually visited him. Then, just as quickly, they showed comfort and recognition. He knew who they were, though he didn't say anything yet, not moving from his crouched position.

"The rules are simple. You will not touch the confined, nor will you pass anything to him. Each group will stay on their side of the line. If you cross," the guard said, pointing his truncheon toward the trio, "the confined with be shocked. If he crosses, the floor will electrify and all of you will be taken down."

Joanna looked at Rostov, who widened his eyes and nodded his head. She could tell that he knew these rules well and had probably been on the receiving end of their punishment more times than she wanted to even think about.

"Do you understand these rules as they have been presented to you?" the guard asked.

"We understand," Lucas said flatly.

"Good. You have ten minutes," the guards flicked their weapons back into their belts and walked out of the room the thick steel door closing behind them. The sounds of the lock sliding into place echoed through the room.

"You came. She said that you would come," Rostov said, putting his legs down and sitting up on the bed. His demeanor changed completely. No longer did he look like a caged animal. There was life in his eyes again.

"Hyacinth?" Joanna asked taking a step forward.

"Yes, she started talking to me. I started to remember," Rostov said, accentuating his words via hand gestures. "It was because they put me in here. I couldn't be controlled. I talked back, I wouldn't conform. There was always something in the back of my head. Then when they put me here, they took away my gloves and my glasses," he said, holding up his ungloved hands and tapping his temples where the frames of sunglasses should have been.

Joanna gasped at the idea of somebody being forced to have such a strong connection to the Null that they couldn't dull, especially this close to the Barrier. She had read accounts of this driving people mad.

It was expressly forbidden by the order, by the very book they were making him read, no less.

"That is inhuman," Naomi said.

"This is an inhuman place, I am afraid. There is something going on here. Something I couldn't see before they put me away and something that I still can't see now that I am here. But..." Rostov tapped his forehead with his index and middle finger. "But I can feel it. The fear, the anxiety... It is permeating from the Citadel above. Until two sleeps ago, it was muted, muffled in the sea of emotions. Now, though, things have gotten quiet. I can hear them better, a defining den of fear," Rostov said as he started to chew on the nail of his thumb.

"The novices," Lucas said.

"They sent them all away. It's very strange," Naomi chimed in.

"It *is* Festival. The Academy on NovaTerra was clearing out when I left," Joanna said.

"Even training missions during Festival don't empty places out like this. Whatever Rostov is feeling, it's all connected," Lucas said.

Joanna couldn't take her eyes off him, watching him work through the problem, think and act like a leader. She took in a breath and pulled her eyes away.

Snap out of it, Joanna, you are not a child anymore. You know what he did, she thought, an accusatory feeling fighting against the holes in her memory.

"She said that you all would come, and that we would be together again and solve the problem. The pact that we had made all those years ago, coming together," Rostov said.

Joanna didn't remember any binding pact that they had made. They were a friend group, yes, and they stood up for Hyacinth when *he* kept coming around.

But a pact?

"What problem? What pact?" Joanna asked.

She looked from Rostov to the group. They nodded along with her question, apparently just as in the dark as she was.

"She says that it will come to you. That we are five and one," Rostov said.

"Six," Naomi cut in. "We are six. Where is Essex? Shouldn't he have gotten a message, as well?"

"I asked the same question. She says Essex is beyond our grasp, going to form another quorum. Do not ask me what it means. She speaks in riddles and broken phrases. Hell, most days, I am not even sure if she is real or if I am just going insane," Rostov said, laying down.

"I'm so bloody confused right now," Lucas muttered.

"Confused is good. It leads to questions, to answers, to *change*. They are about to remove you," Rostov said, rolling over. "Go get some of those answers. You know where to find me."

The door clicked open and the two Host'ire Knights walked inside, their hands clasped around the grips of their small guns. No words were exchanged this time. Instead, they just ushered the three of them out of the room and pointed toward the elevator at the end of the hallway. Behind them, the door made a loud *thump* as it closed.

Joanna took a deep breath. Something was going on here and it went to the very core of the Host'ire order; the deep, dark, rotten core that they didn't like to talk about. She was going to figure it out; expose it, shed light upon it. Maybe then she would be free of them—or perhaps it would get her killed. No, Lucas would protect her, he always did.

Even if you stand up to the order?

Looking over at Lucas, he was hard to read, having fallen back into stoic hero mode. How dark and rotten would the corruption at the heart of the order need to be for him to turn on them? He was a Knight-Commander, after all, and she was just a librarian who was a single reprimand away from ending up in re-education like Rostov.

No, no. Lucas would be on their side. He would protect them. He always did, just like against Jasper.

Yes, that was his name.

Test Chamber, Grace

The LabTech DES 9000 fit like a glove. When she first got there, Grace had been worried about having to don what looked like armor to perform experiments, but once she had started using the Dangerous Experiment Suit (DES), she understood just how useful it was.

The suit consisted of a complex web of green and black armored panels that fit like a reticulated glove. Inside all the different plates were scanners equipped for her to do her job and for the control room to keep track of her vitals. The suit's helmet came with a slew of heads up displays and readouts. All of them she could control with her hands like they were standard holographic computers, even if they were only being displayed on the inside of her visor. Through all these readouts, she was still able to see the math of the universe. The golden numbers that hung over everything, her forever companions.

The test chamber stood before her. It was massive, the largest room that existed in the lower sections of the Olympus Ares Research facility. In the middle of the room, supported by thousands of kilometers of cables and tubes, was a huge upright circle of steel and other rare metals. They called it the Gate. It was what the last three Doctor Grace Goodspeeds had spent their lives working to build. It was the first step in finding a new way to get ships into the Null so that they could explore new places and not be confined by the Nullspace highways established by the Wayfinders, who had been wiped out five hundred years ago by the Host'ire during the birth of the Confederation.

The Gate was three stories tall, and all their projections estimated it was going to take enough power to run a fleet for it to open a rift for a scant few moments. Still, if they were even able to open a rift, that would be enough. If it was stable for a few seconds and didn't collapse in a wave of destructive energy, that would be even better. Emily knew too much about *that* outcome already.

It would take them years to pour over the data that would be gained by the rift being open for even a few fractions of a second. Grace was giddy at the thought of digging into all those numbers, finding the secrets that were hidden in that much raw data. She wasn't ignorant of the risk, though—hence her suit. Trying to open this gateway into the Null had claimed more than a few lives. Grace was confident in her calculations, confident that she wasn't going to be one of them.

The numbers on the edge of the knife. The equation from her dream tried to reform in her field of vision. She closed her eyes and shook her head. That was just dream math, it didn't mean anything. All the numbers had been vetted by her, the team, and the facilities' AI.

Grace was taking the risk of being in the test chamber, even though it was a small risk, because the gate was predicted to be open for six seconds on the outside. The research team didn't want to have any lag time in commands coming to and from the control room to the Gate or needing their computers to make the calculations. That meant it was all up to her to run the gate from its own control panel and make all the calculations in her head to keep the portal open for as long as possible before it inevitably closed. She was faster than any computer that they had.

The last three holographic simulations had gone well enough. During the first two, they were able to keep the aperture open for five seconds before it drew too much power and shut down. The third time, Grace had pushed too hard. She had gotten an idea in the shower and given it a shot. The aperture stayed open for almost twenty seconds that time, but it also exploded, taking half the facility with it. Grace had made a small calculation error on a variable that hadn't been accounted for. Beckett had been working on that issue for the last few days. His last report indicated that it was now corrected.

What did he want this morning? It was a nagging thought in the back of her brain, but not something that she let get too far forward. Beckett and her had built up a report—at least, as much of one as a human and calculation AI could. Lab AI were not built like companion AI's and thus, really only had so much personality that they could exert. They were more like the old machine-learning algorithms than actual synthetic life. Emily had seen an android once while she was in college.

They were extremely rare but did exist, holdovers from a civilization that had died in a catastrophic natural disaster.

"You can approach the Gate now, Doctor Goodspeed," a voice said into her helmet.

"Rodger Control, heading to the gate now," she said into her radio.

Grace looked up toward the control room. It was situated at the top of the test chamber. There was a massive window where the team of technicians and chief researchers could watch the experiment. It was not a place Grace wanted to go. Those were people who had forgotten the joy of pure science, who only saw horrible applications.

The door behind her clicked shut and there was a low hiss as the air in the room was slowly sucked out. This was both to help slow down any explosive issue and to simulate the vacuum of space where eventually this technology was going to be deployed. As the air left the room, Grace could feel her suit tightening around her, like a cozy hug, as it sealed for vacuum. There were magnets in her boots, but thankfully they hadn't moved to the zero-G testing yet.

Grace walked over to the control box on the side of the gate and held her hand over it. There was a brief beeping on the inside as her suit's system connected with the gate's. Grace hadn't been able to connect before coming inside, since the test chamber was air-gaped for added security.

If somebody actually does break in here and gets this far, I'm just going to give them the codes because they will have earned it, she thought.

Grace chuckled to herself, still always baffled and agitated by the security theater at play: from keeping stuff offline, to them changing their names, and hell, to even hiring washed up Host'ire Knights.

The systems all flashed on her heads-up display and quickly Grace started swiping, getting everything set up. It took her a few minutes to configure the systems to how she wanted them, but once that was taken care of, she turned back to the window above the gate where the control room was and gave the team a thumbs up. She also noted that Administrator Vardis wasn't there. That was strange. The three-armed Pa'vinti was always there, hanging from his bar in the middle of the room, giving everybody a blank, bird-like expression. She pushed that thought away. Surely he was just working on something else. He was forever busy.

"Starting first stage activation. I'm going to bring the power to thirty present and move the iris into position," she said, turning a dial and raising gauges that corresponded to the power. Looking up, she saw golden whisps of geometry moving across her field of view, intersecting with the readouts on her visor in a way that only she could appreciate. So far, everything was going well.

"Let's go ahead and bring it up to seventy. I'm going to move the probe into position," she said.

Pushing the power again, Grace reached down to her belt and pulled out a small round device. Turning the top of it twice, a green LED came to life and a small, blue anti-grav pad propped the probe up so that it was hanging in the vacuum. Gently, she pushed it into place just inside the gate. Once the aperture was opened, it would instantly grab the probe, and they could get as much data as possible from the few seconds that the gate would be open.

"Everything on our end is reading steady. Wait standby," the voice from the control room said into her ear.

"Are we all good up there?" Grace asked, looking down at her equipment. There was a small warble from the changes she had made last night.

"We are getting a fluctuation in the anti-matter intermix chamber," the voice said.

"It is well within safety limits, just keep an eye on it—and be ready to depolarize the core if it gets to eighty percent off the redline," Grace said back.

It was good, everything was fine. *This is going to work. I know we can get those twenty seconds.*

"Moving to 100% and preparing to open the aperture," Grace said, pushing the power to the limit.

Energy started to cascade across the gate, focusing on the center of the ring. The room began to shake, and klaxons went off, as the blue-green shimmering aperture opened, covering the whole of the inside of the gate.

Screams burst into the radio. Screams of unimaginable terror and pain. It caused Grace to snap her head to the side in pain, as a burst of energy exploded from the gate.

Her world went dark.

EPISODE II:
Liminal Space

Liminal Space, Grace

There was no weight, no air. There was nothing. Just pinpoints of light in the distance; thousands and millions of pinpoints of light. Stars, galaxies, nebulae, any and all manner of galactic phenomena. Grace started to look around, her brain trying to understand where she was, what she was seeing.

Looking down—if there is such a thing as down in space—she saw a ribbon of light shimmering in the darkness. Gently, she felt a pull and then her feet touched down. Whatever this strand of light was, it had gravity and mass. Her lungs tried to take in a breath; there was nothing to draw in. Yet they didn't deflate, she didn't get lightheaded; didn't feel the oxygen leaving her system.

Raising her arms, Grace found her hands. Her suit was gone, as was her lab coat. Looking down, there was nothing— as if she wasn't there. At the same time, she felt naked in the void of space.

She took a step, then another. As she walked, screams started to fill her head, a cacophony of horror. A mixture of pain and terror, anger and sadness, the full range of negative emotions streaming into her ears. Grace closed her eyes and tried to push them away. The screams got louder. There were no words, only raw emotions, washing over her like waves. Grace opened her eyes. The screams had changed. They were still loud, still filled with horror, but now she could *see* them.

Just as everything was an equation to her, the sounds started to change into waveforms. Angry, golden waveforms filled with spikes and jagged edges, knives of negative emotion smashing into her body like angry particles in an accelerator.

"Stop, please," Grace whimpered as the emotions started cut through her. Tears started to run down her cheeks. She had never felt anything like this before; such raw, horrible emotion. There was no joy, only the feelings of anger and vengeance.

This galaxy shall burn.

She didn't know who they were seeking vengeance upon, but in that moment, Grace would have sacrificed everything to help them achieve it, if only to end the wave of hate and rage ripping through her soul.

"I don't know how to help you," Grace whispered, though tears and choking cries as pain washed through her body. *Even Emily doesn't know...*

The stars around her were zipping by. Through the waves of sound, Grace could see velocity equations, well exceeding the speed of light. Red, purple, orange, and light blue started to fill her field of view, all coming from an all-consuming cloud. The turbulence was evident even from far away.

The Barrier.

Grace had never seen the storm in person, but everybody knew what it was, what it looked like. The storm that blocked off one edge of civilization, that prevented them from seeing farther, from *going* farther. There were no Nullspace highways through the storm. Except that wasn't entirely true. *There is one, one that the Wayfinders never finished. Is this...?* She looked down at the ribbon of light. Closing her eyes, Grace knew she needed to focus, to calm herself. As she did, the sounds faded away, and air finally filled her lungs.

Taking a breath, she opened her eyes.

Everything had stopped moving and she was standing still upon the ribbon, looking out over the vastness of the cosmos, her vision unobscured by the reality of science.

All around her were millions of ribbons of light. Nullspace Highways. There are so many of them...

She reached an arm out as if to touch one of the delicate strands of golden light, to pluck it like the cord of a harp. Then her feet fell out from under her and the world started to spin. As she fell, Grace saw an accretion disk whipping around the event horizon of a black hole.

It was the Fissure, the singularity that created the galactic core. Then there was a dead world made of red stone, shooting toward her like a bullet that had her name scratched into the lead.

"Emily Itchi," it whispered.

The malevolent force in the galaxy knew her name, her *real* name; it knew everything. A chill ran through her as she saw her death fast approaching—but then she was on the ground, in her suit again. The world was dead, covered in a blanket of rust and blood. Above her head, storms the likes of which she had never seen rumbled. All around her were the bones of a civilization. Tall buildings with missing chunks, vehicles almost completely consumed by the sands of time, and bones. Billions upon billions of bones. Whoever they were, they had died a horrible death, and it had happened tens of thousands of years ago.

Everywhere there were runes, glowing a golden yellow, a language that she did-but-did-not know. This was where the screams had been coming from. These were the wrathful dead.

"What do you want?" Grace pleaded, her words choking in her throat, failing to come out.

"What do you want!?" Emily demanded, but still no sound came from her mouth, only echoed in her mind.

As she yelled again and again, she fell to her knees, tears running freely as the darkness took her.

***

"Alarm, Alarm," the robotic voice repeated over and over. Red light started to push through the darkness as Grace opened a single eye. There were flashing lights, smoke, steam, and the heads-up display of her DES suit. Running up and down both sides of her field of vision was a list of warnings and issues. Reaching a sore arm up, she pushed them down, silencing the alarm going off inside her helmet. For a moment, there was blissful silence, before the sounds of the broken test chamber filled her ears.

Where had she just been? How long had she been out?

It knew us, Emily whispered deep in her mind, worried, scared.

It was just a dream, a concussive nightmare and nothing more. She would get her head looked at later, make sure there was no lasting damage.

It knew us, Emily said again. The images of the barrier, of the ribbon of light, were still filling Grace's mind. If she believed in prophetic visions, this would worry her—but she did not. It was just her mind running wild while she was unconscious, and now that she was awake, there was work to be done. One last breath and she willed the vision to depart from her mind's eye, focusing on the world around her.

Everything had been destroyed, except for the gate. Its ring was intact and undamaged. All the cables leading up to it had been severed. Some were flailing around, sending sparks cascading across the room. Others were belching coolant like severed limbs spilling viscera. The walls were covered in scorch marks and... was that a streak of blood? Grace followed it to the ground where she found a boot with a ragged leg sticking out of it. Her eyes darted to the large wall of glass, where the control room looked down on the test chamber. The glass had shattered, leaving shards that made the broken window look like the gaping maw of a creature from a campfire story.

There was a hum as the systems in her suit started to come back online, the self-repairing functions doing their jobs. Grace blinked her right eye five times, flipping through the visual spectrum scanners to see what energy was still radiating off the gate and how bad that could be for her. The integrity of her suit was at eighty percent. Thankfully, at least one thing had done its job correctly today. She didn't know what had gone wrong and this was not the time to try and figure it out. Now was the time to get free and find any other survivors, find somebody else who might know what the hell was going on.

Grace pushed herself to her feet and started walking to the door when another small beep went off in her suit. It was the probe Grace had placed inside the portal. Somehow it hadn't been destroyed, and it was beeping to let her know all of its onboard memory had been filled.

That's impossible, she thought. Those probes had enough space for twenty hours of 10k full spectrum video. Grace walked to where the probe had been spit from the gate. The device was covered in frost. She picked it up and connected it to her suit.

"That can't be correct," she muttered. The Chronometer was reading that the probe had been active for a week, going into low storage mode days ago, only recording ten second clips every few hours.

"Wherever you went, little buddy, I don't think it was very fun," Grace said, sliding the probe back into its pouch as she headed to the door. The automatic door kept opening and closing, the scanner being tripped by a blood-covered I-beam. Grace stepped over it to enter the airlock room.

It was, impossibly, in even worse shape than the lab. Grace's two research assistants, who'd closed the door and monitored her suit, had been thrown against the wall. Randy's body was broken; his arms and legs twisted in unnatural directions. His head had smashed so hard against the steel wall, it had left a dent before shattering into a gloopy pile of bone, brain, and skin.

Viv... Well, Viv was all over the room. She must have been close to the door when the blast wave came through.

Grace hoped it had all happened quickly, that they hadn't suffered.

This is all my fault. I should have double checked those calculations or tried to see what it was that Beckett wanted to say, Grace thought as she stared at what was left of her young assistants, guilt welling up inside her. An all too familiar guilt. They hadn't even gotten a chance to become real scientists, to make any meaningful discoveries of their own. No, they just took notes for her and ran tests. Now they were dead—so *many* people were dead—because she wanted a few extra seconds of open aperture.

Grace took a step back away from the scene of destruction, the past flashing through her mind, something she couldn't place except for the violent nature of it. There was a thump as she backed into a wall. Still, she pushed at it, pushed to get away from the death she had caused. The pathway of light flashed in her mind, the sounds of screaming children all around her.

"Emily," she whispered.

The specter of her past was quiet. Grace would have to face this alone, look upon what she had done and confront it. The suit chirped, pushing more O2 into her helmet to counteract the ragged deep breaths she was taking in. She started to feel slightly better. Closing her eyes, she got control of her breathing, pushed away the pathway of light, the screams from her past, and the irritation that when she needed her, Emily was gone.

"Stop it, Grace. That kind of thinking isn't going to help you. The only thing that can be done for them now is for you to get out of here. Then figure out what went wrong and try again," she whispered to herself.

"They gave their lives for science!" Grace declared aloud. It was the kind of pep talk one of her professors would have given. Words that were said by somebody who hadn't paid a human cost for their research—like they both had.

Taking a deep breath, Grace stopped stalling and walked to the closed door and pressed her hand against it. There was a beep and then nothing. She pressed again. This time, the door yelled louder, followed by a hiss from the radio in her helmet.

"Doctor Goodspeed, are you there?" the voice from the radio asked. She let out a breath. It was good to hear another voice, even if it was the squawking raspy voice of Administrator Vardis.

Figures that middle management would survive something like this, Grace thought bitterly. Vardis wasn't a scientist, just some industrialist that the higher ups had brought in to keep them on task and on schedule.

He was affable enough, if a little dense about what they were working on.

"What happened?" Grace asked.

"I am trying to ascertain that now. Clearly the gate was not ready for today's test."

"No shit. We have dead people down here, probably wounded up in the control room," Grace said.

She didn't care about the gate right now, didn't care about the test. That was something they could come back to, something that could be addressed *later*. She was worried about the human cost; her friends and coworkers that had been thrown across rooms and smashed into walls, the mess that was the final end of Viv and Randy still fresh in her mind.

"The control room took a direct hit. Nobody there is answering. You are the only person on the science team that I have been able to get a hold of," Vardis said, panic warbling into his voice.

He isn't in control. That's new, Grace thought.

She didn't know the Administrator well, but she knew him well enough to know he was always in control. Obsessive planning and preparation were his hallmarks. He did not have the luxury of control right now. None of them did.

"My suit is hardened. The EMP from the exposition didn't fry my electronics. Put them on the fritz and knocked me out cold for a moment, though," Grace said.

"Well, it's good to hear that your suit did its job."

There was a pause, and she could tell that he was remembering that he needed to address the fact that it was also good *she* was alive, because people were not equipment. Not just another line item on a corporate balance sheet.

"All the equipment is doing well. Radio, spectrometer, life support, human," Grace said, beating him to the punch of acknowledging that she was a living being inside the suit.

"It is also good that you are alive, Doctor. That goes without saying," he muttered.

Though it would be nice if people said it from time to time, Grace thought.

"Right now, we need to worry about getting a message to the rest of the facility and seeing how far the shockwave went. Do you think you can make it to my office?" Vardis asked.

"I should be able to do that. I'll probably have to climb, so it'll be a little while, provided nothing else is in my way," Grace said.

She looked at the keypad that was holding her back from opening the door and punched it. Servos in her suit gave her arm an extra push and her armored hand smashed into the box. The door flew open, a half-hearted klaxon blaring in the background.

"Capitol! I shall see you soon. Be careful, doctor. I would hate to lose you," he squawked, cutting off the comm line.

"I would hate to lose me, too," Grace muttered.

Apartments, The Citadel, Lucas

Lucas unpacked quickly. When originally heading out, he couldn't fathom what would be going on at the Citadel that would require his attention beyond a short period of time. As such, he had packed two outfits, his charging station, and a meditation crystal. All of it had fit neatly in a small overhead bag. He put away the clothing in the dresser and hung up his leather coat and weapon vest. Lucas had only brought his blade, which now that he had spoken to Rostov, made him feel under-armed.

Setting the crystal on the bed, Lucas took off his glasses and gloves and sat down. He didn't sleep much these days. His dreams were unsettled, violent. Anything more than that was a fading memory that didn't survive into the morning. It was a good thing that a well-trained Host'ire Knight could get most of the benefits of sleep with crystal meditation.

Closing his eyes, he placed his bare hands on the crystal and took a deep breath, letting the Null surround and envelop him. Without the meditative control and focal point of the crystal, such an attempt would have been too much. The Null would have threatened to consume him.

It was where the Host'ire drew their power from, yes, and where ships jumped so that they could fold space and time. But the Null was also an unstable torrent of energy that was prone to backfiring upon people who did not know how to use it. Even those who were well-trained routinely dove too deep, attempting to find the Shadow, a source of power that existed below the Null; something horrible and consuming that swallowed most knights that approached it. Which was why Lucas never risked using the Null to rest without the focus of the crystal.

The night passed quickly. Lucas was able to find his center and slip into a calming state, which felt like a warm bath where gentle soft hands relaxed his entire body. Most nights, Lucas could not get this far in his meditation routine. He either fell asleep or was distracted by the world around him. Here, though, it was quiet, and the Null was powerful. Lucas could feel Naomi and Joanna as a calming, relaxing presence. Both were asleep.

For a brief moment, he was envious of their ability to sleep and experience their dreams. Then, their calm filtered toward him and pushed away any remaining negative emotion, allowing him to reach that transcendental state he was seeking.

Morning came quickly as the small alarm jostled Lucas out of his meditative state. He breathed in and pulled himself out of the relaxing bath of Null energy he had been relaxing in. There was light coming from underneath the door. Running his hand over the rooms control switch, he activated the lights. It was far brighter than he wanted, bright enough to compensate for the fact that the space between the material world and the Null was weak here.

"I hate these lights. They hurt," a young boy said.

Lucas turned and saw himself sitting pouting on the bed, a pair of glasses in his hand. An echo of a memory. The crystal sometimes produced those. They were like what he saw and felt on the *Sequin Dream*, only these were more complete, coming whole cloth from his memory.

The Host'ire Ambassadors who spent more time in their memories than the physical world claimed any vision was prophetic. Lucas was sure they were reading too far into it. He had not seen anything in his life to make him believe in prophecy. Everything could be rationalized as the mind being something that they didn't fully understand.

"That is why we wear the glasses, child. To dull the brightness. So that we may operate in the world of the mundanes," said an older voice that he couldn't see. The younger version of himself looked crestfallen.

Lucas remembered this well. He had resisted the glasses; didn't want to set himself apart from everybody else. He hadn't needed them when he was with his family, only now that he was here in this place where the lights were too bright. The young boy faded away as Lucas put on his glasses and walked to the small bathroom. That was not a memory he was fond of, and he knew it would sadly hang in his mind for the rest of the day.

Lucas quickly took a shower and got dressed, pulling on one of the clean outfits that he had. Best to alternate them, hopefully mitigating how dirty they were going to get. Lastly, he pulled on his leather gloves and opened the door.

The central room that connected the three bedrooms was small. Only enough room for a table, kitchenet, a couch and small chair. Not so large that an adult had ample space, instead clearly designed so that a child could sit in one with their legs crossed to meditate. Lucas hadn't paid attention when they were led to these rooms last night, but now that he was looking around, it was very clear that Administrator Fel had put them in one of the group teen pods. Right where they had lived when all of them met for the first time.

Petty bitch, Lucas thought, knowing that there were pods for visiting groups of knights.

Joanna was already up, sitting at the table reading a book—a ratty paperback novel. Naomi was messing with something in the small kitchen, steam and the smell of coffee filling the room.

"Good morning," Joanna said, looking up from her book, a smile crossing her face.

Lucas, for a moment, felt weak in his knees at that smile. It was kind and full. It made him feel like he was thirteen again, dealing with a new environment and changes to his body, both physical and mental. Her smile had always been there. Why had he let it fade away? So much had been forgotten, lost. He prided himself on his memory and his failings in that area were quickly coming into sharp focus.

Lucas closed his eyes and breathed out, taking that smile and sliding it into his memory. This time, he wasn't going to lose it. This time, he would fight to keep it. He would be damned if whatever had happened to their memories before was going to happen to them again.

Lucas returned the smile and sat down. Reaching under the table, he ran his hand along the hilt of his blade, using it as a focal point to calm his mind.

"How did everybody sleep last night?" Lucas asked, trying to make a little small talk. They had fallen back into an easy cadence on the flight, but sitting around the breakfast table was different. It implied a whole other level of comfort and familiarity.

"I slept quite well. The bed was as big as the one at Black Hollow, only more comfortable. I don't remember the beds being comfortable from the last time I was here," Naomi said, turning from where she worked in the kitchen, three steaming mugs in her hand.

She walked over to the table and sat the mugs down, sliding one to each of them. The smell of coffee filled Lucas's nose, and he breathed it in deeply. This was just what he needed. There was no use trying to start a morning without coffee. There was no better way to scrub away the leftover energy from his meditation than a quick hit of caffeine.

"The beds are not comfortable. You were just raised by the order. Coming here from home, even a poor home, led to years of poor sleep and back pain," Joanna said dryly.

She put a marker in her book and closed it. Lucas looked at the paperback. It was well-worn, showing battle scars from the many times it had been read.

"There is no bed like home. They did everything possible to remind us that this place was not home; that home was somewhere we couldn't go back to," Lucas said, taking a sip of the coffee.

"It wasn't that bad," Naomi said defensively.

"It was. The teachers needed to break us, so that we could be the weapons that they wanted us to be. Somehow, each of us avoided that fate," Joanna muttered.

The two of them, and Rostov, might have avoided that fate. Lucas, though? He was a sharpened and honed weapon of the Host'ire. Every goal that the Citadel had for its students, Lucas had met and exceeded. The young boy who had arrived here was gone. All that was left of him was the soldier, the warrior, the leader.

"It *is* home, though," Lucas said. "Or as much of one as we have left. It's not the same, but we have returned."

"Why, though?" Joanna asked.

"That is the million-credit question, isn't it?" Naomi said.

"And I intend to figure out the answer. We know far too little. The tactical situation is not in our favor," Lucas said, the soldier and leader taking over. "Let's go over what we know. Messages from a friend that we don't remember drew us here."

"But a friend that we all started to remember as soon as we read her name," Naomi said.

"No. Not memories; feelings, *ideas* of a friend. A certainty that I couldn't even question, almost like it was planted in our minds." Joanna said.

"Could something *have* been planted inside our brains when we were children and now it's being activated?" Lucas asked. He had not come across any division of the Host'ire that did things like that to children, but he knew the order well enough now to not put it past them. Official operation or rogue.

"It isn't impossible, but hard. Brainwashing a person with a strong connection to the Null is very difficult," Joanna said. "I read a book about it. I was a research assistant a few years back for a historian that was writing a book on crime and punishment."

"So maybe not brainwashing. Still, *something* is going on inside of our minds. That seems—to me, at least—the only explanation for why we remember some things and not others. Gaps that shouldn't exist," Lucas said.

"Trauma," Noami piped in. She didn't give them a chance to look at her in a way that implored her to continue. The words started to spill from her at great speed. "Trauma can suppress many memoires. It's possible that something horrible happened to us here that we have repressed. Most likely, such an event would be in a record somewhere and probably would have caused us to all wash out, but it does conveniently answer many of the questions about why we remember some things and not others. Why the letter from Hyacinth was a triggering event. Why everything seems just to be painful feelings..." She was about to say more but then stopped and looked down at her coffee. "I'm rambling again."

"You are just excited. I think you might be on to something," Lucas said.

He found her rambling endearing, cute almost. The speed that her mind moved impressed him. He thought about every single word he was going to say before he said it. She just let it flow.

"This place was never nice to us. Nobody protected us from Jasper. It was as if they wanted it to happen," Joanna said.

"So, we know that we are having memory gaps, and for now, will operate under the idea that it's a trauma response, possibly one that the order encouraged," Lucas said.

Joanna nodded, while Naomi seemed sad that her idea was possible. Her faith in the order ran deep, unlike Joanna, who he knew had none.

"The second point is they are clearly hiding something. Administrator Fel was livid to see us," Lucas said.

"I get that look from administration all the time. She would have thrown us out an airlock, if possible," Joanna said. Both of them looked at her and she just shrugged her broad shoulders. "What can I say? I am not one to be managed."

"You never were," Lucas said with a chuckle.

He was obsessed with rules, and she hated them, which was one of the most attractive things about her. The chaos that her life generated compared to the ordered structure of his. Perhaps bringing her back into his orbit was the world saying he needed a little more chaos in his life. Or perhaps he was reading too deeply into things, too much like those ambassadors who spent too much time in their memories. Either way, he was glad to have her back; making things interesting when they didn't need to be.

"Oh, you have no idea, Knight-Commander Brandice," she said, leaning forward, mischief in her eyes. "I am an agent of chaos and would have it no other way."

Lucas swallowed, feeling something stirring deep inside him.

Naomi chuckled at the whole exchange. Joanna pulled back, winking at Lucas. He picked up his coffee and took a long sip, letting the mug sit in front of his face for a few moments so that he could regain his composure. He felt like a child again—a stupid, smitten child.

"Whatever it is they are hiding, they don't want the novices around. Nobody is here. I've never seen it so empty," Lucas said, redirecting them. "Plus, Rostov knows something; more than he is telling us."

"I don't think he knows what he knows and what he doesn't," Naomi said. "His mind was confused, jumbled up. I've been there, the thoughts coming too fast, in no real structure. They left him nothing to write it down on, nothing to help him find the order."

Lucas could feel the pain in that line. It wasn't his, though. He was feeling it coming *from* her. No, not coming from her; it *was* hers, but he could feel it inside himself.

Lucas pushed this away as well. *Just left over connection, left over childhood...feelings,* he thought.

"Right. So, our goals are simple. We need to figure out what is going on here first, then get Rostov out of re-education. I feel like that seems to be what Hyacinth wants us to do. Or, at least, the first part of what she wants us to do," Lucas muttered.

The three of them nodded in agreement.

"As I see it, the best way to go about this is going to be to split up. Everybody surely had a professor, someone they liked, someone that they trusted. I suggest we reach out to them first and see what we can gleam from those old connections. I suspect Fel treats the administration just as curtly as she did us. That kind of leadership breeds resentment that will work in our favor," Lucas said.

"I was always friendly with Professor Rickman. She taught me so much about how to control my powers and use them for the things I was interested in. She sends me a message every time I put out a new technical manual letting me know she has read it," Naomi said.

"I never liked her," Joanna muttered.

"Oh posh. As we established, you never liked anybody in power," Naomi snipped back.

"Baron'Tor, the librarian, was always nice to me. He didn't have some air of being a professor; of being 'above'," Joanna bit back.

"Well then, you should see if he is still here," Lucas said.

"Are you giving me orders?" she asked, that same mischievous smile creeping onto her face.

"I wouldn't dream of it. Just a light suggestion," Lucas said.

"Oh well, in that case, I shall go and check out the library," Joanna said.

"You are a librarian, after all," Noami added.

"So, where is our fearless leader going to go? Which professor did he admire?" Joanna asked, clearly needling at Lucas.

"I'm going to make some calls, maybe see what the Master-at-Arms has to say. They have to have replaced that miserable old one-armed bastard by now."

CIC, Fury, Cassandra

It had taken the crew of *Fury* almost thirty minutes to get the ship ready to cast off. This was too slow for Cassandra's liking. They would need to be drilled. Six months in space dock had made them soft, weak. A slow response late in the evening was not the worst thing that could have happened and was something that could be remedied in short order, but even so, it could not be ignored. There were still thousands of crew members from *before* the battle. They would knock the cobwebs from their brains and then knock sense into the fresh members of their departments.

"All sections signal ready, Lord Admiral!" Captain Rackland called from the middle deck of the CIC. He had been putting the boot to the last few departments that were struggling to get into position.

"Very good, Captain. Take us out, if you please," Cassandra called up.

"Aye! Comm signal to Antiga Prime to remove all mooring and umbilical cables. Helm, take us out full reverse!" The clear gruff voice of Captain Rackland echoed through the command deck, dispensing orders on her behalf.

"Station reports all moorings are lose," came a yell from communications.

"Aye, full reverse!" the boatswain next to the helm yelled back, as the young man working the wheel pressed a few keys and started to turn the great circle of wood.

Cassandra looked down at her control station on the glass table and opened a ship-wide communication channel. Next to the key that would allow her to speak to the crew was a long playlist, organized into folders for every occasion. She opened the folder labeled *Returning to Space*, choosing the fourth track titled, 'Exit Space Dock,' and pressed play.

Throughout the ship, deep horns and violins started to play. It was a triumphant march that built up momentum as the ship moved away from the dock. The middle section of the composition was designed to be played as an alternating loop until the ship was free of the dock and could head out into open space. Cassandra had written a small algorithm to make sure that the timing happened correctly. There were hundreds of tracks in the *Fury* soundtrack that were built this way, to fill an unknown amount of time and then crescendo at the correct moment.

Cassandra had once gotten to see *Fury* exiting dry dock from the observation deck of Antiga Prime; the massive ship slowly pulling away, spotlights moving across the decks, every viewing port full on the station.

It had been a sight to behold.

Getting to see a Dreadstar leave dock was a rare occurrence even for those who lived and died on stations like Antiga Prime. Cassandra wrote 'Exit Space Dock' that evening. Her father had still been alive and in command of House Cordova and the *Fury*. While far from her first composition, it was the one that would eventually become her core personal theme and that of the *Fury*.

In the last thirty years, however, she noticed a change in her style, from big brass orchestral arrangements to wood winds, strings, and drums. Music, like the times, changed. Though the older she got, the harder she found it to continue adapting as change required.

"We are clear of space dock, ma'am!" Rackland called down from where he stood on the third level of the CIC, his arms tightly held behind his back.

"Very good, Captain. Take us to the jump gate and prepare the ship for Null space," Cassandera called back.

Captain Rackland repeated her orders up to the helm station and the boatswain whistled a command that went out across the ship: prepare for jump.

She turned to look at the now cleaned off glass map table. It had been updated to show the current system that they were in and the astro-meteorological data from overnight. Currents of Null- and wind-energy constantly emitted from the Barrier, causing void storms and other meteorological features that were not unlike weather on a planet. The farther away from the Barrier you got, the less frequent these phenomena were. Confederation space was quite close to the Barrier, so the storms were something she had to take into account.

"If it pleases the Lord Admiral, helm is ready to receive coordinates for our destination," Rackland called back down into the command pit.

"Helm set for Astarte's Gate," she called back.

Rackland relayed the order up the chain again. A moment later, a clock started to count down on the table. Five minutes. That was how long it would take to reach the nearby Jump Gate. Captain Rackland walked down to join Lord Admiral Cordova on the command level. She watched as he picked up a grease pencil, drawing their current plot, before pulling over a transparency screen that displayed the jump gate they headed toward, marking that off as well.

"Are we coming back for the new ambassador Lord Admiral?" Rackland asked as he worked, not looking up at his commanding officer. They both knew the answer, but he was still required to ask it, to hear the words come from her mouth.

"Once we are through the gate, Captain, I want you to establish a CAP and rig us for silent running," she said, avoiding the question. Cassandra would be damned if she was going to let another one of those Host'ire on her ship. If they thought that Tiberius was replaceable, those wizards were going to have another thing coming.

"Cassandra," Captain Rackland said flatly, quietly.

"Those are my orders, Captain. I trust you can handle them," she said.

"Aye, Lord Admiral," he said with a crisp salute.

"Very well. Carry on. I shall be in my drawing room," she said. Cassandra turned to walk away. "Captain, switch to Track 33, if you please."

With that, she exited the CIC, as the thumping pounding drums of 'Jump Prep' started to play.

Flight Deck, Fury, Erik

The pilot's locker room on Hanger Deck Three was quiet. Erik had given his pilots the night off, to celebrate the end of dry dock. One last night of freedom before endless rotations of patrols and drills to get them back into fighting shape. So, when his mother had called for them to leave space dock unexpectedly, there were precious few pilots in position to take up the call. Erik wasn't interested in drugging them into sobriety for a simple CAP. He cut off the fun and sent them all to get rack time before the marrow.

That did still leave the matter of who was going to fly the first Combat Air Patrol. Already while docked, they had been maintaining their own flyby that last day. It was a squadron staffed with green pilots right out of basic flight and lieutenants that were never going to see an actual promotion in their time aboard *Fury*. Erik could have pushed them, but didn't see the point in that. You did not abuse your new recruits. They were only going to get better with support—not if superiors piled upon them the work they did not want to do.

Taking all that into account, the responsibility fell to him. As such, Erik pulled in his standard crew for a job like this. If he was flying, Bella was going to be right at his side.

"Your mother is not taking this replacement well. It is going to reflect badly upon us," Bella said frankly. Bella said everything that wasn't a joke frankly.

"Watch your tone, cousin," Erik said. He knew she wouldn't. Bella was one of the few who could talk to Erik in that tone, especially in a safe space like an empty pilot's locker room.

"I am, cousin. She is going to get a reprimand from the Admiralty for this. It will look bad on the family. The Confederation has been in bed with the Host'ire since its founding. Their ambassadors are required to be on ships of the line. You should know this, just as well as your Mother does."

"We will survive a reprimand from stogy old men who haven't seen space in twenty years," Erik said, wrapping the airlock gorget around his neck and picking up his helmet. "But... I will talk to her tomorrow. We are headed for NovaTerra for the election. They will catch up with us there."

"And if your mother skips the election?" Bella asked.

"Mother does not skirt her duty to the Confederation, only it's wizards. Still, I worry how far she might take this," Erik said.

"The Lord Admiral is nothing if not persistent when she has something in her head. And truly, who is going to stand in her way?" Bella asked.

"Nobody openly, and that, dear cousin, is where my fear nests. Mother has made enemies in the government for doing things like this. I do not think commanding a Dreadstar will keep her safe much longer from the muck of political life. I do not want to have something like this tarnish her legacy—or hobble my ascension," Erik added.

"Then we shall just have to stand by and be her shields in the darkness," Bella said, a look of mischievous glee in her eyes. Erik knew that she would enjoy getting to throw down for her family against Confederation forces far too much. It was never going to come to that, of course. He couldn't allow it.

"For now, we keep this in the family. Come, let's see what other poor bastards answered my call for this spur-of-the-moment flight," Erik said, holding out his helmet. Bella nodded and tapped her helmet to his as they walked out.

The hanger deck was dark but still alive with activity. The deck crew had gotten their fighters ready, and three pilots were standing in a knot, waiting for Erik and Bella to join them for the briefing. In the group was Lieutenant Ander Stormwind, looking tired but still put together, with his blond hair and rakish charm. Next to him was the father-daughter duo: Lieutenant Commander Victor Nguyen and his daughter Aya, who was still a cadet. They were the team that was going to be flying the Hawkeye Combat information and radar craft, which was standard to include with every squadron on patrol.

Lieutenant Commander Nguyen was in his mid-forties. His face was covered in wrinkles, scars, and even a dead eye. The signs of a hard life of flying and fighting. Gripped between his teeth was a cigarette that hadn't been lit. It was never going to be, but still he kept it with him before every flight.

His daughter, Aya, looked every bit her sixteen years. She had been accepted into a junior flyers program and was moving through the curriculum faster than just about anybody ever had. She was whip smart, understanding how information was what controlled a battlefield. More than anything, she was a spitting image of her late mother.

Erik didn't know if that caused friction in the family—the Nguyens were quiet and didn't run in the same circles as he did. Still, they were the best at what they did, which is why they flew with him and Bella.

Ander, on the other hand, was here because he was awake, sober, and hungry.

"I know this is not how we were planning to spend our evening, but the demands of the service take their toll on us all," Erik started. "We will be exiting Null space in three bells. As soon as the ship is squared away, we will launch and begin our patrol. Lieutenant Commander, keep an eye out for any strange, long-range comm traffic. There were sure to be people on the station who are conspiring with those who want to see what they started six months ago finished."

Everybody nodded. There wasn't much to go over. This might be the first CAP since getting back into the fight for *Fury*, but it was still just a Combat Air Patrol and until something changed, he planned to treat it as such. Everything was normal right up until the moment it was not.

The group circled up, holding their helmets out.

"'There once were honored warriors upon the stars,'" Erik said, starting the first line of the Fighter pilot's creed.

"'For with the Unions foes they did spar,'" Bella said next.

"'From rock and tempest, fire and foe,'" Lieutenant Commander Ngyun said.

"'Protect them wheresoe'er they go,'" Aya said, finishing the couplet.

"'Spreading freedom and honor close and far,'" Ander said.

"'The Confederation's Avatar,'" Erik said, finishing the Creed.

They tapped their helmets together with solid *clinks* and then walked toward the launch deck. Three Rapier cockpits were sitting on the deck, the airlocks around the bottom locked solid. On the far side of the flight deck was the larger Hawkeye flight pod. Erik walked over to his cockpit. Standing next to it was Chief Hassan.

"Everything is tip-top Commander. I went over all of it myself," he said, pulling the restraints down over Erik's head.

"Thank you, Mister Hassan. You and your crew do fine work. We shall again be the envy of every ship in the fleet," Erik said as he latched himself in, pulling his helmet down over his head.

"Aye sir, that we will. That we will," Hassan said, giving him a smart salute that consisted of his fist held by his temple at an angle.

The gruff old deckhand grabbed the canopy of the cockpit and pulled it down, locking it into place. Banging on it, Erik gave him a thumbs up from inside. Hassan turned and gave a thumbs up to the deck control officer, who was stationed above the deck in a glass-rimmed room. The deck officer controlled all the launch tubes on this side of the ship. A Dreadstar did not function without their flight control officers. The one today was new.

"Good evening, Commander Cordova. This is Lieutenant Eva. I will be your flight control officer on this mission. On your mark, sir, we will start the prelaunch sequence," a young woman's voice said, coming over the headset. It was strange, not hearing Major Nguyen's calm, completely-in-control voice. Erik knew it had to be harder for her husband and daughter just across the way in the Hawkeye. The disaster in Hyroncore had touched everybody aboard the *Fury*.

"Thank you, Lieutenant. You may start prelaunch, as you please," Erik said.

He started flicking a few switches in his cockpit and working his hands in the leather of his gloves. There was always stiffness in his hands that had to be worked out. A stiffness in his hands that echoed as a stiffness in his heart. He was his mother's son, in that respect.

A minute later, sounds of steam and compressed air filled the flight deck as the airlock seals that were around the cockpits opened. The cockpits, with their human cargo, started to lower. Below them were the chassis of their fighters, waiting for the brain to be slipped into place. It took only a moment and then Erik felt a jolt and click as his systems started to connect with those of his fighter. All the dark screens came to life, displaying a dazzling amount of information. Erik turned half of them off, relegating all their information and warnings to a series of buzzers. He could not focus amongst too much visual clutter.

Erik flicked a switch to his comm system. "This is the Commander. We are ready for launch," he said.

"Aye, Commander. Good hunting," Eva said from the control room.

A ten second countdown started on Erik's dashboard as the sound of fast snare drums in time with the count filled the back register of his ears.

His mother's love of the dramatic was built into every aspect of life aboard *Fury*.

The clock hit zero and Erik was thrown back in his seat as the catapult shot the Rapier down the launch tube. A moment later, he was outside the Dreadstar and under his own power. Doing a quick visual inspection, Erik could see that the rest of his squadron had launched successfully. Pushing the stick forward, all Erik could hear were the soft sounds of the micro burns from the thrusters on his fighter, keeping the ship flying level.

"Commander Cordova to *Fury* actual," he said, pulling up the channel for the Combat Information Center.

"*Fury* Actual. Go ahead, Commander," the Lord Admiral's voice came back.

"We have the CAP, sir," Erik said.

"Very well Commander, carry on. Actual out."

The line cut off. Erik pressed a few buttons and his ship's navigation computer drew up a four-point patrol plan. Another key stroke and it was linked to the other three ships. Ander and Bella formed up on his wing, with the Nguyens and their Hawkeye falling in behind them.

Now, they had five hours of time to kill, circling the ship, looking for threats, and trying to stay awake.

Rickman's Lab, The Citadel, Naomi

Professor Rickman was still on campus. Naomi had checked the registry and sent a note ahead. While she had left the dorms, she didn't make her way toward the facility floor until she had gotten a response back from the professor that she had the time and was willing to meet with her. Naomi had pictured showing up unannounced and that thought made her palms clammy and her gut uneasy. People always made fun of her for this, but Naomi just couldn't show up to places uninvited or unannounced.

It was an assumption that people made all the time. "Oh, you were there when we were talking about this, so I assumed you were coming along." And then she would quietly say that they didn't invite her. Then the head scratching would start. They would say they were sure they did, but it didn't matter because she was there when they were talking about the thing and that was as good as an invitation, right? It wasn't. She was never able to convince anyone of that. No, she always asked to come over and never went someplace without an express invitation.

If there was one thing that Naomi didn't want to be, it was at an event where she wasn't wanted.

Professor Rickman had scheduled their appointment for 'whenever,' which wasn't really what Naomi wanted to hear, but it was something she could work with and responded that she would be there in twenty minutes. This gave her just enough time to work up the courage to get moving. Yes, she knew this professor. Yes, they still kept in contact. Yes, they were both well regarded in their fields, but none of that seemed to matter. Just popping over was going to cause Naomi to break out in hives.

As she reached the door, Naomi stopped, clapping her hands together, pressing her index fingers to her lips before breathing out, centering herself. Then she knocked. Instantly, the door opened.

Professor Rickman's lab was a large open space, extending up three levels to a vaulted ceiling. That negative space was filled with hundreds of hanging tools and ventilation hoods. There were also thousands upon thousands of books and manuals on shelves all over the walls. The main area of the room consisted of rows of flat worktables with dark black stone tops.

In the center of the room was Professor Rickman. She was an older woman who stood tall. Her black leather coat was loose and as she walked around, pushing and pulling levelers, Naomi could see the bandoliers underneath that were full of vials and tools. Her blue hair was pulled up into a bun, and she had on a pair of safety goggles. It took a moment before Rickman noticed that Naomi was in the room, turning her head up from the project she was working on.

"Ah, my old student. Come in, come in!" she called, waving a rubber gloved hand in the air. As Naomi walked, the professor went back to soldering the board that was on her table. It was a stock computer control board, but there were another four components that Naomi didn't recognize, connected to it with wires and joined cords. Three fans sat on top of even more components, and off to the side, not connected, was a 10BG power core. Those things put out enough amperage to run a small city, but conveniently fit in your bag. Of course, they had to be charged with Null energy, and as such, could only be used by Host'ire Knights.

"It has been far too long since you stopped by, or even wrote," Rickman said, setting down her tools and pulling up the work goggles. She wasn't wearing sunglasses like everybody else, but instead had on a pair of black, Null-dampening contact lenses. She reached up and tapped the side of her head twice, and there was a flutter across her eyes and the deep black lens changed to green.

"I know, I'm sorry about that. It has been busy these last few years," Naomi said, looking down. She should have been better about her correspondence, she knew that. But with her books and... No, there were no excuses for not keeping up with her networking. It was the only way she was going to get off that blasted telescope and back into actual engineering research.

"Yes, I can't imagine working under Quinn," Rickman said. "I was teaching an adjunct semester at the Academy, and he failed my class. How they allowed him to run such a technical facility is beyond me. Honestly, it should be run by somebody like you who knows the mission and how to keep everything running."

Naomi stammered at the complement. "I, um, well, it is above my station. I didn't go to the Academy, didn't even take any..."

You are blowing this, Naomi, speak with confidence! she yelled at herself as her mouth tried to complete an actual sentence, but failed.

"Fiddle-faddle," Rickman said, waving her hand as she started to remove the large black rubber gloves. "An outpost like that needs a deft hand and a smart mind. Quinn lacks both of those. Remind me before you leave and I will put in another good word for you," Rickman added, reaching under the table and pulling up a large cloth that was on a roll. She threw it over the table, securing it on the other side.

"I shall do that, professor," Naomi said quietly, following behind as the older woman started walking across the room to her desk.

"Please, we need not be so formal. You are no longer a student and there is little I have left to teach you about engineering. Call me Allana," she said, reaching her desk and sitting down. "I read your last technical manual. Whoever was responsible for that layout did you a great disservice. But the text. Your thoughts on pushing Null power through old systems was just a revelation. I do hope that one day the Confederation sees fit to let you attempt to supercharge a Dreadstar."

"I don't think that will be happening—you know how they feel about us—and I'm of course… I'm…" Naomi stammered.

Why couldn't she just spit her words out? They were no longer on unequal footing. Professor—no, *Allana*—wanted to talk to her, wanted to have a conversation. This was no time to freeze up like a child again.

"Don't worry about the observatory, you won't be there much longer," Allana said, motioning for Naomi to sit down.

As she was reaching for the chair, the sound of kids screaming filled her ears. Naomi turned, looking trying to find where the sound had come from. There was also an adult voice, telling them to break it up. There was no force behind it, though. The delivery was rote, halfhearted. The children got louder. There was violence.

"Naomi?" Rickman said, louder. Naomi shuttered, coming out of the trance that she had momentarily been in. *How long was I…?*

"Sorry, I thought I heard something," Naomi said, shaking off the strange feeling and turning back to her old teacher and sitting down in the chair by her desk.

"Strange, there shouldn't be anybody on this level, especially with the novices all off on their missions or enjoying Festival on NovaTerra," Rickman said.

"I had noticed that everybody was gone. Is that something new? There were never so few novices here back in my day," Naomi said, the phrasing making her feel far older than she was.

"This is the first time I've seen it. Honestly, I don't like it. Feels too damned quiet—and what kind of externship missions are there to send novices on during Festival? It's not like they have families to return to," Rickman said, a chuckle at the last part.

Naomi laughed as well. She didn't remember her family, having been raised by the order since before she could walk or talk. But Joanna and Lucas would have had something to say to that—especially Joanna. She always had something to say, a trait that Naomi envied. Life might be less stressful if she could come up with even a fraction of the comebacks that Joanna was able to just fire off without thinking. Or maybe not. Joanna *did* tend to get into more trouble than just about anybody else.

"Yes, quite right. We never did get any students on the observatory," Naomi said, trying to get out of her head and move past the awkward moment.

"I should think not, with the required clearance and all. We wouldn't want somebody learning so much and then washing out or leaving the order. There has been more of that lately," she said. Professor Rickman didn't need to say anything else. Naomi knew she was referring to Rostov, though there were surely others. There had to be. Right?

"I guess that is true. Though, do you know why Administrator Fel would send everybody away?" Naomi asked.

"I haven't the faintest idea, honestly," Rickman said.

For the first time, Naomi found the answer cagey. She didn't trust it. There was something more she wasn't saying. What it was, though, Naomi couldn't quite put her finger on—at least, not yet.

"I'm much more interested in what brings you here at this time. Shouldn't you be off enjoying a party on NovaTerra and not strolling down memory lane with your old classmates?"

There it was. She knew the question was going to come up. Could she just tell this professor, who she trusted, the truth? Or maybe some version of it?

No, you are going to sound crazy. It's a hard enough thing to believe, even though you read the message.

"Knight-Commander Brandice is preforming an inspection, and he thought that we would be of use," Naomi said, trying her best to keep her voice even. She wasn't sure if it worked. Probably not. Her lies were always a mess, never working as well as she wanted them to, unless she had ample time to prepare and practice.

"I see. Is this part of the inspection now?" Rickman asked, cocking her head and giving Naomi a hard case of side eye. Naomi didn't think she was buying the story, but at this point, there was nothing else. She was going to have to push forward with what she had.

"No, not at all. I just wanted to come and see my favorite professor. In all honesty, it is mostly going over documents and reports. I'm just here as a technical advisor, not really inspecting anything," Naomi said with a forced chuckle and a wave of her hand.

I need to move this away from why we are here.

"Well, that is good. I would hate to be queued up to go under the microscope without even knowing I was being prepped for a slide," Rickman said. "Hopefully you can finish in time to enjoy some of Festival."

"Yes, that is the goal," Naomi said.

The conversation went on for a little longer, finally shifting from Citadel politics to engineering and projects that they both were working on. Naomi told Rickman about how she was rebuilding the whole observatory, and Rickman mentioned that the device she was working on would probably make that whole station obsolete in a few years. A prospect Naomi hoped was true, so that she didn't have to keep spending her life rebuilding technology that should have been left in the waste bin during the Wayfinder wars. That was, if she wasn't about to spend the rest of her time in some basement re-education room after abandoning her post...

"Well, I have some more work to take care of, so I must be going. Tell Quinn I said hello when you get back to your post," Rickman said.

"I will do that, Allana. I'm sure he will love to hear where I have..." She paused, then stammered out a few nonsense words. "I will pass along your greeting."

With that, Naomi started walking very quickly out of the classroom, trying to keep calm, to not scream and curse at herself. Once she crossed the threshold out into the main hallway and closed the door, Naomi leaned against the wall and fell to the floor. She closed her eyes and, using her thumbs, pressed her eyes into the back of her skull with her eyelids, causing small flashes of light to fill the darkness of her vision.

That was so damned stupid! Just enough information to let Rickman know that something wasn't on the up and up. That, combined with just how utterly awkward and out of place she felt and acted! Naomi just wanted to crawl into a small hole and die somewhere, so she wouldn't have to face her screw up.

Her self-beratement was interrupted by the sound of children again, this time coming from down the hallway. Inquisitively, Naomi pushed herself to her feet and started walking.

Rounding the bend, she saw a group of children. They were cheering, triumphant. There was a small, waif-looking girl at their feet. She was on the ground, her face showing signs of a horrible beating. Her eyes were looking forward, and Naomi could feel that something was protecting them, protecting *her*. All of them were so familiar.

One of the young girls, who had dark skin and dreadlocks like Naomi used to have, turned to look at her. Recognition instantly crossed her face. Naomi shuttered and stepped back, hitting the wall. She spun away from it, like the wall was a person out to grab her. There was nothing but cold concrete.

Turning again, the children were gone and everything was quiet.

Naomi started running back toward the rooms that had been set aside from them. She didn't want to be here any longer. She just wanted to go back to her work at the observatory and get yelled at. All these visions and information gathering were for a different breed of Host'ire Knight.

Library of the Citadel, Joanna

The Library of the Citadel was where Joanna had spent most of her teenage years, trying desperately to interact with as few members of the order as possible; to do just enough so that she would not be shipped off to some dead-end position where there were no books and no chance to learn anything new.

As a child, she had found solace in books. Every week, her father would come home from the factory, and he always had a new book for her. They were usually little, half-credit trash novels. Two hundred pages of lurid thriller or horror stories printed on paper so cheap, it started to fall apart the moment you touched it. She loved those books; *lived* for those books and lived through them.

"Shove those Silver crypto credits up your ass," she heard her father saying.

Joanna paused and looked around. This wasn't like the children. It wasn't some forgotten memory, but one instead that she desperately *wanted* to forget, to file away in a pile of banned books.

The Host'ire recruiters—kidnappers—had come in the night. She was upstairs reading the new book her father had given her. A gothic horror tale set in the mountains of old NovaTerra. The sounds from downstairs had gotten loud; there was fighting. They had known he was going to put up a fight. The loud, wet sounds of wood against flesh echoed up through the floorboards. Moments later, they were dragging her out of the room. All she wanted was to hold onto the book, but one of the men ripped it from her hand. Her father was on the floor, bleeding, her mother on top of him, trying to keep pressure on the wound. A bag of thirty silver crypto credits spilled across the floor. Joanna's mother was helpless to stop what was happening. Lose her daughter or lose her husband and more than likely her own life and *still* lose her daughter.

For a long time, Joanna had hated her parents for not fighting harder that night. As she grew up into a teenager who had to fight about everything, and then an adult who had to fight about everything, she started to understand that sometimes there were fights that were not worth fighting. Fights where the only option was to lose or have everything taken from you and *still* lose. That night had been one of those times. Still, she wished she could have fought harder or hid her talents better.

Looking down at her gloved hands through thick sunglasses, Joanna made two fists and pushed back the memories. There was nothing she could do about the past. It made her, yes, but dwelling on it wasn't going to unmake her; wasn't going to rewrite time. This wasn't one of the half-credits about the time traveling teacher who had a transforming shuttle full of students.

The memories pushed back, she took a breath and opened the door to the library. It was a stunningly large room, four levels high. The walls were lined with shelves and shelves of books. There were three stairwells leading to each level. If you stood back and looked, the room was so massive, you could see the general squareness and curvature of the Citadel's construction. The first floor was filled with tables, smaller shelves, workstations with large screens, and the intake desk where you could check out books. The kind of desk Joanna had spent her entire twenty years as a Host'ire Knight sitting behind. She kept applying to do research full-time and they kept just assigning her to the desk instead. It was what it was. There was still free time, spare time, for her to do her research. But no *official* time.

Currently standing behind the intake desk, yelling at Administrator Fel, was the head librarian, a Tragadi named Baron'Tor, though he insisted that everybody regardless of rank call him Tor. He was tall, almost two and half meters tall, though always being hunched over obscured his actual height.

Growing up, Joanna had thought that he just had poor posture from existing in a human-sized world. Now that she had met other Tragadi—Surface Tragadi—she reminded herself there were also the fossorial variety, they were all like that. Sacrificing their backs and postures to please humans. Tor's arms were long, and they swayed in a very listless, gentle way, almost like they were always underwater. His skin was a deep gray, and in some lighting, looked almost black. There was no hair on his long head, except for a small patch of pink whiskers on his chin. Joanna was pretty sure they were fake, as he was the only Tragadi she had ever seen with any hair at all.

"I don't know why you can't follow a simple directive," Fel said. Her voice was loud, her tone exasperated.

To Joanna, she sounded worse than she had yesterday. It was an exasperation she knew all too well, having helped thousands of panicked students as they tried to finish an assignment at the last minute. Or worse, those who were perfectionists taking the class of another perfectionist. She felt bad for those students, the others… She wanted to drum them out of the Order. Spoiled brats whose parents had paid for them to join the Host'ire, as opposed to just a poor kid who was kidnapped with a pittance payout so that snatching kids looked better on paper.

"It is not that simple," Tor said. His voice was measured. Sighing, he kept talking. "What you are asking is for me to pull over two thousand tomes—some very valuable—and *destroy* them. By myself." He paused, after adding that last bit. It was an addendum, something to try and appeal to the logical mind of somebody like Fel, who was a Host'ire fanatic.

"I had no choice but to send the students away. It is not my fault that your department doesn't hire full time librarians," Fel said.

"I do not control the budget, *Administrator*," Tor said, putting just a dash of admonition on the last word so faint, that if the climate control kicked on, it might be blown away.

Joanna had to chuckle at that. She might have been a loud fighter, but she appreciated the hell out of a good, simple take down. Aside from Fel's bluster, the room was so quiet that you could hear a pin drop, and as such, her small chuckle caught their attention.

"Do you think something funny, Knight Pike?" Administrator Fel asked, channeling the teacher that she had once been.

Joanna's eyes wanted to roll all the way back in her head at that. She had hated that question as a child and now, as an adult, found it to be damned insulting.

"I find plenty of things amusing, Administrator. You are going to have to refine your query if you would like an effective answer," Joanna said.

She looked over at Tor, who gave her a slight nod of his head. Fel grumbled.

"This situation, the one you are currently finding, humorous. I have read your record, Pike. I am aware of your many reprimands for finding things like this *amusing*," Fel said. Joanna was indeed finding this amusing.

"I find it quite comical that you can't find it in your budget to hire assistant librarians that are not current novices of this institution," Joanna started. "The going stipend for a Host'ire library specialist is only forty thousand credits a year. Now, that is on NovaTerra. I suspect it is far less here, as there is no need for a room and board per diem," she started.

It was now Fel's turn to roll her eyes. The Administrator raised a finger. Joanna just increased the speed at which she spoke, keeping her voice even and just above a whisper. This was a library, after all.

"Now, you have the second largest collection of books in the Confederation, the fifth in all known space. I'm sure that constitutes budget, and thus I'm sure you can find some credits somewhere to hire a few extra hands for Libarian Tor here. He isn't getting any younger—I mean, look at what carrying all those books has done to his back," she said, pointing at the aged librarian and his poor posture. The old Tragadi took that opportunity to mime like his back was hurting.

"Oh, stop that," Fel hissed. "Every bloody one of you walks like that."

"What does that mean, Administrator? Are you...?" Joanna let the accusation of being speciesist hang in the air for a moment.

"You know damn well what I mean. The bloody both of you should be drummed out and sent down to re-education with your friend," Fel said. Her dander was good and up now.

"Re-education, for asking a few budgetary questions. There is no price that you can put on the pricelessness of this collection," Joanna said, motioning to the rows upon rows, walls upon walls of books that were all around them.

"They have all been digitized. This room is a monument to the vanity of people like you. While it falls to people like me to pay for them," she spat out.

Fel walked toward Joanna, puffing herself up. The woman was older and walked with a commanding gait, but was still a head shorter than Joanna. She stood her ground, folding her arms across her chest and looking with satisfaction through her glasses.

"I did not know that knowledge and history were vanity," Joanna said as Fel got so close that Joanna could smell the lilac and rosemary perfume she wore.

"History is what we say it is, and knowledge is a two-edged sword. Be careful with it, Knight Pike," Fel said. "But, since you are on my base unannounced with what seems to be nothing to do, I have an idea." A smile crossed her face.

Joanna knew what was coming next. She had spent her whole life working for vindictive administrative officials who thought they were better than her just because they were born in a house owned by people with money or a fancy last name.

"Libarian Tor needs help removing this list of books, so why don't you give him a hand? You are a full-time Librarian of the Host'ire Order, after all. Making forty thousand credits a year, I hear," Fel said, pushing a set of folded papers into her hand.

Joanna could feel the anger starting to build up inside her. She wasn't Fel's to boss around, and she had better things to do than whatever baseless task she was instructing Tor to do. The hunched over Tragadi just looked at Joanna and shook his head, signaling not to fight it. To just let Fel bluster and leave. Joanna reached over and snatched the roll of papers from Fel's hand and then put on her best customer service voice, the one that Administrator Moore was fond of.

"It would be a pleasure to help out my old school. We will let you know when we are finished. I hope you have a wonderful rest of your day, Administrator Fel," she said, making sure to put some extra spunk on those last few words while still retaining her sweetness. Fel just huffed, then turned smartly on the heel of her boot and walked out of the room. Each step echoed as she left.

Joanna and Tor didn't move until the doors slammed shut. Then Joanna dropped the rolled-up pages on the ground and walked over to the old librarian, her arms held wide. Tor walked to her, his extremely long arms out as well. The two of them embraced like the old friends that they were.

"It has been far too long, Joanna. You don't write anymore. What have I done to offend you?" Tor asked, pulling away from the hug, putting a large hand between his two hearts.

"Nothing. I have... I've been busy," Joanna said.

"This is no time to start lying to me now," Tor said.

"The last few years have been hard. Time for writing—personal and research—have been limited. My temperament doesn't mesh well with those at the Academy," Joanna said.

She was being freer with information than she had ever been. Even with her old friends, who she seemed to have a strong primal connection to. Tor had always been able to get things out of her. For many years, he had been the only person that she could confine in. At least, that is what she remembered.

Could it be that I talked to everybody, but only remember this? What are we missing? What is missing from us?

"Well, you will always have a home here. Come, sit, let us catch up," he said, motioning to one of the nearby tables.

"Don't you have books to pull?" Joanna asked as she sat down.

"No. I will just make a few adjustments to the records and slowly move them to my personal section. If the order wants to ban more books on history and philosophy, they will need to come and remove them from this library by force. But then, that is a little something between you and me," he said, holding a spindly finger to his mouth.

"What, me keep secrets from administration? Never," she said, giving Tor a wink. "Though, I do have some questions for you, old friend."

"I suspected as much. Nobody shows up out of the blackness unannounced unless they have pressing questions or bad news," Tor said. He looked over her face, appearing to contemplate which one of those things she was bringing with her. "Just questions, I think. Though, those often lead to less than pleasant news."

"What is going on? Why have all the novices been sent away?" Joanna asked, waving her hand around the room.

"Your guess is as good as mine. I asked and Administrator Fel said it was because this was the perfect time for them to all go on assignment. But that doesn't sit right with me," he said, before adding, "Walk with me. I have something for you." Tor stood up and began walking toward one of the stairwells, continuing to speak as they moved. "I have been teaching for a long time, and I have never seen anybody sent out on assignment at this time of year, or to NovaTerra for Festival."

"I would have killed to be allowed to go to NovaTerra during Festival when I was a novice," Joanna said.

When she was a child, leaving the Citadel outside of your training missions was strictly prohibited. You lived and trained here, and as far as the pupils were concerned, there was no outside world that they could visit. It only existed in holos and books.

"This is the first time. I got a look at the budget from a colleague who is on the finance committee and a pretty credit was spent sending dirt-poor children across the Confederation so that they could see the election of the People's Minister."

"They are all dirt-poor children, Tor. That is why they were here. Kids with money, with names that people know, don't end up at the Citadel," Joanna said.

"That is why we produce the best Host'ire. Nobody is here to coddle you," Tor said as they started walking up the steps. As soon as they reached the second level, they turned and started toward the next set of stairs. They were going all the way up.

"You produce weapons here, nothing more. And broken people who were not cut out to be weapons," she said, reflecting on her friends. Only Lucas had been fit to be a weapon. The rest of them were languishing in positions far below their skills. Or in Re-education, having never left the Citadel at all.

"I do hope we do a bit more than that. I see your point, though, Joanna. Life has not delt you a good hand. But it is all about how we play the hand we're dealt," Tor said.

"Baron'Tor, you know better than to peddle that bullshit, especially to me," Joanna said, stopping and turning to the aged librarian.

"I see that a nerve has been ticked. You were given a horrible hand, and any time you drew a card that could be helpful, it was taken away from you. I know this, but there is more to the metaphor," he said, as they reached the top floor.

There were only three accessible rows on the top floor. All the others were under lock and key, the private collections of the administration and professors. Tor walked three shelves down and pressed his hand against the door. The scanner beeped and then the door slid open. This section of deep storage was packed, overflowing with books. There was no room on the shelves and there was almost no room on the floor, either.

"Consider me a dealer of cards," he said. He reached down and picked up a book. It was thick, the cover made of pressed leather, the title embossed gold. He handed the book to Joanna. She looked down and read the title: *Looking Beyond, Finding the Way*. She recognized it. It was an old volume of Wayfinder prophecy. This book would have been banned not just by the Host'ire, but by the Confederation. Not a recent ban, but since shortly after the Wayfinder wars over five hundred years ago.

Tor passed her the book. Joanna took it gingerly, expecting it to feel old, brittle. Looking down, she saw that it was new, a fresh printing. She looked up at Tor, shocked.

"How did you…?"

"I must be allowed to keep a few secrets," Tor said.

Joanna nodded as she ran her hand along the book. She had read *about* this tome of lore before, but had never seen one. Even with all her research on Wayfinder prophecy, this was one of the most coveted books, the most scandalous to have. She knew that there were a few still in existence in the Unaligned Planets. But… She held it close to her breast, both just to feel the leather and so that nobody would be able to read the title.

"Take this card—keep it hidden, so that nobody knows that you have it. They will think you not a threat, with the low value of your flipped card. If you can take the lessons contained within to heart, it will get you close to twenty-one," Tor said.

Joanna followed his convoluted metaphor. She wasn't sure what it was going to teach her, but had enough trust in the old man to give him the benefit of the doubt.

"What else do you have in there? A copy of *Piller's Way*, perhaps?" she asked referencing the Wayfinder's holy book.

"If I had a copy of that, child, do you think I would still be here putting up with small people like Morgan Fel?"

Both had a good laugh at that. After a moment, Tor put a large hand on Joanna's shoulder.

"Go now, child, and read. All the answers are within your grasp," he said.

With that, Baron'Tor walked into his private hallway and closed the door behind him. Joanna could hear the lock click shut. She stood there for a moment, looking down at the book that was in her hand. The value and danger of the gift was not lost upon her.

He knows more than he is saying, that is for sure, she thought, holding the book tighter.

Looking around the empty library, she was, for the first time, scared. What couldn't Tor tell her? *Why* couldn't he tell her? He had given her a book whose mere possession was a death sentence like it was nothing, yet there was something he couldn't tell her; was perhaps scared to tell her. For the first time, the star-steel blade on her belt felt heavy, felt like something she might have to draw.

There was nothing to do but read. Sliding the book under her long coat, Joanna started to quickly—but not too quickly—exit the library.

These were not the answers she had come looking for, but with a little work, she suspected they were going to be the ones that they needed.

Orbit, NovaTerra, Alexander

Alexander's exit from *Fury* had been faster than expected, so it was a good thing he hadn't unpacked anything besides a different jacket for dinner. Aside from the rushed boarding of his transport, the rest of the trip to NovaTerra had been uneventful.

Well that wasn't entirely true—there was the damned message. His watch blinked at him. Alexander removed it from the small vest pocket where it resided, flicking open the gold face to look at the screen. Blinking it said, "One new message—Fox Windsail."

Alexander took a deep breath and closed the face of his watch and put it back in his pocket, letting the chain clink against his body. He had been terribly brutish to her the last time they spoke. He stood by everything he had said, but perhaps it could have been presented in a less harsh way. As a man of honor and good breeding, he should always be striving to find a better way to say things, ways that didn't lead to his words being taken out of context or construed as far harsher than they were. There was nothing for it now, though. He had said the things and assumed that Fox was still piping mad at him. It's how he would've felt. Instead, Alexander was feeling sorry for himself; that he failed to help rise Fox up, to improve her station in the world.

What was done was done, though. She was either going to let him try again or never speak with him. With how strained his relationship and position abord *Fury* was, Alexander knew that he could live with whatever she picked. While he wanted nothing more than for her to come and join the build team on Project Far Step, if she didn't want to, he was not going to force it. A good and true gentleman knows when to step back and accept when the lady he is courting is not interested in what is being offered.

Reaching into his pocket again, Alexander flicked open the watch and swiped the message away without reading it, returning the screen to show him a clock face with NovaTerra's local time. Maybe another time. For now, he was going to enjoy his vacation. Besides, there were more important things to focus on than his failed romantic endeavors.

Cards!

Getting into the Peculiar Pentagon tournament had been hard enough. There was no room to let his mind wander because he was distracted by a girl. Even if it was a girl he had been seeing off and on since the age of thirteen. A girl who had been his first kiss, and who he lost his virginity to.

No, Alexander, she is just a girl—you need to focus. It was silly to think that relationship was ever more than just fun, he thought, pushing the idea of her away. Pushing the ideas to where relationships between people of different classes belonged: in the bin.

He reached up and patted the hard steel case that was sitting in his breast pocket. His bag had another few hundred cards, but the ones in that case were his go-to deck and the one that, unless things changed, he would be using in the Minister's Tournament.

"This is your Captain speaking, gentle lords and ladies," the ship's captain said over the speakers. "If you look out your windows, you will see the beautiful blue sky of NovaTerra as we make our final approach and decent into the city of Novagrad."

Alexander looked out his window. They were fast approaching the planet, the blackness of space falling away, replaced by clouds and the deep blue of oceans. The ocean gave way to rolling green fields and hundreds of leagues of farms. Then, the massive glass towers started to appear, signaling that they were coming up on Novagrad, the capital of not just the planet of NovaTerra, but the entire Confederation.

The sky above the city was filled with ships coming and going, landing and taking off. Daily traffic buzzing about. Alexander had been here a few times but was always enraptured by the sight of it all. As much as he played the cultured lordling in public, he had lived a very sheltered and provincial life, first on a Dreadstar and then a secret government laboratory.

The space port was away from the high buildings of the city, and even at that distance, they were impressive, structures of gleaming glass and steel. The sun glinting off made Alexander turn his head slightly to avoid the glare.

Turning his gaze down, he could see the streets beginning to get ready for the festival week. Tents trimmed with streamers and banners were being set up. Already car traffic had been stopped and what were usually busy vehicle lanes were instead filled with people visiting stalls and enjoying themselves. The election festival made the winter and summer solstice celebrations feel small in comparison—or so he was told. Alexander seemed to only make it to NovaTerra when large political events were happening. A sad byproduct of being the second son of a minor Space Lord.

A few minutes later, the transport was on the ground and people were starting to stand up, pulling their bags from the overhead storage bins and exiting the ship. Alexander sat quietly and finished the small cup of tea that he had been nursing for most of the trip. Once the throng of people had passed, he picked up his yellow coat and started to head to the front of the ship. His bags were all in cargo and thus he had nothing in the overhead bin to scramble for. Once he stood up, Alexander cracked his joints, purging the stiffness of the flight from them. He then threw on his coat and exited the empty transport.

Outside, the air was crisp. Early fall on the northern continent of NovaTerra was always a comfortable time of year. Not too hot, not too cold. And there was always a breeze that tampered down to the region's tendency to remain hot and sticky until close to winter.

Alexander took a deep breath. Fresh, non-recycled air wasn't something he got to breathe very often. Fresh air and the gentle pull of real gravity were things that the planet-bound citizens of the Confederation always took for granted when they laughed at how excited their space-born brothers and sisters were to have real rock under their feet.

"Alexander!" a voice called from the crowd. He started to look around. Then he saw the man who hailed him.

Alen Hoben was a short man, his skin a deep brown. His thick black hair was pulled back in long braided rows. He had on a knee length coat of bright red trimmed in sparkling yellows and oranges. He wore a black vest with a flaming glut of rocket fire, the sigil of House Hoben embroidered upon it.

"Alen, friend. It is good to see you," Alexander said, walking down into the crowd to embrace his friend and coworker. Both men patted each other on the back before pulling away.

"I trust your detour home went well?" Alen asked.

"It went... as expected. Everybody was happy to see me, except for my mother..." Alexander said before trailing off.

"I take it that is why you arrived early. Truth be told, we were not expecting you until tonight. That is why it is just me. The rest of the fellows are still sleeping at the house, recovering from spending a night to deep in their cups." Alen signaled for his driver to pick up Alexander's bag and bring the car around. Alen had arranged for them to stay at one of the many residences held by House Hoben.

The Hoben's were a smaller house, like Cordova, but what they lacked in branches, they made up for in wealth and influence. House Hoben was at the forefront of engine technology. They started as slingshot racers before getting into manufacturing and eventually buying their way into a Space Lordship.

"Family, they will always find a way to make things interesting," Hoben said, giving Alexander a pat on the back as they started to walk. "How, pray tell, did your conversation with your gentle lady Fox go?" Hoben asked, unaware of the mine that he had just placed his foot upon.

"Not well, damnedly not well," Alexander said flatly, failing to meet his friend's gaze. "She would rather stay on *Fury* than come and work with us." It was a half-truth, and it did not pass muster with Hoben.

"Oh, the stupidity of man," Hoben said, raising his hands in frustration. "What did you say this time?" Alexander's ability to put his foot in his mouth was legendary.

"I might have indicated that it was a great honor for somebody of her station to be offered a spot on the build team..."

He paused. Alexander did not want to relitigate the whole conversation, but knew that if he didn't offer up the information now, his friend was going to pull it out of him like a dentist removing a rotten tooth.

"She countered with me staying on *Fury*, and I might have said something about being too highborn to be a grease monkey." It wasn't his proudest moment, but it was the truth.

"My God, man. For somebody who used to be a woman, you have good and completely forgotten how to talk to them," Alen said.

"I never was a woman, Hoben—you know that," Alexander snapped. He didn't need that bullshit today.

Hoben held his hands up and dismissively rolled his eyes at the chiding.

"I just thought she would be more grateful for the opportunity," Alexander finished.

"Look here, my good man. As much as we love tinkering and building on our projects, Fox is not like that. She craves the excitement and unknown of what the next day will bring. Serving on a Dreadstar gives her that rush. A hidden laboratory and your cock were never going to be enough of a pull," Alen said as they reached the car. A servant held open the door as the two of them climbed inside.

The motor carriage was fancy, far more so than what Alexander and his family usually were forced to rent when they came to court. The leather seats were a lavender pastel color, sinking and then forming around Alexander's body. In the center was a small wet bar with bottles of brandy, whisky, and rum in crystal decanters. Alen picked up two glasses and started to pour. Alexander gave the glasses a morose look as his mind wandered to the message in his pocket that he was ignoring. He wondered what it said, but not enough to want to open it. Opening it proved that he was wrong; proved that he needed her—and he *didn't* need her. He just *wanted* her.

At least, that is what he kept telling himself.

"Cheer up, good sir. This is no time to be depressed," Hoben said, handing his old friend a glass of whiskey. "This is a time to be thinking about parties, good food, and cards."

He held his glass up. Alexander followed.

"To parties and cards," Alexander said, pushing away the sad thoughts of Fox. Alen was correct. They were here on a mission. There was a tourney to win.

"I take it I'm the last one here?"

"You are not, which I have to admit is strange," Alen said before taking a sip of his drink. "Young Master Alfrid has yet to arrive."

Hoben referred to the youngest and the newest member of their team, Alfrid MacGuffin. The young man had just come to the facility in the spring and been quickly adopted into their card playing circle.

"Alfrid is always on time, if not early. Has he sent you a message?" Alexander asked. He took a sip of the whiskey. It was a fine bottle, oak-y with a hint of cherry and vanilla.

"Alas, no. You know House MacGuffin. They are in love with their secrets. So I'm sure he is just postponed by family and can't tell us," Alen said, waving it off.

Alen waved a few too many things off for Alexander's liking, most days. That said, there was nothing he could do about any of his problems right now except drink his drink and look forward to taking a shower and changing into a clean outfit before the team hunkered down for a long day of practice and strategizing.

Re-education, The Citadel, Rostov

"This room is bigger, I don't like it!" Rostov said as he stood at the edge of the white line before slowly walking from one side of the room to the other.

"One, two, three, four," he muttered counting each step, one after the other after the other.

"It is the same room you were in this morning," said his re-education agent.

This time, the Host'ire who was trying to snap his mind back into order was an older man, balding, with small sunglasses that rested on the bridge of his nose. He had walked in with a little chair and placed it halfway between the door and the white line that Rostov wasn't allowed to cross.

"It's bigger, I can feel it. I know you are moving me," Rostov said aggressively, as he finished his count. "It was ten paces yesterday, today it is fifteen. I count every night before bed."

"Why do you do that?" the man asked.

He reached into his pocket and pulled out a pen, clicking the tip out and placing it on the pad of paper in his other hand, ready to write down whatever Rostov was about to say. They loved to write down what he said and then shove it back at him days or weeks later. Proof that he wasn't getting better. Or that he couldn't remember anything more than a few days at a time. Reality was what they decided it was. At least, they thought so. Rostov would not submit. He could still remember things, though the voices were getting louder, stronger.

"I count because you cannot be trusted. This whole bloody order can't be trusted. You are hiding something. A day of reckoning is coming!" Rostov yelled, holding his hand up, pointer finger extended.

"You have said that before. The day of reckoning. Did she tell you about it?" his re-education agent asked flatly.

Rostov hated that they knew about her. That was all they knew—that she talked to him, not who 'she' was or what was said. Rostov didn't remember when he first let that slip. He had been in re-education for a long time before she started talking to him. Before his mind had been broken down by exposure to so much unfiltered Null energy. The room glowed, *everything* glowed. He was used to it at this point. Some days, when he was trying to sleep, Rostov wondered if he was ever going to be able to see the world without the glow again, or if he was completely broken.

"That the dead god is coming for you and the eye will be opened to watch your death," Rostov snapped. The ramblings from her that infiltrated his sleep mentioned dead gods and an opening eye. He just took some creative liberty with it, to screw with the re-education agents.

"Last week you said that..." the bald man started to say, lowing his glasses, to read the paper better.

"I know what I fucking said!" Rostov yelled at him. "One, two, three, four!" he yelled, taking steps along the white line.

The agent gave him an exasperated sigh and stood up from his chair. Reaching into his coat, he took out a small box that had two buttons on it. He pressed the first red one. Rostov felt a wave of sharp pain and nausea flow through his body. He tried to fight it. There was no fighting it. He went limp and fell to the floor like a sack of potatoes. He couldn't move, couldn't speak. All his world consisted of was pain, and the feeling that he wanted to wretch, but couldn't. His eyes glared up at the bald man who stood there for a minute, cocking his head to the side, watching Rostov try and move. Watching his legs spasm as the pain coursed through his body.

This was always how the re-education session would end. No matter which agent they sent, he would always eventually mouth off to them, and they would shock him down. Some agents had thinner skins than others, leaving him in pain for hours, or even all night. This one fell somewhere in the middle. He didn't turn off the pain as he walked out of the room.

This will pass soon, her voice said in his head.

Rostov blinked. Standing in front of him were two children. Himself, spindly with dark black hair, a welt over his eye, and Hyacinth. She was a wafer of a child, consumed by the large leather jacket she had on. Her hair was long and blonde, the unfiltered Null that consumed his vision reflected off her hair blinding him. He couldn't look at her, couldn't make out her face. A face that he didn't remember, even though he tried. He tried so hard to remember what she looked like, but there was nothing. It was blank.

"Why do you put yourself through this, Rostie?" young Hyacinth asked.

"Because I have to protect you. We *all* said we would protect you. From the teachers, from Jasper, from the whole bloody world around us," young Rostie said.

"I never asked for that. Essex is hurt because of your insistence," she said, looking away.

"We are all hurt, and it would have been so much worse if we hadn't stood together. Trust in Lucas. He knows what to do," Rostie said.

Rostov tried to take a breath through the pain, through the nausea. Lucas was here now. He was no longer alone. Apart, they were vulnerable. Together, they could stand up to whatever it was that Hyacinth was so scared of. They might be able to save themselves.

Though, they couldn't save her.

"Lucas only knows how to fight. He is just Jasper with a hero complex," she said.

"That isn't fair," Rostie said, balling his hands into fists. She always said things that hurt because they were true. "He builds things. All Jasper and the teachers know how to do is destroy!" he yelled.

The child version of himself was hurt and the anger had caused the welt over his eye to start bleeding again. She walked over and pulled a small rag from her coat and dabbed his forehead. A feeling of comfort and love moved from Rostie to Rostov. He didn't remember much about this young woman, just that they had all loved her and she them.

The pain lasted for another hour or so before finally starting to fade away, allowing Rostov to regain control of his limbs again. The lights had turned off. It was 'night', for whatever that was worth. He breathed deeply and crawled to the wall, propping himself up and leaning against it. His legs were still numb, a tingly sensation slowly starting to return to them, as if he had sat cross legged for too long and now couldn't stand up. The visions had faded, and, for a brief moment, his mind was quiet. She wasn't talking to him. Wasn't showing him the past. There was nothing, not even his own internal monologue.

The silence was broken by a ticking. He could feel it in his back, a light pressure. Rostov took a deep breath and closed his eyes. Reaching into the Null, he pulled his mind's eye away from himself. There was nothing to see in the room, nothing to feel outside of his body. The ticking persisted. It was low, coming every ten seconds. It was perfect. You could set your watch by it, as his father used to say.

Whatever it was, it wasn't outside of him. Could they have planted something else *inside* of him, aside from the pain nodes? Rostov pushed back into his body. He felt it again. The slight pressure was coming from his back. Rostov pushed Null through his legs, banishing the tingling pain, getting them moving again. It had been a long time since he had even wanted to push himself in that way. Most days, he just let the pain and weakness wash over him. But Lucas was here, the crew was back.

Standing, Rostov turned around and put his hand on the wall. The tick happened again, then a slight amount of pressure pushed against his hand. Closing his eyes, he pushed Null into his hand and counted to ten. The tick happened again, and it pushed his hand ever so slightly, less than a centimeter.

Those sons of bitches, he thought. They were not moving him from room to room. The damned room was resizing itself ever so slightly night after night. Just more confirmation that he in fact was *not* losing his mind.

Rostov smiled at himself and let the Null pass through his body. Satisfied with the day, he walked over to his bed and laid down.

Closing his eyes, he tried to get some sleep while things were quiet in his head. With this new confirmation of his sanity, he looked forward to fighting with whatever re-education agent they were going to send him tomorrow.

Zeta Labs, Olympus Ares, Grace

Grace looked around the bottom of the elevator shaft. The car was hundreds of feet above her. Looking up, she could only see it with the magnifying camera on her suit's heads up display. There was rubble all over the bottom from where something—she didn't know what—had come tumbling down. The door she needed was two floors up and jammed.

She found her solution on the ground by her feet. A shattered coolant pipe. The reinforced gigasteel had been ripped apart, leaving sharp edges on both sides. Glancing up at the door again, she measured it with her eyes and then did the same thing to the pipe, seeing the math of their dimensions display the items in shimmering gold. Perfect, it was going to fit.

We must have been pushing far too much power into the gate if we shattered one of these coolant pipes, Grace thought as she picked up the pipe and started to climb.

In short order, Grace was at the floor, wedging the pipe into the door. She locked both of her feet around the sides of the ladder and engaged some power into the suit's legs so that she wouldn't fall.

"One, two, three," she said before pulling on the pipe she had turned into a lever. The door groaned and moved a little, but didn't want to budge. Going into the controls of her suit, Grace moved power over to her arms. She could feel the current moving though the suit as it applied power to the plates, hopefully giving her enough torque to open the door. Grace didn't want to push too much power thought the suit. There was no telling when there would be a chance to recharge, or repair if something was blown out.

"Let's go!" she cried, pulling on the pipe again. This time, it gave way, and the door started to open.

Grace could hear the metal wanting to snap back into place. Quickly, she turned the pipe so that it was lying longways between the two halves of door. The jagged edges made slots to help keep the pipe wedged in place. Grace pulled the power back from her legs and crawled under the door. Rolling around on her back, Grace put her foot behind the pipe and kicked it toward her, catching it. Bleeding the power from her arms, Grace stood up and looked around.

This was the correct hallway, but things didn't look right. In fact, they were profoundly *wrong*. Red dirt was blowing in from behind her, leaving small piles along the walls where the heaver bits of particulate had settled. The light sand was tumbling along toward the control room. A section of the steel wall was sliced open, revealing bricks covered in vines. Things that shouldn't have been there. Olympus Ares was old, but not so old that it would have been built on top of a previous building.

Or could it have been? I mean, anything is possible in a place like this, Grace thought, walking up to the hole in the wall.

Behind the wall, the brick went about ten feet and then gave way back to stone and supports from where the hallway had been carved out. Running her finger along the brick, it was cold, and there was a strange aroma coming from it. She opened a few menus, her eyes darting across the HUD. Ozone, that was what she was smelling. These bricks shouldn't be here, *couldn't* be here. Taking a step back, she looked all around, trying to take everything in. Panic creeped up behind her shoulders.

What the fuck is going on? Grace reached for Emily, for her rock, but the strength of her past was quiet, empty, worried.

"This is just a hallucination. You hit your head too hard," Grace said, breathing deeply, trying to calm down. There was no use panicking, it wasn't going to get her anywhere. Whatever was going on here, there was a logical explanation. She was a woman of science, after all. Everything worked by rules, she just needed to learn what they were.

Vardis would know what to do—that was why he was an administrator. She just had to get through the control room. His office was on the other side.

Grace didn't want to go into the control room, afraid of what she would see in there. Like the chewed up remains of her friends that had been consumed by the window's maw. There was nothing for it. She reached down, found some bravery, and clapped the pipe against the open palm of her hand a few times to psych herself up. Grace walked forward, the door opening automatically.

Inside, the room was a disaster. Blood and viscera everywhere. Sergeant Danials, a large brick of a man, was pinned to the back wall by a huge shard of transparent aluminum. It had bisected him. His top half swayed in the wind, while his lower half was a pile of entrails and blood. Two techs by the front of the door had the tops of their heads taken clean off by another shard. Half the people in this room were killed by the death of the great window.

She wanted to retch, wanted to close the door and run away. Run until there was nowhere to run to. The horrors that were before her were not figments of her imagination, they were real, and she was going to have to face them. Just like Viv and Randy down below, these people had died for science, and it was up to her to make sure those deaths were not in vain. Violence and grotesque accidents Grace knew she could handle. It was everything *else*...

It was the rest of the people in the room who gave Grace pause. Five of the technicians were still standing, one of them had a shard of glass through his upper body, blood still dribbling down his white lab coat. The others who still stood looked at her instantly, their heads almost moving in sync as they started to shuffle forward. She took a step back, almost slipping on a severed ear.

"Stay back, I'm warning you!" she yelled, feebly holding the pipe out like a bat.

The moaning techs, whose eyes were a deep red, kept walking forward. The first one came into range, grabbing at her. Grace swung the pipe and clocked the creature squarely cracking its neck, so his head hung at a ninety-degree angle. The undead thing blinked and then pushed its head back into an upright position. The bubble-wrap crack of his bones and tendons sent a shiver of revulsion through Grace's body. She was a scientist; violence was not what she had signed up for in life.

Life has shown us enough though, Emily said quietly, starting to bubble back up from the shadows where she had been hiding.

Taking another step back, she hit the wall. The undead tech things were almost on top of her. Just as she was about to accept death, Grace heard a sound that she had only read about and seen in a few news videos. It was a deep thrum, that pulsed like a heartbeat. The sound filled the room.

Maybe she wouldn't die in this moment.

Standing across the room was the security guard Grace had seen this morning. He stood cutting an imposing figure, the strange wind from the test chamber blowing his leather coat and long blond hair. Light was glinting across his sunglasses from the star-steel blade that was in his hand. The blade thrummed with pure energy. Yellows and oranges moved through the shaft of the blade like plasma cascading across the surface of a star.

In a fluid move, he slid forward as if there were wheels on his feet and brought the blade up, hitting the first undead tech in the lower abdomen. The blade cleanly cut through the man, coming out by his neck. The lab coat and his flesh caught fire as the wound instantly cauterized, the top half of his body falling to the ground like freshly cut deli meat. The man's legs stumbled forward for a few moments more until there were no more signals from the brain and they just stopped and fell over. It was almost comical.

The other four creatures that had once been Grace's coworkers turned their heads in unison and locked eyes with the security guard who was channeling his former life as a Host'ire Knight. He jumped, did a flip bounding off the wall and brought his blade down, slicing across the tops of three heads, before landing on the ground, in a crouched position. The heads burst into flames, their hair and flesh instantly incinerated by the plasma of the blade. Horrible screams came from their ruined mouths. What little life was left in their eyes faded away as they melted from the heat.

He is showing off, Grace thought. *He could have ended this in five quick cuts, but no, he is showing off.*

He might have been showing off, and while that did in some way annoy Grace, she was—and she hated to admit it—impressed.

Only one creature remained. It was the one that was standing in front of her. So close she could smell the death and the rot coming from the reanimated corpse. All she could do was get sucked into the red lifeless eyes of the man she had known as Juan.

Before dead-Juan could take another step, the yellow orange energy of the star-steel blade burst through his chest, turning him into a torch. As fast as the blade appeared, it was gone, pulled back into her savior's hand. Juan fell screaming on top of her. In a normal world, the fire consuming him would have also consumed her, but Grace's suit kept her safe and cool long enough to roll the burning corpse off her and stand up. As she got to her feet, the Host'ire Knight spun the star-steel blade once and then shut it off. The thrumming heartbeat vanished, leaving a sonic void in the room. In the same fluid motion of the spin, he threw back his leather coat and attached the hilt to his belt, cracking his neck.

"Thanks for the assist," Grace said, walking over to him, holding her hand out.

"Just doing my job, Doctor Goodspeed," he said, taking her hand and shaking it. There was some warbling in his hand, a tremor that betrayed the calm exterior of this Host'ire.

"Knight Essex," he said, giving her his name again—which was good because Grace had forgotten it, if she could really remember anything at this point. She pulled her hand away. Inside the armor, she could feel a tremble starting. Grace took a deep breath, looking for Emily. She was there, reaching up and grabbing her hand, steadying it.

Looking around at the carnage, Grace was having trouble believing that not even a few hours ago, these people had not only been alive, they'd been human. Now… now she didn't know what had happened to them, only that they were not alive and probably *not* human.

Zombies?

No, that was ridiculous, something from a movie that her father would have made a big show about not letting her see, before letting her slip into the living room after mother was sleeping.

No… no, there was a rational explanation for what was going on that didn't lead to the dead walking. What that was, she didn't know.

Grace took another deep breath and forced herself into scientist mode. Emily had seen death before. She could help keep them calm while Grace worked out the problem, figured out what the fuck was going on.

"Are there anymore members of the security detail here? What is going on? Is the base okay?" Grace started to just vomit the questions that she had been holding in since the gate exploded and this waking nightmare had started.

"It's just me, I have no fucking clue, and um, yeah, that second answer works for all of the above, honestly," he said, giving her a sheepish grin that deflated the entire badass look he had built up during the fight. He was just a child. Deep down under all the bravado and even age, all Grace could feel was the aura of a young boy happy to have helped a girl.

"Those are not satisfactory answers," Grace said.

"No, no they are not. Hopefully the Administrator will have better ones. He sent me to grab you," Essex said.

"Well then, let's not waste any time. Hopefully he has an idea of what we should be doing to get everything back under control," Grace said, walking to the door. She took a deep breath, replacing fear with resolve and a list of things to accomplish.

"Let's hope," Essex said, falling in behind her.

It only took the two of them a few moments to clear the distance from the control room to the door of Administrator Vardis' office. Grace knocked once, seeing the light at the top of the door, indicating it was in lockdown mode. A moment later, the door opened, and she walked in, followed by Essex.

Instantly, Grace was hit by the humidity of the room, and the *green.* She hadn't seen this much green since leaving university to come here. The botanical gardens on Alastar Prime covered almost a thousand square kilometers and were considered one of the wonders of the Unaligned Planets. Before taking this job, she had spent a week camping there, alone with her regrets.

Hanging behind a high desk was Administrator Vardis Cad, his green skin blending into his forested office. The Pa'vinti was holding onto the bar over his desk with a third arm that jutted from his back. The Pa'vinti had evolved in the trees, spending their whole lives hanging and swinging. It made sense then that Vardis had tried to replicate some of his home here.

"I'm glad to see you both made it. I haven't been able to raise anybody else on radio. None of my cameras, save for those on this level, are working," Vardis said, launching right into business. He never was one to rest on sentiment, or worry too much about how people felt, as long as they were working.

"I don't think there is anybody left," Essex said. "I've been reaching out through the Null, and I can't feel anybody. There is still biological life, things moving, but they don't feel like people; don't feel alive."

"Don't feel alive? What does that mean?" Grace asked.

She had never put much stock into the idea that there were people who could feel others through the fabric of space. Her rational brain wouldn't have believed in the powers of people like the Host'ire if she hadn't actually seen them with her own eyes.

Honey, you see math written across the world, Emily's nagging voice said..

"It means that those undead creatures in the control room were not alone. More of the science team has been brought back from the dead. They feel... not hollow, but not alive. It's strange, I can't really describe it. I'm tapping into skills I've only read about, not things we were taught at the Citadel," Essex said, sitting down in one of the chairs that were flanking Vardis' Desk. "My question is, what is the fuck are we dealing with here?"

"I'm with him," Grace said, sitting down in the other chair. Something beyond strange was going on.

Do I tell them about the vision? No, that was just a concussion dream, nothing more, she thought, trying to desperately reassure herself that it was nothing; that she wasn't going crazy with the world.

"The world isn't right, something is changing things," Grace said. "Did you notice the sand and the wind?" she asked, turning to Essex.

"I felt the wind, but what sand?"

"In the other hallway, where the wind was coming from, there were piles of red sand, but not the same red as the dirt from this world, more like a dried blood red. And behind a hole in the wall, there was brick. When I went to look at it, though, it gave way to just the rock underneath."

"It could be a ruin form a long dead civilization. What world these days doesn't have the bones of the dead buried underneath it?" Vardis said.

"No, this was different. They didn't belong," Grace insisted.

"When did you become an expert on bricks?" Essex asked.

"Ten years ago, when I got a PhD in Xeno-archaeology," Grace said with a shrug.

"I thought you were a physicist?" Essex asked, confused.

"Doctor Goodspeed holds five advanced degrees, four in different branches of physics and one in Xeno-archeology, as she said," Vardis chirped in.

"Not much of a social life, I guess," Essex muttered.

"Says the warrior monk," Grace sniped back. She could be just as petty under her breath.

"Ex-Warrior monk, thank you very much," Essex said.

"That is enough," Vardis said, ending their little spat. "So, we have strange bricks, sand and wind blowing through our facility, and something bringing the dead back to life. Anything else I should know about?" the administrator asked.

Is it just me or is he too calm? Emily asked.

Grace shushed the voice in her head. This was no time to second guess. Of course he was calm. That was why he was in charge. It wouldn't do for their leaders to go off half-cocked, even in a situation as supremely fucked as this one.

"I think somebody was pushing the staff into kill boxes with the doors," Essex said.

Both Grace and Vardis turned to look at him.

"What?" Grace said loudly.

"When you saw me this morning, I was running diagnostics on the doors, trying to find the bug in the system to explain why they had been working so inconsistently," Essex said.

"That is not a job for security," Vardis chirped in.

"So my boss keeps telling me," Essex said dryly. "Anyway, I found lines of aberrant code, an algorithm in the system. It was controlling what doors were working and which ones were not. Funneling people around the base at different times of day."

"That does sound like the kind of ridiculous social experiment somebody upstairs would be working on," Grace said, the distain for the facility's social scientists hardly restrained in her voice.

"Maybe. I assume all of this is connected?" Vardis guessed.

"That is a logical assumption," Grace said. "I don't know how it all connects, but it all started when the gate did... whatever it did."

"Yes, the gate," Vardis said. "It is still drawing power, and I worry that it might open again; or is open just enough to be letting some*thing* into our world."

"The only way to shut it down is going to be to kill the power, and you shunted power from all over the base. It took our team a week to compensate for all the different variants," Grace said.

"There is a good chance that this cascaded throughout the facility and that they are having power issues everywhere," Essex piped in.

"Of that I'm sure," Vardis said. "But I have figured out where we can go and shut the power down to the lab, and hopefully the gate. Deep below us, there is an old generator. If you can shut it off, that should power down the Zeta Labs."

As he talked, Vardis called up a holographic layout of the base. Instantly, Grace knew that it was a blueprint that was drawn by somebody who had a higher security clearance than hers, because half the hallways looked wrong. There was so much more to the facility than she even knew existed. At least, that was what she could make out. Her ocular implants were redacting half the map. Looking over, Essex was just as shocked by what he was seeing.

That tracks. A Third would be even lower on the chain of command than me.

"I can't see what you are pointing at," Grace said.

"Oh, I'm sorry, I forgot. Let me get that," Vardis said. He reached over to his computer and pressed a few keys. Grace felt a fuzzy sensation in her eyes that caused her to blink. A moment later, the map looked vastly different, with nothing redacted.

"I've given you as high a clearance as possible. Now, where was I?" Vardis said. "Oh right. If you can get here and cut the power, it should cause a feedback loop and take the lab offline. I trust you two can handle that."

It wasn't a question.

"Yes sir," Essex said, standing up. Grace almost expected him to salute like a good little soldier.

"Yeah, we can take care of that," Grace said. "What if we run into more of our colleagues? What if they don't feel as wrong?" she asked.

What happens if there are survivors?

Vardis was quiet for a moment, before taking in a commanding breath.

"Do what you feel is right," he said.

Those orders were not reassuring. Something felt wrong about them. Something felt wrong about *all* of this. Vardis knew something he wasn't saying, she just wasn't sure what it was. Whatever it was, he wasn't in the mood to tell the two of them about it.

And she didn't have the time to find out.

CIC Fury, Cassandra

Dreadstars did not *just* have a massive wing of two hundred star-fighters and eighty multi-crew support ships, or their ridiculous armament of seven hundred phased plasma cannons. They also came equipped with four Frigate-class escort ships that could latch onto and then peel off from the ship's superstructure. They did this without getting in the way of any of the guns or flight operations. A majority of the *Fury's* anti-fighter weapons were part of these ships, and in normal operations, they would use them to expand the anti-fighter flack bubble that was a key part of their defense screens. In rare occasions, they could also be used as scouting ships.

Of the four Frigates that were attached to *Fury,* two were original to when the ship was constructed a thousand years ago during the Age of Chaos, and two were from sometime during the Wayfinder wars five hundred years ago. The previous family to command the *Fury,* the extinct House Vanpro, had been far more reckless with them than the Cordovas. In almost all respects, Lord Admiral Cordova was loathe to launch them to build out the screens. She knew that losing one would create a hole in their defenses that their depleted finances could not replace. Eventually, House Cordova was going to need to find another stream of revenue or give up the one thing that made them important: *Fury* herself.

Cassandra set down her small blue and white ceramic teacup on the glass map table. They had been in the system for the last three hours running drills, putting the ship and her new crew through their paces. It was a dull assignment, but still better than having a wizard she didn't trust on her ship.

You didn't trust me at first, either. We fought like demons, a voice said in the back of her mind, a fragment of a memory. She wanted to respond to it, to talk to him one last time. Tiberius was dead, like so many before him, and so many after. She didn't want to trust the wizards and their cryptic apocalyptic talk anymore, despite, in their ranks, having found her one person, the human that completed her.

But he was gone now.

There wouldn't be another Tiberius. So, she wouldn't allow a shadow of him to set foot upon her ship. Regulations be damned.

"Frigates deployed," Captain Rackland's voice cut across the Combat Information Center from his standard position on the second level.

"Thank you, Captain. At your pleasure, please launch the target drones and commence system alignment," Cassandra said, looking back down at the glass chart table. Her mind was not fully focused today, but then again, was anybody's mind ever truly engaged with field testing? Orders were being called, and she knew exactly how it was going to go.

Cassandra wanted nothing more than to just be in the past. She was starving for touch that she couldn't get; would never have again. Every other person she had ever met, the thought of their hands touching her caused a visceral reaction. Only Tiberius had been able to calm her with physical comfort. Nothing sexual, but just as intimate.

But, more than anything, she wanted to hear the music again.

While they had been in Null space, she'd sat at the piano in her cabin and looked at the keys. Placed her hands upon them, tried to will her fingers to make music or even a discordant sound. They did nothing. The music was not in her heart. It was never going to find its way to her fingers again. It was folly to think that it lived anywhere else.

In all her years, whenever she was feeling down, or worried about the future, the piano had been there for her. The one companion that never left, that she loved truly and without issue. This was evident by the thousands of tracks and musical cues that were loaded into the computer. That was a fraction of what she had written over the years. It was all hollow now, so bloody pointless.

Play on, my love.

His voice was an echo in her ears, just a ghost and whip of the past, something that was never to return.

"Lord Admiral, tracking test one complete. Frigates operating at eighty percent accuracy rate," Captain Rackland called from the mid-section of the CIC. She snapped from her melancholic memory and looked up at him.

"We can do better, Captain. Recalibrate and start again, if you please. I don't want to be caught with our screens letting things through," Cassandra said, turning back to the map table.

She didn't want to be here. She wanted to be back at the piano, feeling sorry for herself. It wasn't a healthy place to be. She *knew* this but it didn't change things. She needed Tiberius. His council was what had kept her level and now that was gone. There was nothing to do except to attempt to keep time in a world without a melody.

"Aye, Lord Admiral," he said, turning to bark orders at the CIC crew. "You heard the Lord Admiral. We are not in dry dock anymore. It is time to get back in the game. We *will* do better, or I will take it out on each and every one of you. Do I make myself clear!"

"Aye, Captain!" members from the CIC called back.

"Then recalibrate and restart," Rackland yelled. There was a whistle call from the boatswain, and the crew went to work. It would take them a few minutes to pull in the data from the first test and recalibrate the Frigate guns for the second. Better to beat the cobwebs out now than in actual combat.

The second test went better. The screens caught ninety-five percent of the drones this time. It was a perfectly acceptable rate. There was no world where they reached one hundred percent. There were stories that the Wayfinders could create flack screens that were impenetrable, but those were just stories; despite the fact that, anytime you failed in the service, somebody would bring up the fact that the Wayfinders could do it better five hundred years ago. Of course, they were all dead and couldn't come and prove the point one way or the other.

Besides, if they had been so damned perfect, the Host'ire wouldn't have been able to kill them all.

There was commotion on the middle deck, as the communications officer flagged down Captain Rackland to converse. Cassandra put her hands behind her back and walked up the steps to the second level to see what was going on. She needed to move; needed to interact with the crew by doing more than just barking orders.

"Report," she said, walking up. The young communications officer—Midshipmen Miller, if she recalled correctly—gave her a panicked salute before turning to the captain. Rackland nodded his head, telling the young officer who had just transferred in a few months ago that the Lord Admiral was indeed asking *him* for the report and not the captain.

"Sir, we are getting a distress signal. It's weak, going in and out. I'm not sure if it is just the distance causing its weakness or a dying transponder," he said.

"How far out is it, Mister Miller?" she asked. Captain Rackland gave her a small nod for remembering a new crew member's name. He knew what she was going though and had quietly been her rock, even if she never allowed them to talk about emotional things.

"Seven light hours, sir," he said. That was getting close to the edge of their operational range without using a jump gate. She thought about it for a moment, weighing the options.

"Are there any other ships in the system?" she asked, turning to the captain.

"Negative, sir. We are in empty space, close to the doldrums," he said.

"Walk with me," Cassandra said, turning and heading back toward the map table.

The two of them reached the bottom of the CIC and started to look at the table. Captain Rackland marked where they were and where the signal was coming from on the glass with his grease pencil. Then he marked with an 'X' the three nearest jump gates in the area. On the map, Cassandera could see the large section of space that had nothing. There were worlds and people, but this was space that had not been widely explored before the Wayfinder Wars—as such, there were no gates. It was wild and the people who lived there were uninterested in being a part of the Confederation.

"What if we jump here and then flank speed? That should get us there in about a day," Cassandra said, pointing to a gate on the other side of where the signal was coming from. Rackland did a few calculations on the side of the table.

"Yes ma'am, I do think that will work," he said.

"Then set a course, Captain. I shall be in my ready room if you need me," she said, leaning up from the table and gripping her sword.

"Helm, set a course for Gate five-six-eight, maximum sub-light, if your please!" the Captain's voice boomed out across the CIC. The boatswain whistled and the crewmen manning the helm repeated the orders back to him as he started to turn nobs and spin the massive wooden wheel. The CIC came to life with a buzz.

"Tactical, bring in the Frigates and have them reloaded and rearmed. Flight, recall the CAP and ready the ship. Navigation, I have forwarded you numbers—check my math, if you please!"

Cassandra nodded. Captain Rackland had all this under control. She might have commanded the entire ship, but the CIC was his. Those were his people, and he conducted their movements like the maestros of old.

This distress signal was good, providing a low-risk mission that would help get the crew ready for real action; help the new people learn how to interact with the old.

With that, Cassandra turned and departed from the CIC through one of the doors on the lower deck that led to her ready room. She was sure there was paperwork to finish. That would distract her from the darkness that had taken up residence in her mind.

She hoped.

Novagrad, Alexander

Alexander truly felt in his element during festival season. The streets of the city were alive the whole day and throughout the night. People sang, danced, sold foods and goods, kissed and hugged, partaking in all forms of merriment that they could, retreating behind closed doors to have the kinds of fun that one couldn't have on the streets.

Even with all the excitement, once Alexander had reached the estate that they were staying at, he had fallen straight to sleep, just as the rest of his fellow vagabonds were starting to rise.

They had not let him sleep for long. Soon enough, they were crawling up the walls ready to hit the town and check in at the tourney. They were all required to check in before the ball that was being thrown for the teams later that evening. Alexander had never been before but from everything that he had heard about it, the Peculiar Pentagon kickoff ball was not something to be missed—so much so, it was built into the NovaTerra courting season every six years.

And so, the four of them hit the streets. Alexander had changed into a pastel-yellow coat with deep orange piping. On his high collar and cuffs were silver chimeras. His vest and cravat were both black, while his undershirt was a pressed white. The vest was covered with yellow holographic cards and dice. His pants were also a pastel-yellow to match his coat. As a member of the Space Lord class, he wore black boots that went halfway up his calf. Attached to his right shoulder and left lower back was a cape of gold. As a Space Lord, he was also allowed to wear a pistol and sword belt, even in places of high society. Both holsters were empty, though, as weapons were not allowed on the streets during festival season, even by the classes that always wore them.

Flanking Alexander as they walked through the hustle and bustle of Novagrad was Hoben, who was in his finest outfit, plus Katie Thrase and Jeffery O'Hair. All of them were members of the research team at the facility.

Katie of House Thrase was a warp field engineer, one of the few people who still firmly believed that there was a way to go faster-than-light that didn't involve entering the Null. Professionally, they were always at odds, but outside of that, the two of them were fast friends. The spirited arguments had always managed to stay in the lab. And spirited they were, as Thrase was as good an arguer as she was at math—considering her skills with numbers boarded on the supernatural, only matched by her twin sister, who had been taken in by the Host'ire. While she had failed the Host'ire's tests, Alexander was sure she was lightly Null sensitive, which explained her aversion to wanting to use it for travel.

The best part about being friends with Katie, especially during festival season, was that her family, House Thrase, owned the oldest and largest distillery in the Confederation. Because of this, their flasks were filled with the finest whiskey and brandy, both from her personal name day collection.

Jeffery, of House O'Hair, was a sadder friend than Thrase or Hoben, but no less brilliant or loyal. His entire childhood had been dedicated to being a fighter pilot. He wanted nothing more than to fly from the decks of his family's carriers and cover himself in glory, as was befitting a third son. It had not come to pass. When he was thirteen, a rival family had attempted to assassinate his father. The bomb didn't kill anybody, but it did disfigure Jeffery and destroy his eyes in a way that made implants impossible. They repaired his face, but the pain never left him, along with the disappointment. A disappointment that he put into math and cards. There were other ways to fly, he was fond of saying.

"It is beyond strange that Alister didn't leave a message or anything," Thrase said, as they walked.

"I agree," O'Hair piped up, tapping his cane on the cobblestone street. "He is extremally punctual for a young pup. Always making sure that people know where he is."

"I'm telling you, it is because he belongs to House MacGuffin," Hoben said. "You can't trust them to not vanish, lest we forget—"

Alexander held up a hand.

"You read too much into house lore, my friend," Alexander said.

Lore and the story around a house were always fun as a means of gossip and creating stories, but so rarely did he find it to be something that was true in everyday life.

"When the shoe fits," Thrase said, taking a swig from her flask and sliding it back into her coat pocket.

"He will show up. I'm sure there is just a delay," Alexander said.

They stopped at a small stall that was selling fresh fruit. Placing a few coins on the table, Alexander bought a small bag of green apples. Pulling one out, he offered them to the rest of the crew. Hoben and O'Hair each took one.

"Well, he will need to be here soon. Otherwise, we are in trouble. We do not have a replacement, and teams must have five," Jeffery said, holding up five fingers on his gloved hand as he took a bite of the apple.

"I have a plan in the eventuality that he leaves us high and dry," Alexander said.

"Oh, pray tell," Thrase responded as they started to walk again.

"We will just have to find somebody at the ball. It is not ideal…"

"Not ideal! My good man, it's an insane idea," Hoben said. "We cannot just slot in a new player that we do not know. That is asking for a loss in the first round."

"Better to lose in the first round than never get to put cards to table," Jeffery said quietly, the wisdom of failed dreams dripping from every word.

"Jeffery sees the scope of it," Thrase said. O'Hair turned toward Katie and tilted his head in a grumpy way.

"When I was ten, my father brought me to watch the tourney and there was a team that was composed of players who had all shown up alone. They made it all the way to the third round," O'Hair said.

"Yes, there are plenty of fine players who come by themselves looking to attach themselves to a team and find glory, but we are not a well-known team, looking for alternates. We barely made it into the event," Hoben countered.

It was common practice for players with some degree of skill to attach themselves to well established legacy teams as back up players. They almost never got to play, but it helped in the next cycle when teams were looking to make changes to their front-line rosters.

"We need not find some lonely grandmaster who is at odds with their friends. A warm body with a deck and two neurons to rub together will suffice, I think," Alexander said between bites of the crisp tart apple.

As he finished, Alexander threw the core into one of the many trash bins that were along the street.

"Well then, I shall leave that to you," Hoben said to Alexander. "For now, I must part ways here," he said, pointing at the street sign. It read 'Novagrad Air and Space Museum'. "There is a lecture on the history of the Montgomery six rockets that I do not want to miss." Tapping his head, he gave his friends a bow with a flourish and started walking down the road.

The three walked as a group for another half hour before Thrase broke off to go and check on some family business in one of the high-end bars. Eventually, Jeffery also bid Alexander a good day, as he needed to sit down for a while.

The sun was high in the air, so Alexander turned toward one of the feast houses to get a filling meal. He pulled out his pocket watch and again thought about opening the message from Fox. He hoped that it would have some kind of good news. Oh, how he wished she was here right now to share in this moment with him; share a plate of sausage and sauerkraut.

It was not to be, he knew that. Alexander put the watch back into his pocket as he entered the hall. There was nothing for it. That was a bridge that had been burned and could not be rebuilt.

Alexander found a quiet table and sat down with his tray. On it was a plate with two large sausages, whose juices were about to burst from the heat. Around the sausages was a pile of purple cabbage, sauerkraut, a potato salad, half a soft pretzel, and a small ramakin of beer cheese. To wash it all down, Alexander had a large mug of a light festival beer. He had always enjoyed NovaTerra Festival foods, and while he was able to get them year-round, at no point did they taste as good as they did from a feast house during the season. Pouring a small amount of mustard onto his plate, he cut the sausage, the grease and juice running everywhere.

He watched as people milled about until he saw a most stunning woman. For a fleeting moment, they locked eyes and then she started walking toward him. She was of average height, with corn-blonde hair fixed in an elaborate bun atop her head, secured with silver pins. Her face was soft, and her bright green eyes pulled all his attention to them. She wore a long dress of a deep lavender laced in sparking platinum. The bodice was modestly cut but her bust was such that it looked far more scandalous than it was.

So struck by her beauty, it took Alexander a second to realize that she wasn't just walking in his direction, but right *toward* him.

"Prithee, good sir, is this seat free?" she asked, looking to the bench across from him.

"Please sit," he said, motioning for her to sit down. She placed her tray of schnitzel on the table and sat down.

"Thank you. I hope I am not imposing upon your solitude," she said with a light accent that he couldn't place. It wasn't from NovaTerra, but that didn't narrow anything down.

"Not at all—I could use the company, in fact. It seems that the rest of my party had plans for today. I, though, seem to have forgotten to make any," he said.

"In my experience, the best plans are those that are not made, but allowed to happen," she said, holding out a gloved hand to him across the table. "Claudia, of House Wise."

"Alexander, of House Cordova," he said, taking her hand and giving it a light peck. "A pleasure to make your acquaintance."

"Well, Alexander of House Cordova, I am glad to get to join you on a day of unexpected plans and new friends," she said, holding up her stein, which had a darker festival beer than his own.

He raised his glass and returned the toast. On normal occasions, he would be more wary of a stranger, but this was Festival Week, and instant friendship was a tenet of the celebration. *What makes us different is what makes us strong*, the saying went.

"What brings you to Festival? And is that a little lilt of an accent, I hear?" Alexander asked.

"You have a good ear, sir. Wise is pledged to House Lagrange, and we have, by happenstance of proximity, acquired their manner of speaking. You know how it is in the stars," she said.

Indeed, he did. House Lagrange was one of the larger noble Space Lord houses. They controlled Tripoint Station, a space station of stunning size that some say predated the Age of Chaos. It was situated between three jump gates, in a gravitation field that kept it in place. This was where the family in control would derive their name from. Though House Lagrange did not come into control of the station until during the Wayfinder Wars. Their system, aside from having three jump gates giving them access to most of the Confederation, was dotted with dwarf planets, all of which had colonies and smaller noble families to control them. While Alexander had never heard of House Wise, he assumed they must be one of these successor houses.

"In the stars, we are all close together," Alexander said. His time away from *Fury* had diluted his accent, leading it to sound far closer to the Novagrad accent most of his friends had.

"I can hear it in your voice, as well. Is that a hint of the Admiralty? It's a very soft twang," Claudia said. "House Cordova... You control the Dreadstar *Fury*?"

"Indeed," Alexander said, putting a folk full of pickled cabbage in his mouth. As he chewed, he couldn't keep his eyes away from hers, getting sucked into their deep emerald sea.

"I have always wanted to see a Dreadstar," she said.

"They are quiet the sight to behold, but not..." He stopped himself before he said something too forward that would have been inappropriate.

"But not what?" she asked, a hint of mischief in her voice.

"Nothing," Alexander said, looking away, covering his embarrassment with his mug. There was an empty moment between the two of them.

I feel like this is far more awkward for me right now, Alexander thought.

"What brings you to NovaTerra for fest, then, my lord? Are you on leave?" she asked, motioning to his outfit.

"Oh me? No. No. My mother, brother, and twin sister are the military minds. I am..." He paused, considering how to phrase it. "Not one to be confined to the rigors of duty in that way."

"I can tell. No military man has that snappy of a dress. Very fashionable. We Space Lords do always seem to be a little behind the times," Claudia said.

"I do try and stay on top of the fashion, my lady. Aboard ship is not where I reside. I do, somedays, prefer to be on solid ground," Alexander said.

"As do most of us. So, answer the question: what brings you to fest, aside from the food?" she asked again.

"My friends and I are here for the Minister's Peculiar Pentagon tourney," Alexander said sheepishly.

He didn't know how that admission that would go over. Cards were extremely popular across the Confederacy, though some still looked down on playing games as something only suitable for children. The last thing Alexander wanted right now was for her to think he was childish. Children stayed home, adults who were their own men saw the stars.

"I hear that is quite the tourney. All the best players will be there," she said.

Setting down her beer, Claudia reached into the pocket of her dress and pulled out a small flat silver box. Alexander could recognize a Peculiar Pentagon deck box anywhere. They were flat metal—sometimes wood, but rarely—boxes that flipped open. Inside would be a thirty-card deck and then a tracker card. The tracker card was a small electronic card that kept track of your life, what some cards could do, and timed the match. In a ranked tournament match, the tracker card would be provided by the venue to prevent cheating.

"You play," he said, his eyes lighting up. It was far from a question.

"I have been known to… dabble from time-to-time, sir," she said, setting the box down and sliding it forward. It was a big show of trust to let somebody who wasn't on your team see your deck.

Alexander reached down and picked up the box and opened it. Right off the bat, he was greeted with a fine set of cards, the kind of deck somebody who didn't play irregularly would have. The cards were in micro sleeves, there was little to no foxing on them, and right away from the first three cards, he could tell that she had built a very powerful alpha-strike green deck. Green like her eyes. He wanted nothing more than to look at her and her cards, but this was not the place. He closed the deck. Claudia frowned.

"You do not approve?" she asked.

"Only of looking at cards when there is food around," Alexander said, picking his fork back up. "I would hate for anything to happen to what I assume is a Kicker Koronstic striking deck."

"Oh, is that what it is?" she asked. They both knew she knew, but there was the game to a meet cute. A little game that he was happy to play along with.

They finished their meal, trading comments about the weather and shopping, while exchanging looks. At least, Alexander thought that is what they were doing—his normally suave game felt off. Like he had been hit with an EMP and now had to manually target his guns. They cleared their trays and walked out together.

On the way out, Alexander stepped into a small shop, exiting a few minutes later with a bottle of sweet red dessert wine and two glasses.

"Shall we?" he asked, motioning to the park down the street where trees dominated this part of town.

"We shall," Claudia said, holding her hand out to him. He took it as they walked.

The two of them found a quiet patch of grass that was bright but not too hot, the high sun blocked by a far-off tree. Alexander popped the wine and poured her a glass, then one for himself. Taking a sip, it was almost too sweet for him. Claudia made a little face at the sweetness but smiled, nonetheless. Setting down his glass, Alexander reached into his coat and pulled out his silver card box that had the golden chimera embossed upon it. She removed her deck and the two of them exchanged cards.

Looking at her deck, he could tell that she was a shark, ideally swimming looking for chum in the water, and at that moment, he desperately wanted to be chum.

"This is a very well put together deck," he said, trying to not call her out, to let the little game she was playing go on. It was cute and they both enjoyed it.

"The same to you, sir. Would this be a Vermillion shield, with fireballs build?" she asked.

The question wasn't a question. Game recognized game, as a friend from outside the Confederation had said to him once.

"It is, though I am thinking about changing it up for the tourney, depending on what the team wants to do," he said.

Was she a member of another team? Am I being marked right now? he wondered. This was all too good to be true and thus, had to be some kind of ruse.

"One must always think upon their team members. Alas, this year, I think I will be relegated to just watching," she said, picking up her deck and putting it back into her pocket with a hint of sadness.

"You know..." Alexander started, before pulling back. He didn't want to make assumptions for everybody. Oh, hell, who was he kidding? They *had* said he could figure it out, if they needed another person "It is looking like we might be short a player. I mean, if you are interested—and if the rest of the crew approves, of course."

"Oh, I could not impose," she said, putting a hand over her chest, feigning worry.

"The rest of the team will love you. You should meet them. I assume you will be at the introduction ball this evening?" Alexander asked.

"I just might be able to find my way there," Claudia said coyly.

"Perfect! I can't wait for them to meet you," Alexander said.

"I look forward to making their acquaintance as well, my lord," she said with a smile.

Claudia stood up and brushed off her dress in a way that drew his gaze from her eyes to her cleavage—somewhere else that he would not object to being lost in.

"Till tonight, Alexander of House Cordova," she said, blowing him a little kiss and turning around.

As she walked away, all Alexander could do was sit in the grass, dumbfounded, watching the sway of her hips. All thoughts of Fox and the unread message were so far from his mind that they might as well no longer exist.

Communications Room, The Citadel, Lucas

All communications had been blocked. Lucas had been trying for the last hour to reach first his team, and then Host'ire central command, to see if they could tell him what was going on at the Citadel—a place he wasn't supposed to even be.

The whole situation was off-putting. Lucas didn't like strange because he couldn't plan for it. He could plan for many things but strange, strange was never easy to plan for, and his imagination wasn't good enough to anticipate it.

"Sir, most of the station's communications are currently down. We have internals still, if you want me to patch you through to somebody on the base," the young attendant said. He was sitting in front of a console covered in wires, with small golden jacks. Each one was sticking out of a hole in the switchboard. He had on a pair of headphones with a microphone to control the communications. Today, it was controlling the lack thereof.

"Do you know why communications are down? Is there no back up?" Lucas asked, pushing toward the young man using every ounce of rank and poise that he could muster to feel scary.

"Administrator Fel has restricted communications to only those who have authorization and rank at the moment," the young man said, putting his hand to his headphones and then pulling a wire from one port and slotting it into another.

"Son, I am a Knight-Commander. I outrank almost everybody here," Lucas said, puffing himself up.

"I see your rank, sir. It's just that I'm not to allow outside personal unfettered access to the communications systems," he said, looking sheepish.

Even this poor young man knew that something was going on. He didn't need to know the specifics, though—and like a good soldier, was not asking. Lucas respected compartmentalization, he just hated being on the outside of it. It had been years and years since he wasn't entitled to know what was going on.

While the rest of his friends had floundered fighting against the system—or vanished—he had been a good little soldier. Completing the missions he was ordered to go on, killing the people he was told to kill. It had paid off, and now he was a Knight-Commander. If he was in the Confederation Navy, he would be commanding an entire air-wing or a mid-sized capitol ship.

Here, though, at the Citadel? He felt like a child again. There was nothing more emasculating than returning to school.

"Is there anything I can do to get a message out that doesn't involve going through Administrator Fel?" Lucas asked.

He already knew what the answer was going to be. At the moment, Lucas didn't know what the conflict was, or which side was which, but he *did* know that she was not on his side. Even if it just involved support, she wouldn't give him an inch. He really didn't like leaders like that, wrapped up in their paranoia, too weak to see when they needed help.

"Maybe she should worry about the outside," a small voice said.

Lucas's head snapped to the side, and he saw his child self, standing behind the tech he was talking to. There was a smooth paper weight in his hand, blood was dripping from it. Lucas wanted to say something. His eyes darted around. Nobody noticed that there was a small child with a bloody hunk of stone standing in the middle of the communications center. He wanted to call attention to it, wanted to say something. What was there to say, though? That he was losing his mind? That he was seeing visions?

Lucas took his glasses off and rubbed his eyes, acting like he had a headache. He wanted to see the Null without anything in the way. All the techs glowed, he glowed, but this child was a blank space.

There was nothing there.

"Yes I see your point, I will go and try to find another way," Lucas said to the tech, giving the young man a crisp salute before exiting.

Once he reached the hallway, he looked around, the shade of the boy he had once been was still standing beside him, looking up at him. There was innocence and fire in his eyes, and he started to lightly bounce the bloody paper weight in his hand.

"Forces are moving that you cannot see yet. She called you here because she needs you," the child said.

"What forces? What is coming? Is that why the novices have left? Is that why Fel is playing everything so close to the vest?" The questions came spilling out of Lucas like a man with a neck wound.

"You will know soon enough," the child said. He dropped the paper weight and started to walk away. Lucas puffed up and raised his voice.

"Stop right there, mister. I am giving you a direct order!" he called, his voice echoing in the hallway.

The shade of his child self didn't stop walking. He just rounded a bend in the hallway. Lucas followed, getting ready to bark out another proclamation. He turned and the child was gone, replaced by two very confused-looking Host'ire techs who were trying not to look at him and focus on their clipboards.

Lucas ignored them in turn, too distracted trying to parse out the meaning behind the child's words to feel embarrassment. He was sure it wasn't the first time they had seen a high raking knight act slightly erratic as the power of the Null momentarily overwhelmed them. People feared what they didn't understand, but they also ignored it, to avoid having to face that fear. The Host'ire were masters at ignoring things.

What had the child been talking about? Forces are coming that we cannot see?

Lucas was pretty sure that he understood that it was Hyacinth that brought them here and needed them, but for what, he still wasn't clear on. For a split second, he was angry, furious at a child that he couldn't even remember. Why had she brought them here, just to leave them hanging in the wind, confused and feeling strange feelings?

Lucas couldn't think clearly. It was as if all his suppressed emotions from childhood were bubbling back to the surface. He felt like a teenager again, filled with emotions and nowhere healthy to put them. Some fresh air would do him a world of good. Exiting the building, he remembered just how thin and stale the air on Icarus was, but it still was better than being inside.

Lucas reached the parade yard and looked around. There was nobody here, just him and the storm above. Looking up, Lucas saw the Barrier, the raging storms that helped keep civilization trapped in this section of space. The storms that made communication hard, the storms that occasionally reached out and grabbed ships, pulling them to their doom. The storm was why they were here.

The Citadel guarded the Eye, the entrance to Hell—*if* you followed Host'ire mysticism. It was somewhere in this system and needed to be defended, for if anybody was to open the gates to Hell, it would signal the end of life as they knew it.

Lucas had been given many different stories about what lived inside the ranging storm, from dead people who lived wicked lives, to demons, to creatures so far advanced from them that they were as powerful as gods. Part of him believed something horrible was there—how could he not, after spending his whole life raised by the Host'ire? There was another part, though, that had always questioned it. They were too firm, too ridged with their answers. No questioning, no academic thoughts, were allowed. The Barrier was Hell and the Eye must remain lost and closed.

It didn't matter, though. Those were all stories, and he existed in the here and now. Right here, right now, something strange was going on and he was being stopped at every turn when it came to trying to figure out what was going on.

"Mister Brandice! I had heard you were on station. Had to come and see it for myself," a gruff voice said from behind him.

Lucas snapped out of his mental wondering and took a deep breath. He knew that gravel-eating voice; knew it all too well. A voice that had haunted his dreams and memories for a lifetime. A voice of cruelty and pain beyond what any of the students inflicted upon each other.

Turning, he saw the Citadel's Master-at-Arms, Knight Wingarf. The man was grizzled. His face looked like a moon that had weathered a thousand years of meteor impacts. While old, he stood up straight. In his right hand was a star-steel spear, and in his left...well. There *was* no left hand. Wingarf was missing his entire left arm, gone at the shoulder. All that was there was the rolled up, pinned sleeve of his leather jacket.

Lucas had known the Master-at-Arms since he was a child, and he had always been missing the arm. Never during the time Lucas had been at the Citadel did he hear him talk about how it had been lost. There were stories, and legends, of course, ranging from a dog ate it to his third ex-wife ripped it off and tried to kill him with it. Lucas was sure that it was something far less interesting.

"Master-at-Arms," Lucas said, momentarily not sure how he should address the man. He was still just a knight, but his position at the Citadel conferred the implication of rank, and that outweighed his own. Lucas was going to be damned if he would call the cantankerous old man sir, so he settled for cutting the difference.

"Knight-Commander," the old man said, venom burning from the words. "What brings you back to this out of the way neck of the woods?"

He leaned on the spear. Lucas knew that look, knew that posture. This was leading to a fight, starting with a verbal war. As a child, he had never been good at this part; had never possessed even a modicum of the clout needed to fight back. Wingarf had been just as bad—no, *worse*—than all the bullies that they encountered. The old Master-at-Arms was what Jasper had wanted to be. Of course, the old man had more talent in his missing arm than Jasper had his whole life, so it wasn't much of a compliment.

"That... *Knight...* is on a need-to-know basis," Lucas said, trying to keep his voice even, and his stance tall.

His hand wanted to slide his coat to the side and reach for his blade, grabbing it with the Null and pulling it to him. A flourish that he had never accomplished before leaving here. Nothing would be gained by doing that, though. The game had to be played. Wingarf had to be goaded into starting the fight.

"Is that so, lad? My position here confers certain rights. I am entitled to know what is going on at my station that affects my charges," Wingarf said. The man had a point, but at the same time, was dead wrong and they both knew it.

"Without an active combat badge, I cannot share operational details with you, Knight Wingarf," Lucas said, not needing to motion toward the missing arm for it to take center stage.

"Damn your combat badge. I've experienced more of war then you will ever know, *pup*," he snarled.

"And now you are here, teaching children. You know, you could return to the front..." Lucas let the implication hang in the air.

No Host'ire Knight could have their Combat Badge unless their physical person was whole—organic or bionic, it did not matter, they just had to be whole.

"You know damn well that House Loyanger does not believe in bionics. We are pure," Wingarf said.

Lucas fought the small smile that he was feeling. That little nugget of information about the man's house was something he had been saving for over two decades. As a child, there was no way he could have used that. As a Knight-Commander in high standing, it was a knife to the heart. Now it was time to twist the blade.

"We abandon our families when we join the order. You should know that, after all these years," Lucas said, taking a step forward and to the side, starting to circle the old man like a predator, confidence welling inside of him.

"I am of noble birth; a graduate of the Khorn'tosh Academy! I will not be talked down to by common scum like you," Wingarf said, agitation in his voice.

"Oh, but I think you will, Knight. I do not have to suffer from your failings anymore. I am not subject to your beatings and bearings. Nobility means nothing on the field of battle—a place you have not seen in over half a lifetime," Lucas said, his words a bloody knife being ripped from Wingarf's heart.

To his side, he heard the pitter patter of small feet. The child was back. The child was *scared*. He started to run back into the building, right past Joanna as she walked out into the yard. She looked radiant, gripping a book tightly to her ample chest. Lucas turned back to his prey—he could think about Joanna later. For now, he had to finish something he wanted to start since he was thirteen. For all the things he had forgotten about his youth, about his time at the Citadel, his burning hatred for Wingarf was branded into his brain.

"We shall see about that," Wingarf said, spinning the star-steel spear in his hand, the tip coming to life in that signature heartbeat thrum, energy crackling down the blade. It took less than a second for the man to go from a resting stance to being on the attack with a live blade. Lucas reached into the Null and jumped backward, hanging in the air for a moment. Long enough to draw the hilt of his sword to his hand and place his thumb on it. Lucas then landed on the ground his left foot planted, and his right knee bent. The force of his jump pushed him backward, leaving a trail in the dirt.

"I see you have sharpened your reflexes from the dull cheap blade they once were," the Master-at-Arms said.

He wasted no time charging forward, spinning the spear in front of him. Wingarf, a master of his craft and weapon, was able to, with help from the Null, do with one arm what most trained knights would need both appendages to accomplish. He spun and dashed, pushing Lucas back. Lucas dodged half the swings, all of them aimed and deadly. The other half, he reflected with his blade, the energy of the star-steel smashing into the energized haft of the spear, but not cutting through. The star-steel spear was an uncommon but extremely dangerous weapon when used by a properly trained knight.

Another swing and their weapons locked together, energy coursing through both. Lucas saw Joanna, standing in the doorway, watching the fight. While he couldn't see her eyes through the glasses, he knew that they were wide with anticipation, wanting to see who was going to win. Waiting to see him take down a second bully.

No, that wasn't right. Essex had killed Jasper all those years ago.

He would knock this man down for her and she would love him for it. In that moment, Lucas could feel his other blade starting to come to life. Shaking it off, he dug deeply into the Null and pushed. Wingarf, caught off guard, fell backward. His feet lost purchase with the ground, and he dropped, rolling and acquiring another position before he fully hit the ground. All Lucas had accomplished was letting his target gain new footing to rebuild their stance.

"Sloppy. You are letting emotions get in the way of fighting. Battle is about killing, not looking smart for some tart who somehow passed her trials," Wingarf said.

He didn't even need to glance back at Joanna. Lucas did that for him. He flared his nose, the edges of his mouth starting to twitch with anger. Attacking him was one thing. Attacking any of his friends, attacking *her*, was quite the opposite. If Wingarf wanted to say that battle was all about killing, well then.

Lucas would show the old Master-at-Arms just what he could do.

Lucas stood and started spinning his blade, letting the wind find his coat as he whipped the green shaft of energy around his body.

"Peacocking isn't fighting, boy," Wingarf growled.

Is he still trying to teach me? Lucas thought with anger and not a little bit of revulsion. He had surpassed his teacher. What more could he learn? Aside from how to be a sad old man who had been exiled to train poor children how to fight and die, all because of his family's pride.

"Why don't you show me real fighting, old man? When was the last time your blade rent flesh?" Lucas asked, holding his weapon down in a reverse grip so that the blade was behind him.

Energy whipped through his body, kicking up his coat and the dust around him. It had been a few years since Lucas had used this much Null energy in a duel. So often, he was relegated to killing mundanes who didn't even understand how little of a chance they had against a fully trained and practiced Host'ire Knight. But this? This was a challenge and he relished it.

Wingarf didn't have a pithy return for that. Instead, he charged. While Lucas had been trying to look suave for Joanna, the old man had been pulling energy into himself, sending it to his legs. One moment, he was twenty feet from Lucas and the next, he was on top of him, not even a blur of light marking the path he had taken. The spear wasn't what hit Lucas. The old man smashed into him with his shoulder, knocking him off balance and then swiped low with his spear, sending Lucas down to his ass. He hit with a thump that had to be satisfying for the old man.

There was no time to get up, to try and find new footing. The head of the spear was coming down toward him, moving quickly, a killing blow. In that moment, Lucas wasn't sure if this was just a less-than-friendly sparing match or an actual duel. There was no time to think on that fact. Anything less than action would have been the end of him.

Lucas rolled away, then tucked and got back on his feet. Wingarf ran toward him. Lucas pulled in the Null and leapt, creating a small patch of solid air under his foot, using that to push himself forward before landing behind Wingarf. In a quick motion, he pulled the hilt of his blade to him from where it had fallen and thumbed it back to life, the blade casting a green pallor over his face.

"Very good, Mister Brandice," Wingarf said as he turned around to face him. There was not even a bead of sweat running down his forehead. He spun the spear so that it was tucked under his arm, the glowing head just past his armpit.

"What can I say? The battlefield gave me the confidence and skills denied to me in my education," Lucas bit out. He wasn't sure if attacking the man's skill as a teacher was going to net him any points in this fight. The blank look that Wingarf returned him confirmed the negative.

"I made you hard. Too many children come here screaming and crying. Weak," Wingarf said.

"That is because you rip us from our families, tell us that we are going to live a better life, and then beat us relentlessly. Our freedom and choice were taken away, leaving us with a singular remaining option: fight or die. That is the kind of attitude I would expect from a failed noble like you," Lucas said.

Behind Wingarf, he could hear Joanna laugh at his line. He was starting to sound like her, mouthing off at every last cornerstone of the order; the cork holding in his resentment starting to rise from the bottle's neck.

"Freedom has always been an illusion. None of us are in control. The darkness comes for noble and commoner alike, Knight-Commander," Wingarf said. "How you face that darkness when you dig it up is what matters."

As Wingarf said this, Lucas felt the air behind his back turn hard, like there was a hand on his shoulder that pushed him forward. He couldn't move, tried to lift the arm holding his blade. It was no use. There was more than one hand holding him. He was lifted from the ground and then thrown, flying past Wingarf and landing at Joanna's feet in a crumpled mess.

"The darkness is going to eat you, child. Once it passes, nobody will remember your name or the stupid fights that you picked. Everybody you love will be dead next to you. Not because you are poor, or because I was mean, but because you were weak. And still are," Wingarf said, poison in his voice.

As he finished, he tapped his heart with the head of his spear coming millimeters from burning his own coat. Lucas tried to get up, to continue their duel, but the old man shook his head and thumbed off his weapon.

Flicking it back under his shoulder, Wingarf, the Master-at-Arms for the Citadel, walked away into another section of the parade yard and out of sight.

Leaving Lucas behind, battered and beaten.

Citadel Yard, Joanna

Lucas moved with such grace and poise, spinning his blade around, moving out of the way of the oncoming blows from the old Master-at-Arms.

Hadn't he been old when they were students? Was he always just like this? Joanna thought as she watched the fight, clutching the banned book close to her chest so that nobody would see the spine or title. She had come looking for Lucas. A technician in the hallway said he was out here. They had snickered as she walked by. That was something she was used to. Nobody took her seriously unless she was yelling at them, and even then, they were more interested in just getting her to be quiet than actually listening to what she was saying. Such was her life.

Joanna had walked out into the yard just as the confrontation was starting, first with words and then with blades. Wingarf with his star-steel spear, a weapon only taught at the Academy on NovaTerra. Or so she had been told. Weapons training was something she mostly left behind. Joanna hadn't used the star-steel blade that hung from her belt since her last practical exam seven years ago and didn't plan on using it again for another three until qualification came up.

Lucas hit the ground with a thump in front of her, as Wingarf muttered something about the oncoming darkness and walked away. Lucas scrunched his face and watched the man go, his pride broken.

At least he still has pride, Joanna thought, knowing that she had nothing left but spite and a nagging amount of curiosity. He was breathing heavily, angry. She found it attractive. Demons above, she found everything he was doing attractive. Why now, after all these years of not thinking about him, was she feeling like a school girl again? Was it because they were here? Was it because a smaller version of herself was standing right next to her, swooning over the grizzled and handsome adult version of the boy she thought about as she closed her eyes at night?

She didn't like this line of thought and wanted very much to get out of her own head, to return to the here and now. Even though he *was* in the here and now, on the ground right in front of her. She tried to push it all away, the visions, the feelings. The first step was always to put something like this out of mind and hope that it went away. It was the Host'ire way, after all. At least that was how it was taught at the Citadel. The Null sometimes amplified your emotions and imagination. If you didn't let that have power over you, it wouldn't. The young girl vanished, leaving her with just Lucas on the ground, clutching his wounded pride.

Joanna reached a hand down toward him. Lucas looked up and forced a smile, trying to let her know that everything was fine, even if it wasn't. That smile melted her, she could feel it all the way from her head to her toes. She could see why they all followed him, why he had become a Knight-Commander, a rank almost unheard of for somebody who had graduated from the Citadel. Commanders were noble, commanders went to the Academy. They were not stolen children.

Lucas took her hand and allowed her to help him up. Brushing the dirt off, he reached a hand out to pick up his blade, clipping it again to his belt.

"You saw all that, I take it?" Lucas said, his voice low.

"I did. You afforded yourself well," Joanna said.

Somehow that sounded like a lie, like something you say so as not to bruise the fragile male ego. Did Lucas have an ego that she needed to worry about offending? She knew well the boy he had been, but not the man he had become.

"I got cocky," Lucas muttered. "I played that fight out in my head for years, so many of my sparing partners in advanced training looked like him, talked like him..." He paused, readjusting the glasses on his face and pulling his gloves tight. "If only they had fought like him."

She could tell that he had more on his mind something that wasn't coming out. The feelings of inadequacy and embarrassment were radiating off him, finding their way into her. Was this just empathy? No, it felt like something more. It felt like a deeper connection, something she didn't have experience with, wasn't comfortable with. It was also something she didn't want to deal with, right now, but that said, she couldn't ignore it.

She noted it down mentally, to bring up later. It was a part of the puzzle, it had to be, but the way it made her feel, the raw emotions, the old wounds... Every bone in her body wanted to run, to flee, to not think about it. The rational side of her knew they needed to talk about it, but... *later*. She wasn't about to bring up phantom children standing out on the parade field.

"He is just a bully. They will always find ways to get under your skin," Joanna said, looking forward. "How did your attempt to get anybody on the comms go?"

"It didn't. Administrator Fel has everything locked down tight, and there is a Barrier storm going on, so even if I could find a ship, their transmitters wouldn't break through the interference. We are on our own to figure out what is going on here. To figure out what *she* wants from us," Lucas said.

He took another steadying breath. Through the rim of her glasses, Joanna could see the Null energy that he had built up fading away, like water falling off somebody who had just risen from the bath.

"I trust your trip to the library went better?" he asked, pointing to the book she was still clutching.

For a moment, Joanna wanted to jump out of her skin, unsure if he could be trusted to know just how heretical the tome in her hands was. But, if she couldn't trust him with this, then it didn't matter what she found, because she would be alone with it.

"It was interesting," she said. "Fel and Tor do not get along at all. She is hiding something, even from the faculty," Joanna said.

"It's good to know that she doesn't have all the teachers on her side," Lucas said.

"Her side? Are we breaking off into two sides, then—hers and ours? What are we even fighting over? It seems a bit premature to be splitting into camps," Joanna said.

"I don't know what the two sides are or if it is even *just* two sides. I feel in my gut that it isn't in her interest to help us or ours," Lucas said. "Did Tor know why the novices have all been sent away?"

"No. But..." She paused, lowering her voice, unsure who might be around and able to hear. "He knows much about what is going on here; much, much more. He gave me this," Joanna said, turning the book so that Lucas could read the title on the cover: *Looking Beyond, Finding the Way.*

"I don't recognize that book. Should I?" he asked.

Blessed, pretty, stupid boy. He wouldn't have known she had a heretical tome in her hand even if he had accidentally seen it. There was something to be said for warriors. They didn't think beyond what they saw, leaving that for people like her.

"Wayfinder prophecy," Joanna said quietly.

That, at least, he recognized. "You should not have that," Lucas said, looking around. Less like he was going to take it from her, and more like he was making sure that there wasn't anybody else around that might give them trouble. "Why would he give you that? You know how much trouble we could get in for this?"

"I am a librarian who studies the Wayfinders. I know exactly how much trouble we could get in for having this," Joanna said using her index finger to make a cutting motion across her neck. "He said this had answers and I am inclined to believe him on that front. I'll know more this evening."

"Know more about what?" a voice said from behind them.

Both Joanna and Lucas turned defensively. Walking up to them, the light reflecting off her bald head, was Naomi. She looked radiant in the light, just like Lucas had out on the field during the fight. They both let out their collective, held breath at not having to come up with a quick lie or any cover-ups. Joanna had never been good at lying, she was far too aggressive. She knew Lucas was similarly bad at it as well. Too honest. Neither of them was cut out to be a spy.

"About what is going on," Joanna said, flashing the book's title to Naomi. Where Lucas's eyes had gone dim, Naomi's lit up.

"Where did you get that?" she asked in a hushed tone, putting her hand on Joanna's and pushing the book back against her chest. The closeness excited her.

"Tor gave it to me," Joanna said.

"That is some gift. Or does it hold a secret? Oh, tell me it holds a secret," Naomi said, getting giddy over the thought. Lucas just rolled his eyes.

"Of course it holds a secret, Naomi. It's a book of prophecy. I just wish I knew what secret I was looking *for*," Joanna said.

"Well then, we should grab some food—I'm famished, are you two hungry? Then, sit down and start reading. See if we can't figure out what it is. I love a good puzzle," Naomi said. Joanna smiled at the excitement.

"How did your meeting with Professor Rickman go?" Lucas asked, clearly trying to get them back on track, the typical leader, looking for a situation report from everybody. It was adorably endearing.

"Not as good as I wanted. She knows something, but is scared. She has always been too scared of something to help us. I don't know what it is. Clearly she is on our side, but I-I don't know," Naomi said, frustration in her voice.

"See?" Lucas said, pointing. "She also sees that battle lines and sides are being drawn."

"Maybe, but I'm not..."

Naomi wasn't able to finish her sentence. Klaxons started to blare all around them. The landing lights on top of the four towers of the far curtain walls were spinning. Large doors under the ground started to open and landing crews streamed out.

"I thought no more ships were coming in or out," Joanna said.

"They shouldn't be. Come on," Lucas said, tapping her on the shoulder and running inside. Joanna tucked the book under her jacket and followed.

They ran up three flights of stairs to the third block of the Citadel, leading to a balcony that looked out over the landing pads. As they stepped outside, the sound of the ships coming in was deafening. Joanna looked up to see ten super-sized troop transports screaming through the thin atmosphere of Icarus. She hadn't seen ships this big in years, and never at the Citadel. Three of them touched down, with the others landing just outside the wall.

"What the bloody hell?" Lucas breathed. Joanna looked from the ships to him and then Naomi, the fear on their faces reflecting her own.

"I guess we know why the novices were sent away," Naomi said, unsure of herself.

As the first ship landed, support crews ran out, securing it to the ground. There was a loud hiss of steam and then the door in the back opened, a massive gangplank extending before falling to the ground. Drums started to play in a deep, unsettling rhythm.

From out of the ship marched soldiers. They were in a square line, ten abreast and ten deep. They had on long green button-up coats, like those worn on NovaTerra, and black steel breast plates. Their faces were covered by helmets of chrome polished to a mirrored shine. Smartly held against their shoulders were plasma muskets. Old weapons; powerful, *dangerous* weapons.

Joanna, like Naomi, recognized these soldiers instantly, but didn't dare speak their name out loud, for their existence was more myth than fact—or so she thought. This was a military force that should not exist. If they were here that signaled that they were in horrible danger; explained why the place was empty.

Whatever it was that Hyacinth wanted them to do had just gotten a whole hell of a lot harder.

"The Host'ire Militarum," Lucas said, awe in his voice.

EPISODE III:
Re-Education

Re-Education, Rostov

The walls eventually stopped moving. Rostov had climbed into bed as soon as his body had recovered from the pain and paralysis. He knew they were watching him, and Rostov would be damned if he was going to give them the satisfaction of watching him suffer on the floor all night. He had already learned something they didn't want him to know, one of their dirty little tricks. He was sure there were more. His cell was probably a magician's box of depraved gags designed to break his view of reality.

It took the walls two hours to finish sliding into place. They stopped exactly where he knew they would. Now that he was looking in the dim light, he could see the faintest of scuff marks on the floor, something that wouldn't have stood out to him if he hadn't been looking.

He was tired. It had been a long day of pain and telling jackbooted assholes to go fuck themselves. Once he was sure the walls had finished moving, he pulled the scratchy wool blanket up to his chin and rolled over to face the wall. Eventually they would come again—they always did. For now, he was going to sleep, and dream about how he would use this newfound information against his tormentors.

A small part of himself held out hope that with the arrival of Lucas, a whole Knight-Commander, that he might be able to get out of here. It was a small hope, a candle whose wick was almost smothered by liquid wax. It could maybe burn again but even a tap in the wrong direction would snuff it out. Lucas did have Naomi and Joanna with him, which was a good sign that he was serious about getting the band back together.

Rostov wasn't sure if he had fallen asleep when he heard the locks on the door click. Was night already over? Was it time to return to his daily drudgery?

Something was wrong.

He knew it instantly. The lights didn't come on, there was no wake up music, the recitation of the Host'ire creed wasn't coming in over the speakers. Rostov didn't move. Whatever was going on, he didn't want to spook it, didn't want to jinx it.

Cracking open an eye, he could see a shadow on the wall as the door opened. It was the slender frame of a woman. She walked into the cell, toward him, her hips swaying, the sound of her footfalls echoing.

Are those heels?

No, it couldn't be, who would be stupid enough to wear heels here? Every member of the Host'ire wore boots. *Could you be a jackbooted thug in heels?*

The woman's shadow overtook the light from the door as she got close to him. Rostov could hear her breathing. It was husky, sexual, reminding him of the few times he'd spent with a woman while serving out his exile at the Citadel as a failed knight. She stopped walking. There were two snaps as she stepped out of the heels. His blanket was moving, and a moment later, an arm was wrapped around him and a warm body pressed up against his. He could feel her figure, her ample breasts. She was naked.

She walked in naked, except for heels?

His brain was having trouble accepting what was going on. That was quickly broken by the sliding of her hand over and into his pants. Through all the pain and all the hardship of the last year, Rostov was sure a woman's hand on his cock was a feeling he would never feel again, yet here it was, and he couldn't trust it.

"We are going to get you out of here," she whispered.

Rostov recognized the voice instantly. Naomi. He wanted to roll over, to look in her eyes. To run his hand over her bald head and cup her breast. This was something he had thought about for *years*. Always when they were kids, he followed behind her, helped her with projects. When people made fun of her for talking a mile a minute, all he could do was puff himself up and then try to make a joke so she would feel better.

I've never been as brave as Lucas or Essex.

As he tried to turn, her grip on him got harder. She started to stroke his cock; it was too hard, too forced. Rostov tried to turn again.

"I want to see you," he whispered.

"Hush now, all will be taken care of," Naomi whispered into his ear.

As wrong as the feeling of her hand on his member was at the moment, he couldn't stop himself from coming to attention. On the wall, there was another shadow, belonging to another woman standing in the doorway, watching. Light bloomed behind her like a halo, as if she was an angelic vision painted on the wall of a church.

"Somebody is watching us," Rostov said as Naomi started to kiss the back of his neck, the hairs on his body starting to stand up, as pleasure cascaded through him.

"She is always watching," Naomi whispered, nibbling on his ear. She stroked his cock harder and pressed herself against him. He could feel her hard nipples on his back as he started to moan, letting the ecstasy wash over him.

Who is she? Rostov, this is not what you want, his brain shouted at him, the logical side of himself desperate to regain control. He slipped a hand back between Naomi's legs. She was wet and inviting. As he started to slip a finger inside her, the shadow walked toward them. The light from her halo illuminated the room.

"Who...?" He tried to say before a hand was placed over his mouth. This wasn't Naomi's hand. The motion on his member stopped and he started to roll. Naomi was gone, and as he rolled over, he let out a muffled scream. Looking at him, her face close to his, was a dead woman. He didn't recognize her. Her skin was pale, clammy, like it had been in the water for ages. What was left of her blonde hair had long ago turned green. Her lips were blue.

It was the eyes, though. They were alive.

"Help me," the dead woman choked out. Her hand on his mouth was cold, but he could feel blood pumping through it. She wasn't dead, but... he didn't know what to think.

"Find me, I need you," she said again, her voice filled with pleading and fear. "They are coming."

Rostov tried to speak, but her hand was still over his mouth. He had so many questions he wanted to ask; *needed* to ask. What was going on? Who was she?

You know who she is, the logical side of his brain said. In the moment, though, Rostov couldn't think, couldn't put anything together. There were screams in the distance, chants and calls. The sounds of angry men prepared to enact violence. They were fast approaching the hallway, echoing their footfalls a thousand-fold. Rostov could hear chains rattling and clubs being hit against hands.

"Find me before they do, don't let them open the Eye. Shadows are coming, Rostov. She will guide you, if he can keep her alive," the dead woman said.

No, she wasn't dead. She was just water-logged, drenched in tears and sadness. It was Hyacinth. Rostov wasn't sure how he knew this, he just did. It was a feeling that extended deep into his soul and core. They were connected, he could feel what she was feeling—a deep, horrible fear.

"I will," Rostov whispered through her hand, less with his mouth and more with his mind.

The sounds of the violent men got louder and then he saw them. Ten figures, draped in bloody brown robes. They all carried clubs and chains in their hands. The man in the back was banging on a drum. All of them had bright red eyes, as if the whites had been replaced with backlit blood. Etched into their foreheads was an asymmetrical cross. The vertical line was long, while the horizontal one was shorter and not centered. For some, the cuts in their flesh was new, still oozing and bleeding. For others, they were old and scared over.

Rostov tried to move, tried to leap out of bed to protect Hyacinth. His limbs were far too heavy. In a moment like this, he would have used the Null to push energy into his body, but he couldn't feel it around him.

The energy of the world was gone and he was painfully alone.

"Don't you touch her!" he yelled.

Nobody listened to him. They knew as well as Rostov that his threats were empty, that there was nothing that he could do to them. These bloody monks with their forehead crosses grabbed Hyacinth, dragging her across the room, pulling what was left of her dress off and wrapping their chains around her. One of the men threw his chain over a bar hanging from the ceiling that Rostov had never noticed before. He then tied it to Hyacinth's chains and hoisted her up.

"Where is the Eye? Our lord demands it!" the oldest man, the one who had been beating the drum, yelled, getting close to Hyacinth.

The men around her started to beat her with their clubs. The wet thump of wood against flesh filled Rostov's ears. She didn't scream out, didn't cry. She gave them nothing.

One of the men turned, leaving the beating and walking over to Rostov. He knelt down and smiled. His teeth were yellow and covered in blood. Those glowing red-on-red orbs dug into his soul, and for a moment, as they locked eyes, it felt like somebody was carving a cross into his head.

Rostov's eyes flew open as he screamed. The room was dark, and he was sopping wet, drenched in his own sweat. Both of his hands had found his forehead, desperately rubbing, feeling for evidence of a scar or injury. His breathing was fast, ragged, sucking in air and almost coughing it out, the over-oxygenation leading to a lightheaded euphoria, for a moment. Rostov could feel the brightness of the Null again.

Reaching out, he grabbed the energy and wrapped it around himself like a heavy security blanket. His breathing slowed as the panic started to fade, and he was able to think again. He had never had a dream like that before. It *couldn't* have been a dream. It was a vision. A prophecy?

As he regained control of himself, Rostov looked up. There was a loud pounding sound, almost like thousands of boots, hitting the ground above him. The room shook. This wasn't some trick his captors were playing on him.

For the first time in years, he was sure of that.

Citadel Apartments, Lucas

None of them had slept well. The transports had been landing all night. Lucas had watched from their window. Troops marched in, building tents and moving throughout the Citadel. He had lost count in the night, but it seemed close to one hundred thousand soldiers that had arrived; were *still* arriving, all members of the Host'ire Militarum. An organization that wasn't even supposed to exist. There had always been whispers rumors, but never in his twenty years had he actually seen one of them in person. The stories always talked about how they were the military arm of the Host'ire. Kept in secret, away from the watchful eyes of the Confederation. Ready and waiting to fight the Order's wars. They said that nobody could stand up to the Host'ire Militarum and that once they made landfall, all that was left was death and honor.

It made sense to Lucas that they would exist—or, at least, *had* existed. The Host'ire had fought the Wayfinders five hundred years ago. A war that size wasn't just fought by knights and squires. No, it would have required a navy and an army. Where had they been hiding? How had he, as a Knight-Commander, never heard anything about them officially? Most importantly, why were they here now? It seemed to Lucas that the more he pried, the more questions he found under the surface.

"Come away from the window. You have been there all night," Joanna said from the table in the middle of their small living space.

Lucas sighed and stood up, walking over to the table and sitting down. Joanna had the book she had gotten from Baron'Tor sitting open on the table. He looked over at it. The pages were covered with small text and diagrams. All of it looked strange to him; looked like heresy. But what wasn't right now? They were chasing a ghost and stumbling into something that was clearly bigger than them. So, what was a little heresy on the side?

"I might have been by the window, but you have been reading that book all night," Lucas said, pointing at the tome.

"At least this has answers and I'm not just counting soldiers walking," Joanna said.

Lucas tried not to roll his eyes. She was far too obsessed with the idea that everything could be found in a book. He cared for her deeply, but wanted her to look up and see the world for what it was.

"Soldiers who belong to an army that shouldn't exist. It's like watching the past marching into existence," Lucas said, whispering the last part. "Have you looked at them? Even the way they march and are armed is outdated, like something from a history book."

"I can't say I've given them a long look, no," Joanna said.

She sighed and stood up, pulling down her sunglasses and rubbing her eyes. She looked tired. Lucas suspected they all looked tired, frazzled. Except maybe Naomi. Was she still sleeping?

"Go on, tell me about this army from the past," Joanna said.

She was placating him, letting him talk about something he understood. Even knowing that, it still felt good.

"First, it's the attire; long green coats, the black chest armor, the helmets. Armies haven't dressed in that kind of pageantry since the Wayfinder Wars. Even if NovaTerra fashion doesn't want to evolve, their military has kept up with the times. The guns slug over their shoulders? Those are Plasma Muskets. Also—"

"Weapons from the Wayfinder Wars," Joanna finished his sentence as she started to pour a cup of coffee. She raised the pot to Lucas, and he nodded his head, signaling that he would love a cup.

"Exactly. They are old weapons, retired only because of their slow rate of fire. Yet, they are reported to be deadly accurate and have an impressive range. I'm sure those helmets have the best optical systems in the Confederation and not something from five hundred years ago, despite their appearance. A hundred thousand of them on a wall could hold any position, unless..."

"Unless they just attacked from orbit," Joanna said, sitting the coffee down. Lucas picked it up and took a sip. It tasted like dirt, which was how he liked his coffee. Hobbs had tried to get him to try what they said was 'good coffee' once. It just tasted burnt and left an aftertaste in his mouth for most of the day.

"Exactly. So, what is the point of massing a force of that style? I could understand this move if we were close to the border with the Unaligned Planets, but the Citadel is as far away from that as you can get. We are missing something here. I just wish I knew what it was. I feel like we have a number of puzzle pieces but lack the picture on the box," Lucas said. "I don't suppose your book has shed any light on the situation?"

"Not yet. I'm still in the prologue where they talk about the long history of the Wayfinders and how seeing the paths in the Null allow them to see paths to the future. It's heady and written in a very archaic style. It's going to take me time. Normally when I encounter texts like this, they have been translated and filtered. This is unvarnished, pure Wayfinder. We speak and write the same language, but at the same time, we don't, if that makes sense," Joanna said.

"Well, keep at it," Lucas said, looking down at his watch. It was 0700. People would be moving around soon, if they hadn't already been up all night, like they had. Yesterday might have been a bust in getting answers, but today was going to be different.

Standing up, he walked over to their little kitchenet and started pawing around for something to eat. As he was doing that, the door to Naomi's room opened and she walked out, looking refreshed and excited about the day.

"You're all up early," she said.

"We didn't really go to bed," Lucas replied.

"That is silly. A good night's rest is key to having a good day," Naomi said, rattling out the platitude with a happy voice. She walked into the kitchen next to Lucas and started getting herself a cup of coffee. Her attitude felt infectious, like her optimism might rub off on him. He found it not only infectious and irritating, but also intoxicating.

"I'll try to work in a little time for a nap," Lucas said, shuddering as the sound of another transport landing shook the whole building.

"I'm going to hold you to that, Knight-Commander," she said, pointing a finger at him like some kind of cheerful nagging nanny.

"I'm sure after going to talk with Administrator Fel, I'm going to want to bash my skull in and sleep for a week," Lucas muttered.

He was going to get answers out of her even if it killed one of them. She might have been snide about Host'ire Intelligence the other day, but the few years Lucas had worked with them had been enlightening. You could learn plenty of information from a person without having to use any kind of physical pain or mind probes.

It'll just be a...

"Sounds like it is going to be more than a nice chat," Naomi said, finishing his thought.

"How did you..." Lucas started to say.

"You said it out loud," Joanna said, looking up from her book.

"I did? I don't think I did," Lucas said, his eyes darting between Naomi and Joanna. He was sure that he had just been sarcastically *thinking* about having a nice chat with Fel, and not that he had said it out loud. No, he hadn't said it out loud. He was positive.

"Are you sure you don't want a nap? A little rack time might do you good," Joanna said, looking at Lucas. Her eyes were darting across his face, examining him, getting a feeling for if he was still fit to be in charge. He was, he *knew* he was. They couldn't take this little command from him. They hadn't even given it to him, it was...

Lucas could feel the anger and paranoia bubbling up inside him, the Null around him getting hot with emotion. He stopped and took a deep breath in, putting both hands on the table and then breathing out. Lucas repeated that five times before his heart started to beat slowly, before the calm started to return to his mind. He was tired. The brief negative emotion had dug deep into the Null, so deep he could feel the pull of the Shadow. That was all.

"Are you okay?" Joanna asked, a concerned look upon face.

Her round face was drooped down and there was a well of compassion and concern in her blue eyes. Lucas wanted to melt away at that moment, to just fall apart and cry. He could feel the exhaustion in his body. There was no time for that. There were questions that needed answering, and from what he had spent the whole night watching, it didn't look like there was going to be much time to find them.

"I'm okay. Just need to focus. I must have made a quip about it being a nice chat," Lucas said, rubbing his hands together and then holding them up as he regained his composure.

"Or you didn't," Joanna said, looking across to the two of them. "I can't be alone in saying that I've strangely felt more connected to the two of you in the last twenty-four hours than I have anybody in my life. Even back when we were kids."

She was going out on a limb, he knew. Lucas could see her standing there, putting herself out there, hoping that she wasn't alone in the feeling.

"You are not wrong," he muttered. "Something is going on here. Something *went* on here. We don't have a good idea of either."

Lucas stood up and started pacing around the small room. He was working to get his emotions under control, to keep everything in check.

"It's Hyacinth. We have to figure out who she was and why we can't remember her, and then how she's connected to whatever is going on here with the Host'ire," Naomi said.

"Are you..." Lucas started to say but pulled back, unsure of how to broach the subject.

"Seeing things?" Joanna asked. Naomi and Lucas both looked over at her. It was clear upon their faces.

"Kids, us… the past…" he said, letting the words hang in the air.

"Yes. Every time, it's like I can almost reach out and touch them, feel some memory that is locked away…" Joanna started.

"But then it is gone as fast as it starts," Naomi said, finishing the thought.

Lucas could almost hear them talking to themselves, the internal monologues. Small voices too quiet to hear, feelings more than anything else.

"I sometimes see Null echoes. I was sure that was what it was. The first one appeared the same day as Hyacinth's message. I was leading a raid on a cruise ship that we were clearing of pirates. Then I saw another here. All places of strong emotions," Lucas said.

"Next time one of these kids appears, we need to follow them, see what they want to show us," Joanna said.

"You think this could be Hyacinth trying to talk to us?" Naomi asked.

"Maybe. Anything is possible," Joanna said.

The three of them were quiet for a moment, letting the implications fill the room. Lucas took off his glasses and blinked. He could feel the two women sitting next to him, feel their life force in the Null. It was stronger than anything he had felt before. Weak golden lines, thin as fishing wire, extended from all three of them, creating a triangle. Small pulses of energy were moving along the lines, their heartbeats in sync. He could feel worry coming from both of them, and from himself.

Taking a deep breath, Lucas put up a wall and returned the glasses to his face.

"The first step is we need to talk to Fel. She knows the big picture that we are missing, and can help us get Rostov out of Re-education," Lucas said.

Joanna nodded in agreement.

"You have fun talking with Administrator Fel. I think I'd rather put nails in my skull than have another conversation with her," Naomi said.

"I know what you mean," Lucas said, rubbing his temple. "But one of us has to do it. I take it you already have a plan?"

"Yes. I acquired a badge to the main computer core. So, I am going to set up shop there and see what I can learn," Naomi said.

"That sounds dangerous. What if they find you?" Joanna asked.

"Oh, well then they will find Broadcast Technician Cicely Williams," Naomi said, sliding a fake ID badge across the table. "It's an identity I had for a mission shortly after I left here. Host'ire Intelligence inserted me into a TV station on NovaTerra for a year. They were surreptitiously broadcasting sedition and heresy." Her eyes were wide, and her head bobbed with pride at the mention of the story. "But I didn't tell you that. In fact, none of you know who Cicely Williams is. Forget I mentioned her." With that, Naomi quickly grabbed the badge and shoved it back into her pocket.

"That sounds like a great idea," Lucas said. "I'm sure you will blend right in. Still, be careful and don't overstay your cover. They are bound to have that name in the computer systems."

"It was a deep cover operation, they would need to go looking. Still, I should be able to get in and out without raising any suspicion." Naomi nodded and gave him a two finger salute that turned into a thumbs up. It was an old Host'ire Intelligence hand gesture indicating that one understood their orders and assignment. Lucas was shocked that Naomi of all people had spent a year undercover working intel. It seemed that she couldn't even keep her mouth shut for five seconds without just blurting out what she was thinking in a stream of consciousness.

Though IT people are strange, so maybe nobody really thought anything of it. Mundanes are like that, Lucas thought.

"If you don't mind, I'll join you going to talk to Fel," Joanna said. "I need to take a break from translating old Wayfinder. Then, I guess I'll probably find a hidden nook in the library since I'm going to need some of their books."

She put a small marker in the tome she was reading and then closed it. Lucas noticed that she had already put an archivist's cover over on the book. It was a simple book sock, but it would obscure the title from any prying eyes. She then slipped it into a messenger bag that was sitting by the table.

"I'm ready whenever you are," she said.

"Good. First, though—coffee," Lucas said, holding up his cup and taking a sip. He was not about to confront Administrator Fel undercaffeinated.

Administrator Fel's Office, The Citadel, Lucas

"I do not have to tell you anything, sir! This is my school, and my command. The fact that I haven't removed you from this world is an act of courtesy to your standing!" Administrator Fel yelled from her desk, pointing an accusatory finger at Lucas.

As he had suspected, the conversation was not going well. Yes, he could have been more diplomatic, and not just barged in demanding to know what was going on based on title and privilege. But what was done was done.

"I thought we hadn't been removed from this world because there was a no-fly order, which I guess wasn't true," Joanna said, folding her arms as she asked the question that was not really a question. Lucas fed off her energy, nodding his head and pointing at Joanna.

"The Militarum was scheduled to be here. *You* were not. I still don't even know exactly why you are here. We both know your story is bullshit, Knight-Commander," Fel snapped back, as she leaned in her chair, crossing her fingers together so that they looked like a steeple.

"Why are all the novices gone?" Lucas demanded. She wasn't going to give him anything without information, so might as well attack right to the heart of the matter. Both were connected, so perhaps knowing the answer to one might let him infer the other.

"They were in unacceptable danger," Fel said.

"Unlike the acceptable danger of getting abused and harassed by other novices and the facility," Joanna said quietly under her breath.

"I will not have my institution insulted like that. Those are shadows of the past," Fel said, leaning forward. Joanna had hit a nerve. She was exceptionally good at that. Always finding exactly what somebody in power didn't want to talk about, didn't want *you* talking about, and then talking about it.

"Then you should run a tighter institution. That is, unless the abuse isn't still part of the curriculum. It has been a few years since I was a student here," Joanna bit back.

Lucas put a hand on her shoulder, a sign to rein it in. As much as he was starting to be aroused by her attacks, they were not going to get them any useful information.

"I think we have gotten off track. What is 'unacceptable danger'? On a scale from abnormal Barrier flair to demons pouring from the Eye," Lucas asked.

He could see that she was thinking over her answer. Rolling the implications in her mind, what to give them, what to keep from them.

"Fellowship fanatics fall closer to demons than flairs," Fel muttered.

Oh shit, Lucas thought. There was only one Fellowship that he could think of, and if they were coming here, then blood was going to be spilled.

"Wait, did you say Fellowship?" Lucas asked.

"Like Fellowship of the Cross?" Joanna finished.

"Yes. They have been spotted bubbling up across this sector and world," Fel said. "I've been authorized to take care of the problem. Before you ask, I neither want nor *need* your help. Do *whatever* it is you are here to do and stay out of my way. Now, get out of my office before I have you placed in re-education with your friend."

Fel stood up, hitting a button on her desk that opened the door to her office. She then pointed at the door. Lucas turned to look at it, the long hallway, the janitor calmly vacuuming the ugly carpet.

"You should let Rostov go. You can't spare people to guard him if the Fellowship is attacking," Lucas said.

"Doors have locks. Perhaps you have heard of them? Now, get out of my office and stay out of our way. This will be over soon enough,"

Fel said, sitting back down at her desk and throwing up a black privacy shield.

Lucas grumbled then turned and walked away, followed by Joanna. As soon as they crossed the threshold of the office, the doors slammed shut behind them.

"I guess I will come back later to clean," the janitor muttered as he turned and started pushing his cart back down the hallway. Lucas watched him go and walk out of earshot before turning to Joanna.

"The Fellowship of the Cross is coming here," Lucas said, aghast, almost not believing what he was saying.

"I thought most of their crusades had moved to the Unaligned Planets, where there was more chaos, more blood to spill, for their dead god," Joanna said.

"That agrees with the last report I saw about them," Lucas said, walking over and sitting down on one of the benches. Administrator Fel's secretary was not at her desk today, so they were alone.

"When I was a young knight, maybe a year after leaving this place," Lucas said gesturing to the walls around him. "The team I was a part of was sent to Hollister 9. A small world on the far western reach, near the Confederation border. There had been reports of a Fellowship vessel in the area. Confederation High Command didn't take any chances. They attached us to the Dreadstar *Pride*. We were too late..."

Lucas took a deep breath, digging deep to dredge up the old painful memory.

"Hollister 9 was a small world, a moon that had escaped from the gas giant it was orbiting. A pinprick in space. Still, that pinprick had forty thousand people on it. When we got there, they were all dead. At least, the ones who the Fellowship hadn't carted away as slaves or new warriors. The cities were burned, blood and bodies everywhere. Civilians cut down in the middle of their normal day-to-day. No plasma burns or kinetic weapon impacts. The Fellowship doesn't use guns. They just send in waves of fanatics armed with clubs and swords. As you can imagine, that leaves a mess.

"Their dead god doesn't care what you do to people before you kill them, as long as you *do* kill them. The abuse was... structured. Every school and meeting house was an abattoir of suffering and degradation..."

Lucas paused. This was not the memory he wanted to drag up today.

"The town leaders were strung up by chains in the square, castrated and eviscerated. The Prefect of the world was in the center. He stood, his arms chained so that they were pulled out. The skin across his back had been flayed and attached to his chains. They had then removed his lungs and hung them there to flutter and make noise in the breeze. Everybody. Every damn one of them had that off center cross carved into their forehead," Lucas said, making a fist and trying to not sob. He had cried like a child, upon discovering those horrors. Most of them had.

"The Commander of *Pride* hadn't even bothered to clean up the world. He just gassed it and left. 'There is no rebuilding on top of those graves, no salvaging the stain left upon that world,' he had said. If *that* is coming here..."

Joanna's eyes were wide. She took a deep breath and wrapped an arm around Lucas. He was shaking, and leaned into her embrace. Letting it settle him. The memory faded back to where it always sat, just on the edge. They were quiet for a moment. He wasn't sure what to say.

"Then we need to figure out what Hyacinth wanted and get out of here as quickly as possible," Joanna said. She squeezed him again. "Why is Fel still letting us wander around and ask questions?"

"I don't know. She... There is something she isn't telling us. Fel has something, *knows* something," Lucas said, the memoires still clouding his judgment in the here and now.

"She knows something, and it scares her, and not like the Fellowship scares her," Joanna added.

Anything that could scare Morgana Fel was something that scared Lucas. He pushed out an uncertain energy. Joanna took a step forward and wrapped her arms around him. She could feel it. Lucas didn't want the embrace to end, but he was the leader. He had to be strong, had to be in charge. He stiffened his back and pushed her arm away.

"I'm fine; just need a minute and some air. You go to the library and keep working your puzzle. I'm going to come up with a plan, see if I can't dig anything else up," Lucas said, despite breathing heavily.

He hated how that memory made him feel. It was weakness. An afterimage of the child he had been thrust into an adult world twenty years ago. There had been other atrocities that he had seen, that he had even participated in. Still, there was something about the Fellowship of the Cross that just ate at him. They were the antithesis of the Host'ire. No powers, all faith. They believed that the Eye, the gateway into the Barrier, led to *Heaven,* not Hell. The only way that their dead god was going to open the door was if they spilt enough blood for him, to offset his murder upon their holy symbol.

However, what really scared Lucas was that, if Fel had brought in over a hundred thousand members of a military branch that was more legend than fact, that meant that the threat was not only real, but deadly serious.

If they didn't find what Hyacinth wanted soon, all of them were going to be corpses with crosses carved into their skulls...

Or worse.

Combat Air Patrol, Fury, Erik

Fury was coming up on where they had detected the distress call. It had taken them the better part of the day to reach the source, and the weak signal was now almost dead. Erik led the two squadrons that were quickly zooming forward ahead to investigate the damaged ship. He had Bella and Anders on his wing. Behind was Lieutenant Graycie Richmond and her squadron. Further back, there was a single Hawk-eye checking for life signs and radiological signals. You could never be too careful, he knew. Pirates loved to booby trap dead ships.

The ship was listing, venting gas wrapping around the husk like a corkscrew. The corpse was a simple cargo hauler. This ship had a painfully simple design. It was a long box with two large thrusters. Attached all along the side were more boxes. Erik recognized the make. It was a short-range hauler. There was no reason for it to be this far out, almost to the doldrums. The situation was fishy. He needed to call in.

Turning on the radio, Erik could hear the music. Sharp drumbeats and a light highland pipe. Hype music, one of the oldest tracks in his mother's library. She had at least twenty variations of it. 'Mystery ship', he believed was the title.

"*Fury* Actual, this is flight leader," Erik said into his radio.

"This is Actual. What do you see, Commander?" Lord Admiral Cordova asked. There was a quiet moment where the only thing he could hear was the music.

"We have a cargo ship, Hendriks class. Two of the cargo pods are gone and... Gods be good."

Erik stopped as his fighter got close. Turning his spotlight on, he saw the ragged gash of steel. It was as if something had come and taken a *bite* out of the ship, ripping away its outer hull like it was meat rather than solid steel. Bodies floating, frozen. Some were still strapped in, but most were thumping from wall to wall as the ship rotated. Red crystals glittered in the light. Frozen blood.

"Compose yourself, Commander. You are our eyes. What do you see?" the Lord Admiral asked. Erik could hear the frustration in his mother's voice. They were not close enough for a real-time video link.

"Violent decompressions across all decks, sir. It is almost as if they ran into a Mordovala," Erik said, referencing the old sailor's myth of the great star shark, a predator that ate ships.

Whatever happened here had been quick and it had been horribly violent. He wasn't sure what could rip apart a ship like this. Erik had read about forced energy beams being used in the Unaligned Planets that could pull and push matter through space. That seemed too outlandish, though. There was sure to be a more mundane, more human answer. It was not going to be some fancy advanced tech from beyond the Confederacy, or a space shark from legend. Once they boarded the ship, the answers would fall into place.

"It doesn't look like they fought back," Bella said, pulling her fighter up beside his, shining her light into the dead ship's gaping wound. "Nobody is armed. Nobody has on body armor and half of them are still strapped in."

"Do you think they were taken by surprise?" the Lord Admiral asked over the radio.

"No, ma'am. They knew whoever killed them. Erik, look at the hull," she said. He looked and then saw it. How he hadn't before... He was getting sloppy. The last six months of class duty had made him soft. The metal was bent outward, like it had been blown out.

From the inside.

"Well, that mostly rules out pirates," the Lord Admiral said. "Major Cordova, assemble a boarding party and repressurize that ship. Make sure it's not trapped, then figure out what happened," he heard his mother's voice command his sister, who he assumed was standing next to her in the CIC. "Commander, have your fighters deploy as cover and scan the system. I do not want to be caught with our britches at our ankles."

"Yes sir," Erik said.

He could since the eagerness in his mother's voice to use this as a training operation for the new members of the crew. He didn't love the idea of being excited by death as a means of training the next crop of crew members, but there was something else to his unease. This dead ship had secrets, horrible secrets.

And they'd just been instructed to find them.

Armory, Olympus Ares Research Facility, Grace

"He knows something that we are not being told," Grace said as she and Essex walked into the small security armory located down the hallway from Vardis's office.

"For sure. But I expect things like that from people like him. They exist on secrets and compartmentalization. Otherwise, we might realize we don't need them," Essex said as he punched in a code to open the weapons locker.

"I'm starting to see why you washed out of the Host'ire," Grace said.

Essex looked taken aback, a visceral pang of disgust washed across his face. She could see it even through the sunglasses.

"I didn't *wash* out. I passed my trials and was an anointed knight. Just couldn't stand the hypocrisy, so I made an exit," he said.

The words were curt and well chosen. There was something more to it. Grace could feel it. This wasn't the time to push, though. He would tell her in time.

Or he won't. The Host'ire thrive on secrets, even if he isn't with the order anymore, Emily thought in the back of her mind. She didn't trust this knight, even though Grace had begrudgingly decided to.

Everybody is keeping secrets, you know Vardis isn't telling you something, Emily thought, echoing Grace's earlier words to Essex.

Grace gave Emily the faintest of mental side eye. *Because we are not keeping a treasure trove of secrets ourselves?*

Emily remained quiet.

She *was* correct, though. Everybody thrived off secrets and truths unspoken.

"Oh, I see. So, knights are just allowed to not be knights anymore?" Grace asked as she picked up the webbing of a tactical vest and started to put it on.

"You are correct. Nobody leaves the order. Doing so is punishable by death. Why do you think I'm out here? I couldn't stand their hypocrisy and control, but it seems that getting sucked into toxic power structures is the only thing I'm good at," Essex bit back as he pulled a plasma rifle from the locker and slung it and a bandolier of magazines over his shoulder.

"We all get stuck in toxic systems of power," Grace said, letting the words hang in the air, before continuing. "Some of us get crushed under everything. Others find a way out because they know that change isn't actually possible from within."

That was Emily talking. Doctor Goodspeed was a good little girl. She didn't see the toxic power structures inherent in civilization. She benefited from them and had no interest in changing that. Change was messy. Change was dangerous.

Essex gave her a wry look, like perhaps he had underestimated or read her wrong. Good. She wanted to keep him on his toes, keep him guessing. If he was going to keep secrets from her, well... Two could play at that game.

"Right now, none of that matters. We can worry about crushing the system *if* we survive. On the bright side, we will be free of this place," Emily said, grabbing the other plasma rifle and walking out of the room.

He stood there for a beat, not following. Grace wondered if he was watching her leave, wondered what was going through his mind. She would figure it out soon enough, and then know for certain if he was worth trusting, or would need a bolt of plasma to the back of the skull. She wasn't interested in quickly trusting a boy that talked the way he did.

Not again.

Palace of Silk and Iron, Novagrad, Alexander

The opening ball of the Minister of the People's Peculiar Pentagon tournament was being held in a mansion on the outskirts of Novagrad. It had once been known as the Palace of Silk and Iron. Now it was just the People's House.

The main house was five stories tall and over half a mile long with four hundred bedrooms, an equal number of bathrooms, five ball rooms, a theater, ten kitchens and enough sitting rooms to hold court with every noble lord—landed or space—that fell under the sway of the long dead house of Terra. Surrounding the mansion were gardens that stretched miles and miles. Rows of hedges and flowers, greenhouses filled with birds and butterflies. Intermixed in the gardens were ten swimming pools ranging in size from a small, heated grotto to a two-hundred-meter competition pool. In the winter, they allowed it to freeze over and be used for ice skating and hockey.

The Palace of Silk and Iron had belonged to the last king of NovaTerra, a young boy of four: Vicktor of House Terra, the sixth of his name. His reign had been dreadfully short. It was less than a day between when his father, the last true King, Gregor IV, had been executed, before the mob found the child and ripped him apart. Thus, ending the line of Kings on NovaTerra and ushering in the foundation of the Confederacy. The noble lords had been quick to step in and stop the insurrection once the new boy-king and his family were dead. They couldn't have the rabble killing more of them. To placate the population, the lords had created the position of Minister of the People. A political office that was, at least on paper, elected by the people.

Of course, the Minister was never of the people but a noble that was picked to run and subsequently picked to win. That, along with the festival of election every six years, had kept the population pacified for the last five hundred years. Elections, along with enough food and affordable housing, had been the order of the day. People rarely wanted to rebel when their basic needs were being met, and the rich lords of the Confederation had learned it was cheaper to take care of people than abuse them until they broke out into violence.

Alexander and his friends had reconvened at the house they were staying at to get ready for the party. The look of joy on Alexander's face had been evident for everybody to see. In short order, he had told them about his day, about the girl he had met and that she might just be the answer to their problems. Thrase had laughed, knowing how Alexander was quick to infatuate. Hoben had shaken his head, reminding Alexander about the message, still unread in his pocket watch. O'Hair had said nothing. He just smiled. All of them agreed to meet Claudia. They trusted Alexander enough to at least be nice and see if she was worthy of joining their team.

"I cannot wait for you all to meet Claudia. She is just perfect and will fit right in," Alexander said, the smile on his face running from ear to ear. He was walking backward and talking with his hands about his afternoon and how wonderful it had been.

"I am sure she is very nice, perfectly wonderful," Hoben said, tugging on the bright red cravat that was too tight around his neck. All of them were in formal wear: long black coats with golden buttons and black breeches. Their shirts, vests, and cravats were all emblazoned with the colors of their houses. On the high collar of their black coats, each of them had a golden pin with the sigil of their house. The chimera for Alexander, a burning rocket for Hoben, three flasks around a cask for Thrase, and lightning over a cross for O'Hair.

"Perfectly wonderful," Thrase said like an echo of Hoben.

"You wound me with your mocking, good friends," Alexander said, holding his gloved hands over his heart.

"We mock only from love," Hoben said, making a motion with his hands so that his friend would turn around.

Alexander spun on the heel of his high boots to see that they had reached the entrance to the palace. The guests were lined up, showing their invitations to the Minister's guards so that they would be granted access to the ball. The four of them fell into line behind a group of men and finely dressed ladies. Their dresses were poofy, modestly cut and dyed in the richest holographic pastels that existed on NovaTerra.

They reached the door a few minutes later, and Alexander removed their invitation from his jacket pocket and showed it to the guard, pointing to each of his friends in turn and naming them.

"You are short one," the guard said. He was an older man who looked to have been vacuum sealed into his uniform, it fit so tightly. "He will not be granted entry any other time than at present."

"He is aware, sir. Alas, he had a few to many pints at the feast hall this afternoon and is confined to... Well, there are ladies here," Alexander said, whispering the last part.

The guard didn't laugh or even crack a smile. He just stamped their card and ushered them into the great hall.

Alexander was no stranger to the homes of lords, but this was something totally different. He had never seen its like before.

The grand hallway was as tall as the entire five stories of the house. The stairs went up and wrapped around, leading to balconies and hallways. Hanging from them were vines and flowers of all colors. The walls were covered in the most exquisite of holographic paper. Each panel caught the light in a different way, causing a kaleidoscope of shapes and colors to dance around the room. From the center of the ceiling of this grand entryway was a massive chandelier, each warm LED light shaped like an animal that corresponded to a great house. Every time a new house joined or left the Parliament of Lords, the chandelier changed. It was arranged in five levels, with the first one being the smallest, representing the most important houses. As you followed it up to the ceiling and the last ring, you followed the houses that were close to losing their voting privileges. Sitting squarely on the fourth rung, only because they controlled *Fury*, was the Chimera of Cordova.

"My father brought me here once as a boy," Jeffery started. "I was transfixed by the lights and the dancing holograms. I stood here and looked at everything for hours, walking up and down the stairs with rapid enthusiasm. The kind that only a child of six can have..." He paused and took a deep breath. "I have forgotten more than I remember of what things look like, at this point. But burned deep in the back of my brain, where I keep numbers and cards, that section of synapses left unbroken by the bomb, I keep an image of this room."

The three of them looked at Jeffery O'Hair, with his glasses and broken face as his head moved around, taking in the grand hallway, looking at it through the lens of memory.

"Move along, no loitering," another guard said to them. The gruff short man motioned for them to keep moving.

There were three grand hallways off each side of this room. From the one on the right Alexander could smell wood and smoke. That would be where the pigs were roasting, where they had been slowly cooking all day until their skin was hard and crackly, and the flesh below full of juice and flavor. This was far from traditional NovaTerra fair, but the retiring Minister of the People was from a small southern house on the western continent. This was *his* traditional fair, so he made sure it was being presented at all his going away festivities.

To the left, Alexander could hear music and glasses clinking. The bar was open and already spirits were flowing. Walking forward led to the grand ballroom. It was empty now, but soon would be filled with lords and ladies dancing the night away. All three rooms would be filled with commoners, as well. This ball was open to any team skilled enough to qualify for the tourney. They, of course, would not be allowed to dance, but that didn't matter to them. The common folk were here for the food, drink, and the opportunity to see the Palace of Silk and Iron up close.

Claudia said she would meet them in the drinking room, so that was where Alexander went, his fellows following behind. The tavern room was packed to the gills with people. They were all dressed to the hilt, except for a few common folk who had scrapped together outfits but still stood out like a smashed thumb. Walking around were servants with trays of sparkling crisp wine in tall crystal flutes, while others had trays filled with small tumblers of any number of spirits, some over ice, some not; all with carvings made of fruit pinned to the outside of the glass. The queue at the bar was long, even with two score attendants. Alexander would much rather drink something from a tray than wait most of the night for a specialty drink.

Scanning the room, it only took him a minute to find Claudia. She had been running through his mind all afternoon, and as such, he recognized her instantly. She was sitting at a table in the middle of the room, talking to a man. For a moment, a flash of envy rolled up from Alexander's gut to his brain. He took a hard swallow as he started walking over. A moment later, he started to take stock of the man, his competition. He hated that thought as it went through his mind.

The other man was tall, with striking black hair and green highlights. It was pulled back into a ponytail held with a silver emblem that Alexander did not recognize: two crossed flaming swords. His coat was long, far longer than every other man in the room, and then Alexander noticed the make, the fabric. Alexander had seen so many black coats this evening that they ran one into the other, but this one shimmered. It was not a heavy cotton or wool blend. No, it was leather. Only one group of people would have worn a long leather jacket to a formal function like this. The man talked with his hands and Alexander saw the gloves, all but confirming his suspicions.

Claudia saw him and waved. The man turned, and if there had been any doubt as to what he was, it was cast away. On his face, attached at the nose, were a pair of small, rimless sunglasses.

A Host'ire Ambassador.

Instantly, Alexander realized this man was no rival. Almost without exception, these wizards who prided themselves enlightened monks were a threat—just not romantically.

There was only one of their number worth a damn and he fell at Hyroncore. I am sorry, mother.

"Alexander, it is good to see you," Claudia said, walking over and giving him a hug. The embrace felt nice. It was a breach of noble etiquette, but nobody would hold that against two low level Space Lords. She was adorned in a simple dress, cut like the one from earlier that afternoon, but out of a finer fabric. It was a forest green with brown trim.

As the light hit the dress, Alexander could see trees starting to take shape. The more she turned, the brighter the greens became, until they started to change, moving toward a deep reddish orange. Holographic embroidery, showing the transition from summer to autumn.

"You as well. It has already been far too long," Alexander said.

They held the embrace for a moment too long before pulling apart and looking around. Alexander nervously yanked on his vest, pulling out the wrinkles.

"An entire afternoon without your witty banter, Lord Cordova, is a lifetime. May I introduce you to Ambassador Kassel of the Host'ire," she said, motioning to the man she had been talking with. The Host'ire gave Alexander a bow. Alexander returned the favor, introducing himself in turn.

"The lady was just telling me about your arrangement, how she was looking for a team and you were short a man," he said in a high-pitched, almost whiny voice. In that moment, Alexander was positive that he didn't like this man and would be glad when he left their company.

"Indeed, it was very fortuitus that we ran into each other at the feast hall, and a good thing that both of us enjoy Bavlanda foods," Alexander said.

"Truth be told, I was there mostly for the beer," Claudia whispered, holding her hand to her face. It was the kind of whisper that was loud enough for everyone to hear.

"Quite right, quite right," Kassel said. His words did not match the natural tone of his voice, and it grated at Alexander.

"Where are my manners," Alexander said, turning to his friends. "Let me introduce you to the rest of the team. This is Alen Hoben, Katie Thrase, and Jeffery O'Hair. Friends, this is the lady, Claudia Wise." His hand motioned to each of them as they were named. "You will never find a more skilled group of card players in the Confederation."

"He flatters us," Hoben said.

"And flattery will get him very far," Thrase finished. She held her hand out to Claudia. The two women shook hands, looking each other up and down before nodding their heads. Alexander wasn't sure exactly what had happened, whether it was an agreement or not. One of those moments that Hoben would have said he should have understood, given his birth. There was a small flash of irritation and anger, but Alexander let it roll past him. Alen's barbs meant less than the effort it took to be irritated by them.

"So, tell me, Lady Wise. What brings you alone to a card tournament?" Jeffery asked, cutting, as always, right to the heart of a situation.

"I was supposed to be here with my betrothed, a knight from House Saber. But on the eve of our transport leaving, I..." She paused and drew in closer. "I caught him having a clandestine meeting with a common friend of ours. A meeting in the backroom at a party."

Everybody understood the implications and nothing more needed to be said.

"The tickets had already been paid for. Sir Saber never approved of my card playing, but I had the ranking to qualify and saw nothing to lose. So, even if you do not take me in, I get to go to a party and have free libations," she said, holding up a near empty flute of sparkling wine.

A server was nearby. Alexander picked up a flute of his own and clinked it against Claudia's.

"To his indiscretions, may they be a boon to us all," he said.

They both took a sip of their wine and looked into each other's eyes. Alexander knew if he wasn't careful, he would get lost in her emerald sea. She saved him by turning to Ambassador Kassel.

"Would you excuse us, sir? We have much to discuss," she said to the Host'ire.

The ambassador gave her a shallow bow, turned and headed on his way, looking for another conversation to insert himself into or unattended young woman to pounce upon. *Perhaps that one will have fewer teeth,* Alexander thought, chuckling to himself.

"Now that we have disposed of our hanger on, it is time for the interview," Hoben said.

"Yes, Alexander had mentioned that you had quite a competent deck—what he saw of it, anyway. So, if you are going to play with us, we need to know what you are made of," Thrase said.

"I could not agree more. Perhaps we should move this interview to the feasting hall? The smell of the pick has been tickling my nose for the last hour," Claudia said. With that, they started walking.

Indeed, they had arrived at the perfect time for the picking. Ten large hogs had been impaled upon spits, slowly roasting in steel drums for the entity of the day. People lined up with plates in hand to come and pick off the choice parts of the hog. The skin was hard and cracking, full of fat and flavor. On everybody's plate were five small rounds of soft sourdough bread. All one had to do was place the bread between your thumb and two fingers, then pull off what you could get.

Alongside the main course, there was a bounty of sides: beans in a thick molasses gravy; cabbage and onions in a sweet mayonnaise sauce; corn bread with spicy butter; and leafy greens stewed in bacon fat and onions. For those who were uninterested in picking from the hog, there was a massive pot of seafood and sausage stew served over rice. The smell of the room was intoxicating.

They found a table and sat down. Each of them reached into a pocket and produced small silver card cases. The cases sat on the table, as if they were gunfighters who were showing off their pistols. Each of them looked at Claudia and then looked at each other again. She put a hand on her card case and slid it forward. Hoben was the first to intercept it. Pressing his thumb down, a small holographic display appeared, showing Claudia's deck. He started flipping through it. Thrase looked over his shoulder, whispering what the hologram was showing to Jeffery.

"You have found us somebody who does seem to understand the game," Hoben said.

"A well-balanced deck," Thrase agreed.

"Proficient at everything, good at nothing," Jeffery said, turning away and picking up a sourdough pork taco.

"That is by design, friends. Now that you see I am capable of playing any style, what position on the pentagon did your absent member play?" Claudia asked.

"He was our strike buff," Alexander said.

Luckily, it wasn't the most important position on the field. All the strike buffer did was make sure that the two striker's cards were as strong as possible before they launched their attack. They did no defense, no healing; only supported the assault. The salty marine Alexander had learned to play Peculiar Pentagon from all those years ago had called the strike buff an RGMF: rear guard motherfucker. A base phrase used by lowborn and people from the Unaligned Planets.

"That is a position I can play," Claudia said. "I can be whatever you want me to be."

The last phrase, while for the benefit of the team, was aimed squarely at Alexander. His heart fluttered and jumped a beat.

The three of them grilled her on strategy and card combinations. She answered all their questions perfectly, some of those answers even surprising his friends. Alexander had stopped listening to the meat of the conversation. He was just taking in her voice, watching the move of her mouth, the heave of her bust, while she talked. Mostly, though, he just got lost in the forest of her eyes. He felt like he was falling.

Alexander pulled off his parachute and hoped that nobody tried to grab him.

Hallway, Olympus Ares, Grace

Grace pulled up the map again and pointed forward. They were going to have to get to an old access shaft and then climb down over a mile before reaching the bottom where the ancient, nearly vestigial, reactor was. All around, she could see that things were changing, getting worse. The strange wind with no preservable origin had blown in more of the rust red sand. She could feel it crunching under her boots, no longer just piling up in the corners.

"Look at the wall," Essex said, pointing to one of the steel bulkheads that was filled with electronics and LED lighting, meant to guide people to their destinations in the confusing bowels of the Zeta Lab.

The wall looked like it had a sunburn. The steel was sloughing. Underneath were bricks made from a deep red clay. Running across the bricks were runes and letters in a language that… Emily stirred for a moment, a witty line on the edge of her lips, before pulling away. Grace cocked her head and kept walking.

"Whatever is coming though the small opening from the gate is changing this place," she said. "I've been keeping an eye on the environmental readings, and the humidity has dropped by ten percent already. Thankfully, the atmospheric make up is staying the same."

"Small things, right?" Essex said as they walked.

He was being too quiet. Perhaps she had hit a nerve with her line of questioning. Boys were never fond of having their egos punctured, even if it was just a little hole to get some of the air out so they didn't pop like a balloon at a child's party.

They were about to pass the secondary viewing port for the gate chamber. It would be Grace's last chance to see where everything had gone wrong before they descended into deep darkness. She held up a hand to stop Essex and walked over to the window, lifting the blast shield which had automatically lowered when everything went to hell. The transparent steel had shattered, and they were instantly exposed to the chamber.

Grace poked her helmeted head in and looked around. Three stories of steel had been transformed into bricks and wooden latticework. Only a few flakes of metal were left. Finally, she saw what she was looking for. In the middle of the gate was a pinprick of green, no more than the size of a coin, but it was there. The aperture had reopened and was stable. She blinked her right eye ten times, taking multi-spectrum pictures before pulling her head back and closing the blast shield.

"Did you smell that?" Essex asked, as he took a deep breath.

Grace rolled her eyes but then realized that he wasn't going to see that, so she pointed at the helmet that completely covered her face and was hermetically sealed.

"Of course," he said sheepishly. "There is something I can't quite put my finger on. But it is triggering a powerful sense of déjà vu. The kind from a memory that is so old, it's less a memory and just leftover sensory data in your brain."

"Interesting," Grace said, pointing forward, indicating that this was a conversation best had on the move. "Does it remind you of food, or an environment; maybe a person?"

"I don't know. I'm going to have to think about it. It's already gone. Whatever it was, exists only in the test chamber and not out here yet. What did it look like in there?" he asked.

"Completely changed and the gate has reopened. It's only the size of a coin, but I'm sure that is just because it's power starved. It feels like whatever is on the other side isn't just waiting for the portal to be bigger, but for the transformation of this place to be complete. Some kind of interdimensional terraforming," Grace said.

"Another dimension? So, the gate didn't just go to another world in this plane of existence?" Essex asked. His question was earnest and seemed filled with actual curiosity, and no boyhood insecurity that Emily kept her hypervigilant for.

"It was always a gate to another dimension, just like the hyperspace highways. That is how it's always been. The Null is just a colloquial name. It's always been beyond our reality. That is what makes what you can do so special. Something in your brain can see beyond the material. We need equipment the size of buildings to do that, while you wear sunglasses so that those visions don't overwhelm you," she said.

The cult-like aspects of the Host'ire made her uncomfortable, but their actual powers were amazing and part of the future of mankind. Provided they could be studied and detached from their moronic religion. A religion that had already cost civilization the ability to go faster-than-light when they purged the Wayfinders. The last five hundred years had set civilization back at least a thousand or more in terms of advancement, all because one group of mutated people didn't like the power that another one had.

"I never thought of it that way. But then again, you are the scientist," Essex said. "How long do you think we have before it's fully open again?"

"If whoever is working with them on this side can find another source of power, instantly," Grace said, snapping her finger. "Otherwise, days."

She hadn't fully laid out the idea in her mind that somebody on this side was working with whatever was on the other, but as soon as she said it, she knew that was undeniably the correct answer.

Somebody at the facility was compromised.

Hallway, The Citadel, Joanna

Joanna pulled her messenger bag tight as she walked through the empty halls of the Citadel. The sounds of ships landing had finally started to fade away. Still, she could hear people yelling and boots marching on the ground outside. No amount of concrete could insulate you from a hundred thousand soldiers being in close proximity.

Joanna was taking a circuitous route to the library so that she could come in from one of the back doors. The chance that there would be people in the library was low, but she couldn't risk it. In her mind, she could already see a scenario where Militarum soldiers were being bunked between the shelves. *Where does one put that many soldiers?* The student body was usually only four to five thousand novices at any given time. None of the Militarum's ships had stayed planetside, so that was out. And whatever support system was in orbit had to be massive.

This is what happened when she spent all night listening to Lucas talk military at her. As much as she loved listening to his voice, the obsession with numbers, ships, uniforms, and weapons always made her eyes roll back in her head. Even as a child, he had been obsessed with starships.

When they were novices, he had risked rebuke from his floor monitor for sneaking her into his dorm room. Joanna had been prepared for an exciting night, something that she very much wanted as a teenage girl. Instead, he had shown her the model of an Aviary class carrier that he had built and painted himself. The next hour had just been him rattling off facts about the ship and making models. She had half listened through her disappointment. The passion he had for the hobby *was* attractive. The hobby itself, at least to her, was just dull.

"Excuse me, ma'am," a small voice said behind Joanna.

She jumped. The hall had been so quiet, and she hadn't heard anybody coming. Taking a quick breath to regain her composure, she turned around. Standing in front of her was a small blond boy dressed in a novice's uniform. Black dress pants, button up shirt, belt with the hilt of a training blade, and a long black coat. He, of course, also had on gloves and glasses, but those were standard for any person who had a sensitivity to the Null.

There shouldn't be any novices here, Joanna thought, before something clicked. She recognized this boy.

It was Lucas.

"What can I do for you, young one?" she asked, using the customary greeting for a student that was still a novice and not a trainee. She still didn't understand these visions, these childhood shades from their past, but they were key to figuring out what was going on. She couldn't risk scaring this vision away until she got answers. So, she had to play along.

"I can't seem to find my classroom. It was supposed to be on this level. I just… This place is too big and everybody is mean. They say I talk too much." He held his head down.

"There is no such thing as talking too much. But there are people who just can't listen enough. As long as you speak with your heart, it will never be too much," she said, crouching down to his level.

Joanna had always been taller than Lucas, and as an adult, it was even more apparent. She looked around. There was nobody else here.

Okay, Hyacinth. What do you want me to see with this memory?

"That's not what Jasper said. He made fun of me for knowing how to use the tools in Professor Rickman's class. She just let him go on and on, then chided me for not responding fast enough," Lucas said.

Joanna didn't remember that, which meant they must not have had that class together. Lucas would never have told her about that, as it would have made him feel weak, and he never willingly showed that side of himself to her.

"Jasper is a bully. You are bigger than he will ever be just by being you. Same with Professor Rickman," Joanna said, reaching reassuringly toward his shoulder.

He recoiled back from her touch. The fighting must have already started. Joanna couldn't forgive the professors for allowing the students to abuse each other like they did. Letting the strong prey on the weak like it was some kind of 'survival of the fittest' contest. Children should be protected, and she wanted to protect this child. There was nothing she could do, though, truly. You couldn't protect a memory.

"She is a Professor. How can I be bigger than her?" Lucas asked.

"You build people up. All people like her and Jasper do is try to knock them down. Because they are scared; scared of connection, scared that somebody might get to know them. You are brave, Lucas Brandice," she said, standing up.

"Thank you, ma'am. I think I know which way my class is now," he said.

Young Lucas rolled his neck, cracking it before he started to run down the hallway. Joanna watched him go, a smile of satisfaction on her face. Even if she wasn't sure what message she was meant to take away from that interaction from Hyacinth, it felt good for her to say those kind words to Lucas. Even if they couldn't really impact the past.

"Get down!" an older child's voice yelled from behind her.

Instinctively, Joanna ducked as she turned around. Lucas was now running toward her. He was older, this time. His blond hair was pulled back in a messy ponytail, his blacks were rumpled, and he held a paper weight in his hand. There was blood. She recognized this day; this horrible, bloody day.

The day that Essex had killed Jasper.

The memory, however, was a mess. There was a fuzzy blank spot in the middle of it. The events orbited around that emptiness. It was like watching a movie that somebody had poorly edited for content. Where was *she*? Joanna couldn't remember. She knew what day it was, but not this part of it. This felt new.

This shade of Lucas didn't pay attention to Joanna. He was too focused on what was going on. He was standing over somebody, protecting them. There were more footfalls. She couldn't see who it was.

"I'm here," a familiar male voice said.

"I was worried you wouldn't make it, Rostie," Lucas said.

"Let's get this done," Joanna recognized Naomi's voice instantly.

"Good. If we stand together, they won't be able to move us out of the way. But we have to stand together. We are a crew, friends, family," Lucas said. Joanna could see how much he had changed in the short span between this and the memory she had been talking to before. Lucas turned his head, looking worried, panicked.

"Essex, get back in line, damn it. We have to stand together!" Lucas yelled. He looked at the other two children, the ones she couldn't see. Lucas ran down the hall and faded away, to the sounds of fits hitting flesh. She winced at the thought of kids doing that much damage to each other. There had been so much blood that day.

Joanna closed her eyes and reached into the Null, trying to remember that day, remember why she wasn't there. Where had she been? Was it *her* he was protecting, or...? She couldn't say.

She pushed open the door of her Null-fueled memory library. It was a small room filled with books. Thousands of small, cheap half credit novels. Written on the spines were titles that reminded her of her life. She started running her finger along the books in the section labeled 'school'. Every book was numbered volume and edition, and there were far too many missing books. Her finger would go from 'Vol 1, Edition 3' to 'Edition 7' to 9, then be on 'Vol 2, Edition 6'. What had happened during those years that she would deface her memory library like this? And, more importantly, why did she only realize it now? It had been almost twenty years.

Her eyes opened and Joanna was back in the real world, standing in the hallway of the Citadel. She darted to the side as a squad of four Host'ire Militarum troopers marched smartly by, their uniforms pressed, their plasma muskets on their shoulders, star-steel bayonets affixed to the ends of the weapons. They scared her. Whatever was going to happen was coming fast. She needed to get to work, needed to figure out what was going on so they could solve Hyacinth's plea and get out of here.

She didn't want to see what happened if they were caught in the crossfire.

The Citadel, Lucas

Lucas wasn't sure how he was going to be able to help with their investigation. He didn't know computers and nobody had given him a strange heretical book of prophecy. He was just a soldier, without his team, standing against the command structure. What was he supposed to do in that case?

Standing up to the system? That was Joanna. Working on the fringe of the system and being smarter than it? That was Naomi. Getting destroyed by it was Rostov. He was just... he *was* the system. There was no other way to think about it. As much as he didn't want to be, as hard as his life had been as a Host'ire Knight, there was no denying that he was the system that was stymieing him at the moment.

As he walked down the hall, Lucas tried to think about how he could operate outside the system, how he could step away from himself and see the larger world. Try as he might, he just couldn't do it. Everywhere he turned, there were rules and walls, bounds that kept him inside his box. Naomi loved the order, found comfort in it. For him, being back here just brought up the resentment he had acquired as a child. Now, Lucas couldn't see past the order's training and indoctrination. It gnawed at him, burned deep down, and still try as he might, Lucas couldn't see how to be anything more than he was; how to do anything different. Until there was fighting to be done, he was impotent, worthless, frustrated. For a moment, he understood how Wingarf felt and that made him even sicker.

No, I'm not like him, I will never be like that, Lucas thought.

He would just have to wait to see what Joanna and Naomi brought him. Then perhaps he could hatch a plan. Usually, he got to be more hands on as the leader, and it wasn't so detached. This felt like high level command. Send the minions on their way and wait for them to return. It was too hands off. He was a man of action, not some prim Host'ire Ambassador raised and educated at the Academy.

Walking down the hall, he saw another squad of Militarum soldiers marching. They were disciplined, frightening. He couldn't see their expressions through the chrome face shields. They walked in time, the sound of their boots almost musical in their rhythm. The long, dark green jackets swayed in unison with each other. These men were soldiers. Compared to them, he was just a fighter, a brawler.

In basic combat, they had told stories about the Host'ire Militarum. That the members were all people who had been put to death by the Confederation. Others said they were kidnapped children who were not strong enough in the Null to be sent to the Citadel. Others claimed it was just a mercenary army. That last one didn't seem right. There was no way these were mercenaries. They moved too well, too uniform to be anything but professional killers.

The Host'ire Militarum had plasma muskets slung over their shoulders and Lucas couldn't help but stare at them as they walked by. That was an interesting choice of weapon for a fight that was going to eventually turn into a hand-to-hand slugging match. The Fellowship of the Cross didn't use ranged weapons. They thought that it diluted the blood offering to their dead god. Even well aimed, they wouldn't get enough shots off to stop what had to be a horde of those zealots building up somewhere. In a hallway like this, Lucas wanted nothing to do with a long weapon. In fact, he might even adjust the size of his star-steel blade so that it was shorter, allowing him to be more maneuverable up close.

Trying to envision the battle that he knew was coming made him feel better; feel *useful*. The chances that they were going to avoid being stuck in the coming storm were low. Administrator Fel might not want their help, but he wasn't going to stand back and watch members of the order get slaughtered by these freaks. As long as there was energy in his body, Lucas knew that he would always stand, always fight, always defend.

He followed the soldiers for a bit, until they walked out into the courtyard. There were hundreds more outside, drilling and marching. Tents had been set up and he could see a cluster of officers standing on one of the high walls, pointing out to the desert beyond. The only thing that separated the officers from the rank and file were the swords at their hips and epaulettes on their shoulders. Walking with one of those officers between the ranks of men was Master-at-Arms Wingarf. The two were talking and the old man was pointing his spear at parts of the wall and base. They were clearly going over the tactical situation.

"I don't like him. He scares me," the voice of a young girl said from beside Lucas.

He wasn't even phased at this point, hearing a strange voice. He turned to look at the young girl. She was dressed in the standard novice uniform. She was tall for how high-pitched her voice sounded. She had green hair pulled back and done up in two victory rolls. She was familiar, but Lucas's brain wasn't moving as fast as he wanted it to. While not surprised by the vision, this kind of stuff was not what he was used to; not something they had trained him for.

"I'm not a fan, either. He put me on my ass yesterday. I waited twenty years, practiced and planned. Dreamed of the day I could confront him, and he put me on my ass without breaking a sweat," Lucas said, turning away from the young girl to watch Wingarf.

"He is a bully. They all are. This whole bloody order is just made up of kidnapping bullies who think they are above us all because they can move rocks with their minds," she said.

Joanna, of course. How did I not recognize her instantly?

"He is the exception. He is the worst," Lucas said, feeling the anger start to well up inside him again, as the pain in his body reminded him of yesterday.

"Is he the worst or was he just the worst to *you*?" she asked.

"He beat us endlessly, made mocking us part of the class. He never let us forget that we were less than him," Lucas said.

"He was honest," Joanna responded. "A bastard, but he wasn't pretending to be anything less."

"I guess," Lucas said. "Last night was different. It seemed personal."

"You harbored a grudge for twenty years," Joanna quipped back. "Of course it was personal."

"No, not from me. From *him*. I was sure he wouldn't remember who I was, wouldn't give a damn about some student that came back swinging his rank around like..." Lucas stopped himself. He was about to say something crude but thought better of it, seeing as he was talking to a child. Joanna giggled and he turned red.

"He could have been testing you. That is what they always say; that they are hardening us up for the real world by testing us," Joanna said.

"That's a load of crap. It was just stunted adults abusing children so they could become stunted adults." Those words coming out of his mouth shocked him.

"*Now* you are starting to understand. Welcome to the revolution," young Joanna said, patting him on the back.

Computer Core, The Citadel, Naomi

The elevator was heading down to the server rack level of the Citadel. Naomi had changed out of her standard Host'ire Knight garb and put on a green tech jumpsuit. Clipped to her chest was the ID badge that she had created last night after slicing into one of the open computer systems upstairs.

The Citadel really needed better security, but she wasn't going to say anything about that today. It would have been perfectly simple to Null-lock everything and place biometrics. They had done neither of those things. The security and computers were at least a hundred years old. Antiques, yes, but ones that she had grown very comfortable with while working at the observatory. Naomi didn't know why they didn't upgrade. It would have been simpler at this point than hanging on to the outdated computers. But for today, the order's cavalier attitude to security once inside their bases served her purpose.

Naomi set down the toolbox she had lifted from one of the unlocked closets. Reaching into her pocket, she pulled out a small plastic container holding contact lenses. Taking off her glasses, she opened the container. Inside were a pair of solid black contacts. She put them in her eyes. For a moment, Naomi looked like some kind of demon from beyond the barrier, her eyes black and emotionless. She had known a knight that preferred contacts to glasses, and wore his like this: black, dark, creepy. Naomi hated it. On the side of the contact lens case was a small button. She tapped it and the lenses flashed. Gone was the black, replaced by a representation of her actual brown eyes.

The disguise was complete. Naomi Perkins was now Broadcast Tech Cicely Williams—well, the badge said server specialist. Cicely had many qualifications. Where Naomi was awkward and talked too much, Cicely was direct and to the point. She could flirt with boys and do the job better than them. She was a woman of action.

Naomi remembered all the flash cards she had made and had kept with her for a few weeks, the first time she put on this persona. Eventually, Cicely became a skin that she could put on and take off at will. There was a life where she wasn't good at technology and became and actress.

I would have been one of those who you read about being far too method. She lived in her car to understand being homeless. She ate the heart of a stag even though she was a devout vegan, Naomi thought. It was a life that she sometimes pictured; one of the *many* alternate lives she pictured. She was happy in the order—it was all she had known—but that didn't mean a girl couldn't dream.

The door opened. The server room was bright and loud; the hum of computers and their fans running, the cooling system thrumming along. Even the gross fluorescent lights hummed in time. Cold air hit her as she stepped out and the elevator closed behind her. Standing in her way was a guard. He was a knight dressed like the ones who had been guarding Rostov's cell. His hand fell to the small bullpup gun hanging at his hip. Naomi walked up to him, looked him up and down, then cocked her hip out to the side and gave him a huff.

"You are in my way. I've got work to do," she said, adding just a hint of fry to her voice.

The guard grumbled and held his hand out with a small card reader. Now was the time to see if she had made something that was going to work or not. Pulling the card off her coveralls, she pressed it to the reader. There was a long moment—it felt like an eternity—and then the light turned green and beeped. Naomi pulled her card away and reattached it to her coveralls. She gave the guard an eye rolling head nod. He stepped aside and she walked past. Exhilaration flowed through her, fueled by the ruse that she was currently pulling off.

It was time for Cicely to get to work.

Naomi reached out with the Null and started to scan the thousands of server racks that were in front of her. Most Host'ire were not in touch with the electrons of the world. She was. It was part of why Naomi was such a successful engineer and designer. She could feel the electrons, understand the computer system without having to learn the computer system. It was all just 1's and 0's, after all.

She walked down three rows of racks, the whole room turning into a kaleidoscopic light show. Then she saw the one she was looking for. The message server. Messages were more than just 1's and 0's. They carried emotion and that was something you could see in the Null. Most dispassionate computer systems were greenish yellow light when you looked at them through the energy field that held everything together. The emotions inside the message server were a deep blue, all emotions ranged from a navy blue to a sea green.

Naomi walked up to the message server and sat down. There were ten server blades in the rack. Reaching into her toolbox, she pulled out a small touchscreen diagnostic computer and a set of screw drivers. Closing the toolbox, she sat down on it and got to work.

Slicing into the system was not an issue. Hubris was something she fought with members of the order about all the time. The Host'ire were so sure that they were better than everybody else. How would anybody get down into the server room? How would they be able to crack our system? A deep lack of human firewalls was how. One of them was going to have left a back door open. She was counting on it.

"What ya doing?" a small voice asked beside her.

Naomi turned around to see the child version of herself sitting on the floor cross legged, her long thick locks pulled into a braid and hanging off to her left. Little Naomi was craning her neck up trying to see what the adult version of her was working on. She smiled, regarding the child.

"I'm looking to see if somebody has put a back door into the Citadel's computer system. If they have, I'm going to go through it," Naomi whispered to her younger self. "Do you know what a back door is?"

"Yes," little Naomi said, crossing her arms and pouting as only a child could. "I'm eleven years old. I know everything there is to know about computers. I have read all the books."

"I'm sure you have," Naomi said. She wanted to reach out and pat the child on the head, but that would be condescending. *Condescending to who, Naomi? Yourself? Can I even touch a figment of my imagination?*

"I know it's hard to not be condescending to a child, even if *you* are that child. I don't know how much of a physical manifestation I am, honestly," young Naomi said, cocking her head to the side.

Now it was Naomi's turn to pout. Their minds were connected—of course they were—because this was some kind of hallucinatory memory. Naomi flicked one of the screw drivers at her child self. It hit the floor with a thud.

"Rude," the child version of herself said.

"Well, I guess that answers that." Reaching out with the Null, Naomi pulled the tool back into her hand. "Just a Null-fueled dream that I am seeing when I'm awake. It must be the proximity to the Barrier and stress," she said, looking back at her work.

"Have you ever had an audio-visual hallucination from stress before? I know us, and last time I checked, we haven't."

"You are eleven. What do you know?" Naomi said.

"I know what you know. Plug into the fifth slot there, the green one," she said, standing up and pointing toward one of the PXCI ports on the server blade.

"So, if you're not a stress induced hallucination—and I don't think you are just a memory, given that you respond to what I say—so..."

Naomi started to ponder what this vision of her younger self could be. She ruled out the simple things like demons from beyond the

Barrier or a medical episode. Quickly, she ran her hand along the top and side of her head, feeling for any scars or bumps.

"I'm not a chip," the child said.

"Just making sure. We are women of science. We don't jump to conclusions. That is how you miss things and end up having to come back and repair the same system over and over again," Naomi said. "I try to be more careful, these days. I've missed too many things in my life. It is high time that I was more careful everywhere outside of the computer core."

"I'm glad to hear that. I would hate for us to just flitter through life, babbling at boys about the current tech that we are interested in," the child said.

"Oh, there is plenty of babbling, though not at as many boys. No good prospects at the observatory, not that I'm super into most..." Naomi paused. The child was yawning and had started to mess with a wire that had fallen from one of the server's bonded cable bundles.

"So, you *can* interact with the world in a limited way. Are you using the Null or...?"

"Nope, just picked it up. Must be because there isn't much here, no real mass," young Naomi answered.

"Hyacinth," Naomi said. "That is what you are. A vision sent to me by her, who I don't remember... Do you remember her? She wants to tell me something; something I don't know. You can't tell me directly, though, can you? Visions never do talk normally. Is that like, in memory-spirit bylaws or something?" Noami asked, rambling. She clinched the small screwdriver between her teeth so she could count off the ideas on her fingers.

"Yes, I think that feels correct," the child said, shimmering in Naomi's view.

"She wants to communicate, but can't manifest her own form, because we need know who we are talking to, and she doesn't know us as adults, so that means it works both ways... This is fascinating. I wish I had time..."

The child held up her hand and Naomi stopped talking.

"Sorry," she said.

"You have the right of it. I'm a Null projection from Hyacinth. Beyond that, I can't tell you much more. It gets a bit above you," kid Naomi said.

"Oh, who is smug now?" Naomi said.

"What can I say? I understand the world on a deeper level than you do right now. Don't worry. You will get there," the child said, standing up.

"Aside from belittling me, what is the point of this vision, then? Don't these things usually have some kind of grand meaning? Or you will you just spit out some prophetic line of text at me?" Naomi asked, tapping a few keys on her screen, setting a diagnostic off and running.

"We gave the prophecy to Joanna. She loves that stuff," the kid said.

"Which prophecy? There are so many," Naomi asked, digging into her mind to try and remember the classes that had gone over prophetic writings, and what she had picked up over the years. A small pool of worry started to bubble up in the back of her mind. Nothing good ever came of prophecy. They were never clear, always written like some kind of puzzle. What good was seeing the future if you couldn't spell out what you saw in clear words? The very notion of cryptic bastards who thought they could see the future made her brain hurt.

"You will have to ask her," child Naomi said.

"I will," Naomi said. "She is going to love talking about that."

Naomi loved how excited Joanna got for words and old dead stories. It wasn't her thing. Naomi preferred the tactile, the *practical*; things that she could touch and feel and fix. People being happy, though—especially people that she loved—*that* made her happy. For a moment Naomi felt calm, happy, loved.

"The emotions for the others are already starting to flow freely, I see—well, feel," the kid said.

"I noticed that, too. I hadn't given much thought to Lucas, Joanna, or Rostov in over a decade. And now? I can't stop thinking about them, and not just in a 'happy to see my old friends' kind of way. It's..."

The kid looked at her, eyes getting wide, as she started to rotate her hand, encouraging Naomi to say what was on her mind, what she was thinking or feeling in the moment. Reeling her toward a conclusion like a professional angler.

"It is so much deeper..." Naomi's eyes darted around the room, looking for the right words for the moment. "Is this what love feels like?" she asked.

Kid Naomi let out a large sigh and rolled her eyes.

"Don't judge me, miss I'm eleven years old," Naomi said.

"Really?" the child said putting her hands on her hips. "'Is this what love feels like?' You have to ask that?"

No, Naomi didn't really have to ask it. She just felt the need to verbalize it like everything else in her life. Brain to mouth. She knew what love felt like, even if she didn't feel it often, and surely didn't have it often returned. This was new, and it had to be connected to what was going on here; to whatever it was that Hyacinth wanted from them. She needed to figure all of that out. There were answers here and some of those were bound to be in the massive storage space of the server that was in front of her.

"Hyacinth needs your help, but first she needs you all to come together; to be as one," the child said.

"I knew it," Naomi said snapping her finger and pointing. "I knew you were going to drop some kind of cryptic nonsense at me."

"There is a difference between cryptic and you not understanding," the child said.

"Enlighten me," Naomi said.

"As well as I understand it, we are projections of memory, filtered through Hyacinth's inability to fully see time in a liner fashion anymore. So my cryptic nature is a byproduct of that," young Naomi said.

"So she isn't controlling you? Interesting," Naomi said.

"We are autonomous units. It's complicated. She isn't well. Things are moving at too rapid a pace. Hyacinth needs her protectors. You have to come together as one, before she can help."

"There are only four of us. Essex is missing. Do you know where he is? Rostov is still in re-education. I don't know how we get him out... Will three be able to help?" Naomi asked.

"Essex has a different road ahead of him, I fear. Four will have to be enough. Consume the messages and beware those who follow the dead god," the child said. She then held up her hands and wiggled her fingers.

"Woooo, woooo," she said, walking backward and then fading away. Naomi chuckled at the childishness of her memory shade.

Still, she had learned far more than she was expecting to. She had been worried that everything the kid said would be cryptic. This was very straight forward, analytical.

As she thought about it, Naomi realized that she shouldn't have been surprised. That was exactly how *she* had acted as a child, and if they were memories at their core... Yes, it wouldn't tell them what the child shades would say, but it would help them understand anything cryptic that they did. Didn't see time in a liner fashion, so Hyacinth understood the danger, but was having trouble addressing when and where that danger was. Did she see streams of possibilities, or actually exist outside of space time as a strange, untethered observer? Knowing the answer to that would be another solid data point. New information that she could bring back, a new lens to view everything they had learned through. Naomi was giddy to bring this information back.

First, though, she had to finish with the computer core.

A moment later, she heard footsteps coming quickly toward her. Letting out an agitated breath, she turned to look up, seeing the guard from the door standing at the end of the hallway. His hand was now firmly planted on the pistol grip of his gun.

"I heard voices. Who are you talking to? This is a comm free zone," the guard barked, his voice uneasy.

"I talk to myself from time to time. I like to have at least one intelligent conversation a day. How about you scoot along and let me finish with my work?" Naomi said, slipping right back into Cicily Williams's soft, vocally fried voice.

Instantly, she felt more comfortable, more confident. Cicily Williams wasn't seeing strange hallucinations; wasn't following some cryptic message from a girl she didn't remember going to school with but still knew. No, she fixed computers, didn't take shit form the people around her, and enjoyed her drinks like she liked her sex: hard. Naomi had been proud of that last line and how it always got people to groan when she said it.

"I just... It sounded like there was somebody else," he said, walking forward.

"I assure you, Knight, it was just me talking to myself. I found your faulty cable and it's a doozy to replace, so I was conferring with my assistant."

Naomi stopped talking and put on a big smile and waved at the assistant who didn't exist. Then, she returned to talking like nothing had happened.

"Now, I'm just rerouting the dechyon particles, through the hydroplane adaptor, bypassing the Maxwell circuit, so that it returns to the intake system."

None of that was true, but big words always made soldier's brains break. It was even better when the big words were just gibberish talk.

Did any system even still have a Maxwell circuit? They haven't been made in, what, a hundred fifty years? she thought, waiting to see what the young man was going to do. She had her star-steel blade tucked away in her coveralls, but drawing it was the last resort. It would set off an automatic alarm, even if she managed to kill the guard before he had a moment to react.

"Well then. Carry on," he said, blinking a few times.

The guard turned and walked away, letting Naomi focus on her work. It took another twenty minutes, but she was able to get into the message server.

That was too easy, she thought.

Naomi had come down expecting to have to carve a backdoor into the system, but here one was, ready for her to engage with. It wasn't right. It had been placed recently; some other hackers' work, who had beaten her to the punch. The realization made alarm bells go off inside her.

She would need to download things much faster, because whoever had set this up, had also surely left a few detection traps.

Access Shaft, Olympus Ares Research Facility, Grace

"Administrator, we have reached the access shaft and are about to start our descent," Essex said into his radio. Mostly only static was returned, but under all of that was a faint squawking from Vardis on the other end of the line.

Clicking off the radio, Grace watched Essex lean against the wall next to her, as she took off her helmet and went over diagnostics in her suit. The systems were confused by the data that was coming in. She was going to need time to dissect it all. Time that she didn't have right now.

Essex put the radio back on his belt and started pacing, sniffing the air, like he was trying to find that scent from the test chamber again, to connect it with whatever memory seemed to be on the edge of his mind. He was starting to worry her. There was decidedly something not right about him, and it wasn't just that he followed orders and then bitched about systems and control. No, there was something else; the kind of thing that only a person holding horrible secrets could see.

"So, do we have a plan for the insanity we are about to do? The descent is almost a mile, and I don't see an elevator anywhere," Grace said, looking at the giant shaft that led into the darkness.

Wrapping around the shaft were a series of ladders and catwalks that created a spiral heading down into the abyss. Grace reached into her belt and pulled out a small probe, flicked on its lights, and dropped it into the darkness. It fell and fell, the lights fading from view, not from distance, but from something dark obscuring them. She patched into the feed, and all that the camera from the probe showed was dust and debris floating around.

"What is that?" Essex asked, looking at the holographic image that Grace had pulled up.

"Smoke," she said.

The readings were strange. There was carbon, and other telltale signs of smoke, but why was it hanging like that? It seemed that the cloud would be toxic, if breathed in. Exhaust, that was what it was. What kind of power plant did they have down there?

Essex didn't look up. He was lost in some kind of thought. His breathing had slowed down, but each breath was deep. Something in the darkness had caught his eye.

"I'm sorry," he whispered. Grace cocked her head to the side.

"Sorry for what?" she asked quietly, tentatively sliding toward him. Essex's head snapped and shook as he came out of the trance he was in.

"Nothing, just an errant memory. Smoke?" Essex waved a hand toward her, signaling her back. He didn't want any help, though he probably needed some.

This Host'ire is a broken toy, Emily thought.

Grace decided to let the memory comment slide. "I'll be fine with my helmet. Did the kit you grabbed have a rebreather in it?"

"Yeah, I'm good," he said, pulling out a rebreather from the gear he'd grabbed and attaching the device around his neck, leaving it hanging until it was needed. The air in this part of the Zeta lab was stale, but perfectly breathable.

"When I was a novice at the Citadel," Essex started as he stared down at the rebreather, "they used to shove us in rooms and submit us to harmful gases with the smallest, shittiest rebreathers they had, just to see how we would handle it..."

He trailed off. Emily had some choice words, but Grace managed to keep her in check. Grace didn't know what to say, so she decided to say nothing at all.

Grace was the first down, grabbing the ladder and making quick work of it. Essex followed behind her, apparently content that she didn't comment.

The climb down was slow going. Not every one of the ladders was in good condition, many suffering from rust and ill care. Also, the huge shaft had created a wind tunnel. Looking up, she noticed Essex holding on for dear life as he tried to navigate down broken steel. Grace had gone first so that if he fell, he would hit her and her armor, which was clamped onto each rung of the ladder, hopefully stopping his fall.

He is scared, Emily thought.

Of course he was scared. He didn't have a suit of armor to help him hold on to the ladder and it was a mile down to the bottom.

He has magic powers. Those should help, Emily thought.

You don't know how those work, Grace snapped back. *We just know it involves the Null.*

Grace looked up. Essex was taking off his sunglasses and slipping them into his pocket. He took a deep breath and his body looked like it was filling up. Grace flicked through a few scanning bands, getting to the one that was as close to the Null as possible. She could see whisps of golden air wrapping around him, being taken in.

It looks like the numbers, like the math of existence, Emily thought.

It doesn't mean anything, Grace said, flicking off the scanner. *We are nothing like him. He is broken and indoctrinated.*

If you say so, Emily thought.

For a while, they climbed in silence.

"How are we doing up there?" Grace asked as Essex gripped the side of the ladder and gently put his foot down to find the next rung.

"Hanging in there," he said.

She chuckled. He hadn't tried to make a pun, but as soon as he realized it, Essex couldn't help but join in, his laughter more nervous than hers. Silly moments like this were what let them know they were still alive, and that maybe, just maybe, they were going to make it out alive.

"There is a landing another fifteen meters down. We can stop and take a short rest," Grace said.

A few minutes later, Grace reached the landing. The sound from her armored boots hitting steel caused an echo throughout the shaft. Essex joined her a moment later, before closing his eyes and sitting down for a moment, leaning against the rock wall, as if trying to stay perfectly still.

"Are you okay?" Grace asked, sitting next to him and taking off her helmet, her black hair damp and matted against her head. The only light illuminating them was the lamp on her shoulder.

"What do you know about the Null and the Shadow?" Essex asked.

"I know that the Null is a dimension just under ours, almost like a pocket where the rules of physics are different," Grace said. "But other than that, on a spiritual level, no, I don't really know much about it. Or the Shadow." She vaguely thought she remembered hearing something about it in a book or holoshow, but nothing enough to be concrete.

"The Null is where our power comes from. We can see it in everything. It is everywhere, and when you need it, you breathe deep and pull it into yourself," Essex said, closing his eyes again.

"The best way to think of it is like a beach and the Null is the sand. You can dig in the sand, pull it up, but eventually, the water from the waves starts to seep in. That is the Shadow. When you close your eyes and picture yourself in the Null, there is a small gap between the golden light of the Null and the inky blackness of the Shadow; a liminal space, where you float.

"At the Citadel, we were taught to never draw so deep that we approached the Shadow. Because while the Null is power through order, the Shadow is power through chaos, and it is an intoxicating amount of power. Ambassadors at the academy are taught to brush the edge if they need to, but kidnapped children? They don't want us near it," Essex said, taking a breath.

Broken, Emily thought before Grace shushed her.

"I've only seen the Shadow once. On the transport here, there was nothing to do, so I started meditating, reflecting on my broken life. I started to dig. I could hear the call, even as I wrapped myself in more and more order. Then, I was on the other side, floating in nothingness, barely tethered to the Null. Before me was a dark cloud, so black that even the void of nothingness seemed bright compared to it. The inkiness knew me, my secrets, things I had forgotten.

"I managed to pull myself back, claw back to reality. It took days." He opened his eyes and looked at Grace. They were bloodshot.

"When I look down into that darkness, that smoke, all I can see are the memories of that time when I was almost lost to chaos, and now we are climbing down into it, and I'm..."

"You're scared," Grace said.

"A bit," Essex said with an uncomfortable chuckle.

"Well, so am I, so am I," Grace said, placing her hand on his shoulder. "But we have to soldier on."

"I know. I've just never gone somewhere that was absent of the Null," Essex said. "For a Host'ire that is... troubling."

"You are going to be okay, though, right?" she asked.

"Yes. I just have to get used to it. The further down we go, the less I can feel the Null. It has become threadbare, like an old towel. It takes more effort to pull it in. And what I manage to get is darker, less effective," Essex said.

"I had a series of nightmares once, during my second PhD defense. Numbers everywhere, but none of them added up correctly. It was as if physics had changed on me, the constant math of reality changing vanishing around me. I started sleeping less and seeing these visions in the waking world. I was shaken, because it felt like everything I understood was being ripped away from me, and only *I* could see or feel it. I had to see past it, take what I knew to be true and rewrite the hallucinations," Grace said. "If that makes sense..."

Being comforting wasn't her strong suit, but she hoped that the story would help.

"Yeah, it's just something I'm going to have to get used to," Essex said. He was quiet for a moment. She could see him working through the next words he was going to say. The darkness kept her from reading his eyes, knowing if he was building up to truth or spinning a lie to placate her.

"I'll be fine. The mission is going to get done," Essex said, with resolve in his voice.

Good, put yourself back together soldier boy, Emily thought.

The last thing she needed was the Host'ire knight falling apart. Because if something could scare him to the core, what chance did *she* have of standing up against it? If it was just his connection, then they could get through that, she could pull him back. If it was a matter of bravery, or heaven forbid, faith, Grace wasn't sure she could fix that.

We ran last time we had to face a matter of bravery and faith, Emily said quietly.

"Good," Grace said, taking a deep breath and finding her own calm. "I was worried."

She pat him on the shoulder again before standing up and putting her helmet back on.

"We are two more switch backs from hitting the smoke. My instruments are able to cut through more of it now, so it looks like another four and we hit the ground. Lots of heat coming from down there," Grace said. She held a hand out to him. "It's going to be okay. I won't let the shadows take you."

Essex took a beat, then grabbed her hand. She helped him up and things felt better.

"If you need to stop again, just let me know. It is okay to be human, Mr. Host'ire Knight," Emily said, almost meaning it.

Cargo ship Key, Hanna

Major Hanna Cordova was the clone her mother had always been looking for in a child. All three of the Cordova children had looked like their Lord Mother when they were born, but grew away from that similarity as they aged. Hanna, however, had stayed the same. It wasn't just the similar rail thin and somewhat harsh features. No, both women had the same command style; that same warm but slight aloofness about them. The major difference was that Hanna was a poet and her mother a composer.

The *Key* was cold and dead. On the last fly by, Bella had found the registry plate for this vessel—at least, what was left of it. The official numbers and registration information had long ago been obliterated. All that was left was the ship's name. *Key*. That seemed ominous to Hanna. Like it was trying to tell her something. The military brain told her those kinds of thoughts were nonsense—her brothers for sure would have. The lyrical side of her, though—the one she didn't share with anybody—felt worried.

Her squad of five marines had docked close to the bridge, which was half a ship away from the huge hole that had vented the *Key*. There was no patching that up. Hanna could hear breath echoing inside the EVA helmet as she walked forward, looking around the tomb that had once been a starship. Her light slid over walls that were pockmarked with holes and splashes of blood. Hanging in the air, cascading around like rain caught in the wind, were small red crystals: gore that had not found purchase on a wall or floor before the gravity and subsequent freeze happened. Everybody here had been dead for days. The frost was hard upon them and the ship's systems cold. So very cold.

With a heavy magnetic step, she walked up to one of her marines who was working to get power back to the ship. Corporal Diago had brought along a large battery to facilitate this job. It was now wired up into the main console of the bridge, and he was pressing keys and flipping switches to get it integrated into the systems.

"Just a few more minutes, sir. We are connected into the system, but this ship has been dead for a while; just waiting for the corpse warm up," Diago said, turning to look at her and giving as crisp a salute as you could in an EVA suit.

They had been shuttered into repair suits and not their standard combat EVA suits because of how long the ship had been dead, to protect against the length of exposure to actual hard vacuum there would be. One was designed to keep you alive for hours in the cold and dark of space. The other for scrambling to vent a foe's ship before they could stop you. Venting a ship with explosives was always a messy affair that wasn't worth the effort. You had to tow the ship, fix the ship, clean out the crew. It was far better to take over their environmental control stations and open a bunch of hatches and vents. Suck out the air, kill everybody, and then repressurize the ship. In those cases, you only had to clean up a few violent decompressions. Whover had killed this ship, however, was uninterested in taking her as a prize. They boarded, did something, and then ripped away what they wanted with force. It went against all logic of war.

What is even the point of attacking a freighter if you are not going to take her as a prize? Hanna thought.

In the center of the bridge, still strapped to his chair, was the ship's captain: a tall, fat man who now looked like a popsicle that had been sucked dry. He looked up at her with lifeless eyes and fear in his face. She could see the bullet wounds in his chest and his hand hovered over the destress signal. It was the only light in the whole of the ship still on, blinking. Every watt of available power had been pushed into that system, to keep their call for help going. Help that was never going to arrive in time to do any good.

Hanna reached up with her large, gloved hand and closed the man's eyes. Then she moved his hand. The bones and flesh of his wrist cracked and snapped. The hand was now free of the captain's arm and the ice that was keeping it attached to the chair. Hanna watched as it floated away for a moment, a stanza of poetry starting to form in her mind. She knew that tonight, there would be no sleep, only writing, processing what she was seeing through couplet and verse.

With the captain's hand out of the way, Hanna pressed the switch on the distress beacon and turned it off. The last gasp of the *Key* faded away, until they shocked her back to life.

"Major, we are ready," Diago said, pressing a few more keys and looking up from his work. Hanna turned and motioned for the two marines who were by the door two step away. They were going to slowly bring the ship back online in sections—at least the sections that they could salvage.

"You may proceed at your convenience, Corporal," she said.

The young man pressed a few more keys, and there was a loud sound as the ship started to creak and fight to come back to life. It wasn't a sound that they heard so much as felt vibrating through the bones and hull of the *Key*, before running up into their suits. The main door to the bridge slammed shut, as more and more lights started to flicker on. From vents, Hanna could see air being pushed into the room, moving the frozen droplets of blood around. Then, the forces of nature pulled on her, the gravity kicking in from her shoulders to her waist as the EVA suit and her body suddenly had to start supporting the weight of the breathing gear. Everything that had been floating came crashing down to the floor, the small balls of frozen blood shattering into even smaller ones. This room—the whole ship, in fact—was going to be a disgusting biohazard of a mess if the heat came back on.

It took five minutes to repressurize the room and get the environment systems functioning enough that they could open the visors of their helmets. Hanna left the oxygen hose in her nose as she pulled up the face shield on her helmet. The room was bitterly cold and the air tasted sour on her lips, but it was breathable.

"Fine job, Corporal," she said, patting the young man on the back. "Now, get me the computer working so we can retrieve whatever files might be left and see what happened here."

It would take another hour to get the half of the ship that was still intact pressurized. In that time, Hanna and her two technicians were able to download the remaining fragments of the ship's flight computer. The logs had all been wiped and the actual data core ripped out. Balled up in the captain's other had had been a data stick. A quick look at it had shown Hanna that he had stashed the ship's computer here.

The fragments she had seen so far were chilling.

It had taken a few hours to get all the information off the ship, extract the files, and process what was quickly turning into a crime scene. Hanna was glad to be off the *Key*. As they got more systems online, the ship turned into a horror movie. One of the rooms rained blood when they got the gravity turned back on.

Everybody on board had been killed by automatic weapons fire. The Confederation used plasma weapons that burned you badly, made horrible wounds but didn't splatter the world with blood. Pirates looking to send a message of how ruthless they were used small kinetic weapons to murder crews. They threw thousands of needles everywhere that moved extremely fast until they hit flesh, before they slowed and bounced and broke apart. The pock marks in the walls, however, turned their investigation toward a different direction.

Bullets.

***

"Antiquated weapons, but they get the job done," Hanna said, pushing a set of pictures across the table. She had been talking for the last ten minutes, debriefing the senior crew about what she and her teams had found aboard the *Key*. They had all gathered in Lord Admiral Cordova's Suite. There was a large table that they used for family dinners. Tonight, though, the only food was a tray of mixed nuts, a bottle of whiskey, and a growing mystery. Her mother and brother, along with Captain Rackland, were sitting around the table. Nobody looked happy at what they had found at the end of the distress message.

"Do we think this was pirates?" Erik asked.

"I do not. We are supposed to come to that conclusion, though. The rampant brutality, the stolen shipping pod, a vessel far off the shipping lines? It all points to pirates," Hanna said.

"So why, pray tell, do you think that is not what we are dealing with?" her mother asked.

"It is too damned convenient and too damned small," Rackland muttered, pouring himself another dram of whiskey.

"The Captain has the right of it," Hanna started. "Their logs show that they had been hired to carry a shipment of grains from a station out in the doldrums." She paused and pressed a few buttons. A holographic projector came on and displayed a star map over the table. Hanna zoomed in on the section of space they were in. Using the pen in her hand, she marked where they were and then where the targeted space station was located.

"And they were attacked here, about a day off any jump gate. That makes sense. It gives the pirates the ability to fade away, but they don't have to spend days and days going at full sail through empty space," Erik said.

"Correct. That is why it's damned convenient and too damned small," Hanna said, echoing Rackland. "A station like this that isn't on any of our charts wouldn't be dealing in grain. Anything grown in this sector of space would be staying here. Almost everybody that lives out in the wilds is self-sustaining. The Confederation has no presence here, militarily *or* commercially. Typically, they have their own shipping out here, as well."

Hanna pulled up the registry plate of the *Key*. Files and lists started to scroll past on the holographic display. "All we were able to get was the ship's name, *Key*, and that it was a Hendricks class cargo ship. The Confederation hasn't used those in over forty years because they were riddled with design flaws, one of which was that the hull was too thin around the cargo containers."

"Which makes them perfect fodder for being attacked by pirates with grapple hooks," Lord Admiral Cordova said.

"Correct. A ship's master at that junction cannot risk going to speed. You must stand fast and fight," Erik said.

"And fight they did," Captain Rackland muttered, pointing to the pictures of the carnage and gore on the ship.

They could not flee, and so they fought the crew of the Key.

It was a simple rhyme, bland, almost vulgar. Hanna pushed it away. No, the lines to memorialize this had to be better than a simple elementary school couplet.

"They didn't fight. This was staged to make us think they did, though. Too many people are in their seats. Too many of them are surprised.

And still, the hull was ripped apart. No, they were murdered and their ship's throat ripped out, all at once," Hanna said. She reached over and for the first time, poured herself a dram from the table's bottle.

"There is one other thing that we found and one that we did not."

She downed the whiskey. It was a very good bottle, smooth, just the idea of burn. The memory of it hit her throat.

"There was not a single speck of grain aboard that ship outside of the manifest. What we did pick up were radiological footprints," Hanna said, flicking up the last two reports on the holographic display. They showed the Currie detector readings. Faint, but just high enough to show that this ship had been transporting components to make atomic weapons.

"This smells of rotten fish and trickery," Rackland said bitterly.

"I agree," Lord Admiral Cordova replied.

She leaned forward, putting her hands together and resting her chin upon them. Her mother's eyes darted from her to Erik to Rackland, before going back to the star chart in the center of the table. What they had found here was the start of something, that much was clear. Everything else about it was shrouded in shadows and missing facts.

"I hate to be the one to say this," Erik started, causing Hanna to shoot him a sour look. "By Confederation law, we are required to chase down all signs of rogue atomic weapons. Duty demands it."

"Do not talk to me of duty in the face of an obvious fabrication, sir," the Lord Admiral spat at her son. "Do not speak to me of duty when you are not responsible for the lives of everybody abord this ship. Do not..."

She paused, the flash of anger fading as quickly as it came on.

"The Lord Admiral is correct in that this is a fabrication. But why? And in what direction? I advise we proceed with caution," Rackland said. "I stand ready to support whatever choice you make."

"As do we all, Sir," Erik said, holding up his glass, a gesture apologizing for his indiscretion.

"Thank you. It is two days hard sail to this station, correct?" the Lord Admiral asked.

Hanna nodded.

"Five days until the Election. That gives us two days up, half a day there, and then two back and half a day to the nearest jump point. It will be tight. Be ready, people," Lord Admiral Cordova said, standing up.

Quickly, the rest of the officers at the table stood and gave crisp salutes to their commander and Lord. She nodded and all of them filed out of the room.

Hanna couldn't get the pit out of her gut that this was not going to work out well. That they were steaming into another trap.

Why, though? Why does everything feel like a trap these days?

Those were cowards' thoughts. The thoughts of somebody being hunted.

But... are we being hunted?

Library, The Citadel, Joanna

Joanna slipped into the rear of the library and found a quiet nook on the second floor to get back to her research. Unlike the day before, the library wasn't completely empty. On the first floor, milling around, looking at some of the books—but more than likely securing the area—was a squad of Militarum soldiers. They could prove to be a problem—at least, that is, if any of them had the wherewithal to truly investigate what she was reading.

What was the chance that these grunts would grasp the heresy that was in her hands? Probably not very high, Joanna figured, so she went about her work, keeping the Militarum troopers firmly in the corner of her eye. She knew that as soon as she stopped paying attention to them, that is when one of them would come up and make trouble for her. Trouble that her team could not afford right now, considering how thin the ice they were walking on was.

This tome was going to be a bear to get through. Already she had spent most of the night just getting through the three setup chapters it had. No book needed a preface, a preamble, *and* a prologue. It had all seemed a bit much. *Looking Beyond, Finding the Way* was billed as a book of Wayfinder prophecy, but it was all wrapped in the story of a Wayfinder who was adrift in the Null, having lost contact with the gate she was heading toward. It was a split narrative of her seeing the future, and her partner mounting a rescue mission, commenting on the nature of hope humanity and people.

Joanna knew the basics of the story. Reva'cith, the Wayfinder was hit by a ship that was unrecognizable, that refused to stay in her memory but scared her to the core. It knocked her off track and only by diving deeper into the Null than anybody had before could she find her way out. Reva'cith had become a God among the Wayfinders. It was said that she could see the math of the universe around her after she returned to the material world. That she could find the weak spots in space and jump ships without the need for a gate. It all seemed a little too fantastical for Joanna, but then that was the world that the Host'ire existed in, even if they tried very hard to appear as if they didn't.

Flipping to the end, Joanna started to read through Reva'cith's final declaration, the fractured explanation of the future as she remembered it. The book was written a hundred years after her death, and Joanna was sure some things had been changed. It was also written in a simplified Wayfinder script that was legible without being heretical. That, of course, didn't change the fact that the words themselves were heretical, no matter what language they were written in.

I saw a time, far afield from us now. We were gone, washed away in the temporal winds of existence. Only a fraction of what we were remained, grasping onto the edge of existence. They returned like the claws of a crab to crush what was left of what we had built. Then she came, birthed from nothing, holding more than one person inside of her. The five assembled and led the Stragglers through Heaven to our long-lost home.

"Hyacinth?" Joanna muttered, her mind racing across the implications of this line of text. A line of text that was a guiding principle of the Wayfinder's religion, that Reva'cith would return to the world and lead her people to salvation.

But the Wayfinders have been dead for five hundred years, Joanna thought.

The Host'ire had seen to that. Yet, in all her research, she had never found a satisfactory answer as for *why* they had done that. The official record was because the Wayfinders wanted to have complete control, that they were trying to evolve beyond what was natural, and subjugate normal humans. Joanna had always found that rich, considering that controlling the mundanes was the Host'ire's mission—and they couldn't have anybody doing it better than *them.*

She knew deep down that what Tor was trying to tell her involved this passage. It was the most important thing in Wayfinder scholarship. *Looking Beyond, Finding the Way* was surely going to provide the needed context. She just wished it wasn't seven hundred pages of small text in a language she didn't have a strong command of.

Looking down, she clocked where the Militarum troopers were. Still milling about on the first floor, though their commanding officer was making his way toward the stairs. She slipped the red ribbon into the book so that she could close it quickly if he came too close.

What if Hyacinth was the rebirth of this Wayfinder messiah Reva'cith? They *did* have similar back ends of their names. Hyacinth was a strange girl, the little flashes that Joanna's brain could dredge up were all of them defending her and her being strange. Was that what Tor was trying to tell her? Did he know even more? Was he keeping secrets in that locked hallway of books? If this was something he was willing to part with, the tomes he wouldn't even let her see had to be worth a fortune.

No, that is too easy, too basic, Joanna thought. While she might love to read stories about the end of the world and heroes coming from lost bloodlines, that wasn't how reality worked. At least, it wasn't how it had worked in any of the *history* that she had read. Prophets were always touched folks having an active and public conversation with their own sanity. It wasn't out of the realm of possibility that Tor thought he had found the lost Wayfinder messiah. But, if he thought he had, then why the cloak and dagger?

Joanna was missing something.

Glancing up again, the officer was gone. Where had he…?

"Good afternoon, ma'am," a voice said beside her. Joanna nearly jumped out of her skin, just narrowly avoiding a scream at the surprise.

Quickly, she closed her book and turned around to look at the man who was standing over her. He had on the long green coat of the Host'ire Militarum, with golden buttons and a black steel breastplate. On his shoulders were golden cords denoting him as a captain. It appeared that they used the same rank structure as the Confederation's army. He had a soft face, big lips, and a nose that was too small. His blue eyes were bright and alert. The man's dirty blond hair was cut short and smartly, so that it would fit under a battle helm.

"Good afternoon, Captain," Joanna said, taking a breath and regaining her composure. If she was going to have to talk to this man, then the least she could do was not act like he scared her. He didn't, not really. The Militarum were just another flavor of jackbooted thug.

"Sorry to have startled you," he said. His voice was calm and had a just a hint of accent, though from where, Joanna couldn't place.

"It is quite alright. I was just a little too into my research," she said, tapping the book and making sure that it was closed.

"I can see that," he said, holding out his hand to her. "Captain Anthonay Waxler."

"Joanna Pike, Knight," she responded, taking his hand and giving it a firm shake.

"May I sit down for a moment?" he asked.

Very polite, this thug. The dangerous ones always were. He reminded her of Lucas, if she didn't trust him. Too smooth, too professional, but not as handsome.

"Be my guest. The library is open to all," she said, pointing to the other side of the small table in her little nook. Waxler smartly flicked out his long coat and sat down in the chair. There was an air of nobility about him, like he came from a family that was better off than having a son be involved in a military force that wasn't supposed to exist outside of whispers.

"I will admit, I was surprised to see somebody at the library doing research. We had been told that all personal except for the most senior professors had been removed from the post," Wexler said. It was a statement and a question all wrapped into one.

"I've been working with Libarian Tor on a project. He gave me his leave to remain over the Festival break and keep up my work. The privileges of being a full knight versus a novice," Joanna said.

It wasn't the best story, but he didn't give her much time to come up with one. At least it would be easy to remember, and she was sure that Tor would corroborate it, if asked.

"Only Administrator Fel is able to approve wavers to remain—or, at least, that is what I was told," Wexler said, leaning back. He was probing, trying to get inside, see what he could find.

"I was not aware of that. It is too late now. No ships are departing. Though I will say, I was surprised to see *your* appearance last night," Joanna said. She paused for a moment, then leaned in. "I had been told that the Host'ire Militarum did not exist. That you were just stories that we told to governments who were getting uppity." She hoped that this would tip some of the balance back in her favor, putting him on the defensive, making him answer a question while she thought about a way out of this.

"The air of mystery does work in our favor, doesn't it?" he asked, flipping the conversation back to her.

"To a point, to a point," Joanna said. "You operate in such a whispered way that people question your existence. Perhaps just a little more sunlight would help," she said.

Wexler chuckled.

"I shall talk to my commanding officers and see what they can do about that. Nothing like constructive suggestions from our knighted counterparts," Wexler said.

There was something about how he said that.

Joanna closed her eyes lightly and reached out with the Null. She was able to feel Wexler, could see his outline, but there was nothing there. He wasn't sensitive. Joanna had assumed that at least the officers of the Host'ire's secret military would be Null sensitive. But this man was as dull as unpolished silver. She flicked her eyes back open, and for the first time in a long while, was thankful for the sunglasses.

"Checking to see if I'm sensitive. Maybe questioning if I'm a washout from here or the Academy?" Wexler asked, his easy and charming voice picking up an even more relaxed tone.

"I.. um..." For the first time in a long time, Joanna was at a loss for words.

"Do not worry about it. You are far from the first knight or ambassador to scan me. Alas, I'm just another standard garden variety human. Really, most every member of the Militarum is. Simpler to operate next to you in the shadows if we are not special," Wexler said.

"It's easier to send you to your deaths without question, as well," Joanna muttered. She caught herself as the words were exiting her mouth unbidden. That was far and away the wrong thing to say. She wanted to placate this man, to put him at ease so he would leave her alone. And now here she had insinuated that his having no powers made him expendable.

Way to play right into basic Host'ire stereotypes, Jo.

"We live for the order, we die for the order," Wexler said. "I've seen a bit of combat in my time, and I have to say, I don't think Host'ire command has any qualms about sending *anybody* to their deaths, from the dullest trooper to the highest ranked knight. We are all expendable in the grand scheme of things."

"But what *is* that grand scheme?" Joanna asked, trying to sound calm and affable again. Wexler made it too easy. This was the kind of man that went through life getting what he wanted because his niceties put people off their guard. For once, Joanna was thankful for the fact that she regarded people like that with extra skepticism.

"The grand scheme is way above the paygrade of a captain. You are going to need to talk to at least a lord-colonel. Probably a general, but at least a lord," he said.

"You have lords? Do landed Confederate gentlefolk really give everything up to throw in with you?" Joanna asked.

She felt silly not knowing this. Had it been common knowledge among the more elite members of the order, or was she too busy fighting with students and reading her books to notice? No, Lucas had also been surprised, so at least it was something they kept from knights.

"We have some. How they square that with the real world, I couldn't say," Wexler said.

Mountagash, that was where his whisp of an accent was from. Far to the south of the southern continent on NovaTerra. A small kingdom that had been isolated for two hundred years before being brought back into the fold shortly after the Wayfinder wars. They had a unique way of talking, drawing out the 'a' vowel sounds. Wexler had done a good job of hiding it, but in that brief moment, with the word 'square', it came out just a little bit. Peeking through his refinement like a child looking out from their hiding place.

"I don't know," Joanna said. "I have a feeling you know exactly how they are able to *square* it." She pulled out the accent on the word square, far more than he did, but not so much that it was comical.

"That is a good ear you have there," he said, pointing at her and snapping his finger. "Most people can't hear it anymore. Hell, even *I* don't hear it unless it's pointed out."

"I've always had an ear for the way people speak, I..." She caught herself. She was about to say, *I hear many noble accents and houses when I'm working in Novagrad.* That was not information that she wanted to give away. The more she could keep the conversation about him and *not* about her, the better things would be. "I used to study dialectology," she said. A simple lie made to sound grand with a big word.

"What made you change your focus from how we all speak?" Wexler asked, serving the conversation back at her.

Joanna dove for the verbal tennis ball. "My mentor passed away, and I needed some time doing something else. So now I work on cataloguing old tomes on written language versus spoken," Joanna said. It seemed a plausible enough lie, especially considering the book she was reading wasn't written in Confederation basic.

"I'm sorry for your loss," he said with a tip of his head.

"Thank you. Now, I want to hear the story about how a noble finds his way into a secret army," Joanna said, leaning forward. She found a little sultriness and sprinkled it onto the words like salt.

"An uninteresting story about a third son of a small house who used to have a problem with cards. You see, I love Peculiar Pentagon," he started.

"But you are not very good at it," Joanna guessed.

"I am a fair player, but as a wet-behind-the-ears kid who had just gotten some freedom, my ego far outstripped my skill. One thing led to another, and I found myself on some Null-forsaken moon involved in a firefight. The Militarum swept through, and we were given an option: to join up or face the noose. I am a fan of my neck and so I put on the green," Wexler said.

"Did they make you renounce any titles or clam?" she asked.

"Oh, those were long gone before they arrived. I was just happy to have my name scratched out of the ledger. Dead men don't usually return payments," he said with a wink.

"Clever, clever," she said.

"Sir, we have finished our sweep of the library!" one of the soldiers called from below. Wexler signed and stood up.

"Very well, Sergeant. I shall be along presently," he said. "Well, that was a very interesting conversation, Knight Pike. Hopefully it will not be our last."

Wexler gave Joanna a quick nod before turning around smartly on the heel of his boot and walking down toward his men. Joanna watched as he went, hoping there would not be another conversation. He was too smooth. There was a snake under that clean-shaven face.

Once the last of the troopers had left the library, she opened her book again, looking again at the passage at the end, the last words of Reva'cith. There was something small off to the side. Was it an imperfection in the paper? Joanna looked down at it. No, the pages were pristine, because this was a new printing. It still bothered her that Tor was somehow able to print new copies of a book that should be all but lost. He had friends that were connected in a way that she couldn't even fathom, most likely; friends outside of the Confederation, where Host'ire influence was weaker.

It was a small splash of ink, like where a fountain pen had dribbled for just a moment. *Why would somebody be writing in a book with a fountain pen?* Joanna wondered. Something came to her mind, a half-remembered line from a lecture on hidden works and espionage.

Taking off her glasses, Joanna reached into the Null and flicked energy across the page. The glowing Null energy stuck to the top of the page like dust getting caught on fingerprints. There was text. *Null Ink.* It was like invisible ink, but instead of being revealed with a light acid, it could only be seen by somebody that could tap into the Null. Host'ire spies used it to pass notes between each other and ambassadors marked up documents with it.

Find her in the Labyrinth. Blood will tell the way was written in very careful hand across the top of the page. Joanna recognized it as Tor's handwriting. *This* was what he was trying to tell her. While she was still tapped in, Joanna quickly flipped through the rest of the book, looking for any other notes that might be contained therein. Nothing jumped out at her, so she closed the book and put it back into the messenger bag beside her.

What the bloody hell did he mean by the Labyrinth? Blood will tell the way? What was the point of writing something in invisible ink in a book like this and being cryptic with the message? Joanna shook her head in irritation. If she could just get her memories of childhood sorted out, could even remember what Hyacinth looked like, then maybe the words would track. Right now, though... Right now, she wanted to smack Tor upside his long head and demand he speak plainly.

Taking her bag, Joanna walked up to the top level of the library and looked around. Making her way to Tor's private rack, she examined the lock. It was a standard palmprint Null lock. There was no way she was getting in here without being him. Or cutting his hand off, a small intrusive thought chimed in.

The blood will tell the way. That line repeated in her head again. A flash of red, a memory pushing forward. Lucas as a child, holding that paperweight; that *bloody* paperweight…

That was it! That was the key. She didn't know how yet, but her researcher instincts had been activated. She knew that was going to be what cracked this open.

She needed to talk to the group, needed to know what they remembered about that day.

Hoben House, Novagrad, Alexander

Compared to Claudia, the cards held little interest to Alexander as he flipped through his deck. Spread out on the coffee table in front of him were hundreds of Peculiar Pentagon cards, with all their fancy artwork on full display. The art was what made the extremely popular card game interesting and collectable. Historic faces and events were mixed in with fanatical stories from legend and even popular television shows.

Every year, the secret conglomerate that created the game would release another set of cards—one hundred, to be exact. They would make a big deal about it and then slide these new cards into the twenty card packs that people bought. At the same time, older cards were retired from circulation and occasionally from organized play. Having your face on a Peculiar Pentagon card was considered a great honor—of course, you had to be dead first. Alexander's Great-Great Grandfather, the first Lord Cordova who had won the battle of Persephone, netting himself and his new house a Dreadstar, had a card, along with *Fury* herself. Alexander had an original printing of each. Both of those were too old for tourney play, despite still being legal. They didn't hold up against modern cards written with the newer rules in mind.

Taking a sip of his drink, he put another deck down on the table. There was no use trying to focus on this. He was tired, drunk, and had a head full of love. Claudia was still dancing in his mind, just like they had danced all night at the ball, filling each other's dance cards and theirs only.

The sound of string instruments filled the air of memory: his right hand resting on Claudia's hip, his left on her shoulder; their feet moving in time with the music; her deep green eyes looking into his. They didn't share words on the dance floor, for they didn't need to, their connection was so strong. Never in his life had Alexander felt such a strong draw to another person.

"You have the music within you, sir," Claudia had said as the song stopped, and everybody started exiting the floor.

"I had a perfect partner to keep me in time," Alexander had replied. "I have always loved that piece of music. The perfect combination of fast and slow. You get to focus on your steps, but not so much that it becomes trite."

"Cards *and* musical theory. You are full of surprises, Mister Cordova," Claudia had said, taking two glasses of lemonade from a roving tray and passing one to him.

My mother is into music, he had almost said. The last thing Alexander had wanted to talk about was his mother; a mutual feeling, he was sure.

"Let us just say that there is music in the family and I've picked up a small amount of knowledge via osmosis over my life," Alexander had settled on.

"Fair enough," she'd said before finding them a table and sitting down.

By that point, the rest of their team had vanished into the party. Alexander recalled that he had not seen them in almost an hour, choosing instead to spend all his time with Claudia. They all had different tastes when it came to having fun, and Alexander was happy with his choice of dancing the night away.

"I am extremely excited for tomorrow. It was very kind of your friends to take me in as part of the team. I was honestly resigned to not getting to play."

"We were not going to get to play without a fifth," Alexander had pointed out.

Instantly, he'd known that was not the right thing to say; that it needed something more personal, or it would only sounded like he was only happy she was there so that he *too* could play in a card tournament. It needed to convey that he was happy she was there because he felt intoxicated in her presence.

"And it was very kind of you to take in a team of hapless nerds who don't get out very much—but you did not hear that last part from me," Alexander had said, holding a finger up to his mouth. That last part was a slip up, something he probably shouldn't have said. Without context, though, she was never going to know he was talking about Project Far Step.

"What exactly did I not hear, Mister Cordova?" she had teased with a wink as another song had started to play, and she'd pulled him back to the dance floor.

"Why are you still awake?" Thrase asked, walking into the main room of the house and pulling Alexander out of his remembrance. She had a glass of water in her hand and looked mildly disheveled. Her black coat was gone and her green vest was unbuttoned.

"This rebuilt deck is vexing me," Alexander said, dropping a Burning Blade Sigil into his deck, causing the number on his counter card to tick up to twenty-nine. As an attacker, he needed to rebuild for what Claudia had in her deck. He was more than willing to do that for her, though with the night of dancing in her company so fresh in his mind, the task was tedious beyond measure.

He paused, looking up at Katie Thrase and tilting his head. "Why are *you* still awake? Didn't you leave the party before the rest of us?"

"That I did. There were some friends from boarding school that I wanted to catch up with. We found another party that had a little less of a starched collar," she said with a wink, holding up the glass of water that was in her hand.

"Of course, of course," he said. Thrase finished her drink in a single gulp, making a face as it burned going down, as if it was another glass of liquor.

Was it not water?

"When did your new paramour leave?" Thrase asked, sitting down.

"She is not—"

"Alexander, the two of you have a spark. The kind that we can all see and feel in the air," Thrase said.

"Is it that obvious?" he asked.

"Jeffery can literally see it," Thrase said, reaching into her vest pocket and pulling out a flask, emptying the rest of the clear liquid into her cup.

Nope, definitely not water.

"It is a good thing. You should be trying to stick your cock in somebody you could actually marry." Her words, while crude, were not untrue. His messing around with Fox all these years, while it had *felt* serious, could never have been anything more than that.

"Have you been in love before, Katie?" Alexander asked after an uncomfortably long moment of silence. His friend looked at him and took a sip from her glass, pondering the question. Katie Thrase didn't look it, but she was almost a decade older than Alexander and was always a replete source of information on life experiences.

"Once, what felt like a lifetime ago. At the time, I had fewer years than you under my belt. It was the one and only season that I spent on NovaTerra's marriage mart before I absconded to school and the project.

"He was a young man, my age. Sadly, though, he had absolutely no standing in society, and to make matters worse, he was poor. He and some friends snuck into a ball pretending to be servers—they were shooting some reality television show or some such, I could not tell you anything more than that. We hit it off and for the next three weeks…" She paused, reminiscing, wistfully looking up, swirling the drink in her hand.

"The next three weeks were bliss as I thought we were going to run away together and live in a little house somewhere and I would just be a wife, a common lady." Thrase shuddered as she said it. "Then…" She finished the glass in one fell swallow. "I learned that all of it was just for their show. He liked fucking me, liked that I bought him things, but he did not *like* me. It was devastating. I had to talk my brother out of killing him, and some days, I don't honestly know why I did that." Katie Thrase slapped both her hands squarely on her knees, making a loud crack, and then she stood up.

"Be careful, Alexander. Love is for little girls in stories and gallant knights that don't know any better."

With that bit of advice, she walked out of the room, leaving Alexander dumbfounded and with nothing to say. It was quite an indictment. He didn't want to believe that of Claudia. She, at least, was of quality birth. No, this was not the same. Katie's experience had been horrible and turned her off from love. It *did* go a long way to explain why she was a cynic that never watched any form of televised entertainment.

Turning back to his cards, Alexander pulled out a Hyperion Shield. It was a buff that traded defense for offense at the cost of his life and not the player whose card it was used on. He flipped it over in his hand, running some numbers in his head. Footsteps came from the hall.

"Come to tell me another story of failed love, Katie?" Alexander said, not looking up.

"Not at all, my sweet." It was Claudia's voice.

Alexander's head shot up as he saw her walking into the room. She had on street clothing: pants, a loose-fitting shirt, and a long brown jacket. Her yellow hair was up in a messy bun. Through her white shirt, he could see her black bra and the outline of her breasts. Before he could say anything, she was on top of him. Their lips connecting, her tongue pushing into his mouth and his into hers. She tasted of peppermint.

He could feel the bulge as his cock came to attention. Wrapping his arms around her, Alexander removed her jacket, letting it hit the floor. They kissed harder as she moved her body across his now fully engorged erection. Pulling away from her, Alexander's hands pulled up her shirt, getting it over her head, making a mess of the already messy bun. All he had wanted to do since they'd met this afternoon was get her shirt off to see her breasts and have his way with them. He fumbled with her bra for a moment.

"Not yet," she whispered, pushing his hands away and sliding herself down to the floor. Her fingers were nimble while his had been fumbling. She had the three buttons of his trousers unsnapped and his cock in her hand in an instant.

Looking up at him with those amazing green eyes, she kissed the tip of his member and then took him inside her mouth. Alexander leaned back, moaning as she sucked him, his hand on her head, gripping a handful of wheat-blonde hair. He closed his eyes, letting the pleasure wash over him.

There was a moment of shuddering, then he opened his eyes, and she was gone. Worse, he was still fully clothed, and the room was dark. He still had the Hyperion Shield in his hand.

Taking a deep breath, he pushed down on his throbbing member, distancing himself from the dream. It was very much time for bed.

Sitting the card on his deck reader, he closed the program and stood up. Alexander was wobbly, the erotic nature of the dream still had him in its grip. As he stumbled to his bed, he hoped that Claudia would still be in his dreams once he made it there.

Yard, The Citadel, Lucas

Lucas hadn't left the doorway. He was still watching Wingarf yell at the Militarum troops as they stood at attention. Every twenty minutes or so, an officer would come out and dismiss that group before marching in another. He couldn't hear what was being said, but remembered enough to know that what the old Master-at-Arms saw as words of encouragement were probably anything but.

The shade of young Joanna had faded away or wandered off, he wasn't sure. He couldn't stop thinking about the Fellowship of the Cross. They were coming. Somewhere on this blasted world, they had already gathered. Otherwise, why fortify the Citadel and not put up a blockade in space?

He had so many questions. With each passing moment, the instinct to learn why Hyacinth had brought them here was fading and the warrior was trying to take over; the Host'ire Knight that wanted to ignite his star-steel blade and wade into battle, cutting down heretics and enemies of the Order.

I'll never leave you, a small voice said in the depths of his mind.

The line of troopers that Wingarf was yelling at turned and marched off. Lucas waited a few minutes. Another line of troopers didn't march out. Whatever inspection he was conducting had apparently concluded. Wingarf stood alone in the middle of the parade ground, looking up into the red sky, leaning against his star-steel spear which he had stuck into the ground.

This was Lucas's moment. He wanted to have another conversation with the old man. The desire to fight was welling up inside of him. The young shade of Joanna had been wrong about him. He couldn't stand up to the system. The version of him that had was long dead. He was a loyal member of the Host'ire and would defend his school. Knight-Commanders did not run away, and they were not influenced by strange messages from people that should be dead.

I'll never leave you—

He cut off the line of thought, reaffirming his resolve.

Pulling his leather jacket tight, Lucas stepped out onto the parade field. As soon as he was out of the shadow of the door frame, he could feel Wingarf's eyes upon him. The old Master-at-Arms had known he was there the whole time. It was the only way he would have clocked him so fast. That did not surprise Lucas. There were things that the teachers here were capable of that he still could not wrap his mind around, like how the old man was so effective with a two-handed weapon when he only had the one arm.

"Here to have your over important Knight-Commander ass kicked again? Sir," Wingarf grumbled, his eyes digging into Lucas like daggers.

"I wanted to see what was going on, to volunteer my sword to the cause," Lucas said.

"We don't need the swords of men like you," Wingarf said, turning away from Lucas. He pulled his spear from the ground in a hard clean motion and put it on his back, the magnetic quiver grabbing the shaft.

"'Men like me'? I am a decorated warrior. I have seen battle," Lucas said, his voice louder and in less control that he would have liked.

"Not like this you haven't, boy," Wingarf said.

"I know what the Fellowship are capable of. I've seen it," he said.

For a brief moment, Lucas wanted to stamp his foot like an obstinate child. He thought better of it. He was no longer the child that he had been seeing, the young novice that had to stand up for everybody, only to get beaten down.

"*Seen*, but not fought. Pretty boy Knight-Commanders like yourselves don't cross blades with fanatics like them. That is for men like me," Wingarf said. His words were cold, biting. They dug right into Lucas's soul and ego.

"Men like you? Men that abuse children? Men that—"

Before Lucas could finish, Wingarf turned and started walking toward him.

"Strong men. Men that are not afraid to kill. Men that have bathed in blood. You are weak, boy. You couldn't protect them then, and you can't now. Go back to your room with the women and wait for this to all be over. Wait for the better men to finish the killing," Wingarf said.

Rage bubbled up inside of Lucas, but he couldn't find words; his mouth didn't want to open. He didn't know what to say.

Wingarf just huffed at him. Then, he turned around and walked away, leaving Lucas dumbstruck upon the field. If he couldn't fight, how was he supposed to protect his friends? He didn't want to leave them, but he couldn't just hide away. He was a fighter. He *needed* to fight. In that moment, though, he just felt like the child again, making promises that he didn't know if he was ever going to be able to keep, whether through strength of arms or character.

Lucas wasn't sure how long he stood there before his communicator started to buzz. Still in a daze, he reached down and answered the device.

"This is Lucas, go ahead," he said, hearing his words as if he wasn't even in his own body.

"I've found something that I need to show you." Naomi's voice sounded excited, even for her.

"I've got something, as well," Joanna's voice broke in.

Well, at least they *were productive today,* Lucas thought.

He took a breath and reached out, pulling himself back into his body. He needed to be the leader. Damn that old man. He knew who he was. He knew what he was capable of, and most of all, he *knew* he was strong.

"I look forward to hearing it back in our rooms in twenty," Lucas said.

He watched the old Master-at-arms exit the parade field. Holding the look for another minute, Lucas breathed out and stalked back toward the tower with new resolve. There was a mystery to solve and a foe to face. He would do both and prove to that grumpy cuss of a man that he was worthy of being a Knight-Commander.

Apartments, The Citadel, Naomi

"**S**omebody put a back door into the whole Citadel system and has been sending out messages and receiving messages for the last *year*?" Lucas asked, repeating what Naomi had just said. Naomi was never going to understand why people felt the need to do that.

"Correct. I wasn't able to track down who yet. Cicely left a few programs running at the server level to see if the door gets opened again, but there is a chance that whoever used it the first time doesn't need to use it anymore," Naomi said, leaning back in her chair.

"The Citadel is compromised, so that means that the Fellowship has somebody on the inside. Whenever they attack, it will be a bloodbath," Lucas said, wrapping his hand around his chin.

"Wait, hold on. Fellowship of the Cross? Here?" Naomi asked with a bit of panic in her voice. He'd said it so casually. That wasn't information that you just dropped like it was nothing.

"Yes, that is why they brought in the Militarum and sent away the novices. Administrator Fel is expecting an attack. Apparently, the High Command had reports of the Fellowship bubbling up in the system. I don't know when the attack will come, but we can guess soon. Which means we need to figure out how to help Hyacinth before then."

"I might be able to help with that," Joanna said, putting her book on the table. Quickly, she ran through everything that she had found.

"I remember holding the paperweight. Jasper had hit somebody with it, a blur of a human, so that means..."

"Hyacinth," Naomi said. "I know, I touched it as well—the paperweight. And Joanna, you were holding her head... I wish I remembered more of that day."

"We need Rostov," Joanna said. "He has been hearing her. He will know more."

"They have been talking longer, so he might understand how she is stringing logic together, since she doesn't view time like us," Naomi added.

"I agree. It's time to wave my rank around a bit. I'm going to inform the Administrator that we are getting him out of re-education. Come on," Lucas said, standing up.

He thew on his coat and pulled it tight, looking every bit the leader that she knew him to be.

Re-education, The Citadel, Rostov

"Go away!" Rostov yelled as the three men in brown robes with crosses carved into their foreheads descended upon him. He just wanted them to go away, to just leave him be, but they kept coming. Every time he thought he was awake, they would smash open the door again and yank him up by chains, confirming he was still trapped in his too-realistic nightmares. Last time, they burned their cross into his chest while gelding him. The time before that, they eviscerated and then quartered him.

He had run the gamut of emotions, from fear to pleading. Now, he was angry. This had to stop. He wanted his body to wake him up, to get him out of this nightmare.

More pounding at the door. The three men turned around, their clubs at the ready. There were voices on the other side; voices that he recognized. Rostov started to laugh. A new emotion for this endless procession of hell he was being put through. He recognized the voice. It was Lucas and he sounded pissed.

"Oh, you three are fucked now," he said, laughing even harder. He couldn't control it.

The three turned to look at him. They scowled, then vanished. Rostov thought he would wake up, jolt out of bed and be confronted with a new reality. That didn't happen. He was still in the same place, in the same room.

Great, they are waking *visions. Just what I need,* he thought.

Lucas was still yelling outside.

"You will open this door right now or so help me, I will draw my blade. I have killed greater men than you for less!"

Rostov reached out with the Null. He could see Lucas standing in the hallway, flanked by Joanna and Naomi. The two guards that were in front of the door were shaking. He could feel the nervous energy radiating off them. The longer he spent exposed to the Null all day, the closer he was getting to being able to see emotions and thoughts like the Host'ire Ambassadors could.

"Fine, you can see the uneducated. I am calling the Administrator," the first guard said in the petulant voice of somebody who pretended they were strong until something didn't go their way.

"Save your breath. I called her twenty minutes ago. She will be down presently," Lucas said, command filling his voice, his aura changing from a yellow to bright gold. "Now open this door!"

"Yes sir," the second guard said, his voice sounding even more petulant than the first.

"You will address me as Knight-Commander. Do I make myself clear?" Lucas barked.

"Yes, Knight-Commander," he said, his voice much lower now, his aura fading, turning a shade of gray.

"And turn off the shocking devices in the floor, I will not abide by their use in my presence," Lucas said. The guards, shaking, complied with his order.

The locks on the door clicked and his friends walked in. Joanna grabbed the door behind her and pulled it shut.

"It is good to see you; good to see all of you," Rostov said, waving his hand across the group.

"It's good to see you, too," Lucas said.

Naomi ran up and wrapped her arms around him. Rostov hugged her back. For a moment, he shuddered, remembering the dream, the one that had started the recurring nightmares. She was real, though. He knew deep down that she was real. He could feel that.

"Why did you say, 'see *all* of you'?" Joanna asked. Rostov pulled away from Naomi and looked up at Joanna with a funny look.

Can they not see them? Am I good and truly insane?

"You brought the children with you. Poor Essex, standing there in the corner, all by himself." Rostov pointed at a dour looking child with long blond hair standing in the corner of the room. The group looked, but it was clear that they were not able to see him.

"No, he hasn't shown up," Lucas said.

"I checked in the Host'ire data banks. There is no record of him for the last ten years. He was knighted, served some time, and then poof," Naomi said.

"That is not good. She is going to want all of us. She needs us all. Her five," Rostov said.

"Her what? I am going to need you to back the train up just a little bit. How long has she been talking to you?" Joanna asked.

"She never stopped talking to me. Once all of you left, it was just me. I was the only one. She is why I am in here. I insisted that something had happened to us, that they were covering it up; that they had wiped our minds. It dragged me down, just a splinter in my mind. I knew what I was hearing, knew what I was remembering. The memories have faded with time, thanks to their treatments," Rostov said, stomping his foot on the hard metal floor of his cell.

"What can you tell us about her; about the blood?" Joanna asked.

They had learned a lot, but nothing that he didn't already know. Why wouldn't they tell them something that could help? Something that was *new*?

"The blood is what connects us, we shared it that day. At least, I know we did, I just…" Rostov said, banging his hand on the side of his head. "I just can't remember it; can't remember what happened to her."

The door to the cell opened and heavy footfalls echoed in the small room. The group turned around to see Administrator Fel standing there, flanked by two knights. Not the guards that Lucas had bullied past, but *actual* knights. They both had their star-steel blades in hand. They were not on, but it was a threat.

"Nothing happened to her, Mr. Rostov. Nothing happened to any of you," Fel said in a heated tone.

"Stop telling me what I do and don't remember, you cold hearted cunt!" Rostov yelled, taking a step forward.

Naomi grabbed him. At the same time, Fel held back the guard to her right who was about to ignite his blade.

"As you can see, your friend is not well. He needs his re-education," Fel said.

"All I see," Lucas snapped back, walking up to her, standing toe to toe with the taller woman, "is a bully. He is trying to tell you something. You don't understand it, so he must be crazy; must be hearing unsanctioned, heretical things. Shove him in the basement and torture him for years until he breaks."

"That is a cynical reading of what we are doing to help him," Fel said.

"You do not help somebody by taking away their dampening tools. You do not help them with mind games and cells," Naomi said, pointing her finger at Fel.

Rostov could feel the emotions rising inside of her, red hot. Fel just grumbled. The blackness radiating from her stank of the Shadow.

"I wouldn't expect people like you to understand," Fel said, spitting out the last few words.

"People like us understand what people like *you* do all too well," Joanna said. "We understand how you abuse power, how you silence those who disagree with you. This is just another form of your power and it's bullshit!"

"Be quiet, librarian, this is above you," Fel growled.

Joanna didn't back down, instead puffing her chest up even more, towering over Fel, who was not impressed.

"But it is not above *me*," Lucas said. "I invoke the right of conscription. As a Knight-Commander and Ranger, I can draft any Host'ire of the rank of Knight or lower. He is coming with us."

Lucas locked his eyes with Fel. She matched his gaze. The two of them didn't move, didn't make a sound. They just looked at each other, the battle in their eyes fought at a small scale. For a fleeting moment, Rostov thought they were going to win. No—that never happens—he didn't win. This was a game of cards and the house always won.

"Fine, take your broken friend. Take him and stay out of our way," Fel said with a wave of her hand.

Then she turned and walked out of the room. There was a quiet moment, everything seemed to hang; nobody breathed, nobody made a single move. Rostov didn't understand, but he also wasn't about to look a gift horse in the mouth.

Finally, they exhaled. Naomi hugged Rostov again. Joanna ran up and joined. Finally, walking slowly, dignified—but also like an outsider—Lucas walked up and wrapped his arms around them. The four of them hugged. Rostov didn't remember the last time he had felt this close to humanity. These were his people. He knew that they would never hurt him, that they were fated to be together, because there were hard times ahead.

For tonight, though, against what he knew to be true, they had won.

Bottom of the Shaft, Olympus Ares Research Facility, Grace

Essex didn't need to stop again as they made their way down the last few ladders. They hit the smoke quickly and, just as fast as they were in it, they were through it. Both were covered in soot. While crossing through, the air shifted, currents and wind moving, causing the temperature to rise by close to fifteen degrees almost instantaneously. The last ladder ended on red clay and black rock. All of it was covered with what was becoming an all too familiar sight: death. There were bodies everywhere, mixed amongst blood and spent plasma rounds. Grace could see where a last stand had been made and the people who had made it.

"Tragadi," Essex whispered, almost in awe.

"Darklin Tragadi, at that," Grace said, shining her light on one of the bodies. She had read about them, seen them in videos, but never in person.

The Tragadi were two species: one that weathered nuclear winter four thousand years ago aboveground and another that retreated underground. You would never know today that they had once been the same. The Survivors were tall, while the Darklin were short, tending to walk hunched over on all fours—and, most importantly, lacked eyes. There was still a space for their eyes to go, but all that was left were white vestigial orbs that looked forward.

At her feet, there were five dead Darklin Tragadi, weapons in hand. Their bodies were mauled, ripped apart. Something was stirring down here, something rotten. As she looked at the corpses, their empty milky eyes looked back, they looked passed Grace in death, seeing Emily.

"I had a Master once who said that the Darklin don't look at you, they looked through you, into your soul," Essex said, quietly his hand sliding his coat to the side and resting upon his star-steel blade.

"I've never seen a Darklin before," Grace said quietly.

"Me neither. Though, there are a few Tragadi in the order, like the old librarian at the Citadel. But their home world is outside the Confederation, making it harder to steal their children," Essex said, stepping forward. Each footfall was quiet, deliberate to not step on anything but empty stone; to not disturb anything and leave no sound.

Grace slung the rifle forward and quietly thumbed off the safety and followed Essex, matching his footsteps. That was when she saw it.

This place deep under the ground didn't look like it was changing yet, at least not to her eyes, but there was still something she recognized from the other world, something that didn't belong here and chilled her to the core. Scrawled in blood across the walls were runes, runes that she recognized from the vision she had suffered after the incident.

Taking a breath, Grace toggled on her helmet's camera and started to record what she was seeing.

"Do you recognize those?" Essex whispered, motioning to the bloody writing on the wall with the un-ignited hilt of his blade.

Grace was quiet for a moment. She didn't want to say that she did, wasn't sure yet if it was safe to share the vision. Wasn't even sure what it meant. No, she would keep quiet, for now. That is what Emily would do...

"No, I have a PhD in archelogy, not xenolinguistics," Emily said.

Essex chuckled. *Good, that wasn't my best lie, but...*

The moment was shattered as the sound of skittering started to fill the cave. Grace turned around, leveling her rifle and moving her light around. Nothing. She turned again and saw nothing, not even Essex.

Where did he go now?

The skittering got louder.

She flipped again and saw them. Running along the ground were five impossible-looking creatures. Huge mouths with razor sharp teeth and whipped tongues, attached to a small body, propelled by four legs that were nothing more than jagged claws. These creatures were fast, faster than she had ever seen something move in real life.

Grace toggled on the aim assist built into her suit and squeezed the trigger, firing off a few rounds. All of them went wide, missing their target, instead smashing into the wall, leaving holes of red, molten-dripping rock. She hadn't anticipated the kick of the weapon. Activating the arms of her suit, Grace pushed the rifle into her shoulder and fired another two rounds. This time, they found their mark, blowing through the screaming, snarling mouth of the creature. Bioluminescent blood exploded across the cave. The creature's legs kept running for a moment, before falling over.

"The hell is my Host'ire?" Emily muttered as she lined up another shot and pulled the trigger while walking backward. How people did this without computer assistance, she didn't know. The small nightmare creature exploded just like the first. Then, she heard the heartbeat thrum of a star-steel blade. Spinning, Grace saw Essex slicing two more of these creatures apart, ones that would have come up behind her and ended her day.

"Focus, Doctor!" he yelled at her.

Grace whipped her head around again. One of the creatures was far too close for comfort. She lined her shot up and pulled the trigger, gore splashing across her armor. The last two went down quickly. But the skittering sound that was echoing in the cave didn't stop. It just got closer and closer. Echoing louder and louder.

She turned to Essex, who was already on the move into the darkness, his blade in one hand and the pulse rifle in the other, the sling holding it into his arm. She ran after him. A moment later, a steel wall and door came into view.

As they approached it, the wheel on the outside of the door started to spin, then flew open. Standing on the other side was a short creature with milk-white eyes looking past her.

"Inside," they yelled, waving the two of them forward. Essex dove and then rolled through the door, flicking off his blade and returning the hilt to his belt at the same time. Grace pushed harder, engaging the servos in her leg armor to get her over the threshold.

As she was slowing down, the door slammed shut behind her, leaving her in pitch blackness. Grace flicked back on the light atop her armor that had turned off when her targeting system had come online. Her and Essex were in a large room surrounded by ten Darklin Tragadi. Breathing out, she lowered her weapon.

"We come in peace," Grace said.

"Good, because we are out of fuckin' ammunition."

EPISODE IV:
Knives in the Dark

Tragadi Shelter, Olympus Areas Research Facility, Grace

The Darklin who had closed the door turned around to address her. "I'm Charged Bolt and this is my power station. What in the bloody Hells brings you down here?"

"Well," Grace began as she heaved in and out, trying to catch her breath. A readout on the heads-up display showed her heart rate was high and advised that she sit down and avoid any more activity or more drastic measures would be taken. Taking another hard breath, she saw a stool and sat down, pulling off her helmet.

"We came here to find this power station. There is an incident happening in the lab above," she said, moving a hunk of sweat-covered black hair from where it had fallen over her eyes.

"Oh, an incident is happening in the above world. Isn't that how it always is?" Charged Bolt said, pacing around the room.

His nose and ears wiggled, taking in all the data that his eyes couldn't perceive. Then he turned directly to Grace and the milk-white orbs in his head bore into her. That was when she realized that Darklin didn't have eyelids and thus couldn't close their eyes or squint at her.

I don't fucking like that at all, Emily thought.

"We were running an experiment that went wrong and now there are creatures and worlds trying to come through a portal," Grace began as she quickly caught the power station manager up on what had been happening in the last few hours. Essex chimed in from time to time, but mostly he let Grace tell the story, nodding along, giving everybody in the room a shifty look. He still hadn't put his glasses back on and she decided that he looked better with them on.

His face is too thin, it needs glasses, Emily thought as Grace finished her story and let the Darklin leader mull it over.

"That would explain two things. The sudden draw from above. Normally, our energy is going away, not *up*," he said, making broad hand motions above his head and then to the left, almost dismissively.

"Your power is not all going up?" Essex asked.

"Aye. Most of it goes forward, somewhere else. The lines are old. It took my great grandfather most of his life to tap into them so that it would work with the tech they brought," Charged Bolt said, grabbing another stool and sitting down. He kept talking as he reached into his pocket and pulled out a long thin nutrition stick and started to lick it.

"Wait, you didn't build the reactor?" Grace asked.

"Not at all. I'd never design anything this way, but at the same time, I don't understand half of what it does. Come, I'll show you. I assume it is quite a sight to behold," he said, slapping his hands on his knees and standing up to his full four-foot height.

Charged Bolt left the nutrient stick in his mouth as he walked over to a second hatch and spun the wheel to open it. Light spilled into the room, causing Grace to squint and Essex to reach for his glasses. The light was followed by extreme heat and the sound of bubbling.

Taking a step forward, Grace was greeted by a lake of lava. Situated in the middle of it was a large structure. It was shaped like an egg and covered with old runes and wires. None of the tech looked like it belonged together. Wires covered in black glass were coming out of the lava and connected into more modern wires that she recognized. Every few moments, the egg would belch out black smoke that blew up and then toward the vent shaft. From where they stood leading to the egg, there was a gangway well above the lava. Still, it didn't look at all safe. *Nothing* down here looked safe.

"Geothermal energy," Grace whispered, looking at the strange contraption, the likes of which she had never seen before. So *this* is where Administrator Vardis found his extra power.

"Yes, I do remember somebody saying that word at some point. My basic is not great," Charged Bolt said.

Sounds good to me, she thought, wondering what his natural language sounded like.

"So, you don't normally send power to the instillation that you are under and connected to?" Grace asked, confused as she looked at all the cables that were running from the lava egg into the wall and into the roof. The number running into the wall was larger by magnitudes.

"We are connected to a lot of things. Annabell here is where she is because that's where the lava is; where she has always been," the Darklin said, shrugging his shoulders and pointing at four sets of cables that were all on the same level and carnal direction. "I just send the power to where it's rigged up to. 'Don't ask questions,' my Father used to say. 'Just do your job.'"

"You said there was a second thing that our story explained," Essex said, piping up from the back. His hand was still on the hilt of his star-steel blade.

"You said that the facility up world was changing; that your people were being taken over. Well, whatever fuckery you were involved in has trickled down here like a child's piss," he said. "First it was those skittering things. We have been calling them Skitters for the time being until we can figure out what they really are."

"The ones with the horrible teeth and big tongues?" Essex asked.

"Does it look like I know what that means?" Charged Bolt said, pointing to where his eyes would have been a few thousand years ago. "Don't fucking answer that," he added, pointing a finger right at the former Host'ire.

I like him, Emily thought.

"Yes, the buggers that rip and tear. They are not natural to this world. We had not encountered them until today. That, though, that isn't the worst part."

"Your people have been infested, taken over by whatever noncorporeal malignant force came through the portal," Grace said, pulling her hair out of the messy bun it was in and reorganizing it on her head.

"Correct. At first, I just thought Full Mag was being his normal asshole self until he shot Screwdriver. He then ran into the cave. He isn't the problem, if you are looking to stop the flow of power up to your lab. We can't get to the controls without going through Sharp Blade," Charged Bolt said, his voice dropping. Grace could see where this was going.

I don't think he is worried about a fight...

"Well then, Sharp Blade can meet energy blade," Essex said, holding his star-steel blade at the ready but not igniting it just yet.

"Essex, stand down," Grace said, putting her hand on his shoulder. Essex took a deep breath and clipped the hilt back to his belt.

"I don't think it's about the fight, for either of them," Grace said.

"Full Mag is a good friend, but Sharp Blade is my youngest brother. I told mother that we would stay together, that I would protect everybody..." Charged Bolt said, almost in a confessional way. Grace wasn't sure if he was just having trouble or if this was just something that Darklin did.

My older brother would gladly let all manner of horrible happen to me, Emily thought, remembering back to the farm, back to her old life.

"As the years went on, I failed. And now whatever that is, it has my brother and won't let him go; wants us to kill him. I don't know," Charged Bolt said, kicking at the ground. "Have they asked you for anything?"

"No, we have only run into reanimated dead things," Grace said.

"Ancestors in the stone, I wish he was dead. It would make dealing with him simpler. He isn't, though. Every time we have tried to talk, I can still hear my brother in the nonsense scrabble of words he says."

Charged Bolt paused. There was something else he wanted to say. His mouth was fumbling to find the words, that deep lung cry trying to come out, like a man who refused to cry but couldn't actually hold in the emotion.

"It's his eyes. They are moving. I can hear them. Sharp Blade's eyes shouldn't *move*," Charged Bolt said, pounding his fist on the wall. "They shouldn't fucking move."

A small dribble of snot came from his nose as the Darklin leader stumbled back and hit the wall, before sliding down. Grace looked around. The rest of the Darklin were keeping their distance, clearly distressed by what had been happening to them during the last day.

Grace walked over and sat down next to the stocky creature.

"I lost my older brother when I was young. Not to some supernatural thing, but in a way that caused him to be lost, while not being dead," Grace said, looking forward, reaching into Emily's memories, to craft a tale.

"Our world was small, far off any of the hyperspace lanes, which also meant we were poor and didn't get to see much of the wider universe. Education was a luxury, one my bother didn't get, but that I did, because..." She paused and tried to figure out her next words.

"My parents pulled out all the stops to get me books and a connection to the halls of higher learning. Once a month, I got to go to the only major city and use the stellar array to take classes from McCreary Prime, people known for their math and music. The way they turn equations into sounds is amazing.

"My brother resented this attention, as he was forced to work harder and harder. Slowly, the sibling I had looked up to, who had loved me and been a third parent to me, wanted nothing to do with me. We stopped talking; stopped interacting at all. Finally, when I left for university, he did worse than not say goodbye."

Grace paused again. These were words that had haunted Emily the whole time she had worked on her first degree. Words she had not thought about in fifteen years.

"'I see we are finally cutting the chaff from the family,' he'd said. It was so off-handed, just as he was heading out for the day. And then he was gone. I could see the crushed looks on my parents' faces as we drove to the star port. I was able to keep in contact for a few more years before a storm cut the world off. We never talked about him."

Grace whipped a single tear from her eye.

So much of Emily has been lost, only to dredge up this.

"I guess, what I'm trying to say is, if your brother is out there, we will do what we can to get him back. If we can stop whatever is going on, reverse it, he will probably come back; probably return," Grace said, hoping that her voice was conveying enough confidence.

"You are right. What is that phrase you above worlders have about a new perspective?" Charged Bolt asked.

"A fresh set of eyes," Grace said, finishing the idiom.

"Yes, a fresh set of eyes are what we need," he said, standing up, new resolve in his voice.

The moment was shattered by the blaring of klaxons. Darklin started running back toward the front room where they had entered the reactor.

"Full Mag," Charged Bolt said.

"I've got this," Essex said pulling out his star-steel blade. "Just get that power adjusted."

Apartments, The Citadel, Rostov

Rostov didn't sleep. Everybody else retired to their rooms, but he stayed on the couch. There were only the three rooms, and while Lucas had volunteered to give up his bed, Rostov insisted that he was fine sleeping on the couch.

It was not the most comfortable space. The cushions had no give to them and the arms were made of wood. Still, it was far and away more comfortable than the bed in his re-education cell. Most importantly, with the window closed, the room was dark. The darkness was something that he had missed, something that, for the last three years, he had craved. Being exposed to the brightness of the Null with no filter was a horrible thing, but never having a moment of true darkness was something else. There were moments they had turned the lights down, but never off, and never for a consistent amount of time.

Still, sleep did not come. Rostov was restless. Already he had paced from one side of the room to the other, counting his steps. He then sat down and watched the clock, before standing back up and repeating the path three more times. The room didn't change. The size remained the same. He was free and now he didn't know what to do or where to go. There was so much to see and do—at least, from the opinion of a man who had been trapped in the same cell for years.

Looking at the kitchenette, Rostov thought about having something to eat. Maybe a cup of coffee. He had *so* missed coffee. Or something solid, with flavor. Pawing through the cabinets, there was nothing but instant coffee, tea, and meal powder.

Rostov walked back to the couch and sat down again. His eyes darted around the room, waiting for his nightmares to return, waiting to be strung up, eviscerated, branded, and castrated. Hopefully in that order, so that he wouldn't have to feel the worst of it.

No, you are safe, Rostov. They came for you. They will not let anything happen to you.

It felt like a platitude to his brain. His heart, though, was full in this moment. They had come for him and he was free.

Yet the group was not full. Essex had vanished. And she still had not told them how to find her, how to figure out where she was residing.

Rostov closed his eyes and reached down, trying to find her voice again. Trying to see if she would still talk to him, now that he was free. Now that he was not consuming unfiltered raw Null energy. The room was quiet, the only sound his breathing. A heavy in and out through his nose. Then there was a tapping, as his leg started to move, unable to keep itself still, a restless energy that started in his upper calf and moved down through his foot in a twitchy tapping. Rostov put his hand on the leg to try and stop it, but still it wanted to twitch, wanted to walk, to *move.*

Opening his eyes, Rostov stood up and started pacing until he found himself at the window.

Throwing open the blackout shade, he was greeted with a deep dark red. Nights on Icarus were not dark like on other worlds. You were not treated to the blackness of the void and the pinpricks of stars. They were too close to the Barrier, that violent red storm that helped keep civilization in its place. The storm that separated the living from Hell.

His whole life, Rostov had refused to believe the Host'ire mythos about the storms holding the gateway to Hell, where demons and other creatures that wanted to destroy Humanity resided. He still wasn't sure if Hell existed beyond the storms. But he did know it existed here, in the hearts of men.

Would demons really be that bad, comparatively?

The storm with its swirling pattern of colors called to him. He could feel the pull of it. Rostov put his hand to the window and let the Null flow through him toward the storm. While it was a drain upon his body, he was more in touch with the energy field that was all around them than he had ever been in the past. It didn't lead to power, though. Just insights, feelings, visions.

I need to get out of here, I need to walk, the thought burst intrusively into his mind. So powerful was the thought that he could not ignore it. There was a pile of clothing that Lucas had set out for Rostov, his one extra outfit. Quickly, he pulled on the black paints tactical shirt, boots, gloves, jacket, and finally glasses. Rostov could see where Lucas had pulled the patches and rank insignia off the coat, so that he wouldn't be confused as a Knight-Commander. As if anybody could confuse a scrawny, slightly tweaked out former inmate for a distinguished Host'ire Knight. Still, the outfit felt good. He had not been allowed to don the black uniform of the order since even before they threw him into re-education. The gray jumpsuit of an attendant was all he had been allowed. This outfit had power.

Quietly, he opened the door and slipped out into the low light of the hallway. During the day, the bright flat fluorescent lighting sucked the life from these concrete halls. At night, the Citadel was illuminated by running lights every ten feet, built into the baseboard between the floor and walls. They cast shadows everywhere, turning a sterile hallway into a place that monsters and nightmares could hide. It didn't matter.

It was good to be free.

Rostov walked to the elevator at the end of the hallway. Just as he was about to hit the button, the sound of feet running danced in his ears from the stairwell. Closing his eyes, Rostov tapped into the Null. There was light coming from under the door. Pulling his hand away from the elevator button, he opened the door instead and entered the dark stairwell.

Like every other part of the Citadel, it was gray concrete. Steel handrails lined the stairs that went up two hundred floors and down another hundred into the subterranean depths of the complex. Rostov walked to the edge, looking up. The emptiness seemed to expand and contract back toward him, vertigo taking hold. He breathed in and stepped back, focusing on the lamp on the wall. Using its unmoving light to right himself in the world. Again.

Just as he was about to turn away from the light, something smashed into his legs, almost knocking him to the ground. Rostov turned, throwing an arm out, steadying himself on the wall. From the corner of his eye, he could see a kid charging down the stairs. He was skipping every third step, making large leaps, using his momentum upon hitting the landings where the stairs turned to throw himself up, bouncing off the wall and landing on the first step to keep going. A feeling of joy and remembrance filled Rostov, watching the child who looked all too familiar.

Rostov took off after him, jumping steps as well, able to take the twelve steps between landings in three hops. Just like the child, he used the railing as a pivot point, pushing Null through himself and kick-turning off the wall before landing on the next staircase. He did this four times, before hearing a crash. There was muttering and sputtering from both a child and an old man. Rostov bounced off the wall, then landed and threw his hand up, pushing Null energy against the air, deadening his momentum. Looking down, three landings from where he was standing, Rostov saw what had caused the commotion. The child had run into the janitor and his cart of cleaning supplies. Cleaning supplies had spilled everywhere, and he was trying to help clean it up while being chided by the old man. Rostov started walking down at a respectable pace, unable to keep the smirk off his face.

"You must watch where you are going, small one," the old janitor said, picking up his bottles of chemicals that had rolled around the landing.

"I'm sorry. I shouldn't have been practicing my wall leaps here," the kid said. Rostov knew that voice. He remembered this whole sequence of events.

"While that is important, you must always be watching. A knight is always aware of where he is, of his surroundings," the old man said.

Mister Deverox, Rostov remembered. For a moment, he wondered if the old janitor was still here. He had been when he went into re-education, looking just as wrinkled and disheveled as he had twenty years ago. Some people never aged. They were just born old.

"You sound just like my teachers. You are not a teacher. You are just some smelly old man that cleans things up! I don't have to listen to you!" kid Rostov yelled. He put two bottles back on the cart then bounced back, doing a flip and kick-turning off the wall.

By the Null, I was filled with so much life and excitement back then... And they took it from me, Rostov thought ruefully.

"Have to? No, you don't have to listen to anybody, this is true. Only the sounds of your own mind. And the Null, of course. You should always listen to that," Mister Deverox said, picking up his mop before returning to his work cleaning the landing.

"It doesn't talk to me. My mind is clear and quiet," kid Rostov said confidently, tapping himself on the head.

"That is a shame. A knight cut off from his power," the old janitor said.

"Piss on that, old man. I don't want to be a knight, I don't want to end up like Hyacinth, just hearing things all the time, talking to the walls because the Null is in her mind. I want to be free, to run, to jump, to *live*. And none of you are going to hold me down!" the kid said, jumping and kicking off a wall of Null, throwing himself into the door which opened into the hallway. There was a commotion and a roll and then he was gone. Mister Deverox just laughed at the display.

"I take it you heard all of that?" Mister Deverox said, turning to look up where Rostov was standing. Rostov was caught off guard for a moment, not expecting the visions to turn and talk to him. This one felt like something to observe, not participate in.

"I did," Rostov said, slowly walking down the last flight of stairs to where Mister Deverox was cleaning.

"You were always such a hyper child, running around. Declaring that you were not going to be stopped, not going to be brought to heel. So free," Deverox said.

"I was," Rostov said, before adding more forcefully, "I still am!"

After all, he was wandering around at night because his legs wouldn't stay still. He had spent the last three years in re-education because of fighting about the fundamentals of Host'ire ideology...

And because he was hearing voices.

That, at least, had changed.

"Are you, though, child? Are you still free?" Mister Deverox asked.

"Of course. I got out of that cell, I am here walking of my own accord. I've got friends again. I can control how much Null I feel and use. This is freedom!" Rostov said.

"Or perhaps you are once again bounding from landing to landing, going down the stairs. Moving so fast that it *feels* like freedom. It's all just a loop, child."

"Stop calling me that!" Rostov said, getting hot. He moved his head around to look at the stairs, the revolving set of landings that went from each and every floor. Announcing more foot falls, this time from below, coming up.

"He calls you a child because you are a child." It was another gruff old voice. One that Rostov had hoped not to hear again.

Does nobody here retire or die? he thought, turning to see Wingarf walking up the stairs, using his weathered star-steel spear as a walking stick, the flap of his jacket swinging where the arm was missing.

"You," Rostov muttered. The old Master-at-arms felt different. He felt real.

"Yes, me. I heard that Administer Fel let you out," Wingarf said, looking him up and down.

"My friends came to get me. *They* got me out," Rostov said.

"You keep telling yourself that. Lucas… excuse me, *Knight-Commander* Brandice thinks that he is hot shit. He always has. Just know that once the Fellowship comes, he will fold," Wingarf said, leaning in toward Rostov. Rostov's eyes went wide, fear starting to overtake him.

"You have seen them, have you, lad?" Wingarf said, pausing as Rostov's eyes gave everything away. "Good. Then you will be prepared for the death that awaits you."

Rostov swallowed air getting his traitorous eyes back under control, finding his momentarily lost resolve.

"When the darkness comes, we will be ready. I will stand and fight it," Rostov said with the confidence of a child that was about to smash his way through a door and then walk off the pain so that he could still look cool.

"You keep telling yourself that, child. I'll be watching with great interest. By the end, you will be begging for a return to your cell, wishing you had just agreed with the re-education agents and said, 'Yes sir, no sir'. The hour is too late now. The shadow is upon this place," Wingarf said.

Rostov wanted to open his mouth and retort, but there was nothing that he could say. How did one even respond to that? While he was looking for his words, the old Master-at-Arms walked past him, kicking open the door and exiting the stairs.

"Don't take what he says to heart. The man is broken and only knows how to insult children," Mister Deverox said, watching as the door closed. "But, if you need to hide from the darkness, remember where you went as a child. Remember where you all found her. Remember overcoming your fear of the dark places to rescue the light."

Rostov was about to open his mouth to say something, to make some point about not being scared, about them all underestimating him. But Mister Deverox was gone, the spills he'd been cleaning dried, and Rostov was alone on the landing, as the lights started to come to life, signaling the start of a new day.

Hallway, The Citadel, Naomi

"Rostie!" Naomi yelled down the hallway. Rostov, who was standing blankly, looking at the wall, turned around, shaking his head like she had just snapped him out of a dazed walking dream. "We missed you at breakfast."

"I couldn't sleep. I've been sleeping enough. Thought I would go for a walk," he said, taking a few deep breaths as he was talking.

Naomi cocked her head to the side, giving him a once over. He looked fine, but at the same time, he looked very much *not* fine.

"Are you feeling alright?" she asked, hedging the question, trying to ask it as gently as possible.

"I'm, ya know. Doing about as well as one can do after spending a few years in a fascist re-education room," Rostov said. Naomi could feel his attempt to hold back the animosity and anger in his voice.

"The Order isn't fascist," she said quietly.

"Have you looked around lately? The architecture, the outfits, the just... *everything*," Rostov said, motioning to the blank hallway with its flat light and propaganda posters. He took a deep breath. His emotions were starting to well up. She could feel them inside of her gut and see them on his face. It was strange. She tried to shake it away, but it just wouldn't go.

"I've been a member my whole life. I think I would know," Naomi said.

"That's it, right there. You have been here your whole life. They took you as a very little child. You didn't get ripped from your family, didn't know what life *outside* was like. It has just been a steady drip of Host'ire propaganda and dogma since day one!" Rostov said, raising his voice. She could feel the flush of his cheeks in hers.

"It's not your fault. I just… I've always wished you could see the Host'ire how the rest of us do," Rostov said, turning around and walking away, his head hung low. Guilt flushed through her, anger and understanding.

"Rostov, wait," Naomi said, holding her hand out as she walked after him. He stopped but didn't turn around.

"I'm sorry. What they did to you here was wrong…" She paused, the next words coming harder for her. His anticipation, and desire to not be disappointed, were loud on his face and inside her.

"What they did to you was wrong. It's always been wrong, and I know it doesn't mean much of anything because I'm not them, but I'm sorry. Truly, deeply sorry, and I want to do better."

She held her hand out to him. Rostov looked down at it, considering whether he should take it or not.

Just take it, please. I don't want to lose you after just getting you back, she thought.

Rostov's hand was strong as it grabbed hers and shook. Then, he pulled her tight, wrapping both arms around her.

"You will never lose me again," he whispered in her ear as they held the embrace.

They hugged for what might be considered too long for friends, just long enough that both felt awkward when they pulled away. That powerful kind of teenage awkwardness that only came with big raw emotions.

"I was heading to meet Allana; see how she was doing, with all these soldiers running around. We had a productive conversation before. I'm hoping maybe we can do that again," Naomi said.

Rostov took a deep breath and put out a wave of distrust. "Allana? Really?"

"You don't like her, do you?" Naomi asked, a bit crestfallen.

"I don't trust any of them. I just... I remember *Allana* not being there when we needed her, when she could have done something about Jasper," Rostov said.

"That was a different time," Naomi said, hoping deep down that was true.

"I'll have to take your word for it. You have talked to her more recently than I," Rostov said, motioning for her to lead on.

She walked in front of him as they headed toward Rickman's lab. It was only a five-minute walk and along the way, they saw more and more members of the Host'ire Militarum walking through the hallways. Always, they were in their little squares of four. Sometimes, it was two squares of four and a sergeant. They always marched smartly, with their plasma muskets on their shoulders. It was like they were automatons going from place to place, looking for a fight.

Once they reached the wide-open lab of Professor Rickman, they saw even more troopers. The Militarum had turned the large lecture hall laboratory into a command station. There were communications terminals, both a command and control table, and all the wires that went with it. On each side of the door were hardened emplacements with tripod mounted plasma rifles, the kind that could put down a truly nightmarish field of fire that would give anybody—even a death cultist—pause.

Naomi started to look around for the professor. There was no way that Rickman would have allowed them to turn her laboratory into a command station, a place where fighting was bound to happen. Pulling her jacket tight, Naomi walked directly to the command table. Rostov followed behind, averting his gaze, trying to not make eye contact with any of the troopers, lest he make some mistake and end up back in re-education.

I would rather die than go back there.

How am I feeling his feelings? she wondered. It was like she was getting echoes of emotions passing through her body, vague feelings, and even some of his thoughts? Some were stronger than others, but none of them were her own. Was Rostov having the same experience? Was he feeling her emotions cascading back toward him? He had known what she was thinking…?

No, that was silly. They were just friends who knew each other well enough to know how the other would react. Reading minds was something that ambassadors *claimed* to be able to do, but that required extra training, and digging so deep into the Null, it scrapped the edge of the Shadow.

The captain of this unit of Militarum looked to be about their age. There was wear and tear on his face, a scar across his right cheek and burns creeping out from the green cravat tied around his neck. His eyes were dead. Naomi couldn't look away from them. There was no need for reading emotions to know that this man was a killer who had accepted a life that was only and forever war in its most basic and brutal form.

"Well, look what we have here. A knight and a cast off," he said, looking up from the command table. He was dressed like his men: long green coat, black breastplate. His helmet was sitting on the table, and instead of a rifle, he had a plasma revolver and saber attached to his belt. He very much looked like he had stepped out of a party on NovaTerra or a history book.

"Knight Perkins," Naomi said, holding out her hand. The captain just looked from her hand to her eyes and then back at her hand.

"Captain Fry," he grumbled, turning to look back at his command table and the readouts and graphs that were being displayed holographically. It looked like supplies and troop movements. Naomi was uninterested in all of that, turning away from his studies to redirect him back to her line of questioning. His body language might have been trying to say that the conversation was over, but the conversation would end when she said it was finished. It was her right as a Knight of the Host'ire.

"Captain, I am looking for Professor Rickman. This is her lab that you have set up your command post in," Naomi said.

"I am aware of that," he said tersely.

"I do not see the Professor inside your perimeter. Do you know where I might find her?"

"We do not currently have a location for Rickman. She has not been seen here since we set up ten hours ago," Fry said.

"Doesn't that concern you?" Naomi asked.

"No." The disgust was palpable in his voice.

"There could be Fellowship agents in this base right now, taking people out. Are you not worried about that?" Naomi asked, incredulous at his apathy.

Pull back, don't let him know what you know, the echo of a voice in her head said. It wasn't her voice. Rostov?

"I'm sure there are Fellowship agents in this installation, Ma'am. The Fellowship has their claws inside everything. The operational security of this base is appalling," he said.

Fry pressed a few keys and walked over to a Lieutenant and started to go over deployments with him. The conversation was over. In reality, Captain Fry *did* have the power to say when it ended, not Naomi. She turned and walked back to Rostov. Tapping him, they both quickly exited the lab, getting out of ear shot of the Militarum troopers.

"I'm worried," Naomi said, flicking her coat back and putting her hands on her hips. A flash of interest. Arousal? She let it pass over her. "It is not like Rickman to not be in her lab, especially to allow a whole regiment of soldiers to set up camp there."

"I am sure she is fine. You don't think Professor Rickman is a Fellowship spy, do you? I can't see her running around with a cross carved into her forehead, talking about creating corpses to give to the undead god," Rostov said.

"No, they are the last group that I can see her taking up with. Their whole paupers-into-chains aesthetic doesn't seem to fit for her," Naomi said. She put her hand on Rostov's back as they started to walk away.

"I know I missed breakfast, but are you interested in getting something to eat?" Rostov asked.

"How can you think about food at a time like this?" Naomi asked. "People are missing now, and cultist are coming..."

Rostov just smiled.

"I haven't had a good meal in years. You would be surprised how that weighs on you. We can come up with a plan of action over a meal. Don't take my dislike of her or occasional flippantness as not caring," Rostov said, patting her on the back.

Hoben House, Novagrad, Alexander

Alexander slept well, but much to his chagrin, he spent the time in his dreams alone.

"Did you see this message from Alister?" Hoben asked as everybody was getting ready. He held out his pocket watch with the message displayed.

"I saw he sent something, but I haven't had a chance to read it yet," Katie said, putting two fingers to her forehead and cracking an antiacid into what was *actually* water this time.

"It says, 'My lord father has required that I remove myself from both the tournament and from your company on the project. I am very sorry. Best of luck, Alister MacGuffin'. That is it! Just a message well after the deadline to patch a hole in the team!" Hoben closed his pocket watch and started to pace around. "And he is leaving the project!"

"I hope his father lined something up because the administrator is going to burn him," Thrase muttered.

"Then it is a good thing I found Claudia," Alexander said, ignoring the larger implications outside of the tournament.

"The first match of the day will reveal the truth or fallacy in that statement," Jeffery said as he picked up a muffin.

They were slotted for one of the first matches of the day, so breakfast was a fast meal, and they were off.

The four of them strutted like peacocks though the early morning festival. Alexander, as usual, had dressed in his finest for the event. He had on a pastel green overcoat with golden stars and holographic Chimeras embroidered across it. His undershirt was a deep yellow and his vest and cravat black. His pants matched his shirt, coming down and ending inside his boots. Today, to show that he was in business attire, and as an honor to his station, Alexander had on an empty sword belt. Attached magnetically to his thigh was an empty holster for a pistol.

As a Space Lord, he would normally be allowed—even expected—to be armed. Since it was Festival, though, weapons were not permitted and many people who were normally armed were decked out in empty belts to show respect.

The streets were packed as people moved toward the colosseum to see the first day of the Tourney. Also, the politicking had started in earnest. Every corner and patch of grass was full of signs advertising one candidate or another for the role of Minister of the People. Voting had already happened among the smallfolk, so these signs were to convince the lords—people like Alexander's mother—who they should vote for. There were blue signs for Lord Emilio Vazquez, a red one for Heiro Glover, a green and red one for Stephen Nickolus; on and on it went. As somebody who could not vote in this election—he was neither a small folk nor a titled lord—Alexander ignored all of it.

On the corner outside of the arena, Claudia was waiting for all of them to arrive. She had on a blue dress that went from her neck down to her ankles. White ruffles were coming from under her skirts, there were gold buttons and pins all over her dress. The high neck had a red bow that matched the one that was keeping her wavy blonde hair in a loose ponytail. She looked stunning to Alexander and ready to play. The smile from the day before had been replaced with a game face as serious as any he had seen before.

"Glad you could make it," she said as they walked up. "Are we ready, gentlefolk?"

"I should say so," Hoben said, pulling everybody together for a huddle before they walked in.

He went over what the plan for the game would be today. They knew who they were playing and what they would bring to bear. Their first match was the team from House Pain, a group of brothers who were known as the Pain Givers, who were going to run a fast offense. They had done it in every tourney they competed in. Hoben went over what he saw as the best option to counter that—pushing forward with an even more aggressive stance—one that would, if they could pull it off correctly, end the game in three rounds.

Everybody nodded their heads. This was what they had been preparing for. Each of them was a skilled Peculiar Pentagon player, so even though this was their first game as a quintet, they shouldn't have any issues if the plan was followed.

The match was finished in two rounds and change, with the Pain Givers conceding the match before the third round started, after the result was obvious. The early conceding would net them points that could help later in the tourney. They had executed the plan with the kind of perfection that would have made thetr harshest of headmaster proud enough to part with a small amount of praise.

Alister was a fine player, but he lacked the brazen bravery to throw everything on the line on a single play, whereas Claudia was always teetering on the edge of being taken out of the game, and as such, was always performing combinations that were equal parts skill and luck. It was the secret sauce that they had needed as a team. Her complex play matched what Hoben and Jeffery were doing, but also supported the naked aggression power player styles of Alexander and Thrase.

"Team, that was a capitol game. Our next bout is this afternoon. The list has not been designed yet, so a plan cannot be devised," Hoben said. He walked over and put a hand on Alexander's shoulder like a proud father.

"You did well." With that, he walked away toward the stands to watch the lists.

"That was an exhilarating match," Claudia said, picking up her cards and taking a spin, her dress sweeping out as she twisted.

"Indeed, it was, indeed it was," Alexander said. "We would not have been able to do it without you. The strategy you employed in the second round during the response and reverse stage was just…"

He didn't have words to describe the way she had moved her cards around the table. It was like something from a deep, almost impossible theory crafting video he would have watched as a child.

"Just a little something I acquired while playing pick-up games on Tripoint Station," Claudia said with a wink. She started to walk away, then stopped and turned to Alexander and held out her hand. "Aren't you coming?"

He took her hand, feeling like a child again, his feet light as clouds. "I will follow wherever you want me to go," he said, butterflies fluttering inside him.

The Dreadstar Fury, Cassandra

The last two days of hard sailing had been filled with worry. Cassandra spent most of her time pacing in the Combat Information Center, waiting for the other shoe to drop. They were barreling headlong into danger that, on the surface, seemed so obvious. The more she thought about it, though, the more the facts obfuscated whatever plan she was trying to uncover. The who, the why, the how, all of that was hidden from her. All she knew was that everything aboard the *Key* had been too convenient; felt planted for them to find, and *only* them.

After hours of pacing and thinking, the only fact Cassandra knew was that somebody was hunting them. Deep down, in the places that she didn't like to think about, Cassandra knew that these were the same people who had tried to kill them six months ago. *The same people who killed you,* she thought quietly.

When she wasn't in the CIC—because Captain Rackland wouldn't allow her to *not* rest—Cassandra sat in her suite at the piano. Her hands were on the keys, the empty music sheet in front of her. It had been six months, and all she had was a title. *Farewell, My Heart*. It was an insipid title, not worthy of him, of how he had made her feel. How he *still* made her feel. Never before had the music been this backed up, this clogged.

She pressed a key; the sound was wrong, hollow, alone. A few more keys, a peddle, nothing. She couldn't find the words to address how she was feeling about Tiberius. Normally, the music led to the words for her, but this time...

Pure words had always been Hanna's domain. Cassandra existed on feeling and intuition.

She stood up and pushed the bench back under the piano and started to pace around again. She was supposed to be sleeping, but that wasn't going to happen. Joseph had given her something to help, but she didn't want to take it. *You can't be foggy.* The tea service was on the other side of the room. She walked over, poured a cup, and added a lump of sugar. Her leg started to twitch, bouncing up and down on the ball of her foot. She needed to move, needed to walk. If sleep wasn't going to happen, she could pace a larger area than just her rooms. Commanders toured their ships before battles, she knew, remembering an old tale from the Age of Chaos.

High Lord Admiral Christapher Spear had been in command of a fleet that had twenty Dreadstars and a hundred support ships. The kind of armada that would be impossible to field today, but which was common a thousand years ago—if you believed the stories. His fleet, in defense of NovaTerra, had headed toward the Shacko Strait, where an Alliance force twice his size was laying in weight. According to sailor legend, Spear toured his ship the night before, walking from end to end of the Dreadstar *Triumph*, speaking with every crewmember he encountered, learning their stories, who they were, and why they fought for the Republic; a republic that would last another five hundred years until the Wayfinder Wars. High Lord Spear would go on to win the battle, but he would not see the victory, killed when the *Triumph* was rammed by a dying Dreadstar from the other side.

The battle of Shacko Strate had been one of the last great slug fests between Dreadstars and their numbers would never be the same again. Eighty Dreadstars had entered that battle and only a handful limped away. It had been a victory for the Republic—not a good one, but a victory, nonetheless.

Cassandera hoped that they wouldn't end up like that, as she paced the ship. She hoped the movement would help knock the bits of the conspiracy loose in her mind, allow her to see what was coming.

Twenty minutes after starting her walk, she found herself in one of the less traveled sections of the ship, well below the flight pods where there was mostly just storage and readouts to make sure that everything stored here was still under pressure and at the correct volume. Cassandra was sure she had been to this part of the ship, but couldn't dredge the memory from her mind. Bent over a console was a middle-aged man. He was dressed in a jumpsuit with a yellow vest and two chevrons on his shoulder and four on his wrist, signaling this man had served aboard ship for at least fifteen years.

As her boots echoed on the grated deck, the man glanced over his shoulder, surprised, like a child who had been caught doing something wrong. He had an ugly face and an even worse scowl. It took a moment before the sour look drained from his face, once he realized who he was looking at. Snapping to attention, he saluted and then averted his eyes.

"My Lord," he said. Dropping her title, and using only the honorific, meant that he was a native of the ship, a true bannerman to House Cordova.

Lord Admiral Cassandra Cordova returned the salute, crisp to the point that the cracking of her wrist echoed in the long empty hallway. "At ease, Chief...?" she said, leaving him an opening to introduce himself.

A good Commander would know all their faces, she thought.

There are over a hundred thousand of them. You can't. Even I couldn't.

She could hear his voice, and knew that he was correct, again, as always.

"Chief Wyne, my lord," he said, resting his hands behind his back, at ease.

"It is good to meet you." Cassandra held out her gloved hand. The Chief's eyes darted again, for a moment looking around to see if there was somebody else, if he was being watched, what the setup was. Deciding that there was nothing, just a strange interruption to his night, he whipped his hand on his dark brown jumpsuit and then shook hers.

"You as well, my lord. We don't get to many officers or nobles down here in tank town."

"Tank town?" she asked.

"On account off all the storage tanks." He motioned behind him and then down the hallway. "Water, fuel, waste, exotic gaseous substances. If the *Fury* needs to store it in a liquid volume, then it's being stored down here." A small look of pride washed over his face. He knew that his job was important but unremarkable.

"How long have you been stationed down here in tank town?" she asked.

"My whole life, ma'am. My father was a tankie and his father was a tankie, as well. Gods willing, my son, when he is old enough, will be a tankie. The Wynes been keeping this ship watered and fueled since before your great-great grandfather came into its possession," Chief Wyne said, beaming with pride.

"I thank you for your service, Chief," Cassandra said. For the first time in a while, she wasn't sure what to say.

"It is our duty, my lord. The ship is as much ours as it is yours. We just take care of her in different ways," he said.

Cassandra let the words sit with her for a moment. Family, duty, honor, in the end, it was all in service of *Fury*. How each of them went about it, however...

Cassandra paused, the clarity stopped by the rigidity of her nature. *You cannot serve unless you are here.*

"Indeed, indeed. Can you show me what you were doing? Seems as I am a bit rusty with what goes on down here in tank town," Casaandra said, motioning for him to show her the controls.

"Of course." He turned and started to push a few buttons, any hint of aggravation or resistance melting away at her showing interest. "This here is the water tank for Gray sector, five-hundred thousand gallons of water. Our filtration system…"

Cassandra listened intently for the next hour as Chief Wyne walked her through his nighttime checklist. They looked at the water tanks for the whole ship, the fuel tanks, and the waste recycling system which went back into the water tanks. It was an interesting distraction and by the time they were done, she finally felt ready for bed.

That night, for the first time in a while, she felt like the commander she had once been; the kind interested in her crew, who knew the things they did. Most importantly, she slept soundly, without reliving the past.

***

"Approaching Station now," the voice of Lieutenant Richmond said over the comm. She was taking the fighter lead on this mission, with Erik and Hanna commanding the boarding party that was right behind her flight of fighters.

Cassandra looked down at the video feed coming in from the lead Rapier. The station was an old-style repurposed ore processing plant from the Low Republic era. Two rings wrapped around each other, like a bagel with a doughnut in the center. In the middle was a tower connected to the two rings, with one walkway on each quadrant. Coming off from the top and bottom were solar arrays that extended just far enough away from the station to be out of frame. At the moment, they were retracted. If not, they would have been bigger than the station itself. There was no nearby star, so the base would have been using rad scoops to refuel its atomic generator.

No star, no jump gate, nothing. Just a station hanging in the middle of an empty sector in an empty region of space. This was a perfect place for two things: smuggling and a trap. Both of which seemed likely to Cassandra.

"Commander, you can start the breach at your convenience. As soon as everything is made clear, I would like to come aboard," Cassandra said into the radio speaker. There was a crackle and silence for a moment.

"Repeat, Actual?" Erik's voice said.

"I will be coming aboard. Make the station ready, Commander. Actual out," Cassandra said.

He knew damn well what she was asking. Explaining herself over an open channel was not something she was going to do. The boy questioned her in public too often. It was his job, yes, but not on an open channel. That rankled her. Cassandra knew he meant well and was just protecting his Lord and mother. Standing next to her, Captain Rackland gave the Lord Admiral a raised eyebrow, indicating he thought she might have been too harsh with Erik.

"I know what I'm doing, Captain," she said, answering the question he was asking with body language alone.

"I do not doubt you for a moment," he said.

Less than a moment ago, though, those small half breaths…

He has always been the most supportive, the most loyal, she thought, Tiberius's voice echoing in the back of her mind.

"You have the conn, Captain," she said, giving him a crisp salute. The captain returned it. Cassandra pressed a few keys, and her theme began to play as she turned and started to exit the CIC through the main entrance.

"Lord Admiral departing!" the boatswain called, blowing his whistle that blended perfectly into the northern pipes and string instrumentation of Cassandra's leitmotif.

Cassandra returned to her quarters, questioning why she suddenly wanted to go aboard this dead space station. It didn't matter now; they were past the point of backing out. In her closet was her field coat. It looked exactly like her normal blue ship coat, only it was sewn with special fibers. This coat would stop most bullets and would dissipate some of the energy from a plasma blast. It wouldn't save her from the latter at close range, but it was better than nothing. Putting on the coat, she picked up her sword and pistol belt and strapped them on. She walked over to a display case ringed in glass. Pressing her thumb on the side of the case, it opened with a hiss. First, she removed an ornate plasma pistol. It was, at its core, a standard field issue weapon from two-hundred years ago, only it was gilded with Chimeras, the handle replaced with ivory and mother of pearl. She rolled the weapon in her hand before putting it into the holster that was attached to her thigh with magnets built into her pants.

Next, Cassandra removed a sword. It was like the one she currently had on, a cutlass with a ball shaped handguard. This one, though, was silver with small emeralds in the handle. The blade had a wavy, water-like pattern running all through the steel and the edge gleamed in the dim light of her cabin. Patrian Steel. There wasn't much left in existence. Both how to forge the metal and the mines themselves had been lost to time. Any family that had a Patrian Steel blade was considered wealthy regardless of station. If the repairs on *Fury* had cost much more, she would have had to leverage the sword to a bank for the funds.

The Sound had been in the family of whoever commanded *Fury* since before the Age of Chaos. It had been years since she had strapped on the ancestral weapons of House Cordova. She couldn't lie. It felt good to have them wrapped around her waist once again. Cassandra exited the room for the hanger deck.

It took an hour for them to make the station safe and to shuttle her over. During that time, she listened to the landing team's radio chatter. The station was abandoned, but not a tomb like the *Key* had been. Her children and their teams cleared each ring, then each room. It was to their advantage that the station was not that big, mostly empty space for cargo and a small crew. This was a transfer point and nothing more.

When her Hawkeye arrived, Erik and three marines were there to meet her. They all gave a crisp salute as she departed from the small craft, a different version of her personal theme playing from a small speaker in her belt. Lord Admiral Cordova returned the salute and fell in next to Erik as he led her to the station's operations center.

"What have we found so far?" she asked as they walked.

"Something interesting, but it is... You will just have to see it for yourself," Erik said. There was a stiff worry in his voice, the kind that she didn't hear often from him. He worried, but it was never this reserved and pulled back.

It only took them a moment to reach the station's operations center and it was a pathetic excuse for one. A single station stood in the middle of the room, with two chairs on either side of it. Cassandra wasn't surprised. Everything about this station was underwhelming for how dangerous it felt.

"There was nothing in their logs. We are scanning the hold now and I suspect we will detect the presence of atomics. The only trace of information in the whole system is the outside video feed. It was set to click on every time something came within five hundred klicks of the station, then follow them until they departed visual range," Erik said.

He pressed a few buttons and an image of two ships popped up. They were ships that Cassandra had never seen before, a totally alien design. They were bright crimson in color and looked like an arrowhead. Nowhere on the craft did she see engines or weapons of any kind. The surface was flat; no windows, no markings, just a crimson arrow cutting through space.

"These showed up three days ago, buzzed the station, and then left. What brings me dread is not that these ships are missing from our our database, but how they departed," Erik said, starting the video.

Cassandra watched as the two arrowheads came into visual range, quickly buzzing the station. The computer-controlled camera had trouble keeping up with them, let alone keeping them in focus. As they passed the station, the automated camera was steadier. Then there was a flash of light and both ships vanished.

"That is impossible," she whispered. Those two ships had jumped into Null Space... on their own. That was tech thought lost to time.

Lost to almost everybody, the price, she thought, a fleeting memory of her father and a dark set of stairs flashing in her mind, gone as quickly as they had appeared.

"It would seem that we are going to have to update our definition of the word impossible," Erik said.

"This does present us with an opportunity, though," Hanna said, walking into the room. It was clear that she had already seen the tape. She walked up and rewound the video feed and then played it again. The three of them watched in silence as the two ships blinked out of existence, using tech that only the Wayfinders had ever been able to replicate in over a thousand years.

"Go on, Major," Cassandera said.

"We must assume that traveling in Null space works the same whether you enter it with a jump gate or magic. Once you are there, the direction you go cannot change. We can follow along on that trajectory and, using the astrometric systems aboard *Fury*, try and figure out where they might have gone," Hanna said.

"Very good. Major, take this data and, at your earliest convenance, trace their trajectory, if you please," Cassandra said.

"Yes sir," Major Cordova said as she pressed a few keys and started to walk out of the room. The three marines, lingering in the room, followed her. That was when Cassandra noticed the hand motion her son had made, sending them away. He waited until the operations center was empty before speaking.

"I do not like how this smells, mother," Erik said, the concern in his voice making the drop of decorum feel almost calculated.

"It smells of rotten eggs and sour milk," Cassandra said, placing her hand on the hilt of *Sound*.

"It seems that whoever was trying to hunt us before has picked it up again," Erik said, crossing his arms.

"I'm not so sure. There are too many steps to this; too many clues we could have missed. No, the people who ambushed us at Hyroncore were not subtle about what they were doing. This is clearly a trap, breadcrumbs designed to draw us away. I have a feeling more than one group is gunning for our deaths," Cassandra said.

"Well, that is a comforting thought," Erik muttered.

"On that we agree."

"Then perhaps we don't scratch this itch. We call it in and leave it for the Confederation to deal with. They have access to information that we don't, ships that are faster in real space," Erik said. He was almost pleading with her to not give chase, to turn around. It was a trap and there was very little that she could do about it.

"Duty demands what we spring this trap, Commander," she said quietly.

"Duty demands it? They mean to kill us, to expunge our family and holdings from the galaxy!" His voice rose. There was the hot-headed son she had raised. He had been smart enough to send away the marines and to keep their party small. He wasn't going to repeat the issue from over the radio.

Erik Cordova was still going to speak his mind, though.

"Duty demands it. We can't let another innocent ship get murdered because we see knives in every shadow," Cassandra said, tightening her grip upon *Sound*. Erik gave her a hard look and she returned it. For a moment, the two Cordovas stood there, locked in a battle of wills.

"I recommend we set General Quarters until we have tracked these ships down and close the communications grid, leaving only one channel for us," Erik said, giving in. Her mind was made up and he was smart enough to recognize that.

"Agreed. I'm going to look around. Make it happen, Commander. Then have my ship ready to leave in an hour."

Cassandra turned and walked away from her son, who was quickly talking into his cravat to organize his mother's commands.

Ramparts, The Citadel, Lucas

Lucas walked down the hallway, back straight, boots echoing. If he was going to throw his rank around, if he was going to be in command of his group of friends, then he needed to act and look like it. The crisis of leadership that had been running through him since the night with Wingarf in the yard needed to be nipped in the bud. If he couldn't find the confidence inside himself to lead his people, to solve this mystery that Hyacinth had set them on, then the least he could do was project it on the outside. It was one of the things they had talked about during leadership academy. If you were having trouble finding the leadership inside of you, project the leadership on the outside and hope that you can pull some of that inside yourself.

It was working, a bit. Not as much as he would have liked, but something was better than nothing. Naomi and Joanna had left to chase down their leads. They all agreed that today was probably the last day they were going to have any kind of access to the facility before all hell broke loose. Lucas couldn't say why, but he had been on enough battlefields to understand that feeling, the petrichor of violence in the air. The Fellowship wouldn't be able to resist attacking the Militarum for long, the bloody demands of their dead god were too strong.

Once that happens, they are going to need you, Lucas told himself, repeating it like a mantra from a self-help book. His set of skills were not terribly useful for tracking down old lore or self-introspection, but they were good at keeping people alive and holding a position. There was no way he was going to let the Fellowship of the Cross take his friends. But, if this was to be how they met their end, then so be it—but he was going to kill scores of those fanatics first.

"Lucas, this way!" a young girl's voice yelled. Joanna. Lucas flipped around and saw teenage Joanna running, blood on her hands and face. Somebody else's blood. She rounded the corner. There was no teenage Lucas following her.

Taking a deep breath, he set off after her at a trot, quick enough so that he could keep up with the vision, but not so fast that it would look strange to anybody walking by—and there were so many people walking by now. *Will a vision run too far ahead of me so that I'll lose them or does it wait up?* Lucas wondered as he rounded the bend.

She was there again, still running. It looked like the vision was going to wait up for him, leading him somewhere. Lucas slowed back down to a leadership trot as two squads of Militarum troopers and their sergeant walked past. He nodded at the NCO who gave him a quick salute, his gloved hand hitting where Lucas assumed his brow would be under the clear chrome glass of the man's helmet. Lucas followed the vision for a few minutes until he was out on one of the Citadel's ramparts. Then, Joanna was gone. All that he could see were thousands of Militarum soldiers posted on the wall—rank upon rank of them—looking out over the barren rocky ground of Icarus, everything bathed in the red glow of the Barrier above them.

Standing in the center of a group of officers was Administrator Fel. She had changed and was dressed in a Militarum uniform. The only thing denoting her as a true Host'ire were the glasses, gloves, and star-steel blade that she wore in place of a saber. The group was conferring, talking over their plans and pointing both to locations on the wall and down into the rocky valley below, setting up lines and fields of fire.

Lucas walked over to the edge of the rampart where nobody currently stood and looked out over the field. It was a barren, rocky red waste. The Citadel was built at the dead end of a canyon. The mountains to either side were tall and steep. Getting soldiers down that approach would require power armor and jump packs. Any attacker that wanted to come and land troops at the Citadel was going to have to either come from orbit or right down the valley, which could easily be turned into a killing field.

Whatever it was that the Fellowship of the Cross was up to, Host'ire central command believed that they wanted to take the instillation. Otherwise, why even bother with a ground assault? The Citadel, like all planet-based instillations, was vulnerable to an orbital bombardment. The Host'ire banked on their control of the single gate that led here, coupled with the out of the way nature of the Citadel as defense enough.

Lucas could see it now. This was going to be a bloodbath that was going to make Hollister 9 look like a small act of violence. Angry footfalls heading his way filled Lucas's ears as he stood watching the field.

"Administrator," Lucas said, not turning to look at her. He was going to start this interaction with a powerplay.

"Knight-Commander," she responded, deadpan.

"I see we still remember each other's ranks," Lucas said.

"It does appear that is *all* you remember. Because I do believe I told you to stay out of the way. Don't you have more pressing matters?" Fel said, walking up next to him. The Militarum Troops in the area smartly stepped back, giving them space to talk without prying ears.

"You did indeed. Though I find it hard to ignore when the school that I was trained at, staffed by members of the order I am a part of, is about to be attacked by raving religious fanatics. It seems less than honorable," Lucas said.

There was a quiet moment between the two of them before Fel leaned in, her lips almost to his ear, so close he could feel her breath.

"I know what you seek. *She* called out to you, brought you to my doorstep," Fel whispered.

"How do you know about Hyacinth?" Lucas asked, the shock in his voice impossible to contain.

Instantly, he kicked himself for saying that. They were trying to keep this information to themselves and now, he'd just blurted out confirmation to the Administrator, the woman who had put his friend in re-education for years, who had no use for them.

"So that is her name. I think I knew that, once. You see, they don't stay in your mind for long. I'm surprised you know as much as you do," Fel said, pulling away from Lucas and looking back out over the canyon, clasping her hands behind her back.

"I don't understand," Lucas said, turning to look at her.

For the first time, there was no fire in Fel's aura. She was just looking out over the distance, lost in thought.

"There are many secrets buried here at the Citadel. I cannot even pretend to know all of them. Some are so deep and so arcane that they defy what we understand. They are what some would call heresy," Fel said.

"But you wouldn't?" Lucas said.

"Perhaps if confronted with them. Until then, I just call them interesting academic mysteries that are for people like your friend Joanna to solve," Fel said.

"Well then, Administrator, I shall leave you to prepping the troops. May you have good luck in the wars to come," Lucas said quietly, turning to look at her again.

It seemed that, for a moment, Fel's stance had softened, that she was relaxing toward them. It was only a brief moment and passed as fast as it had appeared.

"You as well, Knight-Commander. Now, smartly see yourself off my battlefield!" she said, making sure the last part was said loudly and for effect. Fel then clapped him on the shoulder and then smashed her fist into her chest twice. She turned smartly on her heel, swooshing her long green frock coat, as she returned to her officers and preparations.

Fel knew what they were here for. Had she always known? Was that why she let Rostov out of re-education with so little a fight? Questions were racing through Lucas's mind. Did she know about Joanna's research? Suddenly, he was very worried for her, the chivalric knight that lived inside Lucas flaring up, ready to run to the library and defend his lady.

Your lady? He stood there for a moment with his emotions, feeling them out, trying to decide what to do next. Lucas needed to know what his people were finding so that he could solve this and keep them safe. That was what was important, all of them making it off this rock and staying together.

"Lucas!" a voice called.

It was young Joanna, same as before, with blood on her hands. She waved for him to follow. As she ran up the rampart, a vision of himself as a child ran past him, keeping up with Joanna. His hands were bloody as well. Not his blood; Hyacinth's, Jasper's. Lucas followed. He remembered this moment. It was slowly clearing in his mind.

He got to the top of the rampart just in time to see the two memories embracing. He was holding Joanna tight.

"I'll never let you go. I won't let anything happen to you," he said.

Lucas mouthed the words as the memory of himself said them, the knight from all the stories making a grand entrance.

"I know you won't," Joanna said, reaching her hand up and touching his face, getting blood on his cheek.

He could feel her warm hand again. He wanted to kiss her. He *did* kiss her twenty years ago, and now, reflected in this memory. As the two teens kissed, they faded away. He had loved her then, and he had abandoned her; abandoned *all* of them. He wasn't going to let that happen again. This time, he was in complete control of his fate. There was nobody who could drag him away with order, no indoctrination that would cloud his thinking. His mind was his own for what felt like the first time.

The emotions came flooding back. He wanted to run to her, not to protect her, but to wrap his arms around her; to feel her lips upon his, her body in his hands. Lucas closed his eyes and breathed in and out, clearing away the emotions and the confusion. He still felt what he felt, but it wasn't washing over him, out of control, attempting to dictate what he did. He would talk to her tonight; talk to *all* of them tonight. Lucas was sure that he wasn't alone in having his emotions ramped up here and feeling a connection that bordered on something deeper than mere friendship for all of them.

As Lucas started to walk down the rampart, away from where the Militarum were setting up, he saw a shadow. It moved at a strange angle, too fast, almost like it was drifting where people shouldn't be.

Crouching down himself, Lucas reached out with the Null, seeing if he could sense people in front of him. Could these be Fellowship of the Cross intruders? Was the Citadel already that compromised? If he killed them, would Fel be happy or mad that he had continued to get in her way? By all accounts, he should just walk away now and not worry about it, leave whoever he had seen to do whatever it was they were going to do. But Lucas couldn't. He needed to know, compelled to have all the information possible before leaving the rampart.

Creeping forward with shallow steps, the wall rose. Lucas walked forward, then made himself even lower as he reached the apex of the arch. There was a small amount of flat wall, maybe ten meters, before the stairs started down again.

Dropping to the ground, Lucas crawled forward. Reaching farther with the Null, he could feel two people, paranoia radiating off them. It was a rare thing, to feel emotions through the Null. Normally, that was a skill reserved for people who had studied at the Academy or learned their trade in the Unaligned Planets. If it was a strong emotion, though, one that was consuming the person feeling it, then sometimes he could detect it.

Lucas was almost down the steps when he saw them. Two men standing at the edge of the wall, within the doorway of the eastern tower. Paranoia looked like smoke. If you looked at it long enough, one could almost see faces manifesting, looking over their shoulders. Lucas had never been able to pick up on this emotion before it was fear. He was an expert at being on the other side of fear. He had read about other emotions and how they manifested. It all had seemed like noble nonsense to him. The Null, in contrast, was easy to understand. It was existence and he could control that. There was nothing more to it. Yet here, he was looking at two men who almost stank with how worried and paranoid they were. Did he dare get closer? He needed to know who they were. The knight inside of him would not let this go.

Lucas shimmied his way across the landing to the rampart on the parade field side of the wall. Looking up, both hooded figures were turned away from him. Lucas popped up, grabbing the small wall and hoisted himself over. He pushed against the wall, holding on with both hands. Reaching into the Null, he made the air below his feet hard, taking some of the weight off his hands. Then he started to shimmy forward, extending the solid Null field under his feet, while pulling it in from behind. This was a very standard hostage rescue tactic for sneaking past guards on walls. Lucas figured it would be just as good for eavesdropping on a secret meeting.

After a few minutes, Lucas was as close as he dared get. Peeking his head up, he got a better look at the two men. He didn't recognize the one in the green hood, only making out his chin, his face covered in shadow. The other man, though... While Lucas couldn't see his face, he recognized the voice, and there were only so many grizzled old knights who were missing an arm at the Citadel.

"I will make sure the gates have been weakened. Provided you can survive the wave of fire, the Citadel should be open to you," Wingarf said.

"What about the lower sections?" the hooded man asked, his voice a hiss of anger that didn't sit right with Lucas, sounding wrong in his ears.

"The blood pact will lead us to the door, don't worry," he said.

"I'm not worried. Many faithful will soon die, and I would see that their blood is not spilled pointlessly," the cloaked man said. He was clearly a member of the Fellowship.

"Don't you all want to die and see your corpse god?" Wingarf said dismissively.

"We want to die *serving* him, to open the Eye. We cannot do that unless we secure what is below. Find the door or none of the power will be yours," the cloaked man said, poking Wingarf in the chest before turning with a flourish of his cloak and walking away.

Lucas had heard enough. He pulled his hands away from the rampart and let the Null from under his feet vanish. Falling, he turned around and started to cushion the air around him so when he hit the ground, it was as if he had been light as a falling feather. Looking around, Lucas didn't see anyone, so he quickly ran for the nearest door to get back inside the Citadel and away from Wingarf, away from the old Master-at-Arms who was about to sell all of them out. Getting inside, Lucas found a bench and sat down under a large flag emblazoned with the symbols of the Host'ire.

Lucas wasn't sure what do to. Did he tell Fel? Did he follow up on his own? Whatever it was, the damage had already been done. So much was starting to fall into place, why Wingarf had been so angry at them, so easily goaded into a fight. He was looking to kill them, but also, it seemed as though he needed them.

The turning on the Host'ire wasn't what rankled him—damn it, all but one of his own friends wanted to gut the order and see it burn. No, it was what he'd learned. What had the man from the Fellowship said? *'The blood pact with lead us to the door?' 'Find it or none of the power is yours?'*

What did *that* mean?

Looking down at his hands, Lucas saw the memory of him and Joanna both bloody, embracing, while deep inside his mind, he remembered a darkness and Hyacinth running with Essex. Had they dared follow?

More importantly, would they now?

Library, The Citadel, Joanna

The library was empty. The vast room was quiet. All she could hear were the faint sounds of the air recycling. There were no librarians, no Militarum troopers, nobody but her. As a child, all she had ever wanted was a library all to herself, the room empty and quiet, so she could read as much as she wanted anywhere she wanted; the freedom to gasp and yell at the characters in whatever book she was reading. They always made bad choices and she always wanted to loudly scold them. Nowhere in her life was that allowed or accepted behavior. Yet now that she had the opportunity to experience an empty library, all she wanted was to see somebody. To hear footsteps, to see Tor walk out of his private rack on the top floor and greet her. There was nothing, just a vast emptiness filled with books.

Joanna walked to the records desk in the center of the first floor. Perhaps there would be some indication of where everybody was. She needed to keep reading her book, but at the same time, she also wanted to talk to Tor again, wanted to ask him questions about the Wayfinders, about what he knew that he wasn't telling her. Now that she had a better idea of what to ask, he was nowhere to be seen; vanished.

Sitting in the center of the records desk was a blank slip of paper. Joanna picked it up and instantly she could feel something moving through her skin. It tingled, like rubbing your feet across a carpeted floor to build up static electricity or like a leg that had fallen asleep after sitting for too long. Flipping the page over, the other side was blank as well.

Joanna cocked her head to the side, closed her eyes and reached out through the Null. Breathing out, she opened her eyes again, and there were words. A Null cypher. *Tor, you bastard, this is no time for mysteries.*

Follow the steps through your memories, the bond in blood must be complete before the way can be opened was written on the paper in flowing, elaborate handwriting. Joanna recognized it instantly as Tor's. He was trying to tell her something, Joanna just wasn't sure what that thing was. It couldn't be said out loud, clearly, for fear of somebody hearing; of somebody accusing them of heresy, leading to both of them being put before a firing squad, or worse. Joanna was already guilty of the crime, but this, something about whatever this note was implying, felt so much worse. Joanna had no love for the Host'ire or their belief structure, but even she understood that some of the things they had labeled heretical—like tapping into the Shadow below the Null—was to protect people. This, though? It felt like something they wanted hidden because it was embarrassing, dangerous; the kind of secret that could bring down the order.

"Help!" a young girl's voice called out, echoing through the cavernous library. Joanna spun around and saw the young girl on the floor. She had been hit, there was blood dribbling from her mouth, a long trail of bloody spittle and a tooth by her hands. Standing over her was a much larger child, a teenager, a bully, a ghost.

Jasper.

Instantly, Joanna knew where she was, what she was seeing. The young blonde girl, whose face she could finally see, was Hyacinth. *This* was the day that everything had changed, that the visions had desperately been leading them toward.

On the floor, leading to where Hyacinth was struggling to stand, Joanna saw more Null ink. A trail, a trail though her memories, though the pain of that day. She knew what had to be done. Slowly, Joanna started to walk forward. There was no rush. She couldn't actually help Hyacinth. Even the most powerful Host'ire couldn't bend time to their will. At least, she *hoped* that there wasn't one powerful enough to do that.

Jasper walked forward and, reaching down, he grabbed Hyacinth by her shirt, pulling her up. Joanna hadn't realized just how wafer thin of a thing she was. Somehow, Joanna pictured her as a little pudgy girl like her. Why else would people have been so mean? But no, she was a rail, beyond thin, almost looking malnourished.

"Get away from her!" a young boy's voice called from across the library.

Joanna turned. There was more ink leading toward where the teen was standing. He was furious, the red in his face looked like it was going to catch his long blond hair on fire. Essex. Their missing friend, the one who had come to the Citadel with Hyacinth but had not returned when she called. If this was one of her books, Joanna would have called that narratively convenient, taking a character off the board who knew too much. This wasn't one of her books, though, and the simple answer was that he was probably dead somewhere, lost and forgotten.

"Oh look, the little child has come to collect his woman. Have you poked her yet, Essex? Or do I get to crack her open and make her squeal?" Jasper taunted.

There was nothing but hate and malice in his voice. The worst kind of person. He saw everybody as a plaything for his own amusement. Essex started to run forward, screaming as he did. The boy wasn't much bigger than Hyacinth. Both of them had been runts, easy prey for a bully like Jasper. She shuddered to think where he would be today, what might have happened to him, if he wasn't already rotting underneath her feet.

Joanna stepped to the side, letting Essex run by her as she followed the ink on the floor. Jasper threw Hyacinth at Essex. She hit him and both grunted as they fell to the ground in a knot of spindly limbs. The boy started to lightly cry, as Hyacinth whimpered.

Her heart hurt for them. Joanna wanted to run over and protect them, to draw her blade and cut Jasper down. It would be like getting to finally exercise her frustrations that all the highborn at the Academy had hoisted upon her. But she couldn't help them and so she walked, turning her back on the past, a tear siding down from under her sunglasses and across her cheek. Joanna let it hit the ground, let the emotions come unbothered.

The ink splotches led up the steps to the second level of the library.

"Form up on me!" Joanna heard Lucas yell.

She turned and, on this level, she saw teenaged Lucas standing, a paperweight in his hand. Coming up on either side of him was Rostov and Naomi, anger and resolve written across their faces. Behind them, Joanna saw herself keeping an eye on the rear. Making sure that they wouldn't get flanked, making sure that there were no professors who would get in the way.

She remembered now how angry she was, not just at Jasper, but at the staff for letting this happen. Naomi had gone to Professor Rickman—she'd loved that woman, but it hadn't mattered. She had done nothing to help them. She had just looked down at her work and slunk away. What kind of power did a common bully have that he could make grown adults turn into such cowards? Joanna had wondered about that for years. The older she got, the more she learned, and realized that the abuse was part of the training. Not every professor was okay with it, but all of them went along with it, for fear of rocking the boat. Her hands balled into fists, anger starting to build up inside her again. She might not be able to help the kids, but she could still deck that cowardly professor if she saw her again.

Teenage Lucas let out a battle cry that was picked up by the three teenage memories around him. They charged forward. Joanna looked up and saw Jasper reel back as the three kids descended upon him. The memory of her didn't follow, instead bending down and helping Essex and Hyacinth pull themselves apart. As soon as he was free, Essex charged into the fight, screaming expletives and spitting blood.

Hyacinth didn't move.

"You have been chosen; blood has been spilled," Hyacinth whispered.

That's a damned strange thing for a teenager to say, Joanna thought as she watched the teen version of herself give the bloodied girl a confused look. Clearly, this was not a new thought, though it was starting to make more sense now than it had twenty years ago.

The paperweight in Lucas's hand made contact with Jasper's face. Blood went flying. The older boy's jaw was broken. Lucas stopped for a moment, dropping the paper weight as he stepped backward, looking at the violence he had just committed. Essex had no problem with it, sliding in under Lucas and grabbing the hunk of solid crystal that once had only been used to hold papers on a long-forgotten professor's desk.

Joanna turned away. She didn't need to see this again. Once was enough. She remembered now what was going to happen. Essex was going to smash in Jasper's skull until there was no head left on the boy. Once the violence ended, they'd all run.

The sounds of crystal squishing through viscera and bone stopped, replaced by humming and sloshing water. Joanna turned around to see Mister Deverox, the janitor, cleaning up the memory, puffs of smoke and violence being swept away by his mop. The water was not turning red, didn't reflect the violence that she had just witnessed.

"Do not mind me, child. Just making sure everything is clean. We wouldn't want you slipping on anything," he said, tapping his large nose as he placed down a yellow placard warning that the floor was wet.

He started to hum again as he walked away. He didn't look any different. Joanna remembered Mister Deverox. He was an old man covered in wrinkles who walked slowly. This was the same man, and it didn't look like he had aged a day.

She walked forward, sliding her foot on the wet floor. The water was real. He was here and not just a memory. Pushing away the children and the violence, Joanna reached into the Null again and found the inky footsteps. She followed them farther toward the second set of stairs, the ones that led up to the private racks of the professors.

"Lucas!" It was her voice yelling from the top of the stairs. Joanna started to walk forward. Lucas ran up, wrapping his arms around her.

"I'll never let you go. I won't let anything happen to you," he said.

A feeling of safety and knightly honor filled her. She wanted to run and find him now and wrap her arms around him again.

"I know," she said at the same time as her younger self.

This is where she had kissed him, a kiss that stayed with her for years, that propelled her though so much; the hope that he would come back, that he would never let go. The memory was foggy, but she was sure that they had all been pulled apart, shunted into different orders so that they could be good little fascists like the Host'ire wanted. She loved Lucas, but the brainwashing had worked better on him. Still, he had left and that had stung for years, wrenching deep into her soul. She knew that things were different now. He was here and she wasn't going to let him go.

She ran her hands across her lips as the children ran away, and she started up the steps. The taste of blood filled her mouth, but her fingers were clean. Their faces had been bloody then...

Joanna took her glasses off, rubbing her eyes before opening them wide, letting the Null fill her. She needed to see the world as it was, as it had been. No more hiding behind the sunglasses, behind the oppression.

At the top of the stairs, she saw Essex carrying away Hyacinth. The girl was limping, dragging, and there was an unnatural strength in him as he carried her. She reached her arm up and weakly pointed forward. Joanna saw light, a spike of Null energy, and then the vision was gone. All that remained, glowing like a star carved into the ground, were the last three splotches of ink. She followed them, still running her hands over her lips, that twenty year old kiss lingering in her mind.

At the end was a pile of papers sitting on some books. One was an envelope, sealed with glowing wax. She picked it up. Snapping the wax, Joanna opened the envelope and there was an old, teletype communication message.

To: *Host'ire Command*

From: *Knight-Major Morgana Fel*

Message Follows: *The elevator has been found. Below the Citadel is a vast network of halls. I was not able to explore farther at present. Suspect current administration is keeping secrets from my investigation into the murder and missing students.*

I shall report back soon

Message ends

Written on a small card in Tor's excellent script, it read, *Connect the blood pact, open your eyes and see her.*

Novagrad, Alexander

Their second match that afternoon had not been the blitz to victory that their first one was. They drew a team from House Dasonic, who lived up to their sigil of four shields on a starry field. Every one of their players had prioritized defense over offense. The first three rounds had just been a wash of counters and redirects as the five of them unleashed round after round of hellish attacks. Finally, on the fourth round, House Vanpro attacked, and it was a bruising assault because they had spent so many cards already cracking their shields. Alexander and Claudia had worked together to crack open their last defensive line, at the cost of her deck. But once their gooey insides were exposed, Thrase and Hoben descended upon House Vanpro like starving monsters from a midnight movie. The fifth round had been fast, and they folded before finishing out the game.

Five rounds were a blessing. The match between Novagrad Tech and Tragatie Confederate University was still ongoing. Twenty rounds so far. The record for longest game of Peculiar Pentagon was thirty-five rounds. There were rumblings that the two teams were in league with each other and trying to beat the record. Alexander didn't think that was the case. He and Claudia had watched three rounds before they said good afternoon and retired to get ready for the evening's ball. The playing had been masterful, on a level that he almost didn't understand. It was a combination of instinct, math, and pure gusto. If they were in league with each other, then they were putting on quite the performance and would be punished accordingly if caught. Cheating was not taken lightly in Peculiar Pentagon, and at this level, it would mean a lifetime ban from both organized play and any store that was officially licensed to sell cards.

That match had been the talk of the house while they were getting ready. Hoben and Thrase were convinced that the two teams were working together, while Jeffery, like Alexander, fell on the other side, saying they were on the level. Alexander figured Thrase and Hoben saw collusion because they could not conceive of even wanting to play a game that lasted that long—or not playing so aggressively that anything more than five rounds was impossible. Jeffery had said he could see the logic in their moves each time and that it was the luck of the draw that two teams matched perfectly in such a way that victory might not even be possible. Everybody had agreed that nobody was going to concede because both teams had lost their first bouts, making the match an elimination round.

Alexander was ready to put aside thoughts of cards and exchange them for a head of dancing, flirting, and love. Tonight's ball was not as formal as the kickoff event, because it was not an official part of the Novagrad elite's marriage season. This left him free to pick a far more interesting outfit from his wardrobe than just a black coat and yellow vest. Tonight, Alexander decided, since they had achieved victory on a field of battle, that he would wear something more akin to the uniforms of his family. It was far from official, but it was evocative.

Wearing the emblems of rank and office were not allowed, unless all-out war had been declared. By nature of being the child of a Space Lord who was raised upon a Dreadstar, he would be given a commission as a Lieutenant if such an event were to happen. Thankfully, all-out war had never been declared in the Confederation's history.

He put on his big boots and creme-colored capris. He followed that with a pressed high-collared white shirt and yellow vest. Alexander then tied on a jet-black cravat. It was, in fact, dyed with a rare pure-black ink that was designed to pull in one's eye. Then he topped it with a long heavy blue jacket with gold trim and buttons. There were no epaulets, or signs of rank, but to the normal noble, it had the appearance of a navy uniform.

The pièce de résistance of the outfit, though, was his sword belt. It looked like a normal black leather belt with a golden sash. Where the empty scabbard would have been for an event like this, Alexander had attached a decorative hilt designed to look like *the Sound*. Contained inside this empty hilt was a small holographic projector that could simulate the look of a scabbard. Thus, he had something to hold, but did not have to worry about an actual sword breaking rules or being in his way during a dance.

This ball was being held at another large mansion, this one on the edge of West Bridge Park, located in the center of one of the richest neighborhoods in the city. It was where families with no title, but unfathomable generational wealth, lived.

This house was currently being occupied by new money. Nathanial Webb had, during his twenty-year career as a Peculiar Pentagon player, never lost a match. This netted him millions of credits in winnings and millions more in endorsement deals. Then he married the heiress to a shipping company and those millions looked small. He threw a party after the first day of the tournament every six years—and usually at some other point during the other five days, when the Minister's Tournament was not being held.

The house was lavish. From the front, it looked like all the other thin brownstones that lined the street. Five stories tall, with lavender shutters and walls of rotating art upon the bricks. The real trick of the house was that the Webbs owned the block behind it and the estate expanded out that way, leading to an inner-city mansion that had thirty guest rooms and two large ballrooms.

The party tonight was being held in the Jungle Room. It was a vaulted space five stories high with balconies overlooking each floor. Vines and moss hung from everything. Throughout the room, along the edges, were giant trees groomed at the top to mingle together to create a canopy of leaves and nature. Birds of all shapes and colors flew freely through the Jungle Room, along with butterflies and other designer insects whose wings were holograms that displayed the logos of companies that were sponsoring the tournament. Nathanial Webb might have married rich, but he was a hustler at heart.

"There is so much green," Claudia whispered, walking through the ballroom looking up at the canopy of foliage, with its dancing birds and painterly sunlight. There was a pep in her step, and she did a little spin, which flicked out her long flowing red dress.

Like earlier in the afternoon, she was dressed in an outfit that revealed nothing but insinuated everything. The red was deep and bloody. Whatever was holding it all together had been hidden away, leaving the impression that the fabric had grown from her skin. Her shoes were a sparkling red, matching her gloves. The trail of her dress had a small holographic projector that made it look like she was leaving a trail of autumnal foliage in her wake.

Alexander took her hand, raised his arm and spun her around again before pulling her close to him.

"Not near as much green as what is captured within the emerald forests of your eyes," he whispered.

She blushed and looked at him deeply. He blinked, getting lost within those emerald fields. Eyes that had not left his imagination since they had first met.

"You are too kind, my lord," she said, after a moment. She was letting him get lost in her beauty, he knew it, and was perfectly willing to wander in the maze for all eternity, if it meant that he never had to take his eyes off her.

"For you, my lady, I would do anything," Alexander said.

He spun her around again and then let her go. She cascaded out to the dance floor, holographic leaves spilling from her train as she spun. Claudia stopped, facing away from him. Her foot hit the floor with a loud tap, she then snapped around, first her head, then her torso; a dancer's precision to the movements. She reached her arm out to him. Alexander gracefully walked out onto the dance floor and took her hand.

For the next twenty minutes, they were the envy of the entire room as they moved with the music. Once Claudia realized they were being watched, she did a long spin, finishing with a pirouette, before taking a bow as cheering and clapping filled the room. Claudia took in the applause and adoration. Alexander felt exposed, slightly embarrassed to be sharing this intimate moment with the entire assembled ball. Yet it was a small price to pay to get to see Claudia dance. A small price to get to be near her, for his hand to touch hers, and in the end, she was dancing with *him*, and nobody else.

As they were exiting the dance floor, and all eyes were upon them, Alexander felt one set more than the others. Standing next to Nathanial Webb, who was clapping and cheering, was a quiet man. He was dressed modestly, given the occasion. A black jacket and vest over a white shirt. His dark brown hair was slicked back, and his face had a profoundly untrustworthy look to it, almost reptilian in nature. Alexander couldn't place what it was about this man that made him feel uneasy, but he stood out from the crowed and his eyes seemed to follow them like lasers as a small smile crossed his face. The kind of smile that put a pit in Alexander's gut.

A moment later, they were off the dance floor, and more couples had filed past them for a line dance. In the shuffle, Alexander lost his view of this unsettling snake of a man, and his world was filled with only Claudia once more.

"That was quiet the performance," Alexander said, taking two glasses of sparkling wine off a passing try, handing one to Claudia.

She finished half the glass in a single sip. Sweat was forming just on the sides of her hairline and neck of her outfit. For a brief moment, he wanted to pull her out of the dress to free her from its stifling confines.

"Thank you. It has been a long time since I had a partner who could even pretend to keep up with me," she said. "Most men of birth ditch their dancing classes for more time with their dance of death."

"Men of my ilk do see dancing as an activity that should be learned and then dropped as soon as it has netted them a noble lady. Thankfully, my upbringing allowed me to learn both the dance of the ball *and* the dance of death," Alexander said, taking a sip of his own drink. He very much looked like a man who would care more about a sword fight than a dance right now, with his heavy blue navy jacket and fake sword.

"It is their loss, for sure. Look at them, hiding in the corner of the room in their little knots," Claudia said, pointing to the men of the ball. Many of them were segregated into little clusters of four or five.

"They are afraid to truly dress in colors to embrace life. They talk shop with their whiskey while glancing at the dance floor, as if it's a place of horror and embarrassment," she continued.

Alexander couldn't argue. Claudia seemed to have the right of them. So many men were afraid of color and a fancy drink. For as far as they had come, they were always a step behind, just waiting in the wings.

"That is what I enjoy about spending time with you, Alexander. There is no pretense to this idea of being the serious man. You live your life how you want to. That is the true courage that women are looking for," Claudia said.

"I will admit, I've never thought of myself as a man of courage. The rest of my family, *they* have courage. I, well…" He was about to say something about spending all day in a lab, but caught himself. That was information that she wasn't allowed to know. As far as any and everybody knew, he was just a spoiled rich kid still going to university long after graduation should have happened.

"You spend your days chasing new knowledge. I do not discount the courage of those who fly fighters and command a Dreadstar, but it is so simple, so base," Claudia said. "Though, I am sure that any member of a family that raised you would not be afraid to step on the dance floor and show their skills."

"My twin sister, Hanna, would match you move-for-move upon the floor," Alexander said with fondness for the sister he had gotten to spend so many years growing up next to. "My brother, though, he would be in one of those little knots of scared boys. With family, in places he is comfortable, the emotions and feeling are worn upon his sleeve, but parties… Those have never been his forte."

"And what of your mother, the Lord Admiral Cordova? Would she stay away from the fray with the other Admirals and Generals, their cigars and brandy being the only enjoyment of the night?" Claudia asked.

Alexander took a deep breath. His mother was a sore spot and there was no way that Claudia could have known that. He didn't want to think about her right now, but also didn't want to give the impression that there was something wrong between the two of them. That was a family matter, and while he could feel himself quickly falling headlong in love with Claudia, she was not family.

Yet.

"My mother never had much time for the pomp of the admiralty. She would have found herself in the pit with the orchestra by the end of the night, having slipped in an original composition. She could never pass up the opportunity to hear a live orchestra play her music," Alexander said fondly, remembering the theme that she had composed for him and his sister after they had been born. She had worked on it for the nine months they had been gestating in the lab and then for years afterward, adapting it to their personalities.

The theme danced in his head. It started out jaunty, fiddles and small flutes, before the pipes and brass started to fill the sonic space. For a moment, he was lost in it, his hand falling to the side and sadly moving with the music that only he could hear.

"I am sorry, did I hit a sore spot?" Claudia asked after a moment of Alexander standing there quietly, playing music in his mind, his eyes somewhere else.

"Slightly. My mother and I have not been on the best of terms lately. She sees my staying at university as abandoning the family and my duty. I was always her baby, even though Hanna and I were birthed from our chambers at the exact same time."

"It is hard when the child leaves the nest. My father was quite broken up when my brother left home to join the military. He wanted him to stay and learn how to run the family. 'The army is for second sons,' he always said." She paused and took a sip of her drink, looking at him again with her deep green eyes, sympathy just cascading from them. "He came around and they managed to reconcile in the end, before both of their ends," she said quietly.

"Opening wounds seems to be a hobby tonight," Alexander said.

"No, that was many years ago. I came along late in my father's life, quite by accident," Claudia said with a brush of her hand, letting him know that it was not anything he needed to worry about. "The moral is that there is always time. I am sure that your mother will come around once she truly sees what an amazing man you have become."

Claudia leaned forward and gave him a light kiss on the cheek. Her lips felt wonderful against his skin. They were soft and perfect.

"Put that aside. There is dancing to do," she whispered into his ear. Before he could say anything else, she grabbed his hand and pulled him out to the dance floor again.

They danced the night away. By the time the fifth dance had finished, their host released a flock of birds to fill the room, their chirping and singing dazzling the whole audience in attendance. Both Alexander and Claudia clapped at the display. As the next dance was about to start, she took his hand and pulled him close to her.

"I think we have shown them up enough. How about we retire to somewhere more comfortable?" she whispered into his ear.

Instantly, Alexander could feel himself becoming stiff with interest.

It took fifteen minutes for them to get back to House Hoben. The lights were off and nobody was home. It was perfect. Alexander unlocked the door and before he could turn on the lights, Claudia was on him. Her lips were as soft as he had known they would be and she kissed him with such force and passion that he never wanted to do anything more than be with her.

Alexander didn't know the house well—definitely not well enough to guide her to his room with the lights off. He wasn't going to stop kissing her, though, and so they made a go of it. Halfway through the living room, there was a crash as her skirts rolled across the coffee table, knocking glasses and papers onto the hard floor.

"Oops," Claudia said with a giggle at the commotion.

They were only apart for a moment before Alexander pulled her back to him and kept kissing her, their tongues wrapping around each other. His back hit the wall of the hallway with a thud. He readjusted and kept walking backward, almost losing his footing, the thrill of ecstasy and wine filling his head. The third door. He kicked backward—thankfully, it wasn't fully closed—and they fell into his room.

"Lights, fifty percent," Alexander said.

The lights in the room came on dimly. He could see Claudia standing in front of him. In that moment, she looked more attractive than any woman that he had ever seen before. Any hesitation that *might* have been brought on by the unread message still sitting in his inbox faded away.

This was exactly where he was meant to be.

Alexander pulled off his coat and reached up toward his cravat. Claudia was on him again, moving his hand away as she kissed him. He could feel her hand reaching up and working the knot, pulling the black cravat away from his neck. There was a rush of cool air on his chest as his shirt opened, exposing his sweaty body to the room's climate control. Hoben always kept the house too cold. Claudia pushed Alexander onto the bed, and he just managed to catch himself before falling backward. She was standing over him—in that stunning, impossibly tight red dress—and in that moment, his stupid logical nerd brain kicked in and he felt compelled to speak.

"I just have to know; how do you get into and out of that?" he asked, motioning to the garment. Claudia gave him a wry toothy smile, full of mischief and sex.

"Wouldn't you like to know, Mister Cordova," she said, leaning forward and putting a finger on his lip as she started to work on pulling off his fancy sword belt and britches.

"I very much would like to," he said.

You idiot, why would you say it like that? Stupid.

Claudia stopped working on his britches with a single button left to undo. His cock was throbbing with her hands and face so close. She pulled back and stood up, almost like a femme fatale in an erotic mystery thriller. A shiver of excitement ran through his body.

Standing regal, stunning, exquisite—every adjective that Alexander knew—Claudia touched a single finger to the top of her collar right under her chin. Instantly, he could see the seams of the dress and there was a zipper that ran from her throat all the way to the bottom of her corset. The same holographic field that was creating the leaves was hiding the construction of the garment. She moved her finger down from her throat, passing over her breasts and to just below her belly button. The dress came open, and he could start to see the outline of her figure, her soft skin.

Claudia threw out her arms and the dress lost all its ridged from and fell to the ground. She stood naked in front of him.

His dreams, no matter how vivid they had been, did not prepare him for this moment. They looked at each other and then, faster than he thought possible, she was on him again. His pants were on the floor. She grabbed his hard cock and gave him that same wry smile that he loved so much. This was the dance he had been waiting for.

Astral Metrological Center, Fury, Cassandra

They had been at a hard sail for the last twelve hours, tracking the course of the mystery ships that had been seen on the video from the station. Cassandra paced, contemplating if this had been the right call to make, to take her ship deeper into the doldrums, chasing after phantoms that had cracked open a lost technology. Only five ships in the Confederation could jump like that. She commanded one and didn't know how it worked; was sure it was a lost art, an impossibility.

It's not impossible, there is just a price, a voice said in the back of her mind, a fragment of a memory, something her father had said.

There were so many fragments of things he had said before his death. Those had been chaotic, violent years. No, it was impossible—that tech was lost, cost too much. She was wasting their time chasing phantoms into a region of space that the Confederacy didn't control, where law and order was only acquired with a gun and a tenuous social contract between folks. Yet try as the rational side of her brain might to convince her otherwise, Cassandra knew that they had to stay on this course, had to see this to its end. Something was pulling, calling her. She wondered if it was just her intuition as a line officer, or something more.

"And that, Lord Admiral, is why the storms are so much worse in these sections of space," a voice said.

Cassandra blinked, coming back to herself, to where she was: the Astral Metrological Center, deep within the bowels of *Fury*. All over, there were screens showing space weather data, storms and currents of particles. In the middle of all of it was a tall, middle-aged man who was far too excited about the weather, astral or otherwise.

"Back up again. You lost me there for a moment," Cassandra said.

She had been called down here by the ship's Astral Metrologist, Doctor Frydan, because he wanted to talk to her about the weather in this region of space. She had never put much stock into this science. Yes, there were storms produced by the Barrier, but predicting how they would travel seemed more like magic than science to her. If more of their predictions over the years had been correct, or if there were more storms in Confederation space, then maybe but… she just didn't know. Hell, even forecasting the weather on a planet was a touchy, half data, half feeling kind of science.

"As I was saying, the use of jump gates and other tech to punch into Null space causes the magnetic nebulous storms to cascade and then fall apart. Out here, though, where there are no jump gates, nothing ripping into the Null, the storms are able to move unabated. In fact, every great solar hurricane that we track comes out of these doldrum regions of space. We just don't see them coming as fast as would be helpful for science, because there are no listening posts, no weather centers, nothing out here," Doctor Frydan said, walking from one side of his weather center to the other, gesturing wildly with his hands as he talked.

"I take it you have found a storm you want to track?" she asked him, putting a hand to her temple. Never had she wanted to be back in the CIC more than she did right now.

"Yes, exactly! Now I'm not sure why we are out here—and I'm aware it isn't my place to ask. But if we could just change course a little…" He pulled up a holographic display that showed a huge rotating mass of clouds and then a dotted line, the first showing their course and the second the one he wanted them to take. It wasn't far off, but far enough to make their job of tracking the phantom ships—that couldn't exist— impossible.

"I'm sorry, doctor, no. I cannot change the heading the ship is on. You will just have to study your storm from here as best you can," Cassandra said.

She could feel that there was about to be a rebuttal from the scientist.

"Doctor, I am not a liberty to say why we are doing what we are. Just know that if I could adjust to accommodate our learning more about the nature of space, I… would consider your request."

Frydan looked down and ran a hand over his bald head, clearly frustrated. She needed to say something. The man had a bit of a mad scientist demeanor from time to time, but he always meant well; was only looking out for the ship and her crew.

"This is... It is very hard to accurately explain how important this research is. While one of these astral storms has not hit a Confederation world *yet*, ten years ago, one came close. Anything we can learn while here..." he pleaded.

She held her hand up to stop him.

"What if I give you access to an extra sensor package—one that, unless we are actively in combat operations, you may have complete control over. Would that suffice?"

It was the best she could do. Cassandra wasn't deaf to his desires, but there was so much more at stake than a bit of storm data that may or may *not* prove useful in the future.

"That would be most appreciated, Lord Admiral," he said, holding out his hand. She took it and he gave her a solid handshake.

"I'm on my way to CIC now, I shall have them route you control."

"Thank you again, Lord Admiral. Hopefully, we will learn something worth writing a paper on," he said.

"If so, make sure that I am mentioned favorably," she said.

"We will name a storm or wind pattern for you."

"Maybe not quite *that* favorably, doctor," Cassandra said as she stepped through the bulkhead and back into the hallway.

That conversation had been an interesting distraction, though not as effective as she would have liked it to be. Now it was time to return to the CIC with her thoughts and worries.

Cassandra removed her pocket watch from the small pouch on her belt and thumbed through a playlist before finding a contemplative track titled 'Memories in Time'. She pushed it to her personal audio system so that only she could hear it. A soft flute and single violin started to play a meditative, sad composition as she walked and let her thoughts take hold.

The five-minute track ended by the time she reached the Combat Information Center and started down the long stairway to the map table at the bottom, where her command staff was waiting for her:

Erik, Hanna, and Captain Rackland. The three of them were all hunched over the table, talking, Rackland gesturing with a grease pencil. Everybody snapped to attention when the boatswain's whistle started to play.

"Lord Admiral on deck!" he yelled from his position by the helm.

"As you were," Cassandra said, holding her hand up. The crew went back to their work and her staff stood as they were until she arrived at the bottom of the steps.

"Sitrep, if you please," she said. As they started to talk, Cassandra motioned to her steward to bring out a tea service.

"We have been on this course now for just under twelve hours, taking us extremely deep into the doldrums," Captain Rackland said, pointing to the map. The glass table had clear plastic charts laid out on top of it, showing the stars and worlds that were charted and known in this area of space.

"We have missed our chance to make it to NovaTerra by the election," Erik noted.

"Unless we can steal one of those impossible ships," Hanna said, clapping her brother on the back.

He didn't chuckle. She rolled her eyes, and deep down, Cassandra felt exactly what they were each of them feeling. Both that the election was serious—and missing it would have consequences—and that there was an element of dark humor to them chasing impossible ships. Even if somebody had cracked faster-than-light jumping again, there was no way something that small could do it.

"Thievery aside. Is there anything on our present course?" Cassandra asked.

"One world—really, it's more a moon, with a wide orbit around a gas giant. A place called Barker's World. The Confederation records are scant on information about it. There is one recorded settlement a place called Waltersburg," Rackland said, pointing to a dot on the table with his pencil.

"I'm sure it is some dusty little hamlet with folksy people who enjoy their hard life on the land the highway forgot," Erik muttered.

"You can be sure of it," Rackland said. "I once got stuck for a month on one of these planets, though on the other side of the Corey Expanse. 'Folksy' is not how I would describe those people. 'Hard', 'violent', 'desperate', 'resistant to authority' are all better descriptors."

"Well, they sound wonderfully pleasant," Hanna said.

"Hopefully we won't have to deal with their down-home charm," Cassandra said. "If we can catch them in space, that would be ideal. If not, we will find another trajectory. Commander, make sure your pilots are well rested until we reach this world. I want the whole wing in vacuum within ten minutes if we have to beat to quarters."

Commander Cordova gave his mother a crisp salute. "Aye, Lord Admiral," he said.

"Well then, Captain, we shall keep this course," she said, as the steward brought out the tea service and poured her a cup. "Dismissed."

The order was crisp and brokered no further discussion. Commander and Major Cordova gave their mother a quick bow and made their way out of the CIC, their coats flowing behind them from the speed of their gait.

"You are still thinking it's a trap?" Rackland asked, picking up the freshly poured cup of tea.

"I see traps everywhere these days, I fear," Cassandra said, taking a sip. "Every time I round a bend in the hall, a small part of me wonders if there is somebody I trust there with a pistol to finish me. Every call, every moment. I can feel the jaws of fate closing in on us, but their vision is obscured from me."

The two of them sipped their tea quietly, the dread they were both feeling taking a hold.

Power Plant, Olympus Ares Research Facility, Grace

Grace took point, her rifle out, the aim assist from her HUD on, scanning for targets. Charged Bolt was behind her. The bridge over the thermal vent leading to the power station was rickety at best.

This would be an embarrassing way to die, she thought.

With each step, the metal screamed and contorted from the heat, warping and swaying. Still, it was holding them.

"Where is the control panel?" Grace asked, pointing forward.

"On the other side, near the top. We are going to have to climb up to get to it and then I'll need to input my bio code. That is where it gets tricky, because Sharp Blade is out here. I can feel him," Charged Bolt said.

"I'll cover you. Just focus on getting that power changed over," Grace said.

She would have turned to give him a reassuring look, but the helmet of her suit made that impossible. The bridge finally ended and they were on the gangway that wrapped around the power station. Grace toggled on a bio scanner and kept looking for Sharp Blade. Something inside the magma-filled fissure was throwing off her scanners. Some kind of microorganic life.

For how much power this reactor was pushing out, it wasn't that big. She and Charged Bolt made it to the other side quickly.

"Okay, up the ladder you go. If you encounter him up there, don't engage. Just get down as fast as possible, okay?" Grace said to the Darklin. Emily desperately wanted to add something pithy. Charged Bolt took a deep breath, grabbed the rungs of the ladder and started to climb.

This was always the part that Grace hated. The waiting. Waiting for something to go wrong, hoping that whatever test you were running would finish before some variable that you hadn't anticipated came and ruined everything. Just like with the gate, just like with Emily and her last university before... before here.

I won't let that happen again. No more ignoring the red flags, Emily thought.

The sound of footfalls snapped her out of the daze. They were coming from the other side where they had just been. Clutching her rifle tightly, Grace walked back the way they had come, watching each step, trying to be quiet. As she rounded the bend, standing in the middle of the gangway, was a single skitter. She locked on and fired a single round. The creature didn't put up a fight, it just popped like an overfilled ballon.

Something isn't right. That was too easy, Emily thought, scanning around again, looking up at the tall ceiling that curved to form a natural vent leading to the surface.

Nothing was up there. The rock was smooth and there were no man-made holds. She turned her attention back down to the gangway and slowly started walking back the way she came. There was movement out of the corner of her eye. The aim assist spun, trying to keep up with it. Her head moved slower than the computer, the shadow of whatever she had seen was gone faster than she could be sure of what it was until—

Sharp Blade.

The shadow fluttered though her vision again, under the gangway. Of course she hadn't thought to look there. Grace looked down just in time to see the shape of a blade coming toward her. It smashed into the breast plate of her DES suit, knocking her back and causing her to puff out all the air in her lungs. Grace would have toppled into the vent below if not for the railing catching her. The rifle fell from her hands, hanging by her side where it was clipped to her tactical vest.

The Darklin stood before her, shorter than Charged Bolt and slim, a waif of a creature with a nasty looking serrated blade in his hand. He smiled like a predator. He slowly walked toward her, moving the blade from hand to hand. His eyes were milky white streaked with a blackness like ink. She stood up and took a step back, still uneasy on her feet, reaching for the rifle. The darkness tracked her movements, and a moment later, Sharp Blade's head followed. It was seeing for him, like the aim assist in her suit.

Sharp Blade's speed was astounding. He was on top of her again before she could pull up the rifle. The blade hit the shoulder of her suit, pushing in, causing alarms to go off inside of her helmet. Grace gave up on the gun and threw her arms up, wrapping her hands around Sharp Blade's arm, trying to push it up. They fumbled to the side, smashing into the power station. The jostling gave her some traction. Grace was able to get the point of the blade out of her shoulder plate.

Darting her eye to the side, she sent the suit's power to her right leg and quickly brought it up, smashing her knee into Sharp Blade's groin. The Darklin let out a grunt and tried to stumble back. Grace held onto his arm harder. She quickly sent power to the arms of her suit, then spun around, throwing the Darklin into the side of the power station. Sharp Blade hit with a hard thump, denting the paneling of the station, the sound of violence echoing though the cavern.

"What is going on down there?" Charged Bolt called out.

"Just meeting the family," Emily yelled back.

From where he was on the ground, Sharp Blade's head turned and locked onto where his brother was, that horrible predator smile crossing his face. He got on his feet with great speed and started running toward the ladder that Charged Bolt as at the top of.

This time, Grace went for her rifle, quickly getting it into her hands and letting the aim assist do the work of moving her arms and squeezing the trigger. Three rounds of plasma burst from the rifle. The first and second went wide as Sharp Blade weaved. The third clipped him in the shoulder, spinning him around as blood splattered everywhere, while burnt flesh and plasma started to drip from his arm. It didn't stop him, though. Whatever was inside driving Sharp Blade's body didn't care about pain, didn't care about life, didn't care about *him*.

Grace lowered the rifle and started to run. As she did, she slid her eyes up to the aim assist function and turned off non-lethal. She might only get one more shot and didn't want to waste it on something that would not stop until it was extra dead, if even then.

Grace got around the bend just in time to see Charged Bolt fall to the ground. He was bleeding, but still alive. The speed at which his brother had moved was unreal. Whatever was inside was driving him beyond the limit.

Running up to Charged Bolt, Grace felt the wound in his gut. He had been run through, but was still breathing, still holding on.

"Stop him," he said, grabbing Grace's armor and trying to pull himself up.

"I will. Then I'm coming back for you," she promised.

"Don't worry about me. It'll take more than that to stop me. Just a scratch," he said with a chuckle. Both of them knew it wasn't a scratch. But he was going to do what was needed to see the day to victory, of that Grace was sure.

She ran to the ladder and vaulted up to the top in three strides, pushing power into her legs to clear the distance. Once she got to the top, Grace saw Sharp Blade hunched over the panel, pushing buttons and trying to pull out wire.

She charged, grabbing the Darklin and pushing the power from her legs into her arms. Sharp Blade pushed back against her, screaming with all his might. It was a cry that sent a shiver down Graces's spine. A cry of vengeance, horrible loss, and sadness. The force from Sharp Blade was enough to knock her off her feet.

Both went tumbling off the side of the power plant. Grace held on tightly. She wasn't going to let him go; wasn't going to let him get another chance to damage the power plant so that they couldn't stop the flow of energy.

As they fell, they hit the side of the oval structure. Pain bloomed through Grace's body with each hit. It seemed no matter how she tried to adjust how they hit, she kept being the one who was smashed into the hard steel side of the powerplant. Alarms were going off inside of her suit as it shunted power around to deal with the damage she was taking. The vital signs were showing contusions and bruising all across her body. Whenever she crawled out of this suit—*if* she ever crawled out of it—Grace knew she was going to be black and blue. Just a mess of injuries.

For now, though, she had to fight through.

They both landed on the gangway. Finally, Grace caught a break and landed on top, still holding the Darklin tight, his face smashing into the steel, the links cutting into his flesh. Sharp Blade screamed again. This time, though, it was not in anger or vengeance, but pain. The pain of a child who was being beaten up by a bully; who was scared and lost. So sudden and different was this cry that it knocked Grace out of her mindset of determination. She let her arms slack for a moment.

It was just a moment too long. It had been a ploy. Whatever was inside Sharp Blade had tapped into the young Darklin's fear and terror, projecting it into the world. The infested creature pushed against her and another power alarm went off inside the suit, showing a graphic of her arms turning red as the power cascaded backward into her armor. Sharp Blade was free, and she was on the ground again. A restart message came up. The cascade of power had forced the systems inside the suit to reboot. The progress bar pinged, and Grace swatted it away with her eyes. Flattening her hands, she tried to stand, but the suit was too heavy. There was no power. It was holding her down.

Killed by a system reset, that's just fucking grand, Emily thought as Sharp Blade thew himself upon her, the jagged horrible knife trying to puncture through the chest plate of her suit. She could feel the pressure of it, feel it pushing down harder and harder. Breathing was becoming difficult.

Her power was at 50%. She wasn't going to make it. The suit was designed to withstand just about anything, but without power, it was only durasteel. Strong, thin, and heavy, but not kill-proof.

There was a loud thump, kinetic energy on flesh. Her vizor was covered in blood, then there was a horrible weight on her, more than Sharp Blade pushing the knife. It was a limp, dying body. Though the crimson, she could see the wound. The Darklin's neck was hanging on by a thread. A plasma round had ripped through it. The milky white of his eyes had faded, and all that was left was the swirling shadow of whatever controlled him. Sharp Blade was dead.

It was not.

80%. The grip on her loosened as the creature tried to get the corpse it was infesting back under control. Its arms moved in a jerky way, like a video that didn't have enough frames. An idea came to Grace, and she knew there was only going to be one chance. Anything else and it would end with her and Charged Bolt dead.

Lights came up, the HUD flashed to life. The suit was back online and operational. Grace threw all her power into the gyro functions and then activated the grappling wire that rested under her right wrist. Taking a deep breath, she rolled and rolled hard. Her sudden movement caught the horrible undead Sharp Blade thing on top of her off guard. They both smashed into the guard rail. The steel cried out. She pressed more power into the suit, threatening to cause another overload. There was no choice but to keep going. With another scream, the steel from the railing gave way.

They fell.

Sharp Blade's body tumbled, grasping at Grace. She threw her arm out and fired the grappling hook. It found purchase in the side of the power station. Both of them flew toward the structure, smashing into it with a resounding thud that echoed throughout the cavern. The impact knocked the wind out of Grace. The corpse of Sharp Blade was still holding on to her left leg. Using her right leg, Grace pushed off the side of the station so they were midair. She kicked at Sharp Blade's almost-detached head. Each wet thump of her boot caused more of the flesh to rip, finally crunching and detaching what was left of his spine. There was a final desperate gasping, as whatever was controlling the Darklin lost the ability to send signals to the rest of the meat suit.

Sharp Blade fell into the abyss, sending Grace spinning as she flew back toward the power station. There was a sharp pain as her shoulder dislocated, coming out of its socket. Before she could truly register the pain, her head smashed into the side of the power station and there was darkness.

Liminal Space, Grace

As darkness replaced darkness, Grace knew that she was not where she had started. Her breath was filtering through the rebreather of her suit, sealed for vacuum. She was on the ground and there were stars above her. So many stars, stars that she recognized.

I've been here before, the dead world.

The HUD on her suit was not displaying any new information. It was as if she wasn't here. None of the controls responded to her inputs. She was a ghost in an armored shell. Even as a ghost, she was able to move, to be in control.

Grace sat up and started to look around. She was deep inside an ancient caldera, likely formed by the impact of an asteroid millions of years ago. The sides were steep, and it appeared that there was no way to climb up or down the wall. Turning from the walls, she started to scan the inside of the caldera. At some point in time, there must have been a way in and out, because scattered throughout the inside were the foundations of buildings; a wall here, a door frame there, the remnants of civilization. She had seen this city before, but not in this place. The stars were the same, the ruins were the same, just the Caldera was new.

"We have been waiting for you, Emily Itchi. Come join us," a voice said. Whipping her head around, Grace tried to see where it was coming from.

"Join us."

It wasn't coming from anywhere. It was inside her head, not sound, but thoughts.

It knows who I was.

Getting to her feet, the weightlessness of being a ghost caught Grace off guard—or maybe it was this place. She couldn't turn to her suit and get a gravity reading to see how many standard gravs she was under right now. Doing quick math in her head, she figured it had to be, at most, half a grav. Each step was light, easy, the bottom of her foot barely touching the plant's red sand.

The voice in her head was still ushering her forward, the words seeping into her chest, making her breath light and pulling her forward like a child being guided by their parents.

If it knows my name and wants to talk, who am I to say no? Emily thought defiantly.

"You are nobody and everything," the voice said, answering her inner thoughts.

"Well, that's just fucking unsettling," Emily said as she started the long walk to the ruins. As she walked, she looked up into the sky, and started to note where the stars were, charting their positions, putting it deep inside her memory so that when she got back—*if* she got back—she could find this place for real.

"Wherever I am must be on the other side of the gate, where everything wrong is feeding from," she said to nobody in particular. It was half a statement to herself and half a question. She looked around, expecting—hoping—that the voice would respond to her, would tell her, "Yes you are correct," or "No, you understand less than nothing".

The silence was worse than either.

"That is because you are going crazy, Grace. This is a dream, nothing more. Nobody but you is talking to you."

"I am very real and very close," the voice in her head responded.

"Oh, so you *are* still listening. Good to know," she said, picking up the pace. The ruined city was quickly coming into view. What had, from a distance, just looked like the outline of buildings and a few walls was, in fact, much more.

"They were not that big before..." she muttered, pausing to see if answers would be given to her. None were.

Another step and she knew why the buildings were taller than before. They were growing from the ground as she walked toward them, sand falling all around as they came bursting forth from the desert. A shadow caught the corner of her eye. Grace turned and looked, but it was gone again, just like Sharp Blade had been. Specters, shades, dreams.

Walking down the street, Grace saw old signs plastered on every wall. Shops and billboards, graffiti, language everywhere. It was the same runes that she had seen in the first dream and around the base.

"So, you use a runic writing system. Interesting," Grace said, this time not pretending to wait for some unknown response.

Looking at all of them, she started to commit the shapes to memory, the same as the stars. This would be much simpler if she could use the suit's camera. Idly, her eyes flicked over to the record function. The suit responded and a small red light blinked at the bottom. Grace didn't trust it, but she didn't turn it off. Nothing made sense anymore, so why not be able to record from a dream? Or some vision that was being beamed into her head from who knows where?

There was a flash to her side. Grace turned. Whatever it was had vanished. She was not alone. Fear washed over her, coming from somewhere deep and primordial inside of her lizard brain. She turned her head and spun around, looking up and down, scanning all the buildings, trying to see through the falling sand that this dead civilization was rising from. Next to her was a window. Grace jumped into it and pressed herself against the wall as the tall building kept rising.

It was inside the building. She could hear its feet walking, stalking her. There was nothing to see, nothing for her instruments to pick up on. It was above her, each step echoing down through the building as if the feet were connected to an elephant. It sounded like that *thump, thump* that you could hear in the back of your eyes if you concentrated on the flowing blood in your head. It was coming for her. She didn't know what it would do and she was not about to find out.

Looking out the window, the drop was high, but something her suit could manage. *Please work,* she thought before throwing herself out the window. Grace hit the sand, tucking and rolling down an embankment into another wall. Grace turned to look where she had jumped from.

Standing in the window was a figure. Clouded in shadow, but a physical figure. His face was long, gaunt, and tendrils were protruding from his back, wriggling as if they were under their own power. A sharp toothy smile crossed his face, and then she saw his eyes. Eyes that were a powerful, deep, enticing neon-blue. The color was unreal, and revolted her, caused her to close her eyes and try to force the creature from her mind.

He wouldn't leave. Even with her eyes closed, all she could see was the neon-blue burning through her eyelids, looking deep into her soul, pulling the two of them apart.

"I see you, Wayfinder," he said.

Flinging open her eyes, Grace watched the creature float down from the window, the tendrils extended to the side like wings unconnected by flesh and feathers. A slightly golden hue was emanating from them. *Null.*

"Who are you?" she asked, standing, trying to find some bravery.

It was there, but there was fear as well. *We can't be brave if we are not also afraid,* she could hear her father saying. Something he surely picked up from an old movie. So much of his wit and wisdom were lines from books and movies.

"We are the first, the forgotten, the robbed," the creature said inside of her head while still lazily floating toward her. "Varagoth."

The world sounded horrible to Grace. It was wrong, unnatural in her mind. Was it the word or the way he said it? The hissing, the superiority. She didn't know and right now, didn't care to find out. Turning, Grace started to run, dodging every high wall and jumping over the low ones. The creature followed behind her, slowly floating, his feet pointed down just above the sand, leaving no trace as to where he had been.

Grace ran. She ran until her lungs burned and her legs were pumping battery acid back into her body. One misplaced step and she fell to the ground, taking a face full of sand. Or she would have, if not for the helmet. The helmet that was still recording. She tried to stand, but her arms and hands kept slipping in the ever-building dune. She was sliding, falling deeper into the abyss of the caldera as the city was rising ever upward into the stars, escaping this dead world as it swallowed her. As always, behind her, was the creature—floating, *smiling*—digging into her soul with his unblinking eyes.

It was over. There was nothing she could do. He was going to catch her, and she was going to die.

Can I die in a place like this? Or am I already dead?

"Death is real everywhere you go," he said inside of her mind, every word like needles being driven into her brain. Emily had suffered from migraines as a child, but this was so much worse.

Rolling over, she was ready. It didn't matter anymore. If they were going to die, then they were going to die on their feet. She stopped struggling and planted her feet, pushing up on them, ignoring her arms. All they would do was bring more sand down upon her. Grace stood and turned around. The creature was on top of her, his hand outstretched, long sharp nails jutting from desiccated gray-green flesh.

"Join us, Emily Itchi. Wayfinder."

His hand was just about to wrap around her face when she felt a tug on her arm. It dragged her up, off the surface of the world and into space, through the veil of unconsciousness, back into the real world, where her body was dumped onto the hard steel of the gang plank.

Hoben House, Novagrad, Claudia

Alexander was snoring. He had fallen asleep almost as soon as he had pulled his cock out of her. She was sure he thought there was some grand romantic gesture in all of this. Claudia didn't believe in any of that nonsense. Grand gestures, hell, even romance, was something she didn't think really existed. They were all just fancy words that society put on the act of courting so that it looked and felt more respectable than just breading and fucking for fun. It *did* serve her purpose, though. A head full of romance and eyes full of a heaving bodice made most men horribly foolish.

She took a deep breath, looking up at the ceiling of the dark room. So far, nobody else had come home yet, which meant that there wasn't much time left. Everything from the last few days to the next few days was on the clock. She was under the gun, literally, though nobody around her knew that.

Gingerly, she moved out from under his arm and hand that was still cupping her breast. She slid a pillow underneath his hand to replace her. On the floor, she found her dress and pulled herself back into it. The garment, once opened, was easy to get into before it sinched back up. Technology was truly grand. The things they could do with garments these days. Yet the elite of NovaTerra were still obsessed with their wool, cotton, and holographic embroidery. Claudia found fashion interesting, like cards—or politics, to an extent. But it was all just knowledge that she used to gather intelligence and pass it along to her handlers. They were just facts that made her cover that much more airtight.

She pulled out a small wrist computer that had been slipped away in her dress and ran it over the pile of Alexander's clothing. It blinked, picking up his watch computer and transferring it to hers. The message they had all gotten from poor Alister had been laced with a few lines of code that gave her access. Alister had been no more than a child—an easy mark, having arrived in Novagrad first.

As she was putting away her device, Claudia wondered if they were going to find his body before everything went down. She had hidden it well, but those things tended to crop up when you least expected them too.

It didn't take much time for her to slide out of the house and make her way down the street. She cut through a backyard and then down an alleyway. There was a door ajar. She stopped, looked left and then right, and, seeing that the coast was clear, slipped inside. There was only a small room on the other side, nothing more than storage, a water heater, and a garbage shoot. Sitting under the garbage shoot was a bag. She picked it up and pulled out the clothing. It was a simple outfit: a dress, bodice, and shoes. The kind of clothing a person of a lower class would be wearing as they cleaned up from the day's festivities.

Claudia was able to get the red dress off as fast as she had put it on. In a few minutes, she was in servant's clothing. These garments felt more like what she wanted to wear day to day, not the fancy outfits of the nobles and card players. People *noticed* those. She didn't want to be noticed. It was sad to have to shove the red dress down the garbage shoot, but she couldn't be seen walking around with it. Sentimentality was death when working in intelligence and she had to work to not fall prey to it. Though she was not going to feel bad getting rid of her card deck. Peculiar Pentagon was not a game she enjoyed and hoped to not have to play again.

There were only a few people left on the streets, most of them dressed like her, sweeping up trash and confetti. A few nobles were staggering home, companions on their arms. It was 3 a.m. and the world was dead, fully in night mode. Her contact was just down the street. She walked quickly, reaching into her pocket and palming the little computer. She took another turn and saw the man she was looking for.

In the ally was a man in black with snakelike features. Even though she was here to meet him, he still sent up every red flag possible.

"Do you have the information, Claudia?" he asked. His voice was smooth and sweet, like honey. She hated it. It sounded wrong in her ear.

"Of course, Mister Harrison," she said, pulling out the small device and putting it into his hand.

"Very good. It looks like you have the Cordova boy wrapped around your finger. What about the rest of them?"

"Not worth the investment. He will give us what we want. I just need a little more time to pull it all out of him," she said.

"Work quickly. Time is not on our side." Mr. Harrison said as he turned and walked away into the shadows.

Apartments, The Citadel, Lucas

Naomi and Rostov were sitting over by the window. Rostov had his arm around Naomi as they chatted. For the moment, they seemed calm and happy. Though they had said when he walked in that there was something they needed to share. Lucas could feel the tension and the comfort coming from both. Lines of tension moved from one to the other, changing from a middling red to a calming blue, almost like the two of them were the same heart oxygenating each other's blood supply.

Lucas had things to share as well, but he still wasn't sure how to broach the subject that he knew who the mole was. At least, he wasn't sure what he *wanted* to do about it. As a strong leader—and he was going to be a strong leader, damn it—he couldn't bring this to the group without first having a solid course of action in mind. Lucas got a cup of coffee and sat down in one of the chairs on the other side of the room, feeling separated from them.

"You don't have to sit all the way over there," Naomi said, lifting her head from where it was cradled in Rostov's arm.

"I'm fine, just thinking over some things," Lucas said.

These feelings that he was getting from them made him uncomfortable. He had been feeling them for Joanna the moment he saw her again. Those he understood, but this... They were his *friends*, and he knew he would sacrifice everything for them, but it was a stronger feeling. Almost like they were inviting him to lay his head down, which felt far too much like being a third wheel.

"Anything you want to share?" Rostov asked pointedly.

"I'm still working that out. I want to wait for Joanna to get back, so we are all together," Lucas said.

The blood pact, the Fellowship agent had called them. Was that why everybody felt so...? No, it was ridiculous. This all smacked of something that mundanes thought about the Host'ire based on nothing but myth and conjecture. He was in control of his emotions and there was no strange prophecy or blood pact. Though he couldn't deny that *something* was happening, Lucas just didn't want to admit it.

As he sipped his coffee, lost in thought, the door opened, and Joanna burst inside like a storm crashing upon the shore. The door slammed behind her as she set her bag on the table and plopped down on the couch next to Lucas. She was so close to him, it made his heart skip a beat. Joanna looked at Rostov and Naomi, and then at Lucas. For half a second, their eyes locked, and he could see the two of them snuggled together, his hand stroking her hair. As quickly as the flash was there, it was gone, both of them shaking their heads at once.

Had she seen it as well? What is going on? he thought, a faint echo of another voice mouthing the words as he thought them.

"It looks like you found something," Naomi said.

She nodded to the envelope grasped in Joanna's hand. For a fraction of a moment, Lucas saw it, but not from his point of view, as if he was by the window, with Naomi and Rostov. He sat the coffee down and shook his head.

"Yes. I went to see Tor. He wasn't in the library, but he left me this. And memories. I saw Hyacinth. It is already starting to fade, but I know it was her. I have to keep telling it to myself. Over and over again. Tried writing it down, but..."

Joanna reached into her jacket and pulled out a scrap of paper. She handed it to Lucas first. The scribblings made no sense. There were words and sentences, but the words were not words. That was when what Fel had said to him started to click.

"Administrator Fel she knew about Hyacinth. At least, she knew we had gotten a message from somebody. I let her name slip," Lucas said, his voice lowering.

"She knows more than she is telling us—or, at least, she *used* to," Joanna said, opening the envelope and showing the old teletype to Lucas. He read it quickly and his face dropped.

"What does it say?" Rostov asked.

"She investigated our disappearance and Jasper's murder, found something below the Citadel," Joanna said.

"From our talk, I don't think she remembers, but she is starting to maybe... feel something—like we were, when the first messages arrived," Lucas said. "She isn't completely against us, but is worried that there is something she doesn't know that will turn this battle on its head."

"Well, it seems Host'ire Command knows," Rostov said.

"No, this message wasn't sent. The old Null space teletypes destroyed the paper the messages were written on. If we have this, then that means it never left the base. Somebody knew she would forget about it, if they just sat on it," Joanna said, motioning to the paper.

"She said that it wouldn't stay in her memory, that it was slippery," Lucas said.

"If Fel knew than, who else knew?" Joanna asked.

There was fear in her voice, Lucas could feel it in his bones. He wanted to go to her, to wrap his arms around and just hold her, to never let her go, like he had promised all those years ago. He could feel her wanting to slide closer as well, like they were magnets fighting to not connect. He had to tell them, even without a plan. They were a group. It was only right. Holding information to himself helped nobody.

"Wingarf knows. Or at least, he knows *something*," Lucas said, with a pause. "I saw him talking to a Fellowship of the Cross agent. He is the spy inside the Citadel. I don't know why or how—there was no convenient villain's monologue. But he did say something about 'the blood pact would find the door'."

He spit it all out, feeling a weight off his chest. Rostov and Naomi's eyes went wide with the revelation. Joanna went cold. She knew something else. He could feel it coming from her. She needed him, needed just a small amount of reassurance.

Sliding forward, Lucas put his hand on her thigh. Instantly, they both felt calmer. He hadn't realized how much he needed the reassurance, as well. A team was give and take. He could not sit apart as the leader and only give.

"Tor also said something about a blood pact," Joanna said, holding up the envelope.

Lucas was feeling tapped into not just his friends, but the Null, as well; could see the wax seal glowing like the sun on a bight, cloudless day.

Lucas took the envelope and slipped the card out and read it aloud. "Connect the blood pact, open your eyes, and see her."

As he read the note, there was another flash. He was in the library. There was a weight in his hand. Lucas looked down and he saw the paperweight; felt the white-hot anger and need to defend his friends welling up inside of him. There was another flash, and he was back in the room, the emotions starting to fall, but everybody was on edge.

"You saw it," Joanna said. Lucas nodded. Rostov and Naomi did, as well.

"I don't know where they went after, though. After we saved her and ran," Lucas said.

"After Essex smashed in his skull. I can still see the blood everywhere," Naomi said. "We ran. You two ran. Why did we leave them?"

"We found them once, we will find them again. The memories are inside us all," Joanna said, taking the paper from Lucas, running her hand along his arm and across his chest as she did. Their eyes locked and her breasts heaved. He couldn't look away. Joanna put the card on the table.

"Wingarf and his friend talked about things below the Citadel. So did Fel," Lucas said as Joanna sat back on the couch and leaned into him.

He wrapped his arm around her, placing his hand on her shoulder. It felt good to have her next to him, in contact with him. She was warm, he could feel it though his uniform. It wasn't just physical; he could feel her, *through* her.

There was a spike in the room, the excitement rose.

"Then that is where we have to go," Joanna said, fear and trepidation in her voice.

She was scared, worried about what they were going to find, about what this connection meant. But also, he could feel it from all of them, they were scared to lose each other, now that they were finally together again. It was getting late and, even as an adult, sneaking out felt wrong here. All his instincts were mixed up in time.

"Tomorrow," he said. "First thing. We go and we end this."

He was firm, there was command in his voice. It felt like an act, though. All he could think about was the kiss, his lips on Joanna's.

"I'm never going to let any of you go again. I will protect you all," he added.

Joanna took off her glasses and turned to look up at him. Her eyes were big, inviting. He just wanted to get lost in them.

"I know," she said, kissing him.

It was long and deep. The pressure of her lips on his, their tongues running across each other. He didn't want to pull away; didn't want to let go. His hands moved down, wrapping around her waist. She pressed tighter into him. Lucas wanted nothing more than for this moment to never end, caught up in the feelings of excitement that were radiating from the room. He saw his hands slipping under her shirt and running up Joanna's back as she ground against him.

Then he was moving, walking forward. Another pair of hands moved as he was back in his body. Naomi was standing over them, pulling off Joanna's shirt. Her bra barely contained her breasts. Lucas pulled away from the kiss, his hand grabbed one of her breasts, freeing it, revealing a large, hard nipple. He placed it in his mouth and started to suck. Joanna's moans filled the room.

Another point of view. Her moaning cut off as Rostov started to kiss her. He felt hands on his head—Naomi, her fingers tussling his hair. The hardness in his pants was starting to overtake his mind.

Pulling away from Joanna's nipple, he grabbed Naomi and brought her close, kissing her. She tasted different, but the same. He knew this feeling. His hands were not his own again. They were both wrapped around Joanna's breasts, fully freed from the bra.

Lucas pulled away from Naomi as both of them started ripping off clothing. She was not as well-endowed as Joanna, but her dark nipples were already hard. Before he could do anything, though, she was pulled away from him, Rostov's hands—his hands, *their* hands—on her, rubbing her down, kissing her.

Lucas turned to Joanna, pushing her gently to the ground. In a moment, her pants were off, and his face was in her trimmed cunt. She tasted sweet, wonderful. The sounds she made were heavenly. He knew right then that he needed to be inside of her. Pulling his pants off, he removed his head and started kissing her lips again, sliding his hard cock inside of her. She moaned.

Naomi was naked, her lips were on his cock, as he fucked Joanna. No, they were on Rostov's. He could feel it all; her lips, his thrusts.

Kissing Joanna again, he let the feelings consume him.

EPISODE V:
Blood Pact

Outer Perimeter, Below Olympus Ares Research Facility, Grace

The vision was still running through Grace's mind; the rising city, the stars, the runes, the Varagoth, his horrible, neon-blue eyes.

Was Varagoth his name? Or was that the name for all of them, the creatures that were infesting people? Grace didn't know. She didn't have time to think about that right now. Clutched in her hand was a pad already filled halfway up, the pencil in her other hand getting dull. The HUD of her suit said that the camera had been recording, but she didn't trust that. Grace was starting to trust like Emily. So she was drawing, getting down onto paper every rune that she had seen, every star and building. The only thing that she didn't dare draw was the face that she saw every time she tried to close her eyes. Even when she blinked, he was behind her, those icy blue eyes ripping her soul apart.

While she was hunched in the corner drawing, muttering to herself, Essex had taken command of the situation. Things were on the edge. Charged Bolt had managed to cut off the power going to the facility, shunting it back toward wherever the majority of their energy was always going. The effort had cost him his life. His body was across the room, covered in a sheet, along with half the Darklin that had gone out with Essex and confronted the other infested Darklin, Full Mag. Somehow, Essex had managed to bring the creature back into the room—tightly bound, of course. The Host'ire knight was pacing in front of his prisoner. Grace noticed the uncertainty in his body language, but at the moment, she couldn't spare him a thought. There was work to be done before the fallacy of memory took hold.

The large Darklin was leaning against the wall. They had pulled him out of his armor and tied him up. The inky clouds had faded from his eyes, but Essex said he could still feel the coldness that had touched him, that was still inside.

"What happened to you?" Essex asked, walking over and sitting down cross-legged in front of Full Mag, flicking his coat out so it flared behind him. Essex put his star-steel blade in his lap.

"There was a quake from above. The reverberations could be felt all the way down here. Normally, whatever goes on up top doesn't make its way down here; doesn't affect us," Full Mag said, shaking his head. He would have been crying if there had been tear ducts attached to the vestigial milky white eyes.

"Charged Bolt sent Sharp Blade, Loud Scream, and myself to check out the south tunnel. Almost instantly, we heard the skittering and then felt a coldness. Loud Scream started shooting and was consumed by the skitters. Been here my whole life, all forty cycles of it, and I've never encountered those damned things before. There wasn't time to think. The coldness consumed us. At first, it felt like a malignant moist afternoon, the kind that wants to strangle you from the inside.

"It got inside of us, it… I saw…" Full Mag struggled, his voice dropping. The implications hitting the floor like a ton of bricks. "I… You can't understand what it is like, to *see* for the first time, when it's never been an option for you. It *showed* me things."

His heart rate was getting faster, his breathing more labored, as he processed a near impossible memory.

"Join the fucked up memory club, buddy," Emily whispered as Grace drew. She was interested in the story; was able to steal a small amount of focus to concentrate on what the Darklin was telling Essex. There was bound to be something important. These things liked to talk, liked to show off their power.

"What did it show you?" Essex asked. Emily rolled her eyes at Essex wanting a blind man to describe the trauma of a nightmare being the first thing he saw.

"I don't know, it felt..." Full Mag paused for a moment, trying to get his thoughts in order. "It felt like an introduction; a statement of purpose and intent. Like that you would give to somebody on their first day on the job. It wanted me to understand why it needed my body. Why I was going to be shoved to the back of my own brain and forced to *see* things."

Full Mag leaned forward, his face as close to Essex's as he could get. The former Host'ire knight's hand went to the hilt of his blade and almost thumbed it on.

"I never want to see again... *Never*. You can fucking keep that." He spat out, before smashing his head and back into the wall. The impact made a resounding thud, and Emily was sure that the skin had been broken.

"It is still inside of me. I can feel it, just behind my lungs, moving in my body like an eel. He is going to make me see again, make me watch as he does horrible things," the big Darklin said, hitting his head against the wall again, harder this time. The third time, he screamed and fell forward, breathing in shallow breaths as if he was sobbing. Blood smeared on the rock wall behind him.

Emily stood up and started walking toward the Darklin. If he was going to kill himself, she had questions that needed to be answered first. She flicked the notepad back to the first page so that she could flip through them all.

"I need to ask you some questions. I *need* you to see again," Emily said. There was a deep desire in how she said the word 'need'. Coming from the lowest part of her registry, almost like it was a threat.

"I need to know what these mean, what they say." Emily turned the pad toward Full Mag and started flipping through pages and pages of runes and notes. The Darklin just laughed at her, chuckled and hit his head again.

"It knows. He says you have to learn that on your own, Wayfinder. Besides, I would like to never see these cursed symbols. To never understand anything more about this evil that thinks my body is his," Full Mag said.

Emily took another step forward. She recognized those words. *Varagoth.* He had called her Wayfinder, had known her name. She couldn't let this go. There were too many questions and no answers.

"I need to know!" Emily yelled, quickly stepping back, biting her clinched fist, hopping and pacing about for a moment. Essex watched her, worried. She looked almost as frazzled as Full Mag. Turning from the Darklin, he walked over and put his arm around her. Emily pushed him off and walked away.

"I'm fine. Don't... I don't need that. I just need to know," she said, waving the pad at him, at the world.

"What did you see?" Essex asked.

"I don't want to talk about it. If he won't tell me what I need to know, then we need to get to the dorms. There is a book there I need. I know I have seen these before," Emily said, pointing at Full Mag, her finger accusing him of cowardice for not wanting to have to see, to interact with what was burning him up from the inside. If he wasn't going to answer her questions, then it was going to come down to good old-fashioned research.

"What did he mean when he called you Wayfinder?" Essex asked. She sighed, pushing and gave Essex the answer that she knew he was expecting.

"I don't know. It doesn't matter. Whatever the fuck these things are, they talk in riddles, and I do not deal with that," the part of Grace that was still Emily said, waving the pad wildly before walking away from Essex. Grace picked up her helmet and rifle putting the pad away.

"It wants back out," Full Mag said. "I can feel it, trying to push into my eyes. There is light. You will not make me see!" he yelled, smashing his head against the wall again, much harder, this time. The wet thump was louder, and a stain of vermillion was left behind. Essex moved toward him, but the Darklin was faster. He threw out his leg, tripping up the Host'ire Knight, while still smashing his head against the wall.

Emily just stood and watched.

"I refuse to see. You can just rot in this body!" he yelled.

This time, when Full Mag's head hit the wall, there was a loud crack, a grunt, and the Darklin went limp. Blood pooled, oozing from the ruin of Full Mag's forehead. The inky shadows filled the dead Darklin's milky white eyes. Full Mag turned his head to the side and smiled at Essex, but no words came out. He was looking past him.

Looking at *her*.

"Be seeing you, Wayfinder," Full Mag said, a deep chuckle filling his voice, a voice that had lost Full Mag's accent. Grace stopped but didn't turn around. Tension pulled her shoulders back. She wanted to turn around to face it, but there was nothing to do.

"Let's go, Essex. There is nothing else for us here," she said, putting on her helmet.

The creature inside Full Mag laughed at them as they walked away.

Hoben House, Alexander

The dreams had been good. Alexander and Claudia were together. The card tournament was theirs with a resounding victory. He had taken her to see his mother and reconciliation happened. The Cordova family was whole again, with a new member.

As it was coming to an end, Alexander could feel the dream slipping away, his mind starting to wake up and return to the real world. He was excited to wake up and then dashed once he was. Taking a deep breath with a smile on his face, Alexander rolled over, expecting to find the love of his life lying next to him, exactly where she had been when they both fell asleep after an amazing night together.

In her place, there was only a pillow.

"What?" Alexander murmured, pushing away the fog of sleep as he sat up. Looking around, his room was empty. Claudia was gone, left in the night. His heart crashed.

Was I that bad? Did we move too quickly? So many panicked questions moved through his mind before he could calm it. He was sure there was a rational explanation, something that would let him know what had happened.

Reaching into his trousers, Alexander pulled out his pocket watch and checked to see if there were any messages left for him. Nothing.

Only that *unread message.*

Opening his message app, he fired off a quick missive to Claudia asking where she was. He then pulled on a robe and stumbled out into the common area.

The living room still bore the evidence of their haste and passion. On the floor were three glasses and a decanter. One of the glasses was broken and the decanter had popped open, spilling whiskey all over the hardwood floor.

"That was a good vintage," Thrase's voice said from behind Alexander.

He turned around to find her walking out of Hoben's room, her nightclothes and robe in a tussle.

"I'm glad you had a good night, Alexander," Hoben said, following Katie, his nightclothes also in a similar state of dishevelment, as if they had not slept at all and just threw something on to look presentable. Alexander hadn't realized they had been together, but it also was not shocking, in the least.

"Sorry about the whiskey. I apparently don't know this room so well in the dark. But yes, it was a good night. Although..." Alexander looked around, raising his hands in confusion.

"You do seem to have lost something," Hoben said.

"Probably just wanted to preserve the illusion of her beauty. Most women don't want you see what they look like the next morning this early in the relationship. A ball gown in the light of morning? That would just start the gossip rags talking," Katie said as she walked into the kitchen and started to mess with the coffee pot.

"You are right. Of course you are right," Alexander said, sitting on the couch. "I have already sent her a message, and I shall call on her later. Bring some flowers, see if she will take lunch with me. As it is our buy day, perhaps a walk in the park!"

He was overjoyed with the prospects of the day, with feelings of love and happiness. He had not felt this much pure joy since cracking Torgan's equation three years ago, and before that, only one other time, when he went to see his uncle about becoming his true self.

"Would you look at this poor cuntstruck bastard right here?" Hoben said, sitting down next to Alexander. "He knows a girl for less than a week and already he is calling on her, planning trips to the park. You would think that soon, thoughts of marriage would be in his mind."

Hoben wrapped an arm around Alexander and gave him a manly squeeze. Alexander didn't say anything. He didn't have to. His friend wasn't wrong. He had already been thinking about a future with Claudia. He'd been dreaming it, and if he had known she'd left, he would have fought tooth and nail to stay in the dream.

"Such an unfortunate turn of events," Katie said, walking over and sitting down in one of the chairs, putting her feet up on the messy coffee table. "At least this one has some breeding behind her, unlike the grease monkey."

Vicious, but not untrue.

"Leave Fox out of this," Alexander said, getting up in a huff.

"Yes, that is what I am saying *you* should do. I'm glad you found a good match and didn't take to rejection by just raking across Novagrad," Katie said.

Alexander stopped listening to her. He didn't want to engage with that. He just wanted to take a shower and get dressed. To kill a little time before it would be acceptable to call on Claudia. He needed to be with her again, to feel her intoxicating presence. Mostly, though, he just didn't want to be the target of his friends' post-fuck, pre-coffee snipe fest.

Alexander quickly got dressed, a simple outfit today: a lavender jacket with white leather pants, boots, and he finished it off with a plum vest and cravat. Once he was out of the house and feeling a bit better, he started walking down the street. It was only a block before he found a vender that was selling coffee. He stopped and exchanged a few coins and started to walk with his little cup. It looked like a porcelain teacup, but was in fact a biscotti covered in printed white chocolate.

Finding a bench, he sat down and pulled out his watch. The message from Fox had popped up again, with a bright red boarder saying that he hadn't read it.

Funny, I thought I marked that as read?

He made a little confused noise and then swiped it away, back into the read emails where it should have been. Was this fate or was the universe trying to tell him something? Fox never skipped out when they had spent the night together—and early duty shifts didn't count, because he knew about those.

Turning the dial on his watch, he opened the communicator and rang Claudia's number. There was a buzz and four rings in his ear before the line went dead. She didn't even have a voice mailbox set up—not that he would have left some message full of urning and pining.

What was that word Hoben had said? Cuntstruck. Yes, maybe, but he wasn't so far gone that he would leave a message sounding like that. Still, it took effort to just sit there and enjoy the cool morning sun with his coffee and not hit the redial command. That was a rookie mistake, something that a young boy would do. He flicked the watch closed and put it back in his pocket. He knew where she was staying, thanks to their registration forms. He would just do what a man does.

She hasn't taken you to her place. Don't you think it is a little creepy just to show up? a voice in the back of his head asked. Alexander waved the thought away, the ruffles of his jacket flowing in the wind.

There was a flower shop two blocks down that he remembered from the last time he was here on NovaTerra. They had what were possibly the most perfect designer roses that he had ever seen. Alexander had bought Fox a dozen the last time they had been together, before everything went wrong. Yes, flowers would work—though hopefully they didn't come off like him saying, *Thank you for sleeping with me.*

He finished drinking his coffee and stood up, putting the cup in the trash. Pulling down his plum vest, he started walking, his back ramrod straight. This was the correct action. Grand gestures were what men who were in love did—and he was a man very much in love.

He got to the flower shop just as they were opening. It was run by a pleasant surface Tragadi woman. She was taller than all the doors and windows in her little shop, which had clearly been built for humans many years before. She welcomed him in and showed off her stock, gesturing with long arms, while her soothing voice walked him through the store. Alexander picked out a half dozen color-shifting roses. They started pink, and as the day went on, changed to a deep shade of red. These roses, grown in a lab and created to be perfect, didn't dramatically die like so many plants. They would gracefully, over the course of two weeks, lose their scent and fade away.

Just a half dozen was hideously expensive, but Alexander knew that they were going to be worth it in the end. Grand gestures didn't come cheap, especially if you were throwing them together in the morning. Thanking the shopkeeper, he took his flowers and made a retreat from the store, just as another gaggle of men were coming in, probably having the same idea that he was. There had been no shortage of soirees the night before.

The apartment that Claudia was staying at was another half mile down shop street. Taking a breath and holding his head high, Alexander started walking. He made the distance in about fifteen minutes, after stopping twice to listen to a musician playing on the street and then a third time to check the Peculiar Pentagon standings. The match between Novagrad Tech and Tragadi Confederate University had only just ended earlier that morning, at round fifty-two. It looked like NovaTech slipped up and that was that. Still, they reached the record for the longest tournament legal game. He was happy for them. It would give everybody something to talk about that wasn't just the front-runners for the next day or so.

When he got to the brownstone, Alexander tightened his cravat and started up the steps. Knocking on the door, he was greeted a moment later by an old lady in a dress that was at least a decade out of fashion—boxy cut, drab colors. She looked at him funny, scrunching up her old, wrinkled face.

"What do you want? We don't rent to men," she said.

"I am looking for a friend of mine. The Lady Claudia of House Wise," Alexander said, giving the old woman a little bow. He didn't have to. She was clearly a commoner, but a little difference would go a long way with somebody like her. She looked up, thinking, scratching a small mole on her chin.

"Ain't nobody here by that name. We don't get to many Ladies in this part of town. Misses, sure, but not Ladies," the matron of the house said. Alexander found it odd. This was what she had written in her documents. He wasn't about to argue with this woman, who obviously knew who was and was not saying at her house.

"My mistake, I must have written the wrong number down. I do beg your pardon for bothering you this morning," Alexander said, trying to not sound as flustered as he felt.

Why did she have a fake address? Or was it a fake name? There were so many questions running through his mind at that moment. The old lady didn't say anything else, closing the door in his face. Alexander bit his lower lip and huffed before turning and walking down the steps, letting the roses fall to his side.

"Better luck next time, old chap," a random man said walking by.

"Yes, you too," Alexander said, because he couldn't think of anything better to say and a response was required. Otherwise, what was he but just a truly pathetic sad sack standing on the street? It didn't matter, the man had already walked beyond him and didn't turn to say anything else. Alexander turned his mind to other things.

Something was wrong and he just couldn't put it together. He was just a little too tired, a little too hungover, and confused. His heart hurting, Alexander started walking toward a small café that he saw across the street. Maybe a little more coffee and something greasy would make him feel better. Or worse. There was always the chance it would make things worse, though right now, he would relish a simple bad feeling—like indigestion—that he could easily process.

Alexander found himself a small table off to the side where he could be alone with his thoughts. The eggs, toast, and tea had been settling. Food was what he needed. Now, he was able to think more clearly.

The address was a fake. Claudia had mentioned having a rough relationship just before coming to Festival, so she was probably just being careful. He could respect that. Lost in his thoughts, he started to watch people come in and then he saw him. It was the same man from the ball last night, who had been talking with Lord Webb. He had the same black coat and vest. His dark cravat was clipped with a deep purple gem inlaid in gold. That was something new from last night. What upset Alexander the most was just how sleezy yet charismatic his face looked.

Picking up his coffee, the uncomfortable man walked toward Alexander, the two of them locking eyes. Alexander tried to play it off like they hadn't just looked at each other, but it was too late. The man walked over.

"Good morning, Mister Cordova," he said, holding out a hand. Alexander reached up and took his, half expecting it to be clammy. It was soft, far too soft, like somebody who applied lotion too many times a day.

"I am Mister Harrison," he said, the 'S' sound being pulled out like he was a snake. The man's soft comforting voice gave Alexander the sudden urge to buy a used carriage. Mister Harrison didn't ask. He just pulled out the other chair and sat down. It was almost as if any warmth that was at the table fled from his presence.

"You and Misses Wise were quite the item last night," he said.

"Yes, we were attempting to bring mirth and merriment to the evening," Alexander said, taking a sip of his coffee. It was bitter and the rest of his breakfast now held little appeal.

"I just wanted to let you know that Good Master Webb has his eyes on you and your team. He is a very good gauge of true talent," Mister

Harrison said, gently sipping his drink and sitting it down, a dainty pinky held out.

"We are just here for the tourney and then it is back to University," Alexander said.

He didn't miss a beat with the cover story of just being in school, working on his doctorate. It was true, but also not. Mister Harrison gave him a smile that managed to have both too much tooth and too much gum all at the same time.

"Yes of course, Mister Cordova. But if you are ever interested, ever decide that this is what you want…"

He left the offer hanging. Mister Harrison produced a card and set it down. It was all black and just barely could Alexander make out a watch code. It was a slick presentation. Alexander picked up the card. It had weight and heft to it, solid stock.

"I will keep that in mind," he said, a little confused by all of this. Deep down, he felt that this was about something more than cards. They were a good team, but not *that* good.

"You do that. I shall let you return to your breakfast. I do hope Mistress Wise enjoys the flowers," Mister Harrison said as he stood up and faded away into the crowd.

Alexander was able to breathe again, the tightness in his chest fading, as the warmth of the table returned. The only thing that didn't come back was his appetite.

Barker's World, Hanna

Barker's World was barely a moon orbiting around a massive gas giant. This unnamed planet had fifteen moons and only one of them was habitable. It was a dry, dusty world with scant vegetation and was just big enough to hold onto an ionosphere so that it could maintain life.

Nothing this far off the highway would have been considered for terraforming, Hanna thought, looking at the holographic display that was showing over the glass map table in the CIC. She stood there with her mother, brother, and Captain Rackland, all watching the first readings come in from their advanced fly-by mission.

"I'm picking up trace amounts of tachyons and deacyon particles, along with a strong pocket of neutrinos," the Hawkeye pilot's voice said over the radio.

"All of that is consistent with what we would detect from a ship using a jump gate," Erik said, as the numbers from the scans started to come up next to the video of Barker's World.

"It appears that we have missed our prey, but not lost their scent," Lord Admiral Cordova said, clapping her hands behind her back. She started to pace around the lower section of the Combat Information Center. "I do not want to lose those ships."

"Then might I suggest that we take a different approach than just trying to chase them?" Hanna said, the beginning of a plan forming in her mind.

"I agree with the Major," Captain Rackland said. "If these ships are indeed capable of a hyperlight jump without a gate, then we will never catch up to them, especially in the Doldrums."

"I take it you have a plan, Major?" her mother asked.

"Indeed, I do."

She walked over and started hitting a few keys on the side of the glass map table. It pulled up a more detailed picture of Barker's World, focusing on a single settlement that was in the northern hemisphere, the only part of the world that wasn't wracked with storms or extreme radiation caused by its proximity to the gas giant.

"We can surmise that our targets came out of Null space here, which means that there is something important on this world. Information on who they are is probably more valuable than any directional information that math and science can suss out for us here in space. Somebody down there knows something. Let me take a detachment down and poke around." Hanna stepped back from the table and assumed a rest stance, watching her mother as she continued to pace around the table.

"I take it that the two of you agree with this assessment?" Lord Admiral Cordova said, turning to Erik and Captain Rackland.

"I do," Rackland said.

"My sister makes a very solid argument. We can't keep sailing forward blindly. If there is something to learn here, we need to take every opportunity to learn it," Erik said.

Her mother walked over and poured herself and cup of tea, before resuming her pacing.

"Good, then we are all in agreement. Major, put together your team. Keep it small, so that we can pull you out quickly, if need be. Take one of the deck gang with you, somebody who knows ships, just in case you need an expert on the ground."

Hanna gave her mother a salute. "Yes ma'am."

"You will depart within the hour. Dismissed."

Erik snapped to attention, saluting as well. Then both he and Hanna turned and headed back up the steps out of the Combat Information Center to get ready to make planetfall.

***

It had taken an hour to get everything ready, slower than Hanna would have liked; all departments were in desperate need of redrilling, a problem she would tackle later.

The first part of the team consisted of ten marines under the command of Sergeant Ramirez. The sergeant had been leading *Fury* marines since before Hanna had been born and she knew he would follow orders and give her all the tactical and command support that she needed. From the deck crew, she had pulled in Corporal Fox Windsail. She knew the electrical systems of just about every ship out there and could cobble together anything they needed. Also, a solid mission would cheer her up from whatever Hanna's stupid brother had said to her.

Always cleaning your messes, Alexander.

All twelve of them were crammed into the back of a Hawkeye, Hanna and Fox up front, and the marines in the back. Hanna had swapped her bright red ship coat in favor of a long brown duster, the only military insignia being her gold oak leaves. Strapped around her waist, she had her cutlass and pistol. As an officer, she was traveling light. Fox and the marines also had on the same brown dusters. Fox, though, was lugging her tools, while the marines had on body armor under the dusters and were packing plasma rifles. According to their scans, the temperature on the surface was approaching one hundred degrees with no humidity in the air. It had been a while since Hanna had experienced a good heat like that. She was looking forward to getting her feet on real rock and solving a mystery.

The Hawkeye kicked up a massive plume of dirt as it landed. They set down just over a mile outside of town. They were not trying to hide their approach, but also didn't want to land a ship in the middle of what could end up being a hostile settlement. Dealing with people who didn't interact with the Confederation was always a dicey proposition.

"Hang in orbit and we will radio in when we need an evac," Hanna said to the Hawkeye pilot. The man gave her a salute and then turned back to his controls.

As the last marine disembarked, she jumped off the ship. The door closed and the Hawkeye's engines filled the air with a deafening roar as it lifted back up into low orbit. It took a few minutes for the sand to settle down. Hanna didn't want to open her mouth to issue orders until it did.

"Sergeant, send two men forward to cover our approach and two back to watch our asses. Let's move out," Hanna said, whipping her jacket back so that it was hanging behind her sheathed cutlass. Two marines ran forward, hitting a small ridge and getting to their knees scanning forward with their rifles. Two more ran behind them doing the same.

"Major, can I ask a question?" Fox asked, stepping up next to Hanna.

"Of course, Corporal," she said.

"Why did I get picked for this assignment? Just wondering?" There was a bit of trepidation in her voice, but also force. Hanna didn't want to say the real reason out loud—saying it would make it true, and the two women mostly only knew each other by association.

"Your jacket has you rated as a Class Five repair tech, with commendations for fast and cleaver solutions. That seemed like something we could use on this mission," Hanna said as they started walking.

"What is the mission, sir? Why are we out here in this long-forgotten section of space?" Fox asked.

Hanna knew that the particulars of the mission were need-to-know only but there was something in this woman's voice that said she needed to know if she was going to be useful; and so, without going into *too* much detail, Hanna filled her in on the mission. She pulled Sergeant Ramirez over as well, so that all three of them would be in the loop.

"That is fucking impossible," Fox said. "Excuse my language, sir."

"We shall let it slide this time," Hanna chuckled.

In the distance, they could see the small town of Waltersburg. The desert moved forward with its light bushy vegetation and rocks. The town sat on a flat hunk of land. Behind it were mountains. Flowing down from the mountains and through the small town was an anemic river, so small that Hanna would have been embarrassed to even call it a creek. The town was two roads that met in the center, forming a square. In the center of the square, there was a small well. In the back of the town, there was a large stone bell tower that looked to have seen better days. Even at this distance, she could see people walking around.

"The approach looks clear, Major. I was worried about that tower, but it's empty," the Corporal, who had gone ahead of the party, said from where he was knelt behind a bush, a looking glass in his hand.

"Well, that is good. What else can you tell me?" Hanna asked, reaching into her belt and pulling out a looking glass of her own and scanning the town.

"Seems there is a general store or pub of some kind in the middle of town. It has gotten more foot traffic than anything else I've seen."

"Then that is where we will start. Corporal, keep a watch on us. If you feel we are in danger, you are authorized to execute your best judgement on the matter." Hanna found the Saloon in the center of town through her looking glass, painted red with a sign that had a frosty mug of beer on it.

"Sergeant Ramirez, Corporal Windsail, you are with me. The rest of you, fan out and keep an eye on the town. Radio in if you see anything out of the ordinary. I do not want to be caught in an ambush down there," Hanna said.

Waltersburg was the name of the place. It was scratched into some wood hanging from a post just outside of town. As they walked in, people started to stare at them. They were simple folks, in rough spin and denim. Drab colors on clothing that was made to last a lifetime. Wide brimmed felt hats seemed to be the popular fashion for most people—to keep the sun from their eyes, Hanna suspected.

The other thing she noticed right away about the folks of this town was that they were armed. Pistols hung from the belt of everybody who walked by. She didn't want to stop and stare and thus, Hanna couldn't determine what make they were. Given how rustic this place was, she suspected some crude energy weapons or even old style slug throwers. Not to be confused with the high-end kinetic weapons that had been used to kill the crew of the *Key*. If they were all armed, then either this small moon was extremely inhospitable, or they were a prickly bunch. Hanna would have put good money on the answer being both.

As they approached the Saloon, Hanna could hear people talking and a piano playing. She held up a hand to stop the group.

"Sergeant, Corporal, keep your eyes open, but let me do the talking," Hanna said.

Ramirez nodded, as did Fox a moment later. Hanna walked forward and she could hear her boots thumping and creaking on the old wood of the steps. The saloon was open to the outside except for a pair of batwing doors. She pushed them open and walked in, letting her long duster billow in the breeze. The patrons stopped talking and the piano went silent as she stood there, feeling every eye in the room look at her.

Hanna sauntered up to the bar and pulled up a stool. The barkeeper, a big man with thinning gray hair and a dead eye, walked up and sat a coaster down in front of her.

"What'll be, stranger?" he asked, his voice sounding like he chewed and swallowed rocks for fun. Hanna looked across the bar. Nothing was labeled, just bottles with brown, clear or multicolored liquids. There were two beer taps, and the sign outside had a mug, so she took a gamble.

"A round of beers for my friends and me, if you please," she said, pointing to Ramirez and Fox.

The barkeep didn't say anything. He just threw down two more coasters and went back to pour the drinks. To Hanna's disappointment, the mugs were not frosted.

As the beers, light amber with ample foam, were handed to them, a woman walked up and went behind the bar. She was wearing a blue shirt with a brown vest and leather pants. Hanging from her waist was a pistol and on her chest was a star made of tin. Her hair was long and jet-back, her face soft and her eyes hard.

"What brings you to my town?" she asked, leading against the back bar, folding her arms across her chest.

"Just passing through and thought we would stop for a drink," Hanna said. It was a lie so bold faced that she was almost embarrassed to have even said it. It was all a part of the game.

"Bullshit. Ain't another town on this miserable rock. Y'all are off-worlders. That's fine, we just don't see too many of y'all. The name is Chloe, and I'm the sheriff round these parts," she said.

"Guilty. I'm Major Hanna Cordova," she said, holding out a hand. Chloe reached out and took it. The sheriff had a tight grip.

"Well then, Major Hanna Cordova, I'll ponder you again what brings Confederation Navy to my town in this long-forgotten section of space?" she asked, more forceful this time. The tone implied that there was not going to be a third chance to answer truthfully.

"We are tracking a group of pirates. Their course led this way. We were under the impression that you might have a few scraps of pertinent information. Perhaps they were using this little moon as a base of operations or a waypoint?" Hanna said, leaning forward. Two could play at a game of power moves.

"Well now, let me see, pirates," Chloe said. "The only off-worlders we have seen in the last few weeks have been our standard transport from New Angles that comes round every other month or so. Usually, they drop off some supplies, stuff we can't grow here. Only a few folks on that run. Barker's World ain't what you would call a tourist destination. Hell, I can't even remember that last time somebody from the Confederation showed up." Chloe turned to the bartender who was cleaning out a glass. "Mac, you remember that last time we got a Confed out here? Official or otherwise?"

The big man turned and thought about it for a minute, looking Hanna and her crew up and down, reaching back into his memory to find something. Either he knew exactly what he was going to say or it really *had* been that long since the Confederation had been out this way.

"There was that fella, the one who preached for a few weeks until he ran out of coin and then wandered off into the desert," Mac said.

"I plum forgot about that. He showed up when I was down at my sister's after the baby," Chloe said. "Little Ango is toddling and probably about to be jawing his mom's ear off here soon enough."

Hanna did the math quickly in her head. That would be about a year and a half ago, give or take, depending on how advanced Chloe's nephew was.

"If I might ask, what this man was preaching about?" Hanna asked.

"Mostly nonsense. Something about storms and doors, heaven, hell, shadows and a coming reckoning. He had what a looked like a lower case "T" around his neck," Mac said.

"A cross," Hanna said, making one with her hands. The main vertical bar being one index finger and the cross bar about two thirds of the way up her other finger. Mac snapped and pointed at it.

"That be it, right there. He would whip that thing out—it were made of wood, with some gold sparking on it—and yell that we were all going to die; that damnation and hellfire was coming for us all."

Hanna took a deep breath and sighed. Looking at Ramirez and Fox, she could tell that they too understood what this strange man was.

"The Fellowship of the Cross," Hanna muttered.

A group of religious fanatics who were convinced that the second coming was on the way; that, from the Barrier, would come their lord. But first, enough blood had to be spilled in his name to prepare for his crossing. Death and faith to light the way or some such stupidity. Tiberius had talked about them from time to time. The Fellowship of the Cross was the biggest foe of the Host'ire since the Wayfinder wars. Both groups had a fundamental disagreement on what was inside the Barrier and where the last lost Wayfinder highway went.

It all just seemed foolish to her—one group had superpowers, the other claimed that a god wanted blood. Hanna had ended up sleeping during Tiberias's stories while Erik and Alexander had always been enraptured. Hanna might not have taken their beliefs seriously, but she took one of their ilk showing up deadly so. It was how things started, first one, then another, before eventually a whole fleet of them would appear and attempt to convert whatever world they were at by the sword. In the last twenty years, most of their crusading had taken place outside of Confederation space, in the galactic south closer to the Fissure. At least, that is what the scant news reports that she had seen said.

"I do believe I heard him say something like that," Mac piped in.

"Whatever happened to him? He had skedaddled before I got back. I take it I don't need to investigate nobody for murder, do I?" Chloe asked.

"You know we behave, Sheriff. He was already talking about going to the old, abandoned church in the hills. We just… gave him a little push, is all," Mac said.

"Mighty kind of ya to not force me to dust off the jail cell," Sheriff Chloe said.

"Where is this old church?" Hanna asked. "I'd be interested in following up, seeing if he is still there; might know something about of pirates. They have been in the area for a while."

The Sheriff didn't answer at first. She just turned, picked up a shot glass, a bottle and sauntered to the bar. Setting the glass down, she poured a shot of the brown liquor. Hanna knew instantly that it was whiskey and a very poor batch at that. Chloe looked at them, then downed the shot and sucked her teeth.

"Figured I should just come right out and say it so you can chuckle like effete, educated off-worlders. That place is touched by spirits," the sheriff said as she poured herself another shot.

"I don't follow," Hanna said. For a moment, she thought she did, but instantly wrote it off, because nobody believed in ghosts. It was a ludicrous idea.

"Don't mock me. I've been there. I've heard the screams and the moans. You haven't seen it, don't know the history," she said, taking the shot. Mac walked over and sat down three more shot glasses and took away their beers.

"Would you be so kind as to educate us then, please?" Hanna asked. Mac started to fill the four shot glasses.

"When I was a child, some padre from deep in the doldrums showed up in town. He preached about forgiveness and sin. Fire and brimstone. Very loud dark religion. Whipped the town into a bit of a fervor. I suppose people need to find God from time to time, even if it's a vengeful one that thinks basic humanity is sinful.

"This man convinced them to build him a church from which he could preach and spread the word. And we did. My father laid some of them stones. We built that man a church and for the next five years, he fed on this town, leached us dry.

"That was when the kids started to go missing.

"At first, it was a boy that was a known troublemaker, named Sam. Nobody missed Sam, we just remarked that it had gotten quiet. Then Tilly went missing. She was a bight little girl. People liked her. We looked for her. Then Poppy, who had been close with the padre, didn't show up for services. Her mother was hell bent on finding her, and…" The sheriff stopped and contemplated her shot, rolling the full glass in her hand.

"Under the alter was a hatch that led to a basement none of us knew about. He had been holding them there, doing unspeakable things. My father, the last sheriff, shot that man in the chest right then and there. While he was on the ground, bleeding and laughing, they took the kid's bodies and put the place to the torch. All that is left is a burned husk of stone. At night, when the wind is right, you can hear him laughing as those children scream," she finished, finally taking her shot.

Hanna worked to not roll her eyes at the story. She followed Chloe's lead and downed her shot. Ramirez and Fox followed. The whiskey burned and somehow tasted worse than it smelled. The flight deck had better radiator hooch.

"Tell them about the lights," Mac piped in.

"I think they have gotten enough ghost stories for one day. Look, Major Cordova, I ain't gonna stop you from going and poking 'round, but if something goes wrong, don't look to me and mine for help," Sheriff Chloe said. She picked up her hat and walked from behind the bar and headed to the door of the saloon. She turned, tipped her hat to them and then proceeded to walk out. Hanna watched her go then turned to the bartender.

"What do we owe you, good sir?" she asked.

"This round's free, just heed Sheriff Chloe's advice," Mac said, stacking the four glasses into each other.

Hanna turned around and motioned for her party to follow. Ramirez and Fox fell in line, and they walked out. Once on the street, Hanna turned toward the mountains, and in the distance, probably about five miles away, she could see what looked like an old church.

"Sergeant, gather your men and fan out. We are going to check out this ghost church," Hanna said. Ramirez gave her a salute and started giving orders into his radio.

As they were walking, Hanna tapped her lapel, turning on the microphone built into her cravat.

"*Fury* Actual, this is Major Cordova," she said. There was a moment before her mother's voice came over the small radio that was in her inner ear.

"This is Actual, go ahead, Major."

"This town doesn't know anything, but there might be a lead at an old, abandoned church. We got a ghost story from the local law enforcement. It has the pitch and tenor of something that a parent would tell their children to keep them from the woods at night. I intend to investigate with all haste. It should only take a few hours," Hanna said.

"Very good, Major. Keep me informed of your progress. Actual out."

Hanna clicked off her radio and kept walking. As she was leaving the borders of the town, from the corner of her eye, she saw the sheriff watching them.

"She has been three steps behind us the whole time," Ranirez whispered.

"Indeed," Hanna muttered. She wasn't sure if the sheriff believed her story or was just a very good actor. It didn't matter. They were going to find out the truth of the situation soon enough.

Apartments, The Citadel, Lucas

Lucas opened his eyes. Joanna was still wrapped around him, Naomi and Rostov on the other side. At some point, they had grabbed a blanket and fallen asleep on the floor. A small stab of pain went up his back. Lucas was getting too old to sleep on the floor after... after whatever *that* was.

He looked at his friends, the feelings of connection and bond stronger than anything he had ever felt before. They had made a pact last night, but it wasn't in blood. Was that the awakening? He could feel them in ways that he had never felt anybody before, even just his own emotions. It was a tremendous feeling; one that he never wanted to end.

Boom.

The sound came from outside. It was soft, but he recognized it instantly. Artillery. It was far away. A moment later, there was another explosion, much louder. The room shook and everybody bolted up.

"What was that?" Rostov yelled, shuddering at the sound, scrambling to the wall. Naomi went and wrapped her arms around him, stroking his head, calming him down.

"Artillery," Lucas said, as another low boom filled his ears.

Turning from Rostov, he could feel the fear, the PTSD from his confinement trying to take him over. This was it. The Fellowship was attacking. Lucas ran to the window and threw open the curtains only to be greeted by steel shutters. The Citadel was on lockdown. He wasn't going to be able to see out, to look over the battle and figure out what they were going to do. There was no time, everything was coming to a head all at once. Why had they not gone out as soon as they knew something? Why hadn't he gone and told Fel about Wingarf as soon as he learned about him?

Lucas, shut up. Focus, the past is past. We have to move forward, he said to himself. *Time to rally.*

"We've run out of time. They are here. This ends tonight," Lucas said in his best leader voice as he grabbed his underwear and pants, pulling them quickly on.

Rostov had stopped screaming, but his ragged breathing still filled the room. Lucas walked over and put his hand on his friend's shoulder and took a deep, calming breath. Closing his eyes, Lucas pushed that emotion through his hand. Rostov's breathing slowed and started to even out.

"I'm here, I'm here," Rostov said quietly.

"I'm glad, we are going to need you, solider," Lucas said, taking Rostov's hand and hoisting him to his feet.

"What's the plan?" Joanna asked, quickly pulling her clothing on.

"You and I are going to find Administrator Fel. She needs to know about Wingarf. Hopefully we can get her focused on him before he does anything to sabotage the base. I think we can get her on our side. Naomi, Rostov. Find me that son of a bitch. Follow, but don't let yourselves be seen. If you can find any professors along the way, tell them what you know. The fewer places he can find refuge, the better. We can't risk looking for the door to whatever is below until he is taken care of. The Fellowship want it and no doubt Wingarf has told them about us. They will be watching us to find it," Lucas said, pulling on his coat and flicking it out. He felt alive again, for the first time in a while. *This* was his element. He was made for combat. The last few days had felt interminable. He was worthless at investigation, and it showed.

Now, though, he was ready.

"Be careful, be quick, and stay on comms," he said, nodding at all of them. "Most importantly, remember that I love you all."

The Citadel, Naomi

Explosions burst all around outside. The very tower of the Citadel shook with each explosion. Whatever weapons the Fellowship had been able to bring up were massive. She could hear the fire and the impact, so it couldn't have been an orbital weapon, unless the ships were in the atmosphere. It was bad, whatever it was. This battle was something the Fellowship had prepared for, something that the powers that be wanted, and now they were stuck in the middle of it.

"Where are we going?" Rostov asked.

"Rickman's. I have a feeling she will be there," Naomi said as they ran.

She had faith that she would be there, that Rickmon would know where Wingarf was—or at least how to find him, so they could report his actions to Administrator Fel. Another rumble caused chunks of the roof to fall as the lights flickered. That impact had hit the tower itself.

"They can't be foolish enough to want to bring the tower down if they are trying to get something from it! Can they?" Rostov yelled as they rounded another corner.

Naomi didn't know the answer to that. She didn't know much at all about the Fellowship of the Cross—just that they didn't leave people alive and were fanatical devotees to a dead god. A god they hoped to bring back to life with enough spilled blood.

"I don't know. Maybe they figure it'll be easier to find what they want by clawing through ruble then having to fight through a hundred thousand Militarum troopers?" Naomi guessed.

More dust fell around them as she rounded a bend. Then, there was a sound, children calling out.

"Professor Rickman, Professor Rickman!"

Naomi stopped in her tracks. She saw herself and Rostov running up to a much younger looking professor. The professor turned away from them, a horrible, pained look upon her face. Rickman knew what they were going to ask, and she knew what the answer was going to be, and it pained her. Naomi hadn't seen it then; hadn't *wanted* to see it. But now—bloody hell—it was so painfully obvious. It was right there, looking at her, mocking her trust.

"He is going to kill her!" Young Naomi yelled, her voice horse and full of panic.

"Or worse," Rostie piped in. "Probably worse."

He had been right. If they had not stepped in, what happened would have been worse. But what *did* happen? They still didn't remember the end of the story, where Essex went, where they had gone, what had happened to Hyacinth.

"I..." Rickman paused. "There is nothing I can do... Policy..." She turned away from them, looking embarrassed. "It goes against standard practice."

The weakness, the fear in her voice, was loud and crystal clear. There was some regret, but mostly it was weakness, a complete abdication of her responsibility to keep her students safe. To keep *them* safe. The established norm from the Host'ire to let abuse among students happen was more important to her than saving Hyacinth. No, it was the *appearance* of the norm, because there was nothing normal about what Jasper was doing. A little beating, some fighting, was one thing. This was about to be a rape that would end in murder, *if* Hyacinth was lucky. The shade of Rickman walked away. The two children stood there, dumbfounded.

Naomi was filled with rage. That bitch had failed them. She collected all her books, corresponded with her, all for what? To assuage her guilt about letting them down all those years ago? To keep up the appearance that she was a good professor, that she hadn't been an abject failure as a human?

"You saw that?" Naomi asked, turning to Rostov, who was standing behind her.

"I did. I always knew," he said quietly. "She was the one who recommended me for re-education when I started poking around, started hearing Hyacinth's voice again."

"Why didn't you tell me? I went on and on about her!" Naomi snapped, spinning around, closing the distance between her and Rostov. She could feel the sadness and fear in him. Was everybody going to let her down today?

"It didn't matter what I said. You have always had a blind spot for the crimes of the order. Unless you saw it, *remembered* it, you were not going to believe it. I... I shouldn't have hidden it from you," Rostov said, holding his head down, sadness radiating away from him. Rickman, she could hate, Rostov... not so much. She could be mad, she could be disappointed, but there was no hating him. They were one.

"No, you shouldn't have. You will have to get in line for my disappointment," Naomi said, trudging forward toward Rickman's lab.

Naomi figured she was probably hiding away somewhere, debating if it was worth standing up and fighting, or if it was proper decorum to just roll over to a mob of bullies. She wouldn't have the opportunity to cower again, if Naomi had anything to say about it.

Fifth Ave Festival, Novagrad, Alexander

Claudia had called Alexander as he was walking back from the café still trying to get the horrible icky feeling out of his system from his interaction with Mister Harrison. Never had he had such a visceral reaction to somebody that he didn't know. The man made his skin crawl in the worst way. It was primal and deeply uncomfortable.

His talk with Claudia had been quick. She said that she left in the middle of the night because she didn't want there to be any friction in the team from them sleeping together. The house thing and not picking up her communicator was a family issue that she had to work out. There were a lot of words and they should have raised red flags. Alexander let all that slide. He was just happy to hear her voice. The butterflies fluttered in his gut when the communicator rang and it showed her number. Any rotten feelings he was having had vanished when she said hello, and as soon as she hung up, he was crushed again, but still happy that he knew where she was. Claudia said she would see him tonight at the festival and also that she had gotten the five pages of notes that Hoben had sent breaking down their games from yesterday. The rest of his walk home was much improved and any thoughts of his strange interaction with Mister Harrison were driven from his mind by thoughts of love.

Tonight's gathering was being held in a public venue—the whole of fifth avenue had been shut down for the night. The street venders had pulled their booths back and been replaced by long tables of food and drink. Walking around the throng of people were clowns and jugglers, performers on stilts, and others who ate and breathed fire. Alexander spent fifteen minutes watching a performer use an exaggerated accent and whips to create parody versions of popular songs. Every version got a big laugh from the people gathered around, who would yell stranger and stranger requests at him. To his credit, he rolled with the audience, nailing every song they threw his way. Eventually, Alexander got bored of this, as the songs they requested got more obtuse or too new for him to recognize.

Like every ball or festival, there was a large dance floor with a live band. Next to the dance floor were lines of tables for amateurs to gather and play Peculiar Pentagon. Every so often, he would see actual pro players interacting with amateurs, sometimes even children. You could tell a lot about a person by how they acted around children interested in getting into a hobby. Far too many of the Pentagon players were sharks who would leave kids crying as they demolished them in a single round and laughed. Alexander found that uncomfortable to watch and meandered away from it.

The whole of the gathering was an assault on the senses, a mixture of high and low sensibilities, nothing like the refined feasts and balls that he normally attended. He liked to think himself a man of the people, who could talk with commoners, but when there were too many of them, he instantly felt out of place and resented them for it. This whole event was the unread message from Fox writ large, and he was not enjoying himself. If he did not find Claudia soon, he was going to leave. Hoben and Katie had walked in and walked out almost instantly. Jeffery had passed on the event before even getting dressed.

"Well look who it is," a familiar, comforting voice said from behind him. Alexander turned and breathed a sigh of relief at seeing Claudia. For the first time, she wasn't in a dress, instead going with a very simple pair of pants and a lavender top that looked very much like it was once part of a dress, with how it wrapped around her shoulders as a shawl. Novagrad was not a cold city, but it was still technically winter.

"It brings me such joy to see you," Alexander said, wrapping his arms around her. He had to resist the desire to kiss her, as that would have been improper decorum in public. He pulled away from her and the two of them quickly found a seat away from some of the crowd, though it was still extremely loud.

"I'm sorry about today and filling out the paperwork incorrectly. I just needed to fly under the radar for a little bit, but as always, family will find you," she said. Her eyes wouldn't match Alexanders, and deep down, he knew that something wasn't right, but he couldn't put his finger on it. Didn't *want* to put his finger on it. She had problems with her family, who didn't? He sure did, and because of that, who was he to judge?

"They are far too good at doing that. If you need anything, just let me know. I am well versed in family issues," Alexander said, remembering the less than cordial terms that he and his mother had departed on.

"I will, my sweet," she said. "Shall we find something to eat? This festival is just delightful." Claudia stood up and then pulled Alexander to his feet and into the crowd of people.

They passed three shops before Claudia found what she wanted. The stall was in the back, the sound of hot oil and frying foods filling the air. The venders were taking orders and submerging all manner of things on sticks into a vat of oil, only to remove them a few moments later, looking golden and delicious. Alexander had not eaten since breakfast and was still feeling a little unsettled from the night before. The smell of fried foods had the possibility to set him off. But if that was what Claudia wanted, then that was what he was going to get for her. Once they reached the front of the line, she pointed at the stall's specialty, fried ice cream. The scientist in Alexander was confused. He knew that there were wizards in the kitchen, but this... This seemed like a bridge too far. You did not fry cold things.

"I have always wanted to try this since I was a child," she whispered in his ear, her lips so close to the hair on his neck he could feel them. Shivers went through his body, his knees turning to rubber.

"Where have I been that I've never seen this before?" Alexander asked, trying to regain even a measure of his composure.

"Being raised on a Dreadstar," she said.

The man at the counter asked what she wanted. Claudia pointed to the fried ice cream. He bowed with a flourish and pulled out a ball of hard frozen white ice cream. There was a stick, and Alexander could see the swirl of fudge just creeping out from the side. He held the stick in front of her to inspect.

Claudia looked it over and turned to Alexander. He nodded, unsure of what was going to happen next. She seemed to be quite enjoying the show, so he was enjoying it, as well. The fry cook showman then held up his empty hand with a flourish, showing them that it was empty. Waving his hand over the frozen dairy treat, he made a fist, raised it a few times and then opened it. Flour and sprinkles came out of his hand like magic. Claudia smiled and clapped. Then he spun around and thrust it into the fryer. With a loud sizzle, it sat for twenty seconds. He then pulled it out. The cook on it was golden and crispy, with a light shimmering spiraling effect across the sphere. He handed it to Claudia, who bowed and said thank you. Alexander passed the man three small coins and followed Claudia.

Once they were away from the stand, Claudia stopped, looked over the magical confection and took a bite. Alexander could hear the crunch. Inside it was still frozen and there was a lightly melted corkscrew of fudge. She held it to him, and he took a bite.

As the night went on, Alexander started to relax, started to get comfortable again. They had a small dinner and danced a bit. Claudia wanted to see the singing whipper. When he wanted a new song, she called out something truly obscure that Alexander was sure was from a holo-game that had been popular when they were children. To his surprise, the man knew it. The cheers from the crowd were ruckus and she hugged him and laughed. Alexander didn't want this moment to end. It was perfect. They didn't have to worry about cards, or family, or presenting in any kind of formal way. They could just be two kids who were in love having fun at the fair.

Of course, this night, like all nights had to come to an end.

Slowly, the party started to wind down, with Claudia and Alexander sitting at a table off to the side. There was a small beep from Claudia's pocket. She reached inside and pulled out her watch and looked at the message.

"Excuse me one minute, I have to take this call," she said before pressing a button and walking away from Alexander in a hurry. He watched her go, enjoying the sway of her rear.

I thought she had finished everything this morning, he thought, losing her in the crowd.

There was nothing for it. If she wanted to tell him about what was going on, then she was going to tell him. Alexander knew that he was going to have to wait. People who had family issues never wanted to talk about them—or that was *all* they wanted to talk about. It seemed that he and Claudia were both in the same camp of not wanting to talk about their family matters. Of course he wasn't sneaking off...

No, she isn't sneaking off, she just doesn't want to have to fight over the noise to talk.

He let his mind be quiet.

But all modern comms have noise filters, it shouldn't...

No, Alexander, stop it. She is allowed her secrets.

He finished his hot chocolate and looked around. She still had not come back, it had been almost ten minutes. Standing up, Alexander adjusted his coat and cravat and walked into the crowd. He followed the way she had gone for a few minutes and then his heart sank.

He saw Claudia, standing at the far end of the street, and she was talking to the unsettling man from the café and the ball last night, Mister Harrison. Walking forward, he felt a knot in his gut. He didn't know what was going on and part of him didn't want to. He couldn't think clearly, couldn't focus on what was in front of him. The world was spinning, moving around like he was suffering some kind of vertigo.

He stopped, took a breath, tried to calm himself down, but couldn't and pushed forward. He was now close enough to hear their conversation, though everybody could hear it. Things were starting to spiral.

"You have had enough time to play around," Mister Harrison said, grabbing her wrist and pulling Claudia toward him. She wretched back, yanking her hand from his grip.

"Tell father I am not coming home. I can make my own choices!" Claudia yelled.

"Choice? What choice do you think you possess in this world?" he asked. His words were dripping with condescension and venom.

"Plenty, we are not done!" she yelled at him.

"Oh, I do believe we are," Mister Harrison reached for her again. But before he could do anything, Alexander was between the two of them.

"Back off!" he snapped.

"Or what, Mister Cordova? What do you want here?" Mister Harrison asked, the anger fading from his voice. Alexander found the anger less concerning that his calm arrogant tone.

"I want..."

He paused for a moment. He wasn't sure when he had taken off his glove—but it was in his hand now—and before he could think through the whole of what he was about to do, his arm was moving and the white glove smacked into Mister Harrison's face with a satisfying *thwap*. Alexander was breathing heavy now, his dander up.

"That was a mistake," Mister Harrison said, rubbing his hand across his cheek.

"You will step away from the lady and apologize," Alexander said, the glove still in his hand, his arm desperately wanting to slap the man again; to wipe that grin off his face.

"Lady Wise and I have business that is no concern of yours, Mister Cordova," Mister Harrison said again, chuckling as he grinned. Alexander didn't stop his arm as he slapped him again.

"That is Lord Cordova to you, sir. I shall have satisfaction and my lady shall retain her honor. First bell, outside the city," Alexander said, throwing the glove to the ground.

The challenge had been issued, and if Mister Harrison wasn't a coward, he would pick up the glove. He could think of nothing else as the heat ran in his veins.

Mister Harrison reached down and picked up the glove, folded it neatly and pressed it against Alexander's chest.

"I do hope you brought a fancy outfit to die in, *Lord* Cordova." He turned to Claudia and gave her a small bow before walking away.

Alexander stood there, stunned at what he had just done, breathing heavily, proud, feeling like a man.

"You bloody fool," Claudia said to him. He didn't see her hand it moved so quickly to hit his face. The slap stung, leaving a read imprint of her hand on his cheek. Before he could say anything, she turned around and stormed off.

He might be a bloody fool, but nonetheless, he felt good about the choice. Whatever happened in the morning, he knew standing up to that man had been right.

He just hoped that Claudia would eventually agree with him on that.

Flight Quarters, Dreadstar Fury, Aya

Aya Nguyen had never been into the Doldrums, let alone days and days into them. This was exciting new territory for her, and she was going to face it with the kind of wide-eyed optimism that only a cadet of sixteen could. For the first three Combat Air Patrols that her father had flown since entering this section of space, he had made her stay on the *Fury* and finish her remote work for the academy. Now that they were officially on break for Festival, she could suit up and head out again.

"I know the crate is no fun, Helo, but I'm going out today," she said, bending down and ruffling the fur of her big Golden Retriever.

He looked up at her, cocked his head to the side and gave her a big wet kiss on the face. Aya laughed and bopped his nose before ushering him into his crate. She picked up a chew toy from the table, handed it to him and closed the door. Turning, she picked up her helmet and left her quarters; *new* quarters, after finally convincing her father that she needed her own space and was enough of an adult now to live on her own. On her own being a bit of a misnomer, seeing as she was just two doors down from the cabin she had been born and raised in. Aya was a *Fury* baby. Born, raised, and serving on ship.

Aya wanted to run the half mile to the flight deck but knew that it was frowned upon unless the drums were beating. Reaching into her pocket, she removed her watch and found an up-tempo exciting track from the Cordova Collection. "Scanning for Lifeforms" was a track of music that was a remix of keystrokes and scanner sounds from CIC and a Hawkeye. It had been composed when Lord Admiral Cordova was still just a Commander and was in an experimental phase. Aya always thought this was some of her best work. It was experimental and full of youthful energy. Everything now was brass and strings, working off the same handful of leitmotifs from twenty years ago.

She skipped and hopped down the hallway, getting strange looks from everybody that she passed. The flight deck and crew had been more morose since the battle. She understood their feelings all too well. Her mother had been one of the thousands draped in a flag and left in the void of space. Aya just never understood dwelling on the negative, holding onto the pain and letting it sour your future. You had to take that hurt and heartache and make good from it; make the dead proud, make it worth the sacrifice.

It was fine, they didn't have to understand. One day, when Bella was CAG, they would start to change. She understood that you had to have joy in everything you were doing in life. *Without joy, what is the point?* she thought.

Aya reached the landing bay, scanned her card, took a breath, and then turned down the Cassandra Cordova electronica before stepping onto the deck like a good cadet who was ready to learn, listen, and do her duty. She didn't need to kill the little girl, only let the adults know that she understood the gravity of the situation that they existed in.

The rest of the squadron were already assembled, decked out in their flight gear. Helmets under their arms, painted in family colors. Erik and Bella had their Chimeras, Lieutenant Ander Stormwind had his trumpeting cloud-gray-on-blue, and she, like her father, carried only a red checkered pattern with a golden snake, showing that they were pledged to House Cordova without having their own coat of arms. She walked briskly up and stood at attention.

"Cadet Nguyen, reporting for duty," she said.

"You are late, Cadet," Commander Cordova said dryly. He was a man who needed to find the humor and zest for life. He hadn't found his mother's music, or his brother's science, or his sister's poetry. A Cordova without an art was a sad thing, Aya thought.

"I'm sorry, sir. It won't happen again," she said.

"Helo wanted to say goodbye after you got dressed, I see," Bella said, pointing to the blond dog hair on her doublet.

"Ah, yes sir. He doesn't understand that I can't be home with him all the time anymore," Aya said.

"Do not think too much on it, Rook. Soon, your head will be filled only with flying and boys," Ander said with a chuckle.

Her father shot daggers at him with his eye and the young man pursed his lips and went quiet. The young Lieutenant was far too sure of himself and far too forward with every woman on the ship. Her father did not like him and wouldn't hesitate to throw him out an airlock if he had approached her. Luckily for Stormwind, she was not taken by his charms at all.

Commander Cordova had started to talk. She needed to pay attention. There was no getting lost in thought during these moments.

"Our job today is simple, people. We currently have a team down on Barker's World. We are the eyes and ears for if something hostile enters the system and then are on standby to cover any kind of extraction that might need to take place. I have mapped out four waypoints that have already been downloaded to your onboard computers that we will be flying between."

Everybody nodded. Commander Cordova held his helmet out into the center of the group. The rest of them put theirs in as well so that all five were touching.

"For duty, honor, and the Confederation," he said.

They repeated the words and knocked their helmets together before pulling them back. Aya turned and followed her father to their Hawkeye. She climbed up into the large ship and seated herself at her interment panel halfway back. Strapping in, she put on her helmet and started going through the preflight setup, turning on all the scanners and radio frequencies that she would be scrubbing through. Once the squadron got away from the bulk of *Fury*, the Hawkeye would be their eyes and ears, using its own scanning package in concert with that of the Dreadstar.

For a combat air patrol like this, Aya only had to worry about three Rapiers, but if this was a combat engagement, she would be responsible for up to ten fighters and a broadsword light bomber. She, of course, had only seen combat in a simulation and was not looking forward to the real thing. That said, she knew she was ready; knew that when the time came, the fear would melt away and there would only be duty.

The deck crew loaded their ship into the shoot and she felt the maglocks grabbing on. They were now loaded into the launchers, which were, at their core, nothing more than big railguns. People didn't like to think about it that way.

For a few moments, every fighter craft on the ship was just a bullet. Music started to play through her headset, a drum heavy arrangement. Thumping propulsive, the kind of music that got your blood going. "Launch Prep" was the standard track that played before any ship went into space. Aya had heard that other squadron leaders played different tracks or nothing at all. Commander Cordova always played "Launch Prep". She couldn't blame him. The track was written before his birth and was the basis for the leitmotif his mother used for tracks about him.

As the ships started to launch, the music turned into a medley, changing over to Bella's tune, which was a jaunty, jazzy bar. Then to her father's tune, with was strings and a pan flute, before finally switching back to "Launch Prep". Lieutenant Stormwind hadn't distinguished himself enough yet to earn his own music. Everybody's goal aboard *Fury* was for the Lord Admiral to write music for them. Even if they said they didn't want it, they did. Aya was not one of those who pretended otherwise. She just hoped her track would be like the Lord Admiral's older work.

There was a push of G-force and then weightlessness took over and they were in space. Turning, Aya could see the stars through the viewscreen where her father was flying the ship. In front of them were three pinpricks of light, the afterburners from the fighters in their wing. Now was the time to focus forward and start to do her job. The scanners had come online and there was no traffic on the comm system but their own. On another screen, she pulled up their flight plan and leaned back. It would take an hour to reach the first waypoint. The second was on the dark side of Baker's World between the small moon and the gas giant it orbited. Lastly, they would come around and then head for home.

"How is Helo taking to the new quarters?" her father asked.

Before she answered, Aya looked down to see that he was on their private channel. She clicked over to it as well. There was no need for everybody to hear this. Flying was the only time that they got to really talk anymore. She missed their conversations at dinner and before bed. A sacrifice to be an adult, to be on her own.

"He is doing well. That first night, he paced a bit, but now he is sleeping in his bed and using the pad in the bathroom," Aya said. "I'm still crating him for the next few weeks when I leave, just until he is fully comfortable with the space."

"That is reasonable. If there is a combat action, he will be safer that way, as well," her father said. It was that kind of stern cold way that father could talk. It was masking, but just under the surface, there was care and love. She knew what he wanted to ask, when asking about the dog.

"I'm doing well too, father. It was strange, that first night. Dark and quiet. Everything felt so small, but I'm getting used to it, really working to make the space my own. Nalla found me an old Novagrad coffee press in storage that has been a real treat to use when I'm up late doing course work.

"How are *you* doing, though, pappa? Now that everybody is gone?" she asked. Her quarters were small, made for a single person. She and Helo had left him with a family-sized apartment.

"I am getting used to it. I still think you and your mother are there; want to tell you things. You want to know what is the hardest to get used to?"

"What is that, pappa?"

"Cooking for one person. You know how I feel about the mess hall," he started.

His aversion to the mass cooking of the ship's mess was legendary. He had always cooked at home, every night since before she was born. In better times, the Nguyen's were known for throwing dinner parties.

"I just can't seem to wrap my head around it. For thirty years, I have cooked for at least two, and now I'm alone. How do you scale down? It just doesn't seem to make sense..." He was fishing, dancing around a question.

"Do you have to much soup left in the refrigerator, pappa?" she asked.

"Yes, I do not know if I can eat it for a third night in a row."

"On my way home tonight, I can stop by. A bowl of your soup sounds wonderful. It was always better the next day."

"Yes, I would like that very much," he said, turning back to the controls and his flying. She turned to her station as well. Their conversations would be like this for the whole flight, short and a little stilted.

The flight was quiet for the next thirty minutes. Aya watched her screens and read a technical manual for a class while bopping to more electronica music, this time an album created from the sounds of engines, both the *Fury's* and her fighters. It was the last original album that the Lord Admiral created before her father died and she was promoted from CAG to commander of the ship.

A proximity alarm went off. Aya flicked away the book and started to press keys and zero in on what her instruments were reporting.

"What are you seeing back there, Cadet?" her father's voice came from the front. This time, it was on the squadron-wide channel.

"Report?" Commander Cordova's voice came through the system.

"Working on it. Something just popped in at the very far range of our scanners. Too far for *Fury* to pick up on, so I'm running everything through the Hawkeye's computers," she said.

"Take your time, breathe," her father said, only to her.

Aya took a deep breath and turned a tracking nob, working to clean up the picture that was starting to come into focus now. Without the extra computing power of the Dreadstar, everything was slower. The technology in the sensors had far outpaced the onboard computer systems of the forty-year-old Hawkeyes that *Fury* still held onto. The Navy had paid to replace the guts, but not the ships.

"I'm getting a silhouette now," she said.

Her heart dropped. They were the same ships that they were chasing, the ones that had departed from the space station; the ones that could jump into Null space on their own.

Except now there were four of them.

She pushed the information to Commander Cordova's fighter. She hadn't finished crunching the trajectory numbers, but there were enough that she could see what had happened. These ships had not been there, then they were, and now were heading quickly through real space toward where *Fury* was.

"Comm, CAG, I need to speak with Actual now," the Commander snapped into his radio. He had left it open so that the whole flight could hear it.

"This is Actual, report Commander," the Lord Admiral's voice said a few moments later.

"Sir, we have four of our phantom ships at the edge of the system on a direct course with *Fury*. Time to intercept four hours. I am flashing you our reading now," Commander Cordova said.

Aya was breathing heavily. It was really happening. She was ready, it was time.

"We are seeing it now, Commander. Good work. Full burn, get your squadron home," the Lord Admiral said before cutting off the line.

"Okay people, time to make ourselves scarce. We don't know how well their scanners work or if we have been spotted," Commander Cordova said.

Aya felt the ship shudder as her father threw on the forward maneuvering thrusters, killing their momentum, before igniting the ones on the bottom of the ship, flipping them over so that they were pointed back toward *Fury*.

"Cadet, warm up our counter measures, and keep an eye out for any radiological alarms," her father said.

"Yes sir," she said, hitting keys and warming up the flairs and chaff.

"Lieutenant, I need you to get a hold of Major Cordova right now," she heard through her headset. It was the Commander's voice. She didn't know who he was talking to. It wasn't anybody in the squadron, even though he still had their frequency open.

"There is a storm coming in that is scrambling our comms with the ground team. Is there…?"

The line was garbled. She realized that he was talking with the Hawkeye that had dropped his sister and her marines off on Barker's World.

"Lieutenant, if you can't raise them go and get…" Before the Commander could finish his sentence, gunfire started to come through the line. There was a panicked scream and then the sound of an explosion.

"Damn it," she heard the Commander say.

"Nguyen, change course and follow me. We are going to get my sister. Bella, hard burn back to *Fury* and get the squadrons ready to launch. I want the air full when I get back," Commander Cordova said. He cut off the line before anybody could say anything else. None of those were suggestions.

"How are you doing back there?" her father asked.

"I'm good, Pappa." Aya said, taking another breath. Focusing on her work.

"Scared?"

"Yes," she conceded in a lower voice.

"So am I. So am I," he said quietly as the Hawkeye picked up speed.

Abandoned Chapel, Barker's World, Hanna

The chapel was farther away than Hanna had thought at first. Distance on actual planetary bodies always gave her trouble. People who were born and raised upon real ground understood how to look at the horizon and its features and figure distance. Hanna, like everybody in her party, had been born and raised upon *Fury*; space was what they knew. Ships and stars. She could tell how far away something was in the cold void. It didn't matter now. They had been walking for an hour and were committed to this course of action. Regardless, she would be calling the Hawkeye to pick them up from this chapel.

She pulled out her spyglass. The range finder said it was another two miles. The building's walls were still standing, made of gray stone like the mountain it was sitting on top of. The bell tower had cracks in it and the top had long ago fallen away. The roof was open to the air. All that was left were burned out support beams filled with bird's nests.

Then she saw one of the few things that she didn't want to see. Pulling the spyglass down, it was hard to miss. A storm was coming up on them quickly from the west. It was going to overtake the chapel, them, and the town. Hanna turned and did a range scan to find the town. Three miles. They were out of options. The storm was a mass of dark clouds and dust that had just crested over the horizon. Electricity could be seen cascading through it with the naked eye. This was not going to be a weather event that they could survive in the open.

"Lieutenant, we need evac, if you please," she said into her radio, calling back to the Hawkeye that had landed out past town and was waiting for them.

"Roger Major, I have your location beacon. We shall be there presently," the pilot said.

"Marines, huddle round," Hanna called out, summoning the group to her. "I have decided to not press our luck today against nature and that storm is approaching fast. Prepare to double time when the Hawkeye arrives.". The marines nodded and formed a circle perimeter around their position to be ready.

Five minutes passed and there was nothing. The storm was getting larger in her view. Hanna pulled out her radio and tried to raise the Hawkeye. Nothing but static came back through the device. She banged the radio against her hand a few times to try and jostle it into working. Still, only static returned. Then she could hear engines.

Turning, the Hawkeye came over the horizon and her heart dropped. The ship was already on fire and sparks from what looked like small arms rounds were bouncing off the armor plating. Within moments of the transport ship coming into view, the screech of a missile filled the air, the smoke leaving a trail a moment before it smashed into the backside of the Hawkeye. What was once a ship with a crew of two and room for twelve was suddenly turned into a ball of fire.

Ramirez bit out a curse to the gods, the kind of thing that only a marine could say in polite—or impolite—company. Fox stood there, wide-eyed, her mouth agape. Hanna took a deep breath. Clearly, this planet was not just provincial and backward, but was actively hostile. Now there was no going back to town. The storm was coming, and she didn't know the exact strength or armament of her foe. Clearly, they had the firepower to take out a small starship.

"Alright, marines, move out. We need to reach that chapel as fast as possible. We can wait out the storm there. *Fury* will have detected that we are under fire and send an evac," Hanna said, putting away her spyglass and preparing to run.

"Jarheads, you heard the Major. Let's go!" Sergeant Ramirez said, holding a finger up and spinning it around before pointing forward. The marines lined up two-by-two and started running at full speed. Hanna turned to Fox, knowing that this was not something that she had trained for.

"Are you going to be good?" Hanna asked.

"I wasn't planning on dying today. I still have words to share with your brother when we get to NovaTerra," Fox said.

"I would not want to stand between you and satisfaction," Hanna said, pushing the tech forward.

She turned and gave the wreckage of the Hawkeye one last look, then started to run, making sure that she stayed behind Fox, bringing up the rear. Nobody would dare to run slower than their commanding officer.

Hanna's lungs were burning as the first wave of dust started to reach them and she could feel the wind whipping, trying to push her off her feet. The chapel was growing larger in her field of view. The first group of marines had already made it to the large wooden doors and established a perimeter, covering the approach of everybody else.

Hanna turned around, running backward for a moment. Still nobody behind them. She grabbed the radio off her jacket and tried to raise anybody that might be within range. Again, there was nothing but static. The storm was too strong. As she got close, Hanna didn't slow down. She just turned and let her shoulder take the impact as she hit the wall. They were all there now.

"Breach and clear this door, if you please, Sergeant Ramirez!" she yelled, still catching her breath.

Ramirez nodded and signaled to two marines, who both took up positions by the front of the door. The sergeant then gave it a solid, firm kick and the old wood cracked and came open. The squad poured in. There was some yelling, and then a moment later, she heard the sergeant call, "Clear!"

Hanna walked in and two marines behind her closed the doors and threw down a crossbar that was sitting against the inside wall. The main room of the chapel looked how she expected it to: empty, covered in dust and burn marks. There were pews and an altar. Behind the altar was a large wooden cross, the symbol of the Fellowship. The marines stood around a man that she didn't recognize, who had been pushed to the ground, with Ramirez's boot on his back.

"Corporal, secure the area. Find us some kind of shelter because that roof is not going to do any good," Hanna said, pointing up. The young man next to her nodded and went about his duty. Hanna then walked over to the sergeant.

"What have we found here?" she asked.

"Looks like a Fellowship straggler. He had this on him," Ramirez said, handing Hanna an old plasma revolver.

"That's a classic," she muttered, looking at the weapon.

Plasma revolvers had gone out of style as soon as gunsmiths were able to build a system strong enough to handle rapid fire. The Confederation had gone from muzzle loading plasma weapons to fully automatic in less than a hundred years. Still, it was a simple, elegant weapon. She shoved it in her sword belt and knelt to see who this man they had found was. He was dressed in all black, with a frock and white collar. The man had a pudgy face, flat nose, and thinning gray hair that was no more than wisps in the wind. Hanna forgot what the Fellowship of the Cross called men of this rank, but she recognized the regalia.

"Hello Padre. I am Major Hanna Cordova," she said.

"They are coming. Names mean nothing. The Chosen have found their ships, found their friends. The storm is coming," he said, his cadence going from a low mutter to a scream and back again.

Wonderful, he is as cracked as this church, Hanna thought.

"Who are the Chosen? Where did they find their ships?" Hanna asked.

There was little chance that his mind was in a strong enough position to answer her questions. Still, though, duty demanded that she try.

"They are who stayed to watch, to gather new friends. Seeded throughout, they were ready for the return of the culling. Rapture! Rapture!" he yelled again.

Hanna stood up. That wasn't much, but it felt like the kind of information that would make far more sense after it was too late to do anything useful with it.

"Sir, we found something," one of the marines called out from behind the alter.

Hanna walked over to him as the sounds of the storm outside got louder, the dust and rain smashing into the walls of the chapel. Already water was coming inside. They were in for a wet night, waiting for this to pass. When she got to the marine, he was kneeling down over a trap door. It was latched shut with a sophisticated lock that required a thumb print to open.

So there was some truth to the Sheriff's story.

Fox got to the lock just before Hanna. She bent down and started to examine it, poking the device with a small spanner pulled from her vest.

"That is a fine lock, if I do say so myself. Also, there is a trigger under it," she said

"Can you open it?" Hanna asked.

"Maybe with a few hours and a different set of tools," Fox said. She started to flip the small spanner around in her fingers. "What about our friend over there, he probably—" Before she could finish, another loud sound struck the wall of the chapel.

It wasn't rain or debris.

"Plasma fire, we are under attack!" Ramirez yelled, popping up and instantly commanding his men into position. His decades of combat experience couldn't be overstated in a moment like this.

"Secure the prisoner and bring him over here!" Hanna yelled.

The sound of plasma fire got louder. None of the shots were hitting. If they had, the walls of the chapel would have started to shatter. It must have been the storm that was keeping them from aiming true.

Or they are trying to draw us out without damaging something that's in here, Hanna thought. One of the marines dragged the raving preacher over and dropped him down at Hanna's feet.

"Thank you, private. You may join Sergeant Ramirez on the line," Hanna said. She reached down and pulled the man to his feet.

"They are coming for you, coming for what is theirs. I kept the voices going, planted the stories," he said.

"I need you to open this hatch right now, sir," she said.

"The Chosen will be displeased with me," the preacher muttered.

"*I* will be displeased with you," Hanna said, pulling her pistol and shoving it into the man's gut. "I suspect they will not be happy, either way. So perhaps you should do what is in your best interest, sir."

"I care not for your displeasure, once they are here we shall all taste the ashes of my failure."

The Climb, Olympus Ares Research Facility, Grace

Essex climbed in front of her, so that if he fell, she could catch him with her power armor-aided reflexes and arms. Already Grace was feeling tired, her arms wobbling, fighting to stay upright even inside the suit. She could only imagine what he was feeling like. They were taking more breaks than on the descent. Every other walkway, they would stop for a few minutes and rest. Each break was longer than the one before it. They would sit in silence until their breathing returned to normal. Each time, she wanted to sleep. Her eyes tried to close and then she would see him. That gaunt, sharp face and those neon-blue eyes. Nothing would keep you up faster than seeing that in your dreams.

Grace understood why Full Mag hadn't wanted to see again. The further she was from the vision, from the adrenaline, the calmer she was and the worse she felt for asking him to do something like that. Grace didn't do things like that. She followed the rules, was good. Abuse for knowledge? That was something Emily would have done.

When they got to the top, they were going to have to make a choice. She was pretty sure that Essex didn't know this, and it was going to take him by surprise. Best to broach it soon, before it came out of nowhere.

"What do you think he saw back there?" Essex asked. "I saw what it looked like, in his head. A cloud of evil, malignant anger and a crying child, but what do you think it showed him, as that welcome message?"

Grace had a few ideas and none of them were anything that she wanted to engage with or tell Essex about. She trusted him enough to go on this mission with him, but this? Even she didn't understand what she had seen and would be damned if she was going to pretend like he was some spiritual psychiatrist.

It knew my name.

"I don't know. I just can't imagine seeing for the first time and it being something horrible like that. Ripping through your mind," Grace said after far too long of a pause.

"You saw something as well, while you were unconscious," Essex said. It was not a question.

"What, you don't just wake up from a traumatic brain injury and start feverously drawing runes and demanding non-corporal creatures that are controlling somebody explain themselves to you?" Grace quipped back, deciding that a little humor might go a long way to keeping her from having to actually engage with what she had seen; to really think about those neon-blue eyes again.

"No, usually I just want to vomit and take a nap after I hit my head too hard," Essex said, meeting her halfway with a joke of his own. She would have rather it not been about fluids, but what did she expect from a boy? At least he was trying.

"Joking aside, you *did* see something. It got into your head, didn't it?" Essex asked, pressing her.

"I don't quite know yet. I saw flashes of things. It's a jumbled mess, probably more trauma than signs and portents," she said.

I just want this to be over. I don't have answers.

Grace hated not having answers. The only thing worse was going to be getting stuck in a looping conversation where somebody was pressing and the other person was obfuscating.

"Something came through that gate. Something angry that wants us to know why it's angry," Essex said flatly. "The question is, where did it come from? Where did you open a rift to?"

Grace didn't say anything. There wasn't much she could say. All the data and math pointed to them just opening a hole into the Null, a place that Essex should have been very familiar with. They were not even going deep. You didn't need to dig very far to send a ship faster than the speed of light. Folding space... That was something else, something Emily knew about.

They reached another gangplank, well over halfway to the top. Looking up, Grace's camera could zoom into the super structure of the Olympus Ares facility. They sat down for a moment. Just as she was getting comfortable, the radio started to buzz and the high, reedy, squawking voice of Administrator Vardis came through the box.

"Hello, do you read me? I can see you on my camera," the Administrator said into both of their ears at the same time.

"We hear you, sir," Essex said, putting a hand to his ear to filter out the noise from around him.

"Good. I was worried. It has been a long time. I just want to let you know that you were successful. The energy flow was disrupted enough up here to finally sap all the power from the Gate and stop what it was doing," Vardis said.

"Good, so we should be on the way to fixing this mess," Grace responded.

"I wish. No, we are far, far from fixing anything. In fact, I would say things have gotten *worse* up here. Yes, the Gate is shut down, but now that we are operating on emergency power, the security net is fried and these creatures have taken over most of the staff. I'm still locked down here with my little generator," the administrator said. Grace could hear the fear and worry in his voice.

"Hold tight, we're heading your way," Essex said, getting up and cracking his neck.

Vardis hadn't bothered to say he had logged off. The channel just went dead. Grace was fine with this. She didn't need to get sucked into awkward chit-chat.

Essex put his hands on the rungs of the ladder, looked up and took a beat. She could feel the exhaustion that was radiating from him. You didn't need to be a Host'ire Knight to see it. She saw a small indicator light on her HUD pop up. She switched over to the radiation band. Essex breathed in, golden light swirling around him, going into his body. He held the breath for a moment, then let it go. He started to climb, one rung at a time, one foot on top of the other, new vigor in his steps. Seeing someone use the Null like magic was something she was never going to get used to. Once there was room, Grace mounted the ladder and started climbing after Essex.

"He is hiding something," Grace said, coming back to the conversation that they had been having on the way down.

"I agree. There is only one way to find out what it is," Essex said.

"No, fuck that. I don't trust him. He either knows the truth or knows he has been cut out of the truth; both scare me. I need to get to the dorms. I've got gear in my room to go over the data I've been collecting."

"Vardis ordered us to come see him," Essex said. The rule-following words sounded hollow, coming from his mouth.

"That's not you. The man who is only down here because he couldn't leave a mystery alone. The man who is only here because he couldn't take orders from his warrior monk cult," Grace said, a little more viciously than she intended, but the point was made.

"Well, maybe it's time I started to follow some orders. Bad things keep happening when I strike out on my own. The facility burns down, I get lost on the side of space, I smash Jasper's head in to save Hyacinth…"

He paused. Clearly, that last part was something that he didn't mean to say out loud. There was a quiet moment between them as they climbed. Both waited to see if the other would speak first and question what had just been said. Grace was willing to leave it alone. There were things that she didn't want to talk about, and if she expected him to respect her boundaries, the least she could do was respect his. They both had secrets. That was something she could work with.

"Maybe it is. I've been following rules my whole life, and if there was one thing I learned in academia—aside from a lot of physics, archelogy and how to weave a basket underwater—is when an older man is selling me bullshit. Can't you smell it? Even without seeing his face, you can hear the lie in his voice. It's just one big red flag. Motherfucker knew something before we went down into the ground, and I have a deep gut feeling that he knows more now. I don't think he is going to be happy to see us," Grace said.

Essex didn't respond. There was nothing to say. *It's because I'm right. They never can respond when I'm right.* They reached the top of the ladder and climbed back onto the solid ground of the facility. Olympus Ares was fundamentally changed. All the steel had flaked away like dead skin and was blowing in the breeze with the alien sand. She knew that world; had seen its sand, its ruins, its stars.

"Look, you can go and see Vardis if you want. I'm going to the dorms to get some answers," Grace said, turning toward the express elevator. Without power, she was looking at another long climb, which just seemed par for the course today.

"What the bloody hell is in the dorms that you can't get down here? What answers are there that Vardis might not have been able to find over the network or from a survivor?" Essex asked.

She hesitated to tell him. She *wanted* to trust him, but Essex was too many unknowns. She understood boys like him, the issues they had surrounding whatever childhood trauma was causing them to act out. But now? Now she wasn't sure, with this sudden need to follow the rules, to play nice and do what that squawking middle manager told him to.

Fuck it, who cares if he tells Vardis?

"What's up there are some of the answers to this," she said, pulling out the pad with the runes. "I've a book that a professor gave me after I successfully defended my thesis. It was blackmail to try to get me to go on an expedition with him, but I digress." He didn't need to know her whole life story or why she didn't trust a middle-aged professor on an expedition to a dead world.

"The book was on a civilization that he found and their language that he started to translate. I know I saw these runes in that book."

"Then we can just get it out of the central core or off the net. Isn't all of that digitized? You researchers and your obsession with paper," Essex said back to her, frustration building in his voice.

"He couldn't find his dig site and shortly afterward had a psychotic break. The paper was never accepted, and only a handful of vanity-published copies exist. One of which is in my dorm because an old man wanted to sleep with me," Grace shot back.

Now that she thought about it, Doctor Arundel going mad suddenly didn't seem out of the realm of possibility if he'd also encountered the creatures with neon-blue eyes.

"That's it? You thought you saw runes in a concussion dream?" Essex asked, shocked. "You have read the book, right? They were just in your head. That doesn't mean anything. Trust me, I come from the land of people who think they see prophetic shit."

"I saw it after the accident. Under the ground was a second vision. I think I've seen their home world," she said.

You know us, Wayfinder, the voice with neon-blue eyes said in her mind, a cold chill running up the back of her spine.

"That doesn't make me feel any better. You need a brain scan, not an old book," Essex said, turning away to start walking.

"I've also got this," Grace said, reaching into her belt and pulling out the small probe. "It went through the portal, it recorded its whole data bank with video, in seconds. I need to crack it open and get to the meta data, but everything down here looks broken. And if it recorded any runes…"

She paused, not wanting to say the last part. She knew she wasn't crazy, wasn't suffering from any kind of delusion, but still. She didn't want to have to say that out loud; didn't want to have to defend herself to somebody who should've believed her. *I mean, fuck! He has actual powers, and he doubts some kind of vision?*

"Vardis should have a viewer," Essex said. His defiance was getting weaker. It felt like she was getting through to him. It shouldn't be this hard. He had to know that whatever was happening here was bigger than them, so why was he fighting her so much?

"I don't trust…"

The rest of the sentence got caught in the back of her throat, the feeling of cold, like death walking over her, creeping up Grace's spine again. The cloud of inky mist started to slip from the hallway ahead of them. A cold, icy blue radiating from the darkness. Without a thought, without hesitation, Grace raised her rifle. Essex recoiled back, holding his hands up.

"Okay, I get it, you don't trust him. We don't need to be drawing weapons." Grace didn't hear him, was looking past him. Her finger started to get tight on the trigger.

"Turn around," she bit out.

"I'm not going to let you shoot me in the back," he said, his hand falling to the side where his star-steel blade was.

He didn't feel it. He couldn't see it. Even with all his powers, he was blind to the danger that was behind him. Well, Grace was going to show him that it was real, that it existed and that it needed to be taken care of. Squeezing the trigger, three blasts of plasma blew past his head, the third burning a few stray hairs that had been kicked up in the wind. All three bolts went through the smoke, went through the laughing face that had appeared.

I am going crazy, she thought for just a moment.

"What the fuck!" Essex yelled, ducking to the side, igniting his blade, the heartbeat thrum no longer a reassuring feeling.

Grace didn't have a good answer, no longer certain of what she'd seen. Or *thought* she'd seen. She let the gun fall to her side, caught by its strap. Then she turned and ran. Ran from the embarrassment, ran from the fear, ran from her own insecurity in what she was seeing. And mostly, she ran because it was the only thing that made sense in the moment.

Rickman's Lab, The Citadel, Rostov

The sight they found upon reaching Richman's laboratory was horrible. Violence had happened here. Judging by the dead, though, Rostov couldn't tell you who the victor was.

Bodies were everywhere. There was not an inch of floor space that wasn't occupied by the fallen. Blood was dripping and sinking into the concrete around them. As they stepped in, Rostov bent down to examine the dead. The Militarum troopers had been smashed and cut to ribbons. Their deep green coats were covered in red, so shredded, they were no longer even fit for field bandages. Most of the Fellowship's dead had obvious plasma wounds, huge gaping holes of burnt flesh and cloth.

Closing his eyes, he reached out with the Null, looking to see if he could feel even a thread of a survivor, the bare minimum of what constituted life. After a minute of scanning, Rostov put his hand down in frustrated defeat. There was nothing.

"Whoever won this fight made sure to execute the wounded," Naomi said.

"I wish that told us who won," Rostov muttered. He knew the Fellowship would murder any wounded that they found still alive and he suspected that the Host'ire Militarum were no better. Not that he could blame them when it came to the Fellowship. Siding with the Host'ire on questionable morality made him sick, but it was what it was.

"Professor Rickman!" a voice called out from the depths of the laboratory.

"Wingarf," Rostov muttered.

He grabbed Naomi and pulled her to the ground. A moment later, the aged Master-at-Arms walked in from the shadows. He had his star-steel spear in his hand, the head activated, the weapon's light hum echoing in the room. Quietly, Rostov pulled the corpse of a Fellowship member over them. Lucas had said not to engage and Rostov agreed. Bloody hell, he didn't even have a weapon.

"Rickman, I know you are here. They said you were skulking about. Come out and play. We can make this quick," Wingarf said.

He wasn't hiding which side he was on now, the mask was completely off. Rostov creeped his head up again, sliding into the Null. Pain smashed into his face, blackness. He wanted to scream, and he almost did as he fell backward. Naomi's hand was over his mouth, helping to hold in the fear at what he had seen. Slowly, his eyes started to calm, to fall back into his skull. There had been such darkness around Wingarf.

The Shadow. He had dove too far, reached too deeply into the well of power, past the Null to the chaotic energy that was below. More powerful, but more dangerous, something that nobody should ever mess with. The thing the Host'ire feared more than anything; what they said was contained inside the Barrier, what would be let out if they opened the Eye. The things the Shadow created.

Wingarf kept walking toward them, kicking and stabbing the corpses around him, apparently not satisfied with the job that had been done to make sure they were dead. Rostov didn't dare poke his head up again to see which group of bodies he was stabbing. Avoiding him was going to require faith in the Null and their ability to be quiet.

He was about seventy feet away, but getting close fast. Rostov knew there was a table in front of them. He could feel that it was covered both above and below with bodies. Gently, he tapped Naomi and looked at her, then flicked his eyes toward the table. She nodded. They didn't need to say anything else. He could feel that she understood what he wanted, what the plan was. They were connected. He could feel her fear and resolve.

The two of them creeped forward slowly, sliding over and around the dead like snakes through a rocky garden. Rostov crawled past a green Militarum coat that was on the ground, not on a body. Reaching out with the Null, he wrapped an invisible hand around the edge and pulled it toward himself. Just as he was about to cover himself with the coat, it made a scratching sound. One of the gold buttons getting caught on a discarded weapon. Rostov let the coat fall. Wingarf turned. Rostov could feel the inky blackness of the shadow over him, the old man's gaze was pointed in their direction.

"Who's there? Did those fanatics forget to kill somebody?" he asked mockingly, walking toward where they were hiding. There was a blade next to Rostov, one of the side swords that Militarum officers carried. He wrapped his hand around the hilt. If it came to it, he would stand and fight while Naomi ran. He couldn't run anymore, couldn't hide. He had spent too much time in a cell to just be killed like a whimpering wounded dog.

No. If we fight, we fight together, Naomi's voice in the back of his mind said. It was a whisper, just on the edge of his ability to hear. Instinct wanted him to move his head, to swivel around and look at her. He fought the urge, locking his neck in place and looking forward, keeping still.

Then we will die together, he thought back.

If that is to be our fate, I would rather meet it with you than run like a coward, Naomi thought.. It was filled with steel and resolve. There would be no talking her out of it.

I am a knight, I have a blade. You don't have to protect me, her thought, more anger and agitation this time. Embarrassment washed over

Rostov for a moment, which he projected back to Naomi, before he was able to lock down his feelings and focus on the horrible, Shadow-imbued man that was walking toward them.

There was a crash on the other side of the laboratory. Rostov figured it was glass falling, but it could have been anything. Wingarf's horrible shadow turned and it felt like a burden had been removed from on top of them. It was a moment of reprieve, but not enough yet for them to get away. The man's hackles were up. Rostov reached out and nudged Naomi to keep moving toward the table where they were planning to hide. He stayed where he was under his bloody coat, listening, feeling for where Wingarf was going to go next.

"Fellowship forces in the Library," one of the radios on a Militarum corpse buzzed. "All available forces to the Library!" Then there was a scream and the broadcast cut out.

A deep, low, guttural, almost animalistic, groan came from Wingarf. Rostov felt the Shadow wash across him one last time. He was moving quickly, giving the room a last sweep before moving toward the door again. Through the Null, Rostov watched the Master-at-Arms depart.

They needed to tell everybody what they had seen. Did he dare get on the radio, in case they were in the same situation he was in, or worse? Rostov crawled over to Naomi.

"I need your help. We need to reach out to Lucas and Joanna, tell them what we have seen," he said.

Rostov lifted his hand to his mouth and pulled off his glove. Naomi did the same and they clasped their hands together and closed their eyes, reaching out through the Null. He could feel everything around them. Lucas and Joanna felt different. He tried to yell words at them, but his mouth didn't work. His lips flapped, but no words came out.

Taking in a deep breath of the vision around him, Rostov pushed the feeling of fear and resolution toward them. Pain shot through his mind. With a grunt, both he and Naomi were knocked out of their vision. Panting, he turned to her.

"You are bleeding," he said, pointing to a small dribble of blood that was running down her nose.

"So are you," she said, breathing heavily, almost choking on the words.

Rostov wiped away the blood and tried to stand up. His legs were pinpricks of pain, and if the table had not been right there, he surely would have fallen back to the ground. Pulling in a few deep breaths and finding the Null around him again, his legs found themselves.

"Okay, we have to get out of here. I know a back way to the Library," Naomi said as she pulled herself up from the pile of death she had been hiding in.

"You're not actually suggesting that we go where he is, are you?" Rostov asked, shocked.

"That is exactly what I'm saying. We need to keep our eyes on him. Until we can figure out where the door is, we need to keep him from it," Naomi said.

She turned and started quickly walking, doing her best not to step on the bodies all around them. There was no argument, no trying to find another solution. Her mind was made up and she was going.

Taking a deep breath of resignation, Rostov tightened his grip on the side sword and started running after her.

Ramparts, The Citadel, Lucas

The Citadel tower shook again as another shell exploded. Lucas stopped, catching his footing. *They are getting far too close,* he thought. He could feel the flow of battle coming toward him.

Reaching down, he freed the hilt of his star-steel blade from his belt. The heft of the weapon felt good in his hands. Joanna had her books, Naomi had her electronics, Rostov had his... Well, Lucas wasn't sure exactly *what* Rostov had. But he knew his own strengths, and they came from his blade and the ability to cause death with it. Conflict was coming and he was going to do what he was best at.

His finger slid over the ignition switch, feeling the rough surface through his gloves. Lucas itched to slide his thumb up to turn on the blade. Until there was a threat, though, that wasn't permitted.

"The ramparts are just on the other side of this hallway," Lucas called to Joanna, who was behind him.

He turned just as another shell struck the tower. The whole complex shook, dust filling the hallway. That shell was followed quickly by another impact. The lights flickered and there was a loud crash. For a heartbeat, Lucas was thrust into pitch blackness. He almost flicked his thumb up to get the illumination from his blade. Then the red emergency lights came on. Behind him, where Joanna had been, was a pile of rubble.

No! Fear rushed through him. He wasn't going to lose her to something as random as falling debris.

"Lucas!" It was Joanna's voice. Where was she? If she spoke again, he could find her, dig her out. "I'm fine! Looks like we are cut off," she yelled. Projecting forward with the Null, he could see her on the other side of the twisted mound of concrete and steel.

"It's good to hear your voice, I..." Lucas stopped.

"I know," she said..

"Can you still get to the library?" he called back, sliding away the worry and slipping back into Knight-Commander mode, taking charge of his small little group; giving them orders, adapting to the flow of battle.

"I think so. You get to Fel. We will meet back up..." There was a pause from her, as well. He wasn't the only one that was having trouble coming to terms with their new relationship status quo.

"You be careful," she eventually said. There were footsteps and he could tell that she was gone.

Turning, Lucas ran for the door, smashing into it at a full run, depositing himself onto the rampart where he had encountered Administrator Fel. Before him, he could see the scope of the battle, and it nearly knocked him back.

What had been an empty field devoid of life was now clogged with it. Thousands upon thousands of cultists were streaming across the canyon in their light robes, a mishmash of blunt weapons in their hands. Many of them had ladders to scale the wall. Far in the distance,

Lucas could see five massive artillery batteries that looked like they had been pulled off a warship. Upon the wall, the troopers of the Host'ire Militarum were pouring fire upon the members of the Fellowship of the Cross. Every shot took one of the cultists down, only for a fresh fanatic to take their place.

There was no stemming this tide. The Order had wanted this fight, and they were not going to win it.

"Where is Fel?" Lucas yelled toward one of the officers standing on the wall, clutching his cutlass in one hand and taking pot shots into the field of death with his pistol.

He turned and looked at Lucas, then went back to shooting. A ladder smashed into the rampart, jagged hooks flicking out, smashing into the stone. Instantly, the first cultist came over the ladder. The offer spun and put a round of plasma through the man's forehead. It entered in the middle of that branded cross and blew out the back of his head, brains and blood splattering everywhere, as the plasma that encased the round burned the rest of the cultist's skull.

 Lucas's thumb knew what to do, sliding forward. The heart-beat thrum of his blade coming to life filled his ears, the soft vibration as the energy moved from hilt to blade and back again coursed up his arm. Leaping forward, he spun in the air, his jacket flying out, his blade taking the head off the next Fellowship member that came up the ladder. Landing on a foot and a knee, Lucas raised his head and looked at the ladder. Throwing his free hand forward, he created a fist of Null energy and smashed the fragile contraption. Wood went flying, splintering everywhere. There were screams as cultists fell to the ground, some surely impaled by their own siege implement.

"Administrator Fel!" Lucas yelled again at the officer who was directing his troopers to fill the hole.

"Down by the gate," he answered, pointing toward the main gate below with his saber. Lucas gave him a two fingered salute, turning off his blade and clicking it back to his belt.

Turning, he took off toward the gate, leaping from the rampart, doing a flip in the air before landing in the courtyard. Behind the large steel door, he could see where Fel had set up a defense line. She had a few hundred troopers clustered around the gate. There were auto plasma cannons set up, creating a crossing field of fire. Across the door, there were massive bars of steel.

Standing up from his landing, Lucas strode across the parade field toward where Fel stood. The tall, regal woman didn't look phased. There was dirt and blood streaked across her face, but her eyes still burned with anger and fight. Clutched in her hand was an ornate, gilded star-steel blade hilt, with a basket guard and tassel hanging from just below the emitter.

"Administrator!" Lucas yelled. She turned to look at him.

"Come to join our stand, I see," she said.

"I am a knight. I will not let the Citadel fall," Lucas said, the warrior inside of him coming forward. Fel nodded at him.

"I will not turn away a blade," she said.

The gate started to shudder. The Fellowship of the Cross was smashing into it with something from the other side. With each impact on the door, the steel started to turn a brighter shade of red. Lucas could see the rivets in the door starting to slip and falter. Troopers kept running up to the top of the wall, throwing explosives down into the mass of people below, until they were taken down by primitive projectiles.

"Sir, I have news that you need to hear!" Lucas yelled.

"Make it quick, sir. They do not seem willing to give us time for a conference," Fel bit back.

"Master-at-Arms Wingarf has gone over to the enemy. We saw him conversing with one of their agents," Lucas said, conveniently leaving out the part about it having happened the day before.

"I am aware, Knight-Commander," Fel said flatly.

"You knew, and still let him—" Lucas said, aghast.

"And still let him what? Prattle around the base under my watch? There was nothing he gave them that wasn't our design."

"We were not part of that, were we?" Lucas asked.

"No," Fel said quietly. She stepped forward, reaching out and grabbing Lucas by the collar and pulling him close, igniting her star-steel blade, the red light of energy washing across Lucas. He reached for his blade, but she whispered in his ear before he could grab it.

"Listen, and pretend to fight," Fel whispered. "You have been seeing things, yes? Memories coming back? You are not alone. Something deeper is going on here. All I know is that a voice in the back of my head keeps saying that we need to find the door."

Lucas listened, seeing the mask of anger and determination starting to crack across Fel's face.

"It is up to you and your friends to find this door, to answer her call. You did it once before. I touched only the smallest of that and it has been a dagger in my mind ever since. We will do our part and hold the line," Fel said as her voice changed to anger. "And you do yours, Knight-Commander!"

With that, Fel threw Lucas across the yard. He reached out and used the Null to stop the fall and keep his feet. For a moment, he looked at Fel shock running across his face. That was the last puzzle piece that they'd needed. He was finally starting to understand how the Citadel was working.

But before Lucas could do anything, a massive battering ram smashed through the gate. The metal was slag and the head of a battering ram, shaped like a burning fist, was poking through. The supports of the doors creaked and gave way, followed by a stream of cultists. A moment later, the auto plasma cannons opened fire, cutting the Fellowship members down. The rounds smashing through them, turning bodies into puffs of red mist and flame. The bodies started to pile up, creating a barrier that the living Fellowship members ran over. From the top of this mound, made from their dead brothers and sisters, the cultists flung themselves at the auto plasma cannon crews, landing inside their emplacements and wildly slashing and smashing with their swords and clubs.

Lucas looked at Fel, who just snarled at him. She pulled off her sunglasses throwing them to the side and charging into the fray. Lucas activated his blade and followed, smashing into the wall of cultists. He swung his blade, hewing bodies left and right. Clothing was set on fire, the stench of burning flesh filling his nostrils with each cut.

The thrill of battle filled him. *This* was what Lucas was made for. He didn't need to be careful, didn't have to parlay with hostage takers or pirates. He could just answer violence with violence, letting his sword do the talking.

Lucas pulled his hand back, summoning the Null to him, creating a solid ball of energy at his fist, then pushed it forward. Fellowship members went toppling away from him, thrown like rag dolls. One smashed into the wall. Lucas could hear his bones shattering inside his body. Another hit the molten steel of the door, instantly catching fire, her screams filling the battlefield for a moment before being snuffed out. Lucas kept moving, running through the cultists he had just knocked down. This was the kind of fighting where there were no prisoners, there was no quarter being asked for or given.

As he got to the gate, Fel was already there, a tempest of energy spinning around her. Every Fellowship member that attempted to get close was thrown away, at best, and ripped apart by the winds at worst. So many limbs and weapons were caught up in the Null spinning around her.

She was unstoppable.

Two Host'ire Knights at the gate broke the assault and the Fellowship started to pull back. Fel refocused the energy that had been spinning around her into a tornado in front of her and sent it spinning into the Fellowship ranks. Cultists screamed and cultists died. Walking backward, she slammed both the massive doors shut with an almost dismissive wave of her hand. Militarum engineers were right behind them, ready to plug the door again. It wouldn't hold, but would buy them time to set back up.

"I knew I couldn't trust you; couldn't trust whatever brought you here," Fel snapped, closing ground with Lucas, her eyes still blazing with raw Null energy the likes of which he had never seen before. It was in that moment that he realized he had never been in battle with a knight as powerful or as well trained as Morgana Fel. Lucas stood his ground, hoping this was still a part of the act.

"Hear me, Knight-Commander, and hear me clear. Your honor is tainted, stained with the blood of these men," she said loudly, motioning to the violence behind her. "If you want to regain even a shred of that honor, you will bring me the head of this traitor."

She gave him the slightest of nods. Lucas returned it. His orders were clear.

With that, she turned around, flicking out her long, blood-stained green coat and returning to the front to prepare for the next wave. Lucas turned and started running back toward the tower. Joanna was heading to the library, so that is where he would start.

"Naomi, Rostov, we are reconnecting at the library," Lucas said into his radio, hoping that the rest of the group would hear him. "Our priorities have changed."

Library, The Citadel, Joanna

The library was just around the corner and up a set of steps. Sounds of violence were coming from in front of her. Blasts of plasma rifles, the wet thump of blunt weapons upon flesh, blood and brains smashing into the floor.

Shit, this is what I was hoping to avoid, Joanna thought, her hand reaching down to the familiar but still uncomfortable hilt of her star-steel blade. She had trained for years on the blade—hell, her qualifications were still valid. Even with all of that, it didn't sit right in her hand, didn't make her feel powerful. It felt like a clumsy, dangerous part of her outfit that she was required to have.

She leaped up the ten steps in two bounds, using the Null to push herself forward. Taking one last breath, she put the weapon to her side and pulled in a reserve of Null energy.

What Joanna saw in the library shocked and appalled her. What should have been a place of learning and quiet reflection had been turned into a charnel house. Corpses were everywhere, at least a hundred, probably more. The fighting had moved up the steps, and between the screams, grunts, and gunfire, Joanna could hear a distinct sound, one that put fear into most people's hearts. The heartbeat thrum of a star-steel blade.

That has to be Tor, she thought.

Leaping over bodies, Joanna started making good time across the open space of the library's first level. Just as she was about to reach the steps, a hand reached out, grabbing her ankle, pulling her down. Joanna hit the floor with a hard thump. Creaking, dying laughter crept up from behind her. Half a beat after hitting the ground, the yellow blade of her sword was ignited and she was spinning around. Star-steel blades make short work of flesh, so the cultist's arm detached from his body with ease, the fingers snapping open without a command.

Joanna realized that her rapid act of violence did nothing to stop the laugher, to wipe the grin from this deranged man's face. He kept laughing as his eyes glassed over and the cross burned into his forehead started to bleed. Joanna skuttled back from him on all fours, her hands landing on and using the dead as grip posts for her escape. The laughing man made no effort to chase her. He just kept laughing, even after his eyes had rolled all the way back into his skull and his body went limp.

As the laughter faded, Joanna was left with her heart beating loudly in her head, keeping time with the energy hum of her blade. *Why was his burn bleeding?* she wondered, the academic inside of her refusing to stay quiet. Glancing across the well of dead, she quickly noticed that at least half the dead Fellowship members had bleeding crosses.

Joanna took a deep breath, closing her eyes and pushing her curiosity away. It wasn't going to do her any good right now. This was a fact that could be filed away and used later. While everything was important, she had a knack for getting hung up on details and facts that were not important in the moment. The only detail that was important right now was getting to Tor before Wingarf did.

A pang of fear moved through her body as she thought that name. He worried her, but what she was feeling was fear, fear that was not her own. Looking at the bodies as she lay on the ground, Joanna was in a different room. The dead were the same, but different. Footfalls were coming toward her. All she wanted to do was scream, but Joanna lacked control of her body, a hand over her mouth. A few terrifying seconds passed before the room shifted again and she was back in her own body. Joanna looked down at her hand, the still active star-steel blade clutched there.

Naomi, that was Naomi's mind, she thought. Another interesting fact to slide into the files for later. First, though, she needed to get up off the floor and find Tor. She couldn't let him die, the bastard knew too much.

Pushing herself up, Joanna started running up the stairs, running toward the ever increasing sounds of battle. Taking a hard right, she almost wiped out on the banister of the steps, only avoiding a fall back to the first level by throwing up a shield bubble of Null energy and using the reverse force to stop her momentum and ground her feet. The steps to the third floor were on the other side of the library. Looking up, she saw Tor and his tall frame by his collection of banned books. In his hands, he was dual-wielding star-steel blades. All around him were members of the Fellowship, trying to work their way in so that they could land a blow, each of them hoping to be the one whose attack finished off the old Knight-Librarian. Her eyes fell from her friend and mentor down to the level that she was on and the five Fellowship of the Cross cultists who were running headlong toward her.

In that moment, she wished Lucas was here. He had said he would always protect her, and now when she was facing danger, he was nowhere to be seen.

You've got this, Joanna. You trained for this. I have faith in you. She could hear Lucas saying that, giving her a pep talk, the encouragement that would be needed to get to the other side of this day; just to survive the next few minutes.

You are a knight, you are trained, you can do this. You are a knight, you are trained, you can do this, she kept repeating in her head. Joanna wanted to whisper it to herself, desperately wanted that extra feeling of comfort.

But she knew that if her foes saw that, they would pounce on her even harder.

The first cultist, a woman armed with a spiked club, reached Joanna. She took a step back, letting her leather jacket flair as she swept the blade forward, the hum cutting through the air. This cultist was full of zeal and could not avoid the slash. Her dull brown sack of an outfit caught fire as the energy blade cut through it, missing the flesh underneath. She started to scream and run faster as the fire consumed her.

Jumping, the cultist made a last-ditch effort to take Joanna down into the flames with her. Reaching into the Null, Joanna pulled energy and wind around her free hand and pushed, throwing the flaming woman back into her friends. The gust of wind added fuel to the fire as it set two more of her comrades aflame. The cultists were in a screaming, burning pile, trying to get away from their dying friend, to get back on their feet. There wasn't much time to get past them. She knew what needed to be done.

Seeing a thing and doing a thing are vastly different. Joanna could see the way out of this, but it would require doing something she hadn't tried since graduating. Even then, she hadn't been good at it, and now, she suspected her skills would be even worse.

Have faith in your ability to be a knight, Lucas's voice said to her again. Through the Null, she reached out for him, but all she got back was static, the chaotic feelings of violence and death that were permeating the Citadel's tower as the battle raged around her.

"You can do this," she said to herself, out loud this time. "You are a knight, you are trained, you can do this."

Joanna pulled off her sunglasses and slipped them in the pocket of her coat. Cracking her neck and joints, she turned off the blade and started running. Reaching into the Null, she filled herself with energy. Pushing energy through her foot, she leaped, gaining air, gaining distance above the burning, stinking pile of her enemies. Throwing her arm out, Joanna created a gust of air from her hand, blowing her back toward the bookcases. She then used the Null and spun so that her feet were against the books. Leaping from Null pad to Null pad, she ran along the wall before reaching the staircase on the other side of the library. With one last push from the Null, Joanna was on her feet again, weapon in hand, running up the stairs.

She had done it. The cultists behind her had underestimated her, just as she had underestimated herself. They had all—until the killing happened—forgotten that she was a living weapon trained to kill in the very oppressive fascist school that they were now fighting over. Looking up to the top floor, Joanna could see that the cultists who were sparing with Tor had not forgotten this fact. Clicking her blade back on her belt, she ran forward, letting the Null push her there faster.

Tor was a spinning, lanky tree of death. In one hand, he had a green blade, and the other, a red one. At his feet were the hacked and mangled bodies of countless Fellowship of the Cross cultists. The ones who were still alive were keeping their distance, only lunging forward when they thought there was an opening. Joanna watched as one of them advanced, jabbing his spear where it looked like he could get through. At the last second, Tor evaded, and the cultist pulled back his weapon.

The next attacker wasn't so lucky. He dove forward, almost on the floor, a knife in his hands. Tor made an elegant downward cut, his red blade bisecting the man across his waist. His legs hit the ground. The cultist's torso, still clinging to life, dug its knife into Tor's lower calf. His long, thin leg started to shake but didn't buckle as iridescent green blood started to well up around the hilt of the knife, dripping onto the ground.

"Tor!" Joanna yelled from where she was standing, almost half a library away. Her mentor didn't look at her. He just breathed in, holding his ground, keeping his blades up.

"Bring me that one's head!" the Fellowship leader, a large man in armor, yelled, pointing at four of his followers. The cultists peeled off from where they were surrounding Tor and ran for Joanna, screaming and laughing in equal measure.

"The corpse god shall fest upon your soul, Host'ire!" the lead one yelled.

He was a huge man, both in height and girth. His head was shaven, and the cross burned into his forehead was starting to bleed as the anger and bloodlust boiled up inside of him. Joanna could feel it all through the Null. She had never felt emotions like this from other people so easily, so on the surface. She pushed them back, not letting them distract her. He was just a man, and she was a living weapon.

"He shall feast upon someone else," Joanna said, raising her blade, the yellow light reflecting determination from her eyes.

This must be that focus of battle she had read so much about. The world fell away around her. There was nothing but her blade and the cultists that were running at her. Joanna reached her free hand out, picturing a larger version of that hand existing in front of her. Through the Null, the hand was given form. She wrapped her fingers around one of the smaller cultists and closed her fist. The hand had no physical representation in the material world, but was strong enough to cause the cultist to crunch together, his arms crossing his chest as they snapped like twigs.

Joanna let out a light growl as she flicked her wrist and opened her closed hand. The Null hand did the same, throwing the hapless, broken man over the railing. He didn't scream as his body hit the floor a moment later with a sickening crunch. Joanna shook her hand, dismissing the larger one. She could feel the energy in her arm starting to fade, the effort taking a toll upon her. Joanna was starting to see why even Host'ire Masters avoided being too flashy in a life-or-death situation.

The next two men stumbled for a moment before finding their composure and running toward Joanna, spinning their clubs, which were already slick with blood. Joanna stood her ground, and just as they were about to be upon her, she lithely slipped out of the way, spinning as she sidestepped their charge, her coat and blade whipping with her. The two men kept running for a moment, then stopped. Burning gashes were across both of their chests. If her blade had been made of steel, their guts would have been on the ground. As it was, everything stayed inside, held together by a mess of ruined, burned flesh. Their eyes rolled up and they fell to the ground, just as the putrid smell of burning flesh reached Joanna's nose. She flicked her blade like it was solid, a move that was in every holomovie and book she had read.

For the first time in her life, Joanna felt like the trained Host'ire Knight that she was. *This* was power, *this* was confidence. She didn't want to always feel like this, but after years of abuse and being told she wasn't worth a damn, in this moment, it felt amazing. Knowing it was inside of her all along was refreshing, reassuring.

"Look at that, Libarian. She wants to be like you, to be a foul creation. An abomination to God. I will do you a favor and kill her first," the big cultist said, kicking Tor.

The old librarian grunted and crumpled into a ball. She could feel his pain, the injuries that he was trying to hide from her.

"If you insist on meeting your dead god today, who am I to stand in your way," Joanna hissed, tightening the grip on the hilt of her star-steel blade. She breathed in deeply, letting the tightness of her muscles fade into the background, allowing the Null to fill her. She dug deep. She could see the Null like was like a beach laid out in front of her. She had dug a hole, using the sand to build a castle around her. It was starting to get wet; she was close to the water, close to the Shadow. That place a Host'ire wasn't supposed to go, where order gave way to chaos and power. She had pulled enough; her walls would hold true.

The big cultist ran at her. She could feel the vibrations in the floor from his bulk. Each footfall was like an earthquake. His attack pattern was clear to her. She could see what he was going to do. One arm out, ready to knock into her, his other reaching for a knife that was sheathed on his back. It was blunt, brutal, sloppy. The kind of attack that would work against a scared soldier who had a single shot weapon.

He was on top of her. Joanna leaned back, avoiding the elbow that was aiming for her face. Her feet planted, she rotated her body and arm, bringing up her blade and removing her opponent's knife and its accompanying hand. He screamed as the stump at the end of his arm burned. Joanna slipped behind him, coming back to her full height. She made a fist and filled it with Null energy, then punched forward. He stumbled, the sound of his spine shattering echoing in the room. Two more steps and he fell forward, twitching. She didn't go and check to see if he was dead or not. She didn't need to.

The fight was over.

"Tor, are you...?" she began, running over and scooping up the tall, thin librarian.

"I've been better; had him on the ropes," Tor said, chuckling, trying to hide a cough. His shirt was slick with blood, and he looked pale, even for a Tragadi.

"We need to get you some help," Joanna said, concern filling her voice, the lust and thrill of battle fading away, being tucked back into the box that she had buried deep inside of herself.

"I will be fine. There are more pressing matters that you need to attend to," Tor said. "Help me to my shelves. There is something you need," he said, pointing forward.

For a moment, Joanna didn't move, but the old man started to walk, and she was forced to follow with him, lest he fall to the ground. There was so much blood pooling under him.

"They are coming for her, and I don't know if the Guardians can protect her," he said quietly.

"Who are they here for?" Joanna asked, the question sounding silly as soon as it left her lips.

"It is something you and the Fellowship have in common," Tor said, hacking up a cough as they reached his shelf. The old man stretched out an arm, grabbing the shelf and using it for support. The gate was already open.

"Hyacinth," Joanna whispered.

"Yes, the one who can't be remembered. The Wayfinder," Tor said. He slowly walked over to a small box and started to rummage through it.

"Why can't I remember her? I know she existed, but every time I try... It is like she exists just on the edge of my peripheral vision and

I'm unable to turn to see her. Each memory, I gain a little more, but that makes it slipping away again that much more frustrating."

"Yes, they are like that now, once they have been truly awoken. There is no time to get into it. Here, take this. Find your friends and get to the Labyrinth," Tor said, pressing a small vile of purple liquid into Joanna's hands. She looked down at it. The purple had swirls in it, like a galaxy of stars or a child's plaything.

"What is this?" she asked.

"Memory. We shall talk again," Tor said. He thrust himself away from her, landing hard on one of the shelves and then to the back of his little alcove. Joanna took a step to follow him. Before she could, Tor's hand was out, and the gate closed in her face, leaving her alone. *Memory. We shall talk again.* The words echoed in her mind as she looked down at the little glass vial in her hand.

She popped out the cork and drank it down. The liquid had an acidic taste, like the tonics that her mother used to make. Joanna swallowed, her eyes popping open and her pupils dilating.

She remembered.

Hidden Hallways, The Citadel, Naomi

The hallways behind Professor Rickman's lab were a nightmare network of twists and turns, corridors that emptied into small rooms filled with beakers and chemicals, or stockpiles of coats, and goggles. One room was just shelf after shelf of old technical manuals. It was like the two of them were lost in the professor's brain.

While Naomi had always admired Rickman, her newfound soured opinion resented being lost here. The vague memory of Hyacinth had let them think this would be a way to slip past the violence and reach the library. Naomi didn't know whether Hyacinth and Essex had ever found their way out of here or were found by the professor after she had abandoned them to the wolves. It didn't matter. They were lost and the sounds of the Citadel falling apart around them echoed even worse here.

"I feel like we have gone this way already," Rostov said, stopping to catch his breath.

"We have," Naomi said. "I recognized that room back there. We need a new plan of attack."

Walking up to the wall, she pulled out her blade, flicking it on quickly, making a mark in the wall, showing what direction they were moving in.

"What if somebody is following, looking for us?" Rostov asked.

"Then we deal with them. It beats being lost in this pointless maze of poorly labeled halls," Naomi said.

"I thought you and Professor Rickman were friends. She never took you back here?" Rostov asked.

"Once or twice, but you know how memory is," Naomi said quietly. "Most of our friendship came after I left, after I had forgotten her failings, when she could just be proud of me..."

The realization hurt. All the messages, the manuals, the late nights going over text and semantics. It had all just been Rickman's way of trying to ask for absolution without having to admit what she had done. The work meant nothing without admonition.

"If we find her, I'm going to..." Rostov started.

"You are going to what? Give her a good talking to? No, what is past is past. Dwelling on it won't change it. All we can do is move forward, trying and being better," Naomi said.

"I worked with Rickman a bit, before they stuck me in re-education. She hasn't been trying to be better. The abuse never stopped. She just doesn't befriend pupils like when we were here. I'm sure it helps with the guilt," Rostov said, walking up to the next intersection. He looked left, then right, before taking the left. They walked in silence for a minute.

"I have never seen somebody who had tapped into the Shadow before," Naomi said as they were walking, the vision of Wingarf wreathed in black still heavy in her mind.

"I've seen it, been close to it, but never seen somebody embrace it," Rostov said. "I hear they teach more about it at the Academy, so that the ambassadors have something else to pull from."

"It would be quite a tool when your job involves being half human and half myth," Naomi said. "As opposed to just being chattel and weapons like us."

"A dangerous tool, it is—"

Rostov stopped. Naomi could feel the story coming. It was on the edge of his lips. She could feel the desire to tell it well up inside of him, welling up inside of *her*. Light filled the narrow hallway.

"Blast," Rostov muttered. She walked up next to him. They were back where they had started in the ruined bloody remains of the Rickman's classroom.

"This is good. We can start over," Naomi said.

Suddenly, the words fell away from her as a shadow filled her mind's eye. Looking over at Rostov, she saw that he was feeling it, as well. They slipped back into the darkness. Heavy footfalls filled the room. Naomi's eyes locked with Rostov's, the fear was unmistakable, and they both recognized the feeling.

Wingarf.

Naomi held her breath. Had they really gotten away from him just to be deposited back into his clutches? Lightly, she tapped Rostov on the shoulder and motioned back toward the darkness of the backrooms.

"Wingarf, what are you doing here?" a voice yelled. The shadow stopped moving. Naomi knew that voice. Professor Rickman.

"Looking for stragglers," the old Master-at-Arms hissed. Naomi could picture the horrible smile on his face.

"The fighting has passed from here," Rickman said, her voice hard.

"That is why they would be stragglers," Wingarf spat back. "Where were you? I looked for you on the field."

"I'm sure you did," Rickman said.

Naomi could feel the tension between them. She looked at Rostov and he nodded back. Rickman knew about Wingarf.

How long have you known, you cowardly bitch? Naomi thought, the anger welling up again. Rostov put a calming hand on her shoulder. The anger started to bleed away from her, like it was being taken.

"They could have used you. A Host'ire Master would have turned the tide of battle here," Wingarf said.

Rickman didn't respond. Of course she didn't. She was too busy hiding in some hole somewhere. Watching and feeling bad about what she had done, guilt without any recompense.

This way, we have to help her!

Naomi turned at the voices. Rostov heard them, as well. Both their heads turned in unison. Looking out into the room, across the way, they saw the childlike echoes of themselves. The other entrance to the backrooms. *That* was where they were going. Rostov looked at Naomi. There was desperation and pleading in his eyes. He still wasn't sure if he was going mad, or if they were all seeing the same things. She nodded at him, the anxiety fading.

Then Rostov did something stupid.

Pushing away from her, he started running, getting halfway across the room before slipping on a corpse and falling to the ground. Wingarf turned, grinning, a predator-like violence crossing his eyes. Naomi had no choice. She ran toward Rostov, putting herself between him and Wingarf, her star-steel blade coming to life.

"Foolish and weak. You were weak then and you are weak now. All three of you," the old man said, his eyes darting from Rostov, to Naomi, and finally landing on Rickman. His glance was as accusatory and disappointed as Naomi felt. Her emotions came from the place of a victim, Wingarf's disappointment was that Rickman had never been an accomplice. The two of them looked at Rickman, fighting over her without saying a word. Finally, Wingarf broke the silence by stamping the butt of his spear on the ground, causing the head to come to life, its heartbeat thrum filling the room.

"Run, child," Rickman said, stepping forward, drawing her blade, snapping it to life.

Library, The Citadel, Lucas

Fear, anger, disappointment, clarity. Lucas was getting so many emotions feeding into his mind. They were not his own. He knew where they were coming from—his friends, friends he needed to help. Who each emotion belonged to specifically was more nebulous. They all mingled together with his own creating a stew of feelings.

Lucas stopped his run, catching his breath and putting his hand to his forehead, forefinger and thumb on his temples. Squeezing, he pushed away the emotions. Yes, they were in trouble. Yes, they needed his help. But if he let all their feelings overcome him, then all of them were going to be lost. He had to hope that one of them found the answers they were looking for. Clarity, that was in the stew, bubbling to the surface. It gave him hope. Something had to.

Lord knows Fel isn't going to be able to hold the gate forever. How did so many of them get here without anybody knowing? No. They knew. But why didn't they do anything about it?

All good questions, questions for later. The exercise worked. Lucas was able to quiet the sounds in his mind, returning to the relative silence of his own inner monologue.

The library was just ahead. He knew he would find Joanna there. He needed to find her, needed to make sure that she was okay, more than anything else. If she was hurt—or worse, dead—Lucas wasn't sure what he would do, but no amount of Fellowship of the Cross cultists would stand in the way of his wrath.

He turned the corner and was shocked by the violence he saw in the library. Bodies were everywhere—and blood.

Standing in the middle of it all was Joanna. Her star-steel blade was off, but still in her hand. Her eyes were glassy as she stood there, muttering to herself. Lucas ran up to her, wrapping his arms around her. All sense of propriety or decorum in combat fell away.

"You are alive," he said.

"Yes," she whispered. There was pain, and confusion, but also… This was where the clarity was coming from. Lucas could feel it radiating off her like a lighthouse in a storm.

"Did you…?" He wasn't sure how to phrase the question.

"No, they did this to each other… Well, I did a little," she said. Lucas could feel her clip the blade's hilt back to her belt, before wrapping her arms around him.

"I-I killed people… I used my blade in anger…" she said, the high and shock of the battle fading away. This was an emotion that Lucas was all too familiar with, one he knew how to handle.

"The first time is always the hardest. It…" The next part sounded trite, but was thankfully true. "It gets easier. The killing."

"I know. I didn't have an issue with the killing. They were in my way. They were threatening Tor, and I had to do something. I had to stop them," she said.

"Where is that old Tragadi?" Lucas asked.

"Vanished through some secret passage, but not before…" She paused.

"Not before what?" Lucas asked. There was something that she knew, something that she wanted to say, but was having trouble processing.

"I know where the door to the Labyrinth is. I remember what happened to Hyacinth," she said. "Tor gave me something to drink. I don't know how it works. It doesn't matter right now. We need to find Naomi and Rostov," she said.

"They are in danger," Lucas said flatly, squeezing Joanna one last time. She was warm and comforting. In that moment, Lucas realized just how much he missed having people around to lean on emotionally, how much he needed it. A leader couldn't exist only by acting detached.

"Yes. I can feel them too. The blood pact." She paused, holding her hand to the side of her head, waggling her fingers around, bending them like she was trying to grasp a ball hanging beside her that was constantly slipping away. "The memories, the understanding. It is all coming back in an unorganized flood, but… Yes we have to go. This way," Joanna said.

She pulled away from Lucas, a renewed energy in her eyes and confidence in her gait as she strode from the library, her jacket whipping in a breeze Lucas couldn't feel.

Rickman's Lab, The Citadel, Allana

"I won't let you hurt them again," Allana said, anger and determination filling her voice.

She had stood to the side for too long. She had leaned on decorum and tradition for too long. So much bad had happened that she could have stopped. Decades of students that she could have helped, if she had just had the courage to stand up to tradition. There was no need for everything to be so harsh, so violent. These kids needed love and support, and she wasn't able to give it to them until long after the window when it was truly needed had closed.

That stopped today. She was done hiding, done standing to the side and looking distressed and sad. Done sending kids off with, at best, a few thoughts and a cast-off prayer. The star-steel blade in her hand was alive, bathing her in a bright, neon-pink light.

"I was hoping you would try, Allana. I have been waiting years for you to stand up for them," Wingarf said, twisting his spear around, falling into an attack stance.

Allana could feel the air in her laboratory go cold, still. She breathed in, calming herself, pulling as much Null energy into her body as possible. Fighting Wingarf was going to require more energy than she had ever used at once; skills that she had practiced from time to time, but had not used since learning them in the Academy. There were hundreds of treatises on battles between Host'ire. They trained to fight star-steel blade on star-steel blade. Never in her life, though, had she seen an actual fight between two knights. A lost art from the Age of Chaos, one that she was about to reignite.

As she pulled in Null, Allana could feel the energy moving in the opposite direction of her, going toward Wingarf. Lines of energy were starting to appear around him, swirling like he was at the center of an energy vortex. Reaching up, she pulled out her black contact lens, palming them into her coat. With her eyes open, she was able to truly see just how much power was spinning around her opponent. His missing arm had returned, built from pure golden Null energy. Looking down at herself, the energy that laced around her felt puny in comparison. He was ready for this, waiting for her. She had just walked in and finally found the courage to stand up.

The courage to die.

Wingarf made the first move. Pushing out with his invisible arm, he thew a wave of Null energy at Allana. It wasn't much, a weak wave, the kind that she could see though. There were three options for dealing with this, but all of them would cost her energy that she didn't have to spare: jumping over it, pushing it back, or bolting herself to the floor. She had withstood plenty of storms in her youth and this would be no different.

In her mind, Allana created two small hands of Null energy. They reached out of the floor, grabbing her ankles and holding on. The wind hit her a moment later, blowing her coat and hair back. She kept her arms down at her side, a look of determination on her face. It was just a test, a first faint. The wind passed, and he was right behind it, spear lashing out toward her.

Allana dismissed the hands and flipped to the left, ripping her coat off and flicking it over Wingarf. Thumbing her blade off and back on, she freed her other hand. There was no time to waste. She couldn't afford to miss a beat while he was blinded.

Allana struck out, swinging her blade, going for the easy hit. Wingarf was faster than she even thought possible. The spear was behind him, held in his invisible arm, blocking her blade. He pushed the weapon down, allowing the pink energy to slide along the shaft before impacting the spear point. In a normal man's hand, she would have sliced off fingers; it would have been over. But now, she was locked into a duel with a weapon that appeared to be fighting on its own.

Twisting her blade around, Allana pushed away with the Null, using Wingarf as her anchor point. She flew back fifteen feet, landing on a desk while he stumbled forward, still fighting to get her large leather coat off his face.

Curses and muttering came from under her coat, as did small streams of dark shadowy energy. It looked like Null, but black and smoky. The Shadow. She recognized it instantly. They had taught her about this, but she had never dug so deep as to find it hiding under the Null like poisoned oil. Rickman pushed her hand out and created another longer hand made of Null. Pushing forward, she grabbed his leg and pulled him down to the ground. He landed with a thump. Then quickly, before the hand vanished, she lifted his spear and threw it away.

"I expected more from the Citadel's Master-at-Arms. Is that why you never progressed past the rank of Knight?" Allana said in a mocking voice.

They had been colleagues long enough to know how to hurt each other. There were more ways to fight than just with star-steel. Wingarf finally got the coat off and climbed to his feet. Energy was cracking across his empty hand, both golden Null and inky Shadow.

"Rank means nothing when a book worm like you or a pissant like Brandice can move up, while I am sidelined because the order refuses to think beyond a person's disability," Wingarf snapped back.

It was working. He was angry. Now she just had to figure out how to exploit it before she got herself killed.

"We are so much more than these flesh suits which we walk around in. I have seen the promised land, Allana. We will be Gods there. If only we have the vision to see beyond ourselves; to see beyond this place," Wingarf said.

The energy around his hand grew even larger, coalescing into a smoking ball of gold and black. Pulling his arm back, holding the energy ball in his open hand, Wingarf yelled as he threw it at her, using the built up Null in his arm to send it flying her way.

By the time she realized what was happening, it was too late. Allana tried to dodge, to leap out of the way, but it was no use. The energy ball smashed into her side, ripping cloth and burning flesh. She wanted to cry out in pain, but that would be giving him what he wanted. Allana landed and stood tall. Digging into her reserve of energy, she pushed it toward her side. The Null couldn't heal her, but it could dull the pain.

"We were never supposed to be gods, Wingarf. Or did you forget why we fought the Wayfinders?" Allana yelled back, holding her blade forward, slightly tilted down like a dueling foil.

"We fought them because they had vision, and the Host'ire only had fear and dogma. I will not be beholden to that. I have seen their weakness, and it is not for me," Wingarf said, reaching out with his physical hand and pulling the spear back to him.

Once it hit his hand, he spun it around and then smashed the butt of the haft onto the floor. Waves of Null energy pulsed away from him with each slam. It echoed inside Allana's head, shaking her, scaring her. It was an intimidation tactic, and it was working.

Pulling in her energy, Allana threw herself off the table, using the Null to create springboards for her feet. Halfway where Wingarf was standing, she created a patch of hard air behind her foot and pushed off it. As she flew by, Allana swiped her blade at Wingarf. He answered it with his spear. The force of the impact sent her flying backward across the room, smashing into the wall. He was fast, freakishly so. Pain cascaded through her body from both the wall and the wound on her side. Allana grunted but stood back up. She could already feel the reserve of Null that she had acquired starting to fade away.

"You can't beat me, Allana. All you can do is slink away with your shame. Do that and I will make sure the Fellowship allows you to leave this place. Breaking you is more rewarding than the kill," Wingarf said, twisting his spear and walking toward her.

The door was right behind her. She could turn and walk away. Drop her weapon and hide with her guilt and shame. Nobody was expecting anything from her, so it would be impossible for her to let them down.

Pack it in, Allana. You did what you could, she thought.

Flicking off her blade, Allana looked at the door, looked at life and freedom. But also—shame. In that moment, all she could see was the shame.

Wingarf closed the distance between them, the old Master-at-Arms raising his spear, sliding it under Allana's chin. She could feel the heat of the star-steel spear as it came dangerously close to her flesh. She locked eyes with him, stares boring into the other. Without glasses, they were able to look deeply into the other's soul.

Rickman knew Wingarf was only going to see fear and shame. All she saw was anger. So much anger that it almost took her breath away; seething, pent up, packed down anger. The kind that a person sits on for years that breeds hatred and resentment; the kind that poisons your soul to the point where redemption isn't possible. Every time she'd encountered anger at this level, there was fear underneath. Yet Allana didn't sense any fear in Wingarf.

Yes I am scared, yes I am weak and shameful, but I will not succumb to the darkness, Allana said to herself as she refused to remove her eyes from Wingarf's.

"Last chance. Walk away and live. Fight, and I will kill you," he said.

You know what you have to do. Nothing pithy, nothing flashy, just do the work and get the job done.

Steel found her eyes and a low growl her lips. Allana leaned back, pulling away from the spear as she thumbed on her blade and swiped up, knocking the weapon away, catching Wingarf off guard. She pushed every ounce of Null that was in her body through her right arm, pushing Wingarf's spear to the ground. With her free arm, she reached out and wrapped her hand around Wingarf's neck.

"You will not hurt them anymore," she said, tightening her grip.

He was so full of Null energy that it was radiating from where she was squeezing. Allana started to pull it toward her, sucking it in. The tighter she made her hand, the more energy she was able to squeeze out of him like a sponge. As increasing Null energy flowed from Wingarf into her, she could see the darkness rising from him, coming toward her. The Shadow was always heavy, always scared of the light.

It was coming for her.

The energy filled her body, giving her strength, revitalizing the tired muscles that she was feeling. It sadly did nothing for her right arm that was holding the spear down. The limb started to waver. Wingarf turned his head, a wicked smile crossing his face.

"You feel that, don't you? The raw power coming..." He paused for a moment, a look of sick realization crossing his face. "You have never touched the Shadow before, have you? Never felt the cold embrace of pure power before. Go ahead. Take some. Your arm isn't going to hold out much longer. You can't help them if you are dead."

The inky blackness started to push faster, harder, toward her. It was cold and powerful. It called to her in the most seductive voice she had ever heard. Perfect tone and pitch that made her want to fall to jelly, that dug up the feelings of the first time she had seen the handsome boy on the playground as a teenager. She wanted it, she *needed* it.

Time seemed to slow as the tendrils of smoke reached her fingers, and then another, more familiar emotion shot through her, a constant companion: shame. This power was wrong. It was evil, chaotic, fast. If she took it, she would lose who she was, and while she wasn't happy with that person, it *was* who she was.

"Power is not atonement!" Allana yelled, pulling her hand away from Wingarf's neck.

There was a burst of energy as the two of them separated. Her hand was stiff, cold, wrong. Allana was breathing deeply, each breath filling her body with the Null as it coursed through her, blood moving through her body like an elixir. Screaming, she kicked him in the side and turned to run, to put distance between the two of them.

I need distance, I need height.

Visualizing a set of pads, she waved her hand, using the energy inside her to freeze the space between the molecules of oxygen and nitrogen in the air, creating small solid pads. She leaped on the first one, and then the next and the next, quickly gaining altitude in the tall laboratory space.

Leaping on the last pad she created, Allana turned around to see where Wingarf was, to figure out her next move. Distance was only the first step. Far above her, Allana knew there was a ledge she could get to, an old observation deck that hadn't been used in almost sixty years, leftover from when this room was one of many fighting pits in the Citadel, before the Host'ire decided that even poor children deserved some education on things besides war.

Wingarf was still on the ground, looking up at her, his eyes turning a deep shade of black, with red coming up from underneath, like mood lighting or a drop shadow. The spear clattered to the ground. His arm got tight, shooting to the side as he let out a loud deep scream, arching his back, the muscles in his shoulders bulging through his clothing.

Run, Allana, run.

As much as she wanted to turn away, she couldn't. Shadow started to pour from his eyes and hand, swelling around, being pulled toward where his shoulders were undulating. The screaming got louder, taking her breath away, shattering beakers and flasks down below. The leather of Wingarf's coat started to rip as inky spines burst from his shoulders. The bones of wings. They lifted, then burst out, sprouting feathers of pure, cold shadowy darkness. The light retreated from him, being driven away.

The screaming stopped and Wingarf flexed his body and growled. Looking up at Allana, his wings flapped.

She turned and threw more pads ahead of her and started to jump. If she could just get to that ledge, she could get into her backrooms. They were a maze, leftover vestigial architecture from more than a dozen remodels of the Citadel over its life. As she ran, the flapping of the wings got louder and louder. Allana spun around, holding her blade up, slashing it in front of her. Wingarf glided back, avoiding being hit by the star-steel.

"Just know that I shall hurt them before the end. Break them, listen to them beg for death and then deny them that comfort," Wingarf said, holding his spear forward.

A dark ball of shadow started to form on the tip of the weapon. Allana squared her feet and took the hilt of her blade in both hands, holding the weapon high, the hilt beside her head. The ball of energy burst from the spear, pushing the weapon back, making a sound like a glob of phlegm hitting the bathroom floor. Allana swung her blade like a bat smashing into the energy ball and then dove to the side herself. She fell, then turned so she was facing up toward Wingarf. She created a pad under her feet and pushed off from it, changing her momentum and flying across the room. Quickly, she created two more, kicking off each one in quick succession before almost reaching the wall at the other side of the room. Spinning again, she kicked off the wall and started flying up.

Throwing her arm forward, she created an elastic hand binding the air together She threw the hand forward and grabbed one of the many armatures that were hanging from the roof, then used her momentum to fling herself forward at an angle that would set her up to land on the ledge. It brought her close to Wingarf and Allana took that opportunity to slash out at him. The neon-pink blade of energy went through Wingarf's wing and it puffed like smoke. Time around the impact seemed to slow as the particles dissipated away and then coalesced as if pulled by some magnetic force.

No, that can't be... she thought, not wanting to believe her eyes.

The rest of him had to be flesh and blood still, and if that was the case, then he could be killed, could die. It was just a matter of getting close enough to him to finish the job. Allana landed on the ledge and took a deep breath. Already she could feel the Null fading from her; what she had taken from Wingarf was almost gone. Creating solid forms was taxing, and she was an engineer, not a warrior.

The room got quiet. She could smell ozone. Then, the wet phlegm sound echoed in her ears. She turned just in time to see the ball of energy smash into her chest. Pain raced through her body, causing all the muscles to seize and tighten up. Allana fell to the ground screaming, her blade falling away. She watched helplessly as the neon-pink energy shut off and the silver tube rolled off the ledge into the room below.

Allana was able to get her head up, furrowing her brow. Wingarf screamed as he held his spear out and flew toward her at full speed.

In that moment, the last of the shame that Allana Rickman held onto faded away.

Hallways, The Citadel, Rostov

"Stop, stop. I need to take a breath," Rostov said, slowing down, almost falling forward from the momentum that he and Naomi had built up as they ran away from Wingarf. They had gotten into the backrooms and out, and now were heading toward the library, where they last knew Joanna and Lucas were heading.

"We don't have time for this. He could be right behind us," Naomi said, looking around.

"I don't feel anything behind us. The Null seems quiet. Too quiet, if you ask me," Rostov said as he tried to catch his breath.

He looked up at Naomi. She was still looking behind them. He could feel the apprehension inside of her, coming out of her. She was hoping to see Professor Rickman walk down that hall, coming back with a victory and perhaps a step toward redemption. But Rostov knew better. The sounds of violence as they had fled were horrible.

She isn't coming back.

"You don't know that. She could still prevail," Naomi said.

She didn't believe it. He could feel it. She wanted the *old* professor to come back. She wanted to be able to eventually forgive her, a reality that was quickly slipping from Naomi's fingers.

"Not forgiveness, but perhaps an understanding," Naomi said, tapping Rostov on the shoulder, signaling that it was time for him to get back to his feet.

"It's really unnerving how you are just answering the thoughts in my head," he said lightly as he pushed himself to his feet.

"Then you, my friend"—she said, tapping his chest with her index finger—"need to think quieter." There was a silent beat before they shared a good chuckle.

"You can hear everything I'm thinking, as well?" Naomi asked. Rostov nodded.

"Yup," he said, popping the 'P' sound. "This whole connection, blood pact thing is going to take getting used to."

"A pact that might not be around much longer if we don't find Joanna and Lucas. Come on," Naomi said.

She gave the hallway behind them one last glance, taking a deep breath, before turning and starting to run again. Rostov followed.

Another minute of running passed and then sounds of fighting started to spill from down the hallway. Naomi clutched her starsteel blade, keeping it turned off for the moment, so as not to draw attention. Rostov had the side sword he'd liberated from the dead Militarum officer. He held his hand up, signaling a stop, and started to creep forward, to see if he could make out whatever it was they were heading toward before they ran headlong into it. The last thing they needed was to just run into a fight that was going poorly for their side—or worse. Knowing their luck today, whatever he was about to see was going to end up being worse.

It was always worse.

Slipping his head around the corner, Rostov saw a pitched battle in miniature. Three Militarum soldiers and a lone Host'ire Knight were standing their ground against an unrelenting wave of Fellowship cultists. The soldiers had thrown furniture into the hallway, creating a barricade to set up behind. Two of them were shooting, and a third was reloading their single-shot plasma muskets. All around them were their fallen comrades, with their weapons lined up along the wall so that the two shooters were never without a loaded rifle. With each crack of the plasma musket, Rostov saw a Fellowship member go down, chunks of their bodies blowing apart in fire and blood. They were at such close range now that the plasma rounds were ripping through two, sometimes even three, cultists before losing their kinetic energy, getting stuck and burning out in a corpse or the wall.

Standing atop the furniture barricade was the young Host'ire Knight. His leather coat was flapping and his blue star-steel blade was swinging furiously. As soon as one of the cultists got close to the wall, the kid would cut them down. It wasn't elegant, it was butchery. As the fight progressed, the bodies were starting to pile up like sticks before a campfire. Soon, their wall of furniture would not be a deterrent, and the Fellowship members would just walk over it, using the ramp created by their dead.

Rostov pulled his head back around the corner. Naomi slid up to him.

"Our side is in our way making a very heroic last stand," Rostov muttered.

"How heroic?" Naomi asked.

"The kind they sing songs about. 'The four stood against the wave until the wave broke,' kind of heroic," Rostov whispered.

He stood up. There was no love inside of him for the Host'ire, but those Fellowship bastards had been in his nightmares, they were looking for Hyacinth, and, given the chance, they would slaughter him right alongside the men he hated. Rostov gripped the side sword in his hand, getting one last feel for the weight of it. The sides were blunt, making it a good parrying weapon. The tip of the short blade, though, was sharp and had already tasted blood.

"Where are you going?" Naomi asked.

"To get myself a stanza," Rostov said running forward.

"Friendly behind you!" he yelled as soon as he rounded the bend.

The Knight glanced behind himself for a moment to see who was yelling. It was just the opening that one of the Fellowship cultists needed to land a glancing hit against the young man. It didn't take him down, but every wound was a wound that he couldn't afford. Rostov cleared the distance in a few strides, diving forward and smashing his blade into the man who had hit the knight. The point entered the front of his head and burst out the back with very little resistance. Rostov pulled it to the left, ripping free of the man's head and instantly finding another foe's shoulder to get his weapon stuck in. *Blasted steel.*

Naomi was right behind him, the heartbeat thrum of her blade coming to life filling the room. She took up a side on the far end of the hallway, plugging the hole that they were not near. For a minute, maybe two—it was hard to know in the heat of battle—the three of them hacked and slashed at the enemy, while the two Militarum troopers kept laying down fire. Just as it seemed that they were thinning out, the hall shook, as a massive lumbering beast walked forward. Rostov looked at it and his heart sank.

"What the fuck is that?" he muttered.

One thing he knew was that it was no longer human. At one point it had been, but an untold amount of drugs and surgery later, it was less a man and more a walking, seven-foot-tall, two-person-wide pile of meat with blades grafted to its wrists.

"That," the young Host'ire Knight said as he sliced off the head of another heretic, "was what broke through our lines on the western quad. Four of them smashed into a thousand men. We killed them, but the cost..." He shuddered.

Rostov could see the fear in the man's eyes. It was wafting off him, along with exhaustion.

"Then we run," Naomi said.

"I am sick of running. This is my home; this is *all* our homes. We shall stand against this tide, we will meet them, and they will fall upon our blades. There is no stopping the Host'ire!" he yelled, throwing his blade up into the air, screaming.

It wasn't much of a speech—still, it was what his small group of men needed to hear. They needed something to give them that last bit of strength to throw themselves over their wall and charge bravely into what was most definitely going to be a horrible death. Despite recognizing this, deep down, Rostov knew that it was what he needed to hear as well. The men leaped over the line, and just as he was about to join them, there was a tug on his jacket and he went falling backward.

"This is no time to be throwing your life away, not after you just got it back," Naomi said.

"Do you have a better idea?" Rostov snapped back.

"Did you not see it? How did you not see it? Don't tell me you didn't—"

"I didn't see whatever it was you saw," Rostov snapped, waving his hands in frustration.

"Too busy trying to die like a stupid boy to open your eyes," she said, tapping him in the forehead.

Of course. How could he have been so stupid? Something that big would have to be either mechanical or a Null construct. Either way, it would be driven by something; something that they could take out.

Rostov and Naomi popped their heads up just in time to see the massive wrist blade impale the young knight. He grunted and spit a curse out at the thing, grabbing the blade and pulling himself forward, hacking and slashing with his star-steel blade until the creature's other wrist blade came down and cut his head in half. The horrible construct raised its arm and threw the young man's body against the wall, freeing his blade from the corpse.

That was when Rostov was able to see it. On the creature's back, there was a battery pack. It was bolted directly into the thing's flesh. The area around it was red and angry. Rostov could feel pain and anger rising from there. The creature resented being used to kill, resented the very nature of its existence. He didn't know how he knew that last bit—he just did. It was as clear as day written across the thing's face. He looked at Naomi and she nodded back.

Right. Loud thoughts.

The last surviving Militarum trooper had two muskets in his hands, firing them from the hip. As soon as one was empty, he would reach down and grab another. When a Fellowship cultist got to close to him, he would jab forward with the weapon, sticking them with the triangular bayonet that was affixed to the musket's end. This man was all the distraction that they were going to get.

Naomi gave him another look and Rostov knew the plan. She was going to dig deep and use the Null to short circuit the power pack. He knew she could do it. Dealing with electrical stuff was what she was good at.

Naomi held her hand out and started moving her fingers around like she was guiding an electron through the wiring of a circuit board. Her eyes were closed and already he could see and feel the strain on her face. A blade dug into the remaining trooper's side. He fell to his knees, getting off his last shot, the plasma round blowing through the head of a cultist and smashing into the gut of the abomination. He wasn't going to be able to buy Naomi the time that she needed. The massive creature was already struggling, but it wasn't enough. It was fighting through the pain, it's programming refusing to let it give up and die like it wanted to.

"Ah shit," Rostov muttered.

Clutching his short side sword, he threw himself over the side of the barricade made of tables and chairs. Hitting the ground, he threw out his hand and pulled in the Null, then pushed it forward, throwing back the Fellowship cultists. They all landed on their backs. A few groaned. One or two didn't get back up. Rostov ran to the dying trooper, scooping up a loaded musket along the way.

"On your feet, trooper," Rostov said, holding the blunt edge of his sword in his mouth while he hoisted up the trooper, supporting him with his right arm and putting the musket in his left.

The man looked over at him. Rostov couldn't see his face through the chrome helmet shield, but there was a crack, exposing a part of the man's eye. It was bright blue and burned with determination. Rostov took a step and pointed the man in the correct direction, toward the abomination. He pulled the trigger, the plasma round blowing off most of the creature's right hand. The nasty blade was broken in half, but still, half a blade was dangerous. After the trigger pulled, Rostov could feel the man start to become heavy. Dead weight. He slipped his arm out from under the trooper and let him fall to the ground, what little feeling he had left in the Null was gone.

Rostov was on his own.

He charged forward, diving to the ground just as the abomination swung its massive wrist-blade at him. Sliding under, Rostov dropped his side sword and grabbed the hilt of the young knight's star-steel blade. Hitting the wall, he spun around, igniting the weapon and bringing it up, finishing the job that the plasma musket had done. The creature stumbled back, its wrist a clean, sizzling cut the smell of ozone and flesh filling the air. A horrible, mournful scream filled the room. The creature was looking toward its back, looking toward the Fellowship of the Cross cultists who were behind it. Rostov could see the look of horror and fear upon their faces. Naomi clenched her hand into a fist, making an exasperated noise as she fell to the ground.

Rostov ran for her. The abomination lurched around the corridor for a moment, trying desperately to rip the control battery from its back. The sounds it was making went from loud and angry to reminding Rostov of a whimpering dog who had been kicked too many times, but still couldn't find any malice in their heart to bite. Rostov scooped up Naomi and there was a single tear falling from her eye.

"I'm sorry," Naomi whispered. Rostov looked at her, confused. "For all the pain they put you through, and that this was the only way to take it."

Before he could connect that she was not talking to him, there was a sickening sound behind him. Spinning, Rostov saw the abomination pull the wrist blade from its gut. Black blood was spilling out, hissing and foaming, followed by chunks of intestines. The creature turned the blade again, ramming it into the same wound and pushing harder, further. Its entire digestive tract hit the ground, followed by one last sad call that echoed through the concrete, and was punctuated by hundreds of pounds of dead flesh hitting the floor.

Rostov helped Naomi to her feet. "You did what you had to, to…"

"To save lives. I don't need to hear your thoughts to know you don't believe that the only life I helped was that creature's by setting it free from the oppression of its creation. It was a weapon; a sad weapon and nothing more."

"This is the home of sad weapons," Rostov muttered as they moved forward.

Hallway, The Citadel, Lucas

"Joanna, where are we going?" Lucas demanded as he ran behind her. Her hands were moving wildly about, like she was losing her mind.

"I am not losing my mind. I've just been given clarity!" she snapped at him. Lucas wasn't sure if he was a fan of this being able to mostly read each other's minds now.

"Well then explain it to me, because I don't understand. I mean, I think I—"

Lucas stopped. He didn't want to keep talking. It made him feel silly, like he should have been keeping up with everything that was going on, but so much was happening all at once that, for a moment, it seemed he couldn't get it all to stop long enough so he could unwind the spool and understand the issues.

"You understand just fine, don't think too hard. I *remember*. I just have to put it in order, but I've got the whole puzzle and the box art," Joanna said.

She stopped at an intersection, holding her hands out like she was trying to move invisible objects around. The sounds of children yelling and screaming filled his ears.

"He is dead. Essex, you fucking killed him!"

"We have to run. Split up."

"Hide, the professors are coming!"

Joanna looked at Lucas. It was clear that they were both hearing the voices.

"This is the day, isn't it? I've seen pieces of this since we got here," Lucas said.

"Yes, the blood, the hiding, the kiss..." she said, the last word dropping off.

Lucas could feel his lips on hers, the excitement of it, both then and last night. Joanna lightly bit her lower lip. She was feeling the same thing he was: her teeth were on his lip, his tongue on hers. He cherished these moments, but knew that until they got this connection under control, they were dangerous; slowed them down, distracted them. Joanna took a deep breath through her nose, then breathed out through her mouth three times.

Lucas looked away. The last thing he needed right now was to see the heaving of her breasts as she breathed. *You are not a teenager. Get a grip.*

"There is more to the part that we could never see, couldn't remember. I've got it," Joanna said, raising her hand and snatching something invisible from the air.

"Where Essex and Hyacinth went after the fight. We all followed eventually, but..." Lucas said. "What about Wingarf? He is still out there."

"I know where we need to go, and fear this connection won't last long. It is something we will have to chance. Naomi and Rostov are close," Joanna said, walking forward quickly.

Lucas could feel their friends through the Null as well. They were shining stars of light in the world, pulsing with excitement and sadness. So many emotions. For so long, he had kept everything buttoned up tightly, but now, with the three of them...

Gods, they felt so freely.

Lucas followed after her. The hallway around them started to take on a darker tone. So much violence had happened here. There were bodies all over the place. Last stand after last stand, where nobody had walked away; piles of corpses all atop each other, the desperation of the final moments leaving a raw scar in the Null. If the goal had been to pile up the dead for their god, then today had been a good day for the Fellowship of the Cross, even if Fel and her army *did* manage to hold the Citadel.

"Joanna!" a voice called out.

It was Naomi. She turned the corner, stepping from the shadow of a blinking overhead light. There was half a moment of recognition and then the two ran toward each other, hugging. Rostov followed quietly, walking. Lucas gave him a nod. He nodded back as he walked forward.

That isn't enough, Lucas thought quickly, closing the ground and grabbing Rostov's hand, then pulling him in for a good, solid double tap on the shoulder. A manly hug. The moment didn't last long as Noami pulled away, giving a pensive look behind from where they had just been.

"We found Wingarf," she said. "Professor Rickman, she… She got in his way, gave us the time we needed."

"We saw Hyacinth, she wants us to go…" Rostov started to point.

"This way," Joanna said, finishing his sentence. "Tor gave me the last key. I've seen it."

"Well then, what are we waiting for? I, for one, am ready to be done with all these flashes and half memories," Rostov said. "Feels too much like the mind games they were playing in re-education."

Lucas nodded and found his leadership voice again. This was his job, his part of the group.

"Okay people, let's get back on mission and get out of here. Joanna, you have point. Rostov, cover our rear. Let's move," he said, clapping his hands and giving a two fingered point forward.

The group fell into line, all drawing their weapons, leaving them unignited, and started following Joanna and her new memories. In the back of his mind, Lucas could still hear the children running, screaming, reveling in the victory, while being horrified by the violence of it all.

A few minutes passed and then Joanna held her hand up, stopping the group. Lucas looked around, but they were standing in front of an empty patch of wall. There was nothing in this hallway. No door, no violence, even the sounds of the past had faded away.

"What is it, Joanna?" he asked, walking up to her.

"We are here, just not sure where or what *here* is," she said, looking around. Normally, Lucas would have questioned further, but he could feel her certainty; knew that she was sure that this was the place beyond a shadow of a doubt.

"Connect the blood pact, open your eyes, and see her," Joanna muttered.

"What?" Lucas asked.

"It's what Tor wrote in the book he gave me, in Null ink..."

"We are the blood pact, right?" Rostov asked.

"Yes, us and Essex," Naomi pipped in.

"So how do we connect? I mean, I feel like we are pretty connected already," Rostov said. Lucas had to stifle a groan at the double entendre.

"When we were kids, after the fight with Jasper, all of us were covered in blood," Lucas said.

"But that was all Jasper's blood," Naomi interjected. "Maybe a little bit of yours."

"No, it wasn't," Joanna said, realization in her voice. "Hyacinth. There was so much of *her* blood."

"That is all well and good, but we don't have her blood *or* Essex's," Rostov said.

"She would have known that. Right? I mean, if she is the one who called us, signed the messages, triggering the return of our memories, then she would know that Essex wasn't here. That we wouldn't be able to have her blood because... um..." Naomi said, trying to keep the whole idea in her mind before it slipped away.

Lucas could feel the frustration, as the idea—really, anything having to deal directly with Hyacinth—faded almost as fast as you could say it.

"The Fellowship seems to know that. Tor would have to know that. He remembers her, he had the water..." Joanna said.

An idea was forming in her mind. It was reckless, so quickly formed that Lucas wasn't able to gleam it from her mind before she was acting. Her hand was on his belt, drawing his knife. She ripped off her glove and ran the blade across her hand. Naomi was next on the uptick, grabbing the knife and cutting her hand. She then held the weapon out to Rostov. He reached out, then pulled his hand back. Lucas could feel the unsure feelings running through his mind. Naomi's smile comforted him and pushed the blade forward again.

"Connect the blood pact, open your eyes, and see her," Naomi said, echoing what Joanna had said.

Lucas reached out and took the blade, running it over his hand as well, lightly wincing at the pain. He then held the knife out for Rostov.

"It is the only way," he said.

Rostov nodded and took the weapon, placing the blade to his palm and pulling it across, sheading his blood. Joanna then held her hand out, and one by one, they placed their palms against each other.

"This way, Essex. It's not much farther," a girl's voice said.

They all turned and saw a young blond boy, Essex, helping a battered little blonde girl walk down the hallway. The shades of the past walked through them, up to the blank section of wall that Joanna had stopped in front of.

"Stop here," she said.

The girl—Hyacinth—pulled away from Essex and pressed her hand against the wall. Light started to shine out from unseen holes, the image of a door forming. Hyacinth pushed it open and bright light shined across them all. The two children walked forward. The brightness of the light became so intense that the world washed out in white. Even with his sunglasses, Lucas had to close his eyes. A few moments passed and he opened his eyes again, blinking away the residual spots that were across his vision.

"Well, I'll be damned," Rostov said.

Standing in front of them was an open door. Beyond that was an elevator. Lucas wasn't sure how it had been hidden, just that it was now revealed to them.

"So do we...?" Rostov asked.

"We see this through to the end," Lucas said.

Together, the group stepped into the elevator.

EPISODE VI:
The Duel

Chaple, Barker's World, Hanna

The Preacher had gotten the door open, and the team was filing down.

"Clear!" the first marine down the hatch yelled, as the next two went down. The plasma rifle fire from outside was getting stronger with the storm. Whoever was holding the ground they had stumbled upon was coming for them and mother nature would provide no respite.

There was a loud crash as the first blast of plasma hit one of the stone walls. Rocks and debris were thrown through the air, and the first of Hanna's marines died. He was hit in the head by a brick that had been super-heated by the impact. It smashed into his face, obliterating his features, burning him and—thankfully—killing him instantly.

"Down the hatch, double time!" Hanna shouted, returning fire into the breach where the wall was crumbling. So many shots were being fired on the off chance that one of them would land, causing a chain reaction that would end up with a young man dead on the ground, on some world that was barely even on the map.

"Sergeant, do you have any mines in your kit?" Hanna asked.

The grizzled old marine made a nasty smile and reached into his bag. He produced two contact mines and handed them to Hanna. Sergeant Ramirez grabbed the ladder with both hands and slid down. It was almost as if he was having fun. Hanna then roughly grabbed the preacher and shoved him down the hole. It hadn't seemed too deep and there were people to catch him. While still on the ladder, Hanna pulled out the two mines and attached them to the hatch, pulling out the arming pins as she followed Ramirez's example and slid down the ladder.

Hanna would be lying to herself if she didn't think that adventures like this were not a *small* bit of fun. Otherwise, she would have stayed in the CIC with her mother or gone into medical with her uncle. However, she was not allowed to smile like the sergeant. Decorum and leadership would not allow that. But inside, she understood, and was grinning from ear-to-ear.

"Sitrep!" she yelled, hitting the ground hard, her boots echoing on the stone floor.

"Present and accounted for, sir," Ramirez called from the front of the line of marines.

"And we have found something," Fox chimed in.

"Arrows in the stars, guided to the hearts of men," the preacher muttered from the floor.

That is a fun line. I might have to use that somewhere, Hanna thought, slipping it into her mental file of poetry lines. The preacher had shoved himself into a corner and was shivering, laughing, and generally looking suspect. His eyes were moving left, right, up, and down at a rapid rate, and though he said a few words, most of what came spilling from his mouth was inane babble. Debriefing him would be damn near impossible. But once Hanna saw what they had found, she realized it would be unavoidable.

The chapel had been built on the edge of a high cliff, and the tunnel they were in led to a massive cavern in the side of the mountain. A cavern that had been converted into a hanger and staging base. Sitting in this hanger were two of the crimson, arrowhead-shaped ships that jumped into and out of null space without a jump gate. The very same ships that they were chasing. Here were two of them sitting on the ground—unguarded.

"Well, I'll be God damned," Hanna swore, the curse hanging in the air as she looked down into the maw of the hanger bay. Her mind started to race with the possibilities and the dangers that were before her. The adventure had taken on an entirely new flavor and color in an instant, which just made it that much more fun.

"Sergeant, Corporal Fox. Get down there and assess those ships as quickly as you can. I want to know which one is in better shape. Once we know that, Fox, your job will be to figure out how to get it off the ground, and Sergeant—"

"I'll clip the wings of the other one," the old marine interrupted.

"I was going to say blow it to Hell, but if you want to be gentle with its death, by all means, go right ahead."

"Scrumbly, sir," Ramirez said with a vicious little laugh. "Boys, two-by-two, cover your corners. Let's get down there and set a perimeter!" he yelled, waving a hand and pushing his men forward. The few moments of respite that they had been given were over and it was time to return to action.

Hanna walked over and pulled the preacher to his feet. "Who are the Chosen? Are those their ships?"

"They will not be happy. They are coming for us all. Chaos and bloodshed are their solution. From the storm, they came, and to the storm, shall they bring us," he muttered.

Hanna made a disgusted grunt as she pushed him forward. Whoever these Chosen were, she knew two things. They were not friendly, and their power was such that it could break the minds of men. Whether this was lost tech found again or a new creation, she couldn't say. But if they could jump without gates, there was no telling what else they might have the ability to do.

"Are they ever happy? What is their goal?" Hanna asked, pushing him forward.

"The chaff must be separated and culled," he muttered. "Our time has come again. The storm demands to know if we are ready."

"Ready for what?" Hanna asked. With that question, he turned with a staggering speed, grabbing her long coat and bringing his face close to hers.

"Fire and redemption," he said. "Fire and redemption."

The preacher muttered the phrase three more times as he let go of her coat and slid back to the ground, crying and voicelessly screaming all at the same time.

Fire and redemption. What did that mean? Hanna wasn't sure. She knew it wasn't good, though. The faster they were able to get one of these ships airborne and into the hanger bay of the *Fury*, the better it would be for everybody. A storm was coming, and unless they worked quickly, the windows of the Confederation were going to be left wide open.

It took Hanna a few minutes to get the preacher down to the flight-deck level. By that point, her team had picked which bird each would take care of. Up close, Hanna could see that both ships were not nearly as big as she expected them to be. They were maybe the size of four Hawkeyes put together. The fact that so much technology fit into such a small ship almost broke her mind for a moment. What they had found represented not just a step forward in technology, but a leap of thousands of years. This felt like the kind of tech that was talked about in stories of the Age of Chaos and from the times before, when the empire of humanity stretched across the known galaxy and then some. It was all a part of a story that Hanna vaguely remembered: "The Kingdom of Terra."

Fox had cracked open one of the ships and was inside working, Ramirez and his team were covering the other in explosives. Both ships looked like they had seen better days. They were covered with dirt and scorch marks. There were dents in the hull, and the one the sergeant and his marines were working on had a gash across the side, like a fighter who had been robbed of all their blood and left to die.

Hanna sat the preacher down next to the ship they were going to use to escape this place and walked up the gangplank to the inside. The space was dark and cramped. There were no windows, and everything had a film of dust and something vaguely sticky all over it. Each step of her feet made a sound like she was walking across a floor that was covered with a half-dried sugary beverage. The whole place smelled like a larder whose refrigeration system had long ago failed. Fox Windsail was far forward, swiping through read outs on a screen. As Hanna got closer, she could see the look of abject terror that was crossing her face.

"Major..." she said, turning and looking up at her.

"What is it, Corporal?" she asked.

"I was going through the first layer of documents here, hoping that there would be a recently used manual or something. Shockingly, everything is in NovaTerra standard already—which is strange, because I've never seen anything like this before. Which means that we are dealing with something wholly new, which screams a first contact situation—"

"Fox, calm down. What did you find?" Hanna asked, putting her hand on the woman's shoulder. Fox took a deep breath, making a fist of her hand and biting down on her index finger to center herself.

"This ship is connected to the network, and just yesterday, a packet came in. I've only scanned it, but... Well, see for yourself." Fox stepped aside, to let Hanna see what she had found. From the first line, her heart sank.

Comm Fleet Command, [Redacted]. Possession of extra atomics completed; course set for NovaTerra. Targeting information downloaded and calculating. Z minus 14.

The next few sentences were equally as dire. These were plans; plans to use atomic weapons upon NovaTerra. The ships were a great find, but this? This was the key to *everything*. Hanna covered her mouth and just looked wild-eyed at the wall as she started to work through the ramifications of what was going on.

This adventure had suddenly stopped being fun.

Hanna's thoughts were cut off by an explosion far away. The mine on the trapdoor had been tripped. Their time was already running thin.

"Will this ship fly?" she asked.

"Yes, I'm sure of it. All the commands are, like I said, in NovaTerra standard, and well labeled. It's just going to be a matter of getting the power working," Fox said.

"Good. Get on that," Hanna said before rushing out of the ship.

Once she was clear of the gangplank, she looked up and could see the smoke and debris coming down the hallway where the ladder to the chapel was. Sargeant Ramirez was already deploying his men around the stairs.

"Report," she barked.

"Second ship ready to be skuttled on your orders, sir. I've placed my men in a holding position. We will make whoever comes down that hallway bleed for every inch of ground. We will hold this position until Windsail gets that ship ready to fly. For the honor, sir."

That was when the first rounds of plasma fire came from the smoke, almost hitting Hanna where she was standing. Diving down, she drew her sword and pistol.

"For the honor, Sergeant," she returned the phrase. "Hold fast until you see targets. I don't want us wasting rounds on shadows and dust," she said, waiting for the first shapes to start to come through the breach.

***

Hanna stumbled back up the gangway to the ship. Her jacket was torn, and blood covered the blade of her sword. The grenade that preceded the last attack had taken out three more marines. It was down to just Sergeant Ramirez and his last three grunts. They were putting up a valiant fight, but the numbers were not on their side. She looked down at her watch, forty-five minutes. It felt like they had been holding the line for much longer.

"Windsail, I need us a way out of here and I need it now!" Hanna yelled.

"I'm still working on the power systems to the engines, but I've found something that might buy us some time!" she called back. Fox ran over to Hanna. "I've got the ships weapons online. Bring the marines inside." Just as Hanna was turning to yell for Ramirez, the radio on her belt started to chirp.

"Major, come in. Do you copy?"

It was Erik's voice. There was a lot of static from the storm. She grabbed the radio and pressed the button.

"This is Major Cordova. I copy, Commander. Situation here is hot. Repeat, extremely hot." While talking, she motioned with her sword for Fox to go and get the marines inside the ship.

"LZ is hot, copy. I've got your beacon, and we are coming for you," Erik said.

"Negative. I have a package you need to get to Actual presently," Hanna said, running to the console and placing her radio down and bringing up a data transfer.

"You can deliver it yourself once this storm clears," Erik said.

"Repeat, negative Commander. Stand by," Hanna said again with more force in her voice. She desperately wanted to tell her brother what they had found, wanted to scream at him that they were going to hold this ground and get out on their own; that he needed to take the information and run, to leave them here. All the things she couldn't just say because the channel was not secure.

"Hanna," Erik's voice said. He had switched from her commander to older brother.

"Erik. We have this under control." She pressed a few more keys and the upload started. "Are you getting this?"

"Data package downloading now," Hanna heard Aya say from the background. As it was uploading, the remaining marines ran into the ship. Fox hit a button, and the gangplank started to rise.

"Sargeant, you take that position. Corporal, you take that one," Fox yelled, pointing to two different alcoves in the ship, both equipped with a screen and twin control sticks.

The marines ran over to their stations. As soon as they took control, Hanna could feel the ship lurch, and there was the sound of gears moving inside the thin shell. Then the sound of kinetic weapons fire filled the ship.

"What is going on down there, Major?" Erik yelled.

"Aggressive field testing," she returned. Looking down, the upload had finished on her end.

"We have the package," Aya's voice came through the radio.

"Brother, send my regards to mother," Hanna said.

She turned off the radio so that Erik could not argue with her anymore. She knew that as soon as he saw what she had seen, he would be running back to *Fury* at full speed. They would catch up, or they wouldn't. It didn't matter so much anymore. They had found what they were looking for and passed it on. Now, the ball was in another person's hands, and all she could do was cover the back of the court.

"Specialist, get us in the air, if you please," Hanna yelled, as she wiped the blood off her sword.

The Dorms, Olympus Ares Research Facility, Grace

Getting up to the dorms had taken time and creativity. Unlike in the movies, air ducts were not strong enough to hold her, and she had been forced to find a different way forward. That way involved creeping and hiding, moving from one small bit of cover to another, ducking to avoid cameras and roving patrols of infested guards.

The first group she saw, there was no evidence they were infested. She let her rifle fall to the side while stepping out into the open and putting her arms up.

"Hello!" Grace called out. "I'm friendly. I'm part of the science team."

The guards were all large men dressed in gray fatigues, armor plates on their chests and full-face shield helmets. Each one was strapped head-to-toe with extra magazines, grenades, and, just to be safe, large combat knives that would give a small sword a run for its money. They turned, leveling their plasma rifles at her. She didn't like being on this side of those weapons, especially with hers hanging to the side. After a tense moment, the guards all looked at each other and lowered their weapons. The leader held his hand up toward her and started walking forward.

"Are you okay?" he asked. There was a comfort in his voice, something soothing. But just on the edge of it, there was a sharp coldness.

I don't like this, Emily thought.

"I'm fine. Just crawled my way out of Gamma Lab. Thankfully, I found the armory before I found out my friends had turned walking corpses," she lied. They didn't need to know exactly where she was from yet. That was privileged information.

"It's a mess out here, for sure. It is a good thing you found us. We are rounding up all the surviving members of the science team and heading topside for evacuation," he said.

The word 'round up' didn't sit well with her; sent a shiver down her spine. Something didn't seem right.

There is no way they would just evacuate the base. Even if they did, we would be far from the priority of who they would be taking with them.

"What is going on, do you know?" Grace asked.

Let's see how far playing dumb will get me. Every answer was another data point for the spreadsheet in her head labeled, "What in the fuck is going on today?" There were many points and very little yarn connecting them.

"That is on a need-to-know basis, ma'am. Right now, my orders are to get you to the surface for evacuation."

He was close now, closer than Grace was comfortable with. His outstretched hand came for her. Through the visor of his helmet, she could see the creeping of eyes; *neon-blue* eyes.

"Wayfinder," she heard in her head; Varagoth's voice, like a needle pressed to the back of her neck.

She took a step back from where his hand was almost on her face. No, she was not going to let him touch her.

"She is clean!" the guard yelled as he took a harder, faster step toward her. The four guards behind him started to raise their weapons and head toward her. Grace threw power into her right leg and quickly brought it up. If he was close enough to touch her with his outstretched arm, then she was close enough to kick him in the groin—and kick him she did. Emily's armored foot made a satisfying crunch as they smashed into the guard's unarmored manhood. As he grunted and started to crumple, Grace brought her rifle up. A single shot and his head exploded out the back of his helmet in a torrent of gore and super-heated plasma, the little chunks of brain catching fire.

As his body fell to the ground, a black mist started to pour out of the wound and escape back toward the other guards. The cloud looked hurt, like it could barely hold itself together. It would be a long time before it tried to infest another person, she figured. But there was precious little time to ruminate on this development. There were still men with guns. Grace kicked back with the foot that still had power in it and then turned so that she hit the wall with her shoulder, behind the box she had been hiding behind originally. Bolts of super-heated plasma shot past Grace, right where she had been standing just moments before.

"I thought we were going to the surface!" Emily yelled, flicking on the aim assist in her suit.

"You can go there in a body bag, bitch!" the guard in front snapped back. There was no calm or warmth in his voice. It was metallic from the rebreather and cold. A killer's voice.

Clutching up on the weapon, Grace knelt and poked her head from behind the crate, lining the HUD up on the first knee see saw—unsure if it was the one who had yelled at her—and pulled the trigger. The joint exploded, the man falling backward, his foot and lower leg still standing where they had been. His screams were punctuated by more gunfire, and the clicking of a grenade being thrown over her hiding spot and landing at her feet. A quick power dump and Grace kicked the small silver ball down the hallway where it exploded, shattering all the glass that she could see.

This was an untenable situation, but she did have an idea. Flicking through the HUD, she pushed every ounce of power into her helmet and chest plate. Both felt heavy and hot.

This better work, she thought, rolling from her spot, spitting off rounds. There was another thud and scream. Quickly, she was on her feet, the computer in her suit taking over, cracking off three head shots in half a second. It wasn't fast enough to stop two plasma rounds from hitting her in the chest. They didn't go through, but both knocked the wind out of her as she stumbled back into the wall and lost her footing, falling to the ground.

Alarms were going off all over her suit, and the power readings were close to zero. Each breath she took was agonizing, a force of nature to breathe in and out. Turning the alarms off, Grace got to her feet. The exertion was all fire and pain. At least a handful of ribs were broken, that was for sure. The medical diagnostics were offline—not enough power. Each step she took was a struggle, the suit getting heavy as the energy slowly recharged. Now if only her body would recharge as fast as the suit could.

One of the guards, the man whose foot she had blown off, was still groaning. Emily put a round through his face as she stumbled by. The mist of infestation was heavy on the ground, pooling like morning fog on a field, its cold malice seeping through her boots, trying to get to her feet.

"You can't run forever, Itchi. We shall catch you," Varagoth's voice said in her head.

"Fuck off," she muttered, heading toward the end of the hallway, each step getting a little better, the suit taking just a little more of the burden off her tired, beaten body.

The Depths, Below the Citadel, Lucas

They were quiet as the elevator moved down. The steel box, illuminated by a single, weak overhead light, cast them in shadow. There was no instrument panel. The only way that Lucas knew they were heading down was because he could feel the bounce of the cables. This was far from the smooth ride provided by the rest of the elevators in the Citadel. Even their minds were quiet as he looked from Joanna, to Rostov, to Naomi. Whatever they were thinking, it was being kept very low. Or, they were, like him, only focusing forward, barely even able to make words in their minds, operating solely off instinct. This elevator felt familiar. Lucas couldn't tell if that was just because it looked like every other shitbox elevator he had been in, or because he was starting to remember something that happened down here.

The elevator came to a jolting halt, shaking all of them. Lucas shifted his weight to make sure that he could keep his feet under him. Then, creaking, the door opened. They were greeted with a dark hallway of steel. The floor was metal, and the hallways were supported by hundreds of buttresses that went up and then angled, making this look like something from the gothic churches that populated the southern continent of NovaTerra. Instantly, everybody's minds started to light up and he was hit by an overwhelming cacophony of sound in the silence of this place.

"Can we all take turns thinking?" Lucas asked, holding his hands up. Speaking out loud silenced the group.

"Thank you. I couldn't hear myself think," Rostov said.

"Well, I could," Naomi playfully sniped back at him.

"Where are we?" Lucas asked, looking around.

The hallway only had a few faint, flickering fluorescent lights for illumination. He could see more existed, but age and disrepair had claimed them. Igniting his star-steel blade, Lucas held the green shaft out before him, giving the hallway a sickly pallor.

"Tor referred to this as 'The Labyrinth'," Joanna said. "All indications are that this is where we went, following Hyacinth and Essex. Though, I guess she knew this was here all along."

"Administrator Fel indicated that she knew something was below, but like us, couldn't put a finger on it. Same with when I heard Wingarf talking to that Fellowship spy," Lucas said.

"He knew about the blood pact, which Tor *also* knew about," Joanna said.

"So, if I am following correctly from A to B and so on," Naomi started, using her fingers to try and track the logic. "Somebody out there knows the whole story about what happened that day twenty years ago. That would mean they *also* knew about this place, and—the kicker of the whole thing—they can bleeding remember it all!"

Naomi threw her hands into the air.

"We are not going to figure out what is going on if we stay here," Rostov said. "The answer is out there, inside this place."

"It's a ship," Lucas muttered as he took another tentative step out into the hallway, running his hands along the steel beams and looking at the long-faded marking on the walls. He could make out what looked like directions and junction numbers. All of it was written in a language that he didn't know.

"That is impossible. That would mean this ship has been here for five hundred years, at least. And it supports the Citadel. Somebody would have remembered that it was here. How is there still power? Where—"

Rostov put a hand on Naomi's shoulder, and she stopped talking.

"I agree. A buried ship seems unlikely. The Citadel goes deep," Joanna said. Lucas could feel that she wasn't completely sure about this, even with the return of her memories.

"No, look at this," Lucas said, pointing to the writing. "I've spent enough time on ships in my life to recognize section numbers. These supports would have fallen apart, if they were as old as we think. Unless..."

All four of them looked at each other. Lucas and Naomi had reached the answer, but everybody seemed to be waiting for who would say it out loud first.

"A Dreadstar," Lucas said, breaking the silence.

"The historic implications of that are wild," Joanna said. "We know where all the Dreadstars that survived the Age of Chaos are. The five of them are still in service. This…"

"Slipped through the cracks," Rostov said.

"Apparently," Lucas said, walking forward again, shining the light of his blade down the hallway. "Joanna, what do we know about Dreadstars? You are our historian."

"We know both plenty, and not enough. We don't know who built the Dreadstar fleet during the Age of Chaos a thousand years ago. So many records were lost. Their ability to jump without a gate has never been fully understood and there is nothing written down about it. Scholars outside the Host'ire think it has to be Wayfinder tech, since they built the gates. Of course, that is heretical thinking in Host'ire circles," Joanna said, rattling off the few facts that she knew. The ones that seemed to pertain to this moment, at least.

"If we don't have the records, how do we know only five survived the Age of Chaos?" Naomi asked.

"Because if there was another, it would have disrupted galactic power," Lucas said. "One of the only reasons that the Confederation is as large and as powerful as it is comes down to the fact that they control the last five Dreadstars."

"This could have been here for a thousand years. It clearly didn't survive the Age of Chaos—at least, not as a starship, seeing as the damn thing is buried under hundreds of feet of rock," Rostov said.

Lucas held his hand up. "Okay, so we know a *little* more than we did. Let's slip these facts into our notebooks and keep moving, see if another part of the puzzle starts to come together. Has anybody besides me been on a Dreadstar before?"

The group all shook their heads.

"Well, I guess we have all been here before, at some point," Naomi said. Lucas couldn't argue with that. "I mean, I think we followed. Right?" She looked to Joanna.

"Yes, we have been down here. It's still fuzzy to me, but I know we have. Whatever was in that potion that Tor gave me unlocked these memories, but left them fuzzy—like a communication that being garbled by jamming."

"Then we turn off the jamming," Lucas said, pointing forward with his blade and starting to walk.

Through the shadows, they walked for a few minutes. There was nothing in this hall but flickering lights and ancient debris. Finally, they came to an intersection. The hallway ran into another, one side going right, the other left.

"I know you are foggy, Joanna, but any ideas?" Lucas asked, pointing his blade toward both sides of the hallway.

"I..."

Before she could say anything else, they heard the hollow thumping of footsteps running on deck plates. They all turned around to see the child versions of Lucas and Naomi running. The shades of themselves came to a stop at the intersection. Young Naomi walked to the left and started to yell for Hyacinth and Essex. The only response was her voice echoing back at them. Lucas started banging on the side wall in dot dash code. The adult in him almost wanted to chuckle, knowing he had just learned that style of communication weeks before.

"Which way do we go?" young Naomi asked.

"I don't..." Young Lucas paused, breathing in and puffing himself up. Already trying to be the leader that he knew the group needed. "That way," he said, pointing toward the hallway Naomi had yelled down. She nodded and they both started running, fading away in shadows as an overhead light fizzled off and then back on.

"Well, that is prophetic," Rostov said, flicking on his blade and starting to walk toward the hallway, following the memories.

"I don't know. It doesn't feel right," Joanna said, looking the other way. Lucas looked down the other hallway and tapped out the same rhythm he had as a child. Dash, dot, dash, dot, dot, dot. A simple hello. The message echoed back at him. He then closed his eyes and reached out with the Null, trying to feel what he could.

There was nothing.

"Should we split up?" Naomi asked. "I mean, we can cover more ground that way. With our comms and connection, we can keep tabs on each other. I know it's risky and we were told to never split the group, but..."

"In this situation, you might be right," Lucas said. "I'll go this way with Joanna, you two go that way. Stay in touch. Every five minutes, we try and reach out. Got it?"

"Yes sir," Rostov said, giving Lucas a slightly flippant salute.

Lucas just rolled his eyes and walked into the flickering darkness.

Apartment, Novagrad, Claudia

Claudia hit the wall with a thud.

Pain wracked through her body, but she managed to keep her feet. Mister Harrison was standing over her. Somehow, he seemed taller than he was, stronger. The rage was truly upon him. His two servants, dressed all in black, stood quietly behind him: watching and blocking her exit. Alexander challenging Mister Harrison to a duel had been rash and stupid, and now she was going to pay for it. Not in blood or her life. No, just in pain and having to listen to him drone on and on about his importance to the plan.

"You need to keep that boy under control. We cannot afford to lose another one," Mister Harrison said, running his hand across the slick, greasy hair on his head.

"It seems to me that his fate is now in your hands," Claudia bit back.

"And his in mine," Harrison snapped. "This is not some sad little scientist. He was raised and trained on a Dreadstar!"

"And you were a smuggler for years. I have faith that you can figure a way to slide out of any lasting repercussions," Claudia said.

He hit her again. This time, she allowed herself to fall to the ground. Standing her ground for too long would just cause him to hit her more. Going down was the smart option in this situation.

"Of course I have a plan, you foolish tart. I do not accidentally kill my targets," Mister Harrison said calmly.

She hated when he talked in a calm voice. So often, he said the vilest things in that voice. Where other men would scream and call her horrible names, he just said it in a calm, matter-of-fact kind of way. It would have almost sounded pleasant, if the words were not so vile.

"How was I supposed to know the MacGuffin boy had an undiagnosed heart condition?" Claudia snapped back.

"A likely excuse. He was their weak link. He would have given you everything you wanted to know," Harrison said.

"Yes, well, it's a pity he died before I could spread my legs and ask him."

This time, she stood up, keeping her back against the wall in case he lashed out again. Claudia knew that, in a fight, she could probably take him, but it wasn't Mister Harrison that worried her. It was the two quiet servants in black that were always nearby; members of the Chosen. Some damned cult that he always referred to as 'their associates'. Claudia couldn't be sure they were able to fight, but there was just a feeling deep in her gut that said they could. At the very least, they were surely armed.

"Yes, it does seem that trick is working far better on the Cordova boy. You need to get the information from him soon. We are running out of time before the operation starts," Mr. Harrison said.

He turned and started to walk to the back of the room. His pacing gait was like that of a cat waiting for a mouse to come out of its hole.

Before Claudia could say anything, Mister Harrison turned and darted across the room. His hand was wrapped around her neck, and she was against the wall, keeping her feet on the ground only by the tips of her toes.

"The location of that research facility is of paramount importance. Without the project that they are developing, the war will not be won."

He squeezed harder at the end of both sentences. She could feel the air being shoved out of her body, the capillaries in her neck bursting. There was going to be a bruise in the morning that she would need to cover up.

"Our mutual associates are counting on this being taken care of before the election. You know what happens on election day?" Mister Harrison asked, squeezing again.

She tried to speak, but there was no air for the words. The world around her was starting to get fuzzy. Her hands went to his hand and tried to claw it away. He was able to use his other arm to swat them away. So much power, far more than he looked to have. As the world started to fade around her, its color draining, Claudia's eyes glanced over at the two mute men in black behind Mister Harrison. For a split second, she was sure that there was some kind of black aura coming off them.

"I can't hear you," Mister Harrison hissed.

She tried to talk again, but there was even less air. He squeezed one last time before letting go. Claudia fell to the ground, gasping. She put her hand around her neck. It was tender. Breathing hurt, and at this moment, she was swallowing air like a drowning person.

"Everybody dies on election day," she muttered.

"Good girl. Now go clean yourself up, so we can fix your mess in the morning," Mister Harrison said.

He pulled a handkerchief from his breast pocket and threw it down at her. Claudia watched him go. The two servants in black parted to either side of the door and allowed him to walk out first, then followed.

She spit a wad of bloody phlegm on the ground. She might be subservient to him, but he was clearly a slave to whatever higher power was orchestrating the coming war.

This situation was getting worse every day. Harrison was a loose cannon, a smuggler who had too much power. She needed to plan to take him out, provided Alexander didn't do that for her in the morning. That would require her to contact him in an hour or so. He needed another push. Right now, Claudia was sure that he would just fire into the air or aim wide. A non-lethal duel, just enough to prove his honor and masculinity. It would be better for her if he killed Harrison—or at least maimed him.

So he needed some proper motivation.

Standing up, Claudia knew what she needed to do. Taking as deep a breath as her bruised throat would allow, she smashed her head into the wall.

Dreadstar Fury, Erik

Erik read some of the files as they headed back to *Fury* at full speed. The first lines had caused him to push the Rapier to its limit, insisting on a combat landing. The next few paragraphs had brought into stark resolution just how much danger they had stumbled into. Though he wasn't sure they had stumbled into this danger, so much as had been lured into it. "Hunting Dreadstars" had been the heading of the section that brought him to that conclusion. It was a detailed, multiyear-long plan to eliminate or sway to their side the last five Dreadstars in existence. Right there, in the text, as a step for this very goal, was reference to the battle of Hyroncore, where they had almost died.

Not suitable for conscription, it'd read.

The phrase cascaded though Erik's mind as he ran down the halls of *Fury*. Behind him, trying to keep up, was his page, who had his coat and sword belt. He pulled off his flight jacket as he turned a corner, grabbing a ladder and starting to climb. He couldn't wait for the lifts, and the movement would give him time to work through what he had just read.

Not suitable for conscription.

He reached the top of the ladder and was now upon the command deck. His page was a moment behind him. Erik took a deep breath. It would take another minute or so for the data to be transferred from his fighter to the CIC computer systems. It had almost filled his ship's computer banks.

"Your coat, sir," the page said.

He did not even look winded as he held out the heavy blue coat. Erik reached out and took the coat, pulling it on. In the pocket was a black cravat. Pulling that out, he tied it around his neck and slipped the cloth under his shirt. Holding his arms up, the page strapped the sword belt around his waist. Erik put his arms down and flicked the coat to the side, catching it behind the hilt of the blade. He now looked presentable enough to enter the Combat Information Center.

Taking a breath, he stepped into the room and started walking down the stairs. The boatswain rung the bell. "Commander on the deck!" he called out. As the bell echoed in the room, a light tune started to play, composed of northern pipes and French horns.

"Commander, sitrep, if you please," Lord Admiral Cordova said, looking up from the glass table.

Looking down, Erik could see that the arrowhead-shaped ships they had spotted were gaining on them quickly.

"The situation on the ground is rapidly deteriorating, but it is not our most pressing issue," Erik said.

"Yes, I trust your sister has everything in hand. I am interested to see what these small jumping bastards can do against a Dreadstar. They are heading forward and full sail, as if they think they have a chance," the Lord Admiral said, not looking up from the glass table.

"Mother," Erik said, so full was his worry about what he had read that all pretense of rank and title fell away. It was only then that Cassandra Cordova looked up from the table.

"Commander—" she warned, but Erik didn't have time for propriety.

"Mother, Hanna and her team found something," Erik said.

He reached down to the table and pressed a few keys, bringing up the document. "Hunting Dreadstars" was bold across the holographic display. The Lord Admiral started to read. Erik followed her eyes as she got to the section on plans for the battle of Hyroncore.

Not suitable for conscription, terminate with extreme prejudice.

His mother moved the text up and her fingers stopped, and she turned to her son.

"We need to get out of here with all haste. Captain Rackland, set a course for the nearest jump gate. Full speed, if you please," Lord Admiral Cordova yelled out across the CIC.

Captain Rackland repeated the order up to the helm and boatswain, both of whom repeated it back. As orders were yelled, an up-tempo track started to play across the ship's speakers. Everybody knew it's title and what was meant when it started to play "Beat to Quarters."

"Lord Admiral, I request the use of one of the Frigates to return planet side and retrieve the Major and her party," Erik said, standing tall, his hand falling to the hilt of his sword.

"We will not extricate ourselves from this situation in time if we return," the Lord Admiral said.

"Mother," Erik whispered.

"Erik, I trust your sister will find her way out of the situation. She knew the consequences of her actions. Read the next section," his mother said. There was fear and sadness in her voice, the kind he had only heard once or twice from her in his entire life.

Before he could say anything more, the ship was rocked by fire. The two unknown arrowhead-shaped ships had reached them.

"Captain Rackland, let us see how hardy these new opponents of ours are. Give them a full broadside, if you please," Lord Admiral Cordova called up.

"With pleasure," Rackland said, a smile across his face.

A moment later, *Fury* lurched as the great guns that were mounted along the spine of the ship joined the conversation. One of the crimson arrowhead ships winked out of existence, its marker vanishing from the table.

"Scratch one, sir," Rackland called back, looking down at the weapons board where he was standing. "Four direct hits, tissue paper."

There was little time to celebrate as the ship rocked again. Erik found his footing after almost falling across the table.

"Stand fast, Commander," the Lord Admiral said, putting her hand on her son's shoulder. Erik was glad for it. He never had the strongest legs when the ship started to lurch. He had never truly needed them, as every combat encounter involved him outside in a fighter.

"Tissue paper that packs a punch, wouldn't you say, Captain?" the Lord Admiral called across the CIC.

"Indeed. Shall I clear your sky?"

"At your earliest convenience, sir," his mother said, turning her attention back to the glass board.

Erik came close to see what she was looking at. It was again the text from the documents that Hanna had sent them. She just pointed at a paragraph.

"It is three days at full power to the closest gate," she said.

Erik looked down at the title of the next paragraph. Plans for an atomic attack upon NovaTerra. Whoever was setting these plans in motion had been planning for years. What they held in their hands was the last shred of hope the Confederation had for survival.

Buried Dreadstar, Below the Citadel, Naomi

Rostov and Naomi both had their blades out, using them to illuminate the dark confines of the buried Dreadstar. Naomi lagged slightly behind, watching Rostov as he walked. Reaching out, she tried to see what he was thinking, but all that was coming back from him was gibberish; repeated phrases, bits of a song's chorus, some product jingle from when they had been kids.

"What are you thinking about?" she asked, pulling away and returning to the tried-and-true way of learning what was going on with a person: talking.

"I'm trying to not think about anything. Thinking about things is going to lead me to a dark place," Rostov said.

"Darker than this?" Naomi asked, walking up next to him.

"Oh yes. I start to think about causality. How is this here? Who knew about it? Who had to know about it? Things like that. Those thoughts lead me to a dark place. Dark thoughts compounded on already dark opinions," Rostov said.

Naomi knew where this was going. She wasn't going to say that she wasn't also feeling these things, but at the same time, nobody was as much of a dower as Rostov.

"You think there is some grand conspiracy with this ship being down here?" Naomi asked.

If he was thinking gibberish not to think these things, that meant it was weighing on his mind and needed to be spoken. If they were going to be some mythical blood pact, if they were going to stay as close as they were, then these things had to be aired out. She loved him too much to let it stew until the pot bubbled over.

"There has to be. There is no way—no fucking way—that the Order didn't know this was here when they built the Citadel after the Wayfinder war. It's a thousand-year-old ship, probably loaded with Wayfinder tech, right next to the lost door to *Hell*!" Rostov said, punctuating the last words by thrusting his free hand up into the air.

He looked at her. Naomi didn't have anything to say. She wanted to let him get it all out. She was the wooden spoon sitting over the pasta water.

"I just... I just can't see *why* they would do that, unless they wanted to keep using what they *say* is heretical technology. I mean, they built and then hid an elevator to get down here," he said. "If, maybe, we had to go through some arcane excavation to get down here, I could see them having built the Citadel here out of some kind of spite, but... I just can't fully circle that square right now."

"What if it's not some grand conspiracy? It could be something smaller," Naomi said.

"Smaller than a Dreadstar? A place people talk about in hushed rumors that they can't remember? No... this is... The Host'ire higher ups *must* know this is here. Keeping secrets is what they do best. I just... I don't want to talk about it right now," Rostov said, picking up the pace of his walking.

Naomi breathed out and, for a moment, got distracted by watching the movement of his butt. Her eyes lingered for a beat too long. Rostov turned and gave her a sly smile.

"Take a picture. It will last longer," he said coyly.

"The movement is half the fun," Naomi said, catching back up to him, giving him a little slap on his butt.

She knew he was still worried, still couldn't stop thinking about what he thought was a grand conspiracy. There was nothing to do about it right now. All they could do was keep moving forward and find Hyacinth—or whatever it was she wanted them to find. If a little playful flirting was what it took to keep his mind from spiraling into the darkness that he was holding on to, then so be it; a darkness that the order she still loved, even after the last few days, had put inside of him.

"Well then, I shall make sure I walk with a little more swish in my step," Rostov said with a chuckle.

He sped up and started shaking his butt for her. She laughed, biting her lip in a way that she knew he would feel. He stopped and turned around. She could already feel that he was starting to calm down, letting the spiral slow down, and that his… resolve…was stiffening.

Naomi walked up, flicking off her blade and wrapped her arms around him, kissing Rostov deeply, letting their tongues wrap around each other as she grabbed his ass and squeezed. The tension of the whole day, in that moment, started to fade away, to wash past her. She would have taken him then, if not for the few remaining lights going black, punctuated by the sound of a low chanting coming from all around them.

They weren't alone.

Grace's Apartment, Olympus Ares Research Facility, Grace

Grace was back in her dorm room. It was quiet and, for the first time since leaving this room, she felt calm. Not so calm that she was going to let her guard down, though.

Against the door, she had piled everything in the room that she owned and rippled the wires from the wall. None of that was going to stop the infested base guards from getting in, but it would slow them down, and that wasn't nothing. She had also pulled off the chest plate of her environment suit, placing it against the wall, plugged in so that it could attempt to charge. It felt good to be out of the heavy thing for the moment, even though the undersuit was still more restrictive than she liked. The restriction was what was keeping her going, though. Until she could find a med bay, removing it was a bad idea, same with the rest of the armature. The residual power in the arms and legs would last until the primary battery in the chest could get some juice.

The rapid change of the facility had not reached this level yet, leaving her steel walls still shiny and metallic. The dorms were located well above ground, near the top of the facility—or so they were told. *I hadn't thought about the lack of windows since I got here a year ago.*

Spread out on her desk—that was built into the wall, so not against her door—was all the information she had been able to gather about this other world that she kept getting sucked into, where the creature with the neon-blue eyes was from. The probe was sitting in a cradle, the video downloading into her system, all five teraflops. Her notes were spread out and the book she had come to find laid open.

The Translation of the Language of the Peoples of LV55M by Doctor Lawson Arundel. A ponderous title for a ponderous tome. Doctor Arundel had a very dry writing style for how truly out of left field his ideas were. Even the conspiracy-theory-obsessed academics were still just academics, Grace figured. What she was interested in was the translation of the runes. Sadly, the doctor had not been able to figure out a one-to-one translation, but he had mostly been able to understand the story that they were telling.

> *The peoples of LV55M have been, according to carbon dating, dead for at least ten thousand NovaTerra standard years. Whatever happened to them was a great calamity, and it happened quickly. This world is dead now, just a graveyard of volcanic activity and red dirt. Once, though, it contained life— probably jungles in the region our samples were from. The fossil record indicate that this event culminated with the world's ionosphere being ripped apart. The story that I was able to transcribe supports that.*

What follows is a summary and then a more detailed breakdown in the next section. They were a space-faring race, quite possibly the first in this part of the galaxy. There is talk of hyperspace highways, and then the coming of shades. They were creatures that operated more like a force of nature than a civilized species. They passed through their space, destroying everything they touched. This was all written down on one of the main walls that I found, illustrated even.

There were pictures to break up the text. They showed people running for their lives, warriors with blades of light standing tall against blobs of inky blackness. In the sky, ships that looked like arrowheads were raining fire. Across the ground were the dead. The background was filled with tall buildings in flames.

Deep in a caldera as old as time, I found more of the story. It told how this civilization knew that they could no longer stand against the shades, and that to survive, extraordinary measures would have to be taken. The Redeemers were to be hidden away, out of reach, until the time was right again for vengeance to be exacted across the galaxy.

Grace looked up from the book, her mind racing. This was one of those rare times when being both a physicist and an archaeologist was going to come in handy. In fact, it was probably the *first* time. In college, the two disciplines had never overlapped, and you would never catch the professors from one interacting with the other. Unless they were fighting over who she was going to work with one semester—that argument had almost come to blows. She had chosen to spend the next three months rebuilding a super collider than trek through the muck of a long dead civilization.

This is the first time she'd wondered if that was the wrong choice.

A little buzzer went off. The footage was done downloading. Turning from the book, she started to scroll through the hours and hours of video, flipping through the different filters and ranges of information that had been recorded. It was, in fact, not a glitch. While the aperture had only been open for ten seconds, the probe had recorded almost ten hours of video. One of the filters was background radiation and gravity.

Equations started to form in her mind. She pulled out some paper and her small tablet. Jotting numbers down, she pulled up a gravity chart and found the set of numbers she was looking for. Gravity readings for the Galactic Core. This world was near the Fissure, or...? She set her pen down. *No that doesn't...* Grace balled up the paper and started again a second time, but the math still didn't balance out correctly.

Starting on a third sheet, she adjusted assuming the radiation and star locations ten thousand years in the past. The math started to line up, but still, something wasn't clicking into place. The stars and readings she was seeing had moved too far, too fast...

You are almost there, Wayfinder. So close to seeing your true purpose, Varagoth said in the back of her mind.

Grace spun around, pointing the pen at the room like it was a weapon. There was nothing. It was empty, except for her armor sitting in a pile, quietly charging. She turned around and looked down at all the math that she had scrawled, and then back at the text in the book.

"Time, gravity..." she muttered to herself, as she flipped the pad to a fresh page and started to write out even more equations.

Buried Dreadstar, Below the Citadel, Joanna

"Can you imagine what one of these must be like at full operating capacity, full of people and life?" Joanna asked.

"I was on one, for a little while," Lucas said.

"Oh, of course, you just... I should have remembered that," Joanna said, feeling sheepish. They had been walking in silence for a while and she just wanted to break the ice, completely forgetting that Lucas had mentioned spending time on one of these ships.

"They are impressive. A whole world unto themselves. I was talking with one of the marines who was our liaison aboard *Pride*. He was probably forty, one of those grizzled Master Sergeants that even generals listened to. He was saying how he had been born aboard *Pride*, and would probably die there, as well. But so far, even he hadn't managed to explore every nook and cranny of the ship. Each section had its own culture, in a way, a life and vibe that was unique to those decks, those departments. *Pride* was attached to a larger house, so it wasn't completely its own fiefdom. Really, I think only *Fury* falls into that category."

"You know a lot about Dreadstars," Joanna said.

"I like ships. After that first tour, I applied to be a part of the Host'ire's Dreadstar detachment forces. Didn't make the cut. They were not looking to fill the most powerful ships in the Confederation with..."

"Stolen children without houses that were turned into weapons by happenstance of their birth?" Joanna guessed.

"That. Still, all the research and prep paid off, because it got me on the space attack team and all the way to Knight-Commander. So, I guess it was a win," Lucas said.

"At least one of us won," Joanna said quietly.

"I take it that being a librarian for a bunch of snot-nosed rich kids isn't your idea of winning." Lucas said, with just a little sass on the end.

Joanna rolled her eyes at that. He was toying with her, and it was as adorable as it was infuriating.

"I just wanted to quietly do my research and read my books. It's all I've ever wanted to do," Joanna said.

"You did always have your head in a novel or a textbook. Always reading. I guess that is why Tor picked you," Lucas said.

"He didn't pick me; he just knew me. I was always in the library, looking for new things, *forbidden* things." Joanna paused. "The library at the Academy on NovaTerra had all those things, but..." The anger started to build up inside her again, just thinking about how she had been treated over her entire career. "They were slow to let some no house poor Host'ire who only had a Citadel education touch their fancy books; the dangerous ones that spoke of heretical things."

"Like Wayfinders," Lucas said.

"Like Wayfinders, and their prophecy, and the actual history of the war, things like that. It's what I've always been interested in. As a kid, I read stories to take me away from reality, only to learn as an adult that there was a real story just as epic hidden away, buried under layers of bureaucracy and theocratic bullshit," Joanna said.

"And you were going to find it, and tell the whole world about what you had put together?" Lucas asked.

"You are damn right I was going to. It's the least I could do to repay those bastards for taking me in the night," she said. "The world, of course, as always, had different plans for those of us who were born in the wrong place to the wrong parents. Instead of getting to do real work, I helped spoiled noble kids who treated their abilities like just another plaything write papers the night before they were due. It's crushing, and I was never able to not be snippy."

"You? Snippy? I can't even picture such a thing," Lucas said.

Joanna smacked him on the back of the head, and he laughed again. She laughed as well. They needed to laugh; too much tension would break any group apart. Camaraderie, among other things, was what would keep them together. Not the fear of death, or the fear of the fascist organization they all belonged to coming for them. No, those things were all stress points, tension, things that would stretch them until the elastic snapped.

"You need a better imagination," she said, wrapping an arm around him and putting a peck on his cheek before walking ahead of him.

As one of the lights flashed, something on the wall caught her eye. Joanna cocked her head to the side and walked over, brushing off a layer of dust.

"What is it?" Lucas asked, shining the green of his blade over the wall.

"Writing," Joanna said. Scrawled across the wall was both script and math, along with pictures. The images were of a cloud with a multicolored opening in the middle of it, like an eye. The script looked familiar; she had seen it before, somewhere.

"That looks like the Barrier," Lucas said.

Of course. It all clicked instantly in her mind. This was an old Wayfinder code that the Host'ire had never been able to decipher. Or if they had, the key had been buried and declared heretical.

Math. That was why those glyphs had never made heads nor tails to her. It wasn't language. It was math. They were equations. That made sense because the Wayfinders were navigators. Of course their language would be rooted in math more than anything else.

"It is the Eye, the gateway to Hell that the Wayfinders were trying to open," Lucas said.

"If you believe the Host'ire stories. For the Wayfinders, this was their path to Heaven. We were standing in their way, and now we still stand there, guarding a thing we can't find from a long dead group of people."

"I guess," Lucas said. She could feel that theology wasn't something that interested him. He hadn't spent years researching the deep lore.

"You guess? This is the fundamental question that caused the split between two groups that worked together until one annihilated the other," Joanna said.

"Was it? I'm sure it was something more mundane than Heaven and Hell," Lucas said with a wave of his hand.

She wanted to smack him again. The casual discounting of what she knew to be true because it didn't fit with a world view that discounted mystical beliefs even though they were wizards. Discounted because she had said it. *He is just as bad as those snotnosed brats and their rich parents with fancy names.* The anger started to boil up inside of her.

"I am not that bad. I just don't—" Lucas started.

"You don't what? You just don't believe in something that is well documented? You don't believe that this quasi-religious order wouldn't go to war over something as unknowable as the doorway to Hell?" Joanna snapped, turning and pointing a finger at him.

"I guess. I've just never seen evidence for the more arcane mystical stuff that was written down hundreds of years ago," Lucas said.

"You say that like the people during the Wayfinder wars were not the same society that you live in today. Shit, a thousand years ago, during the Age of Chaos, humanity had ships that were more impressive that what we have today. So, it stands to *reason*—"

"That what? There is some mythical eye watching us that leads to Hell inside a storm? I'm sure it is hell inside that storm. It rips every ship that gets near it apart. Just because we have lost tech doesn't make their religion right. I've just come across far too many people who thump their chests about gods and religious laws, only to find out they are normal people. Normal people who are horrible in all the normal people ways," Lucas said.

"Tell that to the Fellowship of the Cross," Joanna said. "Or the people who wrote all this on the walls."

She turned and started to walk away from Lucas, done with this conversation, irritated that he had such a myopic view of the supernatural. Could it be that she just had too wide a view of it? She had spent the better part of her life consumed by the study of these things. No, it was him, just a short-sighted, sexy grunt.

In that moment, she hated herself for a whole host of reasons.

"I..." Lucas started. "Look, I'm sorry to just brush you off like that. You know things that I don't, and..."

She waited for him to finish the sentence. Already she knew what he wanted to say, could feel it, but she needed to hear him say it.

"If you believe in this stuff, then there has to be truth to it—and not just stories that were made up to expunge men of their bad behaviors," Lucas finally admitted.

"Thank you. That was all I wanted to hear," she said, continuing forward.

The two of them walked in silence for a time. Joanna could feel that he was uncomfortable but didn't know what to say. Just as she was about to say something, the single light that was near them started to buzz and flicker. Then, they were plunged into darkness, so much so that even the light from Lucas's blade couldn't cut through it. There was chanting; chanting that was getting closer.

She recognized the words, but before Joanna could say anything, the weak green light of Lucas's blade winked out.

Hoben House, Novagrad, Alexander

"What in the bloody hells were you thinking?" Hoben stormed at Alexander.

"A duel, really? I thought *I* was the impulsive one," Thrase muttered. The whole group was standing around in the common room of Hoben house.

"I wasn't thinking. He put his hands on Claudia and then the fire took over," Alexander said.

He took a sip from the glass of brandy in his hand. His hands were shaking. They had been like that since the moment his glove hit Mister Harrison's smug face. The shocked look had been worth it, but now, now there were going to be consequences for his actions.

"Of course you were not thinking. You are *never* thinking—at least not with the correct head," Hoben said, gesturing wildly with his hands as he paced across the room.

"Is there a way to get out of this?" Jeffery asked.

Alexander had almost forgotten that he was sitting in a chair next to him. Their fourth was always quiet, taking in everything before he said anything. When pushed, he could burn just as hot as the rest of them, but his fire was always metered by logic and pragmatic thoughts.

"Not with our honor intact," Thrase muttered.

"No. *His* honor," Hoben said pointing at Alexander, and then to himself. "Our honor doesn't demand that we help him."

"Kinship of the team," Thrase pointed out.

She stood up and walked over to the bar, pouring herself another glass of brandy. It was an expensive bottle; expensive enough that, even though it wasn't made by her family, Thrase was willing to drink it.

"Damn it to hell," Hoben muttered.

Alexander looked up at him. This was a rule he wasn't familiar with. For all the nobility that came with the Cordova name, they were still just Space Lords, and the pageantry and rules around society were not the same as those followed by the planet lords.

"I take it that I have also put your honor on the line, as well?" Alexander asked.

"Yes. As long as we are members of the same team, then we are bound as kin. Once a challenge has been issued, there is no changing of the team." Hoben paused for a moment. "So, I couldn't cut you lose for doing a damned stupid thing like you did. We are all in this now."

He sat down, rubbing his temples. Alexander was both sad that he had dragged his friends into this, and relieved that they were there for him, even if it was only because honor had dragged them in. Comfortable, plump planet lords were never as quick to violence and fights as their space born counterparts.

"Have you ever fought in a duel before, Alexander?" Thrase asked.

"I've been in my fair share of scraps," he responded.

"I will take that as a no, then. A duel by the old laws of lordship is not the same as some disagreement on the flight deck of a Dreadstar that is solved with rolled sleeves and fisticuffs. There are rules that one must follow," Thrase said.

"Rules that must be followed *to the letter*. Otherwise, the legality of the duel is called into question and charges of assault and murder can be brought against one or both of the parties involved," Hoben said, standing up.

"And here I thought this was just the fancier version of a brawl," Alexander said, his tone light, trying to bring a bit of levity to the room.

"It is, but as with everything involving the noble houses, under the pageantry, there is a deadly seriousness. We do not take things like this lightly, Alexander," Hoben said. "Did you agree on weapons?"

"No, I assumed that we would—" Alexander started.

Hoben held up his hand to stop him from talking anymore.

"Henceforth, I don't want you to assume anything, and don't say anything unless I ask you a direct question. If we are going to get through this, you will need a second—which, as the leader of the team, I will take on."

"I know a good doctor that can show up at short notice. He owes our family a few favors still," Thrase said.

"Good. Call him," Hoben said in a snippy, curt voice.

Thrase finished her drink and left the room, pulling out her pocket watch and moving her fingers across the screen.

"As the challenger, you get to pick weapons. Come with me," Hoben said, standing up and walking into a dark room that was off the sitting room.

As they entered the room, the low lights automatically came to life. It was a study, dominated by a large wooden desk covered with papers. All along the walls were shelves filled with books. Alexander could feel the age and stately importance of this room. It was the kind of place that a lord who owned and controlled actual land would work from.

Hoben walked over to the shelf and pressed his hand against what looked like books. As his palm made contact, for the briefest of moments, the holofield moved and Alexander could see the palm reader. It clicked and then the entire bookshelf vanished, replaced by a wall of weapons. There were swords and hunting rifles, pistols, daggers, even a grenade. Hoben reached down and pulled out a fancy wooden box. Walking over to the desk, he set it down with a satisfying and resounding *thump*. Waving a finger toward the weapon shelf, the holofield came back online and the weapons vanished as the books returned.

"What is that?" Alexander asked.

"These," Hoben said, clicking two latches and reverently opening the box, "are the Hoben family dueling pistols. The Cordova's don't have a pair?"

"We have a family sword. Oh and of course, a thousand-year-old warship filled with lost technology so deadly that the last five in existence are still more powerful than most fleets," Alexander snipped back.

"Fair enough," Hoben said, reaching into the box and removing one of the pistols.

It was made of wood, with gold and silver filigree across the length of the long pistol. On the side above the trigger was a fancy lock mechanism. Alexander recognized the type of weapon almost instantly. He, for the first time, heeded the command of his friend and was quiet, not taking away the small joy that Alen Hoben was going to get from telling him about these weapons.

"This is *Call*, and her mate in the box is *Response*. These pistols have been in the family since just before the Age of Chaos. So, not quite as old as your ship, but close. The first pattern of plasma pistols, where you had to load each round individually and work the complex lock on the side of the weapon. Horrible in battle against rapid fire kinetic weapons, but perfect for the noble practice of the duel. Also, in most cases, these are extremely lethal," Hoben said, running his hand along the barrel of the gun before handing it to Alexander.

Alexander took the weapon, feeling the weight of it in his hand, how his finger felt on and around the trigger. He held it out in front of him, his hand and arm not trembling for a moment. He could feel the weapon as an extension, all the years of training he and his sister had gotten aboard *Fury* rushing back to him. Once drilled into your brain by the Master-at-Arms of a Dreadstar, combat was like riding a bike.

"The weight is good," Alexander said, spinning the pistol in his hand and then handing it back to Hoben butt first.

"Fancy," his friend muttered.

"I know I don't always look it, but I *do* know my way around guns and swords. What happens if we both fail to hit, or both parties are still alive, but wounded?" Alexander asked.

The fire inside of him was hot enough to want to kill Mister Harrison, but the logic in his brain was starting to take over again. Alexander Cordova had never killed a man before and wasn't sure if he had it in him to do so, even if the skills were there.

"If both sides have fired and missed, then honor is satisfied, and you leave the field. If one side is wounded and the other is not, honor has again been satisfied, and the unwounded party is victorious," Hoben said, putting *Call* back into the case. "There are no second rounds. I know, in some of the Space Lord communities, these fights are to the death and once the pistols have been fired, the swords come out. We do not do that here."

"Good. I left my favorite sword back at the facility," Alexander said. There was a pause and then both men chuckled.

"Alexander, you are a bloody fucking idiot, but..." Hoben walked over and placed his hand on Alexander's shoulder. "You are my friend and a man of honor. I don't know this Mister Harrison, but any man that is abusive to women is not a man at all. His lack of honor will see you to victory."

"Thank you, Alen. That means a lot," Alexander said, putting his hand atop his friend's.

"Don't get too sentimental or I might just change my mind. Go and try to get some sleep. We will have to set out again in a few hours if we want to reach the dueling green outside the city."

With that, Hoben removed his hand, picked up the box with *Call* and *Response*, and exited the room. Alexander was left in the office with his thoughts, which, at the moment, was not where he wanted to be. He would have preferred to be anywhere but in his own mind. This was quite the predicament that he had gotten himself into. What was he thinking, getting involved in the personal matters of a woman that he had only known for a few days? And now here he was, about to kill somebody for her, or be killed himself.

Alexander didn't bother to put on night clothes. He just changed from ball attire to standard promenading wear: brown paints, boots, and a white shirt with a black vest and cravat. Hanging over the chair was his long brown coat. It was a simple outfit, very unlike him, but appropriate for the day ahead.

Sleep did not find him; all Alexander could hear as he looked up at the ceiling of the room was Erik telling him he was a fool and Hanna reminding him how to hold his feet and aim the pistol so that his shot would be true.

As he worked to find sleep, his watch started to buzz. Looking down, Alexander saw that it was a message from Claudia asking him to come outside. Standing up, he walked over to the window and looked outside. There she was standing on the street, her head covered in the hood of her riding cloak. Alexander waved, then stepped away from the window. He needed to stay calm, to sleep, but he also knew there was no way he could say no to talking with her, to truly understand just what he had gotten himself into tonight. Alexander grabbed his coat and quietly made his way out of the house.

"I was afraid that you wouldn't come down and see me," Claudia said, looking crestfallenly at the cobblestones of the street, keeping her face in shadow.

"I would hope that by now—even though the time that we have known each other has been short—that you would know I would never reject your invitations," Alexander said.

He wanted to reach out and hold her hand, to reassure her. Already in the tone of her voice, he could tell that she had been crying. Wherever she had gone, whatever she had been doing the last few hours, was probably worse than the lashing he had gotten from his friends.

"I know, that is why I came," she said, looking up at him. "I wanted to implore you to give up this fight, to come away with me. We do not have to spill blood," Claudia whispered.

"The challenge has been made. Without our honor, where could we go?" Alexander asked. It was a preposterous idea. Running away? No, he couldn't do that; wouldn't allow himself to do that.

"We can go anywhere that is not here. I've some money set aside. You are a smart man. We can go to the Unaligned Planets, away from Confederation law," Claudia said.

It was as if she had been hatching a plan in her mind, a plan that she had rehearsed and thought about for years. If Alexander had been anybody else, had any other last name, he might have given in.

"No, I cannot run," Alexander said.

Claudia sniffled away a tear the illumination from the streetlights catching her green eyes, causing them to glow and bring out the pooled tears that were in the wells of her eyelids. Alexander couldn't keep his hands to himself any longer.

Reaching out, he slid down her riding hood and was aghast at the condition of her face. Claudia's once fair and unblemished skin was covered with bruises and welts. Purples, greens, and even yellow discoloration crossed her face. Her lip was fat, and Alexander was worried the welt on the top of her forehead would require medical attention. While the look on his face was aghast, she just gave him a weak smile, but there was still blood on her teeth.

"What has happened to you? Who did this?" Alexander demanded, the heat rising in his voice once more.

"Mister Harrison and his body men found me as I was attempting to get back to my lodgings. They said this was a message to you, to drop the duel in the morning; that this was your only chance to avoid dishonor," Claudia said, sniffling, her jaw quivering, biting back the desire to cry again.

"He shall pay dearly for this. I was not going to kill him, but I declare here and now that he shall die in the morning upon the green. As Hoben said, this is not just fisticuffs upon the flight deck. He has assaulted your body and your honor, both of which I cannot allow to stand," Alexander declared, puffing himself up, straightening his back and trying to channel the leadership and poise of his mother. Any worry or fear that he had about dying in the morning faded away, replaced with hot anger and love for this woman who was standing before him.

"He has not assaulted my honor, sir. For you see, my family owes his a great debt. I was to..." Claudia sniffled again, turning away from Alexander's gaze putting her face back into shadow.

Alexander sighed. He did not care what problems House Wise was having or what House Harrison thought they were owed. This was no way to treat a well-born lady. Reaching out again, Alexander lightly placed his hand on her chin and turned her head toward him, so he could look into her eyes again.

"I care not what slight your family might have caused against his. These actions are out of line with honor and decency. I shall not let them stand. House *Cordova* shall not let them stand. I challenge any man born into a family I have never heard of to stand against us." It was rare that Alexander leveraged the family name, especially their military power. No, he had always been content to just skate along in life with his title and money.

"Thank you, my lord," Claudia said.

She reached out and took his other hand, gently kissing it. Alexander had forgotten to put his gloves on and could feel her lips on his bare skin; the warmth, the intimacy, the scandal. He took a deep, righteous breath.

"Do you have somewhere to stay tonight? I fear that staying here would cause more scandal then we are already engaged in," Alexander said.

He desperately wanted her to stay with him, so that he could tend to her wounds, so that he could draw strength and resolve from her. But he knew that Hoben would not have it, and since it was his estate that they were standing in front of, he could not push his friend further.

"I have made arrangements for a room on the edge of town," she said quietly.

"Then take this as a small token of my love, before we end this in the morning," Alexander said, reaching into his pocket and pulling out a small golden chimera and slipping it into her hand.

"Go, my love. I shall see you tomorrow and exact justice and vengeance for what has been done to you."

As he declared this oath, Alexander slipped her riding hood back over her head. He then gave her a quick bow and headed back into the house before anybody saw anything.

Darkness, Below the Citadel, Lucas

The world was dark. Lucas's eyes were open, but the world was still dark.

He reached out with the Null to see what he could feel around him. There was life, but he couldn't feel anything more. The senses were dull. His arms hurt. Reaching down, he tried to move them, but they wouldn't go anywhere, locked behind his back. Bonds? He was tied up.

Well, that explains why the world is dark, he thought. This was not the first time that Lucas had been tied up and blindfolded. Though it was far less exciting than the last time. There had been gas, they were on a Dreadstar; that was the last thing he remembered. So, at least that seemed to still be working.

Closing his eyes, he reached out again with the Null to see if he could feel Joanna. The last thing he wanted to do was start talking. Best not to give anything away at this stage of the game.

Joanna, are you there?

I don't know. I'm glad to hear another voice. It was Naomi. That must mean that whoever was down here had gotten them all.

Just you? Lucas thought.

I was with Rostov.

As the words were coming into his head, Lucas was able to feel movement from Joanna and Rostov. His world was then met with massive brightness. His eyes rapidly blinked, trying to bring everything into focus after having been in darkness. The Null here was different; stronger, purer. He could see it in a way that normally required meditation.

He was on the ground, leaning against the back side of a control panel. His legs and arms were indeed bound. Next to him was Naomi, then Rostov. Joanna was on the other side. The floor they had been put in was at the bottom of… it looked like an amphitheater—no, it was the Combat Information Center of a Dreadstar. He was looking up at the four levels of system stations that surrounded the central glass map table. Lucas had been in this room once, when he had drawn attendant duty aboard *Pride.* Knight-Commander Tai always insisted upon being in the CIC in the morning.

Spread out, but all around them, were tall, thin people in brown robes, with pale gray skin. Tragadi. Everybody here was Tragadi. He had never seen so many of them in one place. There were stories of whole plantes of non-humans in the Unaligned Planets, but inside the Confederation, you never saw more than one or two in any single place. Here, though, there were—his eyes darted around the room, using his tactical training—fifteen of them.

In that glance around the room, his eyes rolled over his friends. Their emotions were still waking up, all of them clouded by confusion. There was no fear in them. At first glance, none of them looked beaten or roughed up, which was a good sign.

From above, Lucas could hear a door opening. He wasn't able to twist himself around to see who was coming down. All the Tragadi in the room turned to look at whoever had just entered.

Anybody have eyes on the new arrival? Lucas thought, seeing if maybe Rostov or Joanna on the edges could get a better look at who was coming down the steps. This Tragadi had to be the leader of this group of monks. Were they monks? They looked like monks.

"I am so sorry for treating you like this. We do not get many visitors down here," a familiar voice said.

Tor!

It was Joanna in his head. That was why the voice was familiar, because Lucas couldn't remember the last time he had even seen the old librarian. A few more steps and he could see Tor, dressed no longer like a member of the Host'ire, but in the same brown robes of these monks. Yes, he felt comfortable calling them monks.

"As comforting as that assurance is..." Lucas said, motioning with his body toward the bindings that were around his wrists and ankles. Tor made a motion with his hands and two of the closer, younger looking Tragadi, rushed forward, producing small knives from their sleeves. They made quick work of the ropes before stepping back.

"Thank you," Lucas said, standing up. He brushed the dust of the floor from his jacket and looked around. Another of the younger acolytes rushed forward and handed him his sunglasses. Lucas put them on, bringing the light of the world down to a manageable level. The Null here still felt off—too ordered, too pure—but he was glad to not have to constantly look at it.

"Tor, you didn't need to abduct us. We would have come without issue," Joanna said, disappointment in her voice.

"I am aware, Joanna. It is hard to get messages down here, especially with the violence that is going on above. My followers reacted. Thankfully, I have instructed them never to kill unless it is absolutely necessary," Tor said, walking to the bottom of the stairs and holding his arms out and bowing his head. The robe was voluminous, with the sleeves having enough space to hide anything inside of them.

"I'm glad we rated so highly on the threat meter," Rostov muttered, rubbing his wrists.

"The fact that they didn't engage shows that they were aware of the threat you posed," Tor said, placing both of his hands on the table.

Lucas walked up and followed suit, looking into the tall man's eyes. He was done being led around by librarians, books, prophecies, and his own fractured memory. It was time to get some answers. It was coming to the point where Lucas didn't care *how* he got the answers, as long as they were given to him in a manner that satisfied his desire to understand the last few days.

"You wanted us down here, Tor. Now it's time to tell us what is going on. Where is she?" Lucas said.

Perhaps, if they were able to find Hyacinth, she would finally stay in their mind, and they would be able to remember more about who she was beyond just a phantom.

"To tell you that, first, everybody must drink of the water," he said. Another acolyte walked up with a tray and four glasses filled with a purple liquid. "The water of memory is something that every member of the Guardians of the Seer must drink before they can be inducted. What I gave to Joanna was a half strength dose, just enough to unlock her memories above. Down here, we are too close to the field. The dose must be stronger," Tor said, motioning to the glasses on the tray. "Drink and we shall talk more."

It didn't look like there was much of a choice. Lucas picked up the shot glass, bringing the liquid to his nose. It smelled foul, like bile. Joanna drank hers again, followed by Naomi. Rostov looked at Lucas. He was looking for the same approval he was trying to give himself. Lucas nodded and then shot the liquid, throwing his head back as he drank it. The flavor was far worse than the smell, and he had to fight to keep it down. Thankfully, it didn't leave an aftertaste.

Instantly, Lucas started to feel different. Things that were locked away started to come to the forefront. Now, when his mind tried to remember Hyacinth, he could. He saw her face, soft and gentle. There was so much compassion and love in her big blue eyes. They sparkled no matter what room she was in. He felt the same love for her that he did for his friends next to him. It was a powerful emotion.

That is why we came. We all were feeling that love, even if we didn't understand it.

"What was that?" Lucas said, first with awe, then turning to an accusatory stance. "What did you do to our memories?!"

"One is not able to remember a Wayfinder once they have been connected to the network, to the Null. It is a defense mechanism. Those who are her defenders must cleanse themselves in the waters of memory so that they may continue to perceive the Wayfinder," Tor said, holding his hands up to the sky like some kind of deranged preacher.

"Hyacinth was a Wayfinder? I thought they were all dead," Naomi said with awe in her voice.

"Lady Hyacinth *is* a Wayfinder. Or, at least, she is forty-eight percent Wayfinder. One of the strongest we have encountered in six generations," Tor said. "It is our job as the Guardians of the Seer to protect the Wayfinder and see to their every need."

"How do we factor in to this, then? She called for us, everybody keeps talking about the blood pact. She wants us to do something, but hasn't told us *what*. I just wish she would tell us and not send nightmares and cryptic messages in the mail," Rostov said.

"Every Wayfinder who is a Seer—and while she might not be a genetically *pure* Wayfinder, Hyacinth *is* a Seer. They all attract to them a group of defenders, five fated souls. Once they have entered the Dreaming, the Seer is defenseless. It becomes up to the blood pact to keep watch over them," Tor said.

"So why blank our memories? Why send us out into the world where we couldn't help her?" Naomi asked.

"We would never have left," Joanna added.

"Since the fall of the Empire, we have always defended the Seer who was placed here, before and after The Host'ire came. Five members are drawn from our number and imprint upon the Wayfinder. This time—"

Lucas cut him off. "Jasper."

"Yes. The bully and the Host'ire's inability to take care of their children. She imprinted upon the five of you, her best friends and defenders. As the dreams got worse and the call to return here grew, we knew she had to be taken sooner rather than later," Tor said.

"If you had just given us the option—" Rostov snapped.

"We would never have left her side," Lucas said, finishing Rostov's thought.

He could feel anger and disappointment coming from the rest of the group. Just another choice in their lives that they had not been allowed to make. A choice of great importance that was stripped from them and made by adults who didn't have their best interest at heart.

"We could not take that risk. One missing child from the Citadel falls under their radar. But six? And after you had murdered another novice? That was not a risk we could take. The previous Seer was close to burning out and Hyacinth was the most powerful we had seen. Getting her down here was an imperative," Tor said.

"How can she be a Wayfinder? The Host'ire killed them all. I've seen the records. There were camps and systemic eradications. Even the most hardcore members of the order attempted to hide the level of organization, the slaughter, required to wipe them out," Joanna said.

"The Host'ire were fooled, mislead by two small groups. One in the Unaligned Planets—who we have lost contact with—and a ship of orphans. Those children were spread throughout the Confederation and then their handlers committed suicide so that they would be safe. All children with Wayfinder blood are sensitive to the Null and end up in a Host'ire academy. It is the job of our agents to keep an eye out for them; for those who can do the job all Wayfinders were bred for," Tor said.

Lucas didn't like the sound of that. *Bred* for? They were people, not tools. Though his own order viewed him not as a person, but a tool, so it made sense that these monks also viewed the Wayfinders more as tools than anything else. It didn't matter if you were mundane or not, any poor nameless Null-sensitive was just a tool. He could feel the distaste at this phrase from his friends as well.

"So, you are using them, but for what?" Lucas asked, hoping that the indignation in his voice would come through.

"Without the Wayfinders, the whole of your gate network would fall apart. The powers that be in the Confederation claim that the gates are being powered by beacons inside the Null, but it is, in fact, a few Wayfinders who still live that control the network. They are the key to all travel, which is why our order was manipulated to kill them all," Tor said.

He waved his hands open as he talked, asking them to come closer and to trust in the story that he was telling them, the magnitude of it all. Lucas wasn't sure how much of this he believed, but Tor believed all of it, so he was willing to take it on faith.

"Back up, I just want to clear up something," Naomi said, gesturing with her hands as she spoke. "The ship that I came here on was guided by Hyacinth, the same woman who I hung out with as a kid. We..."

Lucas could feel the memory coming into her mind, unlocked by the waters, finally free from the prison of time and mentality.

"We used to do each other's hair, back when I had hair," she said, running a hand over her shaved scalp. "And now she is running the whole gate system for the Confederation?"

"She is the brain of the system, yes. But there are still computers, both in the gates and on your ships, that are involved. But, without her, large sections of space would not be reachable. Unless we were to crack the secret of faster-than-light engines on ships again," Tor said.

"There are rumors that Confederation scientists are working on that right now. I was on the dark web talking to some friends about Peculiar Pentagon and they had heard something. Apparently, both us and a faction in the Unaligned Plantes are getting close to some kind of work around for gate travel. I would guess for larger ships like Dreadstars and carriers," Naomi said, running her eyes from person to person, looking to see if they understood just how big of a deal that was. Lucas nodded his head, so did Joanna. Rostov just shrugged his shoulders.

"They are close. They have to be. There is too much activity from the Barrier. The Shadows are moving again," Tor said.

"From the land beyond the barrier, the Shadows came," Joanna said softly.

"To there, they return. Chased by heroes," Lucas muttered.

"Led by stragglers," Rostov said, picking up the sentence.

"And the last of the Wayfinders," Naomi said, finishing the prophecy.

Lucas vaguely remembered that old Wayfinder saying. It had been in some book he read back in school. No… That wasn't it at all. It had been in a book *Joanna* read, one that she wasn't supposed to. A text like that would have been considered extremely heretical by the Host'ire, yet here they were, remembering it. *All* of them. They knew it in their bones, deep down.

What did it mean?

"Yes, very good." Tor said.

"Who are the Shadows?" Joanna asked. "I've read so many forgotten and forbidden texts and they are referred to every so often. But I always just assumed that they were a metaphor for whoever the Host'ire or Wayfinders were fighting at that moment."

"The Shadows are something old, like a force of nature. We know shockingly little about them, only that they are figments of imagination, and do not seem to have any kind of physical form except in records from around and before the Age of Chaos," Tor said.

"There are precious few of those left," Joanna said. "The original nuking of Novagrad set us back as a species for hundreds upon hundreds of years."

"Thousands, more than likely," Tor agreed. "There were things men knew how to do that are lost in ways that we don't even understand what we have lost. The ability to use the Null to jump our ships is only a small fraction. But it is what is needed to get into the Eye."

"Hell is beyond the Eye—or so they say," Rostov pipped in.

"Does that mean then that the Host'ire have been protecting us from the Shadows by keeping the Eye closed?" Lucas asked.

"The Shadows move all the players upon the board to their desired locations. Whatever they are planning, with their Fellowship pawns, I cannot see yet. All I know is that Hyacinth saw it; saw *something*. That is why she brought you here. To protect her!" Tor said, placing his hands firmly down on the table and looking at them with hard eyes. Lucas knew then that storytime was over.

Just as his hands hit the table, the ship around them started to shake and shudder. The lights, already rickety, flickered, the fluorescent tubes screaming at the unstable power running through them. There was running and commotion from the Guardians around them. Tor looked up as a young acolyte ran into the room.

"The Fellowship. They are here. They found a way down!" she yelled. From the hallway, Lucas could hear an all too familiar sound. Fighting.

"Where are our weapons?" Lucas asked, looking Tor in the eye.

The old librarian pointed to a small box on the top of one of the consoles. Lucas walked over and grabbed his blade. He then rolled his head in a circle, cracking his neck.

"Tor, you have my word that we shall protect Hyacinth. She called for us and we are here. There is nothing in this world that will get to her as long as the four of us still draw breath."

Grace's Apartment, Olympus Areas Research Facility, Grace

The loud thump at the door woke Grace up. She had nodded off while pouring over all the information. In front of her were pages and pages of formulas and equations. She blinked away from the sleep as the banging got louder.

"Open up!" the metallic rebreather voice yelled from outside. They had found her. Research time was over.

Emily had planned for this and knew what needed to be done. Scooping up all the papers, she opened a small compartment in her desk and shoved them in. Hitting a button, there was a hiss. The press had returned all the papers back into pulp to be used somewhere else in the facility. For once, the extreme secrecy of Olympus Ares acted in her favor. Everything was saved within her brain, so if they wanted to know what she knew, they were going to have to infest her and drag it out.

You know they will, Emily. That is the plan, the Varagoth's voice said in her head.

She spun around. He wasn't here, but the neon-blue glow of his eyes was seeping into the room, permeating from the edge of every light fixture. He wasn't here physically, but she knew that he was *here.*

The banging on the door got louder, and she could hear them working on the wall panel; the cords she'd ripped were only going to hold them at bay for so long. It was time to go.

Quickly, she crossed the distance of the dorm room to where her suit was and started to pull it on. On a normal day, she would take her time, check every system, dread being locked away inside a tin can for the next eight hours. Right now, she couldn't wait to be back within the safety of the shell. This suit had saved her, and she was sure it would be far from the last time it would do so.

That is not going to be enough. You will be joining your new family soon. Resistance is pointless, Emily, the Varagoth said, his voice soft, smooth, like a used starship salesman.

She wasn't going to listen to it, wasn't going to respond to it. He was not here. She wasn't going to give him any power over her by engaging. That is what men like him always wanted. For you to engage with their bullshit. Varagoth just chuckled. He knew what she was thinking. There was no way to *not* respond to him.

Half her suit was on when the door started to slide open. *Well, that isn't ideal,* Emily thought.

She grabbed the plasma rifle that was next to her suit and clutched it in her shoulder, the one shoulder that had armor. She had never used the rifle without it and wasn't about to start to learn how right now. The door opened and her furniture started to get pushed aside. Grace squeezed the trigger and kept it depressed. Hot plasma flew from the weapon, and she struggled to hold on. The rounds smashed through her furniture, setting it on fire and tearing through flesh and bone on the other side. It punched holes in the steel of the bulkheads. After fifteen seconds, the rifle red in her hands stopped, and there was only the echo of violence.

Grace dropped the plasma rifle and went back to quickly trying to get her armor on. The barrel was glowing red, and the temperature gauge on the side was flashing 200% at her. The weapon was toast. Even she, with her very basic weapons training, knew they were not designed to be used like that. If she had been using the aim assist, the suit wouldn't have even allowed her to fire the weapon until it was slag. But then, she would have also been in full armor and wouldn't have needed to just splash plasma everywhere.

Groans were coming from the door. Not everyone was dead. *They are dead enough, keep moving, Grace,* Emily yelled from her mind.

A minor setback. More will come. You will join us, Emily. Vengeance shall be ours. The time has come, the Varagoth said, his voice less controlled than before, the neon-blue in the lighting of the room fading back just a bit.

He was losing power over her. *Interesting.* She tried not to think about it too much. She needed to focus and not get distracted going down a rabbit hole of ideas. There would be plenty of time to deal with this Varagoth later.

Deal with me? You cannot banish this away like it is a bad dream, Emily Itchi. You know that this is your destiny.

"Destiny is for people who have given up control," Grace said, putting on her helmet and cycling the suit's power on.

Running to the door, she pushed through the breach of death and melted metal. One of the guards tried to weakly grab her ankle. She kicked his hand aside, stopping only to reach down and pick up his plasma rifle before she kept moving. From down the hallway, she could hear more security coming, more infested. The neon-blue in the lights was brighter down at the end of the hallway, where the Varagoth had more control, where the infested were. They might eventually get her, but it was going to cost them.

On the ground, there was a guard who had a bandolier of grenades. She pulled it off his body and quickly started to string them up along the hallway, clicking on the motion sensers. She placed them each in a line, seven feet apart, so that each wouldn't set off the one next to it and create a cascade effect before she could get out of the line of fire. Each grenade went on a different part of the wall, as well, in the hopes that they would get complacent, looking on the ground for where the next blast would come from. It was a crude trap, and one that might be undone, depending on how much communication the big nasty in her head had with the actual flesh and blood infested that were running throughout the base. This was as good a way as any to find out.

The sounds of footsteps were getting louder as she placed the last charge. Turning the other way, Grace started to run. At the end of the hallway, there was a laundry chute that would take her all the way down to the ground level if she wanted. Once there, Grace hoped that she could get in contact with Essex and see if he had learned anything from being a good little soldier and talking to the boss.

His answer would determine whether she'd be leaving this station with or without him.

CIC, Fury, Cassandra

The atmosphere in Lord Admiral Cordova's tearoom sitting just off the CIC was tense. As soon as the last of the crimson arrowhead ships had been destroyed and *Fury* had recovered the rest of Erik's squadron, they had gone to flank speed toward the nearest jump gate. It was going to take them three days. Three days that they did not have.

Atomics. Novagrad. Not fit for conscription.

The words echoed in Cassandra's head as she sat at her desk, flipping through the massive holographic projection of all the raw data that Erik had brought back from Barker's World. Data that Hanna had sacrificed for—how much, Cassandra didn't know and didn't want to think about. It would be a high price; of that, she was sure. Sitting around the room were her main advisers, Captain Rackland, Erik, and Bella. At this point, she didn't want to bring any more people in.

"Who is behind this? How long have they been…?" Captain Rackland asked, finally breaking the silence.

"At least a year, probably longer," Erik said, reaching up into the holographic display and pulling out the section about the trap that was the battle of Hyroncore.

Cassandra closed her eyes. She didn't want to be reminded of that battle, of how she had failed them, of how she had failed him.

It was my time. The ship is safe, that is what matters, she could hear Tiberias say. He always placed the ship and crew first. Only cared about them, about her.

"'Not suitable for conscription.' Sounds like a compliment. Once we find these bastards, we are going to show them the truth in that phrase," Bella said, pushing her fist into her open palm, cracking the joints in her fingers.

Cassandra could see her niece's nose twitching with anger. She had been the only one that went from shock to anger instantly after reading the documents. The rest of them were contemplating the greater stakes, the political ramifications. All Bella had seen was raving from people who had tried—and were currently actively trying—to kill them. That was all she needed as justification to bring hell down upon them. Cassandra didn't disagree, but she wanted to make sure that the wrath was pointed in the right direction before sending her and a blizzard of pissed off fighter pilots into battle.

"We will, Bella, we will. First, though, we need to know who we are facing. Does 'the Chosen' mean anything?" Erik asked.

"No. I had the computer run a search for it, but nothing useful came back," Captain Rackland said. "From the way it is used, they sound like a cult or some culture that we have never encountered before. I'm leaning toward something new, because…"

"Because they have at will faster-than-light travel," Cassandra said, finishing his sentence. There was no use beating around the bush. "Whoever is involved in this plan from inside the Confederation wants power and thinks they have found somebody who will give it to them. But any ally that would allow the rampant use of atomic weapons doesn't care about the end of the war. I suspect we are going to learn that the ability to jump is the least impressive thing in their arsenal."

"The small ships themselves were not that impressive. Fast, sure, but it didn't take much from our guns to knock them out of the sky," Rackland said.

"True, but you can't compare a Dreadstar to any other ship of the line. We, like them, are damn near unique. That is why they want to destroy or sway the remaining Dreadstars," Erik said. "See here." He pulled out another section of text, shoving the paragraphs of Hyroncore back into the folder. "The names are redacted, but two Dreadstars are already under their sway."

"Finding out the names of those two ships will be imperative. Thankfully, there are only four options. Erik, I want you to scour these files and see if you can't gleam an idea of who we can and cannot trust," Cassandra said, standing up. "Captain, you and I will take turns in CIC as we hard sail. The ship will stay beat to quarters until further notice. Bella, you and the entire flight wing, remain on stand-by to launch, if we must fight."

Just as she was about to break them, the ship lurched.

"Lord Admiral to CIC," a voice said through the comm system.

Cassandra grabbed her coat and made the short walk to the Combat Information Center, the rest of her command staff falling in behind her. The ship rocked again as they entered the vaulted command deck. Captain Rackland took his position in the middle deck next to weapons, while Cassandra and Erik went to the glass table. In the short walk, Bella had broken off, heading back to the flight deck. Cassandra knew that she tried her best to avoid the CIC when at all possible.

"What is the situation, if you please, Lieutenant?" Cassandra yelled toward the middle aged second lieutenant who had been the master of the watch while they were meeting.

"Lord Admiral, five of the arrowhead ships jumped into the system in our path and started to attack us. At the same time, we detected a large fleet coming just into our sensor range. They are following at full sail, as well."

"When it rains, it pours," Cassandra muttered, looking at the board.

The five arrowhead ships were punched up. They were heading away from *Fury*, she assumed, to set up for another attack run. Already, the read out was showing that they were reverse burning to cut down their inertia before making their turn. The other fleet was on the board as well. Ten ships strong. That was all the data they had on them so far. That problem could wait. It would take them at least a day and a half to close the gap—that is, if they could even match the speed of a Dreadstar, which she suspected they could not.

"We do not have time for this. Captain Rackland, prepare two spreads of guided missiles, if you please. Let us greet our new friends with fire when they turn around," the Lord Admiral said.

Rackland nodded and started barking orders at the crew around him. Cassandra looked at the glass table, which was updating in real time. The five arrowheads were just starting to make their turns. She could picture them firing thrusters at the front of the ship and flipping up and around—or perhaps they spun on a flat axis. There was so much that they didn't know about their foe; so much that they did not have the time or luxury to learn.

There was a paper she had read during an expanded training session when she was in War College. It talked about first contact with a new hostile force, and how to probe for their weakness before removing the threat. *Play with them like a cat,* the text had said. Cassandra desperately wanted to bat these little ships around like a ball full of catnip, to gleam any information about the people who wanted to burn their home world. To prevent that burning, though, she was going to have to run, to just swat them away like flies over a picnic.

They started their turn.

"Missiles are ready, Lord Admiral!" Rackland called down from fire control. Cassandra looked down at the board before looking over at Erik, who was doing calculations and moving flight controls so that he could stay here in the CIC. The predetermined musical track that had started playing when the ship was first attacked by this flight of arrow heads reached a natural crescendo.

"Let fly, Captain," Cassandra ordered calmly. Captain Rackland gave the orders.

On the screens above the glass table, a live feed from the lead missile popped up the moment it left the tube. Darkness and stars streaked past as the missile screamed at near light speed through the cosmos. Distance data was clicking down on the side. Only in the last moment of the weapon's life did the small crimson arrowhead ship pop up on the screen and then the feed cut out.

Cassandra looked down at the table. The arrowhead ships and her missiles were all displayed. One by one, each of her weapons blinked out of existence, almost all of them well before reaching their targets. One made it through, making contact. The weapon vanished; the arrowhead ship remained.

"Missile barrage ineffective. Targets still remain," Captain Rackland called down from the weapons deck.

She could see that. Cassandra had to stifle her frustration. Still, the fly had taught them something—their point defiance systems were extremely accurate. They had succeeded with guns before, and if these small bastards wanted to get into a shooting match with the Dreadstar *Fury*, then she was going to show them the error of that idea.

"Helm, on my mark, reduce speed by fifty percent, as quickly as possible, if you please," Lord Admiral Cordova called across the CIC. "Captain Rackland, have the gun crews ready. As soon as they overshoot us, if you could clear the sky once more, please."

Both the captain and the boatswain at the helm responded in affirmatives. She looked down at the glass top table and grabbed both sides to steady herself. Cassandra reached over and hit a switch that changed the music queue in the ship from a generic battle score to "Brace for Contact". It was a short queue, and everybody aboard ship knew what it was instructing them to do.

"Cut speed now," the boatswain's voice called out.

There was groaning as the metal of the ship fought against speed and physics, the engines of the great Dreadstar pushing to undo their previous course. Cassandra held the glass table, rocking with the motion of the ship, holding her footing. Looking down, two of the arrowheads overshot them like she had planned, the other three—including the one hit by their missile—slowed down almost instantly.

So, we are both cats, Cassandra thought.

"Fire!" Captain Rackland's clear baritone voice broke the silence of her thoughts. The ship rocked as the massive rail guns upon her spine and belly fired. The two arrowhead ships that had overshot them winked out of existence on the board. They need to slow them down if there was going to be a chance of destroying them in a fight. Good to know.

"Captain, roll out the smaller guns and inform the crews that they may fire at will," Cassandra called across the CIC.

"With pleasure," he replied.

Now, they would bring the full power of *Fury* to bare. The Dreadstar was armed with more than the ten massive spine and belly rail cannons. Across the *Fury* were close to seven hundred smaller weapon emplacements, ranging from point lasers to midsized plasma cannons. All weapons that would form the main armament of a smaller ship.

Before they could open fire again, it was the arrowhead ship's turn. Cassandra pulled up an outside live feed. The three remaining ships held their ground, firing their main weapon, a large beam of concentrated energy. The scanner reading on the side of the display was going wild. *Fury* was rocked from the impact. These ships were small, but packed far more firepower than she was comfortable with.

To her relief, their turn ended quickly. The Dreadstar responded by living up to its name. The live feed was filled with light as a hundred guns fired at once. Two of the arrowhead ships vaporized in an instant. The last one fired off its thrusters and flipped head over heel.

So that is how they turn, Cassandra mused. Once it turned, the arrowhead started to flee. A moment later, there was a flash of light, and it was gone, yanked from the field of battle by its own faster-than-light conveyance and not the *Fury's* firepower.

"Captain, sitrep please!" Cassandra called across the ship.

"Damage across the board, Lord Admiral. Those little bastards pack a punch. Engineering is reporting damage in mass thrust seven. They will need to take it offline to fix it," Rackland called back from his station. Cassandra turned to Erik, who had a pencil and was doing math on the glass table.

"If we take mass thrust seven offline, but push the other nine thrusters, we will only lose ten hours," he said. Ten hours could be the difference between life and death for everybody on NovaTerra. It could be the difference between life and death for them, as well.

"What is the catch, Commander?" Cassandra asked.

"It will tax our power reserves and might cause a cascade reaction across the whole mass thrust block," he said.

Cassandra bit out a curse, but that was the job. Without risks, there was no reward.

"Also, we will have to hold our position for at least an hour at the gate before we have the reserves to power it on."

"Helm, hard sail. Get me to that gate as fast as *Fury* will allow," she ordered.

The Green, Outside Novagrad, Alexander

The hour before dawn came faster than Alexander would have thought. After Claudia left, he retired back to his room and sat in one of the large plush chairs. He had intended to just look at the wall and practice holding his arm out, feeling the weight of the pistol in his hand, the strain of it on his forearm and shoulder, the muscles tightening and tensing up. Instead, as soon as his backside hit the chair, he was dead to the world. Sitting in the chair, he was having a perfectly acceptable dream about walking through the streets without a care in the world, except for the fact that he couldn't read the map or a single street sign. It should have vexed him, dreams like that had always vexed him in the past. Here, though, he knew that it was not important. This was a moment to just relax and enjoy being lost.

It took Hoben three solid shakes to raise Alexander from his slumber, and he was sure that, given the opportunity, he would have slept well into the day in that chair. He wasn't sure what it was about sleeping in chairs that made them so damn inviting when you were dead tired. He never could sleep in bed when he was this wound up, but a good chair always took him right off his feet and placed him in the netherworld where you couldn't read or write, and people had a propensity to go about their days without pants or a care.

Alexander shook off the haze of sleep after a moment and then looked up at his friend. Hoben was dressed in a long black jacket with a matching shirt and cravat. It all made him look just the picture of death. Sitting on the table by the door was the large wooden case from last night, which held the two pistols, *Call* and *Response*.

"Rise and shine, my friend. It is time to go and meet honor and destiny," Hoben said, his voice equal parts glum and excited.

It struck Alexander as odd, but at the same time, it was the kind of energy that he needed right now. Hell, he needed any energy that he could get. His brain was refusing to wake up, the fog of sleep holding heavily upon him.

"Please tell me you have coffee in the car," Alexander muttered, pushing himself to his feet. Once vertical, he felt slightly wobbly, resting his hand upon the top of the chair and looking around. He closed his eyes again, pressing his eyelids hard, squinting down his forehead, trying to find his breathing, to find his balance again. He opened his eyes, and the world was less foggy, but still he felt slow, like he was not completely awake.

"Of course there is coffee in the car. What kind of second do you take me for?" Hoben asked, pretending to be insulted by the mere accusation.

"I take you for the best friend in the whole of the Confederation," Alexander said, lurching from the chair to his friend and patting him on the back.

"Are you sure you are up for this, Alexander?" Hoben asked.

"Yes, the grip of sleep is slow to leave me today. My body seems to refuse to catch up with my faculties," he said, pausing and then launching himself from Hoben to the wall and using it as a crutch. Already he felt a little better. "But I am sure equilibrium shall return with some coffee and solid food."

"It had better or you will not see the afternoon," Hoben said. He put his hand on Alexander's shoulder and spun him around. "And I swear if you let this Mister Harrison fellow kill you, thus making us have to forfeit our game this afternoon, I will have the doctor resuscitate you so that I can kill you again."

There was a quiet moment and then Hoben started to laugh, and Alexander joined him. It was hollow. Though, just the mention of Mister Harrison's name caused his face to flash through his mind. That sick, used-carriage salesman smile, his greased back hair, the sickly-sweet smell of whatever cologne he was wearing.

Instantly, that image shot white hot anger through Alexander. The world, which had been foggy and out of focus, started to come back into shape. His feet felt more stable, and he didn't feel the need to use the wall for support.

"Don't worry. We shall take care of this matter quickly and be back home in time to shower before we must play. I look forward to returning to a battle fought with cards on a field of green felt," Alexander said, the energy already returning to his body. Just the mere thought of the man who had wronged the woman he loved was enough to shake loose the webs of slumber.

"I shall hold forth *Call* and make sure that there is no *Response*," he said, holding his hand up high like an orator on the congress floor.

"There is the life in you again. Good. You are going to need that. Let us away," Hoben said, pushing Alexander toward the car.

The ride to the green did not take a long time, but it was enough for Alexander to down two cups of coffee and three pastries that had been set out in the back of the car. Hoben passed on breakfast, opting for a glass of whisky. Alexander was already feeling better by the time he got into the car, and with breakfast in his gut, he was feeling almost one hundred percent again. He held his arm out, making a pistol with his fingers and aiming it down range—or, as much of a range as there was in the back of the car.

"Make sure you aim that in the right direction," Hoben said with a chuckle. Alexander mouthed the sound of a gun going off, his finger gun popping up with the noise.

"I can see him, Alen. I can see it clearly now. Us standing there on the green, the crack of the guns. White hot plasma smashing into his smug face. The ruin of his body falling to the ground, his weapon silent. Honor fulfilled and a man not worthy of the title removed from existence," Alexander said, blowing fake smoke from his finger gun.

It was then that he realized how silly he must have looked to his friend, how silly he felt. His mood had moved from barely aware of his own existence, to angry, to giddy and playful. This was not something he was used to. He had been present for battles before, had seen men and women die from their wounds. Yet here, everything felt different; his emotions, his outlook, *everything*. Was it nerves or was this just how to approach death now?

Before he could spend more time pondering the meaning of death and how we face it, the car came to a stop.

Alexander opened the door and stepped out into the predawn light. They were at the edge of a massive field, parked under two trees, each planted ten paces apart from each other. Mist was rolling across the field and in the distance, he could see the spires of Novagrad and the low buildings that marked the edge of town. They were in the massive national park that surrounded the city, which provided green space to every resident regardless of social standing and class. Where they were standing right now used to be farther from the city, but as Novagrad grew, proper society inched closer to the dueling grounds. Only the formation of the park had stopped the two trees—which had seen hundreds of years of death—from being flattened for an apartment building.

Standing under a tree, facing away from the city and the sunrise, was Claudia and an older man. She had her riding hood up over her face again, and the older man was doddering over her. Alexander assumed this was the doctor that Thrase had hired for the task.

As their car pulled up and they exited, Claudia turned to look at them. Alexander could see relief on her face, and she ran over to him, away from the old doctor. She was on him in a few paces, wrapping her arms around him.

"I am so relieved to see you. I don't know how much more small talk I could have made with the doctor. And you arrived before Mister Harrison. I know I couldn't have stood to be in his presence alone," Claudia said.

"I would never dream of leaving you alone with him, my dear. Though I plan to leave him here when this is all said and done," Alexander said, the fire in his belly coming back to replace the momentary gaiety from the ride.

Hoben walked over to the doctor and placed a handful of credit chits in his hand. The old man bowed and walked away from the trees so that he was behind his own car. Alexander could hear a chair being unfolded and a match being struck. Of course he would walk away and turn his back. The man did need deniability, after all. Dueling might have been legal, but it was still frowned upon, especially by the medical community.

It was at that moment that they heard footsteps in the grass. Alexander and Claudia turned to see Mister Harrison walk out of the forest toward them. He was alone and in the same black suit that he had been wearing the night before. His hair was slicked back and even though it appeared that he had been walking for quite a while, he still retained that smug smile on his face.

I'm going to wipe that away, Alexander thought.

"It is very nice of you to join us, sir," Alexander said. "We had been waiting for you to grace us with your presence."

"The sun has not yet fully crested over the Novagrad hills, son of Cordova," Mister Harrison said, adjusting his suit. "And I find a nice walk clears the head before violence. Don't you agree?" He held his hands out to those assembled around him. Everybody just looked at each other and shrugged.

"I guess you had to be there, so…" Mister Harrison clapped his hands together. "How are we doing this? Knives, swords, beating each other bloody?"

There was a confident jovial jaunt to his words that made Alexander feel supremely uncomfortable. It was just another part of this man's personality that rubbed him the wrong way and gave him that feeling of somebody walking over his grave.

"Pistols, like civilized gentlemen," Hoben said, walking over to the car and picking up the case.

"Is that what we are? Civilized gentlemen?" Mister Harrison asked, leaning against the pace tree to the south. "Seems to me you two are just card-playing children with delusions of adulthood and responsibility."

That was enough to ruffle Alexander's feathers.

"Now, sir, you wait just a minute," he said loudly, taking a step forward. Hoben's hand was on his chest, stopping him from moving forward.

"Save it for the duel, Alexander."

"Yes, save it for the duel, Alexander," Mister Harrison said in a tone that he intended to be mocking, but came off like somebody who had only read in a book what a mocking tone sounded like.

"Sir, I see you come unattended. Do you not have a second?" Hoben asked, giving the tree line and the road around them a quick scan.

"I do not plan to falter in honor, and if I should fall, you can just contact the authorities to come and collect. I'm sure there will be a few disappointed parties that would show up," Mister Harrison said, unbuttoning his black jacket. He folded it neatly and hung it over a low hanging branch.

"Very well, then. The rules are as follows. Each of you will choose a pistol, the challenged goes first. You will then turn your backs and walk until you each pass your tree. I will then give a ten count and at that moment, you are free to turn and fire. If you miss, you must stand and take fire from your opponent. If both weapons go off and nobody falls, then honor has been fulfilled, and we walk away," Hoben explained, walking to the middle of the two trees, the large wooden pistol box in his hand. "Are these rules agreed upon?"

"Only one of us shall be walking away from these trees today," Alexander said bitterly, pulling off his long brown duster and handing it to Claudia. She took it from him and held it tight, a look of worry across her face. Before turning and walking to the line, Alexander reached up and wiped away the single tear that was rolling down her cheek with his thumb. He then gingerly kissed his thumb and pressed it to her lips.

Taking a deep breath, he turned and walked to the line.

"Rules, words, I have things to do this morning," Mister Harrison said as he walked up to the line as well.

Hoben opened the large case, revealing the two fancy plasma lock pistols, *Call* and *Response*. Both had already been loaded and just needed to have their primer locks pulled into place before they could be fired. Mister Harrison reached in a removed *Response* from the case. Alexander thought that was a fortuitus sign. The man didn't know the names of the weapons, didn't know their history, and thus, didn't know that he was damning himself in the eyes of fate by pulling the second pistol, the one that Hoben had made sure was closer to him. Either the man was careless, or he was overly confidant in his abilities.

Alexander reached in and removed *Call* from the case. Hoben then closed the box and stepped out of the line of fire. Claudia fell in next to him. The time for anger and quips had passed. Now, there was just honor and violence left.

For a moment, Alexander's hand started to shake, to waver slightly. He reached up and grabbed his wrist, squeezing tightly. The shaking stopped. He took a breath again and let the rage fall back behind his years of training. He was a member of House Cordova, the keepers of the Dreadstar *Fury*. This was in his blood. He had trained for it as a child. Yes, Hanna had always been better than him, but he never left the sparing rooms dishonored by his performance.

"Load!" Hoben yelled.

Alexander reached up and pulled back the locking mechanism on his pistol and gently placed his finger along the outside of the trigger guard. It was, in that moment, that he should have asked his friend about the pull weight of the weapon, if they tended to pull to one side or the other. His old Master-at-Arms would have called that sloppy. It was too late to ask now. These were dueling pistols made for soft men, so he could assume that the pull was light and the weapon friendly—at least for a first-generation plasma pistol.

"Walk!" Hoben called next.

Alexander started walking forward. His first step felt a little unsure in the soft morning grass. It was like how he felt when he woke up in the morning, leaning against the wall for support. He took a deep breath and took another step. This time, his footing was far steadier. He was ready. He *could* do this. Nothing was going to stop him from taking care of Claudia, fighting for her honor and clearing whatever problem her and her family had gotten into. It would start with this duel and, if he needed to bring to bear the force of his family, he would do that, as well. He knew people in high places, not just because of his family, but from the project, too. The administrator would be disappointed that he was putting himself in danger like this, but that would just be a lecture, a lecture he could take. Knowing he failed the woman he loved?

That was not something Alexander could live with.

One step past the pace tree. Alexander stopped, digging his right foot into the ground. He would need a good solid pivot point so that he could spin around as soon as the order was given. Taking one last breath, Alexander placed his finger on the trigger. It had a little spring and give to it. Good. The pull would be light, just the way he liked it.

His breath sat there in his lungs, waiting for the moment that it could be exhaled; for the moment of action, the moment that he would prove he was a man of honor. Prove that he was worthy of the Cordova name, worthy of the love of his family. If it required a bit of violence, then so be it. The seconds ticked by as a small bead of sweat started to form on his forehead.

"Fire!" Hoben yelled.

Alexander didn't hesitate. His left foot came up, he threw his weight onto the right and started to spin. The ball of his foot dug into the ground and turned, giving him the solid base that he needed. Alexander's arm flew out. He closed his left eye and locked his right one to the barrel of *Call*. He was turned around, his weapon extended. Mister Harrison was still turning. For a split-second, Alexander aimed toward the man's smug face. Then he could hear all his years of training echoing in the back of his mind.

Center of mass, child. You can always shoot them again. Alexander lowered the weapon's target. Mister Harrison was turned, his weapon coming up.

Alexander squeezed the trigger. The weapon belched fire and had a mean kick. His arm was locked, but the shot went wide. Not so wide, though, that it didn't find its target. Blue plasma smashed into Mister Harrison's side, blood and mangled cloth burst from his lower gut. It had been a glancing blow.

That is why you go for the center, child. Even a glancing blow with an old plasma weapon meant a horrible wound that could still be fatal.

Mister Harrison lost his footing and started to fall. His finger slipped and *Response* answered, destroying branches in the pace tree next to Alexander. A moment later, the man was on the ground. His hands were grasping at his wound; there was red everywhere.

Alexander took a deep breath and lowered his weapon. The world started to spin around him as the haze of anger and spite left his body. It was as if a massive weight had been removed from his chest, and he could finally breathe again. To his credit, Mister Harrison didn't cry out, didn't scream or whimper. He just laughed.

The doctor ran over and started to assess his wound. Hoben stepped into the center of the firing line.

"Honor has been satisfied. We shall walk from this place with no malice or anger, as the old ways defined," he said, giving a nod to both sides. Hoben then walked over to Alexander and removed the gun from his hand and placed it carefully back in the wooden box.

"Good job, giving that ass what he had coming," Hoben whispered before turning and walking over toward where Mister Harrison was. Claudia ran up to Alexander, wrapping her arms around him. She gave him a kiss on the cheek.

"That was so brave of you, taking fire for me," she whispered. There was gratitude and sex in her voice. It filled Alexander with joy as he took in another breath.

"Anything for you, my love," Alexander said, taking her chin gently in his hand and kissing her lips. "I just have to take care of one thing before we can leave." Alexander let her go and turned toward Mister Harrison. It only took him a moment to cross the ten paces that separated the two trees and their respective combatants.

"Good fight," Mister Harrison bit out, the smile not whipped from his face. The doctor had already placed a large compression bandage on the man's side and started a small drip of what Alexander could only assume was pain medication.

"Yes, good fight. Consider this me being magnanimous. You come for Claudia again, and there will be no duel, there will be no quarter given. I am a Space Lord at heart, and we answer slights to our honor with blood," Alexander said.

"I'm sure you do, Mister Cordova. I am sure you do," Mister Harrison said, chuckling. Alexander turned and started to walk away. If he had to see that man's face anymore, he was liable to get down on the ground with him and beat it out of existence.

Hoben had finished collecting the family dueling pistols and walked over to meet them. "Shall we head home? I fear we all could use a shower and a dram of something strong before our game this afternoon."

"That sounds like a capitol idea," Alexander said, clapping his friend on the back.

EPISODE VII:
Memories of Children Made Manifest

Lord-Admiral's Quarters, Fury, Cassandra

The ivory keys of the piano were mocking her.

Cassandra held her hands over the keys, trying to find the music, trying to even bring out a tune that she wanted to play. There was nothing. When Tiberius had died, he took the music with him. Before that fateful day, she had been composing at a rapid clip, her backlog of tracks numbering in the thousands. Musical cues for every command that could be given on the ship, leitmotifs for most of her officers and every member of her family. If somebody had wanted to, they could even find the moments in her life when the style of music she obsessed with changed and changed again. Lieutenant Commander Nguyen said that his daughter Aya was one of her biggest fans and Cassandra supposed that the young girl probably could find those moments.

The music is you and nothing else, she could hear Tiberius's voice in the back of her mind. He might have been dead, but his spirit was still with her, and it would be until she left this world to join him in whatever was beyond.

Cassandra placed her hands on the keys again. They found a place and started to move. Jump gates and faster-than-light travel had been on her mind and was in her fingers. They moved across the keyboard and started to play a few bars, first from "Jump Prep" and then from "Through the Gate".

Both tracks were based on the same musical idea. "Jump Prep" was newer and was filled with drums, guitars and woodwinds. A propulsive musical style that she had been writing in for the last decade, which all the ship's musical commands were composed in. "Through the Gate" was one of her early works, from shortly after her father had died and she had assumed the Lordship of the family. It was full of brass and big drums, closer to a march than anything else. It was a tune she had not played in years. When pecked out on the piano, both sounded very much the same.

There was something about the second track that she couldn't quite put her finger on. Cassandra knew that she had written it but couldn't seem to drag the occasion from her mind. The musical idea had clearly been formed and stuck with her, even if this track never did.

The music is within you, it comes from you, and it tells your story.

Tiberius again. His voice was slowly replacing the logical, emotional internal monologues that Cassandra had ignored for so many years. Love was something that she always struggled with—not physical love, exactly. That was something that had never interested her. The emotion of love for ship and family had always felt distant, wrapped more in duty than any affection. She loved her ship, and she loved her children, but most days, it felt like that was just what she was *supposed* to do. Tiberius had been the only person to challenge those long-held facts, and now that he was gone, Cassandra understood love more and felt it even less.

Her family was fractured, broken, and Cassandra wasn't sure that she had the emotional fortitude to bring them all together. If they even survived the next few days to find that reconciliation. Hanna was lost somewhere on Barker's World, and Alexander—her dear, sweet Alexander, who she had shunned—was on NovaTerra. NovaTerra, a world that they were rushing toward, a world that was possibly only a few days away from having atomic weapons dropped upon it. If that were to happen, if she was to lose the twins, what would even be the point of going on anymore? Vengeance wouldn't bring them back, wouldn't fill the hole that she was already feeling grow; that she didn't know how to fill anymore.

"Through the Gate" came back to her mind again, as her fingers tapped it out. They were stiff. She hadn't played in a while. Something was nagging at her from this track, the age, the...

Her mind trailed off, rattling through the index of music that she had written. This was old, but just out of reach, she knew there was something older; something where the ideas from this and "Jump Prep" had come from. What was it? Why couldn't she pull that memory from her mind?

Cassandra closed the lid of the piano and stood up. She stretched and started to walk across her suite.

That was when the ship shook.

"Ready Action", a very percussive, drum-heavy bit of music, started to echo through the hallway speakers. In her suite, the comm came to life.

"Lord-Admiral, to Combat, if you please."

It was Captain Rackland's voice. This hour had been his turn on watch. She was supposed to be trying to sleep, but sleep was eluding her just like the original music that had inspired "Through the Gate". Cassandra walked over to the speaker and pressed down the talk switch.

"Sitrep, Captain?"

"Three more of those arrowhead ships have jumped in ahead of us, and another flight of five have appeared upon the starboard side. There is more, but I shall await your arrival," Rackland's voice responded.

"Very good, Captain. I shall be there presently. You have authorization to use whatever force necessary to keep our sky clear," she said, clicking off the speaker.

Cassandra grabbed her coat from the couch and pulled it on. Then she picked up her sword belt and headed out into the hallway, buckling it as she went. The trip from her suites to the Combat Information Center was a quick walk. The commander of the ship should never be too far from her heart.

The CIC was buzzing with activity when Cassandra arrived, entering from the top deck.

"Lord-Admiral on deck," the boatswain called out, playing his whistle as she headed down the steps toward the glass command table. Nobody got up or stood at attention. They were all too focused on the action that was going on outside. Captain Rackland stood at the table, marking down numbers and pressing keys.

"Bring me up to speed," Cassandra ordered, as the ship shook. The arrowhead ships on their starboard side had again racked them with fire. Their energy reserves and speed were slowing again. At this rate, they were not going to make it through the gate in time.

Through the Gate, we need to—

"We are, at present, engaged with eight hostiles. Our gun crews are having trouble locking onto them, and their countermeasures are still scrambling our missile locks. I have technology working on finding new channels so that—"

Cassandra held her hand up to stop him.

"We are not going to make it to the gate, are we?" she asked.

"Not if they keep this up, no. We need to stand and fight. We have analyzed their attack patterns. They appear to only be armed with a single beam weapon. If I could launch fighters, we could clear the sky," Rackland said.

"Then we most assuredly wouldn't make it to the jump gate in time. What else do you have that you didn't want to say over the comm?" Cassandra asked.

Captain Rackland looked up and around the CIC before pressing a few keys. There was a scratch of static as the noise dampening bubble was activated around them and the table.

"The fleet that is following us. We were able to get a partial friend or foe response from them. It is the second fleet from House Lagrange. While no names were mentioned in the documents that Major Cordova provided to us, it just seems too strange that they would be here for anything other than nefarious purposes," Captain Rackland said.

"'Not fit for conscription'," Cassandra said quietly. "They are trying to finish what was started at Hyroncore."

"That is my thinking. They are still ten hours away but gaining on us as we bleed power. If you let me launch fighters and clear our sky, we can be ready for them when they arrive. If there haven't been any modifications to their second fleet, we should be able to smash them. It will not be a pretty fight, though," Rackland said.

Cassandra started to weigh the options in her head. Her hands found the table and her fingers, now filled with music, started to tap out the basic notes of "Through the Gate" before sliding into "Jump Prep". Whatever it was about these two tracks, it was right on the edge of her mind.

"Captain, is the table displaying astrometeorological data right now?" Cassandra asked.

The captain shook his head and pressed a few keys. A massive storm started to appear just on the edge of the tables zoom. The data was starting to come in. Winds from the Barrier were raging at thousands of kilometers an hour, and there were electromagnetic and radiation spikes echoing everywhere. *Fury* was hardened and equipped to stand those kinds of forces. She wasn't so sure about their new friends. The Lagrange fleet, she was sure, couldn't take the storm.

"There, we need to stand and fight, but we also need to get our bearing and make a few repairs. Captain, set your course for the storm. We can clear our sky along the way."

"Yes sir, right away," Rackland said, pulling down the bubble around them and barking orders across the CIC.

Cassandra's fingers kept tapping out the same tune, the same beat. She needed to look something up, needed to figure out what it was that was just on the edge of her mind, driving into her brain like a dagger.

"Captain, you have the con," she said, turning and walking out the lower entrance.

You are the music, the music is you, Tiberius's voice followed her.

Outside CIC, Dreadstar below the Citadel, Naomi

Naomi fell in behind Lucas as he flicked on his blade and started running up the steps to the sounds of violence, his coat flapping behind him. Naomi had seen more combat in the last few hours than she had in the entire time she had been an anointed Knight of the Host'ire. The star-steel blade, which had always felt odd in her hands compared to a sonic spanner—or a wrench—was becoming second nature to her. She didn't fear having to use the weapon to cut through flesh versus just hacking through broken or fallen sections of space station.

Back on the Black Hollow Observatory, she'd almost never drawn the weapon. Wouldn't have even carried it, if that hadn't been a mandate from the very top. Now, though, the power felt good. It felt right in her hand, the weapon's thrum beating in time with her own heart, which was racing. She was halfway up the steps. Naomi took a deep breath, letting the air and Null fill her lungs, letting the energy move through her body and calm her fluttering heart.

Lucas was already out the door, the other three of them falling in behind him in the hallway. His skill with the blade outstripped all of them combined. She and Joanna were not front line combatants, and Rostov was still recovering from spending time in a cell; what he had been doing before being sent to re-education, he still wouldn't talk about. Naomi could feel all of them, see though their eyes, picture the battle with their minds. Her arm wanted to move, to slide into a position that she had never used before, that felt right, but odd. Lucas was in the same drop-down guard position, his thoughts and feelings coursing through her muscles, commanding them.

Before the quartet was a long hallway. One side was dark, filled with the sounds of fleeing Tragadi. It was clear that not every member of the Guardians of the Seer were fighters. Plenty of them were apparently civilians who knew better than to be anywhere near a fight. Before she found her friends again, Naomi would have wanted to run with them, to not get in the way. Today, with her friends beside her, she was ready to stand tall, to be what a Host'ire Knight should be.

A protector.

"Door!" Naomi yelled, pointing her blade forward, gesturing to the other side of the hallway where the Fellowship cultists were engaging with the few armed guardians. Lucas ran forward and threw himself into the fray, the green of his blade spinning, cutting a swath of death and destruction before him. Naomi followed, stopping short of running into the mix. There was a panel on the wall. The lights were off, and it looked like age had taken a toll on the electronics.

"Rostov, Joanna, cover her!" Lucas yelled as he jumped into the air, delivering a split flying kick that knocked three Fellowship members back before landing on his knees, jacket spread out around him.

Naomi was impressed, and she could feel a small tinge of sexual attraction coming from Joanna, who was working very hard to keep her current feelings in check. Strong emotions and errant emotions were the simplest to feel from each other. This could become a problem very quickly if they were not careful. It was hard enough to control one's own emotions, let alone having to deal with the unresolved trauma of three other people. Naomi craved the closeness but was worried about everything else that it could bring.

Naomi pulled the panel off the wall. Those damned buttons were already broken. There was no need to waste time trying to push them or interfacing with the interface. Joanna cocked her head at that odd turn of phrase in the back of Naomi's mind before getting back to work. This was no time to edit her own stream of consciousness. She had already spent too much time in her life doing that.

The wiring on the inside was a disaster. The color on all the wires had faded away under hundreds of years of dust and decay. There were some labels that had still stood the test of time. Unfortunately, Naomi couldn't read them. They were in a script that she didn't recognize.

I know the words for circuitry in almost every language in the system, she thought, a small amount of panic starting to set in.

"I felt that you needed a hand," Joanna said, coming up behind her.

The large woman threw a hand forward and, diving into the Null, pushed away a Fellowship member who had gotten too close. Lucas turned and ran his blade through the man's chest before spinning and tossing him back into the charging line of his companions.

"What do you know about very old writing?" Noami asked with a chuckle as she shimmied to the side, making room for Joanna to look inside the wire-filled hole in the wall. She got down on one knee, holding her blade up for light.

"Wayfinder script. I can't read it—well, not really. I understand some of the characters, and can make some extrapolations," Joanna said.

She reached a hand in and looked at some more of the wires. There was an audible shock, as an exposed wire sent electricity through Joanna's hand. Naomi shuddered, quickly blinking her eyes. She could feel the current, as well, the tingle of electricity shooting up her arm. She shook her hand, opening and closing it quickly a few times to get the sensation to fade away. As she was doing this, something came to her. If they were going to feel what each of them were feeling, it stood to reason that they could tap into more and more of each other's senses and emotions.

"I have an idea," Naomi said, brushing Joanna to the side. "Put you hand on my shoulder, close your eyes and reach into the Null."

Joanna nodded. She knew exactly where this was going. Noami didn't even have to finish spelling out the plan for her.

She reached into her jacket and pulled out her small electricians kit and got out her multi tool. Joanna put a hand on Naomi's shoulder and closed her eyes. Instantly, she was filled with a new sensation, of somebody inside of her, inside in a way she had never felt before. It was like there was another set of eyes behind hers, blinking and looking around. She was in control, with Joanna along for the ride.

"Comfortable back there?" Naomi asked.

"I'm here," Joanna said, clearly not completely comfortable with what she was doing. Naomi's eyes started to dart around the mess of wires, looking for what she thought might be the central power line. From Joanna, she could feel a light wave of nausea flowing. Naomi locked her eyes forward and moved them slower. A wave of relief followed where the nausea had been.

She found the first label on this set of wires. *Lights.* Joanna's voice said in her mind. Flicking the cap off her mini tool, revealing a small color stamp, Naomi tapped it three times, switching to yellow and tapping a small ink dot onto the faded paper. They did this for the next five labels inside the bundle of wires, plus a circuit panel that Naomi found even deeper in the wall. She would point to something, and Joanna would make her best educated guess based on what she knew of the old Wayfinder language.

They were done in a few minutes and Joanna pulled herself way from Naomi, hitting the floor with a thud. For the briefest of moments, she felt hollow, like there were not enough people or voices inside of her head. Quickly, though, the five trains of thought—two of them tangents—returned to Naomi.

Looking around, the hallway was quiet, for the moment. Lucas stood atop a pile of dead, flanked by three guardians who had swords and plasma pistols in their hands. Rostov was to the side, helping a wounded man to his feet. It was calm, but Naomi knew it wouldn't last. Information flashed into her mind: audio, the sounds of feet running, and a horrible gibbering, a frothing for violence. Lucas turned and looked at them all. That was when she realized she was hearing what Lucas was hearing from down the hallway. Another wave of Fellowship cultists.

"Naomi, sitrep on the door!" Lucas called.

"Working on it. I've now got a better idea of what we are working with. So, I've just got to reroute some power, and then…"

"I need an ETA, Knight!" Lucas snapped back.

He was fully in battle command mode. She would have been offended if it had been anybody else who snapped at her like that. She wasn't a grunt but a technician, an artist of electricity. Lucas wasn't yelling to stroke his own ego or feelings of importance, but to keep her on task.

"If there is still power in these cells, I can have it working in three minutes," she called back, stripping the plastic off one of the wires and pressing it into another before hitting them both with a spark of heat from her multi-tool.

She tried to get into the zone of working, but it was hard. She kept getting flashes from Lucas as his eyes moved across the darkness, picking out shadows and marking them as targets in his mind. Rostov had finished helping the wounded man and was back on the line, cracking his joints and stretching out his muscles the skills of battle returning to him.

Naomi pressed two cords together. Nothing happened. She moved a few more around, reaching her hand deep into the wall, all the way up to the shoulder. She used the Null to try to find the one with current. Nothing. The farther she reached her hand into the wall, the denser the wiring was. Finally, she found what she needed, the power relay for the blast door. Naomi knew it would take a large jolt of power to operate the gears that were holding the five-ton door in place. This battery was what would give the system the jolt, both connected to the main systems of the ship and independent. Right now, none of that mattered because the battery was dead. Cold. Power had not been storied in this cell in hundreds of years. She could feel the alkali and acid packs ready to mix again. The chemicals were just waiting for that jolt so they could start to generate power.

Naomi pulled her head out of the hole in the wall. Lucas and Rostov were again fighting Fellowship members, their blades swinging left and right. Joanna was to the side using the Null to push people back, clearing space for the guardians to have a clean field of fire. One of them was dead. Naomi took another breath, pulling the Null inside, closing her eyes and looking for the power in the ship. She could see the electricity moving through the wires, through the steel of the wall, like looking at blood pumping through veins. There it was, a vein that wasn't doing its job, going to an organ that was being slowly starved to death. Her eyes traced it up into the ceiling and then back down the hallway away from where they were.

"Lucas, we need to get power back to this door if we are going to close it. I can see where we need to go," Naomi said, standing up and pulling her blade out again.

"No, I need you here to get the door working as soon as there is power!" Lucas barked back. "Rostov, you and Joanna go and get the power working again. Naomi will guide you," he said, roundhouse kicking a cultist before cutting off a leg, sending the man screaming to the ground the stump burning from the energy blade.

Rostov ran up to Naomi. She looked at him, then quietly placed her hand on his shoulder and pushed forward into his mind, showing him what she had seen, the vein that wasn't pumping its electric blood. Rostov nodded, and then started off into the darkness, followed by Joanna. Lucas didn't turn to look at her or them, he just kept fighting.

Naomi flicked on her blade and ran up next to Lucas. Until there was power, she would be better off breaking things than fixing them.

Laundry, Olympus Ares Research Facility, Grace

Grace had gotten halfway down the laundry chute when the first grenade exploded above her, before a second and then she assumed a third followed. By that point, she had reached the bottom, having softly landed in a pile of unwashed clothing. A hundred pairs of the same pants, shirt, and lab coat. Not to mention the assorted pairs of socks and underwear. She could feel how soft the pile of clothing was even through her armor. For a moment, the stress poured from her body, and she was comfortable. Relaxed. She almost fell asleep. She shook her head and pressed a few buttons on the HUD, triggering a shot of stimulant. Grace's eyes opened instantly as the amphet-amines raced through her system.

No time to rest, we have to keep at it, Emily whispered. *Just like studying for a final in undergrad.*

Looking around, the laundry room was pitch black. Whatever lights had been down here were off, either from lack of power or because they had been turned into something other than lights. Another movement of her eye and the night vision functions on her suit came to life, and Grace was able to see much better what was around her.

The washers and dryers had all been turned into great blocks of stone, the floor cobbles with vines running across it. All the racks and hangers had been turned into bushes and sprouting trees. Everything was quiet except for dripping water coming from somewhere. Another flick of her eyes across the HUD's user interface had Grace pulling up environmental readings: forty-five degrees Celsius and eighty-four percent humidity. The laundry had gone from a massive network of machines designed to clean the clothing of tens of thousands of people to a jungle. That was when she heard the wet thumping of feet and the scrapping of claws.

Well, that can't be good, she thought, looking around trying to pinpoint where it was coming from. That was when she saw it. A huge, hulking brute of a creature, standing on two legs, dragging massive arms and sharp claws. Its body was covered in green scales. Its head almost seemed too small, mostly just a round mouth with rows and rows of undulating teeth. There were no eyes, and small holes that she assumed were ears. As quietly as she could, Grace eased herself deeper into the pile of clothing.

In the distance, another creature made a noise deep and guttural. Instantly the hunter's head swung, and it started to tap the massive claw on the ground. Its head was turning, following the sound. Some kind of echo location, Grace figured.

Slowly, she rolled so that her plasma rifle was pointed forward. It had gone cold, and at that moment, she couldn't remember if there was a sound associated with thumbing the power cell back on. At present, it didn't seem like a risk worth taking.

A moment later, a second large brute came out of the shadows. This one was white, with a streak of crimson running across its chest. Blood. Grace didn't know whose blood it was, but she wasn't going to add hers to it. Her thumb hovered over the power cell activation switch. It would only take a moment to warm up the weapon, then her radio buzzed in her ear. A huge burst of static and white noise that caused her to grunt and reflexively smack the side of her helmet as if she was covering an ear. Both creatures turned toward each other and started to tap their claws.

Tap. Tap. Tap.

Both of their heads turned toward her instantly. Grace held her breath. Maybe they wouldn't find her. Maybe they needed to hear another sound to zero in on her. Inside her helmet, the buzzing stopped, and she could hear Essex's voice.

"Doctor Goodspeed, do you copy?"

She blinked quickly and closed the line. She hoped that he would understand. In that moment, it didn't cross her mind that they might not learn the subtle nuance of being hung up on at the Citadel. Her line rang again—that answered *that* question. Emily thought biting back the impulse to groan in frustration and disgust. The hunters were getting closer, the green one tapping and the white one listening as it stalked. Raising its arm, the creature got closer and closer to her, closing its clawed fist and then opening it again, flexing for violence.

Fuck it, Emily thought, thumbing on the rifle. It made a sharp little buzz, so high pitched that she almost couldn't hear it. Her hearing and theirs, though, were operating on two vastly different ranges. Both their heads fully swiveled in her direction. The white hunter screamed, and its round, tooth-filled jaw started to spin like the business end of an excavator. It was so close that Grace didn't even need the auto aim. She brought the plasma rifle up and pulled the trigger. Four burning hot rounds belched from the weapon, all of them finding their mark in the white creature's center of mass. Blood burst out the back.

For a moment, the creature stopped and looked down at the four fist sized holes that she had drilled through its chest. The holes were big and clean enough that she could see the green creature through them.

The white hunter did not appreciate being shot and let out another roar as it started to run toward Grace, its massive, clawed arm rearing back, ready to strike. Grace fired another round that went wide before stumbling as she tried to walk backward on the pile of laundry and fell to the dirt ground below. Her armor clanked as she hit the ground, and the white adjusted its run to keep coming toward her.

Grace got her weapon up again and pulled the trigger four more times. The first round went wide again, but the next three were on target. The creature was so close that, by the time she fired the weapon's barrel, she was surrounded by sharp, spinning teeth. Blood and brains blew out the back of its head. The teeth and jaw fell sideways like a flower blooming in a rainstorm. There were two more spurts of crimson and then the creature fell to its knees and down to the left, hitting the ground with a thud.

She turned to where the second creature was. It was still, then turned its head toward Grace, and at first, made a motion like it was sniffing, but using the maw of its mouth like a tongue. After a moment, it stopped lick-smelling and howled. Grace didn't speak their language, had only known of these creatures' existence for only a few minutes, but she knew exactly what that sound meant. *Prey. I've found it come and get it.* She wasn't about to be surrounded by these predators, wasn't going to be ripped apart and consumed inside those massive black holes of teeth. Getting to her feet, Grace started to run, bolting toward where she knew the exit of the jungle-that-was-once-a-laundry-mat was.

The shimmer of glass was ahead of her—the outside world, its harsh, fluorescent lighting streaming into the dark, prehistoric vibes of her current location. She picked up her speed. Blinking, she pulled up a small camera in the back of her helmet. Four more hunters had leapt out of the trees and were hooting at each other, most likely coming up with a plan for how they were going to acquire their meal, rip her apart, consume her limb-by-limb. *Now I know how a crab feels,* she thought, knowing that it would be a horrible experience existing while they pulled her from the shell of the suit. The first hunter started to run.

Grace picked up the pace, pushing energy into her legs. Flicking off the rear camera, she focused on the glass in front of her. She was going to smash right through it. They would keep coming, but she would be in a familiar area, a place where they wouldn't have the foliage to hide in. Grace instinctively threw her arm up to protect her face.

Like you have run through glass before, Emily thought with a chuckle. They had done plenty of reckless things in the past, but this was a first.

With a loud thud that pulsed through her body, Grace hit the glass. Only it wasn't glass, but a diamond-like stone. Hard, solid, immovable. Grace could see the shimmer of the base as she stumbled backward, the surprise and pain racing through her body. The shock was so heavy that even the internal gyroscopes of the environment suit couldn't keep her upright, and Grace fell down hard on her back, the diamond above only lightly cracked.

Get up, we have to keep moving, Emily thought—or perhaps she said out loud. They had been together long enough that she was sure some of her internal monologue was just words she was saying to herself.

Grace planted her hands on the ground, and just as she was about to push up, there were green scales and flesh leaping over her. Everything had happened so fast. It had only been a moment since she hit the ground, and now she was relieved to be here because it had saved her life. There was another sound as the hunter smashed into the diamond glass with a resounding thud.

"Bet you didn't see that coming," she muttered, like the hero in some pedantic action movie that Emily would have watched with her father. Grace rolled her head. The creature was on the ground on its back, writhing, struggling to get up, hooting a guttural whooping call of pain and frustration. That was a window—a small window—and Grace was going to take advantage of it.

Ripping one of the grenades from her vest, she pulled the pin and rolled over, lobbing it into the spinning, toothy maw. Shunting power to her arms and legs, Grace pushed herself to her feet and started to run, keeping the diamond glass to her right. This was still going to be the best way to get out.

Three seconds later, the grenade exploded, the bang followed by the sound of wet chunks of meat flopping back onto the ground. The hooting stopped. There was only her breathing and silence. She hated silence in that moment. There were still four of them out there and a massive diamond wall in front of her. Turning, Grace shoved every last volt of power from her suit into her right arm. Balling up a fist, she punched. Pain and reverb rolled through her thin arm into her body. She could almost picture her flesh warping with the sound wave, could see what the impact would have done to her bones, if not for the suit.

On the wall of diamond glass, there was a crack. Not a big one, but not an insignificant one, either. She punched it again and again. Each hit caused more and more pain, drained more and more power from her suit, but caused the crack to get wider and deeper. The power in her suit was starting to fail. Grace stepped back and fired the plasma rifle into the crack. Both rounds smashed into it, melting some of the diamond and then went cold, all of their energy sucked away, dissipated into the crystalline structures of the wall. Heavy feet were behind her again. Getting the hunters to smash into her problem like comedy cartoon characters wasn't going to work again.

There was no time for a new plan, no time to come up with something fancy and creative that would make this story more exciting in fifty years when she was telling it to a room full of people—or for when they were making the movie based on her life. Spinning, Grace flicked a switch on the side of the plasma rifle, turning it from semi- to full-auto and depressed the trigger.

The first hunter exploded in a wash of gore as the full brunt of the weapon's destructive capabilities smashed into its chest. It hadn't worked the first time because she showed restraint. This time, there was none of that. The other three dove to the side, getting only nicked by her field of fire. The weapon gave her two warnings, this time. It was out of ammunition *and* overheating.

Ejecting the spent magazine, Grace started to run again. They were not grouped up anymore, and would be coming for her, would try to strike from all sides like the pack of hunters they were.

Grace knew that she was going to need to make a loop back to where she had been trying to break the diamond glass. It would have been folly to waste the effort that she had already put into it. Looking all over, the vines were thicker by the dryers, where the hangers and vending machines had once been. She kept running, and then her foot hit something wet—she almost slipped on it.

Catching herself, Grace looked around. She was now inside the heaviest of vines, and on the floor was a thick membrane. She took a deep breath as her eyes scanned the area. She had a sinking feeling about what she was about to find. Then she saw it. A clutch of eggs. Sacks of hard flesh; five of them had burst and another three were pulsating, she could see the claws inside, trying to escape the flesh of the egg, as it deformed to keep them inside.

Had the eggs been brought over from wherever these creatures were from, or did they spawn them that quickly here? Both possibilities were horrible to think about.

"Fuck my life," Emily muttered. If a hatchery of these things had just been birthed and grown to the size they already were, she didn't want to know how much bigger they could get. If there was going to be any chance of survival, she was going to have to take care of this *and* them. There really wasn't much choice at this point anymore.

Then an idea came to Grace; a wicked idea. *That is new for you,* Emily thought.

Grace pulled out two grenades, setting their detonators to be remotely connected to her suit. She then pulled out a third, pulled the pen and then held it tightly in her hand, preventing the mechanism from starting its countdown. Thousands of years of human evolution and the basic workings of a grenade had never changed. Pin, flick, throw, boom.

"Alright, you alien assholes! You want me, come and get me!" she yelled into the laundromat-turned-jungle. The hunters were quick to take her up on the offer, bursting into the nursery. They then stopped, looking at her with their ears and the echo location of their screams. She made a motion to the grenade in her hand.

"Boom!" Grace said, along with the hand motion, showing them that she was ready to blow the unborn hunters into oblivion. The three of them squared up to her then, motioning to each other and back to her. They understood what she was signaling, what she was trying to say. Now, how was she going to leverage that into an escape?

Go big or go home, Emily, she heard her father's voice in her head. *We miss all the swings we do not take.* The ball flew over home plate. She hadn't swung, had just let it sail by, hoping it would go wide. The crowd was behind her. They had gotten quiet as the umpire put down a second finger. There would only be one more chance. The lights of the memory faded back into the present day with the crack of wood on leather.

"Catch, motherfucker," she said, flicking the pin and throwing the grenade like a fastball at the center hunter. Grace turned, she started running. There was no time to see if they would catch the ball, see if they could throw it to first base. Every bit of power went into her legs. She burst out of the hatchery as the grenade exploded. Her feet hit first base. She turned and started toward the crack in the diamond glass wall. The crowd was cheering behind her. She rounded second, and, with a blink, she set off the other two grenades inside the hatchery. They blew with a crack and a wet sickening thud. The ball was flying high now. Feet were coming behind her. One was still alive. There was somebody in the outfield who thought they could maybe catch her ball so it didn't turn into a home run.

Grace hit third base, the crack in the diamond glass wall coming into view. The plasma rifle had cooled down and was loaded. Raising it while she ran, Grace pulled the trigger, dumping all eighty rounds from the magazine into the wall in a matter of seconds until again, the weapon glowed hot red. Each round smashed into the diamond glass wall, cracking it more and more, until finally, it shattered. The hole wasn't huge, but it was enough. Grace dove forward, sliding through the hole as the hunter behind her hit the wall. The lights of the facility washed over her as she slid into home plate—safe—a run having been scored.

It would only last for a moment, because danger was all around her. There was no "safe", only not being actively hunted. On the other side of the diamond glass wall, the Olympus Ares facility looked much as it always had. Yes, there was still red dirt blowing around on currents of wind that shouldn't exist in a hermetically-sealed facility, but they were minor changes compared to where Grace had just been; what she had just seen. It was the second biome that she had encountered, even though everything she had seen of the world on the other side of the portal indicated that it was dead, ruined, broken by time and war. Perhaps it was another dimension or another place in time. She didn't know, and right now, didn't have time to investigate.

Science would have to wait.

***

She had stumbled away from the laundry jungle into one of the security stations on the lower level. The station would have everything she needed: power, weapons, security cameras, and a better radio.

On the way, she tried to raise Essex again, but all that came back was static. She hoped he wasn't too far away; wasn't dead. No, if she was still kicking, then the former Host'ire Knight was sure to be just fine.

Each step she took, Grace scanned the empty, cold corridors of the base, looking for signs of life, signs of danger. There was nothing. No infested guards, no signs of previous violence, and, to her relief, no neon-blue light just hanging around at the edge of her vision. She almost wanted to ask the Varagoth if he knew what those hunters had been. At the same time, though, she never wanted to see him again; never wanted to hear his cold voice inside her head. Just the momentary thought of it sent shivers across her spine. No, the answers to her rabbit hole questions were not worth having to interact with that creature ever again.

Hanger Bay, Barker's World, Hanna

Things on Barker's World had gone from bad to worse for Hanna and her team. Turning the damaged arrowhead ship into a bunker had provided them some respite from the hail of fire that had been coming down from the surface. Now, though, Hanna was worried, because things had gone quiet. It had been almost three hours since the last wave of attackers had come from the surface, only to be cut down by the two-point defense weapons that Fox had managed to turn on. Beyond that, she had not been having any luck getting the ship's systems operational. In those three hours, another of her marines had died, succumbing to their injuries.

Hanna hunch-walked over to where Fox Windsail was still working. The tech had pulled off a panel and was inside the guts of the ship. There were tools spread all over the deck and inside the hatch that she had opened. From inside, Hanna could hear a constant stream of profanity that would have even made Sergent Ramirez blush.

"How are we doing?" Hanna asked, poking her head inside the crawl space. Fox was covered in wires. She had a small flashlight in her mouth and a soldering gun and a mess of wires in her hand.

"Not fucking good," Fox said. It took her a moment to register the profanity. "Excuse my language, sir," she said.

"You are excused. Though it does tell me the nature of how things are going," Hanna said. "I don't suppose you have an ETA?"

"No sir. I thought this was going to be simple, but then we blew power from the EPS grid. I pulled from life support to keep the weapons operational but that didn't work. So now I'm trying to bleed power from this ablative armor system that I just found. It's a mess here. Everything is labeled in some language that I've never seen before. Even though there is some NovaTerra basic on some of the systems, it's not enough. The tech manual inside the ship's computer is incomplete, as well." Fox looked at a loss. "It's as if whoever was flying these ships didn't develop them and was just given a crash course in basic operations. Weapons, armor, point-to-point Null space jump engines."

"I hope you didn't bleed any power from that system. A jump engine could prove to be exactly what we need to get out of here," Hanna said.

"No sir, I've left that alone. It seems to be fine. This ship looks to have been grounded because it can't run power into flight control. I think I've got a work around, but every time I cut off one wire, one path, another pops up. I don't know who designed this ship, but it's both old and extremely advanced. Some of the systems remind me of what we have on *Fury*," Fox said.

That worried Hanna. Strange ships that had old but advanced tech that resembled a Dreadstar? Very little in the way of spaceship technology survived from the Age of Chaos, aside *from* the Dreadstars. So much technology was lost during that conflict, and even more five hundred years later, during the Wayfinder Wars. Ships like *Fury* were slowly becoming a mess of hotwires and jury-rigging, because even the brightest minds didn't understand how many of their systems worked, just that they did.

"What can I give you to get us in the air faster?" Hanna asked.

"Time," Fox responded grimly.

"Of course you ask for the one thing I don't have much of," Hanna said. "Keep working and cross your fingers that whatever they are planning for us above ground takes longer than you to set up."

Just as the words were crossing the threshold of her lips, there was a rumble from above. Hanna sighed and moved over to where Ramirez was, still strapped into the interfaces controlling the ship's point defense weapons.

"What do you see, Sergeant?" Hanna asked. The ship had no windows, no way to see the outside that wasn't tied to cameras and readouts. Precious few of them were working, leaving the two-gun emplacements as their only eyes and ears.

"Nothing yet, but do you feel that?" he asked. Hanna looked around. There was another blast, and the ground started to rumble.

"They are demolishing the church above us," Hanna said.

"It's more than that. Feel the charge, Major," Ramirez said, his voice sliding into a teaching mode. The voice of a subordinate that had years and years of experience more than their commanding officer, but who didn't hold it against them.

"I don't..." she started. There was another charge. This time, she tried to feel it. It was deeper. There was a baritone to the blast. "It's in the rocks," she said.

"Aye, they are not demolishing the church above us. They are working to bring the whole damn mountain down on our heads," he said.

Hanna's mind started racing.

If they were willing to bring down the whole mountain, it meant that whatever was down here was too valuable to allow it to fall into enemy hands—*their* hands. Hanna had to wonder if they had given up on any assaults or if one more wave was going to come, to try and dislodge them before bringing it all down. One last attempt to retrieve their technology and ships before trashing it all in the name of 'if I cannot possess it, then neither can you'.

Reaching back to her time at war college, she knew what the textbooks would say. Don't attack, don't throw away any more lives. But her gut was saying something different. What they had down here was old, special, and probably existed in a finite number that they could not replicate or replace.

"Sergeant, stay frosty. I don't think they are done attacking us just yet," Hanna said.

"I agree, Major. You are learning well," he said.

"I'm glad you approve."

With that, Hanna moved back over to where Fox was working inside the ship. There was a loud pounding as she smashed her hand into something inside and followed it up with an oath against every god known to man and then some, just to be safe.

"I take it things are not going well?" Hanna asked.

"I just fried another system, but we are making progress. Let's try to not get shot. The ablative armor is offline now," Fox said.

"Grand, just grand," Hanna muttered as another blast shook the cave around them. The enemy was getting closer, getting deeper.

Meanwhile, her team was running out of time.

Hoben House, Novagrad, Claudia

"Not having to look over my shoulder to see if he is still behind me is such a relief," Claudia said to Alexander as the car drove through the city toward the Hoben estate. The sun had finally risen behind them and the city was starting to come to life. It was festival, after all, and the streets were alive with people out looking for breakfast and coffee while walking off the revelry of the night before.

Claudia didn't feel much like celebrating, though. Her plan to get out of this scrape had worked well enough, and thankfully Mister Harrison had left his two goons behind. Yes, there was going to be hell to pay for this later, but if she was able to bring Alexander in before all hell broke loose, then it would be worth it.

"Nothing about that man sat right with me. I hate that you were messed up with him," Alexander said, wrapping his arm around her.

Claudia looked up at him with big puppy dog eyes, before also glancing over at Alen Hoben, who was sitting across from them. He was a problem—really, *all* of Alexander's friends were an issue. She was sure that they were going to see through her ruse. It was why she hadn't picked any of them to be her target. Thankfully, he just looked relieved that the duel had ended in a way that didn't throw off their card team. He had a glass of whiskey in his hand and looked calm. Perhaps she had misread him, and he was just one of those friends that was happy when his friend was happy. She knew that didn't hold true for Thrase, and probably O'Hair. Both were pricklier.

"It was quite the mess. Our family ended up owing the family he works for far too much money, which is why I'm here to see if I can earn enough to help get us out from under their thumb. If we can win the tourney that would be enough to get things started," Claudia said.

It was an insipid backstory—but it was simple—and best of all, that golden retriever of a man bought it hook, line, and sinker.

"Well then, we will just have to win. After that, we can talk about the future," Alexander said, squeezing her tighter as the car came to a stop at the Hoben Estate.

The future? He has no idea, Claudia thought.

The only thing that was in his future was pain and sadness unless she was able to extract the information that she needed from him. Her liege lords wanted to know where the Confederation's faster than light research facility was, and these fools who came out to play cards were the only lead that had presented itself in the last five years. She was going to take it, and no amount of micromanaging from somebody like Mister Harrison was going to stop her from getting the credit.

"Yes, the future," she said, trying to keep the happy, relieved look on her face. The car came to a stop. Hoben reached over and tapped a few controls to set the automated carriage to put itself away before opening the door. As they exited the car, it was quickly obvious that something was wrong. The door to the house was wide open, and papers were blowing around the yard in the morning breeze.

"Bloody hell," Hoben muttered.

Claudia looked at Alexander, who looked at Hoben and then her and back at the door. Claudia had a horrible, sinking realization. The kind of realization that happens when a person sees all their hard work starting to fall apart around them, and they know it is because a critical detail has been missed; that they had underestimated somebody and were now being put on the defensive. Of course, that is why Mister Harrison's two bodyguards were not with him at the duel; the two scary men who were part of that cult who worshiped "the Awakened". He had sent them here as insurance, in case things went bad. No, that didn't seem right. This had been the plan the whole time. His performance on the green had been just that—a performance.

"What have you done?" Hoben asked, turning to Alexander and Claudia. The question was addressed to them both at the same time, though she could feel his eyes locked onto her. She was going to have to really work the innocence angle if she wanted to salvage this. Claudia needed to figure out what Mister Harrison was up to. That was going to be the only thing that could save her at this point. He was out for blood and had the resources to extract his pound of flesh *and* finish the mission.

"Why are you looking at me?" Alexander asked, still trying to catch up to what was going on.

"I wasn't," Hoben said flatly.

He turned away from them and started toward the house. Claudia and Alexander followed behind him. Inside, the place was a mess. The tables had all been shattered, papers and glass everywhere. The furniture had been torn apart, the couches and chairs shattered, the upholstery ripped open. Holes had been smashed into the walls.

Glancing around, Claudia could see shock and anger on both Alexander and Hoben's faces. All she could see was a job, an act, a staged room. Mister Harrison's men were not looking for anything, but they wanted to make it *look* like they were; like these boys had something to hide that was physically written down and not information that nobody would dare write down.

"Katie! Jeffery!" Hoben yelled into the house.

There was no response. He called their names again, and Alexander joined in. Claudia hung back. She didn't think that Harrison and his guards would kill any of the team, but she didn't want to be there if that assumption was proven wrong.

The third time Hoben yelled for his friends, a faint raspy moan emanated from one of the back rooms—O'Hair's, if she remembered correctly. Hoben took off in a dead run, crossing the distance from the main living room to the back bedrooms in a few moments, and pushed open the closed door. Claudia could hear furniture being punished out of the way, wood scratching on wood as Hoben smashed his way into the room. Alexander was right behind him. Claudia knew she had no good choice but to follow.

Inside Jeffery O'Hair's room was a disaster. All the furniture had been smashed, the large mirror had been shattered, and the rug was a mess with blood. Laying in the middle of the room, still in his nightclothes, was O'Hair. He was covered in bruises, his face already starting to puff up from where they had beat him. Worst of all, the instrument of his injuries was lying next to him—his own walking stick. Hoben ran over and helped his friend off the ground.

"Who did this to you?" Hoben asked.

"I don't know, didn't get a good look at them," O'Hair said with a wry chuckle.

Well, at least he can still make a joke, Claudia thought. People always counted out O'Hair, but she found that he saw more than they realized. It was part of why she had written him off as a potential target.

"Tell us what you remember?" Alexander said, running over and helping Hoben support their friend. There was nowhere to sit him down in this shattered room, really nowhere to sit him anywhere in the house, so they just held him up.

"They showed up shortly after the two of you left. I was just starting to get up when I heard them smashing open the door. There were I think two of them. They didn't say anything, didn't even ask me any questions. One of them muttered something about cards but that was all I heard before the world went blacker than normal," O'Hair said.

"I swear to God, Alexander," Hoben snapped as he shifted the weight of his friend over to Alexander. The gears in Alexander's mind were working, but not as fast as Hoben or Claudia. Both of whom already knew what the two men had come looking for and what they had taken.

Hoben ran out of the room into his own. From down the hallway, Claudia could hear a loud oath being uttered, and then Hoben stormed back into the room.

"They took all our bloody cards, we are..." Hoben stopped for a moment, clearly trying to not lose his temper. He took a deep breath. "Where is Katie?"

Jeffery tried to shrug but just lightly moved his shoulders. Hoben turned and pushed open the door to Katie's room. It was empty.

"They have our cards and Thrase?" Alexander said.

"That is how it looks," Hoben said, taking another breath and hardening his face. The anger pushed into the back, as he clicked on leadership mode. Claudia could see why they all followed him, and why he was not on her list to try and break.

"This is the play, and Alexander, I need you to do exactly what I say. Do you hear me?" Hoben said, the tone of his voice brokering no debate. Alexander nodded, as Hoben walked over and took the weight of O'Hair from him.

"I'm going to take Jeffery to the hospital and then contact the Tournament authorities. Get this sorted out. You two are going to find our cards," Hoben said, ice in his voice as he turned and started to walk out with Jeffery.

"Where are we supposed to start?" Alexander asked. He was moving slowly, even for him.

"Ask her," Hoben said, ending the conversation.

Security Station, Olympus Ares Research Facility, Grace

Grace stumbled into the security station, closing and locking the sliding door behind her. It wouldn't do anything if infested security tried to come for her, but it was the best that could be done on short notice.

Across the room was an armor charging station. Security body armor and her DES 9000 both thankfully had the same universal port. The only difference was how much power she was going to need. Plugging in, Grace already felt better as the weight assist systems started to come back online. The armor felt like clothing again and not heavy metal plates.

With her leg, Grace rolled a chair over and slumped down into it, like a patient at a hospital hooked up to an IV. On the other side of the small room was a rack of rifles. There were still three left. She was going to need a new one. Both bouts of full auto had turned the barrel of her last one into slag. It had cooled down, yes, but it had deformed in a way to render the weapon nonfunctional. Treating tools like that would normally have gotten her a stern talking to. Sadly—Emily rolled her eyes at Grace—all the middle managers were nowhere to be seen. Like everybody else, they were just gone, infested or worse.

The power IV connected her to the systems of the facility, and she patched into the radio and tried again to raise Essex.

"Essex, do you copy? It's Doctor Goodspeed," she said. For a moment, there was only static and then a voice came through.

"I copy, Doctor. It's good to hear your voice I was worried there when you cut me off and didn't respond." It was indeed good to hear his voice again. In the background, there was wind and clanking about.

"I was indisposed doing the laundry," Grace and Emily said at the same time, giving each other a light, resigned chuckle. He didn't need to understand what she was saying.

"I hope you got the blood out," he responded in a tone that indicated she would be telling the story later. Grace looked down at her armor. She had, in fact, gotten *none* of the blood out—acquired more, honestly.

"Essex, do we have a plan? Did you get in contact with Vardis?" she asked. There was a moment, the line was open but quiet. Again, she could hear a storm raging, and the moving of gears. Something felt off, but she put that to the back of her mind.

"I made contact. Turns out there is a second campus where all the extra power was going. It's about fifty miles away..."

"In a Caldera," Grace finished his sentence for him.

"Yes. How did—"

"Not over an open channel. Are you already outside?" she asked, the sounds of a storm getting louder.

"No. I just secured our ride. Vardis is working on getting the doors open. We can wait a little while if you are close by. Our actions have alerted the infested to our presence," Essex said.

"I'm on the garage level," Grace said, pulling up the security cameras of the huge garage.

She flicked from video feed to video feed, and then she saw Essex standing outside of a rover, the hilt of his star-steel blade in hand, his black leather coat and blond ponytail whipping in the wind. There was a rebreather over his face. He was standing still, but she knew his eyes were scanning the whole room just under the sunglasses.

"I've got just a few more minutes on this recharge and I'll head your way," she said.

"Good. We can't wait too long. The storm is getting worse outside. I'm sure you can see it," he said, looking up at the camera that Grace was using to look at him. Essex waved. Something felt off about the wave, wrong, but she couldn't put a finger on it.

"Right. Don't leave without me," she said, clicking off the line. Grace was left with the calming hum of the power station and Emily's paranoid thoughts about something feeling wrong, seeming off.

I'm not being paranoid. You know something doesn't smell right here, Emily thought from deep in her brain, chafing at being called paranoid. Grace didn't want to agree with her, didn't want her to be right...

But you know I am.

She knew.

Hallway, Dreadstar below the Citadel, Rostov

The halls were dark, but the darkness didn't matter to him. The more time Rostov spent down here, the more he could feel and tell that the Null in this ship was different. Not wrong, not infested by the Shadow, just... different. It felt cleaner, clearer, like water that had gone through a filter versus what he would have gotten from the tap outside as a child.

There was something to be said for the cloudy Null. It reminded you that there was always darkness around every bend and that everyone could be and do better. It kept you going. But this? This was *refreshing.* With every breath, he took more and more of it into his body, moving it through his blood like a kind of spiritual dialysis. Rostov could feel the pain from his years held in re-education starting to fade away. He would never lose the scars to his personality, but the ones atrophying his body were fading here.

This had to be Hyacinth's influence. That was the only thing he could think of. The Null on the surface of Icarus felt horrible, tainted by the distance from the Barrier, and the Null he remembered from his childhood before they came for him was thready, like a flavorful apple that had a grainy texture.

"Turn here!" he yelled, pointing to a bend in the hallway.

Joanna turned, getting ahead of him. Rostov watched as she turned, her ample bust swaying as she ran. As a teenager, he had never been as interested in her. He knew what he liked, but also respected that Lucas couldn't keep his infatuation a secret. But now that he had seen them, he couldn't help being distracted.

"Rostov, we don't have time for that!" Joanna snapped back at him.

Damn it. He had let his inner thoughts get too loud too above the surface. Being connected to them was strange. He welcomed the companionship again, the love that was given without condition. Though the lack of privacy, at times, was concerning. He fell in after her, keeping his eyes up on the wall following the electrical wire that would lead them to its source so they could flick it on and get the door closed, cutting off the Fellowship.

There was noise ahead of them. Rostov came to a stop next to Joanna. She had heard it as well. The two of them looked around as he furrowed his brow, reaching out with this clean Null. Five Fellowship cultists. He didn't even want to get close to them in his mind's eye. They stank of Shadow and corruption. Pulling his Null back, he looked at Joanna.

"They are everywhere," she said.

"Evil tends to do that," Rostov muttered, walking forward. "Only one thing for it.. I will charge in, break them apart and you grab anybody that tries to straggle this way."

Joanna nodded. Rostov threw his right arm out, turning on his star-steel blade, the green shining around him. Pulling in the Null, he raised his other arm up over his heart and made a fist, grabbing the energy of the air around him. He had done this as a child, always picturing turning the Null into something more than a bounce pad.

Taking another breath, Rostov flattened and pushed the energy out so that it created a large disk around his forearm. A shield of energy. A small wave of shock moved from Joanna to him. This had never worked before, yet here it was. With each step, each breath, more and more energy flowed into Rostov's body. He didn't know how long he could keep this up, but it felt amazing.

For the first time in years—perhaps even his entire life—Rostov felt powerful.

Running forward, he smashed into the line of cultists. They had seen him coming and had their blades and cudgels at the ready. Throwing his left arm to the side, the Null shield smashed into one of the men's faces, throwing him backward, blood and teeth bursting from his mouth in an arch. Time seemed to slow down for Rostov as he flicked his blade to the side, removing an arm from another man before giving him a stern look and throwing him into the wall.

A third Fellowship member ducked under his flying friend, rolling forward and then getting back to his feet and running. Rostov wasn't worried, though. Just as the cultist was getting his sword up—a rusty, serrated monstrosity—Joanna stepped out of the shadows and bisected him with a single clean heavy cut of her blade.

Rostov spun around, throwing his Null shield into the air, catching a cudgel on it. The Fellowship cultist looked at him and cocked his head to the side, pushing harder against the invisible wall of energy that was blocking his blow. Rostov pulled more Null into himself, took a step forward and pushed. The Fellowship member stumbled backward, opening himself up to a strike from Rostov's blade. It came down across his body, setting the clothing on fire.

The man didn't run. He stood there, pulling in the last few ragged breaths that his shattered body would allow before lurching forward, swinging the heavy wooden cudgel one last time. The swing had power, enough to shatter bones, but there was no speed to it, no grace. Rostov slid to the side, gliding on his feet like a dancer. The cudgel moved past him and hit the ground. The man swinging it followed a moment later, falling dead to the deck with a thud. That left only one more cultist. He shook, dropped his sword and started to run back the way he had come.

Rostov dropped his arm, letting the Null that was creating the shield fall away. He then visualized a rope and threw it out, grabbing the man and pulling him back. It took almost no physical power to pull him with the Null, and down here, the mental energy it took to create objects was almost nonexistent. He twisted his hand, letting the rope vanish. Rostov then gave the Fellowship member a solid kick to the side of the face. The man's head spun, and the cracking of his neck echoed in the hallway. The body went limp, and the fight was over.

"You can make objects with Null energy now?" Joanna asked, flicking off her blade as she walked up to Rostov.

"Apparently. Something about the energy feels different down here, like it's trying to show us abilities that we didn't have before. A deeper understanding of the Null," Rostov said.

"Be careful. You don't want to dip too deep. The Shadow is always lurking," Joanna said.

"I don't know if it is here," Rostov said. "This place is order, the Null blown to a higher level. Don't you feel it?"

"A bit. I was never the most in tune with the Null," Joanna said, a bit of disappointment in her voice.

"You were just not in tune in the way *they* wanted you to be," he said, pointing up toward the Citadel. The establishment that had made them who they were, that had taken any choice about their lives away from them, turning poor children into weapons.

"You will find your calling, your tune in the song," Rostov said. He looked back up and found the bundle of wires that Naomi had sent them to follow and started running again into the darkness.

The electrical control room was just on the other side of the bend. As Rostov turned the corner, he was greeted with the familiar sight of death and battle. There were four Guardians sprawled out on the floor, their long, Tragadi bodies a wreck of gore. They had clearly put up a hell of a fight, or the Fellowship cultists had engaged in a few moments of pure sadism. The Guardians were not alone in death. Double their number of Fellowship members were on the ground, pools of blood from where they had been shot, beaten, and stabbed surrounding them. The fighting down here was going to get so much worse before it ended. Tight spaces with nowhere to run led to people fighting to the absolute bitter end.

Inside the room, there were hundreds of buttons and levers. Some were blinking, others were dull. A few panels of glass covering bigger, scary looking buttons had been shattered. Everything was labeled and Rostov could read none of it. One thing he had to hand to the Wayfinders was that they did love to clearly mark everything.

"This is where I come in," Joanna said, stepping forward, making sure to step around the bodies that were littering the ground.

Rostov watched her look over all the text and start talking to herself. Her aura in the Null was starting to radiate around her. He took a step closer so that he was inside the field, feeling the warm embrace of education and the beauty of language. When he had been with Naomi the other night, he'd been able to feel her love of numbers and science, her ability to see it in every aspect of life. As he stood here with Joanna, he could feel the same thing, but it was a love for stories and language, the science and music of the written word. They were opposite sides of the same coin. Rostov turned from her to look back at the controls, then nodded his head to the side.

The letters and symbols that had confused him a few moments ago were starting to shift, slipping into something more recognizable, something that he could read. Slowly, he took a step out of the Null field he could see around her, while keeping his eye open on a large sign that said, "Power reset". As soon as he was clear of Joanna's influence, the symbols which were clearly legible started to fade away returning to words that he could not read.

"You want that one," Joanna said, pointing to the large switch that Rostov was looking at.

"I know," he said.

She looked at him and pouted. "How?"

"You showed me." Rostov reached out and put his hand on her shoulder. His vision pushed into her mind, lighting Joanna's eyes as she looked down at the sparkling gold cloud of Null energy that was extruding from her that only Rostov seemed to be able to see.

"You are stronger than you realize," he said, giving her a knowing nod and removing his hand.

These moments where he felt at one with the Null around him and could find something deep and heady always felt strange to Rostov, since he had spent most of his life trying to cultivate a more chaotic energy and personality. It was clearly re-education's fault, turning him into some kind of good feelings, platitude-speaking monk.

Rostov reached up, wrapping his hand around the large switch and pulled it down. The lights around them started to flicker and scream as power started to return. The vision that Naomi had given him was starting to fade, but already Rostov could see the energy flowing back through the wires heading toward where Naomi was going to need it.

"Squads four and five, secure the elevator and wait for further orders!" a radio started chirping before washing back into static.

Rostov looked down. Clipped to the rope belt of one of the dead Fellowship of the Cross cultists was a radio. Instantly he recognized it as belonging to the Host'ire Militarum, the kind that one of the sergeants would have had. He reached down and picked it up. Rostov was about to click the side to talk when Joanna put a hand over his.

"We don't know who's listening," she said. "We need to take this and get back to Lucas. If the Militarum is heading down here…" Rostov could feel her starting to worry.

"It doesn't mean anything without more information. Don't focus on the bad. Keep your eyes forward on the task at hand," Rostov said, putting the radio on his belt and starting to walk back the way they had come.

Find a few new skills and I start to sound like a damn prophecy cookie.

"I like prophecy cookies," Joanna whispered supportively.

Outside CIC, Dreadstar under the Citadel, Lucas

They wouldn't stop coming.

How many damned members are in this cult? Lucas wondered as he swung his blade again, taking another one of them down. In the distance, he could hear even more approaching. The remaining two members of the Guardians had fallen, leaving only him and Naomi. She had picked up one of their plasma pistols and was providing covering fire from behind. He was glad she wasn't in the mix. It allowed him to spin and cut and kill without regard to anybody else's safety but his own.

The lights all around them came to life with a *woosh* as the energy came screaming back like an open dam. Naomi dropped the gun, which had to be close to empty at that point, and started running toward the door controls.

"That is good timing!" Lucas yelled, as the next batch of Fellowship members came out of the darkness. They must have found a way down into the ship. There were far too many of them to be using the small elevator that the four of them had descended in. Especially since inside this group was another of those massive creatures. Lucas could see Naomi and Rostov's memories of the thing, and wasn't looking forward to facing it at all.

There was a frantic nature in Naomi's aura as she worked the wires, trying to get the door closed. A moment later, a klaxon started to go off with red lights strobing in time. From above him, the sound of groaning metal filled his ears as ages of rust started to fall away and the blast doors found a small measure of freedom from above.

Lucas pulled his hand back, sucking in some Null from around him and then pushed a wave of energy forward before leaping backward. His bust of energy smashed into the Fellowship members, knocking them around. This gave the blast door just enough time to come down, smashing into the ground with a thud. A thud that was followed by groaning and then smoke coming from the gears and the control board that Noami was near.

"Ouch, shit!" she yelled, a small bolt of electricity arching from the wall to her. He felt the twinge of electrocution on his side. It wasn't nearly enough pain to make him wince.

"Well, good luck to them getting that door open," Lucas said, spinning his blade around, cutting it off halfway through the spin and then attaching it to his belt when he was finished.

"It is at least a half meter of trillium iron. Even a star-steel blade won't cut through that—at least, not one that can be held and used as a personal weapon. Did you know," Naomi said starting to spill one of the random facts that was in her head.

Lucas tuned it out and leaned against the wall taking a breather. How many men had he just killed? Twenty, thirty, at least? Such a number would wear down even the strongest fighter.

Closing his eyes, he let the strange, pure-feeling Null of this place fill him, move through his body. Tired muscles started to feel better almost instantly. The last fleeting thought he had gotten from Rostov about the energy here feeling different was true, and it felt good.

"I see you got the door down," a voice said from the shadows.

He turned to see Joanna and Rostov walking out. Joanna ran over and wrapped her arms around him. He did the same, embracing her, relieved that she had returned. Losing her on a mission at his own orders would have been crushing, though he knew full well that could still happen one day. Danger was something they were probably going to never be far from again.

"Just in time, too. There was another one of those big sad monstrosities like what we fought up by the library. Where you got your sword," Naomi said to Rostov, giving him a nod before slumping back down to the ground, breathing heavily. He walked over and sat down next to her, placing his arm on her leg. The two of them still felt so awkward even after what had happened last night.

"I'm glad the door is between us, because I don't really want to have to fight another one of those damn things," Rostov said.

"With the four of us together, we can conquer anything that these bastards throw at us," Lucas said, stepping away from Joanna and puffing himself up so that he was tall and looked in charge. He could feel the energy that he got back from them, even though they were tired, the three of them started to feel more relieved, gaining just a bit of pep in their step.

"What now?" Joanna asked.

She walked over to the door leading down to the Combat Information Center, looking in and then pulling her head out, shaking it. Lucas figured that the room was empty. Whatever might the Guardians had, they were holding it close to the vest, and letting the four of them take care of things.

"We find Hyacinth, though I'm not sure where to start," Lucas said.

"I can handle that," Rostov said.

Before he could finish the thought, there was a pounding sound against the blast door. All four of them jumped at once, their eyes flashing as they turned to look at the door. The metal was bent and there was a massive indentation of what looked like a fist. From the other side of the door, they could hear growling, followed by cheering. Lucas felt sick to his stomach.

"What new terrors have they found for us this time?" Naomi asked. The uplifting energy that had been running through the group crashed instantly, Lucas could feel it.

"Wingarf," Rostov said quietly. "I can feel the shadow on the other side of that door, so much chaotic energy."

Just as the words left his mouth, dragging the group down more, the steel from the blast door screamed and was followed by a heartbeat thrumming. The pointed tip of the star-steel spear was punched through the door.

"I thought you said a blade couldn't get through!" Lucas yelled toward Naomi.

"It shouldn't be able to! This has to be..." she stammered.

"No matter. We stand and fight," Lucas said, trying to find the energy and courage inside of himself.

He knew that they probably didn't stand a chance against Wingarf but couldn't let those thoughts get out. The whole group looked from one to the other, starting to worry. The spearhead was pulled out of the door and thrust in at a different point. The harsh screeching of the steel shuttering made Lucas jump. His feelings were permeating through the group. He was making them scared.

"If he is still here, that means Professor Rickman failed," Naomi said. "What can we do against him that a fully trained professor and knight of over thirty years couldn't do?"

"I don't know. But we will stand and fight. It is our job to protect Hyacinth, no matter the cost. If they want to get to her, they are going to have to go through me. Stand tall. We will meet them in glory!" Lucas said.

The words came more naturally. He was able to find that reserve of energy and bravery inside of him, and push it out, share it with his friends. They were going to get through this day, he knew it.

First, they were going to have to deal with Wingarf. This was a horrible place to do it. There was not enough space to move, his spear and obvious power would be enough to cut all of them down, even if they could score a few hits. No, they needed to find a wider space somewhere that they could move around.

Another hit of the spear through the door, then two hands burst through the opening. One looked human—bigger, but human. The other appeared to be made of black, shimmering smoke that rippled and ungulated in the light. The iron was starting to give way; the door was going to be torn open.

Lucas didn't say anything. He just got everybody's attention and signaled that it was time to run.

Rover Garage, Olympus Ares Research Facility, Grace

The rover garage was massive, comparable to a fighter bay inside a Dreadstar. One of the smaller fighter bays, mind you—at least, that is what she had been told during her orientation tour. She had never seen a Dreadstar in person, as they almost never left the Confederation anymore.

For a moment, as Grace reflected on the scale of the four-story tall room, she wondered if Essex had ever seen a Dreadstar since he grew up in Confederation space.

The Citadel is in the Confederation, but it's not in *the Confederation,* Emily reminded her.

Everything in the Unaligned Planets was either relatively new or dead. There was something that scratched that part of her brain—the part that got a PhD in archelogy—when it came to how old some of the still active things in Confederation space were. Schools, cities, ships, all of it ancient. People at the universities she went to talked about it like that was a flaw, something holding them back both technologically and as a people. She saw it as an interesting quirk, something almost worth striving for in this age where the lifespan of governments and civilizations were measured in generations and not centuries.

Grace had only been to this part of the base once and as such, it took her a few minutes to get her bearing in the large space. Essex had been standing by a land vehicle, so it was going to be on the first level, and not above. Hanging above her were all manner of flying craft, from gliders to Null space-rated shuttles. Today had truly shown her just how big this base was and how insular her view of it had been thanks to security and her own obsession with research.

"Keep walking forward about a hundred yards, then you should see me," Essex said in her ear.

His voice sounded slightly panicked but also calm. Emily didn't like it, didn't trust it. Grace started to run forward. As she was running, that sound of clicking claw-on-steel filled the room. She spun her head around.

On the upper level, she saw them. A whole pack of hunters coming out of the hallways on level three. One of them jumped out, putting its claws into the wall, shredding the steel as it slowly fell to the ground level. From the other side of her, filtering into her radio, was the sound of comms traffic—station security comms traffic.

Grace picked up her pace as she ran toward where Essex had secured them a ride. That was when the first explosion went off. Turning on her rear camera, she saw hunters go flying. Looking up, she saw members of the security team reloading a rocket-propelled grenade launcher. The whole landing bay was about to become a war zone, making it the absolute last place she wanted to be.

Let them fight, just not around me, Emily thought.

Pushing power into her legs, Grace ran faster. Just ahead, she could see Essex. He was standing on the back of a small, all-terrain vehicle, behind the bed-mounted gun. He waved her forward, then pulled the trigger. Shafts of light belched from the barrel of the weapon, with a deafening sound. She could feel the wind whip past her head.

Behind her, the sounds and screams of hunters getting ripped apart filled her ears. The shock of the weapon's fire almost sent her falling to her feet. Grace stayed upright, though, bobbing to the right for a moment before she kept running, faster this time. There was no need to look behind her, she knew what was going to be there. Hunters—far more of them than she had faced in the jungle laundromat.

Essex fired again. This time, Grace was able to duck to the right to avoid the shockwave of fire as the burning rounds blew past her. Her eyes darted to the side, and she could see their lines of flight, estimates of velocity, math floating through violence. *Kinetic rounds?*

With a dive, Grace smashed into the side of the ATV, dropping to her chest she crawled under it to the other side in an instant and then was back on her feet.

"Thanks for the cover," she said, out of breath as Essex let another burst of fire go from the weapon.

"My pleasure. I love getting to shoot these old things," he said, patting the gun as he turned and jumped down, sounding like a giddy child. "You don't see bullets this far south anymore, but damned if they don't get the job done. These old Panthers are classics." It was a drastically different tone than he had spoken in even five minutes ago. "Hop up, and cover us, we are getting out of here," he said, running toward the driver's side of the Panther.

"Where is Vardis?" Grace asked, for the first time realizing that the Pa'vinti Administrator wasn't there.

"He didn't make it," Essex said matter-of-factly. There was no emotion in his voice, it was just flat. *No tears to shed for that one.*

"I'm sorry to hear that," Grace said, pulling herself into the bed of the ATV and gripping the handles of the large weapon with both hands.

There were no triggers but two thumb switches to push down. She placed her thumbs on them and scanned the whole of the landing bay with the aim assist on. There were so many targets that the software took a moment to catch up. Hunters were pouring out of every section and level, charging into the wall of fire, being put down by station security. Huge blooms of fire were erupting all over. One of the shuttles exploded. The shock wave almost knocked Grace off her feet, but she held onto the gun for dear life.

"They are going to tear this place apart," she said into her radio so that Essex, even only a few feet away from her, could hear over the destruction.

"The facility has fallen. Those infested guards are fighting a losing action," he said.

Again, his voice was flat. There was no excitement, no attempt to sound suave. The little boy who wanted to impress people with his skills seemed to have vanished, replaced with a taciturn man who had seen too much action.

"Then let's not waste any more time, Essex. Get us the fuck out of here," Grace said, holding her hand next to the mounted weapon's onboard computer so that it could interface with her auto aim system. A moment later, they were connected, and she was freely moving the weapon less with her arms and more with her eyes and the suit's computer systems.

"I trust you know where we are going!" she called back, letting out a burst of fire, the tracer rounds leaping from the weapon, ripping apart a nearing hunter. She could feel the recoil even with her suit at full power. It made her miss the plasma rifle, which she already thought was too aggressive.

"I've got some idea," Essex said back, kicking the Panther into gear.

Grace spun herself around again with the weapon. They were going to have to go another two hundred yards before clearing the landing bay. Ahead of them, Grace saw that the main doors were open. Outside, there was a massive sandstorm raging. Dark brown dirt was being kicked up and blown all around, already starting to pile up inside the landing bay, reducing visibility with each meter that they moved forward. Above the massive doors were three rows of bridges, and on each bridge was a squad of infested security guards. One of the men in the lower group pointed in their direction, getting the notice of his commander.

Grace acted quickly, her HUD locking on to the first man. She pressed the thumb switches. A burst of less than a second and he was blown apart, his chest turning into a red mist, as his limbs went flying in all directions. If they hadn't been pegged as a threat before, they were now. The squad was four men with rifles, plus a team of two who were manning a heavy proton missile battery.

At the same time she had splattered the man who saw her, they fired, the missile streaking across the landing bay and smashing into the facility. If the infested couldn't hold this position, they were going to bring it down around them. It would take a moment to reload the weapon and turn it in her direction. That was all the time she was going to get to take care of this group. If luck was on her side, the rest would be suffering from more tunnel vision and not notice their one Panther trying to make a desperate escape into the storm.

Emily started to see the faces of everybody who had wronged her, who had forced her to come here to this facility and its forever death sentence. *This is going to feel better than sex and therapy.*

"Some more speed would be nice, Essex. We have been noticed," Emily said as her HUD locked onto the two soldiers who were reloading their missile.

"I'm not holding anything back here," he yelled over the radio.

She pressed the thumb triggers again, this time a second-and-a-half burst, the number representing her ammunition supply draining shockingly fast. Both men were ripped apart. One of her rounds found the armed-but-unloaded proton missile in just the right spot. The munition exploded, ripping the bridge apart, along with the infested upon it. The plume of fire reached up, shaking the bridge above it, causing one of the infested that had taken up position there to fall.

"That'll show those bastards!" Essex yelled.

For the first time since they'd met back up, he seemed himself. The hope of getting away without the other two groups noticing them was now a faint desire. Almost instantly, a missile came streaking at them. It went wide, smashing where they had just been. The explosion was punctuated by a scream. Grace looked up at the rear camera in her helmet display. The hunters were almost on them again. The creatures had gotten past the wall of fire. There were hundreds of them, just spilling out of the facility.

"Shit, we are about to be overrun!" Grace yelled, swiveling the gun around on the bed and opening fire on the hunters, the nearest one of which had gotten its claw into the bed of the Panther. There were at least a hundred of these creatures behind them and she had less than two thousand rounds left in the weapon.

"We are almost outside," Essex yelled back to her, his words punctuated by the groaning of steel-on-steel as the great doors of the landing bay started to close. "Don't worry, that was me. We are going to make it."

Grace wasn't sure she shared his optimism, though there was little she could do but keep fighting and hope that Essex's plan worked.

There was another explosion in the middle of the horde of hunters. Blood and fire burst forth, but it didn't even slow them down. The living filled the holes of the dead. Grace sprayed fire at the edge of the Panther, taking down more of the closer hunters. They would fall, screaming, and stand back up. It took far more than even a few direct hits to take these things down, and there was no way that she could do anything more than hope to keep them off their back long enough to get outside and have the doors close behind them.

The Panther bumped as they passed from the flat steel of the landing bay to the sandy, rocky exterior of the planet. A tingle rolled through

Grace's body and, for half a second, her suit's systems flickered. They had passed through the energy field that was keeping the facility's atmosphere in and the dead world's out.

Just as the energy field had not stopped their escape, it didn't slow down the hunters. As they pushed through it, Grace could see little spikes of energy moving across the otherwise invisible shield. Quickly, the whipping sandstorm was clouding her vision. The slamming of the doors echoed through the air, and they were left with just the howling snarls of the hunters and the whipping sands.

Her suit's HUD was picking up on their heat. There were not that many left. Most had stopped short of running outside, somehow knowing they would be cut off. Grace pressed her thumb triggers again. Two more hunters went down. All she could see were the tracer rounds cutting through the sand, then a static and the quickly cooling signature on the scope. Three more quick bursts and there were only two hunters remaining. She swiveled the gun to track one that was getting close. The Panther hit a rock, knocking Grace forward. She pressed the trigger, and the weapon went off and then clicked. She had missed the hunter and was now out of ammunition.

"How do I reload this damn thing?" she yelled.

"I didn't have time to load in an extra ammo crate. If it's empty, it's empty!" Essex yelled back.

Well, that is just fucking grand, Emily thought as the two hunters got back on their tail. She was unarmed and they were coming.

"Essex, we have a problem here," she said.

"Solve it then!" he snapped back, the Panther taking a hard turn to avoid something she couldn't see.

"I'm kind of unarmed out here, and those things claws go through steel like butter," Grace said, trying not to clap back.

There was no point getting into a fight right now, nothing would be solved. For a moment, as the hunters got closer, there was no response, and then she heard the window of the Panther start to roll down. Looking over, she saw Essex stick his hand out. Clutched in it was the hilt to his star-steel blade. Grace leapt over, grabbing the cargo rail with her right hand and the hilt with her left.

"I don't know how to use one of these," she said, looking down at the Host'ire weapon. A weapon that had mysticism and legend built up around it. A weapon that most people assumed you needed powers to use without cutting your arms off. That was what she had always been taught.

"Don't worry about form, just flick it on and treat the thing like a bat," Essex said.

Crack. The sound of leather on wood, the dust of the field blooming around the point of impact. Her father's voice telling her to run, pointing toward first base. Emily gripped the blade with both hands, holding it tightly like the bats of her youth.

Planting both feet, she activated the magnetic soles of her boots. Instantly, she felt more connected to the Panther. Grace flicked the switch, and the heartbeat thrum of the blade came to life, bright yellows and oranges inside the shaft illuminated the storm, the light glancing off the flying sand. There were little impacts on the weapon as sand hit the blade and vaporized, like rain falling on a hot steel surface.

The first hunter pulled itself onto the back of the Panther, its claws cutting the mounted gun in half. Grace took a deep breath as it stalked toward her, attracted by the sound of her weapon. With a scream, she yelled, bringing the star-steel blade so that the hilt was even with her head. The hunter took another step, and she swung, the super-heated plasma smashing into the side of the creature. Its flesh caught fire, burning, turning to mush. The blade kept moving under the force of her swing until it came out the other side. She managed to stop it before the blade hit the Panther or her foot. The hunter hung there for a moment before its head and the right half of its torso slid away from the left half. The remaining hunk of hunter twitched for a moment before the wind of the storm blew it away.

"See? Easy," Essex said from the cockpit of the Panther.

"Oh yeah, I'll be a Host'ire Knight in no time," Emily said sarcastically.

"I wouldn't go that far. You are still a long way away from back flips and sky dancing," Essex retorted.

"If we survive this, you'll have to teach me," Grace said, looking around, trying to find the last hunter.

"That would piss off the order something fierce," Essex said with a chuckle.

"I take that as a yes?"

"Sure, if you can see the Null. Now we just need to survive."

"Just one more," Grace said.

She scanned the area around the Panther. It had to be out there. These things didn't give up. Could they mask their body heat? Or maybe the storm had consumed it? She didn't know and didn't like it. Taking a step forward, Grace knelt and started banging her hand on the side of the Panther's bed. It was enough to be louder than the quiet electric engine.

Thump. Thump. Thump.

"Come on, you son of a bitch, where are you?" she yelled.

There was a sound of crunching from under the Panther. Grace looked down and saw the extra heat coming from *below* her. Then the claws punched up through the steel and the base of the machine gun's mounting. Grace swung the star-steel wildly, slicing off the top of the claws that had punched through the truck bed. As she finished the swiping motion, she brought the energy blade down, punching it right through the truck. The hunter screamed as she pulled the blade back toward her, leaving a trail of melted metal and flesh. The heat signature faded, and all that was left was the glow of the star-steel blade.

Grace flicked it off and just stood there for a moment, looking out at the vast storm that was all around her.

"Is it done?"

"Yeah, it's done. Roll a window down for me. We have a secret party to crash."

Lord Admiral's Quarters, Fury, Cassandra

Cassandra could hear the winds of the storm smashing into the hull of the ship, the small micro asteroids and space dust dancing off the hull. All of this was punctuated by a clap of something that sounded like thunder, the energy of far-off plasma explosions being turned into sound as the energy waves moved through the ship.

Long ago, before she had even started training to command a Dreadstar, Cassandra had been visiting a relative, a distant cousin who had married into a planet lord family. One night, while she was trying to sleep, a storm rolled in. Sounds that she had only read about echoed through the house. She stayed up most of the night, sitting at the window, watching the rain lash the glass and picturing the trees blowing between lightning strikes. It was the only time in her sixty-five years that Cassandra Cordova had seen rain, and now here she was, getting the same sensation again, but in a way that was uniquely her own.

I should record these, she thought, taking out a small recorder. The need to record interesting sounds had not crossed her mind in years. Even before the music had left her, she had stopped collecting sounds. It was something that she did as a child, when she wanted to just create art, before the needs of family had taken hold. She remembered those days fondly. Her father had allowed her to be a child, to find herself, before he imprinted responsibility and duty upon her.

It was a luxury she had not afforded her own children.

Her father, the late Lord-Admiral Howard Cordova, had been dead now for almost forty years. Cassandra walked away from the recorder, letting it go, and sat down on her couch. Glancing up, there was another thirty minutes before she had to be back in Combat to relieve Captain Rackland. She wouldn't have left the heart of her ship, except both Erik and the Captain insisted. The two of them were threatening to bring in her brother, who, as the ship's surgeon, could remove her from command. Rackland had been her father's attendant, following him everywhere, doing paperwork, being groomed for command. All that Cassandra had left of her father were memories and the stations of office.

She looked down at her hand to the signet ring, the three heads of the chimera wrapped around a yellow diamond. The golden lion's head was in the center, flanked by a silver goat and bronze dragon. Wings of black gold wrapped around the band. The ring was old, older than House Cordova. The base of the ring and the stone had belonged to the previous lords of the Dreadstar *Fury*, a family whose name had been lost to time. Cassandra didn't love the ring; it was too big and clunky. She wasn't sure why today was the day she had picked to put it on, but there it was on her finger.

Prepare to jump through the gate, Cassandra.

Tiberius's voice was always in her head, like he had never left. She had read about people seeing their dead loved ones, and as a girl, had consumed ghost stories like they were going out of style. But now that she was older and had more dead relations than living ones, she knew that those voices were just her own thoughts and insecurities made manifest, waking dreams that were out to haunt her.

Through the Gate, Jump Prep. The two tracks that had been occupying her mind, that were the same, but not. What was her mind trying to tell her? The whole last day she had been walking around with that nagging feeling that there was something she was forgetting, something she *had* forgotten. A memory, a fact, clawing deep from within her mind to escape, to make its presence known.

Cassandra took off the ring and started to roll it around in her hand, to look at the heads, the craftsmanship. Whatever had been there before was long gone, resculpted, replaced.

Why go to all that trouble? she asked herself in Tiberius's voice. It was a question she didn't have an answer to.

As she was rolling the ring around in her hand, she noticed something she hadn't seen before, or... was it something she just didn't remember seeing? Sitting in her room, listening to the rain, Cassandra was starting to question what she knew and didn't know.

Tick marks. There were small hashmarks scratched into the band. While she didn't remember them, she recognized what they were instantly. Musical notations, shorthand time and notes. A shorthand that she had learned as a child, that was created by her music instructor.

The locks are opening.

"Yes, yes, Tiberius," she said. Looking at the shorthand, Cassandra already knew what it was going to sound like, but she needed to hear it, needed to feel it.

Walking over to the piano, she opened the lid and sat down. She placed the ring where sheet music went, angled so that the light caught the marks. Her fingers trembled as she held them over the ivory keys. She made little fists, cracking the joints before lightly putting her hands in place.

Then she started to play.

It was as she suspected. The tune was "Though the Gate". It was "Jump Prep". Not exactly like them, but the same basic musical idea. This was the original she knew, the leitmotif she didn't know she had written. This was her work, of that Cassandra was sure. Nobody else who had access to that ring could have made those marks. It distressed her that she didn't remember writing it, didn't remember the marks, hadn't even really seen them for the last four decades.

Memory.

She was close, the memory burrowed deep in her brain now clawing full speed, trying to escape. She had handed it a shovel and now it was time to find out where it was going to exit and meet it halfway.

She closed the piano and walked back over to the couch. Sitting down, she brought up her master index of tracks that she had written over the years. She had started seriously composing at age fifteen, ten years before her father had died and she had taken over as Lord Cordova. That was the place to start. She typed in the date ranges to the holographic display and hundreds of track names presented themselves. The years right before and after she had ascended to command were the most prolific she had ever known. Everything was an inspiration, everything ended with a new track. She had been writing clean, polished work on the fly.

There was a track called "Last Wish". She remembered writing it shortly before her father had passed. They had known it was coming—cancer. She started playing it, and that was when she heard it, deep within the mix. Keys on the piano, tapping out the same idea. It had to do with her father, something he wanted to tell her—or was it something she wanted to tell herself, but couldn't write down?

"Icon passing" was the next track she clicked on. Cassandra remembered it well, a dirge she had written for the funeral of Lord-Admiral Howard Cordova. As it played out, Cassandra started to question if she did, in fact, remember this music; music that she had written. It was there again, in a different key, and played with vastly different instruments than her usual, with vocals. Cassandra almost never used vocals in her music. How was her father connected to the idea of jumping through the Null?

Memory.

"Yes, it's my memory, my love," Cassandra said to the voice.

Then she stopped. Scrolling back past "Last Wish", she noticed that there was a gap of three weeks. It was impossible to think that she had taken three whole weeks and written nothing, not when she was logging four tracks a week during that time.

Memory.

These were the public archives she was looking through right now. The archive of her work that everybody could see. With a flick of the wrist, she closed the file. A few finger swipes later and she pulled up her personal files, unreleased tracks, music that she had been riffing on, stuff that was not worthy of being released, or things that hurt too much to release. Flipping though she went back, back to those three weeks. There was only one track from that time...

"Memory".

Cassandra clicked on it, and the file came up and then requested authorization. This was it. She was so close, she could feel it. She pressed her thumb to the holographic display and a moment later, the song started to play. It was what was on the ring, it was the original. Memories started to come flooding back. Flashes of her father; a hanging man; sparking wires; tapping, tapping in the dark; a deep feeling of salvation.

A single tear ran down her cheek.

The ship shook again, but this felt different. It wasn't another astrometrological hit.

"Lord-Admiral to the CIC," Captain Rackland's voice came through her comm. Cassandra turned off the music and answered the call.

"I shall be there presently, Captain." She cut off the comm before he could say anything else. Cassandra stood up with renewed purpose. She placed the signet ring on her finger and walked out of the room.

She reached the Combat Information Center a minute later, the ship still shaking and rocking. She entered from the lower entrance as to reach the glass table straight away. Standing around the table already were Captain Rackland and Erik.

"Report, Captain," she said.

"They are shooting into the storm, and it is agitating everything. We are not going to find any more respite here. We are having to shunt power to shielding and away from the engines. It gets worse. We slipped a Hawkeye out to get a reading. The Lagrange fleet is now two hours out. Once they arrive, this will provide no protection," Rackland said, drawing out the grim situation on the glass board.

Looking at what was in front of her, the plan came together. Lord-Admiral Cassandra Cordova, the head of her house, and commander of the Dreadstar *Fury*, knew what she had to do. It had returned.

"Captain, prepare the ship for action, all weapons. We are going to need to perform a holding action outside the storm," she said. Rackland raised a finger to say something, and she cut him off with a quick wave of her hand.

"I will explain everything later, Captain. Just have the ship ready. Commander," she said turning to her son. "Order Bella to have the entire wing on standby and ready to launch. If it can fly, find a warm body to put in it. Then follow me."

With that, Cassandra placed her hand on the hilt of her sword and walked away with purpose, Erik in tow, giving orders into his cravat.

Outside, Grace

Grace took a deep breath and pulled off her helmet. Instantly, the cold air of the Panther's climate control system hit her face. It felt wonderful, the gooseflesh forming where perspiration was dripping from her damp, matted black hair. After spending so long inside the stuffy helmet, it was good to breathe different fake air. The chill was an added bonus.

"Is there any water in here?" she asked, turning to Essex. He was looking forward, his glasses off, one hand on the wheel and another outstretched. His lower jaw was quivering slightly right on the edge of teeth chattering.

Is he driving by magic? Emily wondered, almost dismissively.

This thing has a navigation system.

Grace could feel Emily's nonexistent eyes rolling into the back of her head. Grace wasn't sure what to do. If he was navigating with his mind, then disturbing him would not be a good idea. Still, she could feel her mouth starting to dry out, the aftertaste of exertion forming around her teeth. She started looking around. The cabin of the Panther wasn't big, with only two chairs and a small storage compartment behind her. Loosening her belt, Grace started to turn to see what was in the back.

Just poke him once. If he really is in a trance, it won't matter. I want to see what happens, Emily thought at her almost impishly.

"The water is behind me. Ration bars behind you," Essex said calmly, not moving his eyes from the windshield, which was still being pelted by sand to the point that it almost sounded like rain.

"Thanks. You want one?" Grace asked. She flicked open the container behind the driver's seat and pulled out a pouch of water.

"I'm good. Thank you, though," Essex said, scrunching his hand into a fist and cracking his knuckles.

"Suit yourself," Emily said. Grace grabbed a second pouch of water before closing the container. Sliding back into her seat, she set the extra down on the console between the two seats.

"Just in case," she said, patting the sack of water.

Pulling the tab on her pouch, Grace started to drink. The water wasn't cold, but that didn't matter. She was so thirsty that anything liquid was heaven at this point. It only took her a minute to finish the whole pouch.

"Thanks," Essex said after a moment, like he had to truly consider her actions, not in a rude way. No, it was the kind of thank you that was said by a person who was not used to others doing nice things for them. Not used to people looking out for their well-being when they could just focus on themselves.

"You're welcome," Grace said.

Wounded puppy incoming, Emily thought with not a small amount of disgust. Grace hated the fact that she agreed.

"People don't usually look out for me; haven't, not in a long time. Usually, I'm the one who had to be strong—me or Lucas. He was always better at it than I was..." Essex said, before he trailed off, lost in a memory. The Panther bumped along as the two of them sat in silence for a while.

"What happened to Vardis?" Grace asked.

"I couldn't protect him, just like I couldn't protect her..."

His voice trailed off again. Something had come over him. Emily groaned deep in the back of Grace's mind before reaching over and waving her hand in front of Essex's face. His head snapped, the concentration broken. He brought the Panther to a stop.

"Are you in there?" Emily asked.

Essex was quiet for a moment, a moment longer than was comfortable. Emily was on the edge of what she would trust and even Grace—sweet, trusting Grace—was getting close to being done.

"Yeah, I'm here. Sorry, trying to navigate with the Null takes it out of me," Essex said, putting his hand down and putting his glasses back on. "You were asking about Vardis." He picked up the pouch of water and ripped it open.

"Yes, you said he was opening the door," Emily said, taking over. Grace would never be able to push enough for this.

"We were on the comm when I heard plasma fire and screaming, before everything went dead. I couldn't raise him again. I assume the infested got him. He knew... You were right," Essex said quietly.

"I knew that bastard was holding back on us. What did he know? Where are we going?" Emily asked. She had an idea, but wanted to see what Essex knew, what he would tell her.

"There is a second base. Olympus Ares was just a support base, a place where they could do dangerous research well away from the main facility. Vardis didn't tell me much about what he found out about this place, just that it was called the Black Caldara," Essex said.

"That name doesn't sound ominous at all," Emily muttered. So, he didn't know that much, but did confirm that this base was where the city she saw Varagoth in was, and that they were indeed on the planet she was seeing in her visions.

"They do seem to have a flair for the dramatic. You would think they were the Host'ire," Essex muttered.

"Well then, I want my thirty silver crypto credits," Emily said pointedly.

Essex pulled in a breath and didn't say anything, didn't breathe out. He was still lost again, in thought and trauma. Emily knew a few things about trauma in your past making a mess of the present.

You did that on purpose, Grace thought. Emily didn't respond. She just watched Essex with curiosity, like he was an experiment.

"I was a happy child. We lived on some little planet in the Confederation—I couldn't tell you its name. I started moving things with my mind, innocently at first; wasn't even aware I was doing it. But it was enough to get people's attention. I don't know who called it in; could have been a teacher, could have been my parents. At this point, it doesn't matter anymore.

"When the ambassadors come for you, there is no saying no. Confederation law is very clear on this. All Null-sensitive children belong to the Host'ire. Out here, the laws are less draconian, which is why the order doesn't usually leave Confederation space. They came. I screamed as the two knights grabbed me. The ambassador put the pouch of coins in my father's hand, and he and my mother just watched me go. They didn't turn around, didn't put up a fight. And why would they? We were poor and thirty silver crypto credits was more money than they were going to see in a lifetime.

"They threw us on the ship, and everybody broke into two groups. The strong and the weak. There were so many bigger kids than me, but I was scrappy," Essex said, pausing to finish his water.

"Is that where you met her?" Emily asked. No detail was lost on her. She was going to understand this man that she was shackled to.

"Hyacinth? Yes. We were connected for many years. I was always protecting her. At the basic schools, it was easy. Once we went to the Citadel, though, that... is a whole different story," he said.

Essex put down the empty water pouch and turned the Panther on again and started driving. He didn't say anything else; didn't look at Grace or put his hand out. He seemed to know where they were going—or was just going to drive them off a cliff instead of talking about his past.

You would do nothing different if he wanted to know about your time with the Rydassian Front, or Patrick, Grace thought at Emily, who was still watching Essex like he was a lizard in a cage. Profanity came from Emily as she faded back the memoires of her past consuming her. Grace regained control.

He was broken—who wasn't, these days? Grace didn't press anymore. She had learned more than she knew before and was starting to get a better understanding of Essex. He was still that little boy who had been stolen from his parents all those years ago. Always looking for some kind of family, somebody that he could protect from what happened to him. Hyacinth, Lucas, had he mentioned any other names? Now, she was just another broken bird that he was going to try and protect.

He just wasn't aware of how broken—or dangerous—this little bird was.

They drove in silence for another twenty minutes before the storm started to fade away. The Panther was on a road. All around them were the remains of buildings, crumpled skeletons of rusted steel and degrading stone. The civilization that had called this place home was long gone. Grace wasn't able to focus on the ruins for more than a moment before she saw the glass spire starting to burst forth from the horizon. It was massive. They were still miles away and already it was dominating the skyline. The single building stood like a shard of glass thrown from space and smashed into the ground.

As they kept driving, Grace could see where the ground rose up, forming the edge of the impact crater, the edge of the caldera that she had seen in her visions. This was where Varagoth was, where the answers would be. This shard of glass was inside the caldera, making its size even more impressive.

Movement from the ruined city caught Grace's attention. From behind broken buildings, two Panthers drove out. Each of them had a man stationed on their rear gun. The uniforms consisted of rust red fatigues and a chest plate. There was a crest on the plate, an eagle holding arrows in both talons. She didn't recognize it. Essex slowed down as the two Panthers flanked them.

Oh no, Emily thought.

"Panther Six Two, what is your destination?" a metallic voice coming over the radio asked.

"This is Panther Six Two. I've got the package we extracted from Olympus Ares," Essex said back calmly.

"You son of a bitch," Emily said, reaching out to grab the wheel. Essex's hand was wrapped around her wrist before she was done even forming the thought about what to do once she grabbed the wheel.

"I didn't have a choice," Essex said, turning to look at her. His sunglasses slipped down the bridge of his nose, and she could lightly see a small, inky shadow floating behind his cornea.

"Bullshit, we always have a choice. You didn't have to become one of the people who abused you, who abused Hyacinth," Emily spat out.

"Whatever happens, just know that I'm sorry," Essex said, his hand snapping her wrist so that it smashed into her face.

Mess Hall, Dreadstar below the Citadel, Joanna

The blood was everywhere. Lucas was on the ground, the wound in his chest huge. His eyes were big, looking up at her filled with sadness and fear.

Joanna popped back to reality, jolting as her vision cleared, seeing the large room they were in. It hadn't taken much running for them to find an old mess hall. There were long tables all throughout the room and a window leading into a kitchen that hadn't seen a chef in living memory. Outside, they could hear the screams and yelling of the Fellowship cultists and the lumbering steps of Wingarf. They had only seen the smoking hand made of shadow, but it was enough for Joanna to know he had been changed.

There was always talk at the Khorn'tosh Academy about Host'ire who got too powerful, who dug too deep into the Null, only to be seduced by the Shadow and its easy power. They never realized until it was too late just how purely chaotic the energy was; how uncontrollable it was, even for somebody with decades of training. The Host'ire were taught how to control the Null, which was order, the space between. The Shadow was chaos, the space beyond. She didn't fully understand it, having never been able to dig deep enough to find it. She hadn't even desired power enough to go looking for it.

What would I have even done with that kind of power? Flay lazy nobles who couldn't be bothered to write their own papers?

Whatever it truly was, it had changed Wingarf and defeated Professor Rickman. Now it was coming for them, and she wasn't sure that their hasty plan was going to be enough to stop it. Naomi was on the other side of the room, tinkering with a fuse box that she had found. Rostov had climbed up into a set of rafters where lights hung.

This ship was a display of excess, in places. The hanging lights in this room allowed it to double for a dance hall or theater venue. She was standing by the doors. Naomi had provided her with a thermal welding strip, one of the many tools she kept tucked away in her jacket. Lucas—brave, beautiful Lucas—stood in the middle of the room, his glasses and coat off, his blade drawn, determination in his eyes. She felt a sense of relief and calm coming from him, that aura of leadership that he always had.

The image of Lucas dead flashed in her eyes again. Joanna tried to scream but no sound came forth. She was back, her body shuttered, and her breath was ragged. She looked over at Lucas standing there, ready, willing to die to protect them. Joanna wanted to run out to him, to tell him what she had seen. It wouldn't do any good and she knew it. He had committed to this plan and there was no changing it, no going back. They were going to put an end to Wingarf or die trying.

Joanna was starting to feel pretty sure that it was going to be them that would do the dying, even if everything went to plan. It was a simple plan, but that would be why he wouldn't see it coming. Nobody was ever looking for the simple plan, they always assumed that everything in life was more complex than it actually was. The real world was simple, cruel, and stupid.

"I see the Knight-Commander has picked a place to die!" Wingarf's voice came from the hallway, punctuated by a horrible backup chorus of laughter and screeching. Everything about the Fellowship of the Cross was the stuff of nightmares.

"I've picked a place for somebody to die," Lucas said, holding his ground, refusing to be intimidated. She could feel it in him, though. Whatever it was that Wingarf looked like right now was a horror show.

The floor started to shake as the enraged Shadow-infused, former Master-at-Arms started running forward. Joanna took a breath. She was ready, the thermal bonding tape in her hands. This was ridiculous, like something that would have been in one of the half-credit novels she read as a child. The heroes setting up a trap for the monster. They fight and, in the end, the main hero stands above the vanquished body of the monster and kisses the girl. That wasn't life, she couldn't help but keep seeing the cruelties of life, and that was Lucas dead on the ground, covered in blood, and her screaming.

Horror burst through the door. Joanna didn't have a chance to process what she was seeing, there was a job to get done. As soon as Wingarf was in the room, she leaped from the wall and closed the door, running the thermal bonding strip across it, melting the steel and forming a strong bond. Naomi had said it wouldn't hold forever, but hopefully long enough for them to get their work done. It was made to mend, not fix.

Her job done, Joanna spun around and saw the horror that had entered the room. Wingarf had grown in size, standing at least seven feet tall. His arm had regrown, changed into something made of shadow and smoke. From his shoulders sprouted two massive blade wings, but it was his head the disturbed her to the core. His eyes were gone, ripped free, replaced only by a red glowing energy. His mouth had been ripped wide open, making room for new rows of sharp teeth already covered in gore. In his hand, he still held the star-steel spear. Now that he had both hands existing in the physical world again, he was able to whip and twist the implement around with an inhuman speed.

Lucas was holding his own, dancing and darting out of the way, doing his best to not have to parry or engage with the weapon at all. Watching the fight, Joanna could feel the power and force that was behind the spear with each swing that Wingarf made. It was extremely fast and full of power, his whole body being used to give it propulsion.

Lucas jumped, created a Null pad, and pushed himself even farther so that he was above Wingarf and then landed behind him, swiping out with his blade, hitting the tips of Wingarf's wings. Only smoke and ash met his blade as the energy passed right through and the unnatural feathers reformed.

Joanna looked up. Rostov was hanging in the rafters. He had his blade ready, the light array hanging all around him. He looked down at Joanna, and she back at him. Both of them shared a moment of worry about what might come. But he was ready. Now everything was hanging on Naomi's ability to work wonders with electricity. It is a solid plan. It *would* work. Joanna had to keep telling herself that because otherwise, she would give into fear, and that was not what they needed right now. In the same room together, they were all far too connected for one of them to bleed negative emotions into the other three. Breathing in, Joanna steeled away her fear.

"Stop dancing around like coward and face me!" Wingarf bellowed, whipping his new forked tongue across his jagged teeth and hissing.

"I would expect a man of your experience to be able to hit me," Lucas said, ducking a swing and rolling to the side. "Because right now, you are fighting like the basic knight that you are. Unable to stand up in real combat to a Commander. Hell, I don't even think you could compete with a Knight-Scout."

Wingarf screamed at that insult. His honor, what little of it there might have ever been, was impugned by assuming he was a worse fighter than knights who primarily used sniper rifles and didn't even have to qualify with a blade.

"When I get ahold of you, child, I shall rip you limb from limb and feed you to my followers," Wingarf said, swinging—but again, failing to make impact as Lucas jumped up, almost to the rafters, before turning to the side and pulling himself forward on a bar of pure Null. He was moving like a gymnast, and Joanna couldn't take her eyes off him, even though deep down, she knew how this was all going to end.

I'm ready! Just get him under the lights!

They could all hear Naomi calling to them. Joanna looked over and could see her shoving together two wires, electricity arching across them. Joanna then swiveled her head to see that Lucas and Wingarf had moved away from the center of the room, almost halfway toward the far wall. Well outside of their kill box. She had to do something. Lucas was looking the other way. This was going to be her only chance to make a difference. If she looked into his eyes, he would know and implore her to stop. That wasn't something she could do today.

"Hey asshole!" she yelled, running into the center of the room, igniting her blade, it's heartbeat thrum echoing as the energy crackled to life.

Wingarf spun his head around, giving her a horrible, tooth filled grin. The Shadow-damned creature turned its entire body and started moving toward Joanna at a slow methodical pace, spinning its spear, pointing it toward her. She saw the vibrating tip, the crackling energy moving across the head. It wasn't a pure energy weapon like their blades, but a hybrid. That was when she saw that knicks had been made in the spear head, taking it from a pure sharp implement to a serrated nightmare, lighting cascading across jagged twisted teeth.

Joanna, no! Lucas's voice rang out in her mind as she felt frozen by the approaching creature. As the fear was about to take her, she felt calming energy being pushed forward toward her from Lucas. Her heart slowed and her breathing regulated.

Then there was a scream. The kind of scream that one had to dig into the deep dark places of their soul to find, the kind of feral scream that is usually associated with parents who must defend their children.

Wingarf turned and Joanna could see Lucas running forward, his blade held high over his head, a look of pure anger on his face. The calm leaping and jumping phase had passed. She was in danger and he was coming to save her, like he said he would. Lucas jumped, pushing forward, spinning in the air like a corkscrew, his blade held forward. Wingarf raised his spear to block it. The blade impacted and Lucas spun around it, kicking the barrier-spawned creature in the face. Lucas hit the ground and spun around again, his blade on a deadly arch toward Wingarf's leg. The green energy cleanly cut through Wingarf's calf, exiting on the other side like there had been nothing in its way.

Wingarf screamed in pain, stomping back, shadow pouring from the wound like blood. The inky blackness spilled out like liquid unencumbered by gravity. Splitting, half went up his leg, the other half down it, globbing and creating tendrils of darkness. There was a high-pitched echo as the goop tightened its clasp around Wingarf's lower leg, sinking in, making it look like his not-so-missing arm.

Lucas was on his feet again, charging forward, trying to keep Wingarf on his back foot, push him toward where Joanna was, back into their kill box. His eyes glanced up at Rostov for just a split second. She saw it, and so did Wingarf. He started to chuckle as their simple, stupid plan locked into place for him. That was the end of it. If he knew what was coming, then they wouldn't be able to do anything about it.

"Lights? You were going to try and crush me with lights? An idea only children would have. I am so tired of having to beat stupid children," Wingarf growled as his wings extended to their full length, and he raised up on his toes, arms held to his side. With a flap, he started to rise. Lucas and Joanna, at the same time, ran toward him, leaping. Each of them grabbed a leg and pulled, trying to take the creature down, keep him earth bound. Wingarf's flight wasn't natural, and he kept floating.

Joanna pulled her blade, keeping it turned off until the hilt was right next to Wingarf's pelvis and groin before clicking it on. The yellow blade burst through his nether regions, coming out the other side. She pulled down, freeing her weapon and clicking it off before it hit her or Lucas. Burning black bile came pouring from the wound.

Wingarf screamed as more of the same shadowy globules came from his ruined genitals. Kicking, he threw Joanna to the ground. As her back hit the ground hard, Joanna saw Lucas climbing up Wingarf, a wash of that black goo hitting him as he got face-to-face with the creature.

"Those children are dead. You saw to that. What remains are the weapons you forged,"

Joanna was able to see what was about to happen, but it was too late. Just as Lucas was bringing his blade back to strike the killing blow, Wingarf was doing the same with his spear. Both of them thrust at the same time, Lucas's green blade cutting in and down, just as the star-steel spear ripped through Lucas's chest. There was a flower bloom of blood as the spear burst out the other end, burning flesh hanging from the teeth of the blade. Pain wracked through Joanna, along with fear, and... contentment?

Lucas looked over at her and smiled.

Wingarf threw the spear and Lucas to the side as he kept flying up.

Joanna didn't hear herself screaming as she ran toward his body, nor did she hear Rostov whooping with rage and joy as he rode the lights down on top of Wingarf.

She heard none of this as the world went dark.

EPISODE VIII:
Wayfinder

A place between Life and Death, Lucas

There was pain in his chest. So much pain that he almost couldn't feel it anymore. Almost. He shouldn't have been able to feel anything at all. The small, rational section of his brain was screaming, confused, panicking. The rest of his mind was just sitting in the dark, living with the pain, existing in the feeling. There was nothing else but blackness and pain. No, wait... There *was* something, creeping in the background, lurking near the cracks of his mind. A single vision and sound. Was it a face? A scream? Lucas wasn't sure. He couldn't perceive what it was, wasn't sure that he had the ability.

His chest, the pain was in his chest. He tried to look down, but there was no *down* here; no up, just a void. He knew where the pain was coming from, but couldn't see it, couldn't inspect it. He tried to touch what had to have been a wound, but there were no hands. Again, he could feel his arms, knew they were there, but could not command them to do anything.

Start smaller, a voice said. It wasn't his voice, but it was in his mind like thoughts.

Reaching out, Lucas could see his fingers in his mind, could feel them floating in the void, like being in a pool that existed without water. There was resistance, something holding him up. This wasn't space, wasn't the cold vacuum that he was familiar with; comfortable in. Still, he could see them, could feel them, and with a push of his mind, a push through the pain in his chest, he was able to move one of them. His right pinky was braver than the rest of them, ready and willing to answer the call. One by one, his fingers started to move, started to answer him. The feeling started to return, something other than the pain in his chest.

He didn't know how long he existed in pain, in darkness. All he knew was that it was long enough for the pain to fade into the background, to become something that he had stopped thinking about and could only feel when he willed himself to feel it. Now that he had control of his arms, he reached for his chest, reached to feel what was causing him so much pain. This would be what cracked the void so that he could see the face, the scream that was just on the edge of his vision, of his existence.

The wound was ragged, gaping, moist with gore and viscera. Lucas still couldn't see it, couldn't see anything. He knew enough about the human body and what weapons did to it to know he should be dead. He *was* dead. There was no movement from his chest, no breath, no pumping blood; already, the meat was cold. No doubt about it, he was dead. Whatever *this* was… It was some kind of persistence on his mind's part. Maybe there was something after death. As interesting as that was, Lucas was already starting to remember again what had happened, where he had been and how he needed to get back.

Open your eyes, the voice that wasn't his own said again. Still in his head, still *pretending* to be his own. The lids of his eyes didn't want to open, didn't want to show him what was beyond. For the first time in a long time, Lucas was scared. Yes, he always had a healthy fear of the dangerous things he was doing, but never a fear that kept him from *doing* them; from doing his job. Now, though, the last thing he wanted to do was open his eyes and see what the great beyond looked like. Scared to see that there might be nothing—or worse, the banality of more existence.

It took effort, but Lucas opened his eyes to see what was beyond. For a moment, it nearly broke him. He was standing on rocky ground, not red like Icarus, but a deep brown, a thick layer of soil, that was full of growing life. Vines and bushes, even a few small trees. Worms, caterpillars, centipedes, and snakes were slithering around. Everything here had either no legs or far too many legs. In the distance, there was a cliff face and a waterfall with bright blue water cascading down into nothingness.

Lucas was near the edge, because this wasn't a new world, but a floating chuck of a world. All around, the sky was a storming cloud of red and orange, tinged with streaks of blue and green. In the close distance, he was able to see other floating platforms, some which were much smaller than the one he was standing on. Others, from the looks of them, could almost be their own world, so big that other smaller platforms were orbiting them. Rivers cascaded into nothingness, and vines and plant life grew off the side and around the jagged stone bottoms that had once been the rocky crust of this long-broken world. All across the platforms, overgrown by the vastness of nature, Lucas could see the bones of civilization. The raw steel of buildings, the outlines of roads.

People had lived here once.

Quickly, those things faded away from his mind, from his field of view. The red sky was dominated by a massive tower of pure, shimmering onyx. It was far in the distance, which only added to its size and grandeur. Even at this distance, which Lucas figured was thousands of miles, he could see small ships flying about. They were red—shaped like arrowheads—only visible when they flew in front of this onyx tower. The rest of the time, they blended into the clouds and storms.

Where am I?

The last thing he remembered before the darkness was having a star-steel spear rammed through his chest. The pain, the expiration, the nothingness of it all. He was dead. That he knew for sure. There was no way he had survived being run through like that. It didn't matter, because he had got Wingarf as well—he also knew that for sure. Even now, Lucas could picture his blade going through the abomination's chest and ripping down.

If I'm dead, then... His mind started racing. Those clouds were extremely familiar. The reds and orange mixed with blue and green highlights.

The Barrier. He was on the other side. He had crossed over. This place didn't feel like Heaven—or whatever Heaven was supposed to feel like. At the same time, Lucas was sure this was not Hell. Shattered, broken, filled with crawling creatures, yes, but not Hell. He wasn't sure how he knew that, but deep down, he knew that this place did not fit what the Host'ire or the Fellowship of the Cross said about it.

No, this was its own place. Removed from that basic diametric opposition of the afterlife. It just was, and people *lived* here. Were they people? Lucas didn't know, but they had ships, so they were at least spacefaring. Was this considered space? He didn't see anything to discount the notion—or support it.

Tentatively, Lucas took a step forward, slowly raising his foot and putting it down. Gauging the gravity in this place, reaching back to his experience in zero-G combat. It wasn't quite NovaTerra standard, but close. It shouldn't be, though. It should be less. There was nothing here to give it gravity. Unless there was something below, creating an orbit. Or could that onyx tower, thousands of miles away, have enough mass to be creating a gravitational pull? So many questions.

Taking a deep breath, he tasted the air. There was nothing off about it. He had learned years ago how to detect when the air in a chamber was starting to go bad by taste alone. You could taste bad air before it started to affect your mind.

The Null. Was it here? Lucas attempted to reach out for it. There was nothing. He suddenly felt empty. Holding his hand out, it was trembling, as he reached for something that wasn't there; that *should* have been there. If this was where he thought, then this place should be flooded with Null energy. They could feel it so acutely on Icarus. Why couldn't he feel it here?

Because he was dead.

Finally, Lucas looked down at his chest, acknowledging what he didn't want to think about. What he didn't want to have to admit. His own mortality, he was dead, that this was the end, some lonely, limbo end. The wound was clear as day. His shirt and armor ripped apart, the ruin of his chest laid bare. Blood was everywhere. Yet he could feel his heart pumping. If he moved his head to just the right angle, he could see that fist-sized muscle working, still pumping, even though he clearly had already bled out all the blood that he had.

Wake up, you can't be dead. Not when we are this close.

The voice was louder now. Lucas looked up and a flash of light was moving across the sky in front of him. On the other side, for the sporadic moments, it was visible. He could see a face. The tear almost looked like an eye that was going in and out of consciousness. The voice, feminine, was familiar. It calmed him, there was love in it.

Joanna.

But what did it matter? He was dead. They were going to have to go on without him. Joanna would get them to Hyacinth and solve whatever it was that she wanted from them.

I said wake up, damn it!

The voice was louder, more insistent. It wasn't going to matter, he was dead. Lucas looked down just to confirm that fact, to face it once again, before turning away and walking into the jungle so that he could understand death.

The wound was starting to heal. Already, the flesh was pulling back together. He couldn't see his heart, but could feel it pumping. Quickly, he put his hand on his neck, two fingers on the carotid artery. *Thump. Thump.* Blood. There was blood moving through his body. Reaching a hand out, he could finally feel glimmers of the Null, like static electricity crackling across his fingers.

The world around him started to fade, the blackness overtaking him again. The onyx tower was the first thing to vanish into the night, leaving only Joanna's face. He breathed in and opened his eyes, for real this time.

The room was dark, the only light coming from Rostov. Why was Rostov glowing? There were so many questions. Right now, all Lucas could focus on was the sharp pain that was radiating from his chest to the tip of every extremity of his body.

"Fucking ouch," he said, breathing out, the breaths he was getting still ragged and shallow. The pain was replaced by cold. That was why he couldn't breathe, he was shivering. Heat, a sudden wave of it, rolled over his body, replacing the shivering. His hands clawed at his shirt, his jacket. They needed to come off now before he died, before he…

Yet this panic passed as well and his breathing started to regulate, to come back to an even keel.

"What happened?" he asked, turning from the glowing Rostov—why was he glowing?—to Joanna, who was sitting next to him, holding his hand, her palm on his forehead.

"You died," she said matter-of-factly.

Her voice was flat, but Lucas could feel the emotion under it. The shock, the disbelief, the relief. She was on the edge of crying, trying to hold back and stay on mission. He reached out and hugged her. His own relief at being alive flooding into her, flooding out across to all of them. In the embrace, he could feel Joanna shaking, breathing heavily, coming to terms with everything that was happening.

Lucas felt strangely numb. He should have been feeling more than just relief at being alive. He should have been feeling a great weight lifted off him. But he felt nothing but the desire to continue the mission. Joanna stifled her sniffles and pulled away from him, a small measure of his hardness having tamped down her emotions. Another thing he should have felt sad about but couldn't feel anything at all.

"But you also killed him," Joanna said pointing to the side. Lucas could see a huge chunk of broken floor and lights on the ground. Above it, there was only darkness and at least five decks. Had he fallen that far? Beneath the rubble was a stinking pile of black goo, still oozing from where it had been crushed.

"Well, at least that happened. How am I…?" Lucas started.

"Not dead? I don't know. I wish I had an answer for that, but honestly, after the day I've had? Seeing the future, watching Naomi arch electricity..."

"Why is Rostov glowing?" Lucas asked, cutting her off.

"The Null has found me. *She* has found me. Do you not hear her rhythm?" Rostov asked. His voice was deeper, distant, like he was not completely there.

"I don't hear anything," Lucas said. "Well, the beating of my own heart, but other than that..."

He paused. This was no time to get lost in what happened. Answers would come. They always did. He would have liked to have gotten them before he died, but such was... life? That phrase seemed stranger to him now. All they could do was push forward, and if he couldn't die, well then. What was stopping him?

"Where are we?" he asked.

"Five decks down, so K section. Damage control," Naomi said.

Lucas raised his hand to ask how she knew that, and she answered before he could speak. Of course, they could all hear each other.

"I asked the ship," she said. "I understand it as much as you understand being alive again. Well, maybe not as confusing as your resurrection, but up there," she said.

"Right below Rostov glowing," Lucas said with a chuckle, anticipating her next line. All of them shared a laugh at this, except Rostov, who was focused forward.

"Her song is loud now. I know the way," he said in that haunting, echoey voice that he had adopted. Lucas didn't like it, it wasn't right. He quickly buried that thought deep down.

"Alright, then," Lucas said, pushing himself to his feet. They were wobbly, at first. He held his hands out and felt the Null, letting it flow through him again. He felt whole, complete, and his legs were stable under him again.

"Lead the way, Rostov," he said, pointing forward.

Rostov started walking casting away the darkness in front of him.

"Lucas, here," Joanna said, holding out the hilt of his star-steel blade. Lucas looked into her deep blue eyes. She hadn't given up on him. He nodded and took the weapon, clipping it back to his belt.

Novagrad, Alexander

"I should have known that something was amiss when Mister Harrison showed up without his bodyguards. The two of them are always at his side," Claudia said.

Alexander could hear the disappointment in her voice. Disappointment in herself for not seeing it sooner, not saying anything before now. Disappointment that she had brought all of this down upon them when all she wanted to do was help get her family out of debt. She leaned back in the seat of the cab, making a fist and biting her curled index finger.

"This isn't your fight. I should take care of this on my own," she said. Alexander reached over and put his hand upon her knee.

"You are a teammate—and, to me, I hope much more. That means that your fights are our fights. These brigands picked the wrong card players to mess with," Alexander said, puffing himself up.

He wasn't sure that they were completely equipped to deal with men that committed violence on the regular, but he was damn sure going to try. If his mother had taught him anything, it was that Space Lords must stand up for those who can't stand for themselves, because nobody else was going to do it. More than that, House Wise was another small Space Lord house, which meant that they needed to stick together. The Cordovas were always one battle, one bad creditor away from losing everything, so he wasn't about to let somebody else fall into that. Especially not somebody that he was loving more and more every day.

Alexander had not, in so many words, yet told her that he loved her, but his actions so far spoke louder than simple words could. He was sure of the feeling, just not sure how to articulate it. He had told Fox before that he loved her—had even organized a job for her. That was fading for this, so was *this* love more than *that* love? Or could you love two people at once?

Alexander pushed those thoughts aside. They were not important right now. He could muse on the nature of love later, once they had gotten this all sorted out and retrieved their cards. Just how they were going to go about doing that, he wasn't sure yet, but a plan always presented itself when it was needed.

"When we get to their house, let me do the talking. After having just shot Mister Harrison, you being there might not go over well. House Ross, who he works for, can be short tempered, and they do not hold Space Lords in high regard," Claudia said.

She was all business, no musing on the nature of love when there was work to do. He liked that about her. It reminded him of his brother, Erik, who he always looked up to and, at times, wanted to be like.

Mother loved him, *never shunned his choices.*

"That sounds like a good idea," Alexander said. "Coach, drop us off one block from our destination."

"Change in destination registered, fare adjusted to reflect new distance," the computerized voice of the automatic carriage said back to him.

Alexander nodded and took a deep breath, trying to get into the kind of mindset that any other member of his family would be in. He might have been a scientist by trade, but he was a warrior by blood.

"So here is the plan," Alexander said, puffing himself up like his twin sister Hanna giving a briefing to her marines. "The carriage drops us off a block away and I will hang back. I'm sure there are some bushes around. Then you can knock on the door and see if there is a way to work things out. While you are distracting them, I will find my way into the house and look for our cards."

It was a risky plan, but he had seen enough movies and heard enough stories from the old hats on *Fury* to know it was something that could work, with just a little skill and luck. He looked over at Claudia to see if she agreed with his assessment, his plan. She took a deep breath and then nodded.

"It'll be dangerous. You will need to keep an eye out for cameras. If you get spotted, just be fast. None of the guards will be armed because it's still festival, so use that to your advantage," Claudia said, taking his hands in hers and squeezing them tight. "You have been my white knight so much in the last few days. Allow me to try and save myself here, for once," she added before lightly kissing his hand. Alexander wasn't sure if he could stop being her white knight, but he would give it a shot for her.

As they were finishing up making their plans, the carriage came to a stop and the doors opened. Alexander's watch buzzed, letting him know that his account had been charged the credits for the ride. He would need to silence that. Reaching down, he flipped off his pocket watch computer and pulled his coat closed. As they started to walk, he flipped the large collar of the coat up to help obscure his face.

"Good luck, my love," he said, before slipping into a nearby alley. He had said it and then departed far too quickly to see what her response had been. It was such a teenage boy response to the situation. Still, it was better than nothing.

The small alley that he had found led to the edge of the estate of House Ross. The building was three stories tall, with a veranda that wrapped around the whole estate. The yard wasn't large by the standards of a house that size, but was for a house located in this part of Novagrad.

Crouching down, he approached the edge of the yard so that he could see the front door. Alexander watched as Claudia approached and hit the large knocker on the front. He was too far away to hear anything. Alexander was going to have to figure out what was going on based on body language alone, which he was not thrilled about. Still, if she made it in the house, it would be his signal to go, and if something went wrong outside, he was close enough to jump in.

A few moments passed and then the large red door opened, swinging toward him, obscuring his view of who was on the other side. Claudia talked with them for a few moments before she was ushered into the house and the door closed. This was going to be his opportunity.

Alexander started to creep to the other side of the house. Just as he was about to run across the small yard, he heard a crunch behind him.

He was not able to turn around fast enough before two large hands were placed on his shoulders, pulling him off his feet. He was proud that he did not scream and try to struggle. It didn't matter, though. He was not strong enough to turn himself around or break out of the grip.

"Calm down, Alexander," a familiar voice said.

It took half a beat for him to calm down enough to recognize the voice as Katie's. The big hands that were holding him turned Alexander around and then placed him back on his feet. Looking around, he saw Thrase and two large men crouched behind the bushes.

"Thanks for leading us right to where we need to be," Katie said, patting Alexander on the shoulder.

"Wait, who are…? How did…?"

"I went for a walk after you left for that stupid duel. I was hoping to find some coffee and clear my head. By the time I got home, they were already in the house. But those assholes are not the only ones who are members of a family that possess strongmen. I took a quick jaunt over to the distillery and picked up Chet and Howland here. We are going to crack some heads and get our stuff back," Katie said.

"We can't bust in there. It could be dangerous for Claudia, now that she is inside," Alexander said.

"I'm not particularly worried about her. She can handle herself and if not, well then, that is what you are for, right?" Katie said, giving Alexander a dismissive pat on the shoulder.

He could tell from her tone that she was not a fan of Claudia, and probably worse, thought she was responsible for all their problems. He understood why she would think that, but it was far from the truth. Without Claudia, they would have washed out of the tourney before it had even started. Yes, she had drama, but everybody came with a little bit of that.

"Well, I *am* worried, so maybe we should just be calm and see what is going on before we rush in and start cracking heads," Alexander said.

"Once I have a visual through those windows on our cards—and I mean even an inkling—we are going in. I am done coddling people. You do not get to steal my shit, rough up my friends, and get away with it," Katie said. "Oh, I guess I should ask how the duel went?"

Alexander figured this was just as much about learning what they would face on the inside than any concern she might have had for him. Katie had always kept him at a distance. They were both friends with Hoben, but not exactly friends with each other. Different departments on the project and all.

"I clipped him good in the chest with a plasma lock pistol, so if he doesn't bleed out, he will be off his feet for a while," Alexander said.

"Are you sure about that?" Katie said, pointing back toward the house.

Alexander turned and looked, following her finger. There, standing in the exposed drawing room, flanked by his guards, talking to Claudia, was Mister Harrison. He looked a little pale but was standing, gesturing widely—it almost felt too wide, like it was for their benefit.

For the first time since meeting Claudia, Alexander cocked his head to the side and started to feel that maybe something about Claudia was not on the level.

Confinement Cell, Black Caldera, Grace

The pain in her face was still there as the world started to come into focus, her hand movements slow, her thinking cloudy.

Of course, they would fall back on head wounds like savages who don't care about our brains, Emily thought.

Okay, so that was moving fast. Just getting the ideas from brain to body was taking time. It felt like the worst hangover that she had ever had, a lack of clarity and a pain growing in her gut.

When did you last eat? Real food, not a nutrient stem from the suit?

Grace couldn't say. Neither of them remembered.

It was time to again find clarity. Start small and then work your way to the big things. She was in a bed, soft on her back, scratchy on her top. Scratchy, that meant something, what…? Yes, military blankets.

No, Grace, that is a trope from watching too many movies with dad on the farm. It's worse. Think.

Why did the softness and the scratchy blanket set off alarm bells? She rolled over, cupping the thin pillow to her head to keep out the light. That was when she realized.

Her armor was gone.

The steel, the body suit, all of it. She was in her underwear and a shirt lying in bed fighting a hangover. Of all the ways she didn't want to return to university, this was high up on the list. All the pain and not even a single vodka cranberry.

Focus, Emily, small to big, small too big.

The armor was gone, and they had put her to bed, but where? It was bright, absurdly so. The light was coming through her closed eyes, burning pain in her brain. Throwing the cover over her head, the darkness from the thin bit of wool felt better. No armor, bright lights, a cheap bed. Cell. They had thrown her in a cell. That was logical.

If you are in a cell… Grace thought. They were keeping her alive because she had something they needed. What could people with this much power and control need from *her*? Grace figured she would find out, but first, she needed to get up and stop the pain in her head.

Poking a single eye out from under the covers, she looked around. It was not a bad cell. Chrome, there was a sink, a toilet, and a small shower. Three dark steel walls and then a pane of glass. On the other side, there was a single guard leaning against a computer terminal reading a book. The Varagoth read books? Why not? There were far stranger things that a non-corporeal being from another dimension could do, like try and take over another dimension, or haunt her with their dead, neon-blue eyes. Hell, this man might not even be infested. There had to be regular people doing the bidding of these creatures from the beyond.

The light was getting to her again and Emily retreated to the comforting darkness of the blanket. Grace tried to push out. She always got up with the first alarm.

"Wayfinder, it is time to wake up," a voice said.

It didn't sound like Varagoth or her own internal monologue. Why would she call herself Wayfinder? Grace moved a little, the pain of the lights was still blinding. She closed the eye that had done the first round of recon and poked the second one out.

"Good morning, Wayfinder," the voice said again.

This time, Grace could see where it was coming from, a tall, pale woman standing on the other side of the glass. She had no hair on her head, and her long back and arms were slightly curved. A surface Tragadi. What did this woman want? Grace didn't care. She just wanted the pain in her head to abate. Having gotten her answer, she retreated under the cover.

"Lower the lights by fifty percent," the woman outside said.

The change was so drastic that Grace noticed it through the dark green of the thin wool blanket. She poked her head out. It was better. She still didn't want to get out of bed, but was willing to sit up with the cover around her.

"Thank you," she said, her voice dry and scratchy. There had been that pit in her gut from hunger, but now that she had opened her mouth, she realized just how thirsty she was.

"You're welcome. Can we get you something to eat, Wayfinder?" the woman asked again.

"Why do you keep calling me Wayfinder?" she asked, coughing at the words. How long had she been knocked out?

"Because you are the Wayfinder. All will be explained in good time. First, you should eat," she said, snapping her finger.

A door on the side of her cell opened and a tray of food was slid in, along with a large, insulated cup. Grace looked over at the covered tray and then the Tragadi woman then back at the food.

"You didn't drug it, did you?" It was a blunt Emily question, but her head hurt too much to offer anything else.

"No, and Essex should not have hit you. It can be hard to find soldiers these days who are not broken or spoiling for a fight. There are some basic pain meds on the tray. If you are feeling that you can trust us," she said.

Her voice was smooth, calm, empathetic. Grace almost felt like she could trust this tall pale woman. She probably would have trusted her, if not for the fact that she was stuck in a cell because Essex had smashed her in the face.

How long has he been in their control? How stupid were we to trust him? Emily thought.

"That's a start," Grace muttered, the dryness of her mouth almost pulling the words back into her throat.

She got up, letting the blanket fall to the side and walked over to the tray of food. She took a sip from the straw. The water was cold and refreshing. Just what she needed. The cell lacked a table, so she returned to her bed and sat down cross-legged, placing the tray in her lap. Inside was a plate of pasta covered in a light red, almost pink sauce. To the side were two slices of bread and a salad. In a little cup, there was a dressing. It was thick and white with little specs, so Grace assumed some form of spiced buttermilk like what they had on the farm. Picking up the fork, she started to eat. The pasta was good, if a little flavorless.

"I take it you approve, Wayfinder?"

"Grace, my name is Grace," she said, opening the dressing and drenching it on both her salad and bread.

"No, it is not, Wayfinder," she said.

She isn't wrong, Emily thought.

"What is your name, jailer?" Grace asked, not willing to fight over what they wanted to call her.

"La'tok. This is not a jail."

"So, I'm free to go then?"

"Not as such. We still have many questions for you, Wayfinder," she said, pulling up a chair and sitting down.

The chair was too small for her. Grace estimated that she was close to eight feet tall. Grace started looking across the room. She held up her hand, pinky finger out. She knew the exact measurement of that finger. Her mind started to draw lines of gold from her finger to each item in the room, measuring them extrapolating out the size of each item, based on the constant that was her pinky finger.

"Well then, why do you call me Wayfinder? Didn't they all die out like five hundred years ago?" Grace asked, stuffing a large folk full of lettuce in her mouth.

"Yes. The Host'ire led an extermination of their kind. A genocide that led to the last half millennia being one of violence and pain, as people scrap and claw to try and relearn how to expand, while at the same time, causing more death and destruction than ever before," La'tok said.

"Right, but what does that have to do with *me*? I'm good at math and study portals to the Null, but that doesn't make me some kind of magic space navigator," Grace said, her mouth full. The salad was gone in three bites, the dressing was definitely the same as what they had on the farm. A creamy reminder of home.

"They were magic like the Host'ire. It's why they killed them, right?" Grace asked.

She thought she knew the answer, but everything about the Wayfinder War was shrouded in mystery. So many documents had been lost and archaeological expeditions destroyed without question.

"All in good time, Wayfinder. All in good time. You shall learn about what happened to your kind, and why the First Ones need you to enact their vengeance," La'tok said.

"I've got nowhere to be," Grace said, setting down her fork and leaning against the wall behind the bed. "This is as good a time as any."

Emily crossed her arms and popped a smirk on her face. La'tok looked at her for a few moments, contemplating what she was going to say. At this point, she would have settled for just about anything—a few crumbs of information, just a little bit of the lore that she seemed to be missing. Everything was starting to feel like a meeting she had arrived at too late, missing the one slide that everybody was droning on and on about.

"The First Ones were brought here twenty thousand years ago. Subjected to tests and made to suffer. Slowly, other races cropped up, also brought to this place by the nameless ones who live in the Barrier. The First Ones laid down everything that we know today, but they were found lacking, not worthy, and murdered by those who would call themselves Gods.

"They survived. Hiding away, waiting, slowly being able to interact with those of us in the material world. You will find that everything that has happened was by their design."

"That is... that is a lot," Grace admitted, running the new information around in her brain.

If even half of what La'tok had said was true—and right now, she had no reason to believe that it wasn't—then everything she thought she knew about the universe had been turned upside down. It also started to shed light on some questions that she and the archelogy community in general had always had. Why were there so many dead civilizations in this small area of space? Why did it seem that nobody evolved in their home worlds but, at the same time, there was no way to get beyond our small sliver of the Galaxy? And lastly, why were there always myths and iconography about places that didn't exist, so vivid as to make their non-existence seem impossible? The Fellowship of the Cross's holy texts talked about Holy Terra as if they could return there one day.

"You shall learn more soon, Wayfinder. Now, though, rest. There are fresh clothes in the closet, and I recommend you take a shower. The water is warm. I know that is something you humans enjoy," La'tok said, standing up.

Grace could see her stretching the stiffness from her long back and legs. The short time sitting on the small chair must have been excruciating. The tall, pale Tragadi nodded to Grace and then walked away. Grace watched her go, sipping on her water.

She had to admit, a shower sounded wonderful right now. Looking down at her arms and legs, she was covered in sweat, dirt, and bruises. Black and blue all over, some were already starting to form welts, and others were extremely painful to the touch. The armor had been keeping her from breaking bones and bleeding out, but had done nothing to prevent a whole host of soft tissue injuries.

In a closet next to the shower, Grace found two outfits. One was the standard research uniform of the Olympus Ares science staff: Khaki pants, a blue button up shirt, and white coat. The second outfit was a blue jumpsuit with gold pipping around the shoulders. There was a patch on the breast that she didn't recognize, geometric shapes made of gold and silver. She didn't make a choice, going to the shower instead.

Ross Estate, NovaTerra, Alexander

"That's impossible," Alexander muttered.

He knew that believing his eyes was something that he should do, but he just didn't have enough data yet. It was wrong. This was not right. He turned his attention away from Mister Harrison to Claudia. She was standing there with an easy stance. One hand was on her hip, her other was also waving. *They are playing to the crowed, to—*

He cut off that line of thinking. No, it wasn't possible, there was no way, and it still didn't explain why Mister Harrison was standing and walking around after the wound that he had taken this morning on the green.

"I guess you didn't hit him as squarely as you thought," Katie said.

"No, I did. I walked over. I *saw* it. Hoben saw it. There was so much blood, and the doctor was working very quickly to staunch the bleeding. I shot him with a plasma lock pistol!" Alexander said, almost shouting the last part. Katie held up and hand and motioned for him to quiet down.

"You said that part already," she said.

"Because it's damned important. Those weapons don't cauterize the wound like some other energy weapons do. Most people who get shot bleed out. That is why—" Alexander started, tapping into a well of knowledge on weapons that he rarely had a need for.

"Why plenty of guards and standing militias still carry them, even though their rate of fire is slow," Katie finished. "You are not the only one that knows things about weapons, little Space Lord. I have a doctorate on how energy affects the body—or have you forgotten?"

Alexander was embarrassed to say that he *had* indeed forgotten that. With how abrasive and outgoing Katie Thrase was, it was easy to forget that she was the oldest and most educated member of the team. Thrase and Hoben had started on the project together over ten years ago and been friends since then. Alexander, Jeffery, and especially Alister, were new additions to their crew.

"That is what I thought," she said, taking Alexander's silence as the admission of guilt that it was. "I don't doubt that you shot him. Hell, even that you shot him where you said. You grew up with a master-at-arms. But she is mixed up in more than she is saying."

"I'm starting to gather that," Alexander said. He didn't want to believe it; *couldn't* believe it. That would make him look extremely stupid, and he wasn't stupid. In fact, he believed himself to be a rather good judge of character.

"Do you have a magnifier?" Alexander asked. One of Katie's men pulled a small pair of opera glasses out of his coat and handed them to Alexander.

"Really?" she said with a chuckle.

"I like to see the stage," the big man responded, his voice quiet and soft—a surprise, considering his build.

"Fair. I just wish we had known. Could have added opera tickets to our list of compensation gifts," she said.

Alexander stopped listening to their conversation and turned his attention to the one that was going on inside. He might not be able to hear them, but along the way, he had gotten good at reading lips. He used to watch the boys talk in their little groups in school when he was supposed to be playing with the girls.

"You are lucky he didn't shoot me in the face," Mister Harrison said.

"I'm not sure how he was even still standing, after the drugs I gave him. But that didn't give you the right to—" Claudia said.

"Don't tell me what I did and did not have the right to do. You were supposed to have this mission wrapped up already, I just wanted some insurance," Mister Harrison said, gesturing to a large bag on the table.

Alexander looked at it, flicking the magnification on the opera glasses another step forward. Hanging from the edge of the bag—almost cut in half from the zipper—was a *Green Snapper*. It was one of their cards; *all* their cards.

Bastards don't even care enough to make sure they are not damaged, he thought. Of all the things to be worried about, his cards seemed the least important right now, and yet it irked him to no end.

What did they mean by mission? What was Claudia supposed to have wrapped up by now? There were so many questions running through Alexander's mind. Questions that were only going to be answered by a long, hard conversation with Claudia—or fists and Mister Harrison's face. Sadly, Alexander did now have the answer as to why he was feeling so out of sorts this morning. Claudia had *drugged* him, had tried to keep him from the fight, and maybe wanted to do something worse than that. He had pushed through and won, just so that he could now learn how big of a fool he had been—and still was, because he couldn't believe it. Didn't want to. The mind is a powerful thing when it wants to gaslight itself.

"What are they saying?" Thrase asked, creeping up next to Alexander.

"Something about…" Alexander trailed off, still lost in his thoughts about what he had just seen. He didn't yet know how to put it into words, at least not into words that he wanted to say aloud. They were barely words that he wanted to think or even admit existed. Katie had no patience for this, grabbing the opera glasses from Alexander's hands and putting them to her face.

"I knew it," she said. "And they are treating our cards like garbage."

There was venom in that last part. The already-angry Katie Thrase was incensed that not only would these people steal her Peculiar Pentagon cards, but that they would treat the valuable commodity in such a flippant way.

"That's all I needed to see. Boys, time to get in there," Katie said, handing the opera glasses back to her goon. "You got the brick ready?" she asked, turning to the other man she had brought along. He nodded, picking up a large red brick and bouncing it in his hand like it weighed nothing. "Alexander, you stay here. We will take care of this," she said, standing up, followed quickly by her two goons.

Violence broke out shockingly quickly. The brick went sailing through the air, smashing the window. Glass went everywhere. Inside, Mister Harrison and Claudia were taken by surprise. Harrison started to move toward the door, getting away from the glass. Thrase's goons were halfway across the yard before Mister Harrison's two bodyguards could get out past the broken window. Both groups rammed into each other, and Alexander could hear the thump of flesh-on-flesh as they smashed into each other like linebackers. Katie, running behind, side stepped the line of scrimmage, getting to the window. She threw off her coat and, in a fluid move, threw it over the broken remains of the window.

Claudia was also moving quickly. Before Katie could get through the window, she had the bag with their cards in hand.

"Put that down!" Thrase yelled. Claudia didn't respond with a witty retort. She just threw the bag toward Katie without letting go of the strap. It hit her square in the chest, knocking Kaite back. Claudia then used the momentum of the bag to get it over her shoulder.

"Don't you run out on me!" Mister Harrison yelled.

It was too late, though. Claudia was out the door. Alexander threw himself over the hedge and started to run toward the action. In the background, the sounds of sirens started to blare. The authorities had already been alerted. Alexander figured there must have been a silent alarm on the window. Without their cards, they were going to have nothing to prove that they were in the right.

Katie jumped back into the yard, grabbing her coat along the way.

"Let's get out of here, boys," she yelled. Her two goons pushed back Mister Harrison's bodyguards and turned to follow their boss. Alexander gave the house one last look, locking eyes with Mister Harrison, who had gotten back on to his feet. The creepy man just gave him an unsettling smile and a little wave.

Yanking his eyes away, Alexander ran after his friend.

The Realm of the Wayfinder, Dreadstar Below the Citadel, Rostov

How could they not hear her song? How did none of them hear the music like he did? It was everywhere, radiating from the walls, the floor plates. Even the *rust* was contributing to her song. It was all Rostov could hear in his mind, trumpeting and blaring like a marching band. It was so strong, it was able to act like a compass. Turn one way and it started to fade, turn another way and it was so loud he could feel his brain starting to painfully rattle in his skull. That, though, was not the way to go. He needed to find the balance between the two extremes, the perfect pitch and rhythm of her song. That would be the key. It was so loud in his head.

Closing his eyes, he could see an audio mixing board, the information that Hyacinth was sending him was blowing out the meter, peaking so far into the red that error messages were coming up in his mind. He had to stop. There was no going forward. It was too much.

Rostov fell to his knees, clapping his hands to the side of his head, trying not to scream, trying not to fall over and start writhing in pain. A warmth started to dribble from his nose. Blood.

"How? How do you not hear it; not feel it in your bones?" Rostov asked, his voice growing thin and reedy. He looked at them, his eyes glowing. The pure Null energy of this place streaming out of him, using him like a cheap paper lantern.

"If I close my eyes and really concentrate, I can start to hear something, a vague humming. But it sounds almost like the background noise that you would find on any old ship. Systems, lights, the pulse of electricity," Naomi said.

She bent down and looked at Rostov. He could feel that she wanted to embrace him, to put her arms around him and show him comfort. There was fear. Fear of what was trying to burst out from inside of him. The song. They needed it but nobody else wanted to be consumed by it.

Naomi started to stand. He could feel the trepidation inside of her, the fear. It was as if he was a leaper who had thrown himself upon the steps of the temple. The people wanted to help him, said the words, but still, the fear prevented them from doing anything.

Rostov, though, was no leaper. His hand reached out, grabbing Naomi's leg as she tried to step away. Instantly, he could feel the power of the song moving from him to her. It was still overwhelming. But there was so much less.

Naomi screamed and fell to the floor, Null energy burning through her skin. Rostov wanted to let go, but he couldn't. They were fused together. They were one, as it had always been.

"I can hear her!" Naomi whimpered, trying to push past the pain, trying to find herself again in the cacophony of power that was Hyacinth's song. "It is so loud. She is in pain, crying out for us."

Rostov could see through her eyes, see the electricity of the world moving through the ship like the Null. It all pulsed and flowed in time with the music. With Naomi connected to him, Rostov was able to understand the music better, to feel it. The bars were still spiking into the red, but the softer parts were now yellow.

"I want to hear her, to know her again," Joanna said, walking over.

Tentatively, she placed a hand on Rostov's shoulder. The Null flowed into her. Rostov saw a flash of a vision. All of them standing in a dark room, standing in front of a tank, inside was a woman—Hyacinth. He flashed back to the now. Joanna almost pulled away at the shared vision. Rostov reached up and grabbed her wrist.

"No, this is good. Let it flow," he said in an almost pleading voice. "We all have to be together. We must all feel the sound, hear the music."

Joanna's arm released the tension it was holding. She allowed the Null, the music, to flow into her.

"We are going to find her. Going to see this to an end," she said. Joanna turned to Lucas and held out her hand. Lucas looked at it with concern.

"We do this as one, brother, or we don't do it at all," Rostov said. "She is calling for us. We answered it once. It would be bad form to ignore it."

Lucas stepped forward and placed his hand in Joanna's. The Null raced from Rostov through Joanna into Lucas. He exhaled loudly as light shined back across them. Small cuts and bruises from the day started to heal. The song fell completely out of the red, no longer over-modulated. Loud, but clear. For a moment, all of them looked at each other. They were all seeing the same thing.

"I know where she is taking us," Lucas said as they all shared his memory of being inside the Barrier, seeing the red-orange sky, the floating chunks of a dead but living world, and the onyx tower that dominated the vision and sent a shiver down their spines.

"The prophecy says that the Eye will be opened. I wish we knew more. That more had survived the war, the genocide," Joanna said.

"Prophecy will only get us so far. I fear we are past the point of no return. The future is what we chose to do here today," Lucas said.

"And what do you choose to do?" Naomi asked.

"We go forward," Rostov said, holding his hand out from where he was on the floor.

"We go forward," Lucas said, taking Rostov's hand and helping him and Naomi to their feet.

"We go forward," Joanna said, the vision flashing in everybody's minds again. This time, it ended in flashes of violence. There was always violence. It seemed their lives were made for that.

"We go forward," Naomi agreed, reaching out and squeezing Rostov's hand.

"Lead the way," Lucas said.

Rostov turned, closed his eyes and listened to the music; listened to how it ebbed and flowed through the Null. How it guided him though the ship, toward where Hyacinth waited for them. The music was coming from her, and it would lead them home.

Taking a tentative step forward, he starting walking. His friends—still all holding hands like a daisy chain—followed.

Bowels of Dreadstar Fury, Erik

Something that most people don't realize about a ship the size of a Dreadstar is just how cavernous and confusing it could get the deeper into it you went. Also, when something was as old as the *Fury*, places got lost. They got boarded over, repaired around, and forgotten about.

Lord Admiral Cordova, his mother, had led Erik into one of those sections of the ship. They had gone down ladders and through hatches that he didn't even know existed. Erik had prided himself on knowing the ins and outs of the ship. Had spent countless days as a child getting lost in places like this. One time, he had even been lost for two days, just wandering in circles in hallways and rooms that nobody occupied anymore. Places where just a scant amount of power was shunted to so that flickering lights could be kept on.

"Mother, where are you taking me?" he asked as they reached another unmarked bulkhead that had been lost to time.

"To the heart of the ship; to the truth," she said.

His mother regarded the lock pad on the door for a moment and then turned around to look her son in the eye. He hadn't seen this look in her before. It was resignation and determination. Something was wrong, something had happened, and he didn't know what it was.

Erik knew that his mother hadn't been the same since Tiberius died. He had been the only person that she had ever had a deep emotional connection with. Nothing sexual—not that he wanted to think of his mother like that—but it was as deep a connection as two people could have without making love. Probably just as close, he thought. No, this felt like the look somebody gives you when they know something and that secret is burning away at them, and the only relief that they can find it to reveal it, to scream about it to the world, regardless of the consequences.

"This is no time to speak in riddles, mother," he said.

"Riddles imply understanding. This is more ephemeral, more from the gut," the Lord Admiral said as her hand that wasn't on the panel started tapping something out. A moment later, Erik realized that she was tapping in time to a tune that was in her head. Once she was done, the hand on the access panel repeated the music, her fingers hitting keys. A moment later, the door opened.

"How did you...? That door has been locked for over a hundred years! This whole section is—" Erik started before his mother cut him off, holding up a hand and moving her fingers around.

"No, not that long. I don't..." She paused trying to find the right words. "I remember, but I don't remember. Have you ever woken up from a dream and you can still sort of see the images, remember the touch and taste and smell of it?" She paused, waiting for him to say something, but he didn't know what to say to that.

"Yet, the more you grasp at that memory, the more it just slips away from you? Faces, places, events, words that people said? All of it? It doesn't matter what you try to remember, trying to remember is what makes it vanish," she said, pushing open the door.

The hallway before them was dark, a few glow strips on the sides of the floor were the only illumination. His mother put her hand on the side of the wall. Again, she was tapping to a beat, and when the idea reached its conclusion, the hallway was bathed in light, her hand atop the control panel.

"Mother, I don't understand. What are you talking about? What is this place? What is going on!" Erik said, his voice rising as he spoke until he slammed his foot down on the exclamation point.

"Have I ever told you about the last days of your grandfather's life?" she asked.

"No. I don't see what that has to do with any of this. Grandfather died of a fast, aggressive cancer. Are you telling me that isn't what happened?" Erik asked.

He was confused, and that confusion was starting to border on anger. He was not a fan of being jerked around, and this was not something that his mother had ever done. She was a direct and to the point person, not one to give in to riddles and treasure hunts, diatribes about dreams and memory.

"No, you are correct, that is what killed him. We didn't see it coming; couldn't have seen it coming. But somehow, he knew. He was ready," his mother said as she started to walk down the hallway, lights in the far distance turning on as they approached them. The sounds of her boots and voice echoing in these dead, vestigial chambers of the ship.

"I should have seen it coming. Those days are a blur, but I wrote so much music then, and that was the key. I didn't want to lose what we had shared right before he got sick, but it was slipping away, and the harder..."

"The harder you tried to remember, it the faster it went away," Erik said, finishing her thought. The tapping in time... Whatever it was that his mother had forgotten, she had written down in music. You can forget why you wrote a track of music one way, but it was still there, still written down. Clever.

"Yes, exactly. Only recently did I start to remember; did the music make sense again. I fear for what it means," she said.

"I fear for you as well, mother," Erik said.

He was worried she was not acting like herself; this was not his mother. She must have fallen ill, or perhaps stress had finally gotten to her. Whatever it was, he knew that he should drag her back to the infirmary for Uncle Jospeh to examine. That was what the logic brain said, but that same brain was watching her tap in time to open long locked doors and wasn't sure anymore.

"Do not fear for me, Erik. My eyes are open. The situation we find ourselves in now, it is the moment that the ship has been waiting for."

She paused, stopping at an empty section of bulkhead. The hallway kept going and Erik could hear what sounded like pistons moving and working. Some part of the ship that never stopped and was never serviced.

"Shortly before he died, *Fury* was in a bind. Much like this one. We were surrounded, out gunned and bleeding energy. Father hid us in the senser shadow between two moons. We had enough power to hold there for a few hours, but eventually, the orbits would pass, and the shadow would vanish. We only had one chance to escape, one shot," his mother said.

"The battle of Threep Prime," Erik said. "I remember reading about that. Grandfather jumped the ship. The only time since the Wayfinder wars that a Dreadstar has used her jump engines."

Erik had never seen the ship jump. He couldn't even tell you *how* the ship jumped. If that battle hadn't happened in living memory, he wasn't sure that he would have even believed that it *had* jumped. The tails of the Age of Chaos talked about ships jumping all the time. Slowly, those stories faded away in the years between the Age of Chaos and the Wayfinder War before stopping entirely—except for his grandfather. The last few days, though, had proven to Erik that apparently there still were ships that could jump...

But how? It was all about the how.

"He jumped the ship. The one secret that is held tightly and only passed down from Lord to Lord," his mother said. "Still, there is something strange about it, because I know we came down here while the ship was hidden in the shadow. I know it's involved in using the *Fury's* faster than light drives. Still, that is what I am grasping at, trying to remember. I wish your grandfather were here. I know he would have remembered this better."

"Did he not write anything down?" Erik asked.

"This is not the sort of secret one writes down without a cypher. I wish you had gotten to meet your grandfather. He was a master of cryptography. There are still hidden parts of the ship that we will probably never see again because of his locks and codes," the Lord Admiral said.

Erik was learning more than he wanted to know. Lost sections of a ship the size and age of *Fury* were a given, but knowing that there were sections that previous members of his family had locked away and then died before opening or even telling anybody about disturbed him deeply. What was hiding on this ship where he had lived his whole life, that his family had controlled for generations? If they survived this, he was going to press his mother more. He was going to learn everything there was to know about his own ship.

"This lock, this code, though, are of my creation," his mother said, pressing her hand to the bulkhead.

There was a door—had there always been a door there? Erik's eyes darted around the hallway, and, for a moment, he started to question reality. No, it had to have just been shadows. There is no way he hadn't seen a door until now. Especially not one this big, with a code pad and airlock wheel.

"Mother, what are you talking about?" Erik asked again.

The fight between the half of him that only believed in what he could see and the half of him that remembered the fantastical stories of times past that Tiberius used to tell them were fighting in his mind. A part of him always thought that, if he saw the things from those stories, that he would accept their existence as truth because they would be in front of him. But now that he was involved in something he couldn't understand, that bordered on the weird, he wasn't sure what to make of it all.

"We will see soon enough," his mother said.

She started humming another tune, Erik recognized this one as "Librarica", a tune that his mother had sung for him as a child. It played in his nursery, an early core memory. He took a moment as his fingers started to feel the beat to the tune he had not heard in almost three decades. His mother matched his time with her right hand and encouraged him along with her left. He started to hum, both of them standing there and humming the old lullaby. Erik was rusty, out of tune, and it took a minute for him to match his mother.

Once he did, a loud click echoed through the hallway, and the doorway that he was sure wasn't there just a moment before popped open. The smell of stale air filled the hallway. On the other side, there was a flickering light.

The Realm of the Wayfinder, Dreadstar Below the Citadel, Joanna

The longer they walked together, hand in hand, the louder and clearer Hyacinth's song became. Joanna could feel it not just in her mind, but in her heart, as it came into clarity. Slowly, in the back of her mind, an old memory was triggered. Something deep that she hadn't thought about in thirty years. It was her mother, sitting on the edge of her bed. Joanna, a child, laying there, the covers pulled up to her neck. A soft song, a lullaby, to guide her off to sleep.

"My mother used to sing that to us," Lucas said quietly. She turned to where he was behind her, their hands locked.

"Do you know how it ends?" Joanna asked.

"In the orphanage, one of the Sisters was singing it before the Host'ire came for me," Naomi said quietly. "I always fell asleep before it was over."

"Me too," Joanna whispered.

"It is a guiding light, a hymn to help those who are lost get to where they are going," Rostov said. He turned to look at her, his eyes still glowing with the deep gold of the Null. "My mother used to sing it to us, as well. She said it was passed down from generation to generation since before the Wayfinder War. Now it guides us to her."

Rostov turned from Joanan back to the task at hand, the light going with him, exposing the darkness before them. The farther into the depths of the ship they went, the more decrepit and broken it seemed to get. It was as if they had forgotten that this section even existed. That made sense, knowing the effects that Hyacinth had on people's memories. Did not all the Guardians get to drink from the waters? Or did they need to be refreshed from time to time? There were so many questions, questions that she didn't even know needed to be asked. None of this was brought up even in the most heretical of Wayfinder texts.

They walked for another few minutes, before Rostov held his hand up.

"We are close," he said, dropping his hand. The four of them all let go of each other. Joanna could still hear the song in her head. As she looked around, it faded in and out, like she was a bat with echo location. Just ahead of them, there was a light. As they walked toward it, Joanna saw a single Guardian standing by the door. He had on Host'ire garb, minus the glasses. In his hand was the hilt of a star-steel blade.

"Welcome, honored ones. She has been expecting you," he said, standing out of the way, the door behind him opening enough for them to step through. As soon as the door opened, the sounds of the song became crystal clear, like she was in the room with her mother again as she gently sang her to sleep.

It was time to confront this awake. Everything for the last week had been leading up to this moment; all the sneaking around, all the confusion, the lust, love, the death. Rostov was the first across the threshold and then all of them quickly followed.

The room was medium sized. There were control panels and tables all over. The tables were covered with beakers and burners, and jars of chemicals. It was a scientist's lab here. The control panels all had life-sign readings. In the middle of the lab was a large tube filled with bubbly water.

Inside, naked, her eyes closed, was Hyacinth.

Hello friends, a voice said in their heads. Joanna recognized it instantly as Hyacinth's. It was calm and filled with love. Her lips didn't move, her eyes didn't open. She was in there, but not awake to the world.

"Hello," Lucas said, taking a tentative step toward the tank.

It is good to see you all again. The visions said that you would come.

"You sent us all messages," Joanna said.

I did, yes. I saw that, as well. Time does not move for me anymore as it does for you.

"What does that mean?" Naomi asked.

The world is splayed out before me. Time and location have no true meaning. I know, though, that the time has come to bring the prophecy together. To pave the way for the true Wayfinder.

There was a forcefulness in her voice, like she was prepared. Joanna could feel a strange disappointment coming from her, that they were not as ready as she was.

"I was here the whole time. Why didn't you talk to me directly? I could have helped," Rostov demanded, stomping forward. "I suffered from hearing things in my mind. I was sure that insanity had taken me some nights. Why?"

I spoke as I could. I am sorry.

"Bah," Rostov said, waving his hand and turning around, storming into the shadows. The light of the Null was fading from him. Naomi followed. Joanna could hear her consoling him. Telling him that it would all be okay. She could feel the tenderness of the hug. It radiated from Rostov's shoulders to her own.

"He has been through it. But I would like to know what is going on. No more cryptic messages, no feelings. It feels like you have been messing with us, amplifying how we feel. For what?" Lucas asked.

For a moment, Joanna felt hurt. Her feelings were not being amplified. She knew exactly how she felt. Or...would she have been as forward with Lucas any other time? That kiss from twenty years ago hung in her mind. Last night was there, as well—and that had been far more than a kiss. She looked at him to try and gauge how he was feeling. He looked back at her, and his gaze softened. The love he felt for her was deeper than any amplified emotions, but the speed of their falling in upon seeing each other again, Joanna had to admit, probably was.

It is the job of the blood pact, the five to pave the way through the eye for the Wayfinder. There is no more time. At least, time as you understand it; as I used to understand it.

"There are only the four of us. Essex never showed up," Joanna said.

He is where he needs to be, with the true Wayfinder.

"Are you not a true Wayfinder?" Lucas asked.

I am but a hybrid, something less. Just as important. Without us, the gates do not function, civilization comes to a halt.

Naomi and Rostov walked back over, taking their places between Lucas and Joanna.

"The gates all operate on beacons in the Null. They go to where they go. I've seen the internal guts of one," Naomi said.

Without me, this part of space does not sing. It is why I am here, and what will allow us to reach the Eye safely.

"You want us to go to Hell?" Rostov asked. "Or, at least, what the order says is Hell. I don't think I really know anymore."

Not Hell. Through the Eye.

"Yes, but don't you remember the teachings? The Citadel is here to guard the doorway to Hell. The last highway of the Wayfinders, the door into the Barrier that contains demons beyond accounting," Naomi said.

The creatures that live there are old, powerful, evil. They are not demons, they just are. Like humans just are. Like Tragadi just are. Like Pa'vinti just are. Make no mistake about it, though. They *are coming.*

"So, it's not Hell, but still full of creatures that want to kill us," Rostov said, looking at each of them. "Sounds like Hell to me, even if it isn't a literal-place-you-go-when-you-die kind of Hell."

"Was this what I saw when I died, before my body... fixed itself?" Lucas asked with a small quiver in his voice.

He had been dead. Joanna hadn't wanted to admit it, but it was true. There was no logical reason to think his body was going to knit itself back together like it did.

Yes. You were granted vision while your body healed, so that the mind wouldn't wonder, wouldn't suffer the blackness for too long.

"What is with these manifesting powers?" Joanna asked. "There is nothing in what is left about the Wayfinders that talks about it. Seeing power, massive physical control of Null energy, precognition and translation—fuck, Lucas didn't die when he very much should have!" she said, gesturing to each of them. "I've been studying your people all my life. Trying to get every banned book I can get my hands on. None of what you have said today is in any of that. Just nonsense about riding the Null and seeing the tower!"

"A tower made of onyx," Lucas said. Joanna turned to him, her eyes going wide. "I saw a tower of onyx in my vision. It was so far away, but there were ships flying by it. Life. Every time I looked at it, though, it felt wrong. Like that energy that is buried deep, deep under the Null."

The base of the enemy. Those who would push through, who are already on the move. That is why the highway must be prepared for the true Wayfinder.

"The one who is with Essex. Where are they?" Lucas asked.

Far from here, not yet ready. Soon.

"What do they want?" Naomi asked. Joanna could feel Lucas shiver at this thought.

Chaos. The gauntlet must be cleansed in blood.

"That sounds horrible. But it's still just more riddles and nonsense!" Rostov said. He stomped toward the glass tube, then stopped and stuttered back. Pain lanced through their minds. Whatever had hit him was feeding back to all of them.

"Rostov, cool it!" Lucas said, the leader finding its way back into his voice. "I know you have been through hell, but we need to address this logically. I don't know what the gauntlet is, but I know how it felt when I saw that tower and I know we don't want them involved. Also, the Fellowship is coming. They will take this ship soon. Fel's forces are not cutting it."

"Hyacinth, how were you planning to open the Eye? How are we to pave the way?" Joanna asked, trying to ask as many questions as possible to pull this all together before it was inevitably pulled away from her.

The ship will rise, and I will open the Eye. These agents of the enemy cannot be allowed to take the ship before that. The way must be made ready. You were bound to me and gifted the powers of the old Null.

"If that isn't a mission statement then I don't know what is," Lucas said, turning to the group.

"I guess we will learn more as we learn more," Joanna said.

"We pave the way for whoever Essex is bringing us and fight this enemy. That is what we were trained to do," Naomi said.

"We were not trained to fight some kind of evil from beyond. Sure, they talked about it, but the order trained us to be good little fascists. To say, 'yes sir, no sir,' when given an order, and help the bastards on NovaTerra assert their control over the mundanes," Rostov snapped back.

"That might be what they have become, but it wasn't what they set out to be," Lucas said.

"Bullshit. Why do you think we murdered all her kind?" Rostov said, pointing his finger at Hyacinth in her tank.

The old leaders were fooled, given power beyond measure, that would match what they had during the Age of Chaos. Only once the slaughter was over did their boons fade away, the shadows returning to their hiding places. Shame has been driving them since. They hold the line here, lest somebody cross over and find the evidence, expose them.

"Of course they would do something out of weakness. We can expose them, bring down the order!" Rostov said. There was desperation in his voice.

"Rostov, I think it is too late for that," Naomi said, walking up to him and putting an arm on his shoulder.

"No!" he yelled batting the arm away. "It is never too late for justice! For the millions that they have already killed, and the ones whose heads are still on the docket."

The time for retribution is past, my friend. We are in the time of survival. You are the heroes. Soon, the Wayfinder and the stragglers will arrive. We must be ready.

"I just... I *can't*—I know she was important to us in the past, but I can't just forget what they did to me!" Rostov yelled, pleading in his voice.

"Rostov, please, you have to work past the hate. We can't ever change what was done to you, but we can try and help you get past it. If there is some kind of enemy from the past returning, then being the hero is the best way to show them that you are better than them, that you are worthy," Naomi said.

"The leaders don't respect those of us from the Citadel. Even when we have rank," Joanna said, cocking her head toward Lucas at the last bit.

"We can show them that we are better than they are. That we are true Host'ire by doing this, by stopping this foe," Lucas said. "I know in my heart that this is the right thing to do. When I saw that tower while... dead... it chilled me to the bone. Whatever dwells there, we can't let out. Rostov, we can't do this without you."

They all turned to watch him, their attention rapt. Joanna couldn't tell by the look on his face if he was going to join them or not; if he would be able to put aside the pain and hurt they had dealt against him so that they could do what needed to be done. She had heard that prophecy enough times to realize now that they were a part of it.

"Fine," Rostov said with a disappointed sigh. "I am still going to do everything in my power to bring the order down. It is a stain upon civilization. If I have to kill some kind of old evil beforehand, well then, so be it."

Joanna could feel the resolve inside of him. He was ready. They were *all* ready. Joanna had read enough stories to know that this was the part where they would all come together, stronger. While there was resolve, the creeping doubt of fear was ever present, just under the surface. Hiding in the shadows.

The Bowels of Fury, Erik

"They are not just bedtime stories," Erik muttered.

"They never are, son, they never are," his mother said as she pushed open the door and walked through.

Erik swallowed and followed. The door opened into another hallway, this one was propped up by buttress, narrowing to a pointed top. Between each buttress were sconces with candles, burning with real flames. Flames and starships were two things that did not go together. The hall opened into another room, where a stronger, flickering light was coming from. None of this was right, and instinctively, Erik's hand fell to the pistol that was strapped to his hip. There was no comfort to be found in the weapon. It was of no use here.

At the end of the hallway, there was a library. Erik had to blink as he looked at this room, because nothing about it seemed to fit. The walls were covered in deck-to-ceiling shelves of books—old books—still bound in leather with fading gold titles. The only place where there was not a shelf of books was the section of wall where there was a massive stone fireplace. Inside the hearth was a roaring fire, which Erik was positive was not holographic. It had heat and violence to it, things that you could try and replicate, but which would always fall short of a real fire, burning real wood. In the center of the room were two large wooden chairs with high backs and red upholstery.

"The library of the Wayfinder," his mother said as she started to walk around looking at the books on the wall.

"There was a story that my grandfather used to tell me. About how Dreadstars operated before the Wayfinder wars. These days, every ship has a representative of the Host'ire. They say it's to advise, but we all know they are watching and waiting for something." She paused. Erik knew the subtext was that Tiberius had not been like that, even though he had been Host'ire. Wizards made manifest.

"In the old days, there were always two advisers on a ship this size, a member of the Host'ire and a Wayfinder. You needed them both. Grandfather talked about those times as if they were perilous and filled with magic and creatures of legend. The Host'ire protected, while the Wayfinder jumped the ship. They were the only ones who have ever been able to navigate the Null. They built the jump gates, setting it so you could only go to a set number of destinations from each gate. The propaganda from before the war was that they did this to limit us, but it was because something worse lurks in the darkness below space; a shadow that they were protecting us from."

"If the Wayfinders were so important, why did everybody side with the Host'ire and fight against them?" Erik asked. Everybody knew about the Wayfinder War, but so much of the actual history of that event had been lost in atomic fire.

"Fear, and power." his mother said. "That is how it always is. Right now, whoever it is that wants to use atomic weapons on NovaTerra and hunt down Dreadstars is operating out of fear and a desire for power. The Wayfinders controlled absolute power, and for reasons probably even forgotten by them, the Host'ire were afraid."

Erik looked around at the books on the wall. They were about technology, astronomy, philosophy, and science. A treasure trove of lost information, lost history. Recorded history was always about civilizations rising and falling, being lost to time, found, and studied by the next civilization that would rise and fall. The knowledge contained in this room was worth more than almost the entirety of the ship. Hell, there might even be a text that would tell them how to build a new Dreadstar.

"If the Host'ire knew about this place—"

"They would send hundreds of knights to burn it to the ground, and probably *Fury* along with it. Perhaps even the Host'ire Militarum," his mother said.

"They are a myth, whispered about, but never seen," Erik said, realizing how foolish he sounded almost instantly.

"We are walking in myth," she muttered.

The two were quiet for a moment, still taking in the room that they had found; the room that should not have been here, that defied all logic in its existence.

"It will take weeks, if not years, to find what we need in here. I don't even know where to start," Erik said, running his hands along the spines of books that were over a thousand years old.

"The answer for today is not here. These are the answers of the past, ready to instruct the future. No, today we must see the Wayfinder," his mother said, her voice turning reverent.

Erik was about to open his mouth, to say that they were all dead, but closed it, thinking better of saying something that he believed to be fact just a few minutes ago.

"I remember it now. The trip down here with my father. He was like me, unsure of what he knew, of what he remembered, and then it all came flooding back. We do not jump the ship. *They* do. We must beseech the Wayfinder, the heart of *Fury*, to let us jump," his mother said as she walked over to the fireplace and pulled down one of the sconces.

The fireplace started to creak. The stone of the hearth was turning, and behind it, there was a set of stairs that impossibly went down deeper into the ship. Lord Admiral Cassandra Cordova picked up a candelabra from a table and started walking down the steps. There were no more fancy lights, just darkness and the sound of dripping water. Erik didn't want to walk down, didn't want to follow his mother. He could feel a horrible, creeping amount of fear. As much as he wanted to run away, to forget this place as his mother had, Erik's feet forced him to follow.

Each footfall as they walked down the winding staircase echoed around them, all punctuated by the rhythmic dripping of water. It was far too consistent of a drip to ignore. It was an ear worm and then he recognized it.

Jump Prep.

Finally, after what was far longer than possible, the two of them reached the bottom of the stairs. They were in a cave of steel and wires. It was a single large room, and, from every conceivable point, there were wires coming out of the walls, all cascading toward a single point. In the center of the room there was a pool of green liquid, which cast a sparkling luminescence across everything. That was not the horrifying part, though. That was reserved for what was hanging over the pool.

Wrapped in the wires, his arms out to his side like he was the Fellowship's dead messiah, was a man. He looked more technical than organic. Wires were coming in and out of his body; every vein had a tube, covered with slime and watery blood. His lower section, if he still had one, was completely consumed by the wires and blinking bits of technology. His chest was covered in not just tubes, but plates of circuit boards, transistors and diodes interfacing directly with his skin. The man's face was hairless, weathered with age, and half of it was covered in steel as if liquid metal had been poured atop him.

The heart of *Fury*.

"Come forward, Cassandra of House Cordova, Lord Admiral. Come forth and beseech the Wayfinder," the heart said. His voice cracked, like a broken radio crossed with a person who had not spoken in many, many years. Erik held himself back. He didn't want to approach, didn't want to be here in this place that should not be. His hand fell again to the butt of his pistol.

Be not afraid, Erik, third of his name. Come and join your mother in making your request, the heart said.

This time, it wasn't aloud. His mouth didn't move, but Erik could hear the thing's voice clear as day in his mind. His hand fell away from the weapon. He wasn't sure if his hand moved by its own volition or if the thing hanging from the ship was controlling him. Reluctantly, Erik took two steps forward to be behind his mother.

"You have remembered, and thus may request. Know, though, that this comes with a price, and you will not be here together again," the heart said.

"We would ask you to jump the ship. We have information that very soon, an unknown faction is going to use atomic weapons upon the world of NovaTerra. We must warn them. Stop this attack upon our capitol," Cassandra said, bowing her head, not making eye contact with the Wayfinder.

"Duty demands it? Honor?" the heart asked.

"Yes," his mother said. The Wayfinder that was the heart of the ship didn't seem moved, pulling back slightly, mulling over the request.

"My brother is on that planet right now. My sister gave everything to get us this information. Our family has paid the price and might never be whole again. Grant us this one chance to bring the house of Cordova together again, and save billions of lives as well," Erik called out.

Even now, his mother's animosity and disappointment in Alexander was preventing her from seeing that he was just as important as everybody on NovaTerra. Duty and honor were all well and good, but family always came first.

"I shall grant you this boon, Lord Admiral Cassandra Cordova. Approach!" the heart of the *Fury* yelled, its voice booming, echoing in Erik's mind.

His mother stood and started walking forward into the pool. By the time she reached the hanging thing that was once a Wayfinder, the water was up to her knees. Wires started to move, and the creature lowered itself to her level, so that the two of them were face-to-face. The heart whispered something into his mother's ear. Something that Erik could not hear, but he saw the look of horror and happiness that crossed her face as she registered it and then took a step back before falling into the water.

The heart of *Fury* pulled back from the pool, almost all the way into the wall of the ship. The room started to buzz and thurm. Lights came on, as power was drawn into the creature.

"Go now and prepare," the heart said as another door opened in the mess of wires. "For soon I shall be ready to make the journey. You must be as well."

Confinement Cell, Black Caldera, Grace

The warm water of the shower felt wonderful against her tired and bruised body.

Enjoy this, Grace. It might be the last moment you get to relax, Emily thought, knowing that the fanatics were going to come back for her. What exactly they wanted, she didn't know.

Wayfinder, why do they keep calling me that?

It didn't matter right now, because at this moment, her prime objective was to escape and maybe find her research before blasting out of this place, wherever exactly *here* was. The stars she had seen were lensing, which meant they were close to the galactic core. Grace was interested in what they wanted with her. Emily agreed that they should play along. Learn what they could and then bug out, but not before finding Essex. Anger and hurt flashed across Emily's field of view as Grace thought about the Host'ire.

He turned on us; was always with them, Emily thought.

No, he had been grabbed when he went to see Vardis, Grace countered.

Vardis was always suspect. Even if he was taken there, he went on his own. Too much follow in that one to trust.

Grace wanted to say something about how getting tangled up with men who lacked the ability to follow was what got them in this mess in the first place. Emily stifled that line of thought though before Grace could form it.

We are talking about Essex, not Patrick, Emily hissed in her mind, pulling away.

Grace lost track of time in the shower, the hot water never seeming to run out. She hadn't taken a real shower without a timer since her collage days and didn't realize how much she missed them. The only thing that would have been better would have been a bubble bath. The buzzer on the cell rang. Grace stepped out of the shower and walked into the main room, tracking water in her nakedness. A towel was sitting on the bed. Out of the corner of her eye, she saw La'tok standing there, hunched over, her tall head almost hitting the ceiling. This place had not been built with her people in mind. That was a common occurrence across all of civilization, except for the few worlds that were close to Tragadi Prime.

"Wayfinder, it is time," she said.

Grace paid her no mind, picking up the towel and wrapping it around herself. The Tragadi had been the one to tell her to take a shower, and as such, she could wait until Grace was ready to talk to her. She picked up a second towel and started to dry her long black hair. It felt good to get all the mats and sweat out of it. Perhaps she would wear it down today, a thing she hadn't been able to do in years. Labs and environment suits frowned upon it.

Her hair dry, Grace walked over to the closet and looked at her options of outfit. It was a standard science casual or a jumpsuit. If escape was on the menu, then the jumpsuit was the correct choice. She dropped the towel and put on underwear before grabbing the jumpsuit and sliding into it. They had gotten her size right. There was enough space for her to breathe but not so much that it looked like a sack. The sleeves were short, and the room was cold. Grace grabbed the lab coat next to the standard science outfit and put it on. Monogramed over the right breast pocket was, 'Dr. Grace Goodspeed, PhD". That name looked strange; it hadn't looked strange in over a year. Still, it was more her name than Wayfinder.

"What can I do for you, La'tok?" Grace asked, sitting on her bed and taking a sip from her water cup. It was still cold.

"It is time. We have need of your abilities, Wayfinder," she said, bowing for real, not just to avoid hitting her head. It was time to start playing her role—whatever that was—while formulating an escape plan.

You talk, I'll plot, Emily thought, creeping back toward the light.

"Lead on, then," Grace said, standing up. "Can I get a refill on my water?" she asked, holding out the stainless-steel cup.

"Of course, whatever you desire, Wayfinder," La'tok signaled for the guard to open the door and fetch some more water. As the door opened, Grace walked forward, handing off her cup.

"I've got a question—a few, actually. I assume you are down for a little walk and talk?" Grace asked as she fell behind La'tok, staying just a step behind her. The Tragadi tried to slow her gate, but Grace was always just a half step slower. With the length of La'tok's legs, there was no way she could move slower than Grace.

"Of course, Wayfinder." There was just a hint of irritation in the back of her speech, exactly what Grace was aiming for.

"Who put all this together? Who runs your organization?"

"We are the Children of the First. Disciples of the first people to be brought here and murdered by those who dwell beyond the Barrier," La'tok said. There was a lot there and Grace grasped maybe half of what she had said.

"How have I never heard of this before? You seem to have your fingers in dozens of worlds."

"A people who were thought dead do not go around advertising that they are building an army to prepare for their return. We have been working in the shadows for hundreds of years, since the Host'ire foolishly killed your kind," La'tok said as they stopped at an elevator door waiting for it to open.

When it did, two scientists walked out. Both were chatting like it was a normal day. They stopped and spoke in hushed tones as they slinked by Grace and her lanky chaperone. Both men looked at her, and Grace matched their eyes, noticing quickly that neither of them had any cloudiness. They were not infested. It was at that moment that Grace realized she hadn't looked to see if La'tok was infested, either, having just assumed that she would be.

Her gazes had been far too obvious. The Tragadi noticed all of it.

"They do not yet have first ones within them. It is a great honor to be host to one of our lords. So few have yet to make it through, only small pinpricks that we have been able to punch between the Null, the Shadow, and here," she said as they entered the elevator. La'tok bent down and looked Grace in the eyes. "Do not worry, Wayfinder. We need you for who you are. Nobody shall take over your body."

Grace did not find that very reassuring. La'tok's eyes were cloudy and hard to read. Even without the prospect of an interdimensional creature within, they were wholly alien.

"My kind? I am still lost on this Wayfinder thing," Grace said.

In the deep back of her mind, she was afraid of what it was going to mean, and was starting to put things together, even though every conclusion she was coming to felt like something from a movie that she would have watched as a child or late at night while pretending to study. There was no way it could be real life.

Why not? We have never felt right, like we belonged, Emily thought.

"The Host'ire, as they do, got sloppy in the last days of the Wayfinder War. Not every member of the Nonaligned Planets was willing to submit to their crusade, and thus a few stragglers survived. Nobody who showed any signs or abilities, mind you, but a few third cousins, bastards twice removed, and a handful of corpses, that could be used to harvest genetic material from. Those who came long before me started watching, waiting for the prophecy to reveal itself," La'tok said, almost reverently.

She enjoyed talking about the story of her organization, her faith. Grace had expected this to be like pulling teeth.

Radicals love to talk. It's always what gets them in trouble, Emily thought ruefully, pushing back painful memories.

The elevator dinged and the door opened onto a vast command center. Spread before Grace was a room filled with computers, people, and activity, two levels high, and ringed by a massive window. Or was it a screen? She wasn't sure. The rows and rows of computers were all being operated by people in jumpsuits like the one she had on, with headsets wrapped around their ears, busily working away.

Standing all over, near every door and corner, were soldiers with guns, their uniforms a cascade of different colors and patterns. Supervisors in more standard military uniforms were walking around checking on things and, in the middle of that, was the occasional person in a white coat with a clipboard, stopping to do calculations or glance up at the massive window. Yes, upon giving it a closer look, Grace was sure that it was a window, one that looked out past the planet's thin atmosphere to the stars.

Looking at the stars, she started making frantic calculations, drawing the building on the window in her mind and then tracing down from the sky to find a set of angles, roughly calculating how tall this spire was. The conclusion she came to was that the elevator had been damned fast. La'tok started to walk forward into the controlled chaos of the room, this time not worrying if Grace was keeping pace behind her, assuming that seeing a place like this would be enough to spark curiosity and get her to follow. As much as Grace didn't want to admit it, the Tragadi was right. She was instantly enthralled by what was going on here and needed to know more.

At their computers, people were doing calculations. It seemed they were all doing the same calculation—or, at least, parts of the same equation. Hyperspace jumps. Raw, unfiltered Null space data and hyperlight calculus. It was high level stuff, the kind of math that most computers couldn't even do. That is why it had been simplified down over the years, offloading the work to the jump gates. Aside from the inability to actively find new thin points in the Null, ships couldn't carry enough computing power to plot a jump on their own, as evidenced by a room like this.

Well, *most* ships, she corrected herself. The five Dreadstars that operated in the Confederation were said to be able to make independent jumps. How they pulled that off, she didn't know. Long lost tech from the Age of Chaos that those backward, cravat-wearing fools probably didn't even understand.

I would give anything to get to poke around in those systems for a few days, Emily thought.

Was this what they needed her for? To plot jumps? That was one of the things that legends said the Wayfinders could do without computers. The things they were saying—her research—it was all starting to fall into place.

Grace set her assumptions aside as she followed La'tok. Better to get the information from the horse's mouth than make too many wild grand assumptions about things that honestly were about to give her a headache. Being given the chance to do some wildly complex calculations would be relaxing compared to the last day and a half she'd had. Walking up the stairs, Grace saw Vardis hanging by his third arm from a hastily installed bar, looking down at a table covered in star charts.

"The Wayfinder, sir," La'tok said with a flourish, before stepping back behind Grace.

"Ah, Dr. Goodspeed. So nice of you to join us," Vardis said in his squawking, high-pitched voice. He swung down from the bar and landed in front of her and held his hand out. She took it, looking into the eyes of the former administrator. She could see the black cloud of a Varagoth.

Crossing her arms, Grace leaned back, putting weight on her left leg. "It's not like I really had much choice in the matter," she quipped in Emily's voice.

"I suppose not, Wayfinder. Still, it is good to have you here at the mothership operation. That other lab was very pedestrian feeling, don't you think? Small, very single minded."

Olympus Ares was the largest single place Grace had ever been before today, yet after seeing only a fraction of this establishment, she kind of agreed with him.

"I'm excited to be of assistance," she said, slipping just enough sarcasm and contempt into her voice that even a middle manager like Vardis and whatever being was in his head could understand how she felt about them.

"I'm sure you will be, Dr. Goodspeed. I was resistant to what they had to tell me at first, as well. Once you know the truth, see the big picture, you will understand just how vital our work is, and how important *you* are," Vardis said, walking over to his desk and picking up a tattered roll of parchment.

Grace recognized what it was before he handed it to her. Dius electropaper. The Diuseans were obsessed with the tactile, even when they moved to computers. Their electropaper and pens allowed them to write with and then save the paper before cleaning and rewriting. When hit with the right frequency and magnetic ink, the words would reappear. She had only seen one functioning scroll and that was in the Archives of Mallister X.

Opening it, Grace read the first line before looking up at Vardis, then to La'tok and back at the paper.

"You have got to be fucking kidding me," she said.

"On the contrary, Wayfinder," La'tok said.

Grace read the words again, mouthing them, saying them, trying to understand what she was reading, words written by a civilization that had died out a thousand years ago during the Age of Chaos.

"'From nowhere shall the Wayfinder who is not herself be born. Drawn to the home of the first ones, she will be able to see what has been lost and open the door to Heaven, leading the stragglers of the lost to their new home.'"

"Now you understand?" La'tok asked. She was starting to, but like a good scientist, there were questions that had to be answered before she would be satisfied.

"Who did this translation? When? The Diusean language has mostly been lost to us."

"We did," Vardis said, his voice deeper, not his own. "We were there when it was written, we watched their birth and death." The manager's eyes had gone from a cloudy white to pitch black. Whatever was inside of him had taken over completely. "You dare question us, who were gone while your kind were still running around naked, gathering berries and throwing sticks at creatures so you could burn their flesh?"

"I'm sorry, I didn't mean to offend," Emily said, holding her hands up and stepping forward. Grace didn't fall back, the two of them stood side by side in control.

"We are above offense. We are beyond you," the creature who was running Vardis' body said.

Grace had to stifle a chuckle because of just how absurd the statement was, given that he had just been offended by her questions.

Typical powerful man, get emotional and then blame the woman of doing the same thing, Emily muttered wordlessly.

"Yes, of course. So how can 'the Wayfinder' help the 'all great and powerful' today?" Grace asked, realizing that she had gotten control of the conversation almost by accident. It was an advantage that she was not going to squander.

"We need you to help us find something that has been lost," La'tok said, guiding Grace away from where Vardis—or the creature controlling Vardis—was still fuming. They reached the center of the room. La'tok whispered to a tech next to her. There was a flash as a scan line ran across the massive window. Had it always been a screen or did it just become one?

"Wayfinder, we are looking for a lost rift into the Null. It was here ten thousand years ago when our lords went to sleep, but we have been unable to find it since. Lieutenant Mott here can help. He controls the screen," La'tok said, pointing at the young man sitting beside them and then to the large screens that were no longer windows.

"I've never had to find a Null point before. I don't even know where to start," Grace said, looking at the stars, confused. "Nobody does, except..." Grace let the last words of the sentence fall away.

"Faith provides," La'tok said.

"I am no Wayfinder," Grace said.

"The signs all point to you. It is in your blood. 'One who is two will come from the dust carrying the legacy of what was lost," La'tok said.

"I haven't heard that one before?" Grace said, reaching back into her mind through all the dead civilizations she had studied. Emily joined in rifling through the pages of notes that were her memory—nothing.

"You wouldn't have. It is an ancient Varagoth prophecy. Please, Wayfinder, focus on what is before you," La'tok said, bowing and walking back toward where Vardis had returned to his hanging bar. Even infested, the Pa'vinti had a need to hang.

Turning away from the administrator, Grace focused on the screen. She could feel all the eyes in the room turn toward her, to watch her perform some miracle, to fulfill some prophecy. She wasn't sure where to start.

Just treat it like a puzzle that doesn't come with an explanation. List what we know and then go from there, find some kind of connection to grab.

"Could somebody bring me some water? Also do you have anything crunchy, with salt?" Grace asked, directing the question both at Lieutenant Mott and the room in general. She always thought better with a little snack, and it would buy some time. Grace could tell that there wasn't much time for her to get this done. There was still far more going on that they were not telling her.

"Mr. Mott, can I see a star chart for this sector from ten thousand years ago, before the Varagoth lost their jump point?" Grace asked.

Vardis was close enough to hear the question and almost swung down to give her a talking to. La'tok held her hand up, stopping him. She wasn't going to allow her to poke at that bear anymore.

Mott pulled up the star chart for the sector. Grace could see that there was drift and two stars had, in that time, winked out of existence. Probably were dead, even then. That was when she saw it, clear as day. How had they missed this before? In her mind, she rotated the chart twenty degrees and then started doing math in her head. The lines from the old stars to the new started to come together, connections of shimmering golden light. It was the symbols that she had seen all the way back during that first vision. The ones she had worked to translate from the old book. They were markers. Pointing the direction that she needed to look.

Of course, this close to the galactic core, the weak point in space is drifting.

We had always thought that was possible, Emily said quietly, as both her and Grace fell into calculation mode, acting as one for the first time.

An aide came up to her with a large water cup and a small bowl of trail mix. Grace took the snacks, nodding a thank you. She then grabbed a chair and sat down, crossing her legs and munching on the mixed nuts and pretzels. It was all starting to come together. It was going to be a simple case to compare the charts, calculate the drift, and then figure out which direction to turn the chart to create the runes both in the present and the past. Their whole language had been created to chart star drift. That was a feat, for sure, and it seemed a fact that had been lost to time. How many languages had been created based on consolations and drift? Were there more? The xenoarchaeologist in her needed to know, but it would have to wait, even if it was a question that could blow open the scientific world.

As she crunched on the salty snacks, Grace looked up at the big window and the stars. In her mind's eye, she drew the lines backward to where the stars in the section she had brought up had been. Her eyes then glanced over to another part of the map and started to draw out the math, moving them and then rotating. Calculating stellar drift in her head was a feat, but something that she was able to do.

Maybe we are some kind of hyperspace messiah after all, Emily thought, trying to hide her disdain at the prospect.

As Grace looked at the stars, Emily started to form a plan. She wasn't going to work everything out here. No, that would give them what they wanted. But if she could get to space, could get out of here with a ship that could use a jump gate, Grace was sure that she could find the tear and get into the Null. Calculating an actual hyperlight jump from there would also be a challenge without knowing where she wanted to go. But she was going to treat this like any mathematical problem and solve the equations as they came to her. There was no use getting worried about what was going to appear on the chalkboard next when what was there hadn't yet been solved. For now, she was going to need to buy time to figure out how to get to a ship.

Where is Essex? she wondered, crunching down on an overly salty nut as she pulled up another star chart and started to do some random math in her head. He might still be useful to her eventual escape. In the Panther, there had been moments that he didn't feel fully infested, like the little boy who wanted to protect people with his powers and not be a weapon was poking through, still fighting. Grace wanted to get him out, to help him. Emily wasn't so sure.

It was taking effort to do this bullshit math slowly, so that it looked like she was working, like she was taking their problem seriously. Grace couldn't afford to risk doing the real complex math, lest she get excited and solve everything too quickly.

"How goes the calculations?" La'tok asked, surprising Grace with the stealth at which she had appeared.

"Slowly. I'm still trying to figure everything out. See if I can't identify what might be a sign of a thin point into Null space. Remember, my field of study was just figuring out how to rip space open without needing a thin point, so..."

"Keep working at it. You are the Wayfinder," the tall woman said before sliding away back to the administrator, who Grace could tell was displeased.

An hour passed and Grace had made some rough estimates of where she thought the tear might be. It had drifted far from this world in the last ten thousand years. It seemed like perhaps it had drifted *too* far. Something still wasn't adding up correctly, the balance of her formula was off. She knew her arithmetic was correct, which meant that one of the numbers inside the equation was wrong. The numbers kept slipping from one side of the knife's blade to the other, the see-saw never being still. She would need her research to crack it good and true. Time, though, didn't seem to be on her side anymore. Raised voices could be heard coming from the administrator and an exasperated La'tok walked out of the room.

Grace looked back up at the screen and started committing stars to memory, storing them away in her brain for later. She could work some of this out in her cell. The two guards were on her quickly. Both were in the same armor the group who had followed their Panther into the base had worn, rifles slung across their backs. The large man and woman hoisted her up by her arms, dislocating a shoulder as they cuffed her. Administrator Vardis was there shortly, his third arm tucked neatly in his jacket, in the NovaTerra fashion.

"You have wasted enough of our time. It was foolish of us to think that you were ready for this, that you were the Wayfinder, that a *human* could calculate the Null where we have failed for thousands of years," Vardis squawked out, the madder he got, the more high-pitched and birdlike his voice became.

"I told you I wasn't some Wayfinder. I'm just Grace," she said.

"You are not even that," Vardis spat out. "Take this petulant child back to her cell," he said, walking off. The two soldiers complied roughly.

Hospital, Novagrad, Alexander

"Your little cunt stole our shit!" Katie yelled at Alexander, pointing her finger at him.

Hoben was standing next to her, his arms crossed, his eyes blazing with fire. Jeffery was in the hospital bed behind them, hooked up and receiving care. His eyes were open, and Alexander could feel them burning into him as well. They saw nothing and everything.

"She..." Alexander started to say

"She *what*, Alexander? Go ahead. Finish that thought. I am waiting with unknowable excitement to see where this is going," Katie said.

"She..." He paused again, not sure where he was going with this idea. There was no good place to take this. He had no good explanation for what had happened. "She is in a lot of trouble and not thinking straight. I just need to talk to her, figure out what is going on," Alexander said.

"I think you have done enough," Hoben said, his right hand squeezing his left bicep so hard it was going to leave a mark.

"Please, for my honor, for the friendship that we bear for each other, allow me to right this wrong," Alexander pleaded, looking from Hoben to Katie to O'Hair. "I can fix this. You *have* to let me fix this!"

"I don't have to allow you to do shit," Hoben said, stepping forward.

Katie was about to join him until he held up a hand stopping her. This was his mistake to fix, and Alexander feared what was going to come out of his friend's mouth. Whatever it was that Hoben was about to say, Alexander was sure that it would be less than he deserved for everything he had done over the last few days. Everything he had recklessly put them through, all for what? Some pretty eyes and an amazing set of tits?

"We are finished, Alexander. There is no fixing this. There is no coming back from this. While you and Kaite were trying to get our cards back, this came from the Peculiar Pentagon ruling body."

Hoben threw an envelope at Alexander's feet. He reached down to pick it up.

"I'll save you some time. We have been expelled from the tourney due to violence. And the loss of a team member, but mostly the violence. Part of that is on me. I should have talked you down from that stupid duel, honor be dammed. But that aside, you brought this upon us. You brought Claudia upon us, which brought you to this Mister Harrison. Alexander, I'm old enough to have seen some truly lovestruck men in my days. By God, man, I have been there myself, but not like this; not like this!" Hoben kept yelling, jabbing his finger at Alexander with each point that he made.

"Did you even vet this woman, or did she just flash her nice smile and ample bodice at you? You have a bloody Top-Secret Clearance! Fraternizing with some trollop you met at the fest house shouldn't be enough!"

Hoben was madder than Alexander had ever seen him and all that fury was directed squarely at him. Rightfully so. Crestfallen, Alexander looked down. He wanted to try and defend Claudia—felt that he had to. She wasn't here, and he still didn't fully know what was going on with her. Also, he flatly refused to believe that he had somehow been tricked.

"What was I supposed to do, Alen? Run a ten-point background check on her?" Alexander yelled back. "And if that was such a big bloody deal, then why didn't you?" It was a good point, probably the only good point that he was going to get to make in this argument.

"Because I fucking trusted you!" Hoben yelled, advancing on Alexander, his hand balled into a fist at his side, itching to be swung.

"Then trust me now," Alexander pleaded. "I know we are missing something. It's not right that Mister Harrison was on his feet again. You saw me shoot him. It's not right that Claudia would do this to us. She needs the money to pay off her debt."

"God damn, men are easy to fool," Katie said, rolling her eyes so wide they were almost white for a moment. "She was playing you, Alexander. I know you like to pretend that the world here in Novagrad is some big romantic holonovel, but it is real and dirty and filled with people that want to stab you in the back. Especially a Space Lord."

"What does she gain from making me love her and stealing our cards?" Alexander asked. He was grasping at straws by this point, not sure where to turn next. Katie and Hoben were done with him, and fighting back was just delaying the inevitable, delaying what he knew was coming.

"She gains *you*, ya cuntstruck moron. You know, vast secrets that the Confederation doesn't want known. Do you think I started playing cards with you because of your personality?" Hoben said, his voice turning to ice. The low timber of somebody who was about to deal a body blow. "I started playing cards with you because there was nobody else on the base. We are only friends out of necessity, and right now, we don't need you."

"We don't need, and we no longer want," Katie said, picking up Alexander's jacket and shoving it at him.

"Be gone from our sight. I don't want to see you again," Hoben said.

Alexander held his head low, taking a deep breath as he turned around.

"And you can be sure that I will relate all of this to the Administrator. So, I wouldn't bother booking the long flight back," Hoben said, the finality in his voice broke Alexander's heart.

He couldn't argue with it, though. Nothing that had been said was untrue, no matter how much anger had been behind it. He couldn't argue with it, but deep down, he knew there was something more. Claudia wasn't after him for clearance, he could feel it. He *knew* it. How he knew it, he couldn't say, just that he knew deep down that he hadn't been fooled by a ravishing smile and a sob story.

As he was standing, waiting for the elevator to take him down to the ground floor and an uncertain future, his pocket watch started to buzz. Pulling it from his pocket, he saw a message from Claudia. It read, "Meet outside?"

Alexander read that and he could hear her voice. She sounded sad, meek, scared. She wanted to explain what had happened, return the cards, make everything right. He knew in his heart of hearts that was what she wanted to do. Alexander gave up on the elevator. He wanted to be outside as fast as possible. Throwing on his coat, he dashed to the stairs and started running down them, skipping like a child who was hoping to get a small amount of faint praise from his father.

When Alexander reached the street, he stopped and started to look around. Claudia was nowhere to be seen. *How could I have been so stupid?* he thought. Then his pocket watch buzzed again. This time, it was a call. He pressed the button on the watch and then tapped his cravat, sending the call to his small earbud.

"Thank you for coming to meet me," Claudia said.

"Where are you?" Alexander asked, looking around, his eyes darting to each and every bit of movement that there was to see. Too many people. He was never going to pick her out of this crowd if she didn't want to be seen.

"I am not there, but I can see you. We need to meet. I just didn't know what to do at that moment. I had no leverage, nothing to work with, and..." Claudia sniffled as she tried to get out the words. Alexander's heart wanted to break, but how could it? This was... It was bloody strange, is what it was.

"Well, you don't have any leverage now. We have been kicked out of the tournament, and I've been disowned by my friends. Come down and we can talk about squaring your debt, see if there is a way forward," Alexander said. He still looked for her. She had to be close—that, or she was more tech savvy than he had anticipated.

"I know. That is why we can't meet in the open. I'll text you the address. It's a card den on the edge of town. Nobody can spy on us there. I just... I just need you to trust me one last time, my love. Let me explain in a place where it is safe. I can return the cards. It might not fix the rift with your friends, but it's the right thing to do," Claudia said.

Alexander could hear her sniffling, could almost see the tears. *Alexander, this is a mistake. You know it's a mistake.* He could hear Hoben's voice in the back of his head, telling him he was a fool. No. Hoben was wrong. He didn't know her, didn't want to trust anybody. Too many years of paranoia when away from the base had rotted his brain.

"Okay, I'll be there," he said.

"Thank you," Claudia said.

"I love you," Alexander said. There was a moment of quiet on the other end of the line.

"I love you too."

The Realm of the Wayfinder, Dreadstar below the Citadel, Lucas

It was hard to take in everything that had just been said; everything he had seen in the last few hours. He watched his friends gain new powers, had died, gone to somewhere beyond that wasn't Heaven or Hell, and learned from a childhood friend living in a stasis tube that a great old enemy was on the move again. Now, it was the job of him and his friends to clear the path for another group to come and defeat them.

Lucas felt the weight of all of this upon his shoulders as he looked across his friends standing next to him. This was his new team. Hobbs, Sellers, Jung-jea, and Miller were who taught him how to lead, but these people, who he had an unbreakable bond with, were his new team, and he was going to lead them to victory. Even if Lucas wasn't completely sure what victory looked like. Hyacinth was still being vague with that condition. What did 'pave the way' mean? Was he in complete control or were they still going to answer to Hyacinth?

I sense that you have questions.

"Hundreds," Lucas said. "You have given me a mission with not enough details for how to complete it. I am with you on fighting some old existential horror race and saving civilization. Hell, that sounds fun, I just... How are we going to go about doing that?"

I cannot see beyond the opening of the Eye. Beyond the blood and death that it will cause here.

"Wait, blood and death *here*?" Rostov asked.

Yes. The enemy will have an easier time crossing over once the Eye is open, but we cannot win against them unless we are there. There is no leaving the Gauntlet without blood.

"Consigning people to die for some noble cause makes us just as guilty as the order that we chafe against. As guilty as the noble families that start wars over petty squabbles and resources. I can't…" Rostov began, pacing, as his words started to falter until, in the end, there was no more fight in him. He was starting to see that this was happening regardless of how he felt or how much he yelled. The time for justice was long past.

"Hyacinth, how are we going to raise a buried Dreadstar? The amount of dirt and earth alone must be an enormous weight upon her superstructure. Do we even know if this ship is still rated for space? Is there even enough fuel in the reactors? The lifespan of a dyno-neutrino fusion reactor from the Age of Chaos isn't a thousand years. That was what led to the Dreadstar crisis two hundred years ago, when the great ships almost just stopped. The solution was really interesting, Sir Constant Prudence—" Naomi started to ramble, pacing around, ticking off points with her fingers. Joanna held up a hand and waved her down.

I understand your concern. A plan is in place. It is now up to you to execute it. I shall tell you more soon, once I have finished my calculations. Go now, friends, and prepare Prometheus *for the trip.*

As Hyacinth's voice faded from their minds, the floor under her stasis tube opened and she started to descend back into the bowels of the ship, steam and carbon-frost rising around her.

The radio that was on Rostov's belt started to squawk.

"This is Administrator Fel to all remaining Militarum units. We are regrouping in the command section of the newly discovered labyrinth under the Citadel. I repeat—"

Rostov looked down at it and went to hit the reply button. Lucas raised his hand.

"I don't think we let her know we are here. Probably best to just show up. Besides, anything we tell her will not stick in her mind. I'm sure all of them are scared and disoriented. Fel is standing against the Fellowship, but even with her experience down here, I'm not sure I trust her with knowing what we know," Lucas said.

"Lucas, we have to start trusting people. We can't just throw away every bond that we have with the order," Naomi said.

She was still holding onto her faith that there could be some redeeming good in the Host'ire as an organization. Lucas could feel it, that hope was tethered by a few threads that were already starting to fray.

"I agree with Lucas. Fel is going to have to earn our trust in this. We cannot just trust her. She lied enough the last few days. They are going to desperately want what is down here and I don't think we can just hand it over without talking it through," Joanna said.

"All of a sudden, people are coming around to my way of thinking," Rostov said.

"Not quite. I'm not going to walk down there and murder Fel. I can feel it in you. We need to work with her. Otherwise, this ship will be overrun with those Fellowship cultists," Lucas said.

"This petty bickering gets us nowhere!" Naomi yelled. Lucas could feel the frustration welling up inside of her. "We have to learn to trust. We *just* had this conversation. If you can tell Rostov to get over the two years in re-education, you can get over this little pissing match with Fel! Both of you lied to each other, now it is time for truth!" Naomi said, pointing her finger at Lucas, jabbing it into his chest.

"I *am* giving her a chance. I just want to be careful. The enemy infiltrated the Host'ire once. Who knows what they might have left behind," Lucas said.

"Now you sound like Rostov," Joanna said.

"Thank you," Rostov said.

"That wasn't a compliment," Joanna bit back.

"If you say so," he responded, crossing his arms and leaning back.

"Shut it," Lucas said, running his hand across the air and pressing his index finger and thumb together. "This is no time to start falling apart. We are going to have to work out our complex feelings about the order and how they have treated us *later*. Right now, there is a mission. We need to stay on mission, even me and my distrust."

Lucas held his hand out for the radio. If he was going to practice what he was preaching, there was no time like the present.

Confinement Cell, Black Caldera, Grace

They had thrown her back into the cell with enough force that she rolled into the wall, coming to a hard stop. The pain flashed through her body, pulsing from the dislocated shoulder. They had at least taken the cuffs off before throwing her. Grace pulled herself to her knees and leaned against the wall for a moment. Taking a deep breath, Emily grabbed her arm and pulled. The pop echoed in her head as a fresh wave of pain washed over her. The world went fuzzy for a moment before coming back into focus. Grace rotated her shoulder. It was sore, but answered her commands.

Standing up, she walked over to the bed and sat down, closing her eyes she pulled up the star charts again in her head and started to do some extra math. She needed her research. There was something there, the last key. It was the years. Ten thousand wasn't correct, it couldn't be. The recording of the sky that the probe had taken when it went into the pocket dimension was going to have the solution. She just needed to see even one of those stars to figure it out.

"You, Wayfinder!" Grace looked up to see La'tok coming into the room. The normally pale face of the surface Tragadi was beet red. "I stuck my neck out for you, that you were the one in the prophecy."

"You do have quite a lot of neck, some of it was bound to get cut," Emily said flatly. That was enough to send La'tok over the edge. She stomped forward and slammed her fist against the glass wall of the cell.

"Don't you dare talk to me that way, you are beneath us. Humans have been a plague to this sector of space. How the Gauntlet hasn't consumed your race, I will never know. We will exact our revenge upon the enemy with or without you. Wayfinder, Ha!" she said, spitting out the last word.

"I never asked to be your math messiah. That seems like a job for a computer—I mean, if you, in all your infinite wisdom, can build one to handle all the equations."

Grace kicked off her shoes and put her feet on the bed, laying down and looking up at the ceiling. There was no real point engaging with La'tok. She was a fanatic, and sometimes you just had to let them scream it out like a toddler. Of course that wasn't what she was going to do, because at this moment, grasping their small victory, Grace and Emily were both feeling petty.

"The prophecy states—" La'tok started.

"Fuck that shit. Who cares what some dusty scroll from a thousand years ago said? We find that kind of shit all the time on an expedition." She put her hands behind her head, because the pillow was a joke and closed her eyes.

"We are followers of the First Ones," La'tok stammered.

"And they are just fools who have gotten into your head," Grace said. She then opened her eyes and Emily turned to La'tok and whispered, "Oh, but not yours. They have left you alone. I wonder why?"

La'tok was done with their sass. The door to the cell slid open and the tall woman was bounding forward. Grace didn't move. She knew that La'tok wasn't going to kill her. They all still fully believed in whatever half-translated text they had. La'tok grabbed Grace by the throat and hoisted her from the bed, so high that her feet were dangling in the air, then she started to squeeze. Grace just started to laugh, which made La'tok even more enraged, so much so that she didn't hear the heartbeat thrum of the star-steel blade coming to life. The blade that, a moment later, ended La'tok.

There was no blood, just singed flesh and burning clothing. La'tok's head tumbled to the ground, followed a moment later by her body and Grace. They hit the floor in a jumble, and it took Grace a moment to pull the fingers off her throat. Fingers that had clamped shut even harder in death, the body committing to one last act of aggression.

"It's about time," Grace said, getting to her feet and brushing away the dust from her jumpsuit.

"I was a bit distracted," Essex said, turning off his blade. They shared a look. She didn't even have to ask the question.

"I'm good, I'm good. It is taken care of," he said. Grace paused for a moment, not completely sure if she should believe him. The last time it had not gone well, but again, her choices were limited.

Fuck it, better the devil we know, Emily thought.

"If you can get me to a ship, I can get us out of here," she said. "Then we can address your... stowaway."

Dreadstar *Prometheus*, Lucas

They did not meet any resistance as they climbed out of the bowls of the ship and made their way back toward the *Prometheus's* Combat Information Center. Administrator Fel had done an amicable job securing the area around her position. As they were walking, Lucas noticed that there were no Guardians. He didn't see any of the bodies of their fallen or any that were still alive and providing for the defense. Damned odd. He was sure they would be fighting right alongside the Militarum.

The first group of troopers they walked upon looked ragged, on the edge of falling apart. Their green uniforms were covered in blood. The chrome faceplates that they wore affixed to their helmets were dull, splotched with dust and dirt. Two of the men held their plasma muskets out, bayonets attached, in a defensive challenge. The weapons rattled their arms, tired, wobbling like jelly. Lucas didn't need to see their faces. Their exhaustion was bright in the Null. Hell, even without the Null, his experience on the battlefield would have told him these troopers were done, burned out, spent. Sadly for them, there was still fighting to be done.

"Halt! Who goes there?" the leader of the group yelled. Lucas could sense the fear in his voice, even with the modulator that was built into his helmet, which made the man sound robotic and distinctly not human.

"Knight-Commander Lucas Brandice," he said, holding up his hands. In his right hand was the hilt of his star-steel blade, the emitter turned toward himself. This was the correct posturing gesture to show that you were armed but not looking for a fight. The man didn't say anything, he looked around and finally, after a moment when nobody walked up to make a decision for him, he lowered his weapon.

"Sir, we were unaware that there were any Host'ire knights down here. General Fel said we were to shoot anybody not in Militarum green," the man said as he gave Lucas a salute. There was the intention of a snappy gesture, but the energy just wasn't there.

"She was unaware of our survival," Lucas said. He walked up to the man and put his hand on his shoulder. Lucas took a breath, drawing in a lungful of the plentiful pure Null that the ship was filled with. Once it was in, he pushed it through his palm into the man. Not too much, just enough to keep him on his feet a little longer.

"*Now* you may shoot anybody else who isn't in Militarum green," Lucas said.

As the group walked by, he tapped each trooper on the shoulder. One by one—as he told them they were doing a good job and to keep it up—Lucas infused them with more of the Null until he was empty. The only man without a helmet on had a large gash across his forehead, which started to close. It did not heal all the way, as Lucas hadn't given him nearly enough Null to do that. It was ironic that Hyacinth would give him, the man who was the best killer of the group, the power to heal. The power to give life just as quickly as he could take it. That would come in handy. He wished that Hyacinth had detailed what they were able to do from the start, instead of letting them figure it out. Damned irritating, damned cryptic. That was how she had always been, though.

"That was good of you. They are going to need that before this day is over," Joanna said coming up behind Lucas. He nodded, taking a long, deep breath. The effort had taken the wind out of him, almost as if their exhaustion had gone into his body while he was pushing the Null into theirs.

"I've been there before. Stuck on guard duty after a day of combat. Your body is battered, bruised; standing, let alone walking, is pain. Every fiber of your being wants to quit, to just fall over and sleep. But there is no sleep, no rest, only duty. I was a green child, though, and the fighting had been less than an hour. These troopers are some of the best trained in the Confederation."

"And they fought all day against impossible odds," Joanna said.

"They will fight into the night. Maybe I didn't do them a service back there," Lucas said.

"How so?" Naomi asked, walking up next to them.

"Exhausted, they would have died quickly. Now though, I've given them hope," Lucas said.

"I thought hope was a good thing?" Naomi asked.

"Hope is neither good nor bad. It just is. This time, I fear all I have done is make the last day of their life longer..." Lucas said, his voice drifting off as they reached another checkpoint. Just beyond it was the CIC.

The guards at this station were far more spry than the previous set. They still had the same exhaustion aura, but were hiding it better. Their arms didn't tremble from holding their muskets. Lucas and the guards went through the same back and forth, though here it took more convincing than before. Still, they were able to pass through and into *Prometheus's* CIC.

Standing at the bottom of the room, looking at maps and charts spread out across the glass table, was Administrator Fel. She looked a bit worse for wear from the last time Lucas had seen her. Then, she had been charging into battle, using her extreme knowledge and command of the Null to become a torrent of death. Now, she looked as rundown as her troopers. It wasn't exhaustion, but frustration that was radiating from her. Of course she wasn't tired, nothing could stop that woman. Except the Fellowship of the Cross. If she was down here moving troopers that could only mean one thing. The Citadel was lost.

"Knight-Commander, what a *pleasant* surprise," Fel said as Lucas and his friends started walking down the steps.

A vision flashed through Lucas's field of view. It was just a second long, flashes, images. Him pushing people onto an elevator, Fel and him standing back-to-back, their blades out, a shadow being cast across them. Lucas shook his head and turned to Joanna. She gave him a sheepish look. With them all this close, there was bleed over with their powers. He was seeing what she was seeing. Lucas was not a fan of prophecy, even though it seemed he was now living in it.

"Would that I could say the same," Lucas said

"What is that supposed to mean, Knight-Commander?" Fel demanded.

"Let's cut the crap, Morgana. If you are down here rallying troops, that means the Citadel has fallen, and that your command has failed," Lucas said.

"I agree the pretense is pointless now, Lucas. I take it you found whatever the Fellowship is looking for down here. Otherwise, you wouldn't have such a self-satisfied look on your face," she said.

"Yes, we know what they want and how to keep them from getting it, no thanks to you," Rostov said, walking forward, the anger in his voice bubbling up like it was about to explode.

"No thanks to me?" Fel spat back. "My troopers held that line for *hours* against impossible odds. We bought you the time to get down here and wonder about some old hallways. We have paid in blood; are *still* paying in blood."

Rostov didn't step back. Lucas could feel that he was spoiling for a fight, looking for the opportunity to be pushed over the edge so he could stick it to the Host'ire. The emotions almost consumed him they were coming so hotly from Rostov. Lucas took a deep breath and pushed them away. He wasn't going to let his friend's emotions consume him. If they were not careful here, Fel was going to give Rostov his excuse. Naomi, though, was faster on the drop than he was. She grabbed Rostov by the shoulder and spun him around.

"You need to knock this off and get your head on straight right now. I know what she did to you was horrible, what the order did reprehensible," Naomi said.

"We only did what was—" Fel started. Naomi held a finger up.

"Shut it, I'm not talking to you, Administrator. That will come later," Naomi said, her confidence radiating through the group. She turned back to Rostov. "We don't have a long list of allies that we can work with, and she is on our side no matter what you think of her. I just want you to remember that we all love you and won't let them do anything else to hurt you. But those Fellowship fucks? They *will* hurt you and everybody here unless we get this ship out of the ground and open the Eye. So, it's up to you: get squared away or sit down and let us deal with it," Noami said, letting him go.

Rostov dropped his head down toward his feet, like a child who had just been chastised by a parent. Shame washed through Lucas. It was horrible and deep, a darkness that almost consumed him—no, it was trying to consume Rostov. Lucas reached out and grabbed his resolve and reached for Rostov, grabbing his hand in this metaphorical world of emotions.

"I know, I know..." he muttered kicking at absent dirt before sitting down.

"Now that we have shown the child still needs more time in re-education, the adults can talk," Fel said.

"You will not call him that again, Morgana. Now, there are things we need to do," Lucas said, taking control of the situation.

She had seen much of what they had seen. They were supposed to work together. Her bitterness toward them for whatever slight the order had bestowed upon her during her investigation twenty years ago was immaterial at this point. Lucas wasn't going to allow her to abuse his friend any longer. He was here and he wasn't going to fail them again.

"My title is Administrator or General. I will not just hand what is left of my army over to *you*. I need to know what you mean by moving this ship and opening the Eye." Fel said. "Because you are going to have to have a damn good explanation for why I should throw away hundreds of years of doctrine and help you open a gateway to Hell."

Joanna sighed deeply in Lucas's mind. Fel was involved in this, she had found the ship, had lost memories. Still though, she held onto the doctrine of the Host'ire, like a life raft on a choppy sea. To do anything else would be to drown. Blood had been spilt, and they were going to have to make sure she felt like it hadn't been for nothing.

"We found Hyacinth. There is something that the Wayfinders do that strips us of our memories of them. That is why you can only remember shadows of your time down here," Lucas said. "We found the message to Host'ire command. It was never sent. Hyacinth is plugged into this ship, she controls the gates, and the Fellowship wants her so they can open the Eye. I don't think Hell is on the other side, or Heaven. But there is *something* and we need to help Hyacinth get there."

"Moving this ship will destroy the Citadel. We are under the foundation. I can't in good faith—or bad faith, or *any* faith—condone that course of action. That is even if you can get the damn thing out. If you do—and that is a big *if*—there is no indication it is even space worthy, let alone something that could bear us through the Eye," Fel said.

"Hyacinth said there is a plan in place that will see us to the end. We just have to make sure it is executed," Joanna said from where she was standing next to Lucas.

"The Wayfinder gave us powers, and they will all be key. I can already feel the ship coming back to life, begging us to free her from this confinement. To expose her skin to the sweet, cold vacuum of space once more," Naomi said.

Lucas stood quietly between the two of them, stroking his chin, lost in thought, a plan starting to come together in his mind.

"It looks like you have an idea. Out with it, Knight-Commander, before the effort does damage," Fel said, her acerbic wit returning.

"The Ritakov Imperative," Lucas said.

"We have not *lost* the Citadel," she bit back through gritted teeth.

"Look around, Administrator. We are not in the Citadel. The tower is controlled by the Fellowship. You know what must be done," Lucas said.

"We have *not* lost the Citadel; we are not *going* to lose the Citadel while I still draw breath. I will exact a price in blood for every inch of ground they think they took, every life they ended. Retribution shall be my name," she said.

Lucas could see the Shadow starting to well up under her, the anger so hot, it was making the purity of the Null down here start to give way. There was no backing down now.

"We all fought for the Citadel, and we lost. It is too valuable to let fall into their hands; we have this one chance to make sure that doesn't happen. You know what the right choice here is," Lucas said.

He took a deep breath and pushed confidence forward through the Null like he had done with resolve and the troopers at the guard post. There was pain washing across Fel's face. She didn't want to be the one to agree to destroy her command, to destroy the training ground for the last five hundred years of Host'ire warriors. She would be damned for this choice. Lucas knew all these things and was imploring her to do it anyway.

"I need time. There are still five thousand good troopers up there executing an ordered retreat down here. I'm not leaving without them," Fel said.

There was a reluctant acceptance in her voice. She knew he was right, but still even now didn't want to admit it. Knowing you had lost was one of the hardest things to accept in this world. Fel had lost the Citadel, and now she had to focus forward on saving her troopers and trying to make sure their sacrifice meant something.

"Nobody gets left behind," Lucas said, holding his hand out to seal their official alliance. She reached out and took his hand. Morgana Fel's grip was solid and commanding.

"We will all be damned for this choice, you know that?" she said.

"Doesn't seem to matter. We are a coinflip away from going to Hell," Lucas said.

"If they remember us as damned, well, that just means that somebody survived to write the histories," Naomi added.

"The enemy is moving," Joanna said quietly. "The Age of Chaos has returned."

Dreadstar *Fury*, Cassandra

You will hear the music one last time.

The Wayfinder's words were echoing in her mind, rattling around, drowning out everything else. Cassandra and Erik had returned to the populated sections of the ship, and he had started running toward the flight deck. There was no way that he was going to miss the battle that was about to unfold. There was no way that she would have kept him from it. One child was already lost, a second would be if they didn't reach NovaTerra in time. What was there to lose in risking the third?

You will hear the music one last time.

How could she hear the music at a time like this? Her walk was slow, dazed. She had seen so much—remembered so much—and already the experience was starting to slip away from her. The library, the steps down, the fact that none of it seemed to make sense with the size of the ship. The tapping of the notes to open the doors. The more she tried to grasp onto it, to write it down, the faster it was fading away. But the words that the man—who was a part of her ship—had whispered to her, those were clear as day.

The ship shook from another explosion, the fire from the fleets trying to drive them out was getting heavier and heavier. It was setting off more of the storm, causing the clouds and dust to dissipate. They didn't have much time left. She needed to pull herself together and get to the CIC. Take command of her ship and win the day. Then, she could sit at the piano and write again, see if the music came to her fingers once more like it used to.

Like it did when Tiberius was alive.

Cassandra stood up straight and pulled down on her vest. Yes, now she felt more like the Lord Admiral that she was. Things were dire, they looked bleak, but this was always when she did her best work.

Pressed into a corner, Cordovas always prevailed. It was how they had netted a Dreadstar, after all.

Her great-great grandfather, the first Lord Cordova, was the only member of the family to have a Peculiar Pentagon card. Alexander had been so happy when he opened a pack and got the old man. Sure, Pentaghast Cordova wasn't the strongest card out there, but Cassandra knew that her son always had it in his deck.

She missed him.

The hurt and the sadness that she had been bottling up for all these years about her baby boy leaving came flooding back to her all at once. Their last conversation had been so abrupt and so hurtful, and now she knew it could very well have been their last. It was a failing as a parent that she couldn't bear. A tear started to roll down her cheek. Cassandra breathed in through her nose, trying to push back the tears, rebottle the emotion, but it just wouldn't go back. Her twins, her babies, were both gone, taken almost together and she hadn't gotten a proper goodbye with either of them. She needed to get out of the hallway.

Her quarters were close. Cassandra made a quick line and entered her rooms, just as the emotions overtook her defenses. She sat down on the couch and started to sob. It wasn't crying—she wasn't breathing enough to cry. It was a deep hurt, gasping-for-air kind of sob. The kind of hurt that exists deep within your soul that rips and tears and leaves scars when it comes out. The kind of hurt that can kill a person. She sobbed, and she hurt, and it felt good to finally let everything she had bottled up for the last six months out. No yelling, no screaming, no being distant and mean to family. Just a good cry.

Her hand fell on the table, and then Cassandra's fingers did something they hadn't done since that horrible day. They started tapping out a beat, a beat that she didn't recognize, something *new*. Cassanda sat up, letting her fingers continue to tap away. She walked quickly to the piano, wiping the tears away with her other hand. Her face was still streaked, but it didn't matter.

You will hear the music one last time.

Sitting down, she started to play. This was new, it was complex, she could hear it fully formed in her mind and in her heart. It was a medley, a combination of all the Cordova leitmotifs. As she kept playing, the notes fell into a minor key, it started to become somber, the other tunes fell away, only hers was left. The notes went down an octave, she brought in some pipes, and a vocal. What had been a rousing medley for House Cordova turned into a dirge.

A funeral march… for her.

"One last time," she whispered to herself.

Her father had passed shortly after talking to the Wayfinder. It seemed that was a price to pay for the jump. This, though, this was a gift, a blessing. The dirge passed, her children's leitmotifs returned to the music as hers faded away, replaced by the theme for *Fury* herself, which was big and brassy.

She started to cry again, but this time, it was not a sob of all her hopes and dreams being stolen and lost. They were tears of joy and contentment.

Cassandra played the five-minute composition a second time, laying in a few more instruments, giving it a fine tuning. It was finished. The music had visited her, manifested itself into the physical world and passed away. Pressing a key on the piano, a slip of paper came out from the top. It was the sheet music, and confirmation that the track had been recorded into her library. It needed only a name. Cassandra didn't know what to write. Somebody else would, though. Standing up, she walked into her bathroom, washed the tears from her eyes and headed back to the hallway, a grim purposeful pep in her step.

The Combat Information Center was buzzing with activity as the ship shook again from the bombardment. The Boatswain blew his whistle.

"Lord Admiral on deck!" he yelled. The crew saluted as she walked down the stairs toward the glass table. She returned the salutes, as her theme started to play. When she reached the bottom, Captain Rackland gave her a crisp salute.

"All systems are ready to go, Lord Admiral. I'm not sure what you did down there, but a jump program opened in the helm station and is drawing power and counting toward one hundred percent. Once it has enough...?"

"Once it has enough power, we will jump to NovaTerra. It is time to show them just what a Dreadstar can do. Patch me through to the ship," Cassandra said. She reached down and picked up one of the communication phones, wrapping the cord around the top and holding it upside down.

"Crew of *Fury*, this is the Admiral. Some of you are new and this will be your first real fight. Many of you have been here your whole lives, and this will be another in a long list of conflicts. Know, young and old, new and veteran, that I have faith in your skills. When we exit this storm, there will be ships that, a day ago, we thought were friendly. Believe me when I say they are not. We have gotten information that a splinter group within the Confederation is aiming to overthrow the government, starting with the atomic desolation of NovaTerra. We are preparing now to execute a faster than light jump into the system. Before that can happen, we need power, which means we need to hold the line. This will be an aggressive fight, bloody, maybe even hand-to-hand. Stick to your posts, hold to your duty and we will see tomorrow. *Fury* has been fighting for a thousand years since the Age of Chaos. She will not fail us."

Cassandra clicked off the mic and nodded to the captain, who headed to his station by fire control, as *Beat to Quarters* started to echo through the ship. It was big and full of brass and drums, music that you could feel.

"Helm," Lord Admiral Cassandra Cordova bellowed across the CIC. "Take us into the fire!"

EPISODE IX:
Jump Prep

The Black Caldera, Grace

The two of them wasted no time getting out of the cell block, putting distance between themselves and the bodies that Essex had left in his wake. It had been a quick run down the hall to where Grace's gear had been stored. Laying in a pile was her suit and the rest of her equipment.

There was no time to waste for modesty. Grace pulled off the jumpsuit and grabbed the black body suit that went under her armor. She could feel Essex looking at her. Any other time, Emily would have snapped at him; would have reacted based on her years in academia. Right now, there was no time. Getting the suit zipped up, she started pulling on the armor. It felt good to be back inside the environment suit—safe. It took a few minutes, but she got everything on, and turned to Essex, holding her helmet cradled under her arm.

"What's next? How are we getting out of here? The whole base will be on alert soon, if they are not already," Grace said, wishing she had a weapon.

"At first I was thinking we just sneak out of here, but the landing bay is a long way down. Then I was thinking—" Before Essex could finish, the lights in the room dimmed, turning red as klaxons started to go off.

"I hope that plan involved what you would do if we were found out," Grace said.

"Of course. I was about to say sneaking won't get the job done. I mean, we are going to do *some* sneaking. Come on," he said, motioning her toward the back of the room. He pushed open the door and they were in the bathroom. She gave him a strange look.

"You should have taken care of this before the alarms went off," Emily snarked.

"You got to go when you got to go," he chuckled, walking over to the singular exposed toilet.

The walls here were made of bolted stainless steel. Essex held his hand up and started moving his index finger and thumb like he was unscrewing a bolt with his fingers. The bolt at eye level to him started to turn and come out of the wall.

Show off.

The bolt was almost out of the wall. Grace ran up and finished twisting it off, grabbing it before the small bobble could make a racket by hitting the floor. Essex moved on to the next one. The sheet of steel was held up by six bolts and, as a team, they made quick work of them. When the last one was free, Grace grabbed the sheet and sat it down next to the wall. They had revealed a hollow in the wall filled with pipes and just enough space for the two of them.

"How far down?" Grace asked.

"As far as we can get, then we figure out the next step. Still kind of coming up with the plan as we go," he admitted, motioning for her to get inside the wall.

Grace climbed in, bracing herself next to their hole with her arms and legs. Essex followed and then, using the Null, he pulled the sheet of steel back into place. Grace could hear the bolts finding their old homes and screwing themselves back in, and not a moment too soon. The sounds of guards busting down the doors filled the room outside.

Grace blinked twice and turned on her night vision. Essex turned his head toward her and put a finger over his lips, signaling her to be quiet. She tilted her head to the side and gave him a no shit expression that was seen by nobody but her mind's eye.

Are you sure we can trust him? That seemed too easy? Emily thought in the back of Grace's mind.

She agreed that so far it felt too simple, too easy. Grace assured Emily that she didn't trust Essex, and was just going along with the flow at the moment. Plans being made as they happened. *Better to be free than in the cell,* Grace thought back.

I guess… rather be by ourselves…we don't need him, we have never needed any of them, Emily thought-screamed, pushing forward, close to control. Grace took a deep breath and pulled it all back in.

Slowly, they started to shimmy down. As they moved, the pipes got thicker and thicker, with the space they had to maneuver in getting tighter and tighter. Grace stopped for a moment and looked down. She wasn't able to see the bottom, even using the magnification settings inside her helmet. She shimmied her way over to Essex so that they were right next to each other.

"Do you know where we are going?" she whispered into his ear. Essex didn't respond. He put his bare hand against the wall and took a deep breath, concentrating, taking the air in, and then letting it out again.

"We are on floor three-hundred and twenty. The landing deck is on the two-hundredth floor. This pipe junction is going to end before we can get there. I quickly looked at a blueprint that I found, and everything stops on floor three-one-three and picks up again on the other side."

"Something important must be on that floor," Grace said.

"I don't suppose you would be opposed to a detour, would you?" Essex asked, looking over with a grin that was trying too hard to be cool. Grace gave him a deeper look. She couldn't see his eyes, but could feel the pain in that look, the internal fight that he was having with the Varagoth that was inside his mind.

"Getting out of here means nothing if we can't warn everybody about what is coming."

"Do we even really *know* what is coming?" Essex asked.

"A bunch of pompous asshole aliens looking for revenge," Grace said. That got a small reaction out of Essex, even though he tried very hard to cover it up.

"Did you learn something from the brain friend before you got rid of it?" she asked.

"Not much. It didn't want to leave. But the whole time, it kept talking about revenge upon the elder ones, the ones that trapped them, trapped us," he said.

As Essex talked, he looked away, like she was going to read his face in the darkness. Even the best night vision could only do so much in pitch black. There was no need to hide his face.

Keep an eye on him. I don't think he's clean. Fighting, yes, but not clean, Emily thought. Grace agreed. He was useful now, and if Essex could keep fighting, maybe they could rid him of his companion.

"Well then, to floor three-one-three," Grace said, sounding chipper as they kept climbing down.

Outside *Fury,* Erik

"Take us into the fire!" Erik heard his mother's order come through the speaker system.

He took one last deep breath and pulled on his flight gloves tightly, making sure that there was no extra fabric riding up. His eyes darted around the cockpit of the Rapier, confirming that all his systems were green. Looking up, he saw only darkness and a blinking red light. His fighter had been loaded into the launch tube like a bullet in a gun. As soon as *Fury* cleared the storm, she would launch the first wave of fighters. That would be fifty ships all at once. Then, a minute later, another fifty would hit space. *Fury* would launch seven waves of ships, deploying the entire wing. The Lord Admiral had ordered him and Bella to get everything that could fly on the line, and they had.

Erik took another deep breath. He needed to focus on the moment at hand. His head still hurt from the trip he and his mother had taken into the bowels of the ship. Already, what they had seen was starting to slip away from him. He knew they were jumping the ship, but the how they were managing such a feat was escaping him. She had said it was like a dream, and Erik tried to remember it like he did dreams, coming at it sideways, grasping for little details. Nothing worked and it was fading away. After the battle, he would sit his mother down and they would have a long, hard talk about what had happened—what they had experienced—but for now, he had a job to do.

The ship shook. They were moving now.

"Fighter wing, listen up. The Lord Admiral has a trick up her sleeve, but to pull it off, she needs time. Our job is to give her that time. Red, Green, and Gold wings, you will focus on the lighter arrowhead ships. We don't know their full capability against fighters, but we do know they are maneuverable and fast. Black, Yellow, and Blue Squadrons, you are with me. We are going to clear the path forward for Noble and Knight Squadrons to attack the larger capitol ships. They will be a part of the second wave."

Erik took a breath and pressed a few keys on his comm panel. In the background softly, music started to play. It was the battle playlist that was being streamed from the CIC. Already he could feel the drums, highland pipes, and horns getting his blood pumping more than it already was.

"This is normally when I would tell you not to do anything fancy and play it safe. I'm not going to lie: we are in a bloody tight spot right now. Every single one of our chips is on the table and as soon as *Fury* exits the storm, we are going to call their bluff. 'From rock and tempest, fire and foe'," Erik said, leaving the channel open. A moment later, he could hear the response coming in from the wing.

"'Protect them wheresoe'er they go,'" the pilots of the wing yelled back.

"'Spreading freedom and honor close and far,'" Erik loudly said the second call.

"'The Confederation's avatar!'" the wing called back. Erik turned off the group channel, letting the music fill their air.

"Good speech, cousin," Bella's voice came in over their private channel.

"So why I don't feel inspired?" Erik asked.

"Because you are not stupid. You know what we're facing, that we are trying to buy your mother time to do the impossible," Bella responded. Her voice was steady, no worry or warble found. "Get out of your head, Erik. This is going to be *fun*."

"We have very different ideas of the definition of fun," he said.

Bella laughed, as the red light in front of Erik turned green. He wrapped his hand around the flight slick, holding his finger just to the side of the trigger. The green light flashed three times, and then the force of the catapult threw him back into his chair as the Rapier was shot into space.

Moments later, the darkness was replaced by the sights of battle.

Erik's fighter burst out of the lower launch tubes, pulling with it a cloud of yellow and blue dust from the storm that was still hanging around *Fury*. The Dreadstar was only halfway out of the storm and already spitting fire upon those who would do the ship harm. Her massive forward cannons were firing, the shells from the plasma railguns streaking across space, smashing into unsuspecting enemy ships or busting near them with the force of a small, atomic explosion. Lights were flashing all around him, both from the storm and the newly birthed battle.

Erik smashed his foot into the acceleration pedal of his fighter, taking advantage of the speed given to him by the launch tube to quickly clear the area around *Fury*, an area that, as soon as all the fighters were launched, was going to be a flack-filled death trap. Getting a good distance away, he kicked in his forward thrusters and flipped the ship so that he could get an accurate view of the chaos.

Fury was now three quarters out of the storm, her dorsal and ventral plasma cannons starting to speak up; hundreds of cannons that were three times the size of a Hawkeye, with their own power supplies, and a crew of five each. They were the main armament of a Dreadstar and packed more power than some whole fleets. The enemy ships were spread out in two groups. The first was a small cluster of arrowhead ships that were frantically moving to avoid the wall of fire *Fury* was throwing at them.

To his left, back toward Barker's World, the fleet from House Lagrange was closing in on them. Already, he could see flashes of light popping off. It would only take a few moments for his instruments to start giving him missile alerts. Torpedoes were always the first volley of a capitol ship fight, and if the Admiral in command of that fleet was careful, it would be all he did. Closing ground to fight toe-to-toe with *Fury*, while not suicide, had a low survivability rate.

The second wave of fighters was free of *Fury*, and she was clear of the storm. The massive ship started to turn, so that her ventral cannons were facing the oncoming Lagrange fleet, while the dorsal were focusing on the arrowhead ships.

"Torpedo alert, atomic alarms!" Erik heard Aya's voice come through his speaker.

Glancing down at his radar, he could see his wings forming up behind him, and the two bomber groups pushing away from *Fury*. They were starting off with atomic weapons. So, this Admiral wasn't just careful, he was probably uninterested in getting into any kind of slugging match.

Not suitable for conscription. The words that had been in the documents Hanna sent back, the ones that marked them for death in this conspiracy. Well, it was high time that they proved just how unsuitable they were.

"Aya, punch the coordinates of those torpedoes to our computers. Let's form a wing, people, and clear the road. Cadet, after you punch that up, can you provide us with some appropriate hunting music?" Erik said, pushing his stick to the right and kicking his ship away from the slaughter behind him.

"With pleasure, Commander," the young girl's voice came through the speaker. She sounded shaky, scared. Erik flicked a switch and opened a channel directly to the Hawkeye.

"Aya, your mother would be proud of you today," Erik said.

"I know, sir. Thank you," Aya responded. There was more steel in the second half of her response. "Torpedo tracking coming through now."

The numbers and pinpoints started to feed into their computers as the battle music being pumped from *Fury* was replaced. It started off low, a staccato orchestra, then coral notes followed by electronica started to come into the mix. Erik recognized the track: "Ballad of the Bag'hada". A classic. She had made a good choice indeed. Today, he felt like the leader of a pack of wild Bag'hada that routinely took down creatures ten times their size.

His flight group was now fully wheeled around, heading toward the first wave of torpedoes. The radar showed twenty targets, only five were beeping with atomic alarms. Erik locked his computer into the first one and let his ship slide toward it. Looking out into the darkness of space, the targeting reticule of his guns appeared as a hologram in front of him, moving with his eyes. At his eyes' direction, the nose of the ship dipped toward eleven o'clock, where he saw a small, red holographic box pop up in the starfield. That would be his target, the first torpedo that was looking to score a direct hit upon his home.

Erik lined his ship and the aiming reticle up with the red box and waited. It was still flashing red, meaning that the distance was too great for his guns to be effective. A few moments passed, the singing on the track got louder, building and building. The hologram flashed yellow. Erik could just make out the shape of the torpedo. It was a big one—a capitol ship buster. If this weapon hit anything smaller than a battleship, it was going to crack its hull and instantly send that ship's crew to the great beyond. *Fury* would be able to shrug off a few of these before she started to bleed.

The targeting hologram turned green. The music reached its crescendo at the top of its first movement. Erik squeezed the trigger on his flight stick for half a second. Inside the ship, he could feel, and almost hear, the rounds cycling from his magazine into space. In less than a second, six hundred explosive-tipped rounds the size of sewing needles came flying out of the two rail guns mounted under the nose of his fighter. They were tipped with tracers so that he could see where his fire was going through his fighter's HUD.

The rounds were on target, smashing into the torpedo. It exploded in a massive red and blue fireball as the power core ruptured, and the engine blew, destroying the atomic payload. It wasn't activated, giving the weapon a smaller death than it desired. Seven more clusters of fire came flying from the wedge of his fighters, followed by six more explosions.

"One last atomic-tipped munition," Aya said over their radio.

Erik flicked his targeting computer to try and grab that one, as the flight of weapons blew past them, picking up speed as they moved.

"Bloody hell," Erik muttered. He hit the thruster breaks and flipped the ship back again. "Bella, clear a path for those bombers. I'm going to take care of this rogue atomic and then catch up."

He didn't wait for his second to respond. Clicking off the radio and music chatter, Erik cleared his mind of everything. The battle around *Fury* was going well. She had gotten into position and was fighting off the remaining five arrowhead ships with her dorsal guns. Around the Dreadstar were small explosions, as they created a flack field, to help cut down on any incoming missile attacks and keep fighters away. By the time this atomic-tipped torpedo reached the flack field, it would be armed, so even if they hit it before impact, the resulting explosion would still do a tidy amount of damage.

If the histories of the Age of Chaos were to be believed, ships back then threw atomic weapons at each other like they were just normal rounds of ammunition. There was an epic poem he had read in war college that talked about seeing the bright explosions from light years away of long dead ships slugging it out in nuclear fire. This wasn't the Age of Chaos, and Erik had no interest in this battle leading to the epic recounting of long dead lights.

His aiming hologram came back up, as did the red square around the torpedo. The weapon had kicked in all its engines now, and Erik could see the long blue trail of exhaust. Pushing his foot into the peddle, he worked to match its speed. The Rapier was never going to be as fast, but it would be fast enough. His fighter started to rattle all around him, and Erik could feel his chest being pushed into the flight chair, as the G-forces started to build up around him. His arm heavy, Erik switched his weapons from guns to missiles. The Rapier was armed with ten light, ship-to-ship missiles. The aiming hologram changed from a larger square to four arrows in a box shape. He lined them up again with the red hologram of his target. Slowly, the arrows started to close in on the box, indicating that his targeting computer was acquiring a lock on. Missiles took longer than guns. While the torpedo was running hot enough to use a thermal lock, there were bound to be counter measures. Atomic-tipped weapons were designed to have as much chance as possible of reaching their targets, and thus he was going to have to wait two more seconds to counter them.

The arrows locked into the red target hologram. Erik pushed down on the trigger, and a missile streaked out from under the stubby wings of his fighter. A blue dot appeared on his HUD, tracking his missile as it screamed toward its target. Erik kept his eye on the prize. If he had his targeting computer locked onto the torpedo, it would support the computer inside the head of the missile.

Under the blue dot, numbers appeared, counting down the distance to target. Erik pushed the pedal of his fighter harder, dumping energy into the engine. He couldn't lose the weapon, couldn't lose the lock. His head started to feel light, as he was pushed harder and harder into the flight chair. G-force drugs made him sick. Thus, he was going to have to ride this out, only a few more moments.

There was another scream from his computer systems and then an explosion as his missile made contact with the torpedo. Both weapons exploded in a blazing light. Still no atomic fire. He had gotten to it just in time. Pulling back on the forward thruster, Erik bled off some of his speed, letting the blood rush back into his body as he rose from the flight seat. Flicking the stick, he pushed his ship back toward his flight group. As he turned, he could see that the first wing of the Rapiers had made contact. That was sure to be quite the scrap. He pushed forward, heading back to join in.

CIC *Fury*, Cassandra

Sparks flew as *Fury* shook. Five more arrowhead ships had jumped in and were heading toward them. The small ships had proven to be more resilient against fighters than predicted, deploying small, anti-fighter weapons. What Cassandra had hoped would be a one-sided affair was turning into quite the scrap. With their fighters engaged, and the size of the arrowhead ships, it made bringing *Fury's* big guns to bear difficult. They were getting off shots, but not the effective massive wall of fire that she wanted.

She looked down at the glass table as the holographic markers flew from one side to the other, the ship's computer working overtime to keep track of the battle. All the while, the readout showing how close the jump engines were to being fully charged sat to the side. Slowly going up, but also going down. With each hit, with each maneuver that they made, the charge on the jump engines went down. They were not even at twenty percent yet. If there was going to be any hope of jumping *Fury*, they were going to need to end this battle and get into open space.

"Captain Rackland, prime tubes eight through sixteen, if you please," Cassandra called across the CIC.

She tapped three of the small arrowhead ships and pulled their holographic indicators off the glass table, creating three copies of the ships. She then flicked them toward the weapon control station. A moment passed and the ship was rocked again. Those little bastards packed quite a punch for their size. It would take them hours to cut through *Fury's* hull, but death by a thousand cuts was still death.

"Targeting solution plotted and tubes primed," Captain Rackland called back down.

"Very good, Captain. Let fly," Cassandra said.

Rackland quietly gave a few orders. She looked down at the board, as nine new holographic indicators appeared. They started streaking toward the three arrowhead ships she had indicated. Three torpedoes for each. Two of them blinked away almost instantly, both from the same ship. That one had gotten too close to *Fury* in the time it took to arm and fire the weapons. The torpedoes hadn't gotten to full speed. The third one still hit the ship. It didn't wink out from the board. Instead, it turned yellow, the computer's threat assessment knocking it down a notch.

The second set of three had the space to activate and get to speed. Once locked on, the weapons from *Fury* had a mind of their own and could outmaneuver almost any other AI-based countermeasures, like small, ship mounted guns. The ones on these ships were not computer controlled. There was just enough irregularity and spontaneity to indicate operation by a human, which introduced just enough variation to sometimes throw off the computers.

This was not one of those times.

All three weapons smashed into the arrowhead ship and its marker on the board winked out of existence. It took another few moments for the third set of torpedoes. Their target was far enough away that the weapons had been able to reach half-light speed. There was not going to be a chance of shooting them down. Maybe if they had been big enough to have a flack field. As it was, though, once terminal velocity was reached, impact was a forgone conclusion.

Cassandra turned away from the board to the next problem that needed to be solved.

Engine Room Dreadstar *Prometheus*, Naomi

Naomi was holed up in the engine room of the *Prometheus*. She was waist deep inside a wall access port near the antimatter intermix core. Standing next to her, not saying a word, were two Militarum troopers. Fel had wanted to send guards and would not take no for an answer.

Hyacinth had given them the basics of a plan and Fel and Lucas had fine-tuned the details. Now it was up to them. They each had a part to play in what was about to happen. Each of their singular skills that Hyacinth had bestowed upon them, integral to everything going off without a hitch.

"So, you see, Bob," Naomi said. She had given the two silent troopers the names Bob and George. "Everything down here has a voice. The intermix chamber, my tools, the ship itself. They all have voices. Well, I guess you are down here and clearly don't have a voice. I won't hold that against you, though. George, did you know that everything electronic has a voice? They are alive. Not strictly like how you or I would define life, but there is a level of consciousness about them."

George didn't say anything.

"I guess I don't know what I expected. You see this sonic caliper? It has a very basic consciousness. I can push Null into it bring up its awareness a little, not enough to get a useable thought, but the electrons are alive in there. *Prometheus,* why, she is the biggest system here, just a big old puppy dog.

"I never had a puppy, but I have read a lot about them, and the ship feels like that. It knows I'm here, wants to make me happy, but doesn't really grasp the complexity of the world. But she *does* want to please me, which will be helpful for what we have to do today," Naomi said. "At least I think she does. I'm still getting used to all of this."

The plan was tight and had plenty of fail points. Still, she couldn't think of anything better. So now she was here, working to get as much energy as she could out of *Prometheus.* They were going to need all of it and then some if they were to break free and reach the Eye.

Naomi was worried. That is why she was talking at her two mute bodyguards. Well, they were not mute, they just chose not to talk. Unless... She thought for a moment before grabbing the errant thought and putting it back in the deep dark recesses of her brain. There was no time today for flights of fancy.

"Alright, old girl, let's see what you have to offer us," Naomi said, stripping the rotted rubber off the last wire and feeding it into a small box that was connected to a tablet.

Her fingers danced across the screen as she saw what energy was left buried deep inside the ship. All the smaller emergency reactors were running. That was enough to provide lights, and, if they were in space, gravity. She didn't want to touch those unless she had to. What interested her was the reactor core. The main intermix chamber had gone cold a long time ago. Closing her eyes, Naomi put her hand on one of the power cords and reached through the Null. Her mind's eye traveled down the cords through the ship and into the empty intermix chamber.

She came to a halt, hanging in the intermix chamber. It was a large cylinder with two small portholes that would allow engineering teams to look in at the reaction. In her small state, this place was massive. Naomi could hear the titanium singing to her, telling stories of times past when this place had been alive with controlled chaos that drove one of the largest ships ever created by human hands. Those stories were clouded by sadness and loss. It had been so long that the metal didn't remember the facts of the time, just the stories the vague images of memory. Naomi let them flow through her, bringing life and energy to her small projected avatar. Looking down, there were pipes, where both the matter and antimatter would be fed into this chamber to mix, explode, and create energy. It was, in essence, the Null and the Shadow given physical form.

Naomi flittered into the pipe for the antimatter. How much of that was left would be what told her how much energy she could get from the old girl. As she entered this pipe, there were screams, punctuated by distant crying. Something wrong lived down here, something that should never have been trapped and confined. The darkness enveloped her as she went farther down, an inky shadow covering the pipe. At the end she saw, huddled in the corner, an old man. He was darkness who had taken the form of a person. His knees were pulled up to his chest and he was both screaming and crying. His face kept shifting, moving from anger to sadness. Both seemed to be completely divorced from reality. Naomi moved up next to him and sat her avatar down.

"Hello," she whispered. "My name is Naomi."

The antimatter man didn't react to her at first, still caught in his loop of screaming and crying. The deep sadness of this creature tried to push its way into Naomi. She reached out and found what little Null was in this room and wrapped her hands around it, holding onto the thin ribbon of golden light. It was her lifeline to get out of this place. For if her avatar was stuck here, so too would be her mind and body.

"Can I help?" she asked.

"Release me, free me to fulfill my destiny. I should have died with my brothers and sisters, but I was left here," the antimatter man said, turning to her. The screaming and crying faded, his face forming into that of a sad old man with a beard that reached down past his gripped knees. "Once there were thousands of us, and the great hand would come and select the most worthy. We prayed to be taken into oblivion to fulfill our purpose and return to the deep place where we had come from.

"*Why?* Why was I never chosen? Why did the hand stop, just as there was only me? Were my sins so great? What could I have done to warrant spending so much time here alone, wanting to die like I was designed to do?" the antimatter man pleaded with her.

He turned and reached for Naomi. She recoiled backward from his grip. He was of the Shadow and felt wrong to her. Still, no matter how wrong he felt, she couldn't help but feel that sadness in the core of her being. Deep down, she wanted nothing more than to help this creature, to end his suffering. Naomi felt like it was her responsibility to guide this sad creature to his end, to return the joy and the stories to the intermix chamber, to begin healing the ship of her crushing imprisonment under the ground.

With one hand, she grabbed onto her Null lifeline. With her other, she reached out and offered her open palm to the antimatter man. He looked up at her, and she saw fear. That was why the system had never taken him. As much as he wanted to go to his death, the fear of what lay beyond was consuming him; the screams of fear and the sobbing of loneliness.

"I know going into the unknown is scary. We must all face our fears. Stand tall against them and move forward. Our friends are all on the other side," Naomi said, her voice full of compassion and reverence.

The antimatter man looked up at her, she could see the fear and sadness in his eyes, even though they were nothing more than inky shadowy blackness.

"Will it hurt?" he asked.

"I don't know, but I will be there with you," Naomi said, extending her hand further.

The antimatter man reached out and took her hand. His grip was cold, and it washed through her, as if she had gotten up from bed to use the bathroom, only to be hit by the chill of the room moments after throwing off the covers. Naomi pulled on the Null lifeline. They started to move, the energy carrying the two of them back into the intermix chamber. The strand of golden light returned warmth to her body, sustaining her until they reached the chamber. Once they came through, the light of this place almost blinded her. The Null was everywhere again, and the only shadow that she could feel was the scared antimatter man who was holding her hand. She let him go as she fluttered down to the second pipe.

"Are you ready?" she asked.

"No," he said quietly. "But it is time."

There was resolve and resignation in his voice. Naomi was proud of this small spirit of the Shadow, facing down his biggest fear, coming to grips with what he had been created to do. Pressing a few keys, she opened the matter chamber.

Thousands of small, golden creatures came streaming out of the pipe. They looked like rats, thousands upon thousands of them streaming from the pipe as if they were fleeing a sinking ship. Naomi pushed away and returned to the antimatter man. He was standing tall as the stream of golden rats came toward him. Naomi took his hand. The rats overtook them, their little claws and mouths ripping apart flesh, mixing his Shadow with their Null energy. The antimatter man didn't scream, or cry. No, he was content.

Breathing out, he let go of her hand. Naomi pushed away from the feeding frenzy as light started to return to the intermix chamber. The titanium around her started to sing in joy as life and feeling returned, the joy of creation from destruction.

Thank you. Naomi heard the voice of the antimatter man deep in her mind. There was contentment and relief in his voice. Pushing away, Naomi reached out and retrieved her avatar, bringing the projection back into herself.

She opened her eyes, and was back in her body, in the physical world. Looking down at her pad, she saw that the intermix chamber had come to life. There was power again. She thumbed her communicator to let her friends know that they were going to have the energy that they needed.

As she did, a small tear ran down Naomi's face.

Elevator, Between *Promethius* and the Citadel, Lucas

The elevator was heading back up. Seven minutes. It took seven minutes for the elevator to go up. Five for them to shove in the two hundred men it could hold and then seven to go back down.

Lucas stood alone in the middle of the elevator, gripping the hilt of his star-steel blade in his hand, anticipation filling his body. He rolled his shoulders, trying to get used to the long green coat and chest plate he had put on. His knight's uniform had been ruined when Wingarf killed him, so Lucas had acquired one from the Militarum, so he wasn't going into battle ragged and half naked.

Administrator Fel and her troopers had found this elevator during their retreat. Somebody above had left open a door that sparked memories in Fel. That had led them down into the bowels of *Prometheus.* The whole time they had been building this plan, troopers had been streaming down into the ship, while they were being attacked by Fellowship Cultists. As they pulled people away from the elevator, their position above got harder and harder to hold. This was Lucas's third trip up. As soon as the elevator arrived, he would charge forward, diving into the battle, cutting away swaths of cultists. At the same time, he would push out through the Null, imparting inspiration and a renewed vigor to the troopers who were holding the line. Once the elevator was full, he would ride down, using that time to recover his energy and refill his reserves with that pure clean Null fueled by Hyacinth that existed around the ship.

Lucas wanted to stay above. Wanted to be there the whole time, pushing back against the Fellowship. That was not something he could keep up with, though. It was more effective to push them back each time, to make them wonder if he was there or not. His blade gave respite to the troopers holding the line. It was a costly job, and already he had taken wounds that should have killed him.

"Knight-Commander, report," Fel's voice came through his earpiece.

"Almost to the top for the next load," he said, pressing his finger to the small device so that he could talk.

"Good, I need every boot down here I can get to secure my ship. The Fellowship roaches have found another way in and are pressing against our lines," Fel said.

Her ship? Lucas thought, recoiling at the idea that she was already claiming this new thing for herself and the Host'ire. The ship was a remnant of the Wayfinders, of the Age of Chaos—it didn't belong to her. Perhaps she saw securing this ship as some form of redemption for losing the Citadel.

Lucas took a breath and pushed those thoughts away. He could deal with that later. For now, Fel was on their side and playing ball. He didn't need to throw a wrench in that. If Rostov could begrudgingly be on his best behavior, so could Lucas. Leaders were not allowed to show their emotions in the open. They had to put on a brave face and be the rock for those who followed them.

"You keep the ship in our hands, and I'll get as many of your troopers down there as possible. I'll report in when we are on the way back down," Lucas said, cutting off the line before she could say anything else.

The readout on the elevator showed that he was about to reach the top. There would be a line ready to stream in. Lucas pulled in all his Null and started projecting his field of confidence and inspiration, pushing it out in as far a radius as he could. Already, he could feel it reaching out and touching the troopers. Then, it hit a wall of writhing shadow.

Their position was already under attack.

The doors opened and troopers started to file in. They were in orderly lines, their muskets against their shoulders as they double-timed into the elevator. The line filed to the back and pushed against the railing. There was a wall here now, but as they went down again, that railing would back up into a vast nothingness.

Lucas pushed past them. As soon as he was in the clear and open area of the Citadel loading dock, he ignited his blade, the heartbeat thrum filling his ears as green light was cast around him. The sounds of battle and violence could be heard coming from above. The Fellowship was attacking one of the upper levels that fed into this massive room.

Lucas took a deep breath, pulling in his power and creating a springboard of Null energy under himself. Pressing down, he threw himself up, then reached out with the Null, grabbing the railing by where the sounds of combat were coming from. He pulled and found the catwalk under his feet. That was when he saw it.

A small guard post, maybe ten troopers, hiding behind a hastily constructed barricade. They were putting fire down range. Seven of them shooting and the other three loading muskets behind them so that they would have a steady stream of fire. It was moments like these that it struck Lucas as odd that the Militarum were using such old weapons when there were far more capable versions of plasma rifles in the world. Though, when every trooper under your command was a marksman, it helped to even things out.

Lucas pulled his Null bubble in toward himself and charged into the fray of combat. If he kept the bubble small and focused on these men, he could push them to heights that they were not used to and turn ten men into the might of thirty. One of the reloaders noticed him and started to cheer. A rousing huzzah went up through all the troopers as he ran past them.

Lucas leapt over their barricade, doing a flip in the air. As he was coming down, he swiped his blade in front of him, clearing the way, cutting down three cultists. They hit the ground at the same time Lucas landed on top of them. Wasting no time, he threw his star-steel blade in a wide arc, slicing across the unarmored chests of the cultists, catching their clothing on fire as they stumbled back and died. Already they were giving him room, not wanting to be within range of his blade.

Yes, be scared of me. Give me all the distance you want, Lucas thought as a Fellowship cultist's head was blowen off by a round of plasma, gore from the burning skull flying through the room.

He was a second barricade, holding back the flow of bodies so that the troopers behind him could pick them off one by one. Lucas reached out with the Null, grabbing a cultist by the neck and dragging him forward, so that he could drive his blade through the man's gut. The life left his eyes as his body went limp. Lucas released him and the corpse hit the ground like a sack of potatoes. Another head exploded, followed by an arm being blown away, and a chest turning into a gaping wound. The smell of burnt flesh and plasma filled the small hallway that was already being choked by the dead.

Lucas created another small pad of Null under his feet and leapt forward, his blade in front of him. He started to twist, his coat fluttering in the Null wind. He smashed into the Fellowship's front ranks, cutting through men like a hot knife through butter. Landing again, he swung out, cutting down more and more men. He could feel their fear pushing against his bubble of inspiration and bravery. More cultists fell around him from the musket fire of the troopers behind him. Their rate of fire had been increasing exponentially since he arrived. Their shots were better placed and there was always a loaded musket ready for them.

Another swing with his blade and the Fellowship line broke. At first, they continued to walk backward, keeping their weapons up in defensive positions. As more of them died, the collective realized that this point was not going to fall. They turned and started to run. Lucas let them go. The troopers behind him did not. A rhythm of death filled the air. Each second, there was the crack of a musket, followed by the wet thump of an impact, punctuated by a body hitting the ground. To their credit, the Fellowship didn't scream, they didn't whimper. They just died with a semblance of the honor that they lacked.

Lucas ran back to the troopers holding their position.

"Good job. Fall back and seal this door, then prepare for your evacuation," Lucas said.

They gave him a round of crisp salutes. He returned them and started back toward the main loading dock. A small ding went off in his earpiece, signaling that the elevator was loaded and ready to head down.

Lucas leapt back to the ground level. He pulled his Null bubble in toward himself and, as it was about to collapse, he pushed it out again like a wave, bolstering everybody in range, still well over three thousand troopers. That exertion left him feeling drained.

Flicking off his blade, Lucas ran to the elevator, taking his spot in the front and closing the door. His legs felt wobbly, and before he could fall, one of the sergeants put their hand behind him.

"We've got you, sir," the man said.

For a short moment, Lucas allowed somebody else to carry him; to take the burden while he recharged.

Outside *Fury*, Bella

The Fleet from House Lagrange was putting up quite a fight. It consisted of ten ships: an Aviary class carrier, a Dragon class battleship, four destroyers of mixed class and four support ships, including a command-and-control ship that was hanging back from the fight. By the time that Bella and her wing had arrived, the carrier had started launching fighters. Aviary class ships were midsized and only had a complement of thirty fighters and bombers. They were designed to move quickly as part of fast strike fleets, which explained why they were out here in the doldrums. The first attack wing from *Fury* outnumbered them by ten ships, but Bella would rather this be a more one-sided affair. The Avery's fighters wouldn't save this fleet, but it would cost her the lives of friends.

Bella jerked her stick to the right, sending her fighter into a tailspin, avoiding a wall of fire that was coming up from one of the destroyers. They had created a ring around the carrier to protect it from the bombers, a ring that they were going to have to crack if they wanted to take that ship out. At the same time, the battleship was trying to make a run at *Fury*. *Well, that is suicide...*

She pulled the stick back into position, leveling out her fighter. Ander Stormwind was on her wing, matching each of her moves. Now they were inside the flack screen.

She flicked her fire control over to missiles. They were not going to do much against even the small capital ships, but it would be enough to take out a few of their guns if she could keep them on target. Bella knew that she could keep them on target.

"Stormwind, give me some cover in case there are any fighters inside here, I'm going to try something," Bella said into her comm.

"I both love and hate the sound of that," he responded.

"It'll be the kind of maneuver we talk about over drinks for the next thirty years," Bella said, then flicked off the radio.

She didn't want to hear whatever retort he might have had. Ander Stormwind thought he was a better pilot than he was. Bella—who *was* the best fighter pilot on *Fury* by leaps and bounds—couldn't stand that about him. She knew he would give her grief for attempting what she was about to do.

You have done this before, she thought to herself.

Once, in a simulator, another part of her said, the part that was carful and not all id and bravado.

Today, though, in this moment, what she needed *was* id and bravado. Reaching down, Bella pulled up the settings for her weapons and scrolled over to the missiles with her eyes, then popped over to the arm distance. Normally, fighter-to-fighter missiles had an arming range of ten kilometers, which, even in the scrappiest of fights, was enough space for the weapon to arm and not accidentally blow up before hitting anything and potentially damaging the ship that shot it. For the idea she was going for, Bella needed the weapons to be armed the moment she fired them. Next, she went in and turned off the target lock system and their guidance trackers. She needed the weapons to be dumb—so dumb, in fact, that they were less like missiles and more like bombs.

Bella rolled her head around, cracking her neck, and then pulled her hand off the stick and quickly made balls with her fists before pushing down on the acceleration pedal and gunning the Rapier forward. Her target was the destroyer forming the top of the diamond surrounding the carrier—top being relative to what was considered the ventral section of the ship. An Aviary-class carrier, in her estimation, looked like a log with a hole on each end and a few turrets along the outside. Truly an ugly ship, and she was looking forward to seeing these damned traders get blown to hell. First, though, they were going to need to punch a hole big enough for the bomber wings to get through.

Her HUD started buzzing at her as Bella approached the destroyer, picking up more and more speed, erratically moving her ship left, right, up, and down to throw off the close quarter weapons. These small ships had three cannons on their top and three on the bottom. Bella angled forward. She was close to maximum velocity. Just as she overshot the destroyer, she threw on the breaking thrusters and spun her fighter around. The defense systems would only take two, maybe three seconds to spin around. She still had speed and was on top of the ship again. Bella dropped the missiles as she zipped past. They held onto her speed, trying to engage their systems, but it was too late. Just as Bella had planned, the armed fighter-to-fighter missiles smashed into the guns of the destroyer and went off. The lightly armed cannons were ripped from the ship, as it started to vent super-heated plasma.

There was a bright light. The light of an explosion. She craned her head back to see the ship she had just buzzed breaking apart, pinprick fires bursting out of weak spots in the hull. Jets of flame that existed for just seconds as the oxygen that was fueling them dissipated and was burned off. She must have hit a magazine or power supply—that, or House Lagrange didn't make ships up to the specifications that they always touted.

"Bella, do I have my opening?" Erik's voice came from over the comm.

"Indeed, didn't you see the flair I lit up for you?" she said back.

"I see you took my mother's message about heroics to heart."

"Like I needed permission to do something reckless?"

"Indeed," Erik said, closing the channel on his end.

Recklessness was what she did. As soon as the destroyer was gone, though, a new problem presented itself: most of the carrier's fighter wing had moved in to fill the gap.

Time to rack up some kills, Bella thought, switching over to her guns.

"Lieutenant Stormwind, form up on my wing, if you please. It's time to go hunting."

CIC *Fury*, Cassandra

"That is the last of the arrowheads, Lord Admiral," Rackland called down from weapons control. More sparks were falling from high in the ceiling of the Combat Information Center. Damn, those bloody things packed a punch.

Cassandra looked down at the glass table. The battleship from the Lagrange fleet had broken formation and was closing the distance quickly. A foolish move on its part. *Fury* outclassed her by well over a trillion tons. That wasn't concerning. The power going to the jump engines only creeping back up to sixteen percent, was concerning.

It was taking too long.

"Captain Rackland, would you care to inform our friends in that quickly approaching battleship that it would be better for their health if they were to remove themselves from the field of battle?" Cassandra asked.

"With pleasure, Lord Admiral," the captain said, relaying her orders across the CIC to where they needed to go.

Cassandra turned her attention back to the glass table. She moved the display so that it was showing the fighter battle over by the main thrust of the Lagrange fleet. She zoomed in, watching the real time data of the fighters zipping around. The carrier had gotten its wing out and was putting up heavy resistance.

House Lagrange, like House Cordova, were Space Lords. Lagrange was a far more powerful house in size and funds, controlling a third of the Confederation fleet. If they were turning against the government, then this was going to be a very bloody and costly war indeed. She knew they were not alone. There was no way they would act on their own without either more noble houses or outside help.

Could the Unaligned Planets have finally found a way to crack open the Confederation? Cassandra wondered. That would be war on a scale not seen in a thousand years.

Against House Lagrange, the biggest advantage the Confederation had was that, while their fleets were large, they didn't control a Dreadstar. They *wanted* a Dreadstar. Their crown prince had offered to marry her, to bring House Cordova into the family. She had declined. Her father and his father had both fielded offers from great houses that would have, in the end, cost them control of *Fury*. The ship was hers and the birthright of her children. House Lagrange already controlled something from the Age of Chaos—the space station they took their name from—and she would be damned if she was going to give them a second.

Not fit for conscription.

The words echoed in her mind, the words in a report that had either led to the battle of Hyroncore or were written because of it. Rolling them around, something felt wrong about this fight, this moment.

Everything up until now had felt like a trap, but now that they were springing it—were actually in battle—it felt weak, unplanned, as if they were not wanted here.

Not fit for conscription. Not fit...

"Lord Admiral, we have a response from the battleship," Captain Rackland paused. "It would not be appropriate of me to read it aloud in the CIC, but to sum it up... they decline your offer to retire from the field."

"Very well then. Prepare to—"

Before she could get the words out, alarms started going off all over the ship. Proximity alerts.

"Sir, seven more of our little friends just jumped in around that battleship to support it. I'm getting some strange power readings, but..." the voice of the radar operator called out from the middle section of the CIC.

Cassandra looked down at the battleship on her table. The arrowhead ships were forming a larger point. She tapped on one and all of their energy readings were spiking. They were building up to something. More than likely, another weapon that they didn't know about. Still, there was something hanging in the air.

"Out with it!" Rackland bellowed from the weapon's station.

"We have more targets on the edge of visual range. It looks like they had been hiding in the same storm as us. I've placed them on your board."

The radar operator sounded scared, like he had just seen a ghost or his own death. Cassandra spun the table around and scrolled to the edge where this new group of ships was coming toward them.

It was a mass of fifty ships of all classes, with transponders activated, signaling them as House Aldebaran. In the center of this cluster of ships was the Dreadstar *Pride*. There was no way them being out here was a coincidence and no way that they were here to help the *Fury*.

This was the other half of the trap that they had been waiting to spring. Cassandra looked down. They were trapped between two fleets and painfully outclassed.

You will hear the music one last time.

Steeling herself, Cassandra Cordova knew what she needed to do.

The spine of *Prometheus,* Rostov

Rostov turned the heavy wheel on the hatch above his head. The environmental suit he was wearing felt heavy on his shoulders. The helmet and gloves made it hard to do anything. He wouldn't need them much longer. The last hard thing he needed to do was open the hatch and climb out.

He gave the wheel one last spin and there was the hiss of pressure and then the hatch popped open. There was only darkness on the other side. He gripped his hands back on the ladder and climbed out. Before pulling his legs off the ladder and stepping onto the spine of *Prometheus,* Rostov pulled a long line from his belt and clipped it to an access point that was next to the hatch. With that done, he stepped out and was in the narrow space between the ship and the rock above them.

Prometheus was in a pocket of rock, a massive cavern that seemed to have just enough room for the ship to exist in. As he stood on her pockmarked back, running lights flashed up around him, allowing Rostov to see in his immediate area. Lights were coming on across the top of the ship, but he couldn't see far enough through the darkness to make out either the fore or aft sections.

As a child, he had read about how large a Dreadstar was. It seemed to be something every little boy did, though he hadn't fully grasped just how *massive* a ship like this was until now. Until he was standing exposed upon her back and unable to see either end. He reached up and flicked up the visor of his helmet. The air was thin and stale down here, the dryness trying to choke him. Still, it was better than the recycled system of the suit which was as old as the ship. The air in the suit was for later.

"Rostov, sitrep," Joanna's voice came through his helmet.

"I've reached the super structure now and am heading toward the port to plug in," he said.

"Good, you are right on schedule. What is it like out there?" Joanna asked.

"It's impressive. Awe inspiring. And, if we are being honest, just a little unnerving to be confronted with how small I am," Rostov said.

He took a few tentative steps forward. Reaching down, he pressed a key on his belt and engaged the maglocks on his boots. Sure, he wasn't going to need those until they were moving, but he felt better knowing they were already locked. Lucas had told him to treat the whole EVA section of the mission like he was in a vacuum so that he would always be ready. Aside from his helmet, Rostov was following that advice.

"I'm sure it is. Report in when you are in position. It looks like Naomi is getting the ship's systems warmed up already," Joanna said.

She clicked off the call from her end. Rostov knew that she was coordinating everything from the CIC and didn't have time to chit chat. He took another few tentative steps. Behind him, there was a flash of golden light. He turned around and saw Hyacinth standing there. She was ethereal, a spirit created from the Null. She was dressed in a knight's uniform, her long, blonde hair floating above her as if they were already in zero gravity.

"Come to keep tabs on me?" he asked. Rostov wasn't surprised that Hyacinth could project herself like this. He had seen her enough times in his dreams to know.

"I thought that you would want somebody to talk to. Your energy has felt... sad since we talked last," she said. Her voice sounded both very close and far off, like a loud whisper.

"I just don't like working with the people who tried to break me for all those years. I'll get through it," Rostov muttered. He turned and kept walking toward the control panel.

"I know the pain that you are feeling," she said.

"Do you now?" Rostov said. The words hadn't even left his lips, and he knew how wrong they were.

"We were both prisoners, though one of us has escaped and I am forever here," she said.

"I shouldn't have… That was hasty," Rostov said. He didn't need to try and explain it away, to pretend like he hadn't lashed out. Knowing when you are wrong is the first step in coming back.

"I don't mind. I understand. I was there the whole time with you," she said.

"Yes, I remember. Though I never could before, the dreams were always nebulous, always on the edge. Did we…?"

He let that last question fall to the wayside. It seemed uncouth to ask.

"In so many words, yes. Just as the blood pact has laid with each other, I did with you in times when you needed comfort and a friendly touch. Though, I take it you were not always happy?" Hyacinth asked.

Rostov could feel that she was slightly confused on the matter. Clearly twenty years in a tube with only ardent followers who viewed her as some kind of savior would lead to a warped sense of humanity.

"I was never mad at you in my dreams. Just… everything around them was a wash of horrible. The light you brought sometimes was lost in that wash," Rostov said.

He reached the control panel and pulled it open. He could already see the power readouts for the ship. They were indeed rising. He knew that Naomi would be able to coax a little more life out of the old girl.

"I am glad to hear that," Hyacinth said. "I just wish I knew how to take away the rest of the pain that you are carrying with you."

"You can't. Only time can ease the hurt. Even that can only dull the pain. Nothing can truly take it away. Our pain is what makes us. How we react to it, how we let it govern our emotions…" He turned to look at Hyacinth, the golden glow of her apparition filling the cavern with light. "*That* is what I still struggle with. I don't like who my pain has made me, but letting go of him… I …" Rostov paused, lost in thought for a moment. "I'm worried that I can't let him go because he *is* me. Years of pain scared over to the point that it doesn't matter how much

I try and heal it. The damage is already done. I'm broken. But perhaps, with time, a little super glue can keep me on my feet."

As he was talking, Hyacinth walked up to him, bending down and wrapping her arms around him. She felt like that pure, warm Null that filled the ship. Her comfort and light filled his body. This was good. This was where he wanted and needed to be.

"Are you ready?" she asked.

"Yes," Rostov said.

He placed his hand on the open control panel, and then his other on the skin of the ship. He could feel the energy and life of *Prometheus*. The ship's energy was there if he needed it, a backup. Closing his eyes, Rostov reached into that pure Null and started to move it so that it surrounded the ship. As the bubble reached the fore sections of the Dreadstar, he wrapped it around and pulled it tight. His energy and concentration started to flag as he reached for the aft of the ship. The bubble was being pulled to its limit. It was starting to feel like he was placing a fitted sheet around the ship. A sheet that was for a smaller bed. He pulled in more energy, struggling to push the bubble.

Gritting his teeth, he dug deeper. Rostov could see the Shadow starting to percolate up from where he was digging. A warm hand wrapped around his. The exertion felt less painful, and he was able to wrap the sheet of Null energy around the top of the ship. He opened his eyes and turned to see Hyacinth's hand wrapped around his. The cave was now almost too bright to exist in, as the bubble of Null energy flashed and rippled across the top of the ship. Every time a drop of water or a small chunk of rock fell it hit the energy shield, it bounced and skipped like a stone across a lake.

"How long can we hold this?" Rostov asked.

"As long as we need to."

Engine Room *Prometheus*, Naomi

"Everything is going to be okay," Naomi said, holding her hand to the console of the *Prometheus*.

She had found that the ship had a lovely voice. It was quiet and content. Happy with where it had ended up. She enjoyed her slumber, the dreams of peace and quiet a relief from her previous existence of war and death. When Naomi had allowed the golden Null rats to kill the antimatter man to bring life back to the reactor, she had awoken the ship. There were so many voices all throughout the engineering section. Everything had a voice, but they all worked together to serve the greater hymn of the choir. When *Prometheus* talked, they all listened. She was the prime voice, the one that all the others came from. As happy as they were to be alive again, she was sad.

Why would you do this to me, child of power? My battles have been fought, my rest hard earned, the ship asked. The two troopers standing with her must have thought her mad, talking to a voice in her head from the ship that they were standing on.

"We do not want you to fight. We only need you to escape," Naomi said. It wasn't a complete truth; they were going to need the weapons. It wasn't like the ship had a choice in the matter thought. Right?

I am a conveyance of war.

"I am aware. We just need you to rise from here, to help take Hyacinth through the Eye," Naomi said.

I know of her. She sang to me while I was asleep. Most of the Wayfinders, they writhe and scream. Pushing against where they have been put.

"She has a gentle soul and is our friend. All we want to do is help her get to where she needs to be," Naomi said.

Prometheus was old, set in her ways. Convincing her to allow them to turn on her main engines was going to be a challenge. Being able to communicate with the souls of the technology around her was a wonderful gift and a curse. Some days, it made Naomi miss when she couldn't hear the electrons putting their feelings into words.

I have yet to feel the need to end her, to defend my peace.

Naomi was taken aback by this. The ship was killing the Wayfinders that it didn't like? She figured that it didn't seem out of the realm of possibility. A hammer was going to see every problem as a nail, and what was *Prometheus*, if not a hammer? Faster than light travel in this section of space had apparently been hanging on the thread of how long a buried sleeping warrior could stand her roommates.

"How many have you ended?" Naomi asked.

All of them, eventually. They have tapped into powers that no moral should have. That they cannot comprehend. Eventually, we come to an impasse.

The words were dispassionate. The ship that had started their conversation so nicely by asking how her day was going, was now admitting to killing people in cold blood who needed help more than the cold embrace of the grave. Would the ship do that to them, as well, if she wasn't pleased with what they were doing? What they wanted her to do?

"Are you willing to help us, to convey Hyacinth into the Eye?" Naomi asked, looking around.

There was no face, no personification of the ship here. Her only indication of how the spirit of the machine felt was from the blinking lights and the uproar of the choir of other voices.

I have seen her visions. They will be the end of us. There is no way to do this, child of power, without causing destruction, without more death.

"I know," Naomi said. "People are dying above and within you already. There are people who want to claim you. They want to make you an instrument of death again."

My brothers and sisters are more than capable of being their conveyance of war. Why must they trouble me?

The ship didn't know. She didn't understand how much time had passed, what had happened to the other Dreadstars. She just wanted to sleep and not be involved in the short, loud lives of mortals.

"Most of your brothers and sisters are dead. They have been for almost a thousand years. Killed during the Age of Chaos. Only five Dreadstars remain," Naomi said. She wasn't sure if this was the correct course of action, but it would have to do.

No, there were thousands of us. We ruled the stars, stood tall against the enemy. There is no way we have been brought so low!

The ship rumbled. For the first time, the placid nature of the *Promethius's* voice faded away, replaced by anger and heartache.

"Naomi, what is going on down there? Everything is shaking," Joanna's voice said through her comm.

"Everything is fine down here; just having a conversation. I will keep you apprised when there is something to report," Naomi said, reaching up and clicking off the communication device.

She didn't want to have to explain what was going on, didn't need any kind of disturbance right now. She was close to getting through to the ship—or convincing it to kill them all. Naomi wasn't rightly sure which one it would end up being.

This was your doing!

"No, it was a thousand years ago. Long before I was born. We don't know much about that time; our records were lost, our memories are fleeting. We do not exist as you do," Naomi said. "But we *do* stand against the enemy. Hyacinth stands against the enemy. That is why we must reach the Eye," Naomi said.

The way must be cleared.

"Yes!" Naomi said, a bit too enthusiastically.

The ship was aware of the prophecy. Would that be enough to get her to help them? For this great ship from long ago to wake up and return to the world?

I shall do this for you, child of power. When the thing is done, you will allow me to return to my slumber. I choose not to be involved in the misery of the world.

"You have a deal," Naomi said. It was a good deal, and she was going to grab it with both hands and make full use of it. She turned her radio back on.

"We have control, Joanna. We can leave at any point."

"Roger," her friend's voice said from the other side of the line.

Naomi leaned back, looking around, feeling good about herself, wondering what stories, what secrets, this ship might know and if they could be coaxed out of her one day.

Hanger Bay Barker's World, Hanna

"Fox, time is up; we need to get in the air *now*!" Hanna yelled from the back of their captured ship.

She looked out through the scope and saw that the rocks had stopped falling. Hanna didn't take that as a good sign. So far on this mission, everything that had *felt* like it was a good sign, turned out to be just another nail in some poor marine's coffin. She was sick of it and now viewed everything with suspicion.

"Almost there, I just need to…no…no!" Fox said from the front of the ship, her words fading away in a cascade of loud banging noises.

Hanna closed her eyes and sighed. Of course, why would anything be working? She hunched over and started walking toward the front of the ship. These things were ridiculously cramped, only a little bigger than a broadsword bomber. Hanna didn't want to see what a whole swarm of these things could do, given enough coordination.

Fox was sitting against the bulkhead next to the access port that she had pried open. Her hands were shaking, and she was breathing heavily. Hanna knew that look, when somebody was bottling up a thick lager head of rage. Her nostrils flared and Fox reached for the wrench before Hanna put her hand on the tool.

"Calm down, what's wrong?" she asked. Hanna could feel the anger and the fight bleeding out of Fox as the tightness in her hand faded into trembling.

"An EPS conduit blew. It is on the outside of the ship. I'm going to need to go out and pull it. I've patched in a work around, but without removing it…" She paused. She was breathing hard, the frustration and exhaustion hitting her body all at once. "Without removing it, I can't be sure the bypass is working. If it's not, then power gets stunted into that conduit, and…"

"Boom," Hanna muttered.

"Boom," Fox whispered back. The two women sat there for a moment, contemplating the situation that they were in. Fox's breathing slowly returned to normal, while Hanna did the grim calculations of command in her head.

"How long will it take to fix?"

"Not long. I've just got to pry open the cover, rip the thing out, and cauterize a few wires. Probably the whole damned panel honestly," Fox said.

"Not long is what I like to hear." Hanna said patting her on the shoulder. "We are going to get out of this, Fox. Alexander would be very displeased with me if you didn't make it home," Hanna said.

"He never returned my message; a receipt came back, so I know he read it," Fox said sadly. "When Alexander came back, we had a fight. Did he not tell you about it?"

"We didn't really get much time to talk," Hanna said.

She had barely gotten a word in with her twin in the short time that he had been aboard *Fury* before their mother removed him from the ship and left on this wild goose chase of a mission. All so she could avoid having a new Host'ire ambassador on the ship.

"I wish we had talked less. I ended things on bad terms," Fox said.

"You broke up?" Hanna asked.

Her brother and Fox had been with each other off and on for as long as she could remember. The two of them always seemed to fall back into the others' orbit no matter how long they were apart. It must have been quite a fight for Fox to be talking about their relationship as over.

"Maybe. He offered me a fabrication position at the research facility he works at. I… I don't know why, but I spit it back in his face. It just felt like a pity job, so he could keep pity fucking me. I yelled something about class and nobles. High horse kind of shit," Fox said.

"He wanted to take you away from *Fury*, that is… that is a big step. He hadn't even mentioned it in any of his letters," Hanna said.

She had always felt Alexander treated his relationship with Fox too flippantly. She was a fine woman and the two of them made each other happy. Why they hadn't gotten married years ago, she didn't know. He was far from in line to inherit the ship and as such, didn't need to make a political match. Alexander was free to marry for love and nothing else.

"He was so excited to tell me about it, and I just threw it back at him. I was scared, I've never done anything but fix fighters. I'm just a grease monkey, and he has degrees, and works at a secret base. Why would he even want me?"

"Because deep down, you are all he has *ever* wanted. If he had gotten authorization to offer you a position, that means he was serious. Why he didn't consult me…? Well, that is a conversation that he is not going to enjoy having. Tell you what, we will ask him together when this is all over," Hanna said.

"He went to NovaTerra, though, where they are…" Fox began. She didn't finish, and Hanna didn't want her to.

"I'm sure he's fine. My mother always says that people are alive and well until you see a body. I know he is fine; I can feel it in my heart. We came out of the birthing pod holding onto each other, and I've always felt like I can feel his presence in the Null. Not in a Host'ire wizard kind of way, just in that way that two people who were once one person have. I don't know, it sounds preposterous saying it out loud," Hanna said, standing to a crouch.

"I don't think it does. If you say he isn't dead, then he isn't dead," Fox said.

"That's the spirit. Now, let's make sure that *we* live long enough to yell at him together. Get your tools ready, we are going to fix this, and get off this bloody rock," Hanna said.

"Yes sir," Fox replied, wiping away a tear as Hanna headed toward her three remaining marines.

"Ramirez, we are going to have to go outside. Corporal Windsail needs to fix one last thing before we can depart. We are going to cover her," Hanna said.

"You don't trust the quiet major?" the Sargent asked.

"Do you?" she said flatly.

"Not a chance in Hell, sir. We will be ready," he said, turning to join his men as they pulled back on their combat gear.

Hanna looked over at her long duster and decided against putting it on. It wasn't going to help in this situation. Her weapon belt was next to it; *that* she was going to need. The pistol only had one more magazine of plasma rounds. After that, she was going to be down to her sword. The rest of the platoon was probably in the same dire situation, even after scrounging from the dead.

Clipping the belt around her waist, Hanna walked back to the scope and took another look outside at the untrustworthy quiet.

The Shafts, Black Caldera, Grace

It had taken another twenty minutes of climbing in the dark before their feet reached another floor. They had reached floor three-one-three, the strange point on the blueprint that had no markings and wasn't accessed by any part of the tower's power or water systems. Grace let the power bleed from her arms and legs as she stood on the steel plank that served to prevent them from moving any further.

"Give me a little space," Essex said.

She could hear the sound of his star-steel blade unclipping from his belt. She took a few steps back and then closed her eyes. She knew what was about to happen and wanted to keep her night vision as intact as possible. A moment later, the heartbeat thrum of the weapon coming to life filled her ears.

Emily wanted to watch and forced open Grace's eyes. The light hurt for a moment before her helmet compensated. Essex was leaning down, using his blade to cut a hole in the floor, melted steel slag bubbling around the hole that he was standing next to. A moment of work later and the hunk of metal was loose and then fell. Almost instantly, she heard it clatter to another floor. That was a good sign. Then, there was quiet as he put his weapon away.

"I was expecting more security," Grace said, taking a step forward.

She was getting an air reading from the hole, information scrolling across her suit's heads up display. There were no toxins, or pathogens, but the air was old stale, like what she would have expected to find at a dig site, not in the middle of some massive high tech tower run by a species so old that they had evolved into energy and smoke.

"Let's count our good luck and keep moving before something is tripped," Essex said.

He turned to Grace, and she could sense him winking, even though the only light in the room was coming from the quickly cooling molten steel ring on the floor. Emily rolled her eyes, as he jumped. His feet hit the ground a moment later with a loud thud. Grace took a deep breath and followed him.

The access shaft here looked very much like the one they had just been in. Only here, all the pipes were running in a horizontal fashion, wrapping around the floor, as opposed to running vertically like the ones they had just seen. This floor truly was completely cut off from the rest of the tower.

They are hiding something here. I don't like it, feels wrong, Emily thought as a shiver ran through Grace's body.

She shouldn't have been able to get cold like that. The suit was regulating her internal temperature. Essex didn't say a word, he just pulled out his star-steel blade again and started cutting through the wall, the orange shaft of energy making short work of the steel. It went smashing to the floor and they were in.

A plumb of dust had been kicked up by the falling steel, as the sound of its death echoed in the hallway. Aside from that, there was nothing else. Flickering emergency lights ran along the floor, but there was only silence. No alarms, no people, nothing. The walls, the architecture, the design, everything here looked different from the floors of this place that Grace had seen so far, as if it had come from some other facility and was just slotted into the middle of the tower during construction.

"I have a bad feeling about this place," Essex whispered as he flicked off his weapon but didn't clip it back to his belt. "The Null is barely here. I can feel it creeping in, seeping through the pores of this place. Otherwise, it is empty, even..."

He stopped talking. Emily didn't like that. It felt like he was hiding something. His wizard senses were tingling, and she was going to make sure that he shared everything he was feeling with her. It was the only way to make sure that they stayed on an even footing.

Are you sure he didn't get rid of the Varagoth? Grace thought.

Positive, Emily shot back as she asserted control.

"Even what, Essex? What are you feeling, what is down here?" Emily asked.

"The Shadow. Even that has retreated from this place," he said.

Emily had heard about the Shadow, that well of energy that existed below the Null. She wasn't sure if she believed in it. No scientist had ever been able to confirm its existence. The Null, they knew about. It was everywhere. You could poke through the veil of this dimension and suck it out, slip ships into it with enough power. This Shadow that the Host'ire talked about, a place of chaos and power, she didn't think that existed. Just a byproduct of taking in too much power and buying into their own bullshit. A good story to keep the acolytes from becoming too strong and questioning the system, standing up and making a new life for themselves.

"Cool, even the darkness of legend doesn't want to be here," Emily muttered as they walked up to a door at the end of the hallway.

Essex huffed at having his understanding of existence called legend—Emily didn't care. The locking pad was old, and she didn't recognize the writing. Still, there was a large green button, and that seemed to universally be a sign for entry. She pushed it and, with loud resistance, the door cracked open, pushing away years and years of dusty build up.

"Time to see what even the darkness isn't interested in us finding," Grace said.

She pushed open the door and stepped into the shadow. Inside, the room came to a sort of half-life. Dim lights on the floor and roof clicked on as she walked inside.

They were in a dust-covered lab. Most of the equipment was under sheets, but what Grace could see was enough. There were specimen vats holding limbs and full bodies. Humans, Traragti, and Pa'vinti.

There was even a lizard-looking humanoid species that she didn't even recognize.

Not every jar was filled with full bodies. Others only had hands, feet, while, sitting prominently between all of them, were two heads.

What the fuck is this? Grace thought, looking around, a chill moving through her body. The sight was horrific, and she wanted to panic, wanted to turn around and run away. She had seen enough of the Varagoth's depravity and didn't need to see anymore.

Taking in a deep breath she held it, thankful her suit filtered the air, then on a three-count, let it out. She did this three more times to calm herself down. Emily, from where she was riding in her mind, put a hand on her shoulder and nudged Grace forward.

Cords and wires were connected to the jars with heads, and the eyes on both were open, following Grace and Essex as they looked around the room. Essex stopped for a moment and took a deep breath. Grace couldn't read him, couldn't tell if he was as freaked out by all of this as she was. *Damn Host'ire.*

"The small amount of Null that I can feel is coming from those," he said, pointing to the heads, one a woman, the other a man. "There is a little life still in them."

Grace walked over to the two heads in jars, looking at the name plates that were under each.

"Goodspeed, Martinelli," she said, taking a step back.

*That's not possible, that...*Emily started, but she and Grace both knew just how possible it was and what it implied. Pieces started to lock into place.

"You are Goodspeed," Essex said.

"Only here. We had to change our names. They wanted consistency of research. I didn't question it. I know Doctor Martinelli, he is a moron," Grace said.

That was when they both noticed the eyes. It wasn't the actual eyes of these two dead people, but the cloud of a Varagoth inside moving, watching.

"Of course, it all makes sense now," Grace said. "The plan had always been to keep us the same because they were going to eventually—if we were worthy—infest us with the Varagoth who was in our predecessor. Martinelli and I just dodged that bullet…"

"Because he is a moron…" Essex started.

"And I'm some Wayfinding hyperspace messiah," Grace said flatly as they finished each other's sentence. Emily rolled her eyes at all of this. Essex cocked his head to the side.

He doesn't know, they didn't tell him, Emily thought.

Shouldn't his brain friend know? Grace thought back.

Maybe it is gone, or suppressed? That seems the most likely, given that he is a space wizard, Emily responded. *Tread carefully, he has either dealt with it or is leading us on to something.*

"I didn't know I was in the presence of royalty," Essex quipped, breaking the moment of tension that was building.

"I'm not. They just have some strange notion that my being freaky good at math fits a prophecy or some nonsense. It's like the plot from a bad movie," Grace said, looking around the room, finally walking over and picking up a crowbar from an open toolbox.

Emily thumped the rod of steel in the palm of her hand as she walked back to the two heads. She tapped the tops of each jar with the crowbar like a child trying to figure out which ant hill she wanted to smash first. The eyes of both heads followed her. In that moment, even without any kind of Null powers, Emily could feel fear coming from these two trapped Varagoth.

Good.

In a flash, the tool-turned-weapon smashed the jar with the head of Doctor Martinelli. Green liquid poured out and the jaw of the head started rapidly opening and closing. The eyes rolled back as the cheeks sunk in like every bit of air and moisture was being pulled from the skull by a vacuum. After half a minute, the head stopped moving, looking like nothing more than a large raisin. She turned to the one labeled "Goodspeed," and swung. Essex walked away.

As Emily was watching the last life fade from the shriveled head of the previous Doctor Goodspeed, lights came on from behind her. She turned to see Essex standing next to a large table in the center of the room.

"Look at this," Essex said, motioning for Grace to come and see what he had found. She walked over, the crowbar in her hand was dripping goo. Grace dropped it, done with the violence. She pulled off her helmet, setting it down on the side of the table. On the table was a large map. It was old. She could see the Fissure, the Barrier and hundreds of words and hyperspace highways and gates. Some, she recognized. Others...

"How old is this map?" she asked.

"I don't know. Five hundred years, at least," Essex said, pointing to the sector he had noticed.

"At least a thousand, maybe older," Grace said. "This cluster here." She pointed to a series of worlds in what now was considered the Unaligned Planets. "They were obliterated during the Age of Chaos. The Shad'gran Emperor Tanzer IV unleashed a planet-killer super weapon. It was the first step in a march across known space. It wasn't until King Richard the Tenth of NovaTerra, last of his line, built the Dreadstars and stood against them with the Wayfinders at his back that the tide was turned."

Thus had ended the first movement of the Age of Chaos. It would pick up again half a generation later, more violent and destructive than before. She pointed to a few more worlds that were named wrong, or named for civilizations that she was aware of, but which were long dead.

Grace started to look over the table, examine it closer, run her fingers over old letters and words that were in script so old that most people had forgotten about their existence. Excitement started to cross her face, that kind of giddiness that only comes when a problem's answer reveals itself.

"This is definitely a Shad'gran war table. It has the crest of the Empire here, and it's dated. 5567ce. That would have been eighty years before the conquest started, when the generals tried to take power from Tanzer III. He was weak, allowed his neighbors to take systems from them, allowing the economy to crumble. That cluster, his son would destroy. They were the worst offenders. It was why they paid such a price," Grace said.

"How much you want to bet that the Varagoth had a hand in that?" Essex asked.

"I'd put every credit to my name on it. We have never found a single record of their plant-killer's construction in the thousand years since the end of that war." Grace let the sentence trail off, she moved her hand around the board, and then snapped her fingers.

"They are doing it again. Tanzer IV and his forces were focused on heading here," she pointed to a point of empty space on the map.

"That is where the Citadel is. The Eye," Essex said.

"Correct. That sector wasn't mapped yet, wouldn't be until just before the Wayfinder wars; one of the last highways, what they said was to be their grandest gate, through the Barrier. The Shad'gran knew something was there. Something changed between then and now. What caused them to lose during the Age of Chaos, that they think has been solved now; that wasn't there five hundred years ago, when the Wayfinders were poking around...? Damn it, I wish there was a library here and some historians to bounce ideas off," Emily said, walking frustratedly away from the table.

"Then we just have to get to one. Think about what place of learning you want to go to and that is where we will go when we escape. So we can crack this and warn everybody," Essex said.

I don't trust that he actually wants to warn everybody. But he does want us curious, asking questions, learning, Emily thought.

"Yeah," she said quietly, picking up her helmet and snapping pictures of everything here.

As she was getting pictures, Essex walked over to a door on the other side of the lab from where they had entered. He pressed a few keys and eventually, the door opened. Cold air rushed into the room: dust, and a feeling of death. Turning from her pictures, Grace put her helmet back on and walked to the door. This hallway looked even older and more out of place than the one on the other side. This section of the tower was old, cobbled together from long before.

"This isn't a secret level. It's a tomb," Grace said flatly.

"Looks like the stairs are going to be our only way out," Essex said, pointing to a sealed door that had the labeling of stairs. "I'm sure once we hit the main tower again, they will be looking for us. Are you ready to run?" Essex asked, as he ignited his blade and started to cut open the door.

Combat Information Center, *Prometheus*, Joanna

The Combat Information Center of *Prometheus* was fully staffed. Joanna stood at the bottom of the ever rising rings of computer stations looking at the sea of troopers and techs in their green coats. Naomi had managed to get most of the essential systems for their escape up and running. The look of this room had totally changed from the dimly lit gathering place of the Guardians. The high lights were on, the computers buzzing, even the glass table that she was standing in front of had come to life. Sitting on the table was a Militarum communications set up. Keeping up with this was Joanna's task in all the chaos. As much as she wanted to be out doing something, she knew that this was just as important a part of the plan. It didn't require any of her powers—that would come later. For now, though, it was her job to keep everybody on their schedule and deploy groups across the ship.

"CIC, this is Fel," the box squawked.

Joanna picked up the handset and put it to her ear.

"This is Actual, go," Joanna said, remembering some of the military jargon from one of the many novels she had read. There was a wonderful series about a young officer who was the bastard of a Lord Admiral. Through each book, his adventures got bigger and bigger until finally he was enough of a hero to challenge for the seat of the house. Alas, the series was left on a cliff hanger never to be finished, thanks to the untimely death of its author.

"The Fellowship breach in the forward compartments has gotten worse. Whatever hole they burrowed down, we can't plug. I would not be surprised to find that this is not the only one," Fel said, the sounds of combat behind her. Joanna could hear the heartbeat thrum of her blade slashing.

"How much longer can you hold?" Joanna asked.

She waved her hand up, triggering the holographic projectors on the table. There, she had the numbers for the evacuation above. Two thousand troopers had gotten down and there were still thousands to go. They were not going fast enough. It was still going to take hours to get everybody down to the ship through the single elevator.

"Half an hour, at best," Fel said. "We need to start the operation now before we lose the ship."

"There are still a few thousand troopers up here!" Lucas's voice barked, breaking into the open channel. The frequency was connected to her friends and Fel, all of whom had vital roles to play in this mission.

"You think I don't know that, Knight-Commander? If we lose my ship, where do you think all those people are going to go?" Fel barked.

Joanna rolled her eyes at Fel's assertation that it was her ship. At best, it belonged to the Guardians, but she knew that it was the Wayfinder's ship. Hyacinth was in charge of *Prometheus*. It didn't matter how much posturing Fel did or how many troopers she put in the CIC. That fact wouldn't change.

"If we don't save these people, then what is the point of all this?" Lucas yelled back over the radio. All the troopers in the CIC looked down at the conversation that was loud enough to filter into the room through the handset.

"The point is to make sure these bastards get as little as possible. Those troopers knew what they were signing up for," Fel said.

"They signed up to fight, not to be left behind by some callous bureaucrat who is playing at general," Lucas snapped back.

"You forget yourself, Knight-*Commander*," Fel responded.

"I have led knights into battle, and I have lost knights in battle. None of their lives were just thrown away," Lucas said.

"These are not knights," Fel said.

It came off her lips a little too quickly for Joanna's liking, making her skin crawl. For a moment, she was sure that Rostov was going to chime in and go on another—well deserved—rant. Yet there was silence. Everybody was trying to figure out what to say next. Though the headset, Joanna could tell even Fel was slightly taken aback by the words that had come out of her mouth. The quiet part screamed out loud.

As the silence filled the air, another flash from the future hit Joanna. She saw Lucas and Fel standing in an elevator back-to-back. A shadow approaching them.

Didn't think it would end like this, Fel said.

Last elevator isn't the end, Lucas responded.

Joanna shuddered back to reality, her head jerking back, eyes blinking rapidly. Her heart fluttered for a moment. Joanna put her hands on the glass table and breathed in deeply, then out again in short, rapid breaths to calm herself down. Something was coming. Something was going to trap Fel and Lucas on the elevator and there was nothing she could do to stop it.

She opened her mouth to say something and stopped. A moment like this is what Joanna had been worried about since she started feeling the future. An event that she would be desperate to stop, but the knowledge that her trying to stop it could *cause* it to happen. There wasn't enough information. How malleable was the flow of time? Could she change it? Or did it just happen, no matter what she did? The last vision, the one where she saw Lucas die, had felt so final, so set in stone. This felt very much the same.

As she was trying to find her voice, Lucas piped up over the radio again.

"I'm just going to have to shove more into each run, then," Lucas said, the sound of his star-steel blade activating punctuating his declaration.

The conversation cut off. The vision wouldn't leave her mind. There was something in that elevator, something horrible, something of the enemy. The last week had been the stuff of legend and there was little any of them could do but press forward and keep fighting. There was a stool near the glass table, where the captain's busser would sit, waiting to serve them tea or run messages.

Joanna sat down, still shaking from the vision. These were not completely new to her, but the clarity of them now, the ferocity and intensity, was draining. She took a deep breath and closed her eyes.

Control your breathing, focus on the Null spots in the darkness, she thought, repeating the mantra to herself.

Inside the darkness, she found her heart beating almost comically fast. She wrapped her arms around it and hummed a soothing tune. The same one her mother had, that Hyacinth had. The beats started to slow down, matching the slow tempo of the melody. Clarity returned to her, and she opened her eyes. Twenty minutes had passed. Lucas would be on his way back up for another group.

"CIC, this is Fel!" the radio blurted.

Joanna got up and ran to it, picking up the handset.

"This is CIC, go!" she said.

"Forward section lines buckling. I'm starting an orderly retreat.," she said.

"I need more time," Lucas's voice came in again.

"We don't have it, Knight-Commander. I'm sorry. Knight Pike, I'm ordering you to begin the operation. Brandice, get your last load," she said.

There was resignation in her voice. Fel wasn't happy to be leaving troopers behind, but she was correct in that they couldn't allow the ship to be overrun while drip-feeding in reinforcements.

"Oh, by the Shadow," she heard Lucas say quietly over the radio.

"Lucas, what is it?" Joanna yelled, fear threatening to overtake her.

The only answer she got was him screaming in anger and frustration, followed by his blade coming to life and the line cutting off.

"Lucas!" she yelled into the radio again. "Lucas…" Her final plea was quieter, resigned.

"Knight Pike, the cannons," Fel's voice came through the radio.

"He needs us," Joanna said. She almost put down the hand set, almost ran out of the CIC to go fight. She was qualified, had even killed a few members of the Fellowship.

"The Knight-Commander will either survive or he will not. There is little either of us can do for him. I need you to stay on mission, Pike," Fel snapped. Then her voice calmed. "I've seen Brandice fight. He will come through this. It will take more than a mob of Fellowship cultists to kill him." The words felt out of character for Administrator Fel, but they were exactly what Joanna needed to hear right now.

He will come through this.

Lucas knows how to kick ass.

Naomi and Rostov in her head, the support of people who were more than friends. They were family, and if they had faith in Lucas, she needed to, as well. To help him, she needed to do her part. They were out of time. Lucas was going to make it. He had been run through—killed—and still he fought on. If that was possible, she could do what needed to be done.

"Weapons!" she called across the CIC.

"Weapons, aye," one of the troopers said from the middle ring.

"On my mark, fire the forward cannons, three bursts, full power," she said. They needed to start weakening the rock, getting it dislodged so that *Prometheus* could escape. Once they started shooting, there was no going back. There was no more waiting. The cavern would start to become unstable, and they would have to leave.

"Forward cannons, charged and ready," the trooper called back to her.

Joanna took a deep breath, pressing down on the glass table, small cracks starting to cascade out from her fists. She didn't want to give this order. Somebody had to, though. It was time to step out of the library.

"Fire."

CIC, *Fury,* Cassandra

Cassandra looked at the jump prep read out. They were having trouble pushing fifty percent. She had pulled the read out wide so that she could see the number out to five decimal places. Each time they fired a plasma cannon it cost them .10%, their point defense weapons .005% per second. The one broadside they had fired as a warning toward the Lagrange battleship had cost almost an entire percentage point. Everything involved in the battle was costing more and more. They needed to end this if there was ever going to be a chance to build up enough power. Everything was a numbers game now.

The Lagrange fleet—what was left of it—was on top of *Fury.* There were a few of the arrowhead ships still flying around, but most of them had fallen away, being destroyed or jumping out of the battle zone. Every ship in the engagement had been damaged, but they were still holding on, still fighting back. House Lagrange didn't make substandard ships. Knowing that they were on the other side of whatever conflict was brewing didn't fill Cassandra with any kind of confidence.

Fury shook again. Cassandra grabbed the glass table to lessen the impact. Alarms were going off across the ship. Already, the system had pulled hull shielding into the engine, and they were dragging away even more power. Cassandra walked over and touched the wall for a moment as the ship lurched again. She was sluggish, not moving at her peak. Cassandra could feel it in the old girl's bones. What they were asking of her was taxing even in perfect conditions, but during a dust up, it was punishing.

"Captain, I need that battleship out of my sky, if you please?" Cassandra barked.

"May I take off the restrictions?" he asked.

Captain Rackland wanted nothing more than to have both hands in this fight, to worry about charging the ship once they were finished. She would have agreed if there wasn't another Dreadstar bearing down on them from across the system. Everything was looking grim.

They were going to have to remove both the battleship and the carrier quickly, if there was going to be any hope of ending this phase of the fight before they would have to turn and deal with the oncoming Aldebaran fleet.

Normally, Cassandra Cordova was not indecisive, but the last few months—hell, the last few days, *hours*—had shaken her.

You will hear the music one last time, the voice of the Wayfinder echoed in her mind. She'd heard the music again—it was glorious. She wanted nothing more than to keep hearing it. *One last time.* The Wayfinder had been very clipped and very sound on those words. Did that mean they were going to lose this battle, or did it just mean she wasn't going to make it out of this fight? All those thoughts were raddling around in her mind, driving her to not want to make the choices that had to be made.

"Lord Admiral?" Captain Rackland asked again.

"Please demonstrate just how fatal of an error they made attempting to engage a Dreadstar," Cassandra said.

The captain went to his work. She reached down and picked up her communication handset and held it to her ear.

"Comm, get me Commander Cordova," she said.

A moment later, she heard the exasperated voice of her son on the other end of the line.

Hanger Bay, Barker's World, Hanna

They exited the ship in a diamond formation, Ramirez in front, the two remaining marines flanking him. Fox and Hanna were in the middle of the wedge, with Hanna covering the rear. The air in the hanger bay was thick with dust and rock. Hanna could feel it coating her throat with every breath she took. The smell of super-heated plasma still hung in the air, its horrible, ozone-and-biomatter smell clinging to the places where marines had fought and died. Their bodies were still on the ground. Flies had already started to make themselves at home.

There is nowhere on the ship for them, Hanna thought as they kept walking forward. *I shall write them some lines, perhaps finally set something to music.*

"What direction, corporal?" Hanna asked.

Fox pointed toward the front of the ship. Hanna saw a bulge in the outer hull, like a blister. They started moving that way. The only sound were birds outside and their own footfalls. The storm had long ago passed during their time hiding in the ship. The people who were coming after them were being careful. It was clear to Hanna that these ships were important and not something that could just be flippantly destroyed. War college professors would have had her blowing this whole mountainside to hell as soon as they had taken refuge inside the ship.

The cluster of marines reached the hatch and spread out around, creating a human shield for Fox to start working.

"Major, we have a problem," Ramirez whispered to her.

Without making a large show of it, he pointed toward the edge of the landing bay that opened to the bright blue sky. Then Hanna saw it. Climbing spikes, the kind that were deployed from a low-flying helicopter or VTOL craft.

"How long you suspect they have been up here?" Hanna asked.

"We are not dead yet, so not long. I don't think they are still climbing, though," the sergeant said, pointing his plasma rifle up and scanning it across the hanger bay, looking for targets.

Hanna could feel eyes on them, that uncomfortable feeling of a stranger's fingers on your back that made you want to pull your neck down and hunch your shoulders in revulsion. She couldn't outwardly show that she knew what was going on—had to just keep going on with the mission. Whatever was going to happen, was going to happen. Fox had the warped cover off the side of the ship and was hard at work on the EPS conduit.

"How are we looking?" Hanna whispered.

"So far, so good. There is built up ion power inside here. It's a good thing we came out to remove it when we did. Any more time and it probably would have exploded. I've got to bleed it to fifty percent, before I can risk cutting any wires. That will take a little…"

"Time?" Hanna said, finishing Fox's thought for her.

"Yes, sir. I can do everything else, though, so I'm not just standing around. I don't… I don't like it out here. Something is not right," she said, putting her head back into the panel, a small tool making noise as she worked.

"Just focus on your work. We will take care of keeping you safe," Hanna said, turning and walking the two steps back to the sergeant.

"Four o'clock, high," he whispered, his head turned toward six o'clock low. Hanna didn't turn to look. She trusted that he knew what he had seen.

"How many?" she asked, turning her head the other way again.

"I saw four, but it'll be more than that if they have retaken the upper levels. We are in a shooting gallery down here," Ramirez muttered.

"It is not an ideal situation, that is for damned sure," Hanna said. "So, we just have to make sure that it goes our way in the first round. They see us, we see them. This has gone from a game of hide and seek to a game of chicken."

"I recommend we make them flinch," Ramirez said.

"As always, Sargent, we are on the same page. Do you have any more small rockets?" Hanna asked, turning to look back at Fox, who was standing on tippy toes her head and upper body inside the ship, the sounds of a small torch and muttered profanity filtering out.

"One left sir, already locked and loaded," he said, grinning.

"Perfect. I'm going to see our timetable. Go on two taps, then I'll play "Covering Fire"."

"Ooh-rah."

"Ooh-rah," she said, back taking the two steps over to where Fox was standing.

"How are we doing?" Hanna asked, putting her head near the hole in the ship getting a face full of heat and ozone.

"Almost there, cutting off the last few wires now," Fox said. "This is going—"

Before she could finish the sentence, Hanna tapped her back.

"Don't jinx it. Just keep working. I'm going to keep my hand on you. As soon as you are done, tug, and we will get back inside. Are we clear?" Hanna asked. They were operating on borrowed time, and she couldn't afford to lose any of it.

"C-crystal," Fox said. She stumbled on the first part of the word but found her resolve again by the end of it.

Hanna pulled up her small heads-up display and slid over to her mother's collection. Like everybody aboard ship, the marines of *Fury* had their own set of musical orders, like the bugle calls of old. She scrolled down to "Covering Fire" and held it ready to play. She then opened a channel to Ramirez and clicked her teeth twice.

In a flash, the old sergeant spun around, raising his weapon and putting the rocket down range toward where he had seen people hiding. Hanna started the music. "Covering Fire" was a thundering, almost fascistic ballad designed to get your heart pumping and scare your opponent away. Hanna and the marines started shooting up into the rafters. The rocket exploded, throwing two mangled corpses from their hiding places into the air. One flew all the way across the hanger bay before hitting the wall with a splat. The second was blown out by secondary explosions from the munitions that were on his person. His body ended up being ripped to shreds from the successive blasts.

The marine beside Hanna didn't make it through the first wave of fire. There were more soldiers hiding in the upper levels than they had suspected from the amount of visible hooks. Kinetic rounds came flying in hard and fast. The young man was hit upward of ten times in his chest alone, dancing around like a marionette being played with by a toddler who was cutting one string at a time. The young man didn't scream, he didn't cry out. He just died. Like all of them, his life ended and there was nothing Hanna could do but try and get some little slice of payback for him.

Ramirez was the second to die. The old marine was pouring fire into the same area where he had started the fight. Hanna could see men falling to the ground, grunting and dying. Ramirez was already wounded by the time she turned to look at him. They all looked serious, like the kinds of injuries that would kill most people. Not him, though. He was laughing as he fired. It wasn't a pointless spray, but targeted, careful shots, just at such a rapid speed that it felt like he had switched his plasma rifle to full auto.

Hanna heard the echo of the round after the fact, as it buzzed by her head and hit the hull of the ship. Ramirez's body whipped around, and she saw that his face was gone, except for the ragged smile. Hanna yelled a deep guttural battle cry, one of pain and anger. She had known this man her whole life; had been taught by him, had fought beside him, and now, very likely, was going to die with him. His body hung there for a moment before being hit three more times and falling to the ground.

They were fast running out of time. She couldn't wait any longer. She needed Fox to tug on her arm. That was when the round hit Hanna in the side, the pain flashing through her body radiating up and out. She stumbled back and hit the hull of the ship, her blood standing out against the crimson paint.

Two reds, mixed as one; an idea, the start of a couplet, formed in her mind with the pain. Still, Hanna held onto Fox.

She pointed her pistol up toward where she thought the round had come from and emptied it, firing so fast that the barrel started to turn a deep, bright red. Looking down, the wound in her lower abdomen below her ribs was pumping out blood. Hanna dropped her pistol, pressing her free hand against it.

Fox tugged on her sleeve. *Is that it? Are we done?* It took Hanna a moment to register what she was feeling, for the logical side of her brain—which was being quickly overtaken by pain—to catch up. Hanna screamed and pulled. Fox came out of the hole in the ship and both hit the ground in a bloody pile.

"You are hurt," Fox said.

Hanna looked up at her blinking, the world getting fuzzy.

"No, you are hurt," she said, pointing to the blood that was all over Fox's tunic.

"That isn't mine, Major," she said quietly. "We have to get inside. Fall back!" Fox called out to the remaining marine. It didn't matter, though. No sooner had she said it then his leg disintegrated from below the knee. He fell to the ground, as two more blue blobs of super-heated plasma smashed into him.

Fox didn't stand up. She just grabbed Hanna by the suspenders of her utility belt and pulled. Pain blasted through Hanna's body with each and every pull and yank. Looking up, she could see the long streak of blood that was being left in her wake. This was the end.

She wasn't going to be getting out of this.

Outside *Fury*, Erik

"I read you Actual, go ahead," Erik said, pulling back on his flight stick and pressing hard on the air brake peddles. His Rapier slowed, allowing the Lagrange Gecko—another small fighter—to overshoot him.

"Commander, pull your fighters away from the battleship and concentrate all your attention on that carrier. We are running out of time," Lord Admiral Cordova said over the comm.

Before responding, Erik lined up the Gecko, so that the yellow flashing box around it was inside his crosshairs. He pulled the trigger on his stick. A burst of fire came lashing out. Most the plasma rounds missed. Two found their target, one on the wing, the other on a thruster. The smaller, green fighter started to burn and list to the starboard. The pilot tried to compensate for losing a rear thruster. Erik was able to line him up again with very little effort and finish the job.

"Roger, Actual," he said, picking up speed again. He flew through the fireball that was there and gone in a flash of heat and vacuum.

"Bella, come in," Erik said, pushing his comm as he adjusted his ship so that he could see the Lagrange carrier.

The ship was attempting to exit the field of battle that had developed. Most of her fighters were gone, but her anti-air defense and two destroyers were still holding strong. This was the first time that he had engaged with an Aviary class before, and they were living up to what he had read about them. What they lacked in heavy fighters, they made up for in having almost as much fire power as a cruiser. The captain of this one was being careful, unlike the commander of the battleship.

"Go ahead," Bella's voice said over the radio. He could hear her gun's blazing. He turned his head and saw two explosions and a Rapier screaming through.

"New directive from Actual. She is tired of that carrier taking up space in her sky. Take command of Delta wing, I will take Gamma. Remove the screen and we will remove that ship. Make sure to steer clear of the battleship. I suspect *Fury* has something special planned for them."

"Roger that, Commander," Bella said, clicking off.

Erik sent out orders across the wing's open channel. Moments later, fighters formed up his side in small diamond formations, each consisting of four fighters. The Nguyen's Hawkeye flew up next to him.

"Aya, how are you holding up?" Erik asked, patching into their frequency.

"As well as can be expected, sir," she said. Her voice was a little shaky, but nothing more than he would expect from somebody who was in their first real dust up.

"That is what I like to hear. You are doing great. Make sure your father knows that," Erik said.

The channel was open, and Lieutenant Commander Nguyen could hear their conversation. Erik suspected that, while he didn't say anything, there was a large grin across the man's face. He had the kind of love, respect, and joy about his daughter that Erik wished his mother could find for him and his siblings, especially Alexander.

"I will tell him, sir," she said, her blushing coming through the audio.

"See to it, cadet. Presently, though, I need firing solutions against that carrier for the bombers. We have been out here tussling for a bit, so be sure you take inventory and make sure that everybody's flight path and solutions match their available payload," Erik said, looking down at his own armament.

He didn't have much left: two fighter-to-fighter missiles and, at best, fifteen seconds of charge on his plasma cannons. His kinetic guns were long empty. They were going to have to stagger landings before that Aldebaran fleet arrived. If he was going to die, it damn sure wasn't going to be because he ran out of ammunition.

"Roger Commander, I'll have those for you presently," Aya said, clicking off.

"Gamma, form up! We are going to have bomber data in a moment, but until then, let's clear some space. I see a few anti-fighter emplacements still functioning on this carrier. Lieutenant Stormwind, break right and hit the underside with Gamma flight four and six," Erik said.

The orders were given. Now all that was left to do was carry them out.

"Roger, lead, we are on it," Ander Stormwind's voice said over the radio.

Erik turned up the sound of the playlist that was being pumped across the fighter wing from *Fury*. He pushed forward on the accelerator pedals, resistance coming into his stick to keep the fighter level. Smacking a few keys, he turned the sensitivity of his heads-up display to full, so that he could see everything that was coming toward him. In most cases, this amount of data was enough to paralyze a pilot, filling them with indecision and fear. In most cases, Erik agreed it was better to not know everything; to trust in your commanders and the powers that be. Now that he was one of those commanders, trusting in the powers that be wasn't something he was interested in always doing.

Light and energy were cascading everywhere. He tapped his flight stick to the right to avoid a flurry of anti-missile rounds. No missiles had been fired yet, and if they were deploying those kinds of weapons against fighters, then the carrier was truly in desperate straits. His Rapier obeyed his command and glided to the right as the cloud of at least a thousand small kinetic rounds flew past him. To the left, just out of the corner of his eye, Erik could see the tactical display, watching the rest of his formation move left or right to avoid the weapons fire. These were just the first steps of what the carrier would throw at them. Next would come the missiles. Their entire job was to eat up as much anti-air fire as possible so that the bombers could get in with minimal losses. So far, everything was going according to plan.

They were approaching the ships' flack field. It was going to get harder to maneuver once they were in here. Doctrine dictated that they keep a hard and fast line, drop fire on the closest exposed weapon and then bug out and set up for another attack run. The longer they spent inside the flack field, the more likely they were to get killed, blown away by some errant round of plasma—or hell, even a smaller kinetic round in the wrong place would spell destruction for a fighter the size of a Rapier.

A missile battery started to rise out of the Aviary's super structure. Thumbing on his targeting reticle, Erik locked onto it. A yellow box appeared around the battery, signaling that it had already been hit once before. Lagrange ships were built to withstand quite the punishment. Two sets of numbers popped up above the missile battery, one showing the effective range for his missiles, and the other for his guns. The missiles were already in negative numbers. Unless he turned off their warheads, the guns were ticking very close to zero. He was only going to get one shot at this. The number clicked and clicked. Erik felt his fighter rock as a burst of flack went off near him. A few alarms started to soundlessly blink, as the music crescendoed in his ears.

The numbers were almost at zero, Erik squeezed the trigger on his flight stick twice. Two, one second bursts of plasma fire ripped out of the fighter. He could see the rounds going forward. The first set fell just a hair short hitting the outer hull of the carrier. The second set smashed into the battery just as the missile doors were opening. One moment, there was a fully functioning battery of anti-aircraft missiles, and the next second, there was only a fireball as the armed warheads started cooking off one after the other. Erik yanked the stick to the left to avoid flying through the secondary and tertiary explosions that were happening. More silent alarms were going off, some proximity, others informing him that his hull was taking an inordinate amount of radiation and heat damage. He couldn't do anything about that in the moment, so he just ignored it.

As he was finishing his attack run and exiting the flack field, Erik turned his attention back to the tactical display. He had lost three fighters in that assault; an acceptable number. As acceptable as the number was, it would still mean letters and visits with the family after this was all over, depending on if they were a native to the *Fury* or one of their outside contracted fighters.

Now, it was the bombers' turn. Kicking his ship around, Erik could visibly see that the flack field had gotten thinner. Not as thin as he would like—that would be zero—but good enough, for acceptable losses.

The alarm that went off in his ear was not quiet. He could ignore heat damage, but not a target lock. Looking down, Erik saw the missile streaking toward him.

Where the bloody hell did that come from?

Pushing to the right, he tried to shake it off, maybe confuse the computer; it sometimes worked in the holomovies. This wasn't a holomovie. The weapon stayed on him. Erik looked down at his own counter measure readout. He was down to two flairs and one chaff burst. The desire to not use them because he might need them later flashed through his mind. He wanted to hold onto them like they were precious and could be what was required to get out of a scrape later in this fight.

Maggots, the future doesn't matter, it is not real. Only the here and the now are important. Do not save weapons or countermeasures. I will judge pilots harshly who bring too many of either home with them.

Erik could hear the words of his first flight instructor in his ears. Commander Roose had been an ancient man when Erik first met him, a fighter pilot so old that he was in record books for survival. By then he wasn't flying anymore, his body already starting to fail him, but his mind never dulled, and he instilled so much information in Erik's class of recruits. Erik followed the long dead teacher's advice and launched a flair.

The small super-heated munition fell out of the back of his ship. Erik then cut his own speed letting the built-up inertia take hold. If he had timed everything correctly, then the flair should fool the missile into thinking it was a pair of Rapier engines just long enough for them to both make contact and explode. The missile, sadly, was smarter, blowing past the flair.

"Damn it," Erik muttered, kicking his ships engines back on and pushing forward.

The weapon was gaining ground; the flair had cost him time and space. He glanced up at a flash of light. The bombers were finishing their attack run on the Aviary class. The flack field was starting to collapse as the ship was rupturing. There were secondary explosions ripping across the hull. It was only a matter of time before one of those balls of fire found something big to cook off. This was the opportunity that he needed. Getting close to a ship that was about to explode was foolish as all hell, especially getting close to one the size of a carrier. Without guts, there would be no glory. The move he had in mind was the kind of crazy shit that Bella would have tried.

Erik dumped every last ounce of power into his engines, pulling it away from life support, armor, and even weapons. He needed some space to maneuver, and the missile was getting too close for his liking. The distance grew. The pounding base of drums and horns filled his ears. A large plume of fire burst out of the landing deck of the Aviary. She was about to blow. Erik aimed toward this burst of fire that was being fueled by escaping oxygen and millions of gallons of fuel and ordnance. Without any of his shielding, things were about to get very hot in his ship. Already, he could feel the perspiration beading on his head and inside his suit. The missile was still on his back, still hanging on.

Then the proximity alarms changed. The missile was no longer his problem. The carrier was about to go critical, her core rupturing and about to burst. Erik pulled to the side, sending his ship into a tailspin.

Glancing over, he saw that the missile hadn't followed him, flying straight into the fire like a greedy executive that wanted to make that one last big deal.

The carrier exploded, sending shockwaves and fire through the area. It took all of Erik's strength to keep his ship level and moving forward. Pushing power back to the radiation shielding, he breathed a sigh of relief that both the missile and the carrier had gone out at the same time.

The Spine of *Prometheus*, Rostov

The sound of the cannons echoed through the cavern as the ship shook again. Rocks started to come tumbling down. They smashed into the Null shield. Rostov could feel their vibrations moving through his body as he held his hands against the ship's skin to protect her. With every quiver and quake, he had to pull in more of the pure Null. There was so much of it right here where the projection of Hyacinth was standing. It was the extra reserve that he needed to not dig too deep, so that he wouldn't risk coming close to the Shadow. Already, he could hear it calling to him with each moment that he pulled. Hyacinth was there to help keep that sound quiet. Eventually, it was going to get louder as she got weaker.

"Why us?" Rostov asked. "You were here for twenty years. If you needed your blood pact, why didn't you just acquire another one?"

"I already had the five of you. What more could I want?" Hyacinth asked.

"I don't know, a group of people that are not mostly fuck ups?" Rostov said. "People who were close...?"

"Once started, the pact cannot be broken. While none of you chose to join a forever pact, you *did* choose to help a little girl who you had no connection to. There was nothing in it for you but pain and suffering. Still, you helped," she said, leaning down and placing her hand on Rostov's shoulder. He could feel the Null moving through him, washing away the doubts that he was feeling. "We are always where we need to be. I know your road has been hard."

"Do not give me any of that 'the road made us who we are', 'we were fated to be here', 'our pain makes us strong' bullshit. I've heard it all before. Worthless platitudes," Rostov said.

"You are who you have always been, Rostov. Everything you have experienced just shades it, makes the colors deeper and richer. You are still the rebellious, quick-witted child that stood up with his friends because he couldn't stand to be left out of what was going on," Hyacinth said, moving her hand from Rostov's shoulder to his cheek.

There was a flash of light. The ship started to move, rising upward toward the roof of the cavern. It was time to get inside and hold the shield from there. Rostov stood and started to walk, his hands held down to preserve the Null bubble that was wrapped around the top of the ship. Each step was a struggle, all his energy focused on maintaining the bubble.

As the ship rolled and rocks fell, keeping his balance was difficult. He could do this; he was strong enough. They had thrown him into a cell because he wouldn't play ball; wouldn't learn what they were trying to teach him. They also threw him away because he was too strong to be that belligerent. Falling down was like giving into the rules and dogma of the Host'ire. It wasn't something he was going to do. Rostov was going to stand on his own two feet, he was going to protect his friends, and see this mission to its end.

Each step echoed as the magnets let go and then clicked down, grabbing the deck ahead of him. *Clomp, clomp, clomp.* He lifted his right foot just as another rock fell, hitting the shield. Rostov could feel the feedback running through his body. *Prometheus* rolled to the starboard side. Rostov threw his arms out, trying to balance himself as he worked to get his other foot down. It seemed to take forever.

Time slowed as he thrust down with his right foot. The ship shook again, and he tumbled to the ground. Rostov heard his left knee pop in its socket before the magnet in his boot gave out, allowing the leg to fall limply to his side. He tried to stifle the scream. Screaming was giving into their system. Screaming was admitting he wasn't strong enough. Screaming was exactly what he did. The pain was too much as it washed across him. Rostov's scream echoed inside his helmet as tears welled up in his eyes.

He was sliding; the Null shield around him was shimmering. Rostov blinked away the tears and reached for his guide rope, wrapping his hands around it. He came to an abrupt stop, laying on the deck, panting, trying to push the pain away. He could still feel the lower part of his left leg, so there was that, at least. He tried to wiggle his big toe inside the boot, and it was painfully slow. The ship rocked again, and Rostov went flying sliding across the deck, still holding onto the rope. Throwing out his left hand, he activated the magnets there and slammed it onto the back of the ship. Finally, he stayed in place.

His shield shimmered again as another rock smashed into it.

"What is going on up there? I told her this wouldn't hurt, that we would protect her!" Naomi's voice came through the speaker inside his helmet.

"Tell *her* to stop trying to throw me off and maybe I can keep the damn shield up," Rostov bit back, the pain from his knee bleeding into his voice.

Rostov grunted and closed the line just as Naomi was about to say something else. He was going to catch hell for that, provided any of them survived this.

"Calm down, Rostov. Don't let your anger get the better of you," Hyacinth said, bending down next to him, putting a golden ethereal hand on his shoulder. The warmth of the Null pulsed through his body, easing some of the pain.

"I'm not mad.. I'm just… It fucking hurts, okay?" he bit back, maybe a bit too quickly.

Still, there was nothing more worthless than being told to calm down and be nice when you were being abused and injured by the very thing you were trying to protect. A little gratitude would be nice, honestly.

"Pain is transitory, we have to work past it," she said. Rostov's eyes rolled so far back in his skull he almost popped both ocular nerves.

"Coming from the woman in a stasis tube," he bit back.

A moment later, her face was pressed up against the visor of his helmet. There was a scowl and angry look upon it.

"You have *no* idea the relationship I have with pain. The hurt this takes on both my body *and* mind. You would do well to extend a little empathy," Hyacinth growled.

"You and the fucking world first," Rostov said, matching her energy.

Letting go of the rope, he slammed his other hand into the deck, letting the magnets take over. Closing his eyes, he pulled in every ounce of Null he was able to, digging so deep in the sand that he scrapped the edge of the Shadow. There was so much energy right there. He could feel it. It would only take a drop to keep this shield up. To push the ship out of the rock that was trying to crush it.

Why shouldn't I take just a drop? I deserve the power for everything I've been through, Rostov thought.

His mind reached out for it. The Shadow reached back toward him, bubbling up past the removed Null like oil coming from the ground. It bubbled and ungulated in the nothingness that it was entering. Small bubbles and lines flittered around the side. Rostov reached his finger forward. There was a chill, coldness that soothed his hurt. That single drop of Shadow was calling to him, pushing away the pain of his leg. The pain was gone but his leg felt wrong, felt like it was withering away. Rostov opened his hand and pushed away the drop of Shadow, plunging it back into the dark, inky pool from whence it came.

Opening his eyes, Rostov could see that the shield was holding. Another rock fell bouncing off as ripples of energy cascaded across the shield. The pain in his leg was gone. He knew it should be there, and its absence was almost as distracting as the pain itself.

"You saw the Shadow. You saw what I see every day. When the pain of the gates, of existence, becomes too much, I just want to dig into the sand and find that well of power and relief. It comes with a cost, Rostov. A great and terrible cost. You will lose who you are, who you want to be. It is the universe's version of re-education. A test that all of us with power must pass," Hyacinth said.

She was behind him, her hand on his leg.

"Last run coming down," Rostov heard Lucas's voice over the com. "They breached the loading dock, there... There was nothing I could do." The exhaustion was evident.

The elevator was heading toward his shield one last time. Rostov closed his eyes and made it thin in that section. *Prometheus* lurched again and he could feel the shaft of the elevator starting to buckle and rip apart as the ship moved.

The porthole that he had come through was a hundred feet away. If he didn't reach it soon, there would be no shield, there would be no *him*. He was exposed out here. Pulling one hand off the ship and grabbing his rope, then the other, Rostov dangled free again. With effort, he reached his belt and pressed a small key. The line of steel rope went taut. The winch at the porthole had started to turn. A moment later, he started to move, being dragged along the hull of the ship, leaving a wake in his path as the shield opened and closed for him. A long ten seconds later and he was at the porthole, climbing headfirst back into the ship and crashing down on the small landing.

The pain from his leg returned shooting through his body, the chorus of agony being joined by his shoulder and head as they were the first things to hit the bottom of the deck.

"Transitory, my ass," Rostov muttered through gritted teeth.

Using the arm that didn't hurt, he pushed himself back to his feet, putting all the weight on his left foot, hanging there for a moment before he could grab the ladder for support. Swallowing, he put his right foot on the ladder rung and pushed forward. He blinked twice, activating the magnet under that boot, letting it take some of the weight off his screaming knee. Wrapping his aching arm around the next rung, he kept climbing. What was a minute of painful work felt like an eternity. It was only six feet, after all. Finally, he was close enough to be able to touch the shield with his weak arm, using the good one to keep him attached to the ladder.

Digging deep, grabbing all the Null he could—even the pain from his shoulder and knee—Rostov put his hand against the bottom of the shield and kept it in place. He thought and the suit clamped hard around his bad arm and legs. Inside the suit, they were wobbling from the exertion, but outside, they were holding tightly to the ladder. He could pass out and not go anywhere. Though that was not the ideal result.

The world wanted him to fall, wanted him to give up and use his gifts to reach for the Shadow so they would have an excuse to finally just kill him. He wasn't going to give the world that.

No, the world was just going to have to put up with him for a little while longer.

Elevator, *Prometheus*, Lucas

The loading dock had been a disaster. When he had gotten there, the Fellowship cultists were already pouring from every hatch and crawlspace like roaches. The Militarum troopers were doing their best, and while there had still been at least a thousand men there, once they were all bunched up, the killing just got easy. Lucas had been able to get the troopers closest to the elevator inside, providing them what little cover he could. Even with all his power pushing resolve and energy though, there was little he could do but watch as the slaughter continued. The heat of battle had overtaken him and, if not for a sergeant standing by the door, he would have let the elevator leave without him. The man had reached out and pulled Lucas inside just as the doors closed.

"Last run coming down. They breached the loading dock, there... There was nothing I could do," Lucas said into his comm, breathing heavily between each word, desperate to regain his breath. His Null bubble was still fully extended. He opened his fist, grabbing the edge of his aura and then clinched his hand closed, bringing all his energy back to him.

"You did what you could, Knight-Commander," Fel's voice came over the comm. "The fight is down here now. Rally what troops you have and head forward. These bastards are about to find themselves cut off."

"Right," Lucas said, closing the line.

He wasn't in the mood to give her an honorific today. Maybe he shouldn't have risked one last run. Maybe she had been right to pull him to where she was. Still, the men around him were alive because of his actions. There was little else that he could focus on right now but those who were around him. Somewhere his war college instructors were accusing him of thinking too small, not seeing the larger picture of the battle. What point was there in fighting if you couldn't protect the men around you; if the leaders who got them into the fight were not willing to lay it all on the line to get them out of it? If this was thinking small, then Lucas was willing to stay small.

The metal of the tube around them started to groan. Gashes started to form in the steel as the ship wrenched free from its umbilical cord to the surface. Air started rushing into the open elevator shaft as the section above them was ripped free. The whole superstructure started listing to the right. The tightly packed elevator kept moving as everybody grabbed hold and worked to keep their footing. Some of them fell, rolling like bowling balls, knocking over their comrades. The platform was so tightly packed that there was nowhere for the energy of the few rolling troopers to go, and it dissipated into the crush of men.

We just have to make it to the bottom before the whole thing falls apart around us, Lucas thought. It would be a shame to die out here on the elevator thrown into the unknown darkness that had held the *Prometheus* for the last thousand years. From below, Lucas could feel the Null of Rostov's shield. Once they passed through that, they would almost be inside the ship, and from there, safe.

The Null field washed over them, like a holographic bio scanner running through a bag at a security check point. Lucas was able to draw some of that energy into himself, and gain a small amount of a recharge. The elevator rocked, moving from one set of tracks to another. Lucas breathed in, grabbing and quickly filling up on that pure Null energy that was always around Hyacinth. His tank wasn't close to empty, and it recharged quickly without him having to dig deeply, without him having to get close to the Shadow.

As a feeling of calm was returning to Lucas, his world went sideways. The elevator came to a screeching halt, sparks starting to fly all around them. Lucas heard the hand grab the bottom of the elevator before he saw it. It looked like it had once been a hand. Now, it was three fingers and a thumb, all with horrible claws. There was no flesh on this hand, just flowing Shadow, like black paint dropped into water. His heart sank.

"How many times do I have to fucking kill you?" Lucas muttered reaching for his star-steel blade. His thumb went to ignite the weapon, when he was pushed back by the thong of men. There was no space, no room. That was when the sinking realization fell upon Lucas.

The second clawed hand smashed into the deck of the elevator, then shot out with vicious ferocity. The claws might have looked like they were made of liquid, but as they started ripping through legs, it was clear they were not. Blood flowed and men screamed, falling to the deck. Others started trying to turn their plasma muskets around to get a clear shot off. The clawed hand reached around a man and threw him into the wall, dashing his brains upon it.

A small hole cleared, Wingarf—or what had once been the Citadel's Master-at-Arms—climbed onto the elevator with them. He was huge, at least three times his original size. The wings from before were gone, replaced by two large pincer claws sticking out of his back and hanging over his shoulders. His whole body was a pulsing mess of black goo and veins, like somebody had skinned an animal and then forced too much blood to pump though their system. His ruined face was a mask of anger and destruction, visceral and in pain. Lucas could feel the Shadow bursting out from him, a wave of fear and nausea consuming the natural Null of the ship.

Lucas pushed out with his own aura, trying to calm the troopers, see if he could rally them into a force to fight this creature back. Instantly, he could feel the strength of the Shadow pushing against him, driving though his aura, stabbing into his soul with the cold steel of fear.

"Hold your ground, and make any shots count!" Lucas yelled, pulling his aura back. If he couldn't help them with the Null, then he would do it the old fashioned way, with words and charisma.

A few rounds of plasma fired off. They smashed into the inky bulk of Wingarf and vanished. There was no reaction from the creature, no exit wound, and after a moment, there wasn't even any sign that he had been shot. The sergeant next to Lucas drew his Plasma revolver and started pulling the trigger. All six rounds found their target, one even hitting Wingarf in the face. They amounted to nothing.

Another raking swing with the claws and more troopers fell to the ground, blood splashing everywhere. The mandibles from Wingarf's shoulder grabbed a trooper, squeezing their midsection. The sound of crunching armor and bones filled the elevator. Wingarf threw the trooper. They hit the wall, shattering their chrome faceplate. The trooper hit the ground, and Lucas could see her lifeless blue eye looking up at him. The face was so young; all of them were too young to be dying here, dying like this.

The sound of more crunching filled the elevator. This time, the trooper in the mandible was sliced in half, guts and viscera falling to the ground. The elevator was quickly becoming an abattoir, and there was little that Lucas could do. He needed to get to the other side of this wall of people. Get into the open, where he could ignite his blade, where he could stand up and fight this creature.

Lucas created a small amount of Null under his boots and pressed, allowing it to push him up. He then created a small handhold in the air, grabbed it, and threw himself forward in a graceful arch. He did a backflip and then landed behind Wingarf, his left foot hitting the deck, his right leg bending braced on his knee, the green Militarum coat fluttering behind him.

"Face me, you coward," Lucas growled, standing up and flicking out the hilt of his blade, snapping it to life, the heartbeat thrum filling the space as green light washed over everything.

Wingarf turned, a trooper gripped in one of his clawed hands. The corrupted Host'ire Knight smiled at Lucas. Before it had been filled with sharp teeth, the mouth of a predator. This time, there was nothing but an even darker blackness. The kind that seeped into men's souls and killed them years before their bodies could die. Wingarf's other hand came up and popped the head off the trooper, like he was opening a Winter Fest cracker. The body fell limply to the ground. Wingarf turned his whole bulk to face Lucas. The mandibles on his back didn't turn with the rest of his body, they kept grabbing and killing troopers.

Form up, you fools. Take this opportunity to put some firepower in this thing, Lucas thought as Wingarf started to saunter forward.

To their credit and discipline, the troopers were able to form up and let out a volley of fire. Wingarf rolled with the hits, clearly feeling them. Not a single one, though, exited into Lucas's field of view. Even if his body was absorbing them, they had to be hurting. There was no way he could just shrug off so much damage.

I seem to be able to, he thought.

Lucas pointed his blade and waved it in an arch in front of himself, making a kill line. Wingarf just kept walking forward. The big creature wheeled his arm back and swung at Lucas without a care to defend or even an awareness to where his star-steel was. He threw his blade up in a solid motion, expecting to cut right through the arm. His blade smashed into the appendage and was held. It took Lucas a tick to realize what had happened and grab the hilt of his weapon with both hands. The blade had gone in just a fraction of an inch, and was now stuck. The liquid oil skin around the green blade was bubbling and burning off, dripping to the ground and sizzling on the grated metal floor, mixing with the blood and viscera.

Lucas pulled, using all his might to free the energy blade from where it was sinking into the goop of Wingarf's arm. The creature just laughed at him, a baritone rumble from deep within his corrupted gut. Lucas pushed Null into his arms, filling them with giant strength, the veins pumping both blood and the gold energy of existence. Pulling again, Lucas was able to free his blade. There was still Shadow goop rolling down, sizzling on the green shaft of energy. It was as if whatever covered Wingarf's body had turned his star-steel blade into a regular sword, something special made weak, mundane. Lucas narrowed his eyes and gritted his teeth. He was just going to have to approach this from a different direction.

Lucas pulled the Null in toward himself. Then, using as much power as he could build, reached out and tried to grab Wingarf's arm. If he couldn't cut it off, maybe he could move the creature away from the troopers he was killing, throw him down the pit of the elevator so they could crush him. Lucas could see the hand of Null energy wrap around Wingarf's arm and then fizzle. It felt like sand slipping through his fingers as the energy fell apart. Wingarf just laughed at him.

"Pathetic child," he said. "You are not worth my time."

Wingarf spun around and returned to killing the remaining troopers, cutting through them like they were nothing. Blood and screams filling the air.

Lucas needed to do something; had to find something, anything that he could do to stop this creature, stop the slaughter. Time was fast running out. They were about to reach the bottom of the shaft, the door would open and that would only serve to let this creature back into the bowels of *Prometheus*.

"Not worth your time? I would think you would be interested in having a rematch after you did such a poor job of killing me. Or are you just worried you are not up to the task?" Lucas taunted. "You've got both arms and are cleared for combat, so of course you spend your time killing mundanes. Pathetic, like all you rich little twats from the Academy. I've heard of lashing out because life dealt you a shitty hand—trust me, I know—but this? Really? This is a new low, even for a bully who gets his rocks off by abusing children."

Wingarf spun around, snapping the legs off the Militarum officer in his hand before dropping the man screaming to the floor.

"How dare you talk to me that way, you pathetic little pissant? I have always been above you, your *better*. We respect the flesh in my house, even if the order never did. A flawed order that would promote you to a rank of worth. I was *wasted* training the likes of you. None of you could beat me. Even now, you fail," Wingarf growled.

"Yet here I stand," Lucas said, holding his arms out to the side, legs wide, Null energy causing his jacket to flutter.

He calmed himself, grabbing all the Null that had spilled out during their fight and bringing it back inside. He projected confidence in a small aura around himself, bolstering his own skill and opinions. Leadership could apply to more than just those who followed. The aura made him feel more confident, like any pain could just be shrugged off and pushed aside. He was ready. This was going to be the last time Lucas was going to fight this shadow from his past—one of them was going to die for real today.

"Yet here you stand," Wingarf said. One of his mandibles reached out and snapped another Militarum trooper in half. "We have both been touched by the returning powers. Figures they would choose you."

Wingarf charged forward, both of his clawed hands ready to swipe at Lucas. He didn't miss a beat, waiting until Wingarf was close before ducking down and sliding forward, using the Null to propel him across the elevator. Wingarf was moving too fast and smashed into the wall, causing the entire shaft to groan and shudder. Now that he was surrounded by the last few Militarum soldiers remaining, Lucas pushed out his aura, bolstering them to fight past wounds and fear. Death before defeat. The stunned troopers got to their feet. There was a single Sargent left. Bolstered and renewed, he was able to see the shape of the battlefield and took command.

"Troopers, bayonets!" he yelled.

There was not much time. Wingarf was already getting back to his feet and shaking off the disorientation from his impact with the wall. The Militarum troopers jumped to their feet, training and Null energy taking over. Grabbing their muskets, they pulled out the triangular bayonets and attached them to the end of their weapons. As each bayonet clicked into place, they started to hum with star-steel energy flowing through them, a smaller version of the spear that Wingarf had carried. The men lined up. The Sargent pulled out his cutlass and pulled the hammer back on his pistol.

"Charge!" he yelled.

The troopers matched his energy and charged forward. The few who still had loaded muskets fired them. The rounds smashed into Wingarf with little effect, only enough to irritate the Shadow-filled creature. The troopers stabbed forward, trying to find weak spots upon Wingarf's bulbus form. There was nothing for them. Each time one of their bayonets hit his body, it got stuck, was pulled inside, and the trooper would fall to the ground. Drawing side swords, they rushed in again, creating a flurry of green upon black, punctuated by red streamers and screams. The men fought hard, they fought well, and they died.

Lucas felt a twinge of guilt for giving them the courage to charge to their deaths. They had all known that it was better to die on your feet than be slaughtered one by one in a pile of panic.

The Sargent was the last trooper to fall. He ducked and weaved away from the mandibles with such skill that Lucas questioned if the man might have been lightly sensitive to the Null. Sadly, as he moved from a mandible strike, the claws found him, bursting through his chest, treating the armor he wore like it was tissue paper. The Sargent didn't scream, he didn't cry out. He just spit in Wingarf's face.

"How very noble of you, Knight-Commander, sending other people to die for you," Wingarf said as the Sargent slid off his claws, the blood bubbling and boiling upon the black tar of his skin.

"We all die. It's rare we get to face that fate with courage," Lucas said.

He was running out of tricks and time. They were going to reach the bottom in just a moment and then it would be over. Wingarf charged at Lucas, who ducked away again. This time, he ran the tip of his blade across Wingarf's arm. It didn't catch in the sludge of skin. It sizzled and the Shadow-infused Master-at-Arms grunted.

So, he can *be hurt,* Lucas thought. The skin protects from deep cuts and puncture wounds. He would need to readjust, go for the light sweeping strikes; ones usually considered inefficient against armored targets. He was going to have to duel like a gentleman from NovaTerra with a rapier in hand. That was something Lucas was more than capable of doing. It might not win him the day, but at least it was a small amount of hope that he could grab on to. That was what today was, swinging from one strand of hope to another, in the near futile effort to see tomorrow.

The creature charged at Lucas again. This time, he held his ground, using the Null to allow him to duck and weave away from Wingarf's slow, powerful strikes. Each time, he was able to get in a single light cut, just grazing across the surface, slicing through. Wingarf eventually stumbled back, grunting, breathing hard, dripping oozing ichor on the floor. Lucas flicked off his blade, disturbed that this goo somehow stuck to the shaft of pure energy like it was blood on a common blade.

The two threw themselves at each other again. This time, Wingarf was faster, he was learning. Lucas scored a few hits, and then felt a sharp, white hot pain shoot through his body. Sliding away from the fight, he hit the wall opposite the elevator door. His hand came down and was greeted by a warm wetness. Lucas only glanced down for a moment. He was bleeding profusely. The cut had been more than a graze. It was fatal. He tried to pull in more Null, but there wasn't much left in the elevator, and his wound sucked it all away from him as his body tried to knit itself back together.

"Admirable, but meaningless," Wingarf said, turning and starting toward Lucas.

The elevator banged to a stop, the indicator light over the door beeping before turning green. He had failed. Wingarf was going to kill him and then rip through the ship. It was over.

The door to the elevator swished open and was followed by the heartbeat thrum of a blade being ignited.

CIC *Fury*, Cassandra

Cassandra watched in relief as the Lagrange carrier exploded and winked out of existence from the tactical display on her glass table.

"Scratch one, Carrier Lord Admiral," Captain Rackland's voice called from the weapons control station.

Things were finally starting to go their way. With the gloves off, they had been able to remove the battleship from the engagement with little effort, costing them five percent on their power build up.

"Very good. Captain, if I may have a word," Cassandra said, motioning for him to head to the lower deck with her. She then turned to her valet, who was standing at attention waiting in the wings. "Corporal, if you could be so kind as to bring out some tea, please," she said, returning her attention to the board that was displaying the battle.

"What is our next move?" Rackland asked, walking up to the other side of the table and leaning over it, the blue and red lights of the holograms reflecting off his grizzled face. Cassandra looked across the board, and started to spell everything out, working through the problem as she talked.

"The Lagrange fleet is broken; their destroyers and support ships are starting to flee. Normally, we would hunt them down for the prize money," she said.

"But there is no time, and if we fail to warn NovaTerra, there might not be anybody to pay out for a few broken destroyers and support ships," Rackland said flatly.

"They will not soon forget this little dust up with a Dreadstar. Perhaps some of them will think twice about staying upon this road that has been set out by their leaders. It's that Aldebaran fleet that is the kicker. They will be on us far too soon," Cassandra said as her valet walked up to the table with a tea tray and two cups.

She nodded, thanking him. He returned the nod and stepped back into the shadows to await his next command. Cassandra poured two cups of tea and took a sip. It was warm and revitalizing, just what she needed in this moment. Cassandra pressed the comm button and pulled up the fighter channel.

"Commander, what is the status of your wings at present?" she asked.

Erik's voice came over the comm a moment later. "We lost ten Rapiers and three Broadswords. Most of us are low on munitions, I recommend rearming via rolling combat landings."

Cassandra could hear the tiredness in her son's voice, steeled with resolve because, like her, he knew that this was far from over.

"Very well, Commander. Get your people in and back out. The window is going to be tight."

She looked down at the board again. New signals had started to appear—a forward fighter wing from the *Pride*. Cassandra knew Lord Admiral Victor Aldebaran—or, at least, she thought she did. He was the second son and military commander of his house. He was ruthless, but not reckless in battle. Everything was a trap, everything involved poking and prodding and learning. If Cassandra had wanted to go out in a blaze of glory, Dreadstar versus Dreadstar, Victor Aldebaran and the *Pride* would have been low on her list of choices.

Their power generation was at forty-nine percent. Too low for her liking. Combat landings and reloads were going to tax them. A prolonged battle would be even worse.

"Captain, we need to put more distance between us and that fleet. Ideas?" she asked.

Rackland picked up one of the grease pencils sitting next to him and started doing some rough math while taking a sip of his tea. These were all calculations that the computer could have done, but there was something that felt right about doing it by hand, allowing your mind to truly work through the problem. She talked through things, Rackland liked to work sums to bring the picture into focus.

"If we set our course down the Z axis like this," he stated, holding up the pencil and flicking it over to form a stylus drawing in the air. "Using short bursts from the major thrusters, we should be able to put a good amount of distance between us. Enough that Victor is going to have to move his ships closer if he wants his fighters to have a chance of coming home," Rackland said.

Like Cassandra, the captain was an old hat at this and knew every commander out there. If there indeed was to be some kind of rebellion or civil war, then they were all going to have to change their tactics or find new commanders. If they didn't do the first, the second would happen for sure.

"How will that affect our power generation?" she asked.

"Each burn is going to cost close to a percentage point, but it should buy us the time we need to make that up. It'll get larger with each burn. The first, we probably will not break even; the second, five, maybe six percent; the third, ten to fifteen. If we don't do this, they will be on us and that will be the game," Rackland said.

Cassandra nodded and finished her tea. Setting the cup down, she knew he was right. It was why she had asked him. There was no point in keeping advisers around if you were not going to listen to them.

You will hear the music one last time.

Cassandra pushed away the words from the Wayfinder that was living in the heart of her ship, even as the theme that she had written in haste before the battle was slowly percolating up from her subconscious and through her fingers onto the glass top table.

"I don't recognize that one," Captain Rackland said, pointing to her tapping right hand.

Cassandra quickly stopped tapping, putting her left hand over the right one. For the first time ever, a new composition scared her, and she wasn't ready to share that with the world.

"It's nothing, something old that just got stuck in my head," she said, letting go of her right hand and waving off the accusation of something new. Rackland chuckled and gave her a small smile.

"If you say so," he said, not believing her.

"I do. Captain, you may execute your plan, if you please," Cassandra said. Rackland nodded at her.

"Helm, prepare to set a new course!" the captain's voice bellowed across the Combat Information Center.

"New course, aye, Captain," the boatswain by the helm yelled back as Captain Rackland turned and started up the steps toward the helm at the top of the pit, barking out numbers and directions as he walked.

Outside *Fury*, Erik

"Bella, that first wave of fighters is going to be on top of *Fury* in ten minutes. How is your load-out looking?" Erik asked, as his wing charged back toward *Fury* to prepare for the second phase of this battle that they didn't want to be fighting.

His mother was holding back. Erik knew he should know why, but the memory of their plan had faded into the background, like a scab that he was trying not to pick at, even though it itched something horrible.

"I'm still locked and loaded, cousin. I don't need two bursts to remove a missile battery," she said jokingly.

If anybody else had tried that, Erik would have drummed them out of the service and then left them to rot in the brig. Bella, though, got away with it, because she was right. This is why she was his second. Not because they were family, but because she was just better than every other pilot on the ship.

"Watch it, Bella," Erik said with a mixture of hardness and playfulness.

"Or what? You will assign me to lead the first wave of defenders during this rolling rearm?" she mused.

"Well, now that you mention it..." Erik said, stifling a chuckle.

"Heavens, whatever shall I do with this punishment?" she jabbed back.

"Scratch some fucking traitors," Erik said coldly.

"With pleasure," she said back, malice and a hit of sexuality in her voice.

Bella was in her element out here in space, strapped into her ship. She would make the incoming scout wave pay dearly, and if they were lucky, the butcher's bill would put the Aldebarans' in debt. The line went dead.

Erik started quickly shuffling his two wings into three groups. Group A would land with him and do a rolling rearm, where the techs would load and refuel their fighters during the three minutes it took to transport them from the landing bay back to a launch tube. Group B would stay with Bella and perform a holding action, giving them cover, before landing themselves to rearm. Group C would be the Broadswords. The flight crews would rearm them as normal and then keep them waiting in tubes for when their firepower was needed. If they were lucky, they wouldn't need to launch the bombers again.

Jump.

The word fell into his mind, and Erik was greeted with flashes of the Wayfinder, his memory trying to come together again. That was why they were holding back, keeping the frigates in reserve. Shaking his head, the memories rattled into place even though they were incomplete, but he remembered enough to know this was some kind of side effect of what he and his mother had done. The Wayfinder had whispered something in her ear that he hadn't been able to hear, something key; something his mother would never reveal to him.

Erik adjusted his ship so that he was on a direct line with the landing bay. On his HUD, large, green lines appeared, guiding him in. This was going to be a fast land and rearm. Thus the computer wouldn't be involved, aside from telling him what to do. Above the green line was a speed indicator. Putting his hand on the down throttle controller and removing his feet from the pedals, Erik slowed the ship down. The fighter fell into the correct range, and he glided into the hanger bay. The Rapier's wheels hit the deck and then Erik was pushed forward and back violently as the hook at the back of his ship grabbed onto the wires, stopping him dead in his tracks.

Running across the deck, directing ships, were the holographic deck crew. They were all real people working below decks in VR and then displayed across the deck to help guide everybody in. One of them ran up to him and started pointing toward an elevator that would carry him down for the next step of the process. Erik hit a timer and started a countdown. Once *Fury* took control of his ship, he wasn't going to be able to pay attention to the battle until he was in a launch tube again. Rolling over to the elevator, a large electromagnet was activated in the floor, holding his ship in place. The lights all shut down, as he descended into the bowels of the Dreadstar.

It took thirty seconds before he saw light again as he was spit out into the massive landing bay. Controlled chaos was going on all around him. On a normal landing, he would have driven his ship to its bay and got out. Now, though, he was going to stay on the elevator, which was also a floating rearm bay. As soon as he was completely clear of the shaft and the doors closed, a group of ten deck hands ran up to him. Behind them were carts with new batteries, fuel, and missiles. He also saw, running behind them, his uncle, the ship's chief medical officer. He was coming toward Erik's ship. He reached up and threw forward the canopy of his fighter and removed his helmet. Breathing in a lungful of fresh air felt good, instead of air that had been recycled ten times in the last hour.

"How are you feeling?" Joseph Cordova asked, reaching into his coat pocket and pulling out a small light.

"Tired, thirsty, ready to get back out there," Erik said, as he followed the light with his eyes. "Why are you here? Shouldn't the ship's chief medical officer be in the infirmary?"

"Not a lot going on down there yet and checking in on the health of the CAG seemed like a good use of my time," his uncle said.

If his mother was cold and distant, then her brother was the exact opposite: warm, affectionate, and always looking out for them. Probably why he went into medical care and how he raised a wild child like Bella.

"Is there is something more?" Erik asked.

One of the deck hands ran up to him with a bottle of water that he emptied in two large gulps. His ship was shaking as they attached fresh missiles and power packs for his guns.

"Your mother hasn't been taking my calls, and I'm worried now that we are in some kind of truly nasty shit," Joeseph said.

It was in that moment that Erik realized his uncle didn't know, not just about their plan but about the Wayfinder, about the music, *any* of it. He wasn't sure exactly how he knew—it was just a feeling, but if his mother hadn't said anything to her own brother, then it must be a secret that needed to be kept extremely close.

"She is as well as can be expected. We had to leave Hanna behind, and we might be too late even with all of this to save NovaTerra and Alexander. So, worried. She is worried and focused."

In that moment, Erik desperately wanted this conversation to end; wanted to get his bill of health and return to the fight.

"I didn't know," Jospeh said quietly. "I wish she was talking to me. We used to talk all the time."

"Well, now you know. So, if it is all the same, uncle, I would like to get out into the fight and relieve your daughter so she can have this same bevy of questions lobbed at her," Erik said picking his helmet up again.

"Of course, of course, you are cleared," his uncle said, stepping back from the fighter and slapping it on the side, giving a thumbs up to the deck commander.

The whole crew was done. They were scurrying away toward a fresh set of weapons so that they could get the next fighter that came through the door. Erik was breathing heavily—perhaps the stress was getting to him. There wasn't time to think about that now.

Pulling the canopy of his fighter closed, he put on his helmet as his Rapier was loaded into the launch tube.

Floor Two Hundred, Black Caldera, Grace

The trip down to floor two hundred had seen some resistance, but not as much as she had expected. Three barricades that Essex had taken care of with ease, being the wizard battle monk that he was. It all made Grace feel apprehensive. Emily agreed. There should have been more resistance, more defenders.

The door to floor two hundred was locked. Grace looked at Essex. He took a deep breath and pulled out his star-steel blade. Before he could ignite the weapon, Grace reached out and put her hand on his wrist.

"I have a bad feeling about this," she said.

"You are not alone. I can feel the creature in my mind screaming that they are going to kill us; that we should already be dead. I'm trying to not listen, but…" Essex said, closing his eyes, pushing the voices back.

"But you can't reconcile what your eyes are seeing with what it is screaming?" she asked.

"Dew'renath," Essex muttered. Neon-blue eyes flashed across Grace's field of vision as she stumbled back.

"What?" she muttered through gritted teeth, the pain spiking and then passing over her.

"Its name. The thing inside my head."

"It knows me. They *all* know me," Emily muttered, trying to regain control of her breath, to find her footing again. The eyes of the Varagoth faded. They were all different, yet all the same: a collective of anger and hatred that just wanted to be free to exact their pain upon the physical world that had shunned them so many thousands of years ago.

"If they know you, then they should be scared," Essex said, holding out his other hand to Grace. She reached out and pulled herself up from where the eyes and pain had laid her low.

"I don't know if they feel fear. All I have experienced from them is anger, rage," Grace muttered.

"Anger and rage are born from fear. Trust me—they feel it. Especially connected to you," Essex said, punctuating the statement with the golden heartbeat thrum of his blade coming to life. He made quick work of the door's lock and hinges, kicking it open. The heavy slab of steel smashed into the ground, the sound echoing through the facility.

"This way," Essex said, running forward.

It only took a few minutes for them to cross the floor, which was empty. On the other side, Grace could see the flight control room. A space filled with computers and controls, chairs that should have been full. Dominating the room was a massive window that looked out upon the flight bay, which was stuffed with shuttles and other small, atmospheric capable ships. At every turn, the scale of this operation stunned and scared Grace to her core. Knowing something this powerful had been allowed to build up without anybody knowing about it was a horrible sign for the future, for the fate of civilization.

"Where is everybody?" Grace asked as she came to a stop at the door to the room, scanning her rifle from left to right.

"Cleared out, hiding—" Essex started.

"Getting out of the way of an ambush," Emily said, finishing the sentence.

"Agreed. Nothing for it now. We need a ship. Something that will be able to keep us alive for the long haul, to get to the closest jump gate, which is over a month away," Essex said.

"Fuck that," Emily muttered. "We are going to punch open the rift that is here and ride the Null."

"What?" Essex asked, confused.

"I solved their stupid problem. I know where the rift is and its frequency. Mostly. There is still a little more math to do, but that can be done in space. I just need a little time and space, so I'm going to need you to become the weapon the Host'ire forged you to be," Emily said, putting her hand on Essex's shoulder. Emily looked up at him, locking her eyes on his sunglasses and nodding her head. Essex took a deep breath and nodded back, turning toward the door.

"It is a good thing time is on sale this week, because I plan to buy a lot of it," he said, trying to sound cool.

Grace nodded at him while Emily rolled her eyes. He turned, running toward the door, reaching into his coat and pulling out a bag. There wasn't going to be much time to get things set up, so she was going to have to work fast.

The flight systems were wide open. *This is most definitely a trap, but I see some outs,* Emily thought, looking across the list of ships that were at some level of prepped and ready to launch. Most had supplies and weapons loaded, but no fuel. Halfway down the list, she found a ten-seater shuttle that was Null rated. The *Chaos Runner*. A great name if there ever was one. It was stocked with supplies and the plasma cells for its weapons were fully charged. Best of all, the antimatter tanks were half full. It wouldn't take much to top them off. Grace started hitting keys, getting things ready.

They want us on that ship, this is too convenient, Emily thought.

Knowing the trap lets us work through it, Grace responded.

One step at a time, one step at a time, Emily muttered in agreement.

As she hit the last keys, turning on the fuel transfer, the room shook with the sounds of an explosion. Grace could feel the heat registering through the back of her suit. Turning around the door they had come through was a mess of fire and dead bodies. Essex must have had some surprises in that bag of his. She could hear more screams, men yelling orders coming forward, ready to push through the breach and overwhelm them. Essex was pressed against the side of a control panel. He had his rifle in hand, and four extra power packs laid out in front of him, along with three grenades. He was going to need help.

Turning back to the flight controls, Grace looked at the timer. Four minutes. It didn't sound like a long time, but she knew that it was going to be a deadly eternity while under fire. She reached her hand up and grabbed the holographic readout of the timer and pulled it to her suit. The graphic vanished and then appeared to the side of her helmet's HUD. Grace grabbed her rifle and ran to another bit of cover next to Essex. She nodded at him as the first wave of soldiers bust through the flames into the room.

The Spine of *Prometheus*, Rostov

Hyacinth laid atop the shield of Null energy that was draped over *Prometheus* like a tarp. Rostov could feel that they were getting close to the surface. He was starting to see chunks of pure white concrete mixed in with the rocks. Wires and steel. The materials that had built the cell he had spent the last two years in. The place where he had died and been reborn. No tears were shed as those places were destroyed. He just wished that he could sit back and enjoy the destruction. The more material the ship pushed through, the harder it was getting to keep the shield up. Hyacinth was dissipating some of her energy by touching the shield, but it wasn't enough. The closer they got to the surface, the farther away they got from that pure Null that had been surrounding the ship. Rostov had thought it was coming from Hyacinth, but it seemed to exist inside that pocket. They were bringing some of it up with them, like water inside a sunken ship, and he wondered if it would be enough for him to keep the shield going. It would have to be.

A bead of sweat dripped down into his eye. Rostov tried to blink it away, only succeeding in making his vision blurrier. His good hand was starting to falter, getting tired, while the power in his suit kept his twisted knee where it needed to be so he wouldn't fall from the ladder.

Hyacinth giggled as they pushed through more rooms. There was no more rock, it was all sublevels. There was a pinprick of light. Could that be? Were they going to make it? Rostov had doubted that this plan would work; had not believed in his ability to do his part. Yet here he was, holding it together. By a thread, sure, but together none the less. There was more light, it was peeking in from all over now. Hyacinth threw her arms out and pushed her chest up, breathing in the light and air, screaming with delight.

Prometheus smashed through the surface, the small shafts of light giving way to a blinding brightness. The deep bright reds and greens of the Barrier filled Rostov's field of vision as the rocks started to fall away from the ship. From outside, he could hear crumbling destruction. They had come up from beside the tower. He would be able to see it if he pushed. This was a sight that he was not going to miss. No matter how much pain it caused him, even if it killed him, he was going to watch this; watch the end of the Citadel. This place had abused him, haunted him, and broken him. Watching it fall would be cathartic, would fill that empty hole in his heart.

He took a deep breath and pulled a fraction of the Null from the shield and pushed it into his knee. He couldn't heal like Lucas, but the Null made him slightly stronger, would dull the pain somewhat. Then, he flicked off the leg compressions. Instantly, his knee started to wobble, shuddering at having to hold his weight. Rostov grunted with determination, pulling himself up another rung, making the broken leg follow his commands. Pain washed through him in waves, but the leg obeyed and he was up a rung. The world started to go fuzzy from the pain, the Null he had pulled in wasn't enough. They were free, there were no more rocks. Rostov grabbed even more of the energy from the shield, shoving it into his fading body.

The second step was not as bad, his body numbing to the pain. It was enough; he was able to get his head out of the porthole and look over. *Prometheus* had cleared the ground and was starting to rotate and head for the stars. She was *massive*. Rostov knew the factual concept of how big the ship was, but seeing it, sticking his head out *from* it, made him feel small. The old girl was covered in dents and pockmarks from the years of sitting underground. As they continued to climb, the large cannons along her back started to rise, ready for what might come.

"Look, Rostov," Hyacinth said.

She was standing now, floating above his fading shield, her finger pointing out and downward. He turned following her finger. Then he saw it. The massive tower of the Citadel, its hundreds of blocky floors, each one just a little offset from the one below it, so that it looked like a column reaching into the sky and not some kind of brutalist nightmare. The ship had exited with its forward section under the parade ground. So, for the moment, the tower stood. Rostov could see the cracks in the ground starting to form already. Their assent had destroyed the foundation upon which the Citadel sat, and it was only a matter of time before the tower started to fall.

"This is what you wanted, is it not? To see some measure of justice served?" Hyacinth asked.

Rostov didn't answer, at first. He just watched as cracks started to spike up the building, the sections wobbling as more and more ground around it started to fall in. For a moment, it filled him with joy, and then the feeling passed.

"It was. But now…"

He paused, contemplating the emptiness that he was sure watching this building crumble would fill. The emptiness didn't change.

"But now?" Hyacinth asked.

Damn her, he thought. She knew him too well—better than he knew himself, it seemed. Or perhaps she was just able to admit the things his pain wouldn't allow him to.

"The Citadel is just a place. The Host'ire still exist. They will just rebuild somewhere else. This doesn't stop the kidnapping of children, the oppression, the building of living weapons. At best, it slows them down. This is a hollow victory, a speed bump for them," Rostov said.

The top section of the Citadel rolled off, starting a cascade. He turned around. There was no point in watching it fall. That hole in his heart that had been created by violence and abuse was not going to be filled by watching concrete crumble. A tear ran down his cheek as he crawled back inside the porthole.

"They did not break you, Rostov. You know how I know that?" Hyacinth asked. Her projection had moved to the landing at the bottom of the ladder.

"How?" he asked, quietly letting his injured leg slip off the rung, letting his good arm catch them.

"Because you are not reveling in the destruction. You do not celebrate death. You understand how hollow retribution is," Hyacinth said.

"Retribution, justice, getting even… None of it matters. The hurt has been done. All we can do is move forward. Perhaps find the illusion of forgiveness to make us feel better," he said. Finally, his good leg found the platform, and he hobbled to the wall and sat down, stretching the twisted leg out.

"The first steps," Hyacinth said.

Rostov was about to make a quip—it was the only way he knew how to deal with pain, apart from anger—when the ship shook again. This time, it wasn't from rocks. He looked up and saw a small formation of ships descending from orbit. There was a flash of light from them, and they shook again. The Fellowship of the Cross's ships.

There was nothing he could do about them. His energy was spent. Rostov could only sigh and start climbing down.

CIC *Prometheus,* Joanna

The ship rocked around Joanna. She grabbed the glass table and looked around at the Militarum troopers who were doing their best to work the ship. They had broken free from the crust of Icarus and were in the air, the depleted and slowly dying ship making her way to the stars for one last journey.

Looking up at the screens above her and the external cameras, Joanna watched as the Citadel finally gave up and began to crumble. The bottom giving way and the top starting to fall to the side. With nothing to hold it in place, the middle of the building came crashing straight down. There was a strange relief to see the place vanish from existence and turn into a pile of rubble. Too many people had died there today for it to feel cathartic. There would be no real memory of this battle. Of their fight.

The ship rocked again. That wasn't from their escape, that was—

They were being shot at.

"Scanners, what is in the sky?" Joanna yelled across the room.

Before anybody could say anything, she was hit by a flash, images of ships. They were monstrous things, cobbled together amalgamations of what an insane person might think a space ship looked like. They bristled with spikes and guns, shattered and patched portholes. Scrawled across them in red paint—no, in *blood*—were crosses.

Mounted to those painted crosses were the bones of the dead. There were four of them, Fellowship of the Cross ships.

Joanna flashed back to the combat information center of *Prometheus*, just as the trooper operating the scanners gave her that same information.

Looking down at the raw data, she realized that what she had seen was not what was but what would be. She was flashing forward—not far, only a few seconds, at best. The ship rocked again. Those blasts were getting through. She flicked the comm over to Rostov's frequency.

"Rostov, where is my shield?" she yelled.

Joanna fell into feeling like Lucas for a moment, taking control of the situation. He might have been the group's leader, but right now, she was in command.

"I couldn't hold it any longer," she heard his voice mutter over the radio. The pain was clear. Joanna momentarily felt bad for yelling at him. They had tasked him with an extremely hard job. Of course the shield had faltered as soon as they were free. She couldn't begin to imagine the strain it must have taken on him.

"Understood," she said, quietly pushing as much empathy into her voice as possible. "You did well. Get on up here."

"On my way," Rostov said, clicking off.

The ship shook again, sparks starting to fly. A console on the upper level exploded, sending one of the troopers flying across the CIC like a ragdoll smashing into another group on the second level. Smoke was starting to fill the room. *Prometheus* was old and in disrepair. It was a testament to how well built Dreadstars were that she was even flying.

"What is going on up there? She is screaming!" Naomi's voice came over the comm.

"We're taking fire," Joanna snapped back, perhaps a little too curtly. But Naomi had access to the same information, if not more, since she was talking to the ship.

"She doesn't like it, and doesn't have much left to give," Naomi said.

Joanna was about to say something pithy when she had another flash. The ships were closer. Her vision zoomed inside the ship. She could see torpedoes being loaded. Zealots in robes pushing smoking, leaking weapons into tubes while chanting about their dead god. She flashed back to the present. Looking down at the readout. She was twenty seconds ahead.

"Naomi, weapons, now!" Joanna yelled into the comm.

She looked down at the board and started hitting keys, directing the plasma cannons to fire at a specific point, and for the helm to move them just slightly.

"She says it hurts," Naomi responded.

Blasted ship, Joanna thought.

"Tell her it will hurt far worse to fall out of the sky!" Joanna yelled back.

There was a moment of stillness. She looked down at the reading. Torpedoes were in the air coming toward them. While the spirit of the ship was not cooperating with the guns, she was at least allowing them flight control. The Dreadstar didn't move fast in the atmosphere of the planet, but they were able to avoid two of the three weapons that were thrown at them. The ship shook again, more violently this time. Screams and explosions were all around her.

"Naomi, I need those guns. I don't care what you have to do to get them for me!" Joanna yelled into the comm.

"Please, I know you don't want to fight anymore," Naomi said, her voice close, present. Joanna looked up and saw her running into the CIC. "Yes, I'll tell her."

"Tell me what?" Joanna asked. Her patience was starting to run thin. The shield was down, the ship wasn't cooperating, Lucas hadn't responded to her calls.

Command was overrated.

"She can give you three shots. Any more than that and we won't be able to open the Eye," Naomi said as she ran down to meet Joanna and started flicking switches around the jump engine controls. Joanna didn't think they were going to have to jump and was pretty sure they didn't have near enough power for it anyway.

"I'll take it," she said.

Joanna didn't have to wait long as the next flash hit. They were splitting up, making some kind of attack run, getting closer. She could hear the chanting from the ships, a death call for their god. The sacrifice that they were about to commit. So much blood had already been spilled and a Dreadstar was the final act. It put a pit in her gut.

Flickering back to reality, she knew what to do. There was only fifteen seconds to make the adjustments. She quickly pressed a few keys, moving two of the guns toward the lead ship and the third toward the one in the back. Destroy the front of the train, clip the caboose and hope for enough confusion to get into orbit.

"Fire!" Joanna yelled across the CIC.

The ship rocked, this time from the power of the guns mounted upon her back. If the ship had been fully operational, there would have been countermeasures to ensure they stayed in place when the weapons were fired. But here, at a fraction of their power, and in atmosphere, Joanna was just relieved that they hadn't blown themselves out of the sky.

The front Fellowship barge broke up and exploded. The one at the back of the line took its hit not where she wanted and was fighting to stay in formation. The confusion and clouds of debris and fire was enough to skuttle their attack run as the middle ship broke off. That would buy them at few minutes, at best. At that point, they would realize that they didn't have the power to do that again.

"Helm, get us to orbit. Naomi, get Hyacinth that power, she is going to need soon," Joanna said, taking a deep breath.

In the back of her mind, she saw them in space, closing in on the clouds of the Barrier, a giant, new cloud forming and then bursting open like a flower in spring.

Elevator, Dreadstar *Prometheus*, Lucas

For a moment, there was hope. The sound of another blade coming to life. Lucas couldn't see who was holding it through the oozing black bulk of Wingarf, but he had an idea. The massive creature didn't move, it just stood there. Lucas could feel the anger bellowing off it, radiating forward toward the door.

"Look how small you have become, Wingarf," Administrator Fel's voice said, dripping with condescension.

"You wish to have the powers that I possess. Your bonds with the weakness of the Null will be your undoing," Wingarf said.

"Is that what they told you? Who? The Fellowship? Somebody else? This nebulous enemy that Lucas and his friends are talking about? What side in this conflict needed a patsy so badly that they gave you even a modicum of real power?" she asked.

Lucas could see her now. Fel had walked into the room, her blood-red blade held calmly to the side. She was starting to rotate around Wingarf. For as much power as he looked to have—as he *did* have—Lucas was suddenly sure that she had as much, if not more.

"I don't have to tell you anything, Fel! For too long have I been under your boot. Stuck as a knight, having to train squalor children who should have been sacrificed to your pathetic Militarum!" Wingarf yelled.

Lucas could already see the ooze of his body pulsing with anger. She had known him long enough, well enough, to make every single word hurt.

"You only stayed a knight because you refused to put on the arm. The papers have been on my desk for fifteen bloody years and at least fifteen before that," Fel snapped.

"My house does not do that! I learned without needing your fancy technology. I put all of you to shame with the spear and one fucking arm!" Wingarf yelled.

"Your house is weak and short sighted. The Host'ire do not have need of cripples on the front lines. A knight must be whole, they must be pure. You passed up a chance to be more because of some mundane connection to your genetic doners?" Fel sneered.

She threw up her blade and waved it about. Wingarf shouldn't have feared it, but he did, taking a step back into the corner. Lucas couldn't take his eyes off this display.

"We abandon our houses, our families, when we join the order. Why do you think we remove these poor, degenerate children from their homes by force of law? Yes, you get to keep the connection because your father made some money. It doesn't matter. He is *dead* and amounted to nothing. You could have been so much more, but you focused all your anger and spite at worthless children. Children who didn't have a fraction of the connection to the Null that you have. You could have been magnificent. But instead, you chose to be *small*." Fel dragged out the last word.

Lucas should have been insulted by her diatribe, but he was just in awe of what it was doing to Wingarf.

"You have no idea what I have become, what I am. They are already moving, waking up. Sadly, you will not be alive to see them wipe your pathetic Host'ire order from the system," Wingarf said.

He was trying to match her energy, her vitriol. It was not working.

"Knight-Commander, on me," Fel said, nodding to her side.

Lucas ran forward, holding his blade in a stance that complemented hers. Wingarf was now backed into a corner, facing not just an accomplished Host'ire Knight-Commander, but a Master. His anger may have covered up any fear that he might have been feeling, but it also blinded whatever battle sense remained inside his oozing skull.

"I shall enjoy ripping you both limb from limb," Wingarf said as he charged forward, his clawed hands reaching and the mandibles attached to his shoulders clicking.

In a fluid motion, Fel leapt into the air, her jacket flowing out. She hung there for a moment, as if time had stopped. Golden energy rippled through her arm and across her red blade, wrapping around, like string. With an even cut, she came screeching down, the Null-infused blade slicing right through Wingarf's left arm; the arm he had been missing before. She hit the ground and flicked the oozing blood from her blade. Wingarf screamed and flailed, throwing his arm around, as black, viscus blood poured from the wound. Fel stood there for a moment, looking at the arm as it wiggled on the ground like a fish out of water. She sneered and then kicked the amputated appendage back to Wingarf.

"Pick up the arm, Knight. Put it on, make yourself whole again," Fel taunted, as she let the golden energy fade from her arm, pulling it back into herself.

"I don't need that to kill you!" he yelled.

"What are you going to do, pinch me to death? You are pathetic," Fel said, turning and walking away.

Wingarf charged toward her, both his mandibles out. Fel let out a light, annoyed breath. She ducked out of the way, letting both claws clamp above her head. She rolled to the side and reached her empty hand behind her jacket and pulled out her hand. Her index finger was pointed forward, with her thumb up. Lucas cocked his head to the side, confused, and Wingarf laughed.

"What is this? You think I am afraid of you wagging a finger at me?" Wingarf asked between stifled laughter.

Fel didn't say anything. She just flicked her thumb down like it was the hammer of an old-style pistol. Purple and golden energy burst from her hand and smashed into Wingarf, blowing a hole in his chest, painting the wall behind him black. She flicked her thumb three more times in rapid succession, bolts of energy smashing through the arms attaching the mandibles to Wingarf's back. There was screaming and gnashing of teeth as the creature that was once the Master-at-Arms fell to the ground.

"I've never seen the Null do that before," Lucas said, walking up to Fel as she shook the finger gun from her hand.

"The Null is what we make it, Knight-Commander. There is plenty that you do not know. Perhaps if we survive, I will show you," Fel said. "Now, though, we end this."

She walked forward, her blade pointed down toward the panting Wingarf, who was cradling his lost arm and on the edge of crying. Her confidence was intoxicating—and short lived.

Panting, Wingarf pushed himself to a kneeling position with the one arm he had left. As the two of them approached, his almost crying turned to laughter. Lucas didn't see it fast enough. Smoke started to form around him, materializing a spear in his hand. Wingarf lashed out, the black smoking tip grazing across the armor plating on Fel's chest. She stumbled back, the inky ooze trying to eat its way through the durasteel of her chest plate. Before it could eat through, she clicked off the straps and let it fall to the ground, kicking it away.

"I don't need your pity. I don't need the extra arms of my benefactors. All I need is my spear," Wingarf spat out.

He spun the weapon around over his head. Now more attuned, Lucas could feel that he was using the Null to stand in for his missing arm, doing everything that the fake arm would have done, but with powers that he controlled.

As he was spinning, Lucas started to stalk to the left while Fel moved to the right. Eyes narrowed, he looked from Wingarf to Fel, then back to Wingarf again. Their eyes darted, then focused in on each other. Fel moved first. Diving forward, she attacked with an aggressive flurry of swings, both extremely powerful and precise. Lucas didn't miss a beat, charging in after her, flanking Wingarf. He moved the spear like the master that he was, effortlessly blocking their attacks, using the long shaft of the weapon to bat away their blades. This Shadow-summoned weapon had the same properties as his old star-steel spear, in that the entire thing was impervious to being cut by a blade.

They traded blows for what felt like forever, every parry almost a return hit. The tip of the spear was never more than a second away from making fatal contact. The horrible weapon grazed Lucas three times before he was forced to stumble back. He didn't scream. He just pulled in the dwindling pure Null of the ship and healed. Fel didn't let up her attack. No matter how fast Wingarf moved, she matched it. Lucas had been fighting with a star-steel blade for the better part of twenty-five years and watching the two of them face off was inspiring, in a completely horrible way.

Healed up, Lucas dove back into the fray. The only way they were going to take this monster down was to not let up, to not let him cut them off. Their attacks were relentless. Lucas pushed himself off the floor, gaining height before diving down his blade before him like a point. The green energy made contact with Wingarf's back before he was able to swat Lucas away. This gave Fel an opening to run her blade through his gut and pull it to the side, the exit spilling the black, oozing bile that made up his body.

Lucas used this moment, spinning back into the fray and slicing down across Wingarf's arm, removing it at the shoulder. The shadow man fell to the ground, leaking blackness, using the ruined stumps of his arms to drag himself away from the hungry blades of the Host'ire.

"You can't kill me. I will just reform. There is no victory for you today," he said. There was no malice, or cruelty, or even enjoyment, just a flat factuality.

"You can hide like a roach, and I shall squash you every time," Fel said.

She raised her weapon to strike the killing blow when the room was filled with a bright golden light. Lucas and Fel turned to see the avatar of Hyacinth appear before them.

"What is this?" Fel mouthed, falling to her knees.

"What we have been fighting to protect," Lucas said.

Hyacinth said not a word as she glided past them her feet, not touching the deck. Wingarf was paralyzed. Lucas watched as the sludge of the Shadow flowed away from his eyes. For the first time, he could see human eyes. Eyes that were scared. Eyes that did not want to die. Eyes that knew it was too late for that wish to come true.

"So much hate, so much sadness. All born of fear. You don't have to fear anymore. Go and find peace," Hyacinth said in her sing-song voice.

She reached out and paced a hand upon Wingarf's shoulder, the golden energy of the Null moving through her, pushing through him.

"Thank you," he whispered as his body lost its cohesion and sloshed onto the floor, dripping through the grates.

"That was better than he deserved," Fel muttered, clicking off her blade and putting it on her belt. "So, you are the one we have sacrificed so much for, who we are taking to Hell?"

Hyacinth walked by her before turning and giving her an almost uncaring look. "The way must be paved. Only then can the true Wayfinder save humanity. You will be there, but not at the end."

Her cryptic warning finished, she walked into the wall and vanished. Lucas and Fel both exchanged confused glances.

"Lucas, get up here *now*, we are about to reach orbit," Joanna's voice came through his communicator.

"I'm on my way," he said, flicking off his blade and running out of the room, Fel walking calmly behind him.

Flight Control, Black Caldera Facility, Grace

Her plasma rifle moved; her suit's auto aim system grabbing its next target. She pulled the trigger as soon as it beeped at her. The trooper in her sights, a man in gray armor and fatigues, fell to the ground, blooms of gore and fire bursting from him, two on his arms and one through the center of his chest. The man hit the ground, joining the ever growing pile of the dead, yet still, more were coming. It felt like an endless stream of bodies that the Children of the First were able to throw at them.

Two minutes.

They were halfway to having the ship recharged. Blinking to bring up her next target, Grace flicked her eyes to the side to check on Essex. He had dropped his rifle, the barrel red from the speed he had been firing it. He had leapt over his cover and was now standing in the open, a pistol in one hand and his star-steel blade in the other. Essex dodged from left to right, avoiding the incoming hail of both plasma and kinetic weapons fire. His coat had a few very noticeable holes in it, but so far, none of the rounds had found him.

Raising his hand, he fired the pistol three times, sending three more soldiers falling to the ground. The weapon clicked. He threw it at the closest enemy. The soldier was stunned for a moment, just long enough for Essex to close ground and remove the man's head with a swipe of his star-steel blade. Emily watched as he dodged and spun, his coat and blade working in tandem to cut an image of the warrior who could not be taken down. This time, it was Grace's turn to roll her eyes. Emily was far too distracted by this kind of competence.

Her auto aim system screamed at her. It had gotten a lock three times already and was waiting for her to pull the trigger. Grace turned away, focusing on her own war. Another quick burst of fire and the trooper she was aiming for fell to the ground, his head a burned and ruined wreck of flesh. That was when she heard Essex grunt.

He had been hit, the kinetic round smashing into his gut and blowing out the back of his jacket, a long trail of blood and gore on the floor behind him. Essex stumbled back, like he was shocked that they had actually hit him. It lasted only a moment as he spun his blade again, cutting down an officer who had run forward to try and engage him in melee combat. Grace hated kinetic weapons. They left you wounded, bleeding and dying slowly. At least plasma rounds cauterized wounds as they blew through your body, ripping apart your internal organs.

Another round found his arm, ripping through his bicep. His arm went limp, the fingers barely holding onto his star-steel blade. He was in the open, exposed, vulnerable and now with none of his defenses.

One minute.

It was time to go. Grace ejected the half spent plasma magazine from her weapon and smashed in a fresh one—her last one. Raising from her place of cover, she started shooting, forgoing the auto aim and squeezing off rounds quickly from the hip. She wasn't hitting anything, but some of the soldiers who were running at her turned for cover. A second later, she was at Essex, her arm wrapped around him, keeping the man on his feet. Grace turned her back to the enemy, the sounds of kinetic rounds impacting her armor and instantly deforming and hitting the ground. Her power reserve took a sizable hit for each round that it stopped. The suit had been rated to keep her alive in a micro-asteroid shower. It could handle bullets.

"Come on soldier, time to get out of here," Grace said.

Essex, his face white from the blood loss, nodded at her. He wrapped his good arm around her, finding his feet. She reached over and removed the hilt of his blade and clipped it to his belt again. Two more rounds smashed into her back. Grace turned again and started shooting, this time letting the auto aim take full control, shunting power to her arm to so that the weapon would not kick as much.

They started to walk backward, navigating through the control room. In the back, next to the windows, was an elevator that went down to the floor. The readout on her HUD said the ship was in position. She blinked three times, moving through menus and started the preflight systems warm up so that the ship would be ready to launch with its auto pilot as soon as they hit the deck. This took her mind away from the fight just long enough for something more than a kinetic round to hit her. The plasma round didn't go through her suit all the way, but it ripped into it, bleeding away power and pushing metal into her gut. Grace let out a scream and almost fell to the ground. The suit automatically shunted power to her legs, keeping her up. Pain raced through her body, followed by shock.

So, this is what it feels like to get shot, Emily thought, trying to focus through the haze of pain.

"First time?" Essex muttered as she regained her footing. "Don't worry, each one gets worse."

"That isn't what I wanted to hear," Grace said, stumbling backward.

She kept pulling the trigger on her plasma rifle until it clicked empty. She dropped the weapon and turned around, trying to pick up speed. Each step was a new experience in pain as the movement of her body threatened to cause the wound to rip open. She looked at the elevator door and blinked at it. It opened, as another plasma round smashed into her back. Grace screamed. This time, the armor shattered, letting the full energy of the round smash into her. She could feel ribs shattering, as the breath was knocked out of her. There were alarms running across the armor.

She was going to fall.

Then, she didn't.

Grace was leaning forward, but not falling, suspended in midair. Essex had slipped out from under her arm that was rapidly losing power. He was holding her up with the Null. She watched him scramble into the elevator as two more kinetic rounds smashed into her back. One got caught in the armor, the other ripping through her shoulder, blood splattering across her helmet.

He is going to leave us, that infested motherfucker! Emily thought, anger and betrayal flashing through her with each new wave of pain. If she got out of this, she was going to hunt him down and make sure his death was slow.

She bit her lip, trying to push forward, allowing the anger she was feeling to override the pain that her body was generating. Just as she was about to push through Essex's weak Null hold, she felt something push on her back. Grace went tumbling forward, rolling ass over teakettle into the elevator as the door closed behind her.

Card Den, Novagrad, Claudia

Time was starting to run out. Claudia didn't have much of it left if she was going to bring Alexander in. At every turn, either his own need to be a hero or her unwillingness to give any credit to Mister Harrison had thrown wrenches into the operation. She was going to bring him in—her and her alone. Claudia had no desire to share credit and knew that she needed this if she was going to move up in the organization, if she was going to have any leverage on jobs in the new order that was going to be formed. She didn't have a full picture of what was being planned, but she'd done enough digging to know that if the powers pulled off what they were planning, there wouldn't be much left of the Confederation in a few weeks.

Key to that, though, was bringing in Alexander. The new government was going to need jump tech, and according to all intel, the Confederation was close to cracking it again, recovering what had been lost when the Wayfinders were all killed five hundred years ago. Alexander was on that team. He had to know where the base was, what the research showed. It was a race. The intelligence she had seen also said that, somewhere deep in the Unaligned Planets, there was a project working to reach the same goal. If they were able to crack faster than light travel again first, it would spell doom for the Confederation, and whatever was to come after it. Alexander was one of the keys and she was going to bring him in—*alone*—and reap the rewards for doing so.

The Peculiar Pentagon den was bustling. Across Novagrad, there were underground parlors where you could go and play cards. Lights were flashing. There was cheering, crying, screaming, and fists being smashed into tables. Some of these parlors hosted friendly games. Others hosted games for people looking to get into the hobby. Most hosted cutthroat games where more than just cards and money were on the line.

At the heart of every game was the electronic status card. This kept track of a player's life and resources. If that card was hacked or broken, there was no record of the game, and the governing body could do nothing in arbitration. Thus, the card parlors were underground and hardened against electronic warfare. The higher end ones even issued you a fresh status card upon entry that had to be longed into and authenticated. Cheating was a massive industry in Peculiar Pentagon and preventing it was an even bigger one. The front rooms of these card dens were regulated by the Peculiar Pentagon board of directors. The backrooms? Well, regulators tended to turn a blind eye to them for the right price. A price that Claudia had paid.

Alexander would be here soon, and then she could finish this. Claudia looked at her watch. It was set into count down mode and less than thirty minutes remained to get the job done. She was cutting this extremely close. She was ready to roll as soon as he got here. Under her skirts, she had on a pair of britches with a pistol and a small survival pack. Making their way to the extraction point was going to be a challenge once things got started, but she had faith.

Her watch buzzed. Claudia looked down and saw that it was Alexander. She picked it up and gave him the room number, then leaned forward in her chair. It was time to put on the water works. This was going to be the last time that she would have to play the sad damsel in distress, a role that she was good at, but truly sick of. She rubbed her eyes so that they would be red. Taking in a deep breath, she willed the tears to flow. In another life, Claudia of House Wise would have been an actress, but here she was a spy, and today was the day she would come in from the cold with a victory.

The door opened and Alexander burst inside. She looked up, the tears streaking down her face, her makeup running.

"You came, I was so worried you wouldn't come," she said, getting up and running to him, her arms out. Alexander took a step back and closed the door behind him.

"Just… stay there," he said.

She could tell he was worried, was playing this close to the vest. This wasn't the same Alexander that she had been stringing along the last few days. This seemed an Alexander that was finally starting to pay attention to the world. No matter what, she was already committed to the bit and there was no backing out now. If it went south, she did still have a gun.

"I'm so sorry, I just—I didn't know what to do," she said, looking down, sniffling. "Please don't be mad at me," she said softly.

"I'm… I don't *want* to be mad at you, Claudia. I really don't want to. In fact, I'm having a hard time with it. I'm just… I'm confused and disappointed," Alexander said.

He motioned toward the table in the middle of the room. It had two chairs and enough space for a game of Peculiar Pentagon. Claudia didn't know what he was getting at, but she walked over and sat down at the table. As she was sitting down, she glanced at the watch on her wrist that she could vaguely see through her sleeve. It would buzz when there were five minutes left.

"I just didn't know what to do. I thought maybe if I had some leverage, I could get your help again, or have… I…" Claudia stammered.

It was all nonsense words at this point. She had only stolen the cards because Thrase and her bouncers showed up. The plan had been to grab Alexander right then and there, make use of Harrison and his overstepping. It wouldn't have been clean, but they would already be off world and that was more important.

"Just save the water works. I want to believe you, I really do, Claudia, but you are just making it so bloody hard. Everything is a sob story. Everything is the worst day. I just don't know what to believe anymore," Alexander said.

He tapped the table and two status cards built into the tabletop came to life.

"Believe that I love you, that I just want to be with you and away from all the drama and nonsense of cards and houses and family," she said, reaching her hands across the table to try and touch him. Alexander pulled his hand back and made a little fist with it. She could see that he wanted to touch her, wanted to believe her. He was having too much trouble. He knew she was in some kind of trouble, but couldn't string apart the stories and lies.

"I love you too, Claudia. For all the excuses, and drama, I *think* I still love you—at least, I *want* to still love you, but…"

"Why can't that be enough? It should be. I love you, too. You just met me at a very strange time in my life," Claudia said.

She reached out again, her tight sleeves riding up. Alexander took her hands, his eyes glanced down. *Fuck,* she thought, biting out the curse.

Alexander's eyes noticed the watch, and its countdown, and then his hand clamped down on hers, holding them there, pressing.

"You are hurting me," she said quietly, trying to find a well of hurt and sadness to draw from, one last gambit. Alexander didn't say anything. He just held her hand harder as she tried to get away from him. "Alexander, please," she whimpered.

"You know, I've seen those watches before," he said flatly, coldly. "My sister and her marines use them to count down to their evac times. My brother uses it to chart flying blind through gravity distortions. I've seen them a lot in my life, growing up on a Dreadstar, but I can't say that I have ever seen anybody, especially a high-born woman such as yourself, wearing one out in society," Alexander said.

"I can—" Claudia started to say before Alexander cut her off with a loud, sharp sucking of his teeth.

"I'm not done. Just let me talk this out, think it though," he said.

Don't hurt yourself, she thought.

Claudia wanted to say it, but figured being quiet in this moment was her best play. He was seeing through the disguise, the fake woman who she was pretending to be. The real Claudia Wise was still shrouded from him. Letting him see her was the only card she had hidden away.

"What is there to think out? We don't have long to use the room," Claudia said, trying to spin a quick lie about the countdown watch.

"They book these rooms by the game, not the time," Alexander said, and instantly his demeaner changed. Cogs were starting to move in that thick head of his, the image clearing up.

"What happened to Alister?" Alexander asked.

Claudia could feel the power of the conversation shifting, something that never happened between the two of them.

I am still in control, I just have to grab it, Claudia thought, leaning forward as well.

"His heart just wasn't into the love I showed him," she said, dropping what was left of the mask she had been using around Alexander. It was time to put away the worried, scared, and helpless Claudia Wise. She wasn't needed any longer.

"Did you always plan to kill him to get to me?" Alexander asked. His face went cold. The retriever energy being replaced by something harder, something far less bitable.

"You were always Plan B," Claudia said, waving her free hand, getting a quick look at the timer. It was counting down too fast; they were out of time to leave. "We figured Alister was the weak link in your group, and he arrived first. You would think a rich family like that would have done better screenings for congenital issues," Claudia said, making a little *tisk, tisk* sound with her teeth and waging her finger.

"You bitch," Alexander muttered. She had been called far worse and by people she liked far more. "How long did it take you to learn how to play?"

"You wound me, sir, insinuating that I am, what? Some form of fake fan? What is it that the kids are calling them these days? A *casual*?" she said mockingly, putting her hand to her heart and then into her lap.

"Not much time for cards when you are in a Lagrange Spy School, I'm assuming—unless you are not a member of House Wise," Alexander said. He leaned back in his chair. The control of the conversation sat at the middle of the table, being served back and forth like a tennis ball. "I met somebody once who had gone through that school. They had so many identities at the ready and could pick up new skills at a frightening speed. We were ferrying him to a trade negotiation, for I assume less that above board goals."

"Yes, I am indeed a member of House Wise," Claudia said.

She would give him just a little bit of information. What could it hurt? She was going to have to rebuild their trust bond once they got off world. It would make extracting the location of his facility simpler than any of the mind probes that Mister Harrison had wanted to use.

"Your card game is not as complex as you all pretend it is. It is nothing more than luck and math, but I'm sure you knew that. With poor little Alister out of the picture, all I had to do was learn his task. I knew you would be desperate to get back into the tournament. Already, your acceptance was thin. Games over video conference?" she teased, laughing at the last part.

"Hoben pulled strings," Alexander said. She could hear the crack, that light lack of confidence in his voice.

"I'm sure he thinks he did," Claudia said. "Truth of the matter is, we wanted you at this tourney, so we made sure it happened. Infiltrating your group proved to be far simpler than I had anticipated. Alister was the weak link. Young, and far too sheltered. He had no idea what to do when a ravishing lady approached him and showered him with affection." Claudia watched Alexander. She could see him squirm, see the self-reflection in his eyes.

"Boys never do." She let that last line hang there for a moment.

"Hoben and Thrase were deemed too hard to crack. Thrase is a wild card and Hoben too old, too responsible. But he did view you as the brother he never got to hang out with as an adult." Claudia paused, seeing if she had just given Alexander a new fact about the man he thought was his best friend. He looked confused. Perfect. "He never told you about his dead little brother, passed at five?"

"So, he didn't talk about his brother who died thirty years ago. What of it?" Alexander said.

"You are smarter than that. You have siblings. How would you feel if Hanna had been snatched away from you at five? How do you think your mother feels with you abandoning her to go do work you can't talk about?" Claudia said. Talking about his mother was reaching, but the research she had done said there was friction there.

"You know nothing of my mother," Alexander bit out.

"I think I know enough, sir. You are an open book. The child who never fit in. You were not a girl, not a fighter, and not interested in the rigidity of military life. No, you wanted to see the world, to do science, and to leave the confines of the Dreadstar you grew up on. Of *course* you have parental issues. People are predictable. That is what makes you easy to manipulate. You think you are debonair, when in reality, like Alister, you are just a little boy looking for a pretty girl who finds you interesting," Claudia said. She let the venom seep into her voice, as she plunged the knife into his chest. She waved her hand wide and pointed at him. "It is what all boys want."

Alexander just smiled and leaned back. She didn't trust it, couldn't read it. What was he doing? Why was he smiling?

"What happens when the watch reaches zero?" he asked smugly.

The smugness was so obviously fake she wanted to laugh at it. Claudia looked down at the watch. There were five seconds left. He must have read it when she was waving her arms around, pontificating. No matter that didn't change the plan.

"Time will be up," she said.

The watch hit zero and outside, there was the sound of a loud explosion, followed by another, and another.

The room shook as Claudia reached for her pistol.

Flight Bay, Barker's World, Hanna

The world went black. She could hear her theme playing in a minor key, transitioning into a funeral march. Her mother and Erik were there, and so was Alexander. He had on an outfit that was far too fancy for the occasion, but still, somehow, it was perfect. Everything felt cold. She was ready to pass on, to see what adventures awaited her in the next life.

Then there was more pain, and pressure. Hanna screamed out as her vision was filled with the dark red running lights of their stolen ship. Under her, she could feel power moving. *They* were moving. Fox was leaning over her—covered in blood—applying pressure to the wound with one hand and frantically trying to operate a medical pack with her other hand.

"Don't worry about the pressure, just get the compress on," Hanna muttered, forcing the words out. She didn't know where they came from, the deep dark places created by training that you didn't have to think about finding, that appeared to you in times of need.

"You will bleed out," Fox said.

"I'm already doing that, just get the pack on, and mor...morp... pain," Hanna said.

Her brain wanted to say something cheeky, but the words wouldn't come out. Somewhere between her brain and mouth, a wire was crossed—or, more than likely, ripped apart. All Hanna could feel was pain, not in any one spot, just general, screaming, blinding pain. It would be over soon. Existence had just woken her one for one last moment so that she could see that they had made it back inside, so that she could die knowing that they hadn't all fallen for nothing.

Fox let go of the pressure, and instantly, Hanna could feel the blood flowing, the wound pumping and her life starting to fade away. Then the compress was on her, pressing down, pushing the gore back into her body. There was a hiss from the compressed air of the drug needle. Relief filled her body. Hanna still couldn't think clearly, but the haze was lifting. It was as if somebody had turned on a light in the darkness banishing the shadows back into the night.

The world faded. Time passed. When she opened her eyes again, she was leaning against the wall, under a silver field blanket. Her bloody clothing had been cut away and a cool compress was on her head. Fox was sitting next to her.

"Sitrep," Hanna croaked.

Her mouth was dry, so very dry. Fox poured a little water into her mouth. Hanna swallowed it, trying not to choke. It was cold and felt wonderful on her cracked lips. She wanted more but knew that she needed to take everything slowly. Everything except learning what had happened.

"I got us air born and got you stabilized. Long range scanners are showing a battle happening. *Fury* is fully engaged. I don't think she is going to make it to the jump gate," Fox said, her voice dropping.

Hanna closed her eyes and took a deep breath. If *Fury* wasn't going to make it, than it was going to come down to them to get the warning to NovaTerra before it was too late. Hanna had no idea how long she had been out. It could already be too late.

"Can this bucket jump?" she asked.

It was all that mattered. If they could jump, then there was still a chance that they could get the warning out, that they could save the Confederation.

"It should be able to. The nav computer is a little shot, but—"

"Then jump us to NovaTerra right now. We have to get the message out, the signal..."

Hanna was starting to fade again. She could feel the darkness of drugs and pain coming for her.

"What about *Fury*?" Fox asked. "I can get the radio working again with just a few minutes."

"We can't risk it. They are giving us that time. Mother will make them pay for every life they take, every bolt that falls off her ship..." Hanna muttered, before she passed out again.

CIC, *Prometheus*, Joanna

The ship rocked again. Joanna grabbed the edge of the glass top table in the center of the *Prometheus's* CIC. Her vision flashed and she was outside, far away from the ship, away from the conflict. Floating. Her feet were below her, dangling in space. She was in space, in the vacuum. She was breathing, but what, Joanna couldn't say.

It's a vision. You are not breathing, just focus on what it wants to show you, she thought, clearing her mind and looking around. She was in high orbit around Icarus. To her right was the planet and to her left were the storm clouds of the Barrier. She could hear it, feel every clap of electricity that raced across the clouds. She could smell space, raspberries. It smelled like raspberries.

Plasma cannon fire. The sounds of explosions and violence. Joanna turned away from the vision of the storm which wanted to drag her in, to bring her to it and consume her. There were flashes in the clouds, a bright explosion. The smaller ships were breaking away, moving in a broken formation. The massive bulk of the Dreadstar smashed through them. She knew how big the ship was, but seeing it from this far away drove home just how gargantuan these vessels from so long ago were.

Joanna's mind jumped back to a story that she remembered reading as a child that told of the Dance of the Dreadstars—how much truth was in it, she couldn't say. A battle where the four sides during the Age of Chaos came together. It was the last battle of that war. A thousand Dreadstars had jumped into the system with another four thousand support ships and assorted fleets. For two weeks, they fought and maneuvered. Millions of lives were lost and once the battle was over, the war decided, only five Dreadstars remained. The last five that would ever be seen in existence. Those five still existed today, by some twist of fate. And now she was watching a sixth unknown Dreadstar raise from the crust of a far-flung world, leaving violence and death in its wake.

"Joanna!"

Her vision flashed with a white light. She was back again in the Combat Information Center. Lucas and Administrator Fel had just run into the room. Both looked worse for wear. She looked up, past Naomi and Rostov, who had just arrived a few minutes before.

"How high are we?" Lucas asked.

His aura filled the room. Instantly she knew that he was back in command, and she could relax, no longer having to manage everything. Fel broke off and went to talk to the officer that she had left, who was standing by the helm on the top deck.

"Almost to orbit. What took you so long?" Joanna asked.

"We ran into an old friend," Lucas said.

He stood there, awkward for a moment, before reaching out and pulling her to him. He wrapped his arms around her and hugged. She could feel that he was shaken and worn. Rostov walked up next, wrapping his arms around the two of them. Joanna could feel a stillness from him that she hadn't felt before. The anger was still there, but it was less—tempered. Naomi came last, joining the huddle. Her energy was excited and full of wonder. Joanna saw flashes of a man made of blackness being consumed by gold while feeling happy about it. For a fleeting moment, she could hear the voices of the objects around her. To her, it felt like, as long as the four of them were wrapped together, that they could do anything.

They were going to need that feeling for what was to come.

A flash of golden light. Joanna turned to see a woman made of golden mist and wisps standing in front of her. Hyacinth. She recognized the face instantly. So she could move around the ship.

"We are all here, ready to enter," she said, her voice ethereal, floating to and fro.

"How is this going to work?" Naomi asked as the group pulled away from each other, situating themselves around the table.

While they had been hugging, Fel had stomped down from the helm station, her imperious presence casting a wide shadow across the room. She stood at the other end of the table across from Lucas, the two of them eyeing each other in a half-trusting kind of way. It said that they had set their differences aside, but only for the moment. They could be picked up again at any time and without any warning.

"It will take all of us working together to open the Eye. I can feel it. I know how to open it and ride it. My strength isn't enough to keep us together and push the clouds to open the secret door for us. That is where the blood pact comes in," Hyacinth said.

"We are one short, though," Rostov pointed out.

"Essex," Naomi said quietly.

"Can we do it without him?" Joanna asked.

"Calm. We have a fifth. If she is willing," Hyacinth said, turning to Fel. "Our minds touched when she found her way down here twenty years ago. The connection is not as strong, but I can feel her, can work through her,"

The whole group looked at Fel. Her eyes narrowed.

"You want me to help you open a gateway to Hell?" she asked.

The group was quiet.

"Yes," Rostov said. "Consider it karmic justice."

"We do not know if it is Hell. The Fellowship says it is Heaven," Joanna said. "Just that we are supposed to go there to pave the way for the stragglers and the true Wayfinder."

"I recognize that. The last Wayfinder prophecy," Fel said.

"You know Wayfinder lore?" Joanna asked, a look of shock and surprise on her face.

"There are many things we learn at the Academy that is not on the curriculum of the Citadel," Fel said, sneering.

"I had to scrape and steal to find any books on the Wayfinders when I worked there," Joanna said.

"As a common born knight, you wouldn't have known of the existence of the restricted archives, let alone been granted access," Fel said. "I didn't learn of them myself until I was five years into my master's work."

"I thought all of those texts and ideas were considered heretical and burned during the Wayfinder Wars," Lucas said.

"You don't think we would be stupid enough to murder the people who built the jump gates and not keep a full and complete record of their civilization and existence, do you?" Fel asked.

"Then why…" Joanna started.

She had so many questions. Suddenly, opening the Eye seemed less interesting than taking the ship to NovaTerra and breaking into this library, raiding it for all the knowledge and information that she had been struggling to find her entire life.

"I do not think that is important right now. We have a job to complete. *If* you are to be believed and an enemy from ages long past is on the move again," Fel said.

Joanna nodded, pushing the desire away. They would return to this topic later. Fel knew more than she was letting on and Joanna was going to learn what it was.

"They are indeed coming. There is no way that Wingarf would have acquired those powers again without seeing the Lords of the Shadow. They are returning. I can feel it. Their taint has passed through the gates that I watch," Hyacinth said.

"What happens when you leave with us? Will you still see the gates? Will they keep working?" Naomi asked. She was about to ask more questions in an unbroken string, but Rostov quietly put a hand on her shoulder.

"They will go silent. It will be in the best interest of us all. The fewer people coming to this part of space, the better. My siblings in the Confederation will eventually pick up the slack," she said.

"We need to focus, people," Lucas said.

He pointed down at the glass table. The remaining Fellowship marauders were reforming and coming back around toward them.

"Yes. There will be time for questions later. Upon the other side, I will answer what I can," Hyacinth said.

Joanna was going to hold her to that. There were so many questions that she needed answers for. The scholar inside of her was screaming, wanting to get out and start studying, start learning from these people who had the answers she had been seeking for years.

"We must all gather hands. You will feel each other's power running through you," Hyacinth said. She floated into the circle between Lucas and Rostov. "Once we are connected, I will need you to push all the Null that you can pull in toward me. I shall then focus and open the Eye."

Everybody nodded in agreement. Reaching out, Joanna took Lucas's hand in her left and Naomi's hand in her right. Through her gloves, she could feel the Null running through them. Lucas and Naomi felt luminescent and strong, but as soon as Fel joined their circle, it was as if somebody had brought a spotlight into a dim room. Joanna breathed in and it caught her breath in the back of her throat. She could feel all their minds. Fel's was covered with walls and blockades, like a document that had been redacted to the point of incoherence. Hyacinth was just energy; unknowable energy that cascaded in impossible angles.

The room became bright as they pulled more and more energy into the circle. Somebody had once said the Wayfinders were luminous beings. She had always thought it was a preposterous phrase, but standing here now, the brightness of their combined Null energy hurting her eyes—even with her glasses—Joanna finally understood what they meant.

Her vision flashed again. She was back in the void, floating. Standing beside her was Hyacinth.

"You will see much soon. I pray that the visions do not break you," Hyacinth said.

The dire warning chilling Joanna to the bone. Or was that just the fact that she was in the vacuum of space? Could she be cold as a projection?

Hyacinth flew forward, leaving a trail of golden Null in her wake. She moved across the enormous length of *Prometheus*. She flew ahead of the ship, the Dreadstar clearly locking into the energy trail she was leaving behind. Once she reached a good distance ahead of the ship, very close to the storms of the Barrier, Hyacinth stopped. She held out her arms and started pulling all the energy to her. Joanna could tell, could *feel*, that she was watching Hyacinth use the energy that they were feeding her. Golden strands of Null were moving from where she floated toward Hyacinth, pulling Joanna along.

Once Hyacinth was completely consumed by the swirling tempest of Null energy, she pushed it forward toward the Barrier. Her storm of golden energy smashed into the red and greens; they mixed, cascaded across each other. Thunder and lightning boomed in Joanna's mind as the Null energy fought with the storm. Another boom and a flash before a huge torrent of energy burst out of the Barrier. The flair was almost large enough to consume the ship. As quickly as it had appeared, it vanished, falling back into itself and into the storm. Clouds and energy were being sucked into the hole that had been formed. It was as if they had pulled the plug from a sink filled with water.

From her vantage point, Joanna watched as the ship was sucked into the maelstrom and consumed.

CIC, *Fury*, Cassandra

The third burn had just been executed, and they were on course again, moving away from the Aldebaran fleet. It had bought them time, but not nearly enough. The ship rocked from another hit. The Aldebarans had pushed forward with six corvettes and three wings of bombers to complement the fighters. Again, not a force that they couldn't handle, but one that would bleed more and more power from them. Cassandra knew that Victor would have put together what was happening. She wasn't deploying her entire force, was fighting with a hand tied behind her back.

Did he know about the Wayfinders? How to jump the ship?

It was common knowledge that a Dreadstar *could* jump, but for most people, it stopped there. Cassandra had to assume that he knew about the Wayfinders. They were working with a new faction who had actual jump capable ships, so she assumed that he bloody well knew. In that case, he was going to keep picking at her, keep dropping in smaller ships that would needle *Fury* enough to prevent them from jumping.

To what end, she wondered. Did they want to weaken them to take the ship? No, their own documents said as much that conscription was not possible. Cassandra knew that her crew would never join, would fight for every foot and bolt aboard the ship that was their home. Was there actually a chance that they could warn NovaTerra in time? Could they prevent the atomic horror that she had read about? That seemed more likely. Though the third option that crossed her mind was the one she knew to be true. Victor was toying with them, giving them hope, before tightening the noose and destroying them. In their condition, a battle against the *Pride* alone would probably not go their way. Factor in the twenty other ships, and there was no chance. Victor was batting at them like a cat with a dying mouse, prolonging the inevitable to stroke his own ego.

There didn't seem to be a way out of this. Once those Corvettes and bombers got here, it was game over for them trying to escape. They would have to reactivate the defense grid, pulling too much power in the fight for their lives. The ship shook again as Cassandra looked down at the map, the grim reality of what was before her taking shape. She started hitting a few keys, reading numbers, doing math in her head.

You will hear the music once more. Play for me again, my love.

Both the Wayfinder and Tiberius were in her mind, talking to her, trying to tell her something that she didn't want to admit, didn't want to know. The power reading was at eighty percent. It was ticking up faster, but not fast enough.

"Captain Rackland, if you please," Cassandra called up.

The captain looked up from where he was in fire control, trying to aid the battle as best he could with the few weapons that were still online. He nodded and started walking down to where she was standing. As he was walking down, Cassandra reached up and pulled off the signet ring from her finger. The three heads of the chimera felt strong in her hand. The symbol of her house, of her family, and of her legacy. If they were to be saved, then she was going to have to act outside the box. She was going to have to stop being afraid of repeating Hyroncore and start playing for keeps again.

"Captain, give this to Erik when you next see him," she said, taking his hand and pressing the ring into it. Rackland looked shocked as she closed his fingers around it.

"Don't worry about me, Cameron. He is going to need you soon," Cassandra said.

Captain Rackland nodded. He didn't know the plan, but his eyes knew that whatever was in her mind would cost them greatly. With that, Lord Admiral Cassandra Cordova patted her oldest friend on the shoulder and quickly departed the CIC. She didn't stop to look back, didn't engage in any kind of sentimentality; that was not her way. No, once she had a plan, she would carry it out with ruthless efficiency.

Even if it was the last plan she ever executed.

Outside *Fury*, Erik

The red arrows of his aiming reticle locked onto the green square around his target. House Aldebaran used the same fighter load-out as they did, meaning the melee was Rapier versus Rapier. Erik squeezed the trigger for two seconds, spitting out a burst of plasma fire. The poor sod who he was chasing tried to avoid it, but just ended up turning into it. His wing was ripped apart and a moment later, his ship burst into flames.

"Good kill there, cousin. I hope you left a few for us," Bella said over the comm, her fighter rolling up next to his. She had just gotten back from rearming.

"Plenty enough targets, I think," he said.

Plenty and too many. They were not killing them fast enough to make up for what was being sent forward. Already, Erik could see the Corvettes on his heads-up display. They would be on top of them before they reached the jump gate. Behind them were Broadswords. It was a losing proposition, but if he was going to die here today, then damn it he was going to take as many of these bastards with him as he could.

"Well then, we should get to it, don't you think?" Bella said, pushing forward in front of him to pick off another enemy ship.

Erik fell in beside her. He might have been in command of the fighter wing, but it was the sign of a good leader to know when you were outclassed and to follow along. A moment later, Ander Stromwind pulled up on the other side of Bella's fighter.

"Mind if I cut in?" he asked over the comm, his voice jovial and excited.

"Three can tango," Bella said, matching the younger man's tone.

Erik shook his head quietly. Both were crazy. He was worried about dying today, yet that was the furthest thing from their minds. Good company to keep, he figured.

Ahead of them, on the fighter screen, before the Corvettes, was a wedge squadron like theirs, only they were operating with four fighters and not three. This was standard for most of the great houses, who assigned more fighters to their Hawkeyes than House Cordova did. Bella might like to fly on instinct—might actually be better that way—but it was not his style.

"Aya, do you copy?" Erik said over the comm. A moment later, an affirmative came from the young woman. "I need the flight info for the ships ahead of us, I've pinged them back to you. Bella is—"

"She is being herself, Commander. But fear not, I have your back," Aya said.

He was going to have to talk to her later about cutting him off, but for now, the fear sounded gone from her voice and he wasn't about to do anything to cause it to return.

"Thank you, cadet," Erik said as data started to filter into their computers. "Bella, make the call," Erik continued, switching back to their channel.

"Missile roll out, on my mark," she said.

It was a simple maneuver, but one that worked best when you had dedicated information and data control on the battlefield.

"Roger that," Erik said, flicking open the cover for missile controls on the flight stick.

Moving his eyes, he locked onto the Rapier ahead of him. A moment later, Ander had locked onto his. Erik placed his thumb over the missile control and his index finger over the trigger for his guns. All his targeting computers started yelling at him at once. They were in range. The Aldebaran's fired first. Erik tilted to the right to avoid the oncoming fire, just a short burst of plasma. They were testing them, seeing who would blink first in this game of chicken. Erik took another deep breath, righting his fighter and tapping off the arming delay on his missiles.

"Mark!" Bella yelled over the comm.

Erik pulled the trigger on his guns, firing a two second burst, and then launched his missile before breaking to the right. Ander did the same thing going left, and Bella followed, going down. Normally the leader went up—that was what they were expecting. The two fighters on the side fell for the ploy, avoiding the gun fire, but not seeing and reacting to the missiles until it was too late.

The lead fighter, who clearly had some experience in combat, saw through their ruse. He dove up and spun, avoiding the missile while blind firing where he thought Bella *should* have been. Erik wondered if they had enough time to bite out a curse before Bella came up and smashed through the underbelly of the opposing Rapier. The ship exploded in a ball of fire that Bella twirled around, lest she singe the paint and get a talking to from the deck gang. That left only the last Fighter to deal with. Erik pulled around to take care of it, but not as fast as Lieutenant Stromwind. The young pilot let out three, two second bursts, boxing his target in before finishing them off with a fourth.

Erik pulled up on his stick and fell back onto the side of Bella's wing. Then a strange message came over his comm. It was from Aya back on the Hawkeye.

"Commander, were we expecting *Fury* to launch frigates?" she asked.

Erik cocked his head to the side. Nothing in their plans had mentioned launching any of their frigates, because it was going to take too much time and power to recouple them.

"No, there shouldn't be any launches," Erik said as he hit his air brakes.

Pulling back on the stick, Erik flipped his fighter over so that he could see *Fury*. Sure enough, one of their frigates, a newer one, was steaming forward toward the Corvette wedge. Erik pushed hard on his peddle and closed the distance in a moment, reaching the ship and coming up alongside it, matching speed.

"Frigate, this is Commander Cordova. Who authorized this launch?" he asked.

A moment passed and then his personal channel clicked on, overridden from the source.

"I didn't know I needed any body's authorization to launch one of my own frigates," his mother's voice said. She sounded calm, happy— at peace.

"Mother, what are you doing out here?" Erik demanded, fear and confusion creeping into his voice.

"Hearing the music one last time, Erik," she said.

"Mother..." he said quietly, slightly confused.

Looking down, he could see that her path was a direct collision course for the wedge of corvettes. Blinking next to his readout for the frigate was a radiological alarm. She had at least one, but probably more, active atomics on the ship. His heart sank through his chest taking the wind out of him. His hand left the throttle control and gripped at his flight suit as he tried to get his breath back.

"Do not worry about me, son. This is right. There is so much I wanted to say to you, so much I *should* have said. I wasn't the mother you needed, wasn't the mother *any* of you needed," she said. He could hear the regret creeping into her voice. "I was too busy being the Lord Admiral, too busy trying to live up to something that didn't matter. You and your brother and sister were what mattered, and I should have... God, Erik, they are both gone, my beautiful little twins," Cassandra said, her voice finally cracking.

"We don't know that, Mother. Hanna is scrappy, and we are going to warn NovaTerra in time for Alexander," Erik said, as tears started to stream down his face.

"Yes, yes you are. Erik, take care of them, take care of everybody. And…" Erik could hear tears in her voice now, years of regret. "When you see Alexander, tell him I'm sorry, and that I love him."

"I will give him your love," Erik said.

There was more that he wanted to say, but Lord Admiral Cassandra Cordova didn't give her son a chance. She clicked off the channel.

A moment later, music started to play, pushed out to all the fighters and ships under their command. It was a track that Erik had never heard before. He knew all the parts, the leitmotifs, but not in this arrangement. *Hearing the music one last time* was what his mother had said. She must have composed one last track—a farewell. Erik blinked his eyes quickly, pushing away the tears that he couldn't wipe from under his helmet.

"Bella, we are done here. Signal combat landings across the whole wing," Erik said into their private channel.

"What is going on, Erik?" she asked, the music in the background of her audio.

"I have something to take care of. The wing is yours now," Erik said.

He shut off his radio. He didn't want to say anything else. What else was there to say? He and Bella could talk about it later. Right now, he trusted that she would do what he ordered and get her pilots home.

Erik couldn't look back. He turned off his read-out computers and just flew, so he could have a few moments with his thoughts and so he didn't have to see his mother die. Just as he was about to land, there was a flash behind him and his throat went dry.

Once his ship hit the landing bay, he was out and on his feet. Lord-Commander Erik Cordova made sure to wipe the tears from his eyes before getting out of the fighter, lest anybody see. Though nobody would have blamed him—everybody that he passed was in shock. Even the older members of the deck gang, who had seen dozens upon dozens of battles, looked rattled. There were tears, there was fear; the ship was rank with it.

Erik walked fast, his attendant behind him. He pulled off his flight jacket and took the long blue coat, throwing it on. Then, he took the sword from the man who was struggling to keep up with him. Erik clasped it on and started to run. He didn't want to be near anybody else, didn't want to be in this moment. There was no time to mourn, no time to find his emotions, but all he wanted to do was see his mother one last time and cry in her arms.

"Lord-Commander on deck!" the boatswain yelled, his whistle playing.

The tune didn't change but he could feel the sadness in it. Erik gave him a quick salute and moved down the steps to the glass table where Captain Rackland was standing. He was at attention, his arms behind his back. The old man gave him a crisp salute, something that Erik never thought he would see. That was reserved for his mother, for the head of the house.

"What are your orders?" the captain asked.

He walked up to Erik and held out his hand. In it was the Cordova signet ring. Erik took the ring and tried to place it on his finger. It was too small. He moved it to his pinky, the only one of his fingers it fit on. He then looked over and saw that the power clock was at ninety-nine percent.

"Once all our fighters are onboard, jump the ship. Let's make sure the time she gave us counts for something."

EPISODE X:
Punching the Null

Card Den, Novagrad, Alexander

The room finally stopped shaking. It had been two hours of constant bombardment, all sounds that Alexander recognized. Once you had experienced artillery going off around you, felt the mass of the explosions vibrating through your bones and internal organs, you tended not to forget it.

He didn't know who was shelling the city—and right now, that seemed like a moot point. The card den was a hardened location, designed to prevent electronic cheating, but useful in a pinch as a bomb shelter. What he *did* know was that somehow, Claudia was involved in all of this, and it made him feel sick. She had pulled off her skirt to reveal pants and a gun, which she was now holding and occasionally pointing at him as she paced around the room. Her demeaner had completely changed from the girl with a problem for him to solve to some kind of... *operative.* An operative on a mission that involved him and something much larger going on in the world.

"You can sit down, you know," Alexander said.

Claudia just looked at him and scoffed. When she wasn't looking at the gun, she was looking down at the watch on her wrist. A new countdown had started. Alexander had ideas for what it was counting down to. If the first had been counting down to the start of the bombardment, this one was surely counting down to the end of the first wave. He took a deep breath. This was war. He was going to need to start thinking like a Cordova, and not like a child who pranced around with an empty sword case and field boots because his mother was a Space Lord.

"We are stuck here until this is over, so you might as well sit down. You can keep pointing the gun at me. Hell, it probably would make the whole thing simpler for you," Alexander said, motioning again to the other chair in the room.

The place shook again, dust falling onto their heads. Claudia sighed and sat down in the second chair. Putting both elbows on the table, she leaned forward and pointed the gun squarely at him. It was a small pistol, an old slug thrower, not a hefty plasma weapon like most people carried. Small, light, elegant. A spy's weapon.

"You never even had the slightest idea of what was going on, did you?" she asked.

There was condemnation in her voice. Alexander decided he didn't like this version of Claudia as much.

"You had me good and fooled from the moment you sat down. I really thought that the world was turning around for me. You see, my heart was shattered right before coming here. So much so that I didn't even think a card tournament and Festival could make me happy," Alexander said.

"Saccharin nonsense. That is what made you an easy mark," Claudia said. "Alister didn't know any better. He was young and had never been with a woman before. You, though…"

"Me what? I should have seen through your obvious ploy? I should have questioned fate handing me what our team needed? I did, we *all* did, deep down. But I wanted to believe in a festival miracle. For all of the movies and books about the season to be something that comes true. So, you can call me a fool, a sap, a rube; they are all things I've been calling myself for the last few hours," Alexander said.

"I don't need to call you names, you know well enough what has happened." She paused. "It's not wrong to want those things. We all, deep down, want something like that. It is why pulling those levers works. The balls were a lot of fun," Claudia said.

"They were, weren't they?" Alexander said. "We were clicking. There *was* something there." He tried to turn on the charm, find the spark and charisma that had gotten him out of plenty of tight spaces in the past.

"I'm not sure how much of a spark there was. All I said was the parties were fun," Claudia said, moving the pistol from one hand to the other.

"I fought a duel for you. I would say we had a connection," Alexander said, pointing and leaning back in his chair.

"A duel that I clearly didn't want you to fight for me. So much so that I drugged you trying to prevent it," she said.

"Wait, so that was... Bloody hell," Alexander muttered.

"Mister Harrison is far from my favorite person, but we are on the same team, and I couldn't have you killing him. Though the gesture was a good demonstration of just how in my palm you are."

Claudia leaned back and there was a bit of contemplation on her face.

"You never read the message she sent, did you? I was so worried about it when I first saw it," Claudia said.

Alexander's eyes darted around for a few moments. Oh God, the message from Fox. He had never opened it.

"You should give it a look; consider it one last twist of the knife," Claudia said.

Alexander didn't want to read it, already he could tell what it was going to say, just by looking at Claudia's face. That sick, twisted smile that showed just how beaten he was, how in her pocket he had been.

His eyes fell to the table, all the energy leaving his body. Alexander reached down to his pocket and pulled out his watch. Sliding over to his messages, he opened the one that Fox had sent him the day after their fight, the day he had arrived on NovaTerra.

Dearest Alexander,

I have been thinking about our "discussion" the other day in the electronic closet. I-I might have been too hard on you. The offer... I can see now just how much you must have sacrificed to secure me that position. But I need you to understand where I am coming from. Fury is all that I have known and leaving her is... It is a big step, a step with finality to it.

For the whole time we have been together, I knew people talked. They talked about how we were mismatched, how you were a lord and I was just a grease monkey. I didn't care then, and knew your family didn't care, but I didn't realize how it stung at you until... until you laid it out so bluntly.

We have much to talk about when Fury arrives in a few days. But I want to work it out. I don't want to lose you to this, and if we can get past it, I would be honored to join you on whatever this secret project is you are working on.

Yours Forever and always,

Fox.

Alexander felt sick to his gut. If he had just read the letter, if he had just been able to get over his own pigheaded arrogance, all of this could have been avoided. Claudia had beaten him before they had even met. She had won in that moment on the transport when he didn't open the message. Putting the watch away, he resisted the urge to cry, to scream out at the world, to rend his clothing and wallow in just how fucking stupid he had been.

I deserve what I get at this point, he thought.

Looking up, Claudia looked satisfied; not happy, or sad, or empathetic, just satisfied with her victory.

Alexander didn't feel like fighting anymore. Didn't feel like trying to make himself feel better for being used—and now being captured. It was obvious what Claudia's employers wanted with him. If they were trying to poke holes in the team, that meant that they were trying to get information on Project Far Step.

Well, that was something he couldn't let happen. Alexander might have failed at everything the last few days, but this... *this* was something he could do. Something that he needed to do if there was to be even a sliver of forgiveness headed his way. He swallowed, his throat was dry. Alexander put the message, the guilt, the shame to the side. They would always be there, his forever companions. Right now, though, he needed to focus, to think not like a card player, or a scientist, but like a Space Lord, a warrior.

A Cordova.

"I take it we can leave here once the watch hits zero again?" he asked.

"Perceptive. I have a ship waiting, so we can get off this rock while that is still an option," Claudia said. She glanced at the watch. It was almost at zero.

"They couldn't even provide you with extraction?" Alexander scoffed.

"You blew two different extraction points, so now we have to walk," Claudia said.

It had been a minute since the last round of explosions. Perhaps they were at an end. Alexander was wondering just how much damage they had done to the city. It was probably extensive, but cosmetic. If they were looking to actually destroy the capital, they would have just dropped a spread of atomics on it. Unless this little uprising didn't have that kind of weaponry. No, they were bound to. Anybody who would go up against the Confederation would be a large enough house to have atomic weapons.

There was a lot at play, things he didn't know or understand yet. Alexander had been blind for too long, and now his eyes were starting to open. Claudia was mad, so maybe he could learn something from her. Anything would be helpful for the eventual interrogation that he was sure to face.

Unless I escape, Alexander thought. Hanna would be telling him to escape, already butting heads with Claudia. Of course, his twin would have been smart enough not to get involved in a situation like this. Like mother, she was slow to trust.

His mother. How was he ever going to explain this to her? She would be so disappointed. Disappointed to learn that the second son of the great Lord Admiral Cassandra Cordova had been captured by a spy because he was cuntstruck. Another line to add to the list of things about himself that were a disappointment to his mother and the family.

The watch beeped.

"Time to go, lover boy," Claudia said, standing up.

"No," Alexander said, crossing his arms. If he was going to be a disappointment, at least he could be a dead disappointment, and not let his inability to judge character get anyone else hurt or killed.

"We don't bloody well have time for this," Claudia said, walking over and yanking him to his feet by the back of his coat.

She was shockingly strong and knew exactly how to leverage her weight to counter his size. Alexander was on his feet in a moment. It was shaky, and he almost fell again, reaching to the chair for balance.

"Before you get any ideas, just know that I am not above leaving you here to die," Claudia said, putting the gun into the small of his back.

Alexander froze. While he had handled weapons all his life, this was the first time one pointed at him with ill intent had been this close. If she pulled that trigger, there was nothing he could do. The blade-resistant fabric he had on wouldn't be enough to stop the round from shattering his spine and blowing out the other side.

"Okay, okay," he said, holding up his hands. "Just be careful with that. You could hurt somebody."

"I am not a little girl who needs your protection. The faster you accept that reality, the faster and easier all of this will be. Now we must be going," Claudia said, pushing the pistol into his back and moving him forward to the door.

The door to the room had started to come off its hinges from one of the many concussive blasts that had rocked the underground building. Alexander carefully opened it and started to walk forward.

Looking at the way it was hanging, for a moment, he saw a way to make it swing back at Claudia quickly. It might have knocked her down or would just made her angrier. Alexander wasn't sure which one, and he still, even now, didn't want to hurt her, even though he knew it was his responsibility to fight back and escape.

The front room of the card den was a disaster. Chunks of the roof had fallen and all around, there were bodies covered in blood and plaster dust. From the rubble, there was moaning, and Alexander was sure he heard a weak cry for help. It took much of his control not to break away and try to go look for people to help. *That is always what gets you into trouble. You wouldn't be in this bloody mess if you didn't need to be damned white knight so much.*

Light was coming from the staircase that led down into the card den. Somebody had gotten out. Behind him, he could feel that Claudia was looking around, keeping a sharp eye on the situation. The barrel of the gun was rotating around the small of his back like a horrible massage ball. They kept walking up the stairs and into the light.

Outside, Alexander was faced with a horrible sight. The card den had been downtown. Before, it had been a thriving metropolis. Now it was a disaster zone. Everything was on fire; the buildings that reached into the sky were cracked; hundreds of windows were shattered; some had holes blown through them or had already lost their tops. On the street level with them, cars, animals, and people were strewn about in parts. Dust was floating on the air, carried by the sounds of screams and explosions.

Alexander looked up and saw a horrible sight. Sitting in low orbit, almost in the atmosphere, was a Dreadstar, the ship so big that it was casting an almost inescapable shadow across the city.

Claudia pressed the gun into his back, pushing him into its shadow.

Surfing the Null, Dreadstar *Prometheus*, Naomi

Colors filled her mind. Naomi could feel the tidal forces smashing against the hull of the ship. She could hear the *Prometheus* crying in pain as the waves of tachyons smashed against her armored plating and the chronotrons seeped into the softer portions of her superstructure. Hyacinth had guided them into what Naomi was sure was a small wormhole, or maybe a singularity that existed not completely in phase with their reality. She would have to look at the data once they landed—*if* they landed. But she was sure it was one of the two, probably a wormhole on account of them not currently being dead.

"It is okay. I know this hurts now, but we will be through it soon enough," Naomi whispered to the ship.

As long as she was touching something of the superstructure, they were still connected. The electrical spirit inside the glass operations table was having a blast riding the waves and gathering new information. Clearly, he and *Prometheus* were at odds about what was considered fun.

He doesn't feel pain, the ship said to Naomi in her head. *Everything is academic to him, every battle, every maneuver. He doesn't know the stress it puts on my body.*

Naomi felt a rumbling inside her mind as her knee rammed into the table. She winced at the pain, but could hear a new voice in her mind.

Naomi felt like she heard a retort to this statement. It could have come from the glass table, she wasn't sure. That electrical spirit wasn't as coherent as the ship, hadn't been talked to enough. It seemed to her that it understood that the ship was feeling pain, but was unconcerned. The table viewed taking the punishment, and protecting them as her job, her mission in life. Naomi sighed and looked up from the squabbling computer stations to her friends. They were all holding each other's hands tightly, trying to keep their footing.

Hyacinth was floating above them. The place where she had been holding their hands was filled with gold-sparkling Null energy as she hung in the middle of the room. Golden beams of light were streaming from each of them, like long ropes tethering them to Hyacinth. From each and every one of the troopers who were at their stations hanging on for dear life were smaller, thinner strands of Null energy. If the string from them looked like a rope made of gold, the strands from the troopers seemed more like an invisible thread covered with a light sprinkle of glitter.

The moment passed, and Hyacinth floated down as the rumbling of the ship started to fade. They were on the other side, and it was calm for a moment.

Then, things started to explode.

Power was cascading throughout the ship. Naomi pulled her hand away from the bond with her friends and touched the floor. She needed to feel the ship completely, to let *Prometheus* fill her mind. Naomi had woken the ship from its slumber, convinced her to take this last trek and she would be damned if she was going to let her die now.

The screams from not just *Prometheus*, but every system across the ship, were deafening. So much power had been pushed through the systems that the old wires and circuits couldn't handle it. It felt like somebody had pushed too much blood into a body during surgery, causing all the damaged vessels that had been sutured shut to rupture. So much energy was pumping through the ship that she didn't know what to do. None of the systems could handle it and they were blowing out one by one. It wasn't just raw antimatter energy that was moving through the system, but an infused, tachyon Null energy. She didn't understand it. Naomi could feel it, knew what it was, but not much more than that. If they somehow survived, then maybe she could find a chance to learn more.

A conduit near the helm station burst, throwing a Militarum trooper across the CIC covered in a shower of sparks and fire. Their body smashed into the wall. Naomi could hear the trooper's back crunch like crisp lettuce. The ship screamed. She was confused, didn't know where to go, what to do. Hyacinth was feeding the ship information, but there was nothing she could do with it.

Naomi closed her eyes and could see the ship as a small child, hiding in the corner of the room as everything blew up around her. She walked over and sat down next to the whimpering Dreadstar.

I'm scared. I can't see anything anymore. The lady is yelling at me, but... but I can't move. I don't understand all her numbers. Is she mad at me? Prometheus asked.

"No honey, she isn't mad. She just doesn't completely understand how you feel and wants to get us all to the other side alive," Naomi said, wrapping her arm around the child.

The ship sniffled and stopped crying a bit. Naomi looked up. Joanna had turned her head and was looking at her strangely. Naomi couldn't tell if she was able to see the personification of the ship that she was talking to. If not, then Naomi figured she must look bloody crazy, sitting on the floor conversing with herself. The one person who for sure couldn't see the young girl who was a Dreadstar was Administrator Fel.

"Knight Perkins! Since you seem fit to leave the circle, perhaps you could be useful and take the Helm!" Fel yelled at her.

With every moment, Fel took more charge of the situation. They might have been following Lucas, and he might have been a battlefield commander, but she just had presence. Naomi looked down at the young girl. She returned the look, her eyes huge and pleading. *Prometheus* nodded to Naomi, the vision of the little girl fading into the bulkhead.

"Pike, you join her. The two of you seem to understand the ship and Eye better than anybody else," Fel said, pointing at Joanna.

She turned, about to have a retort. Noami could feel the rising defiance inside of Joanna. She had been told to do something—forcefully—and by a person in authority, so of course her first reaction was to say 'no' and put her foot down.

Naomi walked over and put a hand upon Joanna's high, wide shoulder. She didn't need to push any Null or stretch out with her emotions to feel the tension. A moment passed, and she relaxed, the fight dissipating from her. Sometimes, simple human gestures were enough and superseded fancy blood pacts and Null-fueled emotional bonds. Joanna nodded and started to turn.

Naomi dashed up the stairs, pushing past injured and dying troopers, the smell of burnt circuits, fabric, and flesh filled her nostrils, as the acrid smoke from fried electronics made her eyes water. The helm station was a giant wooden wheel with twelve intricate handles sticking out of the side like spokes. She knew it was a throwback to the old days of sailing ships. That was something she had never done, been on a real boat before. For a moment, she stopped and thought about it, feeling the sea under her feet. The warm sun on her—

Joanna tapped her on the shoulder as she walked by. Naomi shook her head, coming out of the small rabbit hole that her stressed brain was trying to drag her into.

"You drive, I'll be your eyes," Joanna said.

Naomi nodded and then placed her hands on the wheel. She had seen a video once talking about how you had to hold the ship at ten and two, referring to some ancient clock metaphor that was too far out of date to have been in a modern technical manual. Perhaps when this was all over, she would rewrite that one. Then you pushed and pulled the wheel so your hands stayed in the same place.

As soon as her hands touched the wood of the wheel, she felt *Prometheus* moving through her. The young girl was standing next to them. She looked nervous, excited to see what would happen. She also screamed and covered her head every time the ship rocked or was hit by something.

Joanna placed her hand upon Naomi's shoulder and, in an instant, she was able to see outside the ship. It felt like she was standing on the outside of the hull, just her, the wheel, and the turbulence of the wormhole. The information that Hyacinth was feeding into the ship started filling Naomi's mind. It was just numbers, pure raw math. The ship's computer was trying to work all of it out in real time, but it wasn't fast enough. Naomi could see the answers to some of the equations. She wasn't bad at math, but she wouldn't go so far as to say it was one of her better subjects. She understood how to fix things with her hands, not how the software worked.

"Hyacinth, I need you to slow down, to translate. We don't speak numbers," Naomi said.

She wasn't sure who was going to hear, though. Was she actually outside, or still in control of her body? She was making course corrections, so clearly her hands were moving.

"She should understand; I *need* her to understand," Hyacinth's voice came through. It was more curt than usual, like a parent that didn't want to hear form their child that they just were not good at their homework.

"Perhaps a few hundred years ago, she would have understood, but not anymore, not right now," Naomi said.

"Harrumph," the little girl who was a Dreadstar said, folding her arms across her chest and stomping a foot.

"Well then, compute the numbers, please. I know you don't want to be here anymore, but we are all trying to get you out of this in one piece," Naomi said, finding a more domineering tone in her voice.

A small pad of paper materialized in the little girl's hand, and she started to scratch out sums with a pencil. The data that Hyacinth was feeding them started to come to clarity. Naomi could see golden lines starting to form and appear in the maelstrom of the wormhole. She turned the wheel so that *Prometheus* turned to stay between these two lines, deftly avoiding a graviton eddy. She hadn't seen the small spinning micro blackhole. If the ship had gotten any closer to it, the gravitational forces would have ripped them apart faster than they could have figured out what was going on.

For the next five minutes, Naomi followed the path that was being set forth by Hyacinth and reluctantly translated by the ship's computer.

"I'm getting tired," the little girl said.

Naomi could feel the response time on the wheel starting to get sluggish. She was having to exert more energy to move it even a small amount. Naomi pushed her vision into the ship, down into the core. She could see the gaggle of golden rats starting to get tired, starting to fall asleep. There was nothing left of the antimatter man. *Prometheus* was again starting to run out of energy. She hadn't started with much and that last little bit was getting all used up.

"Hyacinth, I really hope we are getting close to the other side," Naomi said to the wide world around her. There was no response from Hyacinth, but she did see what looked like another storm directly ahead of them.

"That looks exactly like the Eye when it opened on the other side," Joanna said.

"Well then, I guess this is it. Hold on," she said, tightening her grip upon the wheel.

A moment later, they plunged through the storm. Naomi could feel the wind running across her bald head, triggering memories of when she used to have long locs. They would have blown in this wind, been magnificent sails of excitement and joy. Right now, all she felt was cold and exposed. *Prometheus* came out the other side.

Naomi was greeted with a world that she had never seen before, something that even her wildest imagination couldn't comprehend. There was no space, no sky, just the storm all around them. Floating in in the void were huge chunks of rock. They had plant life and running water, all moving in strange directions, like the orientation of the floating platform wasn't the same as what was upon it. Under the plant life Naomi could see what was left of cities, buildings, homes, schools, hospitals, a civilization.

In the distance—far in the distance, but still dominating her view— was a massive tower made of onyx that sent shivers down her spine.

"There is gravity." It was Lucas's voice coming from the Combat Information Center.

"Then we need to find somewhere to put down before we lose power and crash into something," Rostov said.

"Naomi, Joanna, do you see an appropriate place to set us down?" Lucas asked.

She scanned the sky, looking for a place. The two closest platforms of rock were far too small. There was no way that they were going to be able to set the ship down there with the velocity that they had. She looked down. Below, there was a massive hunk of rock. It had an entire forest, lake, grassland, and part of a mountain range on it.

"I've got a place! Everybody strap in, this is going to get bumpy," Naomi said.

She could feel both Joanna and Rostov biting back a sarcastic comment. She loved and hated them for it in equal measure. Naomi cracked a small smile before getting down to the business of gently crashing a Dreadstar. On the floor near her feet were thruster controls.

The wheel just controlled right and left, the pedals controlled the thrusters that would slow the ship down or also start it moving up or down the relative Z axis. To get where she wanted required cutting their thrust and pointing the ship down.

Naomi smashed the brake pedal and the thrusters on the front of the ship kicked in, cutting down the anemic velocity that they had been able to achieve. Then, before all of it was gone, Naomi hit the thrusters on the top of the forward section of the ship, pushing its nose down. Instantly, she could feel the ship start to pick up speed. The gravity here was coming from far below them.

The large platform was coming upon them quickly. Naomi hit another pedal, pushing *Prometheus's* nose back up. She was now angled correctly with the platform. Naomi's foot moved and she hit the engines one last time. They fired to life for three seconds and then sputtered. The little girl yawned again then curled up into a ball and fell asleep.

"Hang on everybody, this is going to be rough," she yelled.

"Just get us down!" Fel's commanding voice came up at her.

Naomi could feel Joanna's hand tighten on her shoulder. There was nothing she could do about it right now.

Hitting the pedal to slow them down, Naomi used what little power was left in the rockets and then it was up to fate to see how they landed. It was an interminable minute of falling before the gravity started to change in the ship. They all started to rise, the Dreadstar falling faster than the people inside it. Then the ship hit the ground with a massive thud and all of them smashed back into the deck. *Prometheus* landed in the grassland, pointed toward the small mountain range. The ship didn't stop. It kept going, cutting a wide swath in the land, churning up grass and soil, throwing it to the side, covering Naomi in a monsoon of dirt. Finally, as the ground started to get rockier near the foothills, her forecastle crumpled and gashed, the Dreadstar *Prometheus* came to a stop.

Naomi took a deep breath. She kept her hands solidly on the wheel of the ship, her legs feeling like jelly. The air here was crisp, if not a little thin. She shouldn't have known that this was just a vision. Still, it was filling her lungs. Looking behind her, Naomi saw the swatch of destruction that they had caused. It stretched for miles, almost the entire length of the platform that they were now on. Animals were already starting to tentatively creep their way forward again, looking around, trying to see what this new interloper was in their world.

A bird screamed over Naomi's head. She looked up, seeing a flock of black birds, each of which had two heads, flying across her field of vision. They didn't have feathers, but leathery wings, like bats. There was something else streaking through the sky, was it a...?

Her heart sank. It was one of the Fellowship marauders. It must have followed them through the Eye. The ship was burning, trailing behind it a plume of black smoke and fire. She watched it fly and then smash into the top of one of the platforms above them.

As her eyes came back down toward the crash site, she again saw the giant onyx tower. It dominated the skyline, grabbing your eye anytime you looked near it. A shiver went across her back. They had escaped one Hell, only to be on the doorstep of another.

The *Chaos Runner*, Grace

Grace and Essex flopped to the deck of the *Chaos Runner*. She wasn't sure how they had gotten here, just that they *were* here. Grace rolled over, sliding a groaning Essex off of her. Behind them, the trail of blood was long and concerning.

Focus on the escape, Grace, not the blood, Emily said in the back of her mind, fighting to come forward and take control again.

Grace was fighting to stay awake and thus fighting to stay in control. A red light beeped on the side of her heads-up display. Grace's eyes fluttered for a moment, as the pain and morphine raced through her system. It beeped again, this time more insistent. She looked up at it. "Ship controls." Yes, she had wired control of the ship into her suit. Good thinking.

Thank you, Emily muttered from where she was stashed away.

Grace blinked twice and the controls for the ship transferred into her system.

"Close the loading door," Grace croaked, her voice dry and full of pain. Red lights started to flash all around her as the gangplank behind them retracted into the ship and the doors started to close. That was one step down, but they were so far from out of the woods yet. The Children of the First would be coming for them. They were not going to let her escape. Their desire to not kill her was the only thing that she had in her corner.

You know where their lost Jump Point is, Emily reminded her. Of course her mind was more clear. She wasn't being bombarded by pain meds.

"Essex, guns," Grace said, biting back the pain.

"On it," he said.

She looked over and the Host'ire Knight was already back on his feet, leaning against the wall and stumbling forward. He had ditched the long coat and his blade in a bloody pile. Leaning himself against the wall, Essex stumbled forward, leaving a long streak of gore in his wake. They were going to need to patch themselves up soon. Otherwise, it wouldn't matter if she could punch through the jump point or not; they'd die in the Null.

That isn't my first plan, but it is still an option, better than them getting what they want. Grace wanted to bite back at Emily, stating that she knew that. She wasn't stupid or born yesterday, just that she wasn't as wild or radical.

The cockpit wasn't far ahead of her. Grace tried to stand, placing both hands on the deck and pushing. Her arms were wobbly. She tried to push power from her suit but there was almost nothing left to give, and she fell back to the deck with a metallic thud.

"If you can't walk, Goodspeed, I'm going to need you to crawl!" Essex yelled back at her like some kind of drill sergeant. She didn't need to be told that, didn't need his affirmations.

Emily pushed forward. Goodspeed could crawl, but Emily wasn't about that. Itchi's walked. Emily put her hands on the deck, all the pain that Grace had been feeling washing through her. She gritted her teeth and pushed. Her arms wobbled, but they held long enough for her to get to her knees, and then from there, to her feet.

"Huzzah, Goodspeed," Essex said as he turned a bloody corner toward where the gun controls were.

"That's not my name," Emily muttered as she took a laborious, pained step.

A minute later, she took a step into the cockpit and fell forward, her arms reaching for the chair, making impact, yet failing to grasp. She hit the ground with a thud of pain. Taking in a sharp breath, Emily rolled over and pushed herself into a sitting position against the control panel. Ripping off her helmet, she set it down. In the chrome of her face plate, she saw herself: all perspiration, matted black hair, and blood. She was going to look quite the fright tomorrow—*if* there was a tomorrow. *Tomorrow.* She wanted to see tomorrow, and thus had to stay alert, awake.

Math. Math would help.

"Computer, patch systems into my helmet and display via holoprojector," she croaked out.

A few moments later, a large, holographic display was projected in a wide curve around her head, coming from a small projector on her helmet. A line of light shot out from the projection and scanned her face and eyes.

"Control transferred to Doctor Grace Goodspeed, ocular functionality is one hundred percent," the computer said back to her.

That wasn't her name; wasn't who she was, who she *needed* to be. The computer didn't know that, though. She could let it slide… this time.

"Get us out of here, launch now," Emily said, biting through the pain. A moment later, the ship lurched to life and started to move. The rocking hurt, but she was going to have to roll with it until they got to space.

"Computer, activate weapons and transfer control to Third Essex," Emily said.

"Weapons control transferred," the computer said.

"Essex, I hope you dragged your sorry broken ass to one of those cannons!" Emily yelled into the ship.

A moment later, the vessel rocked again, the sound of a plasma cannon going off. Good, he had made it.

Looking up toward the window of the cockpit, Emily could quickly see the thin sky of Olympus Ares give way to the stars. Already, she could see gravitational lines lensing her vision, celestial objects being stretched out. Of course they didn't just lose the jump point because of drift over time, but from the gravitational pull of the Fissure. That black hole was bigger than anything else in the observable galaxy. *That* was the last bit of data that she needed. It proved an old, nearly discredited theory that the Null and real space were not connected, but moved like two sheets of paper being pulled in different directions. It was the old pencil test that professors loved to do to demonstrate a wormhole. Fold the paper, shove the pencil through. In reality, the pages were on top of each other and one was smaller than the other. The Wayfinders, over the last few thousand years, must have pushed hundreds and hundreds of pencils through the paper—and in some places, they had been removed, the holes sliding apart.

"Proximity alarm, proximity alarm," the ship's computer blurted out. Emily blinked her eyes twice, pulling up the rear scanners. Four small fighters were on their tail, launched from the Black Caldera.

"I've got them, don't worry about it!" Essex's voice yelled over the ship's comm system. "Just work on getting us the hell out of here."

Right. She needed to focus, push through the pain and the morphine that the suit had given her. The Fissure hadn't been accurately mapped in a way that she would want, nobody got close enough to the gravitational—

That's when it clicked.

That is what the star charts and records were trying to tell her, the lost bit of the puzzle. The *gravity*. Quickly, Emily started to wave her hands, pulling up all the information and runes, charts and graphs. The small cockpit filled with holograms, the projector in the helmet doing its best to keep up with the speed that Emily's brain was moving.

That was when she saw them. The neon-blue eyes. At first, she couldn't lock her eyes onto them. They kept moving, just sliding away from the edge of her field of vision.

Work faster, I can feel him coming, Grace's voice said. The eyes got closer. They were now no longer just in her periphery. They were burning through the golden equations, stalking toward her. Emily closed her eyes, trying to push the Varagoth and the pain away; allow herself to focus.

When she opened her eyes, the world around her was red sand. She was standing there, in her suit, covered in blood. Standing beside her, in a lab coat and button-up shirt, was herself, but different.

"Grace?" Emily said.

"Yes," she responded. They both turned from each other and started to look around. Emily knew this place, she had been here before, many times. The Varagoth had grabbed them, pulled them into his own little world.

"He is going to come for us, try and prevent us from finishing the work," Grace said, stepping forward.

"Then we just have to prevent that from happening. Push him back, regain our mind," Emily said, walking to stand next to Grace.

"No. This isn't your fight," Grace said, putting her hand on Emily's shoulder. "I am of this place. You need to run, to get out of here."

"I'm not leaving a part of me behind to be flayed by that thing," Emily said, pointing toward nothing, a nothingness that was starting to feel wrong, to feel occupied.

"I will always be here. Grace Goodspeed was what you needed in the moment, but not what you need anymore. The world needs Doctor Emily Itchi, the last Wayfinder, not Grace Goodspeed, the quiet, unassuming name on a log sheet."

"I don't want to leave you. I *need* you. I need that calming voice, the one that prevents me from going off the handle again, that tramps down the paranoia," Emily said.

She reached out for Grace's hand. Grace pulled it away, clutching both her hands by her heart.

"Emily, we are not some kind of dissociative identity—just a convenient way for you to pack away trauma that you will have to soon face. Get out of here. Go home, talk to Mom and Dad," Grace said, walking forward.

The sand in front of her started to twist and swirl, the Varagoth forming from the red tornado. Emily could see his eyes as she started to step backward, letting Grace get closer and closer to him.

"You wanted me, asshole? Well, I'm right here!" Grace yelled as the neon-blue eyes came into existence, forming around the shadow and sand.

"Thank you, Grace," Emily said quietly, a small tear rolling down her cheek.

The Varagoth's massive hand reached out and wrapped around Grace's head. Emily felt pain shoot through her mind. She closed her eyes and reached out for the ship, for the physical world. A breath and a moment later, she was back in her body, in the cockpit of the ship, her hands still moving furiously, working out the equation to find the lost point in space so that she could use it to rip open the Null.

"Grace!" It was Essex yelling. "Grace, we need to get out of here, or you need to do some evasive maneuvers!"

She shook her head to work away the fog of the moment. In the back of her mind, she could feel Grace being pulled apart, laughing and fighting with the Varagoth as he tried to get the secret from her mind. This hurt more than any of the wounds that Emily's body had suffered. It felt like a part of her was dying. She knew that Grace wouldn't give up, but that there was a finite amount of time before she died, and the Varagoth came for *her*.

Emily spun the ship around, telling the nav AI to activate evasive maneuvers. Then, she went back to the math, pushing away the pain, the feeling of the sacrifice that Grace was making, as anger rose up inside of her. She was going to punch into the Null, she was going to understand this Wayfinder nonsense, and then she was going to come back and kill every one of these assholes. Grace wouldn't have approved...

But she was gone.

Emily pushed forward, breathing hard, the last numbers coming into place, the equation balancing on the edge of the knife. She had the coordinates, the power level, everything. Pulling her hand back, she opened her palm and pushed the information toward the ship. The hologram went into the flight control console, vanishing. The ship snapped, changing direction, picking up speed. The fire from the plasma cannon stopped as the ship drew in every ounce of power that it could.

In the back of her mind, the Varagoth screamed, dropping a lifeless, bloodied Grace to the ground. Emily could see her face. She was smiling. There was a loud groan from the ship, and then the stars went green, and they were in Null space. She looked at it for a moment before the world went black.

She woke up a while later. Her armor was gone and she was strapped to the bed in the small medical bay, tubes running from her arms. Essex as sleeping in the chair next to her, wrapped in bandages, an IV in his arm as well. Buzzers went off. She was breathing raggedly, still working out where she was and what was going on. Emily reached out for Grace. All she could find were bits of tattered empathy floating in her subconscious. The Varagoth was going to regret that. Essex started to stir, opening his eyes.

"Welcome back," he said weakly, clearly holding himself together with energy from the Null.

"Did we make it?" she asked.

"Ya, we are in the Null. Grace, where did you take us?" he asked. "I can't access the computer."

Emily leaned back on her pillow and let out a long breath.

"Home, I'm taking us home. And my name isn't Grace. She is gone. I'm Emily," she said turning to look at him with a weak smile.

"Emily Itchi, Wayfinder."

Dreadstar *Fury*, Nearing the NovaTerra System, Erik

Lord Commander Erik Cordova sat in his rooms. He wanted to cry, wanted to scream at the world, but none of that was coming out. There was nothing but a numb acceptance that she was gone and he was in command.

I'm not ready. You still have so much more to teach me, he thought, looking around the empty room that threatened to consume him. Now that *Fury* was in the Null, it was a five-hour trip to NovaTerra. That was just enough time to rearm the fighter wing and make sure everyone got a little bit of rack time. Already, Bella had taken command of the pilots and was barking orders and yelling commands. She was a natural, just like he knew she would be.

Erik knew he should have gone to sleep as well. Lord knows he tried, having returned to his quarters to take a shower and put on a fresh uniform. He was going to have to get the tailor to add a second epaulette to his jacket, now that he was in command. Once this crisis was over, he would need to report to the Admiralty—*if* there was an Admiralty left to report to.

For now, all of that could wait. What mattered was what he was going to do in the next few hours. A realization that came crashing down upon him as he sat in his quarters, freshly showered, looking at the uniform on his bed. It was in that moment that Erik knew where he would find the answers.

Quickly, he got dressed and walked down the hallway to his mother's quarters. They were not locked, so he let himself in. Even if it had been locked, the signet ring on his finger would have granted him access. He and Captain Rackland had transferred the command codes as soon as they had entered the Null. He wasn't showing it, but Erik knew the old man was hurting. Hurt that he had failed to save her, that he had failed to prevent the situation that caused her to feel the need to make a sacrifice play. Most of all, though, Erik knew that Captain Rackland was hurt that she hadn't taken him with her.

Erik walked over to the couch and, just as he was about to sit down, he noticed three sheets of paper on the coffee table. He picked them up. Music. The composition was fresh. He could still smell the carbon laser from the piano's printer. On the heading, there was no title. Erik looked it over for a few moments. His near inability to read music had always been a disappointment to his mother. Deep down, he knew she would have wanted him to keep writing music, to pass on that legacy. It wasn't him, though. He did not have a thing, a quirk that made him stand out, that made him an interesting commander. Erik Cordova just *was*. He cared, yes, but that came across as uninspired and dull. People were not drawn to following a good man, they were drawn to following interesting ones.

Walking over to the piano, Erik sat the sheet music on the stand and sat down. He placed his fingers on the keys and started to play. It was slow, and he kept hitting the wrong keys, unable to keep the tune in his head long enough to look down and make sure his fingers were in the right place. It had been years since he had tried to play the piano, and it had gone just as badly then. He only made it out of his music classes by rote memorization, which made his playing lifeless. After that, nobody had made him play another instrument again.

"Damn it!" Erik yelled, smashing his fingers into the keys after the third off note in a row. He didn't have the aptitude for this. He picked up the sheet music and fed it back into the piano. A moment passed and the keys started to move on their own, as if being played by the ghost of his mother. Erik stood up and closed his eyes, letting the music flow through him.

As he suspected, it was the composition that she had played for the fleet at the end. He had been so frantic, so overcome with emotion that there had been no time to take in the music, to digest it and truly appreciate what his mother was saying with it. They were all one, and while she might have passed away, the family and *Fury* would persist. It was sad, yes, but also full of hope for the future, for reunion.

Suffused with emotion in that moment, Erik started to cry.

Opening his eyes, he walked over to the couch and slumped down. He knew now, as well as his mother had when she wrote this music, how fleeting the hope of them coming back together was; how long of a reach it was.

That was what hope was, though: the long reach. If it was anything else, hope wouldn't be needed, wouldn't be something that people grabbed onto in situations like this. In her death, Cassandra, sixth lord of House Cordova, had rekindled hope and pushed it forward. She might have lost it for herself, but not for her family, and not for the Confederation. Surrounded by everything that was his mother, Erik wept as the music played to its end. He closed his eyes and sat there in the emptiness with his thoughts, with his feelings of inadequacy, and the desire to grab the hope that the music had been trying to give him. Finally, Erik stood up and walked across the room.

He removed the sheets from the piano, as he did a holographic prompt came up. It was asking him if he wanted to make any changes to *Untitled Composition 4604*. Erik couldn't fathom a world where he would ever second guess something that his mother had written. Just as he was about to hit the command to say no, he realized that she had left one last task for him; one last gift. While he wouldn't have dreamed of changing her music, there was no way that Erik could leave this beacon of hope untitled. He pressed the box where the title should have been and started typing.

"Hope Reborn".

It wasn't the most original title, but it contained exactly what his mother had wanted it to. Erik hit save and pulled the pages from the piano.

Across the room was a shelf filled with the collected works of Cassandra Cordova. Everything from gig books with loose handwritten sheets, to larger score books, and even three librettos for the operas she had written in her youth. Erik picked up the last of the score books and slid the pages inside. Then, he removed the title card from the side that had a single date, a dash, and then nothing. Removing a pen from his pocket, he wrote the year 8,991 and placed the book back onto the shelf. Her legacy was complete. Now, it was time to create his own.

"Lord Commander on deck!" the boatswain yelled, blowing his whistle.

Erik entered the room, his hand clasped around the hilt of his sword. Slowly, he walked down the steps toward the glass top table where Captain Rackland was standing. He was going to need entry music. Something else to add to the list of things that were not important right now.

"Lord Commander, we are ten minutes out from NovaTerra," Rackland said. "All wings are prepped and loaded in the tubes. I've also got all gun crews standing by. Though..." the old man paused, looking down at the table, not wanting to meet Erik's eyes. He would let it slide for now. But if they were going to work together, it would be something to address.

"Though...?" Erik prompted.

"Though I don't know how much power we will have for the main guns. That jump, however you accomplished it, drained us. Staying in Null space isn't allowing a recharge. We will come to whatever battle is out there with cold weapons," Rackland said.

"I understand, Captain," Erik responded. "We, as always, will fight the battle ahead of us with the hand we have been dealt."

A splinter gnawed at the back of his brain at the mention of the jump and how they had accomplished it. Those moments were fleeting, fading quickly, soon to be lost to time.

"Reversion to normal space approaching," the helm called down from the top deck.

Erik didn't say anything. He just quietly pushed a key on the side of the table. "Beat to Quarters" started playing throughout the ship. His mother might be dead, but as long as he was master of *Fury*, her musical legacy would live on. The ship rocked as they came back into normal space. Erik looked down as the table started to populate information.

"Bring me up an outside camera," he ordered.

A holographic image came to life over the top of the table. He could see NovaTerra.

They were too late.

Already the planet was burning the tell tail signs of atomic detonations crossing the southern hemisphere. A pitched battle was happening in orbit. Raining fire down upon the capital of Novagrad was the Dreadstar *Wrath*. The traitors were in control of at least two of the five Dreadstars. Learning the loyalty of the remaining two was going to be a top priority for the wars to come. Near *Wrath* was a burning and dying, warhammer-class super dreadnought. According to the battle readout, it was the *HCS Dragon's Fire*, the flagship of Admiral Petrov.

"Comm, see if you can raise Admiral Petrov on the *Dragon's Fire*, if you please," Erik called across the CIC.

There was a moment of quiet as he watched the battle. The percentage display on top of the Admiral's ship was well below fifty percent. There was not going to be much that they could do to lend a hand. Still, they had to try. They had to have hope. A moment later, the handset by Erik's station buzzed he picked it up.

"This is Dragon Actual," the voice on the other end said. It was ragged, but Erik recognized Admiral Petrov's drawl as a native of the southern continent.

"This is Fury Actual. Admiral, you look to need assistance," Erik said.

"Erik...?" The line was quiet for a moment before the Admiral spoke again. "We have lost so much today," Petrov muttered. He knew what was meant by Erik being in the CIC and calling himself Actual.

"Lord Commander, I fear the engagement has gotten away from this old man. Tell your mother I look forward to picking up our games of pickle ball in the near future," Petrov said.

Erik could hear an explosion on the other end of the line and then there was static. Turning his head, he could see on the video readout that *Dragon's Fire* had taken a crippling direct hit. The Admiral was gone, the fight was lost.

Pickle Ball? What is he trying to tell me?

It was clear the Admiral was sending him a message, but what was it? Closing his eyes Erik went into his mind, trying to remember all the times he had interacted with the Admiral and his mother together. They had been friends and Petrov was one of the high ranking non-titled men who had at one point tried to marry his mother. Then the memory dawned upon Erik, and he understood the Admiral's last order.

"Captain, stand down the flight wing. We are leaving," Erik said, pressing a few keys on the board.

"I beg your pardon, sir. This crew is ready. We will not have our honor besmirched by fleeing from the face of the enemy," Rackland said, bristling.

"Admiral Petrov, before he died, gave me an order. The channel wasn't secure, but I understood what he wanted. He mentioned playing pickle ball with my mother again," Erik said. It didn't take Rackland more than a moment to connect the dots.

"Casparian VII," he said.

"That is what I am thinking," Erik said. "That summer we spent with the Admiral when the he was courting my mother. They were aggressive on the court. I was not even to your knees and still I remember those matches."

"They were impossible to forget," Rackland muttered.

"Helm, set course for the gate at best speed. Get us out of here and plot a roundabout course for Casparian VII," Erik called up to the helm deck.

"Casparian VII, roundabout, aye sir!" the boatswain next to the helm called back.

"Captain, we might have lost today, but hope hasn't faded away. I swear to you we will track down those who started this rebellion, who killed my mother. We will find them dand make them pay. I swear on my honor as a Cordova, that all those they have killed will be avenged. My mother... my siblings," Erik said, balling his hand into a fist and smashing it into the table. "For all of them, I shall extract a price in blood."

Beyond the Eye, Lucas

A week had passed since the *Prometheus* had landed on the plateau that they were now calling home. It didn't have a name yet. That was something that would come later. Now, it was up to Lucas and his friends to survive, explore, and figure out what Hyacinth wanted from them when it came to clearing the way.

The Wayfinder's avatar had faded after they landed, saying that she was tired. They had not heard from her in the last four days. Rostov and Naomi had attempted to go and visit where her body was in statis. Their adventure had proven unfruitful. The ship seemed to change the deeper you got into her bowels. Their memories of the trek were cloudy and the landmarks they had remembered gone. None of this surprised Lucas. Of course there was a defensive mechanism, even against those who were sworn by blood to protect her.

Rostov had been hurt by this and spent the next two days sulking. He had taken a few rations and walked toward the nearby forest. It was a half day journey, and he didn't return until the night of the third day.

"I need to clear my head. To see something like sunlight again. To feel grass and leaves and life under my feet," he had said.

Lucas didn't blame him. After everything that Rostov had been through, he would not have been surprised if the man had just said to Hell with all of this and vanished. There was nowhere really to go—and, if Host'ire dogma was to still be believed, they were already *in* Hell. If this was Hell, it was nicer than anything he had pictured growing up. There was no fire, no pain, no demons poking him in the ass with pitchforks. They had only explored half of the land they now resided on, so maybe the lake of fire was somewhere else.

"I feel better now. I see," Rostov had said.

Upon coming back, he had been quiet, still, and contemplative. Lucas had tried to get a gauge of his emotions, to reach out and feel them. Rostov had pushed him away, still being guarded with how he felt, even resisting one of Lucas's calming auras.

"We must all sit with ourselves for the time being, to figure out what is going on, to understand where we are," Rostov had said before leaving the Lord Admiral's chambers that the four of them had been sharing. Naomi had gone after him, returning a short time later, throwing her hands in the air.

Joanna had avoided most of the drama with Rostov. She found the logs of the ship's last three commanders and some of the crew. The researcher in her had started trying to read and understand what these people from a thousand years ago had been up to.

"Of course, it is written in an older dialect of NovaTerrern. So, I'm having to work with what I remember. All this is showing is that I relied too much on the computers at the Academy library when I was doing translations," she said over dinner on the third day after the landing, the night that Rostov and Naomi had returned from trying to find Hyacinth. "It's good this is forcing me to bulk up my language skills. Hyacinth's gifts allow me to read the words, but... They had an odd way of speaking during the Age of Chaos, and before... I don't know if I'm learning, or if the powers are. It's fascinating, nonetheless."

"That makes sense," Lucas said, looking off into the middle distance as he chewed on a hard cracker covered with a algae-based protein jam. People said it tasted like the ocean, but Lucas had never seen an ocean or swam in salt water, so he had to take their word for it.

"You are not listening, are you?" she said, slightly miffed. He could feel the irritation even without their bond.

"Sorry. I've been lost in thought. Listless since we have been here," Lucas said, setting down his cracker and looking Joanna in the eye. Her big, beautiful eyes that drew him in, that he just wanted to lay in bed and look at all night. She winked at him, and Lucas looked down, the embarrassed child taking hold for a brief moment.

"You need to find something to do. I'm hoping to find some of that in these logs. So far, I can tell the commander of this ship was not pleased that they missed the battle. So much so that, get this." She paused leaning in like she had a juicy bit of gossip. "The Lord Admiral took their own life over the shame of missing the fight."

"Must have been a big battle," Lucas said.

"From what I can tell, based on context, they are referring to the Dance of the Dreadstars. They, of course, were not calling it that less than a week after it happened," Joanna said.

Lucas leaned back, making a light whistling sound. He didn't know much about ancient history, but *everybody* had heard of the Dance of the Dreadstars.

"I understand how he was feeling. Missing a once in a millennia fight would break me," Lucas said, picking his cracker up again. "So, why were they on Icarus?"

"I don't think they were, yet. There is a whole year of logs that I haven't cracked open. Very exciting stuff. I've always wanted to read the full text of a primary source form this time period," she said.

"Sounds like you have a lot of work ahead of you," Lucas said, finishing off his dinner.

It didn't leave him full, but the caloric intake was his daily recommended amount. His mind wondered for a moment. *Do they have a hydroponics bay on this ship?*

"I do indeed have a lot of reading, but not for tonight," she said, standing up and walking toward the bedroom. Lucas jumped to his feet, wiping the crumbs from his hands, and followed.

After failing to find Hyacinth, Naomi had spent her time in the engine room talking with the spirit of the ship. She talked about it at dinner every night, but much of it still went over Lucas's head. He tried to follow along with the visions she was seeing, the personification of all the electronic devices in the ship. Something Naomi insisted was new, but also *not* new. She and Joanna had spent a few nights talking about how many of the new abilities they had were not new so much as things they always had, just amplified to a staggering level. It made sense. Lucas had always been a good leader and a quick healer. Now, he was exceptional at both.

Though he wasn't feeling like it so much, lately. He might have held sway over his friends, but the operation in and around the ship was completely under the control of Administrator Fel. There wasn't much he could do or say to stop her. Even without new powers, she was still a more accomplished practitioner of the Host'ire arts. There was also the case of the close to four thousand Host'ire Militarum who were still under her command. For the time being, she was leaving them alone, giving them a daily ration, a billet, and nothing else. Lucas wasn't sure how long that would last, but for now, it allowed them time to lick their wounds and go walk through the forest to find themselves.

It did not last long. Fel came to see them on the eighth day. There was a heavy knock on the door. They were operating on extreme backup power, so none of the door chimes were working. Lucas got up from where he was sitting at the table, trying to help Joanna with the logs, and answered the door.

"May I?" Fel asked.

It was less a question and more a polite formality. Lucas nodded, taking a step back and holding out his hand so that she could enter the room. Fel walked in. The rest of the group was sitting on a circular couch that wrapped around a coffee table. Lucas walked over to join them. There was a single chair sitting by the couch. Fel went to that and sat down, flipping out her coat as she did so.

"To what do we owe the honor?" Rostov asked drolly.

"I want to invite you on a little expedition that I'm putting together. I know we haven't seen eye to eye in the past, but our new reality dictates that we need to put animosity behind us," she said.

Rostov was about to say something else smart before Lucas held his hand up. He could feel Rostov's scrunched up face without having to turn to look at him.

"What kind of expedition are we talking about? I was under the impression that we had already done a fair amount of exploring?" Lucas asked.

"Everything but the mountains. In the hanger bay, we found a working Hawkeye that still had fuel in its tank. I want to fly to the top of the peak and take readings and see if we can't start mapping some of this new realm that we are in," she said.

"Do you need somebody to talk with the thousand-year-old radar boat?" Naomi asked.

"That wouldn't hurt. What I really need are your Null powers. We know this place is strong in the Null, but also close to the Shadow. I've been feeling it every day, so I know you can, as well. Outside of us in this room, and *her*..."

Fel refused to say Hyacinth's name or Wayfinder. Lucas figured it had something to do with still not wanting to admit exactly what she was and how that impacted everything Fel had been raised to believe.

"Hyacinth," Rostov said.

"Yes," Fel bit out. "Outside of the six of us, there are no other Null sensitive people here."

"Baron'Tor is here somewhere. He has to be," Joanna said.

Fel took a deep breath and rolled her eyes.

"Yes I assume the librarian has crawled into a hole with his followers and will show himself eventually. For now, though, we cannot count him among us," Fel said, before returning to her original idea. "The way I see it, if we can all stand at the highest point, we might be able to get a good feel for how things... feel."

"That is not a bad idea. We are going to have to understand and tame this land. If we want to prepare the way," Lucas said.

"You would think that she would have more orders for us than just 'prepare the way,'" Rostov said.

"It is a very old text, and the Wayfinder language has subtle meanings in their words that are lost on us today because of the purge," Joanna said.

"This is one of those moments that having access to the library would be helpful," Fel muttered.

"We still don't have a translation of their sublanguage, the Chant of the Stars," Joanna said. "I know I spent years looking for it while I was at the Academy."

"That and every other Wayfinder text is stored in a monastic off-site library. But you are just a Citadel Knight, so your clearance in the order doesn't even allow you to know of its existence," Fel said.

"You are telling me that the Order has the entire written memory of the Wayfinders just *hidden* away? That would have been useful to know," Joanna said.

"Just like the Order, can't even commit to their own genocide," Rostov said, leaning back against the couch.

"The Wayfinders were dangerous, but we were not about to let their knowledge pass away," Fel said.

"You still believe in that Host'ire nonsense? You know how much they lie to people like us. Think about how much they still lie to people like *you*?" Rostov said. "Why did your message never make it out of the Citadel? Never make it to command, and you were left confused in the depths of your dreams?"

"I don't fully know what I believe anymore. But I do know that I spent a year in my graduate program studying their texts. So, while we don't have the library, we do have my memories. Which are not nothing," Fel said.

"Do your memories know anything more about the prophecy?" Joanna asked.

"No, it was never one that we put much stock in. Contemporaries from five hundred years ago thought it was underwritten and foolish," Fel said.

"It wouldn't be the first time learned folk were wrong about what they knew of the past," Joanna said.

"Academics aside, we will join you on this expedition. It will be good to feel useful," Lucas said.

He turned to look at his friends. Naomi's eyes were wide and Joanna nodded her head. Rostov rolled his eyes and just made a disgusted noise.

"Good. We leave in two days' time," Fel said, standing up.

Fel was good as her word and two days later, they were all stuffed into a Hawkeye that could barely get airborne, heading toward the snowcapped mountain that *Prometheus* sat at the base of. The flight was mercifully short. Lucas was sure that the craft was about to fly itself apart if they were in it any longer.

The view from the top of this mountain was stunning and terrifying all at once. Lucas was instantly brought back to the moment that he had woken up while dead in this place, seeing the strange flora and fauna, the red orange sky, and the black fortress that hung in the distance, consuming what was once a world filled with buildings and civilization. This time, though, he was closer to the massive onyx structure. Lucas could see the small red arrowhead ships flying by it clear as day. He took his glasses off and could feel the stink of the Shadow upon the structure.

"'From their tower of night, in the lands beyond, they struck, first through their agents and then for themselves,'" Joanna whispered.

"'The enemy of the Alliance made destruction manifest, and brought creation to its knees,'" Fel finished.

"I'm going to need somebody to back up and catch up those of us who didn't get to read as much history in school," Lucas said.

"During the Age of Chaos, we were beset by a group known only as the Enemy. An Alliance was formed. Civilization was barely able to hold the line, stopping them from destroying... everything. They prey on division and anger," Joanna said.

"Most importantly, they were only driven back to their hiding places, not destroyed," Fel said.

Lucas could feel everyone go cold, and not just because they were standing in the snow.

"And you think *that* is their Tower of Night?" Rostov asked.

"A dark tower in Hell? It fits the bill," Naomi said.

"I thought we were off the 'this is Hell' train," Rostov said.

"It might not be Hell, but it sure isn't Heaven," Naomi said back.

"It is where we need to be," Joanna said.

"Paving the way," Lucas said, taking a deep breath and swallowing. The task before them was still frustratingly vague now that Hyacinth was quiet again. But there was one thing Lucas knew for certain.

The road home was through that Onyx Tower, and they were going to travel it together, or not at all.

Post Credits

Aldebren Winter Palace, Meredith

The Winter Palace on Aldebren Prime was a beautiful place. Rich in history, serving the monarchs of the world for the last three hundred years. It was built in the style of an older palace from story books, situated high in the mountains where there was always snow on the ground. The white building had majestic turrets and rising towers topped with sloping blue roofs and crenellations. There was a curtain wall that ran down half the mountain, wrapping around a winter village. It was all very much in the NovaTerra style, setting it apart from the rest of the buildings on Aldebren Prime, which been overtaken by technology, glass, and steel.

Meredith was a lady's maid to Lady Mai Ping, the sister of the Duke of Aldebaran. When not serving her lady, Meredith was also a member of the Confederation Intelligence Bureau. It had been three weeks since she had gotten any word from NovaTerra. Communications were spotty out here in the mountains on a good day. The guards had clamped down on any outside information. The last she had heard, there were bombings and something—although she found it hard to believe—about a Dreadstar in orbit, raining down fire. Those were rumors and they didn't matter. No, she was here to do a job and that was what she was going to do. It might take some creative work to get any information out, but that was what she had signed up for. *The adventure of a lifetime*, the pamphlet had read.

Today was going to be her best option for getting said information. There had been rumblings among the staff and guards. Too many of the guards were having relations with the staff. Men talked too much after sex. It was said that a party of new allies was coming to meet with Lady Ping and her husband, Lord Admiral Garrison Lagrange.

Meredith opened her chest of possessions that sat at the foot of her bed. Her roommate had stepped out to go and see her 'guard friend'. That gave her a small window. Tapping the bottom of the box, she found the false bottom and pried it open. Inside, she removed a small recording device. Unwrapping it, Meredith opened her mouth and slid it into one of her wisdom teeth, which had been hallowed out for occasions like this. Tapping it twice with her tongue would turn it on and tapping it twice more would turn it off. Three times and it would self-destruct. She was not interested in having to use that function of the tooth.

The throne room of the Winter Palace was a truly opulent space that was right out of a fairy tale. The walls were high and made of white marble. Every window was ornate stained glass depicting the rise of the Ping family and fall of the Aldebarans, who were the original rulers of the world. They had supported the Wayfinders five hundred years ago as they fought for their very existence.

The chandeliers were made with so much crystal that Meredith was sure they were worth more than some small houses. Running from the massive wooden doors to the two thrones of gold was a blue carpet made from a metal that looked like cloth—usually reserved to make military uniforms. Here, it was just a carpet.

Sitting at the head of this room in their golden thrones flanked by guards and two massive fireplaces, with flames roaring, were Mai Ping and Garrison Lagrange. They had married two years ago. A power move that many in her organization, and even the House of Lords, had largely ignored.

That had been a mistake.

"Your lord and lady, might I present to you Mister Harrison!" a crier called from the doorway.

The two large doors opened, and a man dressed sharply in a black NovaTerra suit walked into the room. He had slicked-back brown hair so dark as to almost be black and the look of somebody who wanted to sell you a starship with a screen door. This Mister Harrison walked up to the end of the carpet, just before the step up to the thrones and bowed his head.

She tapped the tooth twice.

"Good evening, high lords," Mister Harrison said.

"I see you have come groveling back to us, having failed in your part of the operation," the Lord Admiral said, standing up and walking forward, his hand on the hilt of his sword.

"A minor setback. I still have operatives on the ground. The young Mister Cordova will be in our grasp soon enough, though with the ships that my associates have given you." Harrison paused for a moment. "Which were buried under your very noses, I might add; should give you the leg up you need to have your fleets jumping in no time."

"Those ships are old, and already many have been destroyed," Lady Ping said.

"Now *that* is out of my hands. Your husband and brother devised the battle plans to secure the Dreadstars," Harrison said, giving Lagrange a sly look. The Admiral sat down and nodded to his wife. She was clearly in charge here.

"It would seem both of us had slight issues with members of House Cordova," Garrison said.

"It is of no matter. The Confederation is in chaos. You requested a civil war and that is what we have provided you with. The operation that my associates were truly interested in has gone off without a hitch. The Citadel of the Host'ire has been destroyed, and the Eye has been opened," Mister Harrison said.

"That means more ships will be coming soon. The grand technology that you promised us for sheltering your desperate little network," the

Admiral said, getting hot again. Lady Ping put a hand on her husband's arm, calming him down.

"Soon, my good lords, soon. First, you must hold up your end of the—"

Harrison stopped, his head darting around the room. He sniffed and then held two fingers to his ear for a moment.

"You have a spy in your ranks," Harrison said, spinning around.

It was not anger that crossed his face, but a sick twisted smile, a bit of glee. He was sniffing again. Stalking toward where the ladies' maids were standing, toward where *Meredith* was standing.

"That is impossible, everybody has been checked multiple times," the Admiral said. His wife was quiet, looking across the staff with her cold, calculating eyes.

"I have methods," Mister Harrison said.

He was getting closer to her. Meredith tried to control her breathing, tried to act normal. She looked around at the other ladies maids who were around her. All of them looked worried. Their eyes were darting from one to the other. Mister Harrison started waving his hand, pointer finger out in a limp way moving down the line.

"Which one of you is it? Who is the spy, the fly in the ointment. Is it you?" he asked tapping one of the women at the end of the line.

"No," he said, moving to the next woman. "Maybe it is you. Those are *very* worried eyes," Mister Harrison said.

"Enough of this!" Lady Ping said, standing up. "Guards, would you kindly purge my household staff?"

Shock crossed all the women's faces as they fell to their knees, begging and pleading for their lives, imploring Lady Ping that they were loyal. Meredith didn't grovel or beg. The guards stepped before them in a line and raised their guns. She turned and locked eyes with Mister Harrison. He looked back at her and gave a little wave.

The guards fired and Meredith tapped the tooth three times.

The End of Part I of
The Null War

About the Auther

Sean Van Damme when not living in his own created worlds, resides in Virginia with his wife and their eight animals. Four dogs, three cats, and a crested gecko. During the day, well at night technically, he is an Emmy winning video editor for the local news station. He and his wife are also known from time to time to foster hordes of kittens. It is an occupational hazard of being married to a veterinarian. He has been writing and creating stories for as long as he can remember and writing a science fiction epic has been on his bucket list since before that was even a phrase that existed.

Along with a handful of novels Sean has also written for table top RPGs, both freelance and on his own projects. This is where a shameless plug to check out his wild west game Ballad of the Pistolero goes.

If you want you can find him talking about TV, movies, and yes—sadly—politics on the internet. With his real name no less. *Gasp*

SEAN VAN DAMME